TREAD SOFTLY
ON MY
DREAMS

Gretta Curran Browne

Wolfhound Press
& in US and Canada
Irish American Book Company

This edition 1998
Published by
WOLFHOUND PRESS Ltd
68 Mountjoy Square
Dublin 1
Tel: (353-1) 8740354
Fax: (353-1) 8720207

Published in US and Canada by
The Irish American Book Company
6309 Monarch Park Place
Niwot, Colorado 80503
USA

First published by Headline, 1990

British Library cataloguing in Publication Data
A catalogue record for this book is available from the British
Library.

Wolfhound Press receives financial assistance from the
Arts Council/ An Chomhairle Ealaíon, Dublin, Ireland.

ISBN 0 86327 648 2

10 9 8 7 6 5 4 3 2 1

Cover Design: Slick Fish Design
Cover Photograph: Slide File
Printed in Scotland by Caledonian Book Manufacturing

Acknowledgements

For permission to publish an extract from 'The Three Flowers' by Norman G. Reddin, I am indebted to Waltons, Dublin.

For their kindness and for procuring rare books from all over the world for me, I am indebted to the staff at my local library; and to the staff of the National Library of Ireland and all the other reference libraries in Dublin.

For endeavouring to help me in various ways, I am most grateful to John Larkin of the Public Records Office, Dublin; Fergus Gillespie of the Heraldic Office; and Dr Philomena Connolly and David Craig of the National Archives in Dublin Castle.

For their encouragement and advice I would like to thank Marie Ayee, Mary Keegan, Betty Kelly, David Roe, and Marie-Jo Milnes. Also, especially, a very warm thank-you to my husband Paul, who during the four years it took me to research and write this book gave me constant and invaluable assistance.

The bibliography at the end of the book lists only a small number of sources of reference, but I would like to acknowledge my debt to the works of two nineteenth-century historians, Dr R.R. Madden and Brother Luke Cullen of the Carmelite Monastery, Clondalkin, who sought, found, and interviewed some of the principal people who took part in the events.

Author's Note

Although presented here as a novel, and cloaked in the style of fiction, this story is a true one based on recorded fact. Most of the characters are taken from history, and all the chief episodes, as well as many minor ones, are based on documented evidence.

Letters from the National Archives in the Irish State Paper Office at Dublin Castle are reproduced herein by permission of the Director of the National Archives.

I have spread my dreams under your feet.
Tread softly . . .

W. B. Yeats

PROLOGUE
1778–1794

Chapter One

The cold weather and bitter winds that had frozen Dublin all winter were hardly noticed in the elegant Georgian mansion on St Stephen's Green. In every spacious and sumptuously furnished room fires were constantly attended by servants who ensured they blazed fiercely by day and smouldered redly at night.

Now it was mid-March, spring was on the wing, and the house was beginning to feel slightly overwarm.

In the drawing-room, the mistress of the house, Elizabeth Mason Emmet, stood alone by the fireplace, her eyes on the burning logs in the grate, her hand gripping the white marble mantel as another pain encircled her lower body. It was a pain she recognised like an old familiar adversary, a pain she knew well, for this was her seventeenth pregnancy in eighteen years of marriage.

A boy. She knew it would be another boy. The woman from the hills had told her so.

But would he live? That's what she wanted to know – would he *live*?

'Let him be born first,' the woman from the hills had said, 'then we will see and then we will say.'

Her eyes remained focused on the fire as she wondered what her husband would say if he knew she had consulted the woman from the hills. At best he would be deeply disappointed in her – at worst he would be utterly appalled.

So it was fortunate that he would never be troubled with the knowledge of her small lapse from good Protestant behaviour, for not one of the male servants knew her secret, only the housekeeper and the maids and, despite the common male view that a wild stallion could be harnessed more easily than a

3

female's tongue, in certain matters women could be relied upon to join forces and close ranks like one silent and secret army of sisterhood.

Most certainly they could.

She stirred her thoughts, then her body, and moved slowly away from the hot fire to the window. Although the pains had started there was still plenty of time. The midwife was already in residence, had been for five days, ready and waiting to carry out the duty which would pay her so well she would be able to keep her own brood in food for maybe three months.

The Emmets always paid their servants well.

She stood by the long window and looked on to St Stephen's Green, truly the stateliest square in Dublin. Really it was a park, a lush emerald-green park edged with trees and faced on all four sides by the red-brick town houses of the Protestant nobility and the Protestant rich.

How peaceful the Green looked, she thought. How utterly peaceful and untroubled it looked. If only the whole of Ireland could be as peaceful as St Stephen's Green. But that was impossible, that was a dream. For, beyond this affluent area, just a few miles from this very house, there was a different Ireland, a different world, a world where brutal oppression and dire poverty abounded. A world that had to be changed.

Another contraction gripped her body, sharper this time, squeezing the breath out of her. She realised suddenly, with the wisdom of experience, that there was not plenty of time after all.

She wiped the beads of sweat from her forehead and slowly turned her back on the window and the world outside that had to be changed. Only the imminent birth of a child could make a woman think such futile thoughts. What could a woman like her do about changing anything? She was not even expected to change the flannel napkins on her own baby. Indeed, no! The rules for a gentlewoman were firmly set down in three simple duties: to marry within her own class, to keep a good house and well-ordered servants, and to bear children.

And she had done all three, and would continue to do the last two to the best of her ability, only this time – if it was a boy, and if he lived – her child-bearing days would be ended. At the

4

age of forty-three, some might say, she was already over the age of decency to be giving birth.

So it was fortunate that she was never deeply troubled by what others might say.

After another gripping pain, a determined look came on her face and she moved across the long room towards the laborious task awaiting her, pausing momentarily to pull the bell-rope by the fireplace to summon the servants, then proceeded towards the door. Despite her bloated body she carried herself with a gracefulness that, if she had not actually been born with, had been bred into her from the day she could walk.

Elizabeth Mason Emmet was a lady of the highest class.

So thought the midwife as she pulled back the rose-scented sheets and helped 'Madam' to bed.

'Don't be afraid, madam,' she murmured gently, 'for I'll take very good care of you. Indeed I will. Now, do you wish me to . . . send for Dr Emmet?'

A spasm overtook Elizabeth Emmet. When she came out of it she smiled wanly at the midwife.

'You ask me that question every time, Mrs Nolan, and my answer is always the same. I have no need or desire for any male doctor, not even Dr Emmet, not when I have a very able and experienced woman like you to attend on me. I have every confidence in your wise and tender expertise.'

'I thank you kindly, madam, I surely do,' the midwife muttered, tears of gratitude glistening in her eyes, for it was no small honour to be called in to attend on the wife of the State Physician of Ireland.

But then Dr Emmet was a man, and Mrs Emmet was a lady, and no true lady would ever allow a man to witness her in the agonies of childbirth.

The child was already born when Dr Emmet came home a few hours later. A tall, dark man, forty-eight years of age, he listened calmly as Simmins, the butler, excitedly gave him the news, but his dark eyes sparkled.

He hurried up to his wife's bedroom and knocked on the door. It was opened by Mrs Simmins, the housekeeper, who dipped a curtsy and whispered gleefully: 'Praise God, sir, 'tis a boy!'

His wife was sitting up in bed, bright-eyed and flushed, the baby held unfashionably in her own arms and not in the arms of the nursemaid who stood beside the midwife.

'Beth . . .' he walked across the room towards the woman he adored and placed a kiss on her smiling face. Seconds later the door clicked behind the midwife, nursemaid, and housekeeper, who had scurried out.

'May I?' he asked.

She handed over the swaddled bundle, but instead of drooling over his new son Dr Emmet carefully opened the cashmere shawl and expertly examined the child's stomach and limbs, his hand cupping each ankle and bending each leg at the knee, all done so swiftly and gently the baby did not cry.

'He seems well,' he said, wrapping the baby up again.

'We are both well,' his wife said.

'Then it is a wonderful day,' he said softly, his eyes now carefully examining her face to ensure that her bright-eyed pinkness was indeed happiness and not the beginning of child-bed fever.

'Oh, Robert!' she said laughingly, 'can you never stop being the doctor?'

He smiled and looked down at his son. 'Now I can,' he said, touching the tiny cheek. 'What name shall he be called?'

When she made no reply he looked from the child's face to her face and saw a certain sadness had dulled her eyes.

'You have no need to ask that question,' she whispered, reaching to take the child back into her arms and pressing him into her as if fearing someone might snatch him away at any minute. 'His name shall be Robert . . . just like all the others.'

'Yes,' he said. He tried to say more, but felt a rush of tears to his eyes and a lump in his throat. His eyes spoke his tribute to her.

Out of the sixteen other children she had borne, thirteen had died within a few months of birth. Four of them had been named Robert.

Their first-born, Christopher Temple, was now a fine young man of seventeen; then two dead babies, before Thomas Addis, now fourteen and almost as tall as his brother. Of the seven who had died consecutively after that he could remember little, just babies, born healthy but dead soon after, until the miracle of little Mary-Anne who was still thriving at five, and who could yell louder and stronger than all the other babies put together.

Then his wife developed an obsession – to bear another boy, another Robert to take the place of the one who had died aged two months, another Robert to carry on her husband's name.

The next three babies had all been boys, all had been named Robert, and all had died days or weeks after birth.

Now here was a fifth Robert . . .

'Will he live?' the question rasped out from her.

'Beth . . .' he put his arms around both her and the child. 'I promise you that I will do everything within my power as a father and as a doctor to help the child to live and thrive.'

She nodded. Her eyes were on the child. She dared not look into her husband's face and show him her doubt, her uncertainty. He had done everything in his power as a father and as a doctor with all the others, but they had still died.

'Will he live?' she asked the woman from the hills the following night.

The woman had spent an age inspecting the boy, the crown of his head, the soles of his feet, the palms of his hands.

'What have you named him?' she asked, her eyes still on the child.

'Robert.'

'No other name?'

'No, just Robert . . . Robert Emmet.'

The woman drew her eyes away from the palm of the tiny hand she held in her own and looked at the mother of the child with cool blue eyes. She was not ancient and gnarled like most of the old crones who claimed to have the Celtic gift. She was young and dark and beautiful.

And as she had done on her previous visit, she spoke coolly and without excess of words.

'He will carry the name into manhood,' she said, then rose and swept out of the room.

Mrs Simmins, the housekeeper, rushed after her and propelled her towards the servants' door that led down the back staircase to the kitchens and the back door; for if Dr Emmet were only to catch a glimpse of this creature draped in amber beads and coloured ribbons plaited in her long hair flying loose to her shoulders, he would put two and two together to be sure.

Dr Emmet hadn't a clue as to what had lit up his wife so brightly when she later summoned him to her room and exclaimed joyously: 'Robert! I want you to write the boy's name in the family Bible – this very night. And tomorrow you may put his name down for Trinity.'

Before he could reply she added: 'And dearest, do see that the servants celebrate.'

She seemed strangely overexcited. He peered suspiciously into her face for signs of child-bed fever, but there were none. Again she laughed at his scrutiny. 'Perhaps it is well that you have taken the habit of looking at me with the eyes of a doctor, for if you were once to look at me with the discerning eyes of a stranger, and he a man, then you would see only the lined face of a matronly woman beyond her prime.'

It was true. She was no longer the pretty young woman he had once written passionate poems for, but she was still his wonderful Beth. He kissed her then, reverent and tender.

Later he appeared in the kitchen followed by his two sons, Christopher and Thomas, who in turn were followed by Simmins carrying a large silver tray on which stood half a dozen bottles of brandy for the men and the same in port for the females.

The servants were delighted to learn they were to drink the child's health – and wasn't it just like Dr Emmet to allow them to do so in their own domain, too! So many masters celebrated family events with their household servants by summoning them into a line in the drawing-room or hall, then stiffly standing by while all sipped a small half-glass of sherry in uncomfortable silence, before being ushered below stairs again as quickly as possible.

In every other household Dr Emmet's attitude towards his servants was considered at best somewhat eccentric, and at worst rather 'radical'; but who would dare openly to criticise the son of Rebecca Temple Emmet, descendant of Sir Thomas Temple, and kinswoman to Lord Temple who was now helping Mr Pitt to govern England.

Dr Emmet's two sons, Christopher and Thomas, were equally pleased to be allowed a whack below stairs. They seemed as relaxed down there as the servants, for neither boy was above having an occasional loll at the long kitchen table enjoying the Irish humour of the staff.

But only they could be totally at ease in the presence of the master and, realising as much, after five minutes Dr Emmet left the servants to it, pausing near the doorway to speak a few words to the midwife who was still in residence, two of her own children sitting on chairs beside her.

'Well, Mrs Nolan, what say you on the state of my wife and child?'

'I'd say both were well as could be, sir,' she cried, putting down her port and straightening her hat as she sprang to her swollen feet. 'Well as could be, I'm thinking.'

The doctor nodded. 'My wife has high praise for your skills.'

'I thank her kindly, sir, I surely do,' the midwife muttered, tears of gratitude glistening in her eyes. She sniffed loudly and straightened her hat again.

Dr Emmet looked at her thoughtfully, his eyes gentle and dark. It was a hard thing to believe now, that in his youth he had despised these lowly born Irish. He had even once shrugged, unconcerned, when he learned that one of his ancestral relatives on his mother's side, Sir William Temple, had been military chaplain to Cromwell. Now that knowledge shamed him to his very soul.

A light of memory filtered into Dr Emmet's mind as he made his way to the library, an unforgettable memory of a dashing young blade riding around his native Cork and thinking the world was his for the taking. And when in actions and in speech he had despised the lowly born Catholic Irish, there was nothing so very terrible about it, he was simply behaving in accordance with the expected standards of the time. The same standards that still prevailed today.

Six hundred years previously, at the time of King Henry II, his Emmet ancestors had come to Ireland from England. They had settled in Tipperary and had fared well, as the English always did in Ireland, for they were the cream of the world's people. But although generation after generation were born in

Ireland, living well off the rich Irish land, they still considered themselves English.

In truth, it had disturbed the Emmets slightly when Queen Elizabeth took a notion to send her army to Ireland to divide up various counties which were then given as gifts of gratitude to a number of her faithful lords. The Irish owners who had lived on their lands for centuries had been naturally furious at being turned out of their castles and country mansions and a number of small wars had followed. But the power of England had soon crushed them, and Lord Wicklow, Lord Meath, Lord Mayo, and Lord You-Name-It were soon reaping great financial harvests from the land they rarely even visited.

And the Emmets did think it somewhat immoral that the wealth reaped from that land was always invested in England while Ireland grew poorer and poorer. But still they clung proudly to their English origins and allegiance.

Until Cromwell came.

Dr Emmet's great-grandfather, a good Protestant and a devout Christian, had apparently wept in shame at what Cromwell had done in Ireland in the name of God and England. Thousands upon thousands of Irish Catholics slaughtered in their homes and fields. Thousands driven from their land which was then given as victory prizes to Roundhead soldiers. Thousands of babies and children put to death by swords when the fanatical Cromwell commanded: 'Kill the nits and there will be no lice!'

That had been the turning point for the Emmets; when Cromwell had come to Ireland on what he called his 'Divine Mission', holding a sword in one hand and a Bible high in the other as he ordered the extermination of the Irish people.

Oh, how the Devil must laugh in triumph when men kill and torture and basely degrade their fellow men, then declare they are doing it in the name of God! How the Devil must laugh, and laugh, and laugh!

It was then that the Emmets decided they owed some form of allegiance to the country they had lived in for five hundred years. Other members of their class felt the same, and within a generation many of the old Anglo families were acknowledging the fact that they were now Irish.

10

Of course, the status quo had to be maintained. The Protestants must remain on the upper floor of society and the Catholics below. And the old affection for England would remain; not even Cromwell could destroy that.

Dr Emmet suddenly recollected himself as he entered the library. So lost had he been in his thoughts that he had to stop and remember why he had come here. Ah yes! His beloved Beth wanted him to record the name of the new baby of the house.

He took the huge family Bible out of its case and sat down at the desk. As he leafed through the pages the history of his family lay before him; the marriage of his father Christopher Emmet to Rebecca Temple. The Emmets had sold their land in Tipperary by then and moved to Cork.

He leafed through the pages until he came to the newspaper announcement of his own marriage, dated 22 November 1760: Robert Emmet, Esq., of Cork, Doctor of Physics and member of the Royal Academy of Sciences at Montpelier in France; to Miss Elizabeth Mason of Kerry.

Like all the young blades at that time, it was fashionable, despite the fading memory of Cromwell, to despise the lower-born Irish. And he had gone along with his set; mimicking their bowed servility and stupid superstitious sayings, laughing at their ignorance without taking into account that England forbade them to be educated. He had only learned their language in order to throw an order to a servant, for most of the lower order in Cork spoke only Gaelic. A ridiculous language! Until you learned it, then discovered its form and beauty.

His new bride had been appalled at his attitude. She might be a Protestant she told him heatedly one night, but she was also *Irish*. And not only did she love Ireland she also loved the Irish people – 'Yes, I *do* mean the Catholics! To me they are people, poor downtrodden people, not jokes!'

He calmed her and cajoled her and thought her the sweetest and most loving girl ever born, even if she was a bit silly.

Perhaps he would have gone on despising them, too, had he not chosen to become a doctor. Naturally his healing powers were intended only for the members of his own class, until the evening that his wife made a very pointed suggestion: 'Physician, heal thyself.'

11

So, in love, he agreed to do a certain amount of *charity* work just to satisfy her. And then he saw the poverty, the suffering, the sheer hardness of life that for him would have been beyond endurance. In utter shame, then, had he recalled the days when he had stood nonchalantly back while other young blades had mocked these people, calling them filthy names then laughing uproariously when they kept touching their forelocks and apologising.

True, there were many who stood tall and refused to kowtow or apologise for what they were; young peasant men and women with bodies lean and strong from hard work and a contemptuous proudness in their posture and eye, and who always forgot to touch their forelocks when a gentleman of the ruling class rode by.

But he did not see them.

A doctor sees only the weak and defeated. He saw children die from starvation, women from poverty and men from the harshness of backbreaking exploitation. But it was the children that touched him most. It was the children that helped him discover his humanity, his soul.

Many he saved but many he lost. And every one that he lost he mourned, until he learned that a doctor must master such emotions, must come to hard terms with constant death. He saw lovely young women age rapidly before his eyes as baby after baby died. Sometimes he denied his own distress by secretly blaming them for their own misfortunes – convinced they had not followed his orders, not kept everything clean, not allowed fresh air to enter their miserable cottages.

Then he had watched his own babies die, and knew he could no longer blame the peasants for anything. For if the baby of a doctor, born into a life that provided every comfort – even to the administering of medicine with a sterilised silver spoon in his mouth – still died, then what chance had the poor lowly born Irish?

No one was to blame but the times they lived in, rampant with all kinds of sicknesses and diseases. But what few doctors there were were only available to the rich, and there were even fewer scientists. What was needed was more scientists prepared to devote their lives and talents to the invention of effective cures for the usual sicknesses that could take a newborn child as swiftly as a thief, not to mention the mass killers named tuberculosis, smallpox, and cholera.

He turned a page and his eyes rested on the tragic record of his own children:

Christopher Temple	born 1761	
Henry	born 1762	Died young
William	born 1763	Died young
Thomas Addis	born 1764	
A still-born child	born 1765	
Catherine	born 1766	Died young
James Mason	born 1767	Died young
Rebecca Harriet	born 1768	Died young
Anne	born 1769	Died young
Elizabeth	born 1770	Died young
John	born 1771	Died young
Robert	born 1772	Died young
Mary-Anne	born 1773	
Robert	born 1774	Died young
Robert	born 1776	Died young
Robert	born 1777	Died young

He lifted the quill, dipped it into the inkstand, and made the new entry.

Robert Emmet	born 1778

As he stared at the entry, the ink still black and wet, he hoped fervently that *this* time, with *this* Robert, those two terrible words would never have to be written against his name – Died young.

Chapter Two

On the beach at Sandymount on a summer afternoon in 1791, Robert Emmet and Richard Curran ran down the stretch of sand towards the sea. The lower parts of their slim young bodies were dressed in knee-breeches for, unlike the peasant lads, young boys of the gentry never swam in the Adam.

Robert was thirteen years and four months; just one month younger than Richard. He led the race towards the sea, looking over his shoulder and smiling with excitement, until he saw his friend lagging behind.

'What slows you, Richard?' he called.

'It's farther away than I thought,' Richard said in a voice that sounded regretful.

'You're not thinking of turning back are you?' Robert exclaimed when Richard slowed to a halt.

'Who? Me?' Richard stammered. 'No, no . . .'

'Then come on,' Robert said impatiently. 'It was you who said you could swim like a rockfish.'

He turned and sprinted on, splashing into the water and sending up gasps of delight as the cold salty water flared around his body. When it was deep enough, he fell forward and began to swim.

After a few minutes he halted his strokes, turned and looked at his comrade who was still standing near the water's edge, looking somewhat knock-kneed and nervous as he stared at the waves lapping at his ankles.

'You look nervous!' Robert said in surprise.

'I am not!' Richard cried. 'I'm not afraid of anything! The water's colder than I thought, that's all. I need to get used to the coldness. Is there any harm in that?' He glared indignantly at Robert, the nostrils of his nose expanding angrily.

Robert stood up in the water that reached his chest. 'It's fine and warm once you're in.'

'Are there any . . . jellyfish out there?'

'No.'

'Not that I'm frightened of jellyfish, you know,' Richard said quickly, 'but I'd loathe to be stung by one.' He looked down at

14

the water then, fearing his friend might think him a coward if he delayed any longer, took a number of tentative steps forward.

'Oh you devil, Emmet!' he cried in a thin pitch, jumping about and splashing frantically. 'The sea is alive with them!'

'Nonsense,' Robert laughed. 'That's seaweed you can feel. Anyway, most of you is wet now, so let's swim.'

Richard shuddered as he looked out at the treacherous ocean, panic whitening his face.

Robert stood watching him silently, water glistening on his black lashes. He had intelligent eyes of the darkest brown and his long hair hung in black streaks around his shoulders. Of the two, both dark in looks, he was the more slender, and much quieter in speech and manner.

'I *can* swim, you know,' Richard insisted. 'Like a rockfish, actually. The water is just rather cold . . .' Again he shivered as he glanced over the ocean, although the air was very warm.

Richard's blue eyes were smaller and lacked the gentle intelligence of Robert's eyes, but few people noticed, for Richard had taken to wearing an arrogant expression which dominated his whole face, especially when emphasised by his newly acquired habit of expanding his nostrils.

The two boys stood looking at each other. They had been friends for over two years, from the time they had left their family tutors to attend Samuel Whyte's famous preparatory school on Grafton Street – famous because Whyte had once declared Richard Brinsley Sheridan to be 'a most incorrigible dunce', and he was now a leading playwright and politician.

The situation was becoming intensely embarrassing. It was a great shock to Robert to discover that Richard couldn't swim. He looked beyond him to the beach, then suddenly pointed across the strand.

'There's a rock-pool back there, behind that large boulder. Shall we go and search for crabs?'

'Crabs? I love crabs!' Richard cried, then shot into a sprint back across the strand, relieved and delighted to be safe on dry land.

On a sand-dune guarding the boys' clothes, Lennard, one of the Emmets' servants, sat tee-heeing gleefully to himself. He had wagered himself a glass of poteen that the Curran boy couldn't swim like a rockfish or even a tiddler. Boasters were always only quarter what they said they were – and that's why he had slipped upstairs and filched two pairs of young Misther Robert's breeches then, instead of driving the two boys out to the Curran house at Rathfarnham, he had made a detour to a deserted part of Sandymount and wondered if the boys might like a swim.

Oh, it was funny! – the sight of young Curran's face, protesting they could not swim in their clothes, and definitely not in the rude; then the shock on him when the two pairs of extra breeches were thrown down.

Lennard tee-heed again, his shoulders jumping on his small body as he watched the boys running towards the rock-pool behind the boulder.

Lennard was the Emmets' gardener and odd-job man, a real jack of all trades, and a wiry little man of not more than five foot three inches high. No one had ever managed to find out how old he might be, so they hazarded a guess that he must be coming up to forty. His square face, red as a berry with bushy brown eyebrows, sported a thick bulb of a purpling nose which was usually poked in everyone's business.

He was playing solo with a pack of cards when the boys returned later, frowning at the cards laid before him on the sand. He looked up, then stared at the two in exaggerated astonishment.

'Back from yer swim already, are ye? Begor, but yiz are great swimmers and no mistake! One minute ye were at the water's edge and next I looked yiz were nowhere to be seen. Oh, bejabers, I sez to meself, they've swum out o'sight – faster than any rockfish. And right trouble I'll be in, sez I to meself, if they don't turn back afore they reach America.'

Richard flushed crimson, but Robert ignored the nonsensical little man, stripping off his wet breeches and changing back into his clothes.

Richard threw himself into the business of copying him, relieved that Lennard had not seen them abandon the sea for the rock-pool.

'America, I sez to meself, that's where they'll be heading, swimming like rockfish to America.'

America . . . Robert Emmet was sure that America was the

16

first word he ever learned, so often was it said in the nursery or any part of the house where the servants roamed. Even his parents spoke often about America.

America had won the Revolution.

And apparently the cheers from the servants' quarters in every house in Ireland had been heard above stairs when the news became a certainty back in 1783. In all the taverns ballads had been sung and toasts drunk to the glorious victories of Saratoga and Yorktown, for such a predominate role did the Irish Volunteers play in the American army, that Lord Mountjoy confessed in the British Parliament: 'We have lost America, through the Irish.'

'And no better country could yiz have swum to,' Lennard continued in mischievous cruelty, 'if 'tweren't for the ding-dong I'd've suffered when your fathers found out yiz had gone there instead of Rathfarnham. How far had yiz swum when ye decided to turn back?'

Richard suddenly found a snag of thread in the knee of his breeches and gave it all his attention, his head bent low. Even now he couldn't be sure if he had fooled Emmet at the water's edge, and the fact that Emmet was not answering the servant gave Richard no further clue. He wished now he had gone in further and made a bigger and longer splash of it, just so the servant would see. Servants were notorious gossips.

'Rot me if they don't come back, I sez to meself. What will I tell their fathers – 'cept I never knew they truly could swim like rockfishes and go so far so quick. One minute at the water's edge then out with me cards then *troth* – where are they? Where were ye?'

Still fingering the thread at his knee and head bent, Richard shot an upward glance at Emmet to see his reaction, and saw him staring thoughtfully out to sea as he buttoned his velvet waistcoat, completely ignoring the servant's chatter.

Richard felt a rush of gratitude. Emmet was a brick, actually, A solid brick of a friend. Of all his schoolfellows Emmet was the only one who did not make him feel intimidated. So many of his other schoolfellows possessed a subtle cruelty and a constant need to display the arrogance of the superior male. They had invoked in Richard a terror that he might be a coward, the most unmanly of all faults, yet Emmet never made him feel that he might be a coward, Emmet never made him feel uncomfortable in any way; he was the most understanding and reserved boy in prep school.

And there was the rub – why did the roosters not crow at Emmet? Why did they not taunt him for his gentle ways and shy smile and treat him so finely? What was it the roosters saw in him? He was sure he had never seen Emmet fiercely expanding his nostrils, so it couldn't be that.

Of course, when it came to mathematics the fellow was a ruddy genius, but then other swots excelled in other subjects and the roosters did not spare them . . . One poor fellow suffered the most constant jibing simply because his name was Vivian.

'Nay, not France, I sez to meself. They wouldn't be swimming to France, I sez. If they once landed in France and spoke in their lah-di-dah Irish voices, I sez, why, the Frenchies might think they were sons of some lord that rides around on the back of the poor. And then there'd be a right who's-yer-father I can tell ye.'

And it was then, as the servant's words sank in, and Richard straightened up, a sudden intelligence came into his eyes as he stared at Emmet.

His coat by his side, Emmet had sat down on the sand-dune and was gazing out to sea, leaning back on his elbows with one knee raised. As young as he was, his posture was so languid, so graceful, it contained that quality found only in true aristocrats and that class of society that never knew what it was to go short of anything.

By George! That was it! Why had he never thought it, for the roosters must have often thought of it – the Marquis of Buckingham, formerly known as Lord Temple, had twice been Viceroy of Ireland in the past ten years, the highest seat a man could hold in Ireland, and he was a kinsman of Robert Emmet's father, Dr Emmet.

Indeed, Richard's own father, who had worked his way up from rather lean beginnings in Cork to be the most sought-after lawyer in Dublin and who truly liked Dr Emmet, had nevertheless once said that it was a bald fact that Dr Emmet owed half the posts he held, including that of Governor of the Hospital for the Insane, as well as Physician to the Viceregal Lodge, purely to the patronage of his noble kinsman at Dublin Castle.

And that was why the roosters never crowed at Emmet, Richard decided grudgingly. A fellow didn't need flaring nostrils when he had the greater weapon of true *class* – O God! Would the fellow never shut up?

' 'Tis a simple question, I reckon, a fair question, and I've asked it more than once so why won't ye answer it – how far out to sea had yiz swum before ye decided to swim back when I was not looking? Was it the Head of Howth? Or was it that little island near there called Ireland's Eye?'

Richard glanced redly at Robert to see how he would respond.

Robert responded by continuing to ignore Lennard completely, rising to his feet and picking up his coat, then slapping a cloud of sand out of it and making sure a good part of it went in the little man's direction.

'Eh! Mind what yer doing!' Lennard cried angrily, starting to his feet and jumping about like a grasshopper. 'Ye've near blinded me!' He pawed at his eyes. 'By the hokey . . . isn't this a murky way to treat me after I bringing yiz out here so's ye could swim like rockfishes. And all I *asked*—'

'Oh, look there,' Richard cried, hoping to distract Lennard, 'look at that poor creature.'

'Eh?' Lennard turned his head and saw an old man bobbing towards them. He was tall but bent, with long white hair, and dressed in a medley of rags that were miraculously held together by yards of string lassoed around his body.

Young Emmet stared in disbelief. Never in his life had he seen such an unspeakable concoction of rags on a man. His long coat had obviously been bequeathed to him by a lifelong tramp; it contained so many patches that if he lay down on the street a child could play hopscotch on him.

'Faith, but he's in poor trim,' Lennard muttered.

The old man was almost level with them before he saw them on the sand-dune. He paused uncertainly, then stopped altogether and stood motionless, staring at them with his mouth open. His face was so emaciated his cheekbones stood out like sharp ridges.

19

When it seemed as if he might stand and stare at them for ever, Lennard blithely wished him, 'A long life to ye.'

The old man seemed to take heart from the greeting. He slowly held out his hand and said in a weak voice: 'Food?'

'Got none,' Lennard replied flatly.

'Food?'

'Got none,' Lennard repeated louder. 'We come for a swim not a picnic.'

'Food?'

'Have ye tried the Quakers up the road yonder? They'll likely give ye food. Lovely charitable people is the Quakers, even if they are a bit prim. But failing that, if ye nip round that big rock there, ye'll likely find some crabs.'

The old man began to babble and shiver. Then pulled in his hand and shuffled slowly away. The three of them watched him go.

'Did ye ever see such a sight,' Lennard murmured. 'I wonder what hole he dragged himself out of? Sure now, looking at him puts me in mind of all this talk I'm hearing in the taverns about Habeas Corpse. Mebbe that's him himself, wha'?'

'I feel sorry for the poor old beggar,' Richard said in genuine pity. He turned to Lennard. 'Don't you?'

'By the hokey, I don't,' Lennard declared. 'If ye want my honest opinion I think he should be shot.'

'Shot?' Richard looked aghast. 'But he's one of your own people!'

Lennard was not at all impressed at being reminded that he was one of the lower order.

'He should be shot,' he repeated with dignity. 'Dirty oul skunk with his hand out. 'Tis the likes o' him that brings disgrace on us. 'Tis the likes o' him that made that Englishman say he never knew what the English beggars did with their old discarded rags, until he came to Dublin. In all the papers it was, and can't ye hear the English laughing still? Dirty oul skunk going round like habeas corpse and bringing shame on us.' He turned his mouth sideways and spat on the ground emphatically. 'One of me own people? Who sez? 'Tis following the example of the people of America and France me own people 'ud be if they got the chance. Huh! Ye wouldn't catch me begging food like him.'

'Perhaps if he was as well fed as you, he wouldn't be caught begging food either,' young Emmet said quietly.

'Eh?' Lennard pitched his brows and peered into the dark eyes of his master's youngest son who was the same height as himself, then the meaning of the words sank in. He jumped back furiously.

'Oh, so ye've found yer tongue at last, have ye? And not content with near blinding me sightless with sand, now ye seek to insult me.' He hitched up his breeches and looked about him with an air of colossal outrage and injury. 'By the hokey! What next?'

'Come now, Lennard,' Richard said sternly, 'I'm sure Robert was only seeking to remind you of the charitable principle of "There but for the Grace of God go I".'

'A holy sermon is it now?' Lennard cried. 'O Gawney, I'm off!' He pivoted sharply on his heel.

The boys looked at each other, then shrugged and followed in his stomp, listening curiously as the little man dug his hands into his pockets and grumbled angrily, not quite to himself.

It soon became clear that his chief grievance was against Robert for taking the side of that begging oul habeas and not himself – a rare oul didley it was when a walking corpse, and a stranger at that, got more consideration than a true and devoted servant of one's own household, wha'? And as for the other one – preaching to him like a Protestant!

Just the thought of it let loose some terrible fury in Lennard that demanded to be relieved. So much so that when he reached the carriage and climbed up to his driver's bench, and after the boys had climbed inside, he twirled his whip like a gladiator preparing for vengeance.

Robert had just closed the carriage door behind him when the horses bolted forward in response to Lennard's lash, sending him toppling over Richard.

'Oh, the devil!' Richard exclaimed in shock, then hung on for dear life as they sped over the roads at breakneck speed with Lennard shouting at every horseman to 'Gesh outa the way of me chariot!'

Only when they reached the winding country road that led to the Currans' house at Rathfarnham, and the carriage slowed to a reasonable trot, did Richard find his voice again. Even then it came out on a croak.

'I say, Robert, the rascal should be f-f-flogged! He could have killed us.'

'You damn well might have killed us!' Robert fumed up to Lennard after springing out of the carriage.

'Me? Tried to kill ye?' Lennard was all innocence. 'And what gave ye a mad notion like that? Did I go a bit too fast for ye or something?' He sniffed blithely at the fear of young boys. 'Nay, ye can take it from me, Misther Robert, just as surely as me mother was married, I was going no faster than I thought I was. As I'm alive I was—'

'We will see how alive you are after my father hears about this. We will see how *employed* you are.'

'Eh?'

Lennard hadn't thought of that. All the pleasure of the drive seeped out of him.

O Gor-a-war . . . Lennard began to tremble with guilt as he thought of Dr Emmet who had always been so kind to him, and placed such trust in him to take good care of his youngest son.

When Dr Emmet finally spoke to Lennard about his youngest son, it was in the farthest region of the garden, late one evening. An hour earlier Lennard had fallen asleep under a tree after a succession of sleepless nights and even more slugs of poteen to get him through the days. But sharp as a fox, as soon as he heard footsteps, then saw his master, he sprang to his feet and pretended to be industriously weeding round the cherry tree by twilight.

But when he looked up warily the light was bright enough to see that the doctor's face wore an expression of deep disappointment.

Lennard was so terrified he missed the first few sentences, but when his brain cleared and the words began to sink in, he was equally mystified.

'He is too diffident, Lennard, too shy for a boy. I sometimes fear that if he remains so reserved in his personality, he will be unable to make his mark on the world.'

'Eh?'

22

From under bushy brows Lennard looked at his master with eyes slightly bloodshot. For days he had been waiting for Dr Emmet to lift his crop and make his mark on *him*. The anticipation of waiting for the ding-dong that would send him packing was driving him more and more to the secret solace of alcohol, not to mention all the mint leaves he had to chew to cover the smell of it.

'Did he tell ye, sir?' Lennard suddenly yelled, his nerves ready to snap. 'The waiting is slowly killing me. Sure I may as well get it over and be hanged now than spend another day jittering at the foot of the scaffold. Did he tell ye?'

'Tell me what?'

'About the day at Sandymount?'

'Sandymount . . . ? Oh yes, he did. Rather took it upon yourself, didn't you, Lennard? Landing the boys at the seaside of Sandymount instead of the countryside of Rathfarnham.'

'Eh?'

Lennard blinked in confusion. Dr Emmet didn't look at all annoyed. Hope sprang so suddenly in the servant's breast that he unwittingly broke all the rules of social and class etiquette and clutched wildly at Dr Emmet's arm.

'Did he not tell ye how I annoyed him and why he raged at me?'

'Raged at you?' A look of pure astonishment came on Dr Emmet's face as he deftly removed his arm from Lennard's grip. 'Then you must take it upon yourself to annoy him more often . . .'

Dr Emmet looked up at the darkening sky. The night was very clear and any clouds that hung were very white and very high.

'That is my complaint, you see, the boy is too diffident in every way. He lacks fire, he lacks vanity, he lacks any display of the courage that a man must possess if he is to survive in a man's world. Sometimes I even fear that he may remain too reserved to stand up for himself on a matter of principle – and that, God forbid, would mark him as a coward . . .'

He turned his head swiftly and looked at Lennard. 'What did you say, man? Robert *raged* at you?'

'With words spitting threats and eyes flashing fire,' Lennard said indignantly.

Dr Emmet smiled in an upwelling of good humour. 'Why, I

have never once heard Robert's voice raised higher than the polite. Why did he rage at you?'

'Why?' said Lennard startled. 'Why, why . . . Oh, ye mean *why?*' He stood blinking as he searched around him for an answer. Then the puzzlement in the doctor's question hit him with all the certainty of day following night – he hadn't squealed on him – young Misther Robert hadn't told his father the all of it – oh, the darling lad!

'Well?'

'Well, 'tis not my place to tell ye, Dr Emmet, not if he chose not to. But 'tis hard for a man to hold his laugh when young Misther Curran brags he can swim like a fish but when it comes to the test it turns out he meant millstone.'

'And Robert . . . ?'

'If ye want my opinion yer worrying unnecessarily about that lad, sir. He may be a shutmouth but at least he's not a squealer. Squealers is worse than cowards in my opinion.'

Dr Emmet frowned. 'Do you think he might have a tendency towards cowardice, Lennard? You seem to have taken to watching his every move. Be truthful with me now.'

'I don't know nothing about him being a coward, Dr Emmet, but I does know this: a quiet lad may grow up to be a quiet man, but a squealer grows up to be an *informer*.'

Dr Emmet hadn't a clue as to what squealers and informers had to do with the subject, but he did see some logic in Lennard's reasoning.

'You speak with some wisdom, Lennard. A caterpillar may change into a butterfly, but apart from a few exceptions, a loathsome child usually grows into a loathsome adult, unless he or she is checked in the process while growing. It is too late to wait until the bud has finally bloomed. Faults may be concealed by fine clothes and polished manners, but in the end the worth of the man comes through.'

'Young Misther Robert isn't lodesome,' Lennard said, his voice fired by a new loyalty. 'Not a bit lodesome in my opinion.'

'Indeed he is not.' Dr Emmet smiled warmly. 'He is the apple of his mother's eye. And, I must admit, in his schoolwork he shows the promise of excellence that Christopher had, the energy for study that Thomas had, but after that . . . I don't know what to think about the personality of the boy. I love him dearly, but I confess . . . I find him a total enigma.'

Once again Lennard had the impression Dr Emmet was talking to himself, but nevertheless, that was going too far – calling the boy names!

Lennard was a man capable of appalling cheek due to a lifelong possession of an awkward disposition and a mischievous nature. But sometimes his cheek was stirred by deeper emotions, and this was one of those times; for as devoted as he was to his master, he had a genuine affection for his master's youngest son, although he had never quite worked out why. The lad was unfathomable – a mystery – so how could he hammer the nail to it? But at least he could put up a few words in his defence when the lad's own father sank to calling him names. A total inigma, wha'? A fine tale that would be to tell to his pals in the card schools.

For one regretful moment Lennard wished fervently that he had not made that oath on the Bible never to disclose to anyone the private business or conversations of his employers.

'Ye asked me for the truth, Dr Emmet, and when it comes to speaking the truth about a person, ye know I'm not the sort to go behind a wall to say it. So now then, if ye want my opinion, 'tis the gentry is to blame and no one but the gentry.'

Dr Emmet's head shot up from the depth of his thoughts. 'Gentry? What are you talking about, man? The gentry are to blame for what?'

Everything, in Lennard's opinion, the robbery of Ireland for a start, but he managed to stick to the subject he had started.

'They want it both ways, the gentry, and I mean no offence to yerself, Dr Emmet, fine and decent gentleman that ye are, but 'tis a rare oul confusion when a child is banished to a nursery for years at top of a house so he won't disturb the peace, then when he's let down to eat with the grown-ups, what happens then? Why, he's told he must only speak when spoken to, and never interrupt his elders' conversation. How many times have I heard it in that house there, by that nanny of a nursemaid that's gone now: "Children should be seen and not heard. Children should be seen and not heard." Troth, 'tis a wonder they don't grow up dumb! Then when they do grow up to a reasonable size, what happens then? Why, they're expected to turn into blathering orators overnight. A rare oul confusion in my opinion.'

Dr Emmet had listened, half annoyed and half amused, but now he had heard enough. Lennard's audacity he had long been used to, and only tolerated it because of the man's incredible loyalty. His devotion to the Emmet family as a whole had always been staunch and, of all the servants, if a secret had to be entrusted to one of them, Lennard was the man to keep it safe, despite his non-stop chatter and incessant opinions.

'Yes, well, perhaps it is time we said goodnight, Lennard. I have a feeling we have both overstepped our boundaries and said too much already.'

Lennard shrugged. 'Sure, where's the harm, Dr Emmet? Ye know nothing ye ever say to me will go further than me own ear'oles.'

Dr Emmet nodded and turned away, then after a few steps paused and withdrew something from his pocket. 'Here, I almost forgot to pass these on to you.'

'Oh, be Janey!' Lennard wiped his hands on his breeches then took the packet of expensive playing cards. 'Thank ye, Dr Emmet, the boys will be delirious. Only last week Ha'penny Hallett asked me if you'd given me another pack lately.'

Dr Emmet was already walking away. Lennard watched him go with a mixture of relief and affection. Relief because his job was safe, and affection because of the pack of cards. The gentry never used playing cards more than once or twice before opening a clean pack, then the second-hand pack was usually given to the butler and valet. But Dr Emmet always shared this perk with Lennard as well as Simmins. Aye, a lot more perks, too. Simmins was not the only one who had the occasional unwanted Christmas gift passed on to him by the master, if he only but knew it.

But then very few people knew of the *real* charity of the Emmets, which went far beyond the passing on of gifts and playing cards. In Tipperary, whence Lennard originated, Dr Emmet still owned some small parcels of lands in Raheen, Crossoel, and Boherorow, from which he exacted a minimal rent from the tenants and out of which he always helped the most distressed of the poor by the payment twice yearly of one guinea each to thirty families.

And the doctor was not the only Emmet with a kind heart. His son Thomas Addis had a few years ago inherited other land in Kerry belonging to his mother's people, the Masons, who were of the first rank in the county; and he was even more generous with his bounty, not only giving the same regular twice-yearly payments to the poor families of the countryside, but also starting a number of secret charities for the relief of the poor people of the town of Tralee itself, a town he felt a special affection for, simply because his mother had grown up there.

Lennard then began to think of his own bounty – the one he would surely win at his next game of cards. He tee-heed to himself and shoved the pack of playing cards in one pocket of his coat and withdrew a flask of poteen from the other. Then, after a deep gulp, he wiped his mouth, tee-heed again, and began to sing to himself.

'Sez the Queen to the Jack yer only a knave, so give me the diamonds and ye keep the spades . . .'

Dr Emmet was not feeling quite so happy. Something in Lennard's words had prodded a blister of guilt in him. He had always considered himself to be a kind and loving parent, but perhaps . . . perhaps he had neglected young Robert without realising it . . . But when a wondrous light beams brightly before a man's eyes, he is apt to be blind to those standing quietly in the shadows.

The light that had blinded Dr Emmet for so many years was a brilliant young lawyer, his first-born son Christopher Temple Emmet. At the age of only eighteen he had been called to the Irish Bar, and within a very short time proved himself to be one of the most eloquent speakers ever to stand in the Four Courts, Ireland's Hall of Justice.

The Emmets were generally regarded as 'Castle people', part of the elite clique favoured by the masters at Dublin Castle, the seat of English rule. But it was through no string-pulling that, by the very young age of twenty-five, Christopher Temple Emmet had already taken silk and become King's Counsel. His knowledge of all the intricacies of the law was so superb, some predicted he might even surpass John Philpot Curran as Ireland's leading lawyer.

He was clearly destined for high judicial office, until he began to show signs of rebellious tendencies, openly confronting many of the ignorant and prejudiced judges who were not averse to letting the occasional piece of evidence, which would prove a defendant's innocence, slip by unnoticed when a humble peasant stood in the dock.

He further shocked the establishment, but earned the applause of his delighted father, when he wrote an allegorical poem entitled *The Decree* and dedicated it to his kinsman the Earl of Buckingham, in which he warned that the future eminence of England would be tarnished and imperilled if she did not abolish those penal laws still suffered by the Irish Catholics.

Dr Emmet had been so proud of Christopher, so proud; then tragedy struck without warning – during a trip to Munster to represent a client Christopher Emmet suddenly collapsed in sickness and five days later he was dead.

Smallpox! When it struck the results were always unpredictable. A poor child might survive it but a strong young man of twenty-seven, overly fatigued by a mountain of work, could die.

Smallpox! If only an effective vaccine could be found for it.

Many had been surprised at the quiet and dignified way Dr Emmet had taken the death of his eldest son, but he had long mastered the unreadable face a doctor must present to the world in the face of death.

Then the second blow had struck.

His second son, Thomas Addis, had been the hope of his heart. While Christopher had been enthralling the legal fraternity, Thomas had been studying medicine at Trinity. After taking his degree, he went to Edinburgh University and secured his MD. And it was while Dr Emmet was basking in the thrill of his son following in his footsteps and becoming a fully trained doctor, and while Thomas was in France furthering his medical studies, that Christopher died.

Thomas had rushed home. He grieved in private with his

parents, but seemed to prefer to spend most of his days in the company of his younger brother Robert whom he had always adored, despite or because of the fourteen years' difference in their ages.

Then Thomas had faced his father with the truth he had kept buried in his heart for years.

'I don't want to be a doctor, Father. I want to be a lawyer.'

'You . . . want to follow in Christopher's footsteps . . . and not mine?'

Dr Emmet could not believe it.

'I don't want to follow in anyone's footsteps, I want to tread my *own* path! I have always wanted to be a lawyer, from as far back as I can remember. But before I could tell you, Christopher had already put his name down for that role in the Emmet family. It was my love for him that prevented me from speaking my true feelings about my desired career. And it was my love for you that made me choose the alternative career of medicine.'

And it was Dr Emmet's love for his son Thomas that had made him accept the news with grace and eventually give him his blessing. Although he felt it necessary to warn: 'You will never outshine your brother at the Bar. You do realise that.'

Thomas had stood there, a tall young man of six foot, as fair as his mother and twenty-five years old. The glow of the candelabrum on the desk had shown up his lean, overstrained face as he looked back at his father with his mother's gentle but determined blue eyes.

'I have no ambition to try and outshine Christopher, believe me, Father. I just want to become a lawyer, and a good one.'

And he had done just that. He went back to Trinity and after only one year sat for his degree of LLB and achieved it; evidence that medicine was not the only subject he had studied in former years. From there he went to the Middle Temple in London where he met another young Irishman also studying law, named Theobald Wolfe Tone. They became the very best of friends, and eventually returned to Dublin together – where Thomas Emmet proved himself a very able lawyer and not at all the disappointment everyone expected.

He had none of the oratorical powers of his brother, all

admitted, but his steady, relentless argument was almost as effective.

And now he was betrothed to be married to a pretty young lady of eighteen named Jane Patten, niece of the Governor of the Bank of Ireland.

Dr Emmet had been pleased that Thomas had done so well and, indeed, that he had found such a charming and lovely girl to marry in what was clearly a love-match, but the thought of Thomas leaving the family home after so recently coming back to it saddened him. Until he came up with an idea.

The house on St Stephen's Green was so big, with so many rooms, that both Thomas and Jane agreed they would be very happy to live there after their marriage in the forthcoming spring of 1792.

So now, in the summer of 1791, Dr Emmet had finally turned his fatherly attention to thirteen-year-old Robert, only to discover that Robert was already beyond his influence or moulding. While all his attention had been focused on his two elder sons and no one else, Robert Emmet junior had been quietly growing into a self-contained and self-reliant young boy. But Dr Emmet, for all his mature wisdom, could not see that.

Dr Emmet had never seen the adoration or the plea for recognition in the large brown eyes of the little boy sitting beside his grown-up brothers. His glance had passed over the boy as quickly as it did Mary-Anne, for Mary-Anne was a girl and therefore her mother's domain.

By the time his eyes were ready to rest with interest on his youngest son, the plea for recognition in the brown eyes was gone, although a great deal of love was still there, if not adoration.

But Dr Emmet was not looking for adoration, he was looking for something else, and what he saw disappointed him; for all he saw when he looked at Robert Emmet junior, was a boy with a face that radiated kindliness and gentleness, and the mildness of manner of the very shy.

Poor qualities for a male. Hardly the stuff to make a man respected by other men in a man's world. But now Lennard said the boy had *raged* at him.

Dr Emmet brooded a minute.

Then he smiled. He didn't believe a word of it. For all his loyalty, Lennard possessed a capacity for colossal exaggeration.

'Don't ye care that yer father's greatly disappointed in ye! 'Tis true, only a few weeks ago he comes to me, and not a word of a lie – he was almost crying his eyes out with the shame of it.'

Robert didn't believe a word of it, and laughed. He looked up from his book at Lennard. 'The shame of what?'

Lennard stared at him wearily. For weeks he had followed the lad around to the point of persecution, endeavouring to bring him out of himself and make him talk more; for since his conversation with Dr Emmet he now considered it his true occupation and paid calling.

'Have ye not been listening to me at all? The shame of you being as quiet as a girl and not talking like a man.'

Robert leaned back on the garden bench and looked thoughtfully at Lennard. 'Is that what makes a man, then? The constant loudness of his voice?'

Lennard nodded emphatically. ' 'Tis the law of the jungle. 'Tis only when ye hear the roar of the lion can ye be certain that yer looking at the king of the beasts.'

'Then perhaps I am in the wrong jungle,' Robert said. 'In the eastern jungles of Siam, the Buddhists believe that hurried actions and loud chatter are the ways of monkeys, not men.'

Lennard sniggered. 'Troth, Misther Robert, but ye will have yer jest. Now why don't ye jest like that with yer father now and again?'

Robert looked at him seriously. 'I was not jesting.'

'Well there ye go, that's what's wrong with ye.' Lennard wiped a hand across his face and sat down on the bench, then spent some moments looking about him with an air of despair. ' 'Tis like I sez to Simmins the other day, 'tis not that the lad's stupid or anything, I sez, far from it, I sez, 'tis just that he's an old woman's child.'

Robert glanced at him darkly, but Lennard was miles away in thought.

'And an *only* child, too – if ye consider the fact that the others were old enough to be thrashing corn when he was only born. But now then . . .'

31

He turned to find Robert had vacated the bench and was strolling across the garden, still reading his book.

For a thoughtful moment Lennard watched him.

He wore a white frilled shirt and rust-coloured suit of well-cut breeches and coat. His long black hair was caught back at the nape with a black silk ribbon and the buckles on his shoes were silver. And all hand-picked for him by a mother who doted on him as if he were her last and favourite child.

Lennard jumped up and scurried forward to continue his mission, and fell into step with the lad who ignored him. His fidgety temperament and wiry little body had not been designed by nature for strolling languorously around a lawn, but he clasped his hands behind his back and attempted the posture which did not blend at all well with his bandy-legged gait.

From under his bushy brows he peered sideways at the book Robert was reading. 'Into the French again, I see,' he remarked blithely.

'Latin,' Robert corrected.

'Oh.' Lennard peered again. 'So it is.'

The funeral pace continued for some minutes, until Robert glanced round irritably. 'Well?'

'I was just thinking,' Lennard piped up. 'Isn't it funny that I'm the Catholic and don't know a word of Latin, and yer the Protestant and read it as well as a priest.'

Robert looked at him with interested dark eyes. 'Would you like to learn Latin?'

'Indeed I wouldn't!' Lennard was about to cry – but then, on second thoughts, it might do his image a power of respect in the taverns and card schools if he were to throw out the odd bit of Latin now and again.

'Well, if 'tis offering to teach me ye are, I reckon I wouldn't mind learning a word or two here and there. Just a word or two though,' he added quickly. 'Until I see how the Latin rolls around me tongue.'

'We will start with just one word shall we?' Robert suggested. 'I have an easy one here that I think will suit you very well.'

'Aye?' Lennard said, grinning eagerly. 'What is it then? Say it slow.'

32

Robert said the word slowly.

'Igno – ram – us.'

Lennard repeated the syllables with the same slowness, blinked, then jumped back furiously.

'The Divil damn me brogues if that's not an Irish word! And every *ignoramus* in Dublin knows it!'

Robert smiled, and left him alone with his fury.

Chapter Three

Round the dining-table in the house on the Green, one spring evening in 1792, two guests had joined the family for supper: Theobald Wolfe Tone and Thomas Russell.

The soup, the fish, the meat, and the sweet dishes were over, so Mrs Emmet and nineteen-year-old Mary-Anne withdrew and left the men to enjoy their brandy and port.

Thomas Russell, a young army captain formerly stationed in Belfast, was a little disappointed when Mary-Anne left the room, for she was a dark and pretty girl who betrayed a great deal of intelligence in her conversation, something he found rather novel; most young ladies of the gentry were advised that the display of intellect could only be considered a handicap if they ever wished to infatuate a man into a husband.

A butler brought a tray of long-pipes and a dish of tobacco to the table, but none of the young men smoked, preferring instead to apply themselves directly to the brandy.

From his seat at the head of the table Dr Emmet was looking with silent interest at the two guests. Thomas Russell was over six feet in height with a face of exemplary handsomeness, dark regular features, and a head of natural black curls. At twenty-three he already had five years' foreign service behind him, and was reputed to have admirable military talents, but his manner was reserved and courteous.

Theobald Wolfe Tone, on the other hand, had a witty and boyish directness which endeared him to most men he met. Eloquent, reckless, and impatient, he had an overflowing sense of humour that could be as scathing as it was amusing. But at heart he was a serious and sincere young man of twenty-eight.

Dr Emmet turned his attention back to Russell who, although an intimate friend of his son Thomas, had never before dined at the house on St Stephen's Green. He then asked Tone, whom he knew well, how he and Russell had become acquainted?

Russell laughed at the memory, and Tone obliged the doctor by relating the incident just as it happened.

'My acquaintance with Russell here commenced with an argument in the gallery of the House of Commons. He was at that time enamoured with the Whigs, but I knew those gentlemen a little better than he. We were struck with each other – notwithstanding the difference in our opinions – and we agreed to dine together the next day in order to discuss the question further. Well, we met and we dined and we discovered that we liked each other the second day better than the first, and the third day better than the second, and every day since has increased our mutual esteem. And, I may add, he did not for long cherish his view of the Whigs.'

Russell smiled wickedly. 'Don't believe a word of it.'

'He is also a great fool and I have trouble to manage him,' Tone said in mock weariness, 'but he has promised to behave himself tonight.'

'And may I propose a toast, sir?' Russell politely asked Dr Emmet.

'Of course.'

Russell raised his glass. 'Gentlemen – to the Whigs!'

Amidst laughter the toast was drunk by everyone except Tone, who refused to be persuaded.

'And why, Mr Tone, do you resent the Whigs so?' Dr Emmet asked.

Tone shrugged. 'I don't resent them,' he said mildly. 'I simply do not hold enough respect for them to lift my glass to them. The Whigs may bleat on and on about the degraded state of Ireland, but all their cleverly worded outrage is nothing more than hot air from an overblown set of bagpipes.'

Russell tried not to laugh at Tone's description, but in the end his face collapsed.

The conversation moved on naturally to Irish politics, and Dr Emmet in general supported the younger men's radical views. How could he not? How could any *decent* man not feel outraged at the present state of Ireland.

In 1789 the Marquis of Buckingham had been succeeded as Viceroy of Ireland by Lord Westmorland, and from that time, and even before, session after session of the Irish Parliament conducted affairs in an atmosphere of appalling corruption.

In Ulster the Test Act, and the system of rack-renting brought in by Lord Downshire, was driving as many Presbyterians from their holdings as Catholics. Other landlords had followed Downshire's lead and year after year as the rents went up and up to an unreachable high, middlemen moved in and seized the farms on behalf of their masters and relet them to other farmers on shorter leases and at even higher rents. This, along with so many other inequitable policies suffered under the Anglo-Protestant administration, drove the Presbyterians – most of whose ancestors had fled Scotland due to English religious persecution – to look down on the native Catholics with a more sympathetic eye; and now Belfast was such a hotbed of political speeches demanding constitutional democracy, it had acquired the nickname of Little Boston.

But for the Catholics in the rest of Ireland the situation was even worse than that of the Presbyterians in the north. No Catholic farmer could earn more than a third of the value of his crops; and every Catholic farmer had to pay one tenth of his income for the maintenance of the Protestant church and clergy. From the little he had left in his pocket, he was forced to pay impossibly high taxes to a Parliament that did not represent him or his interests in any way, for no Catholic was allowed either to sit in Parliament or to be represented in Parliament.

'So, Mr Tone,' said Dr Emmet, 'you have told us your views on the Whigs, but what are your feelings about the Tory Prime Minister?'

'Pitt?' Tone smiled negligently. 'What can one say about young Mr Pitt?'

'They are calling him the Jesus Christ of Britain,' Russell said in an amazed tone. 'Yet they are sending the French to the Devil for their impiety.'

'The Tories have always believed that God is a Tory,' Thomas Emmet said wryly.

'In his own party and in his own country, William Pitt may be considered a political genius,' Tone said. 'And I don't begrudge him that. But he has never even seen the country of Ireland, and shows no desire to remedy the matter. It is not Pitt's policy on Ireland that is at fault, because he obviously has no policy on Ireland. England is Pitt's only concern. And while it remains so, Ireland is tucked away in some drawer in his desk until the day or decade when he finds time to give it his attention. Meanwhile the Irish are suffering like Jews under the rule of his own henchmen at the Castle.'

After a murmur of assent, Tone continued: 'It was our own statesman Henry Grattan, along with the Irish Volunteers, who finally compelled the relaxation of the Penal Laws – but that callous system was in force for over a century, reducing the great body of three million Catholics, morally speaking, below the beasts of the field. And who imposed and continued to sanction those horrible laws on the Irish people? The British Parliament. And now their lackeys in that brothel of corruption most charitably referred to as the Irish Parliament continue to wield the whip on the people they pretend to govern.'

Thomas Emmet agreed wholeheartedly as he refilled the glasses. 'Henry Grattan is still doing his best, but the Irish Parliament is a savage dog that has interbred with its own kind for too long. Grattan and his reformers will never win the fight. The powers of corruption are too great. Even now, those who formerly supported him are slowly and slyly being bought off with Castle money.'

'Then let us hope,' said Tone, 'that the United Irishmen can keep their eyes fixed openly and steadily on the noble goal ahead, and that the colour of the Castle's money will never make any of *us* cross-eyed.'

Dr Emmet could not help but smile. Theobald Wolfe Tone was the most honest of men, and therefore the most controversial and interesting. But he was obviously not a man who lived by words alone.

While still a student at Trinity, Tone had eloped with a young girl of sixteen. Now he had a young family to support from his earnings as a lawyer, which were not very high, due to his showing a great deal more interest in politics than law. He had been one of the first Protestants to join the Catholic Committee and that alone was enough to damn him in the eyes of the Castle-appointed judges on the bench.

Then, just a few months ago, Tone had formed the Society of United Irishmen with the aim of promoting political union between the oppressed Catholics and dissenting Protestants in order to achieve parliamentary reform. Thomas Emmet and Thomas Russell were among the founder members of the United Irishmen, whose publicly declared aim was to bring about 'an equal representation in Parliament of all the people of Ireland of every religious persuasion'.

The English executive at Dublin Castle and their employees in the Irish Parliament had laughed at this – until Tone wrote a widely publicised political pamphlet, entitled *A Review of the Conduct of the Administration*, that shook them to the tips of their silk-tasselled shoes.

We have lived to see an Administration commence and proceed in an uninterrupted career of the most wanton extravagance, the most impudent prostitution, and the most gross and *avowed* corruption; and without even an attempt to varnish over the rottenness of their proceedings, and in complete defiance of public censure, or public infamy.

And will the people of Ireland be thus governed? There is no more fatal delusion in politics, than to mistake a state of *lethargy* for a state of *rest*. The fermentation will begin. The people will not always be defied. They are slow to anger, but they are not the mule beast that will bear any burden provided their long ears be scratched, and provided they are indulged in the sole liberty of braying. They will see *who* they are that rule them with a rod of iron; and they will look among themselves for the remedy.

37

When once a government becomes contemptible in the public eye, its strongest pillar is shaken. Slavery in any shape is dreadful, but slavery to these men is adding insult to misery.

It was clear that Tone's legal career at the Bar would soon be over. Dr Emmet was sure of it. And Tone was too intelligent a man not to know it also. But if Tone felt any regret about this, he did not show it. His dedication to the cause of democracy seemed to mean more to him than any personal advancement in his career. And there was no hope of any halt put on his determination by his lovely young wife. From what Dr Emmet had seen, and from what his son Thomas had told him, young Matilda Tone supported her husband's views totally. And, if his career at the Bar were to suffer, Thomas was convinced that she would quite happily live in a mud hut on a hill with him if necessary.

'How is your young wife, Mr Tone?' Dr Emmet said suddenly. 'Her health was a little delicate when last I saw her.'

Tone smiled. 'She is as beautiful as an angel and as healthy. Thank you for your inquiry. Russell and I took her out to the seaside at Irishtown for a few days, and the three of us had a wonderful time.'

'We did indeed,' Russell confirmed, smiling. 'Even though we lived simply, and Tone and I were forced to help in the preparation and cooking of our meals.'

'They were delicious days,' Tone said dreamily. 'And my wife was the centre and soul of all. I scarcely know which of us loved her best; for her goodness of heart, her never-failing cheerfulness, her affection for all. Now she loves Russell like a brother, just as I do.'

The most honest of men, Dr Emmet thought again as Tone turned to Thomas Emmet and continued the cheerful tale of their seaside idyll, the afternoon walks, the discussions they had as they lay stretched on the grass, the ballads and poems each scribbled up for amusement after dinner.

'I wish you could have been with us,' Tone said to Thomas Emmet, 'then I could have wished for nothing more – my wife, my little children, and the two friends I esteem most on earth.'

Thomas Emmet smiled – he knew very well how much Tone esteemed himself and Russell. Since going to the Temple in London, he and Tone had been almost inseparable as friends, and when Russell came along, he simply completed the harmony. Each had a quality the other two lacked, and each served to fortify the three; and now there was no sacrifice that friendship could ask that one would not make for the other two. Their sentiments agreed exactly, though every discussion extended their views; but as their conversations always returned to the political, so they did again now, to matters relating to their own Society of United Irishmen, which had been established for the propagation of the principles and ideals to which they were all devoted.

At his place beside his brother, young Robert Emmet sat in absolute silence, his arms folded and his face showing no expression but for the concentrated interest of his dark eyes as he listened and watched Tone, Russell, and his brother.

He observed that all were Irish, all Protestants like himself, and all fired by one principle: that the vast majority of their countrymen should not continue to suffer under a system that was inconsistent with human dignity and the fundamental rights of man.

From a very early age Robert Emmet had acquired from his mother and father a deep love for Ireland. But it was firstly from his brother Thomas, and later from listening to Tone, that he acquired an understanding of the three-class system under which Ireland lived.

First – the Protestants, a small body of no more than 450,000, comprising the major part of the aristocracy, supported by England. Their own class, who controlled every appointment in the church, the army, the revenue, the law, as well as possession of the greatest part of the land and property.

Secondly – the Dissenters, a slightly larger body, who formed the main proportion of the middle ranks of the country, and who had settled mainly in the north.

And, lastly the Catholics, who were the Irish, properly so called, numbering over three million.

But amongst this third and lowest class were the descendants of the historic Irish families who had once owned the country, a fact they would never forget or allow to be forgotten, insomuch that it was a regular occurrence for a gentleman's labourer to leave to his son, by will, his master's estate.

When it came to their degradation, Robert had made his own inquiries and formed his own opinions. He had studied almost every page of Ireland's history. He had walked the streets dressed in clothes borrowed from a stableboy and seen for himself the slums reported to be 'the worst in the Western world'. His disguise had not fooled the urchins of the streets; they had known instantly that he was not one of them. They converged around him, half-starved and half-clothed, begging for money, begging for food, then drenching him with contemptuous insults. He had regarded them, too, with absolute silence, and they had eventually fallen away. Perhaps he had been saved from danger by the appearance of their mothers, proud but equally poor women, who first chastised them, then declared they would not allow their children to beg of anyone, not even a Castle spy dressed in the clothes of a stableboy.

Then, and only then, did the truth of the American Declaration of Thomas Jefferson, and the French Declaration of the Rights of Man, bring fire to his soul like a naphtha flame.

Men are born and continue free and equal in respect of their rights. And these natural and unalienable rights of man are liberty, equality, property, security, and the right to resist oppression.

'What say you, Robert?' Dr Emmet suddenly asked. 'Do you have any views on the evening's conversation?'

Seeing all eyes turned to him, Robert coloured slightly, then smiled in such a way that his father's heart sank in the certainty that the boy was going to mutter some shy response. He was fourteen; almost a man! And high time he learned to stop blushing like his sister!

Dr Emmet wearily lifted his brandy glass when Robert's calm and confident answer almost made him drop it.

'As the Dissenters in the north are fairly strong in their numbers and courage, and the Catholics in the south are even stronger in their numbers and misery, and if they were to forget their dissensions and discover their mutual interests, then I think Mr Tone is right when he suggests in his pamphlet that the Irish people should look at those who rule them with a rod of iron, and look for the remedy amongst themselves. Only I would change the last word to *ourselves*, for Protestant we may be, but after six hundred years I think we, too, are entitled to regard ourselves as Irish.'

Dr Emmet was speechless with shock, but Thomas Emmet did not look at all surprised as he smiled at his young brother. Tone and Russell were also smiling.

'By God,' said Tone in blunt honesty, raising his glass to Robert, 'it is penny plain that you, boy, behind that shy smile and disconcerting glint in your dark eyes, are a kindred spirit to myself!'

Lennard had also spent time in the company of a kindred spirit that night. The square was in sleepy darkness as he turned into the Green, but, as always when the drink was in him, he felt the urge to sing.

> 'On a stone wall outside O'Hara's hillside cabin,
> Sat a sweet maid with her red skirts aflappin'.
> And her long black hair – ablowin' in the wind.'

A window screeched open. From somewhere above he heard a rasping voice. 'Quiet, man! It's after one o'clock!'

'Eh?' Lennard glanced up.

'Stop that damnation singing!' the voice whispered harshly.

Lennard stood squinting up from window to window but could see no sign of a face. He looked down at the basement windows, then up again at the windows of the second and third storey of the house from which the voice had come, but not a mortal could he see. He blinked in confusion, then strained back his head to the fourth-floor windows where tutors and their ilk usually had their schoolrooms and bedrooms, but all were shut and black.

'Musha,' he declared in puzzlement, ' 'tis a voice with no head!'

'Sh-sh-sh!' The voice belonged to the head of a butler at one

41

of the higher fifth-floor smaller attic windows, which were set slightly back and beyond view. He rasped down irritably: 'The entire square is abed and asleep!'

'Where are ye? Show yerself, ye coward!' Lennard demanded, the drink as always giving him the courage of ten men. 'Air yer grievance like a man!'

After a short pause, he heard what sounded like a window closing again. He drew his sleeve across his eyes, blinked, shrugged, then sauntered on his incorrigible way, and started up another bit of a song.

> 'She was only forty-two, and very hard to please,
> Not a man could be found, to put her at her ease.'

By the time he reached the College of Surgeons he had regained his good humour when, sharp as a fox, he realised he was on home ground and clamped his mouth shut. Only a bridle lane separated the College of Surgeons from the Emmet house. He took a few steps forward and craned his neck, observing with satisfaction that the house was in darkness, before meandering down the lane towards the stables and his room above the coach house.

More than halfway down the lane, he paused to take a slug from his poteen flask, then looked leisurely over his shoulder towards the walled garden and the rear of the house – 'Eh?'

There was a light burning in one of the rooms on the third floor, in the ante-room of young Misther Robert's bedroom.

Lennard pulled a face, his bushy eyebrows dropping over his eyes like ragged curtains. Over the months he had developed a standing grievance against the master's youngest son, who always managed to win their many battles of words although he said the least.

He took another slug of poteen, then stood sucking his lips as he squinted towards the window.

'A rare oul time for him to be still up, wha?' he muttered suspiciously, then his brows shot up and his eyes became alive and happy with sudden wisdom. 'He's fallen asleep again reading one of them books of his.' He chuckled and continued down to the coachyard. 'And won't he feel stiff and sore and scratchy when he wakes up in the dark and cold and finds his fire and candle have gone out.'

It had been after nine when Robert reluctantly left Tone and the others in the dining-room, to go and study for his exams which were held quarterly. On the sheet-covered desk in the ante-room he spent the rest of the night experimenting with chemicals, becoming so engrossed that he did not realise he was falling back into his old habit of biting his nails every time he paused in thought before writing his notes on paper.

He was oblivious to the jovial departure of the guests, oblivious to the sounds of the family going to bed, unaware that the entire house had fallen asleep while he continued working. Science was a branch of undiscovered knowledge that fascinated him, a field of careful and systematic study, observations, tests and conclusions, which could change the world of medicine.

He might have worked on had he not been suddenly seized by violent stomach pains that doubled him over. They held him paralysed for some seconds, but no sooner had he got his breath back than the pains jolted him again, so intensely that the room went hazy. He put a hand out and clutched at the desk, then realised what was happening – while chewing his nails he had unconsciously swallowed traces of the chemical he had been handling.

Although quite aware of the danger he was in, it did not occur to him to wake his father, or to disturb anyone else in the house.

Quietly and quickly he made his way down to the library in search of his father's medical volumes. He swiftly ascertained that the one he needed was on the very top shelf of the floor-to-ceiling bookcase. He grabbed a chair and climbed up, gasping with the pain in his stomach as he tugged at the heavy volume. Carrying it down to the desk he located the section on poisons. Then he went to his father's small medicine room and found all he needed to make the antidote – except chalk.

He looked around him frantically. Where the damnation would he find chalk?

Then he remembered that he had earlier that day seen

Lennard using chalk in the coach house. Grabbing up the lamp again, he stumbled out of the house and down through the back garden until he reached the gate that led out to the lane and the coach house. He knew the coach house would be locked at this hour, and groaned inwardly at the thought of Lennard's grumblings when he roused him for the key.

The coach house was unlocked, one of the wide doors hung open. He held the lamp high and moved forward cautiously, entering to find Lennard sprawled on a bale of hay.

'Eh?' Lennard raised his head and peered, then sat up with a bleary eye and took the straw out of his mouth.

'Why, Misther Robert, what are ye doing here-along? Why, I was only saying to meself just a while back how ye must be tucked all warm and cosy in yer bed. Ah, couldn't sleep and come to see yer old friend Lennard have ye? Well isn't that *handsome* of ye!'

Robert saw instantly that Lennard was happily drunk. 'Chalk?' he gasped. 'I came to find chalk.'

'Chalk?' Lennard sniggered. 'What d'ye want to do with chalk at this hour?'

Robert held up the lamp and began to search around. 'Where is the chalk that was here earlier?'

'Gesh along! 'Tis too late to be drawing with chalk. And 'tis too late for ye to be annoying a weary and overworked man who might be in his bed now but for the misfortune of falling over a bale of hay which I reckon someone must've moved deliberately—'

'Devil take you for a gossoon!' Robert snapped. 'Stop your geese-gabble and find me the chalk!'

'A gossoon?' Lennard cried, cut to the quick. 'Is it a gossoon ye'd be calling me now? Is it insulting me ye'd be again?' Furious and indignant he got to his feet and put his hat straight.

'What ails ye?' he said suddenly, taking his first good look at his master's son. 'Why are ye shivering and bending over like that? What's wrong with ye?'

'Corrosive sublimate poisoning,' Robert rasped. 'I was experimenting, and careless, and now it's burning like a fire in my stomach.'

44

The drink went dead in Lennard. He sobered instantly with fright.

'Chalk is part of the prophylactic for corrosive sublimate poisoning,' Robert whispered, closing his eyes in pain. 'Lennard . . .'

'Aye! Aye!' Lennard scurried to get the chalk. Two big slabs of it from a box at the back of the coach house. 'Will I come back with ye? Will I get yer father?'

'No, I'll be fine now. Don't disturb or say even a word about to this anyone.'

'But ye look in bad pain.' Lennard said in deep distress, 'and yer father after all is a doctor.'

'Not anyone,' Robert warned again, then slid away leaving Lennard in darkness.

Even half an hour after he had taken the antidote to neutralise the poison, the pains in his stomach were so violent that tears were shimmering in his eyes.

He looked around him. He needed something to divert his mind, concentrate his thoughts on something other than the pain, something demanding.

He removed all the chemical bottles and apparatus, put them neatly away in the wall cupboard, ripped the sheet off the leather-topped desk, then sat down to read a book on mathematics. He sat with both hands on his stomach as he studied the mathematical science of number, quantity, and space.

As butler and valet, Simmins's first job in the mornings was to send up the maids to stoke and build up the fires; when this had been attended to, he himself would march upstairs to brush and lay out his master's clothes in the dressing-room, then, having brought up hot water for him to wash, he knocked on the bedroom door and quietly informed him of the hour. This done, he moved on to do the same for Thomas and then Robert.

When the maid entered Robert's ante-room to attend the fire, she found him slumped in sleep at his desk.

Five minutes later Mrs Emmet rushed in followed by the maid. She bent over and placed a gentle hand on his shoulder.

'Robert, are you awake?' She spoke in that soft gentle voice

45

which the maid noted she reserved exclusively for her last and favourite child. 'Are you awake, darling?'

Slowly the eyelashes lifted and he looked at his mother's face, tight with worry.

'You have not been to bed, dear?'

'No.' He sat up and blinked.

'You look – are you ill?'

'No, Mamma, just tired.'

'Robert . . .' her voice was very soft, 'you know it is foolish to burn the candle at both ends. I want you to go straight to bed, dear.'

'No, I am well – and I have to go to school today,' he said suddenly, moving to his feet and standing upright as if testing his fitness.

'You *have* to go? Why do you have to go?'

'I'm down to play in the hurling match set for after first class.'

Seeing how unwell he looked, his mother was about to protest, but then she remembered how much he loved the hurling games.

'Then you will oblige me by coming straight home afterwards and forgoing the afternoon classes?'

He gave her his first 'Yes' of the morning and smiled at her. She did not smile back. She sighed softly and turned her face to the maid.

Dr Emmet could not believe what Lennard babbled out to him. 'Cosive something poisoning, sir. As I'm alive that's what he sez. He told me not to say nothing to nobody, but, sure, he's only a boy, and all the livelong night I've been awake and edgy thinking o' him.'

'Corrosive sublimate poisoning? Good God, man, the pains would have been excruciating. Are you sure you are not exaggerating again?'

'Who, sir? Me? Exaggerate? Why, I've never exaggerated in me life!'

There were footsteps in the hall and Robert came into the morning-room freshly washed and fully dressed. He carried a great sheaf of papers which he placed in a leather bag that sat on a chair near the door.

46

He looked round and saw his father and Lennard staring at him. Robert looked back at them with eyes large and dark from a face drawn and yellow.

Dr Emmet did not need to ask if it was true. When Lennard had been ordered out of the room he asked his son quietly: 'Why did you not rouse me as soon as you realised what was amiss?'

After a short hesitation, Robert answered truthfully that it never occurred to him to wake anyone at that time of night.

'Did you not think it quite justifiable, whatever the hour, to rouse myself or even a servant on a matter concerning your health and comfort?'

'No, sir.'

'Good grief, boy! Why?' Dr Emmet's voice was getting high with frustration. 'Was your reasoning based on pride or humility?'

'Neither,' Robert replied. 'It was a disaster caused by myself alone, and affected myself alone, and I knew that if I took the prophylactic quickly I would suffer no greater ill than discomfort.'

At fourteen Robert was as big a mystery to his father as he had been at thirteen, but now Dr Emmet was discovering something new. The boy had courage.

He looked at his son's face, drawn and yellow, and imagined how dreadful the pains must have been. 'You're my son, Robert,' he said wearily, 'but there's no knowing you. Sometimes I think a man could live in the same house with you, the same room even, for years, and never discover what you thought about yourself at all.'

When Robert made no answer, he persisted the point, his eyes hurt and puzzled. 'Why do I feel I don't know you at all? Why did you not come to me last night? Why do you never *confide* in me?'

Robert looked at him in amazement, as if the answer was obvious. 'Because you have never invited me to confide in you.'

'What?' His father stared at him, stung. 'By the heavens!' he roared. 'Are you accusing *me* of being at fault?'

'No, sir, but I don't see how you can expect to know me to any intimate degree when I have spent the most part of my growing years without your guidance and without your notice.'

47

His father just stared at him again, unable to believe the matter-of-fact calmness of the words when his own emotions were so deeply disturbed; for only now did he truly understand the reason for the boy's self-reliance, and why he had simply and quietly got on with his own life and studies.

He turned away and walked over to the sideboard, lifted a silver lid and pretended to busy himself at the dish of fried kidneys.

'Boldness,' he said, 'boldness last night with Tone, boldness in your sickness, and more boldness with me now ... And I always thought your quiet diffidence was based on weakness, boy, may I be hanged for a fool.'

Robert looked curiously at his father's back, for there was a strange catch in his voice of which he could not be sure the cause; was it laughter, or was it anger?

It was neither.

When Dr Emmet turned round his face wore the impenetrable expression which he had developed over years of constant practice.

'What time was it, do you know, when you were seized with the pains?'

'I can't recall, sir.'

'Might you still have been at your studies at midnight?'

Robert looked vague. 'I have no idea of what the time might have been. My clock is in my bedroom.'

'You did not pause to go and check the lateness of the hour?'

'No, sir.'

'Then perhaps you had better have this,' Dr Emmet said, unlooping his fob-watch as he walked across the room.

Robert stared at the watch his father held out to him. It was of the purest gold, intricately engraved, with the second dots consisting of minuscule rubies. It had been presented to his father only two years before, by his colleagues at the College of Surgeons and Physicians after he had written an excellent treatise on gynaecology.

'Come, take it, my son. It might help you keep pace with the time and hopefully get you to bed at a more respectable hour.'

Robert couldn't take it. It was too valuable, and too precious to his father who had beamed with pride on the night he had received it.

'I thought . . . I thought I once heard you say it would be bequeathed to Thomas in your will.'

'Well, I have changed my mind, and decided to give it to you. It should go to you, after all – see, it is inscribed with the name *Robert Emmet*. And that is your name, is it not, as well as mine.'

Robert was overcome with confusion. 'But . . . why give it to me now? And not later, as a bequest?'

Dr Emmet smiled sadly, his eyes liquid and dark with emotion. 'You're my son, Robert, and anything I can give to you, I would like to give to you now. Maybe I just reason that a gift from a living father might express more love than a bequest from a cold corpse who needs it no longer.'

And with those words Robert understood the desperate plea in his father's eyes as he silently urged him to take the watch. It was a plea to be forgiven, if not loved.

And so unnecessary, for he had always loved his father, in his own quiet and undemonstrative way, always.

He reached out to take the watch and, as it passed from hand to hand, he knew that he and his father had come together at last.

Chapter Four

The Glen of Imaal lies high in the Wicklow Mountains. A lush and large valley of green pine forests, golden cornfields, and clear mountain springs. It was May 1792. Maytime of the lark song and white hawthorn blossom that smothered the hedgerows along every country lane and hilly path.

Inside the Dwyers' farmhouse at Eadstown, in the west of Imaal, Anne Devlin and her cousin Cathy Dwyer crouched on the hearthmat hissing at a big black buck cat that was renowned for disliking females of the human kind.

'S-s-s-s-s-s-s!' Anne hissed, her own hair as black and her eyes as green as the cat's.

The big buck cat sat with his paws drawn under him, looking straight into the flames of the fire as if the two girls did not even exist.

'S-s-s-s-s-s!' Anne hissed, her small white teeth showing aggressively.

The buck cat merely slanted her a contemptuous glance, then turned his eyes back to the flames of the fire.

'Where did you get this vain thing?' Anne snapped at Cathy.

'Michael bought him in exchange for a hen,' Cathy said. 'And Michael is the only one he shows any respect to.'

' 'Tis a well-known fact that female cats is the best,' Anne said authoritatively. 'Why did he choose a buck?'

Cathy shrugged. 'All Michael's animals are bucks. And he reckons this cat has already been chosen by all the other cats in the glen as their king.'

Anne opened her mouth to laugh, but Cathy insisted wide-eyed. ' 'Tis true! Michael says that every so often cats hold a meeting to choose their king, and the one they choose stays their king until he dies in battle. But he says this one will never be beaten in battle.'

'S-s-s-s-s-s!' Anne hissed challengingly at the buck cat who did not blink an eye.

'He don't seem that fierce to me,' Anne said dismissively.

'That's what you say now – but just ye wait till you hear him hiss and snarl and see him spring to his feet with his back high and his tail standing as stiff as the handle on a shovel.'

'And when does he do that?'

Cathy let her eyelashes fall down over her narrowed eyes in the same way her brother Michael had done when she had asked the same question, and answered in the same quiet and slow way he had. 'When he hears the sound of a rat, or the call of other cats on the wind, or when . . . the moon's riding high.'

'God save us!' Anne stared at her cousin with eyes like saucers, then slowly turned her gaze to the black buck cat that had to be the biggest in Ireland, still sitting motionless with paws drawn under him and staring into the red depths of the fire.

'What is he thinking?' she whispered. 'Sitting there staring into the flames. Begor, but to look at him you would think he knew all the dark secrets of the world and was content to sit dwelling on them.'

'Aye,' Cathy whispered. 'And Michael says when this black cat strolls out at night along the lanes of Imaal, he is without a doubt the king of all the buck cats and the hero of all the she cats.'

'Indeed.' Anne was staring with a new respect at the black buck, for if Michael said all that, then it must be true.

'But he won't court no scrawny or screaming vicious type of she cat,' Cathy added seriously. 'Michael says this cat likes his females soft and gentle and purring like a kitten, just like any buck would.'

'We have to be going, Anne,' Mrs Devlin called from her seat at the table in the centre of the room.

'Going?' Anne's head shot round. She stared at her mother, then at her Aunt Maíre. 'Can't we stay a while longer?'

Mrs Dwyer smiled at her niece. 'And risk being stopped by the militia on the long journey back across Wicklow? Nay, alannah, 'tis best you reach home afore dusk.'

Anne took a deep breath, then another, her eyes frantic as she tried to think of some ruse to delay longer. She wondered if she should pretend stomach cramps, or maybe flop down in a dead faint?

Before she could decide which, her mother said again that it was indeed surely time to be making the journey back across Wicklow to Croneybeag, and Anne did neither. She simply jumped up and sped out of the house on twelve-year-old legs that moved as swiftly as a setter's.

She fled across the farmyard and up the bohereen away from the house and the homing fields and the acres planted with barley and corn, until she reached the open sheep pastures. Clutching her skirts to her knees she ran as eagerly as a hound after a fox until she reached uncultivated ground filled with the scent of the yellow gorse and purple heather on the mountains.

When she thought her legs were about to give way and wouldn't take her much further, she paused and looked down in horror at her Sunday-best shoes all scuffed. 'Holy St Patrick!' she whispered, then instantly forgot her shoes as she looked up and saw a young man with black curling hair

51

strolling down on the road, his hurley bat over his shoulder, whistling to himself as usual as he mused the journey homewards.

'Michael!'

He glanced up, stopped whistling, and watched her with cool hazel eyes as she ran down the hill. His expression remained cool and wary as she slipped over the stone wall and panted up to him.

'What's wrong?' he asked.

'I was afeared I'd miss you,' she gasped.

He stared at her. 'Is that all? Nobody sick? Nobody seriously injured? Nobody dead?'

'On with you!' she smiled impishly up at him. 'We've been hours at your house and I was afeared I'd miss you betwixt us leaving and you coming back from the hurley game.'

'And that's why you came running so far abroad? Just to see me for the fun of it?'

'Just for the fun of it!' she confirmed stoutly. 'Did Wicklow win the hurley game?'

He cracked a sunny smile. 'Aye, we did. We beat Kildare handsomely.'

Anne looked up at him with devoted eyes. Michael Dwyer was the eldest of the Dwyers' seven children, her first cousin, and at eighteen he was her very ideal of a man. He was tall, five foot eleven inches high, with a body strong and lean from hard labour. But what Anne liked about him most was his cheerful and fearless disposition.

'Was Hugh Vesty in the game?' she asked as they strolled on.

'He was. And playing like a hero.'

Anne smiled proudly. Hugh Vesty Byrne was her cousin also. Their three mothers were three sisters who had married three Wicklow farmers; Brian Devlin, John Dwyer, and Sylvester Byrne.

'Can I carry your hurley bat?' she asked as they strolled along.

He looked at her sidelong and smiled. ' 'Tis usually the male that asks the female if he can carry her comb for her. You have a lesson or two to learn, young lady.'

'Ah, go on, give us a swish of it.'

He swung the bat down and handed it to her, then watched her affectionately as she joyously slashed away with it, right and left, running from side to side of the road. She was like a little gypsy, all black curls and wild as the hills at times, like himself in many ways.

'What business brought you over to Imaal?' he asked.

'No business other than it being Sunday and my mammy wanted to see your mammy that she hasn't seen in three months of Sundays.' She placed the bat across her shoulder like a gaming-gun and linked his arm. 'I was the only one allowed to come with Mammy. Da said as always that work on a farm never stops, not even on Sundays. Did you know that we got another cow?'

Michael was about to answer when he glanced up at the sound of a horse approaching. A second later the rider came into view. For an instant Michael did not recognise him.

'Another cow?' he said in a tone of sudden interest as he manoeuvred Anne to the side of the road in one swift movement. 'Where did your daddy get her?'

'He bought her from Uncle Pat Devlin over at Cronebyrne. Now that Aunt Brigid's dead and in heaven, himself and Big Art can't manage the cows so well.' She frowned and added scathingly, 'Seeing as they think milking is only female's work.'

'Well,' Michael said, as the horseman clopped by, 'on a farm everyone must do their allotted tasks—'

'Halt!'

'And the world would be a strange place if females took on the hard job of threshing corn in the fields while big strong men stayed behind sitting on stools gently milking cows, or wearing aprons as they fancily slapped the butter.'

'I commanded you to halt, Dwyer!'

Michael halted, then turned his head very slowly over his shoulder with an air of intense weariness. It was not the first or even the hundredth time that some pipsqueak on a horse had commanded him to halt.

'How dare you forget to touch your forelock when you pass an officer and a gentleman!'

'An officer and a gentleman?' Michael looked around him searchingly, then returned his gaze to the rider, contemptuous

53

humour in his eyes as he looked at the pimply faced fifteen-year-old boy whom someone had recently dressed in a red coat.

'Stand up straight, boy, when you are being addressed by an officer of the King's forces.'

Boy! Anne's eyes moved indignantly from her cousin, who couldn't stand any taller than he had been from the start, to the squeaky-voiced boy dressed in a scarlet coat which was at least a size too big for him.

Michael suddenly started in mock surprise. 'Well damn my eyes – if it isn't young Mr Never-as-long.'

'I see you are as insolent as ever, Dwyer. You know perfectly well my name is Nethersolong. *Ensign* Nethersolong.'

'Ensign?' Michael said curiously. 'Is that your rank?'

'It is.'

'What happened? Did your father buy you a commission?'

'In the 38th stationed at Hacketstown.' Unconsciously the boy beamed. 'Pity I missed the Yankee business though. Wouldn't have minded a crack at those traitorous rebs.'

'Ensign?' Michael repeated. 'What kind of rank is that? I always thought an ensign was a flag.'

Ensign Nethersolong looked uncertainly at the tall youth in high buckskin boots who stood looking at him with eyes smiling. Michael Dwyer always brought out the worst in Nethersolong, for he had a way of looking at a man that made him feel even smaller than he actually was, and Nethersolong was not very tall. He knew he would never have dared to check Dwyer on the road but for the height of his new horse and the power of his new red coat and the protection of the new brace of pistols at his waist.

He sniffed airily. 'Smart-tongued as always, Dwyer. It is a great puzzle to me why you have not yet been flogged. Well let me tell you, boy, I may be a subaltern now, but many ensigns have ended up commander-in-chief.' On that he sat up ramrod stiff in his scarlet coat as if hoping he looked fearsome.

Michael's grin could no longer be contained.

The youngster jerked in his saddle. 'Why are you grinning like a damned cat? I demand to know. And when you reply have the manners to address me as *sir*.'

'Well, sir, 'tis like this, sir, I couldn't help wondering why an officer and gentlemen like yourself, sir, could be so unfortunate as to have a name longer than himself.'

'Why, you ruddy upstart!' Nethersolong dragged a pistol from his belt and waved it in the air. 'If you were a gentleman I would call you out for that, Dwyer!'

Michael looked at the gun, then looked suitably abashed. 'Then 'tis very lucky for me that I'm not a gentleman.'

'Damned lucky for you,' Nethersolong sat waving the pistol in the air a while longer. Eventually he put it away. 'Believe me, Dwyer,' he said loftily, 'it would give me great pleasure to shoot you down for the peasant that you are, but I could not allow you the honour and respect that such a calling-out would give you.'

Michael cracked a smile. 'Sure now, 'tis grateful I am to you,' he said softly, 'for I would hate to be shot into respectability.'

The mockery was lost on the ensign who really was very stupid between the ears. 'Do you know how to handle a gun?' he queried.

Michael shrugged. 'I know that if you cock the hammer and snap the trigger a bullet flies out.'

'What about your aim? Do you know how to aim? Any fool can snap a pistol. It's the accuracy of the aim that is vital.'

'Is that right?' Michael replied with intense seriousness. 'Then I tell you what, you do lend me one your pistols for a minute, and I'll try out my aim, shall I?'

The ensign stared at him, and saw his eyes were smiling in that unsettling way again. He broke into a squeaky laugh to cover his sudden nervousness. 'A fine old fool I'd be to do that, Dwyer. You might aim the ruddy thing at me.'

'Only if you called me out in a duel,' Michael answered, 'but sure, not being a gentleman, I'm spared that danger.'

'Yes, well, there it is, there it is. You may carry on now, Dwyer, carry on your way,' Nethersolong commanded, turning his horse around. 'And you, girl, stop staring at me like a cod-fish! Anyone would think you had never before seen an officer of the King's forces.'

Anne continued to stare after him as he bobbed away on his horse. The feeling inside her was so strong that she thought she might truly be physically sick at any minute. When she turned back to Michael her eyes were blazing.

'Why did you do that?' she stormed. 'Allow that turnip in an oversized red coat to talk down to you – and threaten you with a gun?'

He looked at her in amusement. 'What else could I do?'

'You could have done something!'

'Oh come now, Anne, you saw how fearsome he was.' Michael began to shake with laughter, but Anne was red-faced with rage.

'And I thought you were the king of the bucks, never mind your blasted cat! And as for that pimply faced varmint asking you if you could handle a gun! Sure the fool was so blinded by his own importance he didn't even see that you were wearing a pistol-belt around your waist, even if the gun was hidden under your jacket.'

'He didn't see, did he?' Michael said, then hooted with laughter as he walked on down the lane.

'Here, carry your own blasted hurley bat.' Anne was so disgusted she would not even look at her cousin as he retrieved his bat, his eyes still smiling and hers still blazing.

'Look, Anne,' he said reasonably, 'there's men and men, and if it was a man that had spoken to me like that, I would have reacted like a man. But, for heaven's sake, he was just a boy in a grown-up's coat, and worth no other emotion than amusement.'

Anne was not convinced. 'Maybe you can't shoot as well as Cathy says you can,' she said suddenly. 'Maybe 'tis all talk and bragging on her part, same as you brag about that cat that sits so still he might be in a coma. And why do you wear that pistol-belt anyhow?'

'Well, I'll tell you the truth,' he said confidingly, linking his arm in hers and walking her on, 'but promise me you will tell no one else.'

She shook her head gravely. 'I promise.'

'I wear the pistol-belt for nothing more than show. For the same reason that little varmint wears that red coat. To make me feel fearsome.'

'Is that right?' Anne's heart sank down to her shoes as she

looked into his serious face. 'Oh, Michael, then everything I've ever been told about you over the years was lies – you can't shoot a gun?'

'Not very straight,' he confessed sheepishly.

Her face went from white to red and back to white again as they walked on in silence.

'Do you still like me?' he asked quietly. 'Now you know.'

She thought about it honestly for some minutes, then gave him a wide generous smile. 'Sure I do,' she said truthfully. 'You're still my favourite cousin.'

'Even though I'm not king of the bucks?'

'Even so.'

'Even though I'm no longer a hero in your eyes?'

'Even so,' she said firmly, beginning to feel shamefaced at her own anger.

He smiled at her, and they walked on in the late afternoon sun, arm-in-arm, talking and laughing quietly until they reached the Dwyers' farmlands at Eadstown, where Anne fell into a sudden silence as they strolled down the blossom-covered bohereen that led to the homing fields and the farmhouse where Cathy was wandering searchingly around the yard.

'Oh, Gawney,' Anne muttered nervously. 'I think I'm in the stew-pot.'

'Why so?' Michael asked.

'For doing a runner when it was time to leave. Is Ma dancing with fury?' she called to Cathy.

'What?' Cathy looked up. 'Ach no, herself and Mammy guessed where you'd gone. Can't you hear them still talking like good-oh. 'Tis the black hen I'm looking for. The black hen's gone missing, disappeared entirely, and she on the point of laying chick-eggs after mating with the rooster.'

Michael was almost at the farmhouse door, looking over his shoulder at the two chattering girls, when a shadow in the sky caught his eye. He looked up, then swiftly down and around the first field beyond the yard in sudden alarm.

'Look there,' he said in a low voice. 'Don't speak; just look.'

The girls looked to where he pointed, high above them, and saw the dark outline of the hawk that hung in silent stillness as he watched his prey down below: the eccentric little black hen who had once again wandered from her nestbox in the henhouse.

Cathy's hand flew to her mouth while Anne stared in frozen horror at the waddling hen, knowing that in seconds she would be twisting backwards and forwards inside the hawk's claws.

The predator watched and waited, his great wings fluttering slightly as he prepared to make his attack. Cathy let out a scream as the hawk suddenly dived into a swoop, but the blast from the gun drowned the sound. The hawk crashed to earth only inches from the little hen who was flapping and screaming hysterically.

'God save us!' Anne cried, then turned to Michael and stared at the gaming-rifle in his hands.

'Good thing this was already loaded,' he said in a tone of relief, then turned and placed the gaming-gun back on the wall just inside the farmhouse door.

His mother and Mrs Devlin followed him back out and stood staring at Cathy who was chasing the little black hen as she flapped and ran in all directions, still screaming hysterically.

Mrs Dwyer clucked. 'That will teach her not to wander from the roost in future.'

Her sister disagreed. 'Hens have got no brains, I reckon.' Mrs Devlin pursed her lips. 'We've lost three to hawks and six to foxes in the last six months alone.'

Meanwhile, Michael's dog, an ageing pointer, appeared from nowhere, bounded across the field and came back with the dead hawk in his mouth. He dropped it on the ground of the yard, then stood with tongue hanging and tail wagging, waiting for his master to give him his rightful praise.

Michael patted his head and fondled his jaws, then commanded: 'Now stay back!' Next minute he had overtaken Cathy in the chase. The little black hen was beginning to stagger, almost senseless with fright when Michael scooped her up under his arm.

'Huerta, my crazy girl,' he said soothingly to the hen that made querulous little clucking noises and still trembled with fear.

'She's an awful tiring nuisance,' Cathy said impatiently, for the care of the hens was her job. 'When she's not vainly arranging her feathers in front of the rooster, she's wandering off to have his chick-eggs. Still, crazy and brazen as she is, I would have hated the hawk to get her.'

Anne stood in the yard and stared down at the hawk slowly being circled by the black buck cat, who sniffed once or twice then strolled off languorously, no longer interested now the kill had been made.

Anne looked at her Aunt Maíre. 'He shot the hawk – bang on!' she cried.

'Sure he did,' said Mrs Dwyer. 'And why wouldn't he?'

'He told me he couldn't shoot straight!'

Mrs Dwyer laughed, greatly amused. 'On with you, Anne Devlin, why would Michael tell you that? Sure now, hasn't he been coursing game over the mountains since he was ten years old, and how old is he now – eighteen. And why do you think he always wears that pistol in his belt?' Mrs Dwyer looked at her sister. 'Many a fine pheasant and rabbit he's brought home to us – after one of his strolls up the blue hills yonder.'

'I can well believe it,' Mrs Devlin answered. 'Many's the time a rabbit or pheasant has crossed my path and I strolling across our own hills, and me wishing I had a gun to shoot it and bring it home for dinner.'

'Not to mention the gamecocks Michael brings home when he goes coursing with his gaming-rifle over the hunting-grounds at Aughavannagh,' said Mrs Dwyer. 'The only game he would never kill, though, is the red deer.'

Anne was fidgety with confusion. 'But why would he lie to me like that? I ask you, why would he lie to me with a face as serious as a priest's?'

Anne's mother sighed as though she knew the reason why, but didn't have the heart to say it. So her sister said it for her.

'I'll tell you why, Anne,' Mrs Dwyer said gently to her niece. ' 'Tis because you make a passion of treating Michael like some hero, and that's a tiresome game for any young man to keep playing.'

Anne's face flushed crimson. Indignation and mortification struggled inside her, and indignation won, surfacing to its height just as Michael strolled back into the yard still holding the hen.

'You shot the hawk's eye out!' Anne stormed. 'Look at him now – he's a one-eyed dead bird.'

Michael looked down at the hawk dispassionately, then looked at her sadly. 'So he is.'

Anne followed him over to the corner of the yard where he dipped his hand into a sack of corn and let the hen feed from his palm. The little black hen had regained her confidence; she strained her neck down and took a grain of corn daintily in her beak, swallowed it, then jutted her neck sideways and blinked twice at Anne before straining down to peck another grain.

'You shot the hawk bang on,' she said.

'What else could I do?' Michael murmured. 'I had to try and save this purty little black hen.' He looked at her sidelong and smiled. 'Seeing as she's the rooster's favourite and all.'

'Got him in mid-swoop,' she said.

He shrugged. 'A lucky shot.'

'Lucky?' Anne stared at him. 'Lucky?' She looked away from him to the hawk, her face moving in the way that females' faces always move just before they start to cry. Suddenly she bent over, almost double, clutching her stomach and rocking slowly as she made a terrible rumbling sound that got louder and louder until Michael dropped the flapping hen on to the sack of corn and reached for her in alarm.

'What ails you, girl?'

Anne waved him aside with her hand, rocking slowly until the awful rumbling noise rose into a great bellow and he suddenly realised she was laughing. When she finally looked up tears were sparkling in her eyes.

'O God,' she gasped, 'but doesn't that take the oatcake and no mistake! That little tom-tit in his red coat saying it was lucky for you that you weren't good enough to meet him in a duel so's he could shoot you down . . .' Her voice broke into a heaving sort of bellow and Michael turned up his eyes as she did, again, her imitation of a cow giving birth.

'Here's Daddy,' he murmured, looking up at the high meadows where his father and younger brothers were hurrying down towards the homing fields. 'The sound of the shot must have carried to them.'

'The lucky shot,' Anne said, and went into another spasm

that brought her mother and aunt to her assistance. She was still laughing ten minutes later when Michael bundled her on to the seat of the cart and Mrs Devlin lifted the reins.

' 'Tis her age,' Mrs Devlin said sagely to her sister and brother-in-law, John Dwyer. ' 'Tis that funny age she's coming to when maids don't know who or what they are and laugh at nothing and everything.'

'I know what I'm laughing at,' Anne protested. 'I surely do! You tell them, Michael my cousin and hero, you tell them all about that little earwig in a red coat that asked you if you could aim a gun—'

The horse jolted forward so suddenly that Anne almost toppled backwards into the cart.

The hills were filled with blue shadows. The mountain peaks covered in white mist. All birdsong had ceased and the sleepy stillness of evening had fallen over the Glen of Imaal. All around the meadows and farmland at Eadstown not a sound was to be heard but the eruptions of laughter that came back on the soft wind from a wild Wicklow girl journeying away from the glen and home to Croneybeag, fifteen miles away.

Chapter Five

John Philpot Curran sipped his brandy. It was his fourth glass. The first two he had gulped frantically, the third more steadily, but now as he slowed to a moderate sip he began to feel the numbing terror in mind and body at last starting to thaw.

He was still wearing his barrister's black gown, having fled from court the moment he received the message. Hours had passed since then; long, tense hours since he had rushed into The Priory, his home in Rathfarnham on the outskirts of Dublin.

He was seated at the desk in his study, his private sanctuary, staring unseeingly out of the long window at the expanse of green lawn and thinking life could be such a swine of a business. He'd thought it many times before, said it many times before, and only yesterday had been forced to reprimand Gertrude for saying it too.

Gertrude! A sharp pain pierced his chest.

He took a steadying breath, lifted the decanter and refilled his glass, sipping slowly as he relived that terrible moment when he had been given the message, the moment after his triumph. For over an hour he had relentlessly bullied and tricked and confused the main witness for the prosecution until he had broken him, not allowing himself even a small smile when the admission of perjury came, not until his eyes finally met those of the judge and he had smiled, sardonically.

Then he had been given the whispered message by one of his junior counsellors.

'. . . an accident. Gertrude leaning out of the bedroom window . . . fell . . . seriously injured, unconscious . . .'

She was still unconscious. The only external injury a broken ankle. Strangely, not even a bruise on her lovely beloved face. Must wait for her to regain consciousness, the doctor had said. And so he was waiting, waiting with a decanter of nerve-steadying brandy, to find out if his twelve-year-old daughter was going to live or die.

Gertrude! Astoirin!

His eyes moved to the calendar on his desk. May 1792. He felt still young, but the calendar told him he was now forty-two years old; and if not all, then a great part of his happiness had been the last twelve years. From the day of her birth he had known a delight and love for the child he had never felt for his other three children. Not for Amelia, his first-born, nor Richard his son, not even for Sarah, the youngest and prettiest of his daughters. Hard as he had tried to love them all equally, Gertrude – wild and tomboyish wonderful Gertrude – was the bright star in his sky.

But such a reckless child! He had warned her in the past about leaning out of the bedroom window, though until today he hadn't known her quest had been to prove herself braver than her brother, braver than any boy in breeches, by climbing out from the top floor and scaling down the ivy to the ground.

But it had rained in the night, the ivy was wet, and she had fallen.

His eyes moved from the calendar and rested on the crow-feather quill on the inkstand, black and crisp. A lawyer's pen. Gertrude had given it to him only two days ago, for his birthday, wrapped in a fine linen handkerchief on which she had painstakenly embroidered his initials.

'Would you have preferred one of goose-feather, Papa?'

He saw again her wide eyes anxiously searching his face. And the delight in her eyes as he had unfolded the handkerchief and gazed at his embroidered initials, the J much larger than the small p and crooked C. A disgraceful attempt, even for a twelve-year-old, but she had smiled smugly, waiting for his praise, which he had lavished unashamedly.

Did that happen only two days ago? After the tension and terror of these last long hours, it seemed a lifetime ago.

The brandy was making him feel hot, feverish, but a cold shiver ran clear through his body as he recalled her small white face on the bed upstairs and realised that if she died, if his child died, it would have been a lifetime ago.

Again he reached for the brandy, drinking quickly, waiting for the slow burn of the liquid to revive the corpse of his heart, bring back the glimmer of hope. And there was still hope! Oh, yes indeed! How many times in court had he, John Philpot Curran, turned the tables with what even his enemies described as devastating legal brilliance, and his client had been reprieved, to face life, not death.

Only one person now could turn the tables for Gertrude – the Great Almighty Judge Himself, and He was reputed to be merciful.

Silently he prayed for some of that mercy, for himself, for his child . . . A thought suddenly struck him. A comforting thought. The daughter of Jairus in the Scriptures . . . she, too, had been twelve years old! He closed his eyes and relished the sheer relief as he imagined how it must have been, and how that man Jairus, fearing his daughter's death, must have rejoiced in the words of Christ: 'She is just asleep.'

'Your daughter is dead, Mr Curran. I am deeply sorry.'

He had not heard the doctor enter the room. He opened his eyes and looked coldly at the man who had read his thoughts and decided to play such a cruel joke on him. An incompetent old fool, always joking, and never ever funny.

'Why did my wife send for a fool like you?' his voice was no more than a hoarse whisper. 'Why are you allowed to practise at all? Diagnosed indigestion as heartstroke . . . she lived fifteen more years . . . my mother . . . fifteen healthy years . . .

'Your daughter—'

'*Is only twelve years old!*' His fist smashed down on the desk. 'Still unconscious from the fall. *Asleep!* Do you hear me?'

The old doctor stood shocked and trembling, staring in fear at the dark-haired lawyer. John Curran was the most brilliant and amusing man he had ever met, but when his passions flared, only fools dared to cross him.

Eyes dark and brooding, John Curran lowered his gaze to the black crowfeather quill on the inkstand.

'Perhaps, Dr Sheridan,' he said softly, 'you would be kind enough to ask my manservant to ride again into Dublin and see if Dr Emmet has returned yet from his calls. Dr Emmet, if anyone, will know how to bring Gertrude out of the coma.'

Dr Sheridan stared at him, aghast; but could do no more than contort his mouth in a swallowing motion.

'And, Sheridan, be sure to close the door quietly as you leave.'

'Mr Curran – John – as painful and unbearable as the truth must be, it is my duty, not only as a doctor, but as a friend, to convince you—'

'*Out!* Before I kill you.'

When the door eventually closed John Curran continued to wait. Somewhere in the waiting the daylight turned to darkness but he did not notice; not until someone carrying a candelabrum entered the room. In the yellow glare he saw the pale, beautiful face of his wife, saw her lips move, saw the clutched handkerchief moving from breast to eyes, from eyes to mouth. Somehow he realised she wanted him to answer her, give a sign that he'd heard her.

'Leave me,' he whispered finally. 'Leave, leave, leave . . .'

She moved a pace or two forward, the yellow gleam of the candlelight wavered and fluttered, then finally receded with her footsteps, only a shade slower than the doctor who had scurried like a rabbit.

He sat motionless in the dark for a long time, seeing nothing but images of his twelve-year-old daughter move before his eyes – hair flying like a black silken mane as she clutched her skirts and ran over the lawns like a young filly in flight, vaulting the garden bench in a whirl of frills and white stockings, turning to him breathless with laughter, delighted at the triumph of her own daring. He smiled back at her . . . impossible to chide her.

'What am I, Papa?' she shouted. 'As brave as they come?'

'No.'

'No?'

'*Caileen duv macree*,' he answered, smiling. Dark girl of my heart.

The images began to move past his eyes in faster and faster motion until a voice outside in the hall made him blink in confusion. A young girl's voice that jolted him out of his seat and his nightmare. All a nightmare.

'Papa! Papa! Papa!'

He moved quickly around the desk, towards the door, out of the darkness into the light of the hall. At the foot of the main staircase Mrs Jessop, the housekeeper, stood with arms around the sobbing girl. He rushed towards her, then stopped dead – not Gertrude at all, just young Sarah.

He stepped back and slumped against the wall, blinking rapidly in an attempt to stem the tears he had managed all day to keep in check, but now they burst their dam and blurred his eyes as he stared at the cold truth of it: the bright star in his sky had fallen, would never shine for him again. It was over. The magic that had been Gertrude was over. Verdict unanimous, no chance of an appeal, no hope of a reprieve. A day for the black-hat judge after all.

Mrs Jessop turned from the sobbing girl and mumbled an apology.

'Your daughter is very upset, Master.'

'My daughter is dead,' he informed her in a tear-drenched

65

whisper, then slowly turned back to his study, back to the darkness.

Oh, the pain!

Mrs Jessop was a big, red-faced woman in her fifties with greying black hair that always had strands hanging down from her cap. She ushered Sarah down to the kitchen where a huge fire blazed in the hearth.

'Some hot milk, acushla,' Mrs Jessop said, sitting Sarah down on a chair and reaching for a pan. 'Hot milk and sleep is what you need, my pulse.'

To the left of the wide fireplace, Keegan, the butler, sat on the settle. A short, stocky man with a head of grey hair tied at the nape with a black ribbon.

'Not yet eleven years old,' Mrs Jessop said, speaking of Sarah as if she wasn't there, 'and all confused in herself. And God love her, everyone upstairs too upset to have any time for her.'

'Mistress is in a bad way,' Keegan said. 'In a bad way. And Miss Amelia not much better.'

'Didn't I know something was going to happen,' Mrs Jessop declared in a tone almost akin to satisfaction. 'Didn't I say so to you only last night, Mr Keegan, when that picture fell down in the drawing-room. The divils are out, sez I. Something bad's afoot.'

Keegan, in perfect imitation of his master, responded with a cynical lift of his eyebrow but made no comment. Mrs Jessop was always going on about the divils, though how she knew so much about them Keegan often wondered.

Mrs Jessop poured out the milk and gave it to Sarah. 'There now, darling, get that down ye, my purty, and I'll take ye back to bed.'

'How's the master now?' Keegan asked. 'He sent Dr Sheridan running like a hare afore the hounds.'

'That oul bag of bluff!' Mrs Jessop tutted, her cap-ribbons shaking with indignation. 'Master wanted Dr Emmet to come, not him. But out on his calls Dr Emmet was, and no doubt attending on some bigwig suffering from no more than too much grub. Bless us all, but it makes you think, doesn't it?'

'About what?' Keegan asked.

'About my Malachi,' said Mrs Jessop spreading her bulk over a chair while Sarah obediently sipped her milk. 'I remember the night my Malachi went as clear as if 'twere only yesterday. "Poll," says he, "Poll," he says, "I think me time has come." And me laughing and telling him not to be such an old woman, for a great moaner he was about his aches and pains. But then that's men for ye, babies, every last one of them. And my Malachi was a big soft baby. Bless my soul, but could he whine! "Poll," says he, "Poll," he says, "you'll be sorry when I'm gone up-along, hard woman that ye are, you'll be sorry when I'm gone with the angel Gabriel." And dang me, but I was ... for he went only an hour later, and me not a bit expecting it.'

Keegan made no comment. Sarah sat mute.

Mrs Jessop sat back, her massive arms folded. 'Sure how was I to knowed he was telling the truth for once, and he a genius of a liar all his life. But it makes you think, doesn't it?'

Keegan didn't ask about what. He said quietly: 'Dr Emmet wouldn't have been able to do any more for Miss Trudie than old Dr Sheridan did. The master was very hard on him, very hard.'

'Still, 'tis sorry for the master I am,' said Mrs Jessop in a mildewed voice, her pink jowls quivering and her cap-ribbons shaking again, 'for he's taking it that bad. Heartbroken he is, heartbroken and crying for poor little Miss Trudie.'

There was a long silence while butler and housekeeper, both watery-eyed, sat glooming into the fire.

'Richard's all in a daze,' Keegan said. 'All in a daze. Good thing he has the Emmet boy for company.'

Mrs Jessop frowned, then bustled around on her chair till she was looking puzzled at Sarah. 'Listen now,' she said, 'has the Emmet boy got a tongue in his head at all, do ye know? I can ne'er get a word out of him no matter how.'

Sarah stared at her wide-eyed, but made no reply. The Emmet boy rarely spoke to her either.

In Richard's bedroom at The Priory, the two boys sat facing each other on the window-seat, both gazing silently through the glass at the night sky.

'How could Gertrude have been so silly?' Richard whispered, wiping a hand over his wet face. 'Climbing out to the ivy just to prove she was better than me.' He looked pale and frightened. 'Such a stupid, *stupid* thing to do, don't you agree?'

Robert made no answer, he was still too shocked by the tragedy of it all, and the biggest tragedy was that Gertrude should have felt the need to prove herself braver than Richard, for Richard had no bravery in him at all. A weak and timid boy who allowed others the amusement of bullying him at school, then strutted around at home like an arrogant young buck in pathetic imitation of those he despised. A common error of human judgement made by both Richard and Gertrude, to mistake arrogance for strength, and gentleness for weakness.

'I shall miss her,' Richard sniffed. 'She was just like a brother.'

A silence hung in the room again. Then Richard said wistfully: 'It would be so good if you and me were brothers, wouldn't it?'

For a moment Robert looked at him with silent affection.

'We are friends, Richard,' he said softly, 'true and genuine friends. And that's almost as good.'

Throughout the following day Sarah spent every opportunity watching the study door, crouched behind the cloakstand in the wide panelled hall. At not quite eleven years old, for her the death of Gertrude was still a confusion. She could not fully comprehend the sudden extinction of life in her sister. All she understood at this moment, was that her papa was going mad.

At the rustle of skirts she moved on to her knees and peeped through the folds of a cloak. Her mamma was coming down the hall dressed in a black gown which contrasted sharply with her pale skin and red-gold hair. Even in sadness, Sarah thought, her mamma looked beautiful – in a cold sort of way.

Some time ago it was now, since her mamma and papa had stopped loving each other, and Sarah had often puzzled on the why of it. Of course, in front of the children they had tried to hide their coolness; but even to Sarah's childish eyes the difference was obvious; a *sudden* difference in Mamma who had changed from a warm and happy mother and wife into a chilly, disdainful woman, even though Papa still often referred to her tenderly as 'My divine Sarah'.

It was while sitting, unnoticed, on the stairs leading down to the kitchen, that Sarah had got her first clue as to her parents' estrangement. She had overheard Mrs Jessop talking about some beautiful actress the master was supposed to have fallen head over heels in love with. He had even written a poem about her, a poem that had fallen into the hands of some lout working backstage who had made it public. The Dublin wits had loved it; declared it to be the great lawyer's most eloquent words ever – but the public slight on his wife . . . !

' 'Course it isn't true, asthore!' Mrs Jessop had declared when Sarah timidly questioned her. 'Your dear papa is a good man, a fine man, and don't let the lies of some spiteful people make you believe otherwise.'

'But the poem—'

'Was no different from what any gentleman who loves the theatre would write after seeing a great lady perform on the stage. You see, Miss Sarah,' the housekeeper explained wearily, 'all the world loves a lover and a rogue. And all Dublin loves your papa, and some let their silly imaginations run away with them, making him out to be more than what he is. And not a dang do they care what trouble they cause. And a nice bit of trouble they've caused this time! But ye take my word on it, acushla – 'tis your mamma he loves, and no mistake!'

Sarah was inclined to believe it, especially when she had scrambled back up the stairs into the hall and saw her papa standing by the drawing-room door, his hand on Mamma's arm, speaking to her softly, his face full of tenderness.

'The truth,' he was saying, 'is that her real secret lover, is the Viceroy of Ireland.'

Sarah almost clapped her hands with delight – now Mamma could stop being so jealous and spiteful.

But then she saw her mamma whisper something inaudible as she looked up into his face with an expression of icy dislike.

After that her papa seemed to spend a great many more evenings at the theatre and, much to Mamma's fury, occasionally took Gertrude with him. And Gertrude had loved every wild and wonderful minute of it . . .

A funny buzzing noise came into Sarah's head. It came into her head whenever she allowed herself to think of Gertrude. She blinked the noise away, and concentrated her eyes hard on the figure of her mamma who was knocking on the door of Papa's study.

'John!' she said, in her usual frigid tones.'Have you consideration only for yourself? I, too, am grieving for my child.'

Sarah nervously bit the mound of her thumb as she watched her mamma persistently knock on the locked study door, but receive no answer.

Later that afternoon, Reverend Sandys called, and Sarah peeped through the folds of the cloaks as her mamma tried again.

'John! Reverend Sandys is here to make the arrangements. Gertrude must soon be taken to the churchyard.'

Within seconds the door was yanked open. Her papa, unshaven and heavy-eyed, spoke coldly to the clergyman. 'Do not think, sir, that you are taking my daughter anywhere.'

Reverend Sandys looked confused. 'The child must be buried.'

'She is staying here.'

'What . . . what are you proposing, sir?'

'I propose nothing. I am stating that my daughter will be buried here, in the garden of The Priory.'

Her mamma gasped, stared at him in disbelief. 'You have truly gone mad!'

Reverend Sandys stammered a few words, clutched at his throat, then made a fresh attempt to speak. 'Mr Curran, with all due respect, I must point out, your daughter has to be buried in consecrated ground.'

'Consecrated ground?' A strange smile flitted across her papa's face. 'Then the solution is quite simple, dear man. Find whatever section of Scripture is relevant, and have the grounds of The Priory *consecrated*!'

The door slammed hard.

Sarah saw her mamma, near to collapse, reach out to Reverend Sandys for support. 'He must not be allowed to have his way,' she cried. 'He cannot do this to my child!'

'He is obviously demented,' the clergyman decided, leading

her solicitously to the drawing-room. 'Perhaps his relatives will make him see reason?'

'Yes, oh yes, you are right, Reverend. He would never dare to cause such offence to both of our families.'

Sarah abandoned her post behind the cloakstand and wandered through the house out to the garden. Her eyes were turned up to the sky as she neared the orchard, watching the evening flight of the swifts, chattering and whirling in the air.

When she entered the apple orchard she saw the Emmet boy lounging against the bole of a tree, his head lowered as he plucked at the petals on a sprig of apple blossom. Richard sat at his feet with his back to her and she could hear the continual low murmur of his voice.

'Hello,' she said.

Richard's head shot round. 'Oh, go away, Sarah,' he said tiredly. 'Can't you see that we are talking.'

'Why can't I stay and talk with you?' Sarah asked.

'Why can't you go and talk to Amelia?' Richard asked. 'What I'm saying to Robert is . . . is . . . for nobody else to hear.' He sat glaring at her with a sullen, resentful expression on his face.

Sarah made a 'poof' sound that expressed exactly how she felt about Richard's resentful expression. He was always very possessive about the Emmet boy whenever he came to The Priory, refusing to allow even Gertrude to talk to him. No wonder Gertrude had lost her patience and pushed Richard on to the compost heap.

'Sarah, please, go away,' Richard pleaded. 'Just, just . . . go away!'

Two spots of mortification coloured Sarah's cheeks as she stood her ground in nervous silence, clutching the lace-frilled sides of her white starched pinafore. Beneath her auburn hair her skin was a mixture of cream and roses. For the first time she looked directly at the Emmet boy, her eyes all open and bright and blue, to see if he too wished her gone. But all she saw in his eyes was a kind of desperate pity, which made her feel even worse.

'Did you know that it's bad luck to do that,' she said in a wavering kind of voice, pointing to the apple blossom in

71

Robert's hand. 'The little people get very angry with anyone that breaks the blossom.'

He smiled as he looked into her earnest pretty face. 'I don't believe in superstition,' he said.

'You don't believe in the leprechauns?'

He shook his head. 'No, Sarah, I do not.'

Her rosebud mouth rounded into an 'ooo' of horror. 'They'll trip you up!' she warned gravely. 'You'll keep falling over and you won't know why, but it'll be them, the leprechauns, fleeing across your path faster than you can see, paying you back for disbelieving and for breaking the blossom.'

'Leprechauns be hanged!' Richard cried, springing to his feet. 'I declare but you must be the most silly and insensitive creature ever born, Sarah.'

By nature, Sarah was as weak and timid and cowardly as Richard, and normally she would have run away in tears, but a streak of vanity prevented her from doing that in front of the Emmet boy.

'Insensitive!' Richard remonstrated. 'Up there is our sister lying dead and in there is our mamma grieved to distraction – and all you can do is worry about apple blossom and leprechauns!'

Sarah tried desperately to rally her courage, but her lips trembled in spite of all her efforts.

'By the deuce!' Richard declared, beginning to pace up and down in pettish fury. 'Have you ever known anyone to be so silly, Robert? So utterly selfish?'

Sarah looked at the Emmet boy, who clearly resented being drawn into the matter, but after a moment's hesitation he answered the question and agreed with his friend.

'No, Richard, I can't say I have ever known anyone to be as silly and utterly selfish . . . as you are being now.'

The colour in Richard's face faded slowly and he stopped pacing. He stared at his friend as if he were Judas himself, but the Emmet boy, still plucking at the sprig of apple blossom, was gazing across the orchard as if seeing some far distant memory.

'Heaven be praised,' he said softly, 'that my brother Thomas never shouted at me in such a way or shoved me aside when I was ten years old and Christopher died. Not even when I spoke my thoughts about everything in the world except the one thing that grieved me, the loss of our brother.'

For a moment Richard's nostrils quivered dangerously, but then, red-faced, his shoulders slumped in genuine shame, for underneath all his mock male bravado, he was a good-natured and decent fellow at heart.

'Yes, I own the fault, the selfishness was mostly mine,' he admitted meekly, rubbing his nose. He looked at Sarah and now he was all softness and humility. 'You will forgive me, will you not, for being such a pig?'

Sarah only stared at him, speechless.

'Robert is right,' Richard insisted earnestly. 'In times like this we should all try and help each other. Well at least we can try – I should like to try.' He gave her a smile then, so full of sweetness it was impossible to resist, and Sarah nodded her agreement and forgiveness.

'Oh, rats!' Richard said in relief. 'That's settled then! You can go and search out Amelia now if you like.'

With those words, Sarah realised, as young as she was, they were back to where their disagreement had started in the first place.

She smiled suddenly at the Emmet boy, still feeling a thrill of gratitude that he had indirectly spoken up for her, and murmured a few words of thanks; but the Emmet boy seemed to have reverted to his usual shyness, looking away in embarrassment and offering no reply.

So off she went to find Amelia, who told her to go and search out Richard. She went instead to her mamma, who told her to go and search out Amelia. Her papa was still locked in his study, so she carried on down the hall to the green baize door and stairs that led down to the kitchen, only to find Mrs Jessop elbow-deep in flour and soda, busily shouting orders and complaints as she prepared the mountains of food that would be needed for all the people that would be coming back after the funeral.

Her last hope was Gertrude. She turned and was about to bound back up the stairs when she remembered, remembered that she would not have needed to go in search of anyone if her sister Gertrude was not . . .

73

The inner workings of her mind began to buzz loudly and fog darkly under the weight of loneliness and misery that the memory of her regular playmate brought. Her breathing became rapid and laboured. Then, quite unconsciously, she repressed all thoughts of Gertrude; slowly her breathing eased and her mind cleared, and she wandered out to the garden and began a search for lucky red ladybirds instead.

At seventeen years Amelia Curran appeared older, having a matronly air about her. She had neither the delicate beauty of her mother and Sarah, nor the dark striking features of her father and Richard. Even her personality lay somewhere between the ice and fire of both parents.

It was the following evening and Amelia felt tired and irritable as she brushed the long strands of Sarah's auburn hair. The rantings of the relatives against her father had gone on since the morning hours, and had only recently ended. It was with relief she heard the front door closing and carriages rolling down the drive.

'Amelia dear,' her mother appeared in the doorway, 'please ask Keegan to have this card delivered to the Emmet household in the city. No point inviting others.'

'Has it all been resolved now?' Amelia asked.

'Yes.' Mrs Curran looked very white, completely drained. 'Your father is not to be reasoned with. The burial will be tomorrow. In the garden, directly beneath the window of his study.'

Life at The Priory changed drastically from then on. The enchanting little country estate with its glorious view of the Dublin and Wicklow mountains no longer rang with the laughter of houseguests as it had done so often in the past. Some of the most distinguished people in Ireland had dined there. The excellent wines and good food, spiced with John Curran's wit and drollery had served to make The Priory one of the most entertaining houses in Dublin county.

Now silence and gloom pervaded the house as even the servants tiptoed in and out of the elegantly furnished rooms for fear of disturbing the master. For weeks his grief had bordered on

74

insanity. Day after day he sat motionless by his study window, staring down at the little grave surrounded by black railings.

No relatives, no visitors whatever were allowed to enter The Priory. Only Reverend Sandys was granted frequent admisson, after insisting to John Curran that his poor wife was in dire need of spiritual healing and consolation.

As the months passed John Curran slowly returned to health, then to his work in the courts. But, behind his dry wit and pleasant demeanour in public, only his wife witnessed the black melancholy and the insomnia which drove him to his study in the night.

'And no sympathy does he get from the mistress either!' Mrs Jessop complained angrily to Keegan. 'Nor will he, poor heartbroken man, not while that smarmy parson keeps coming here and whispering to her all the time. Whispering, whispering, nothing but whispering. Lord's my life, but it makes you think, doesn't it?'

'About what?'

Mrs Jessop folded her arms and regarded the butler with an expression of foreboding. 'Mark my words, Mr Keegan,' she said ominously, 'but you'll find the divils are out when there's a whisperer about.'

Chapter Six

The jury had been sworn in the previous day, and now the twelve good men and true filed back into court, ready for another exciting day. The clerk rapped with his gavel and everyone stood as the Lord Chief Justice entered, bowed solemnly to the court, and took his seat.

The case itself would have been rather dull, a foregone conclusion, had it not been for the man chosen as counsel for the defence. It was generally agreed that John Philpot Curran was the most talented lawyer at the Irish Bar, knew more law than any judge and, if provoked, never hesitated to expose in court their lordships' ignorance. Especially if the judge was the one now sitting.

Lord Clare, a grey-eyed man with an arrogance of manner, lifted a delicate lavender-soaked handkerchief and dabbed it to his nose as he disdainfully eyed the defence lawyer.

This simple act produced great excitement amongst the gentry in the spectator benches, who knew all about his lordship's hatred for the younger man. Whenever John Curran and Lord Clare met in court the most deplorable scenes took place, disgraceful scenes to witness in a court of law, and so they flocked to witness them with delight. It mattered not to them whether the accused was hanged or acquitted, as long as they were entertained.

But to the poor people sitting silently and nervously in the back row, clothed in their Sunday-best, the family of the young man accused of treason, the trial held no amusement. All their hopes were fixed on the defence lawyer, hoping he could defeat not only the prosecution, but the judge. Lord Clare made no secret of the fact that he despised not only the lower orders, but lawyers who successfully defended them.

All eyes now watched Curran as he rose to speak. Yesterday his lordship had listened to his arguments with open contempt, made occasional sarcastic observations, then feigned sleep during one of his speeches.

Today he contented himself drawing long-whiskered cats with his pen while waiting for an opportunity to pounce.

The lawyer, eloquent as always, proceeded with a detailed argument on the facts, more interested in scoring a verdict in his client's favour than a verbal duel with the judge – although victory with one was victory over the other.

Very soon he had the rapt attention of the court. Not for him the droning of dry legal jargon which went on and on like a swarm of bees. Curran brought life to every word with a vengeance until, finally, even his lordship stopped drawing and looked up.

He listened for some minutes with an affectation of deep puzzlement, then sighed loudly and sat shaking his head from side to side.

Curran paused, glanced at the bench, then smiled at the jury. 'Gentlemen,' he said, 'you will have observed his lordship shaking his head while I have been speaking, but I assure you there is nothing in it.'

Amidst the grins and suppressed laughter Lord Clare sat stony-faced. He was used to Curran's wit and refused to be intimidated by it. He gaveled for silence, then asked the recorder to read aloud the last statement made by the defence before the interruption.

When the words were repeated, Lord Clare gave a dismissive laugh and flicked his lavender-soaked handkerchief.

'If that be the law, Mr Curran, then I may *burn* my law books!'

The lawyer paused a moment, as if to think about it.

'Far better to *read* them, my lord,' he suggested.

Delighted laughter from the spectator benches. Curran had scored again.

Further down the hall in Court Number Two another lawyer was also having trouble, not with the judge but with his client the defendant.

Thomas Emmet was standing with blue eyes fixed furiously on the man in the dock. The case was of a contested wine bill, during which it was alleged that the defendant had consumed twenty-four bottles of claret in one night.

'It is impossible for one man to consume such an amount of liquor in one night,' Emmet insisted in his client's defence, only to be shouted down by the defendant, purple and indignant, that twenty-four bottles may be impossible for lesser men, 'But not for Finbar Phelan the *T'urrd*!'

'Are you saying the allegation is true?'

'True enough, Mr Emmet. I couldn't lie now. Not after swearing to tell the truth. Twenty-four bottles of claret. No more and no less.'

Appalled, Emmet stared at his client. 'Come now, Mr Phelan, no man could consume that amount on his own. Did you have any assistance in drinking the claret?'

'I did.' The defendant smiled sheepishly. 'I had the assistance of a bottle of brandy.'

The case was soon disposed of, and Thomas Emmet, furious at himself for accepting the fool's brief in the first place, gathered up his papers and strolled towards the doors and the more airy hall of Dublin's Four Courts. He wondered how the case in the Chancery Court was going. Packed on to the public benches of the court he had just left were the rabble, but inside the Chancery Court the spectators were of the higher class. Ladies of quality fluttering fans and gentlemen busy with snuffboxes. Was Curran giving them value? Thomas wondered.

He slipped inside the Chancery Court to see his lordship's face flushed and angry as he interrupted the defence in mid-sentence.

'One would presume, Mr Curran, that all present in this court, and more so the witness who has sworn his sacred oath, understands the meaning of the word perjury. Pray spare us a sermon on the subject.'

'Forgive me, my lord,' Curran answered the judge while looking straight at the jury, his face full of surprise, 'but in points of defence, of trial, and of judgement on my client who stands at risk of his life, I dare not *presume* anything.'

Standing by the door, Thomas Emmet smiled at the skill of his colleague. John Curran was a genius when it came to handling juries, and this particular jury was clearly enraptured with him.

'History,' he told the jury with a sad sigh, 'has taught us the folly of presuming a man to be everything he says he is. History has shown us bishops who have not always believed in God, and judges who have not always believed in justice, and witnesses who have not always believed in their sacred oath and have occasionally lied!' He faced the bench. 'I would remind his lordship of the recent case of the Crown versus—'

'Yes, yes,' Lord Clare cried impatiently. 'Go on, Mr Curran, go on with cross-examination.'

Thomas looked at the accused in the dock, a lad of about eighteen with a face as sweet as a choirboy's. Hardly a rebel, but then rebels came in all shapes and styles these days. This one was probably the poetic type of rebel, songs and poems, but little else. He stood in the dock as if in a dream, stunned at finding himself in court charged with treason against the King.

Thomas then eyed the witness in the box. He recognised him as one of that battalion of witnesses maintained in Dublin Castle and employed as government spies and informers. The Castle had a simple method of dealing with suspected rebels – if a prosecution witness could not be found, they bought one. Then used him again and again to dispose legally of undesirables.

James O'Brien was such a man, Thomas knew, but he wondered if Curran also knew it.

John Curran did, and now his aim was to ensure the jury knew that O'Brien was a Castle parrot. He walked slowly towards the witness box, flapped his black gown behind him, then stood with hands behind his back while he thoughtfully studied the alcoholic face of the witness. Best to simply confuse the rascal, he decided.

'Mr O'Brien, whence came you?'

'Whence?' The witness looked at him suspiciously. 'Speak in a way I can understand you.'

Curran stepped closer to the witness box. 'By your oath, Mr O'Brien, do you truly not understand my question?'

'Well, I think I understand it.'

'Then answer it,' Curran snapped. 'Whence came you?'

'From the Castle.'

'The Castle!' Curran managed a tone of awed astonishment. 'Do you live there?'

'No.'

'So why did you come from there? Are you an excise officer?'

'No.'

'A revenue officer?'

'No.'

'Have you ever passed yourself as an excise officer?'

'I never did pretend to be any kind of officer!' exclaimed the witness.

'Did you ever pass yourself for a revenue officer?'

'I answered that before.'

'I do not wish to give you unnecessary trouble, sir. Treat me with the same respect I shall treat you. I ask you again. Did you ever pass yourself for a revenue officer?'

The witness looked long and nervously at the lawyer who was renowned for doing painstaking research before a case. 'I never . . . barring, maybe, when I was in drink or the like.'

'Was it in drink that you passed yourself as an excise and a revenue officer?'

'I can't say what I might have done when I was drunk.'

'Are you in the habit of being drunk?'

'Not now, but for some time past I was.'

'Very fond of drink?'

'Very fond of drink.'

The witness mopped his forehead and looked around him as a lady's small laugh came from the spectator benches. 'I'm no longer a drunk!' he shouted. 'And I was not drunk when I signed the charge.'

'Of course you were not drunk,' Curran said gently, moving to rest his elbow on the edge of the witness box and giving O'Brien his most sympathetic smile. 'And now, Mr O'Brien, you have the opportunity to prove to the court that you were not drunk. Simply answer truthfully each question I put to you, and justice will triumph.'

The witness nodded, relaxed slightly. Then Curran fired each question with the speed of a bullet zapping from a gun.

'Were you drunk when you sat near the accused in the public house?'

'No.'

'Were you drunk when you heard him talk treason?'

'No.'

'Were you drunk when you agreed to prosecute?'

'No.'

'When you took the money to do so?'

'No.'

'Not drunk?'

'Not drunk!'

The court sat in utter silence. O'Brien blinked, then looked about him with a confused eye, realising he had been tricked. An immense burst of cheering came from the relatives in the last row.

But now the witness had been ensnared, John Curran decided to finish him so completely he could never enter a witness box again.

He resumed questioning at the same speed and O'Brien found himself admitting that by posing as a revenue and excise officer he had extorted money from tradesmen, blackmailed friends and swindled women, until his credibility as a witness was in shreds.

Counsel for the Crown continually made protest, which his lordship upheld, but Curran carried on relentlessly, reducing the jury to helpless laughter as he mimicked O'Brien's answers and held them up to the wittiest ridicule.

'If you continue like this, Mr Curran,' shouted his lordship, 'I shall commit you!'

The lawyer half turned to the public benches and said in an undertone: 'If you do, then I shall console myself that I am not the worst thing his lordship has committed.'

'What? What was that? I did not hear you, Mr Curran.' Lord Clare was half over the bench, hand to his ear. 'Please repeat?'

'I am sorry, my lord, I was merely thinking aloud,' Curran explained as he smiled pleasantly at the man he hated most in all the world.

The public benches were buzzing, the gentry delighted with the entertainment. The courtroom might not be a theatre, but occasionally it was better, and the ending was always real.

Thomas Emmet could not condone John Curran's behaviour with his lordship, but he understood it and sympathised. The two men had despised each other since the days when Lord Clare had been plain John Fitzgibbon, the Attorney-General whom Curran had defeated time and time again. But since his ennoblement and rise to the bench, Lord Clare had made it quite clear to the legal fraternity that Curran would win no victories in *his* court. And so, every time they met, the lawyer had to fight the judge with everything he had.

And he had destroyed the witness, beautifully. O'Brien stood in the box looking somewhat punch-drunk from the blows received in the verbal sparring-match.

In his closing speech, the jury sat spellbound as Curran risked a charge of treason himself by ferociously denouncing the government's practice of using bought witnesses, and the despicable character of such a witness, who supplied false testimony at a price.

'I have heard of assassination by sword, by pistol and by dagger, but here is a wretch who would dip even the saints in blood. If he thinks he has not already sworn his victim to death, he continues to swear without mercy and without end. But do not, I beseech you, continue to allow him to swear his oath on the

81

Bible. If he must swear, let it be on the *knife*, the proper symbol of his profession . . .'

It took the jury five minutes to return with a verdict. Lord Clare addressed the foreman. 'Gentlemen of the jury, how find you? Is Patrick Finney guilty of the crime he stands charged?'

'Not guilty, my lord.'

Another tremendous burst of applause rose up from the back of the court. Lord Clare threw a venomous glance at the defence lawyer, who was already instructing his junior counsel to submit a motion for perjury against James O'Brien.

Thomas Emmet found himself pushed and shoved as many from the back row attempted to reach the defence lawyer and shake his hand, but John Curran was standing with a puzzled expression on his face as a stocky grey-haired man clutched his arm and whispered urgently to him.

Thomas recognised him as Keegan, one of the servants from The Priory. And once again John Curran rushed out of court and into a waiting carriage, still wearing his black gown.

Since entering Trinity College at the age of fifteen, Richard Curran spent most of the week at the Emmets' house in the city, returning to Rathfarnham at weekends, two days which seemed to drag on endlessly, for he was only really happy in the company of his friend Robert Emmet, whom he adored unreservedly.

The two boys were strolling through the college courtyard, their studies finished for the day. It was September 1794, and the second week of their second year at Trinity.

'I have to go home today,' Richard said. 'Left two of my maths books there at the weekend. Will you come with me?'

Robert, conscious that to appear reluctant would hurt Richard, gazed straight across College Green to the columned building of Parliament House while he considered his answer. The Priory was no longer a happy house and, surprisingly, the tense atmosphere seemed even worse since the birth of Mrs Curran's new baby.

'It will be just a short visit,' Richard said swiftly. 'A quick in and out. We would be back at Stephen's Green in time for dinner.'

A little under an hour later they strolled up the lane which led to the rear of The Priory, then ventured inside through the door of the orchard. On reaching the garden they stopped and stared at each other: sounds of hysterical screaming were coming from one of the open bedroom windows.

'It sounds like Sarah,' Robert said.

Richard sprinted towards the back of the house and down the stone steps to the basement. In the narrow passage he almost collided with Mrs Jessop as she came out of the kitchen carrying a glass of purple liquid which he recognised as one of her strange herbal brews.

'What's going on?' Richard asked.

' 'Tis Miss Sarah. No one can console her. Not even me. And who could be blaming her with all the shenanigans in this house! The master ranting and raving at the mistress last night, accusing her of the most shameful things—'

Richard rushed past her and took the stairs up to the ground floor two at a time. He pushed through the green baize door into the hall and was about to mount the main staircase when he met his father coming down. He was almost afraid to ask the question.

'What . . . what's happened?'

'Your mother has gone.'

'Gone?' Richard moved his head from side to side in bewilderment. 'Gone where?'

'The letter she left behind omitted that particular piece of information. All we know is that she has run away with her paramour – the pious parson.'

'*What?*'

A baby cried above them. A housemaid was coming down the stairs carrying the small whining bundle. Mrs Jessop panted into the hall and waddled up to the maid, exchanged the glass of herbal sedative for the baby which she cuddled in her arms.

'And what's to be done with this poor little fella?' she asked her master. 'He's fretting himself sick with the hunger. Na na na na darling . . .'

John Curran stared at the child which he refused to accept as his.

'And not only has your mother deserted you three, Richard, but she had the audacity to leave her cuckoo in *my* nest.'

Mrs Jessop had been racking her brains since last night, and she, too, now believed the master was not the father. A

83

passionate man with an eye for a beautiful woman he might be –
Lord! he'd even been accused of having affairs with some of those
actresses on the stage; in particular, the famous Elizabeth
Billington – but even he was incapable of fathering a child by
proxy, during a two-month visit to London while his wife
remained at home – and this was no seven-month babby!

But still, a helpless infant was a helpless infant.

'Mr John, acquanie,' she said in a coaxing tone she rarely
dared to use. 'You'll not be turning your back on the poor abandoned little mite, will you now?'

John Curran sighed. 'Of course not.'

'God bless you.' The housekeeper smiled. 'You'll look after
him then?'

'No, Mrs Jessop. You will.'

One week later, when Robert Emmet returned to his home on St
Stephen's Green, he found Richard Curran waiting for him in
the ante-room to his bedroom.

Robert was not in the least surprised. Every day since that
terrible evening when he had left Richard standing in the hall of
The Priory staring at his father in disbelief, he had returned
home from college to find Richard sitting waiting for him.

'Has your mother come back yet?'

'No. And Father wouldn't let her back now anyway.'

'Are you all right?' Robert asked, concern in his eyes.

'No, I'm not all right! Father intends to give that swine of a
parson an unholy legal thrashing in court. And now he says he
wants me to give evidence in the witness box, supporting the
charge of my mother's adultery.'

'What?' Robert looked appalled. 'Is he asking you to lie under
oath?'

'He's asking me to tell the truth under oath.'

Robert stared at his friend who suddenly appeared much too
knowing for his sixteen years. 'And do you *know* the truth of it?'

'Yes, but don't ask me the details or whys or wherefores,
please. Events which puzzled me at the time are now beginning
to make sense.'

Robert sat down in the armchair opposite. 'How awful for
you.'

'Damned awful!' Richard was almost in tears. 'I always imagined my first official appearance in court would be as a lawyer. Not as a witness against my own mother.'

'You don't have to go into court,' Robert told him. 'Not if you don't want to.'

'He wants me to do it.'

'But what do *you* want to do?'

Richard closed his eyes. 'I want to die.'

After a discreet knock, the door opened and a wiry little man scurried in carrying a silver tray. Robert gaped at him.

'Lennard! Since when did you become butler? Where is Simmins?'

'Indisposed for the minute,' Lennard explained with a toothy grin, 'but I knew ye wouldn't want to be left waiting for the tea to be brought up.'

'Did you now,' Robert said wryly.

'And is it young Misther Curran that's here again, wha'?' Lennard asked. 'Sure I didn't know ye for a minute and you looking so pale. Has yer dear mother been sighted yet or no?'

'Lennard!'

'Aye, Misther Robert.' The haughty young face glaring at him warned Lennard he was overstepping his very wide mark. 'Sure, wasn't I only asking out of politeness,' he muttered, backing towards the window and clattering the tray down on Robert's desk.

In the following silence Robert watched with amused eyes as Lennard foosthered with the china and spoons, finally resorting to pouring out the tea himself while his eager ears waited for the conversation to resume. But Richard waited until Lennard had at last sauntered sulkily out of the room before saying in a voice hoarse with emotion, 'How could she do it, Robert? *How?*'

Robert didn't know the answer. He thought of his own mother who to him personified everything tender, loving, and faithful, but a comparison between the two women was impossible. His own mother was nearly sixty years of age, nothing at all like the exquisite Mrs Curran.

'God rot her in hell!' Richard cried, his lips back on his teeth. 'God damn her for what she has done to us!' He banged his clenched fists down on his knees. 'The bitch! The selfish hateful bitch!'

A long heavy silence brooded in the room.

Richard lifted his head and stared at Robert. 'I'm sorry,' he said.

'Don't be. I understand.'

And Robert did understand. He had always known how proud Richard had been of his beautiful mother, but every evening for the past week Robert had watched him moon around in utter confusion; Richard's love for his mother losing out in the raging battle with his newfound hate for her.

'How are your sisters taking it?' Robert asked.

'Oh, Amelia goes around grim-faced and saying little, but it has broken Sarah badly. Father has always been her favourite, but after Gertrude's death, when she lost her playmate and he wanted nobody but his dear departed, Sarah seemed to cling to Mamma, and now . . .'

He sat back in the chair and sighed. 'Sarah is being sent away,' he said. 'Your father is at The Priory now. He says she needs a complete break from that house, a complete change of atmosphere. It seems she is very ill, suffering from some sort of mental breakdown.'

Robert drew up a recollection of a pale but pretty little girl with long auburn hair. How old was Sarah now? Twelve or thirteen? So very young to have a breakdown.

'Where is your father sending her?'

'To a Quaker family in Cork – friends of his. They'll treat her kindly, he says.'

It was better than a sanatorium, Robert supposed. 'When are you returning to college?' he asked.

'I had an idea I'd maybe go back tomorrow.'

'A good idea. Exhausting your mind with academic toil will safeguard it from gloomy introspection.' Robert half smiled. 'Always works that way for me, anyway.'

'But I won't be able to stay here on week-nights in future,' Richard said. 'Father says I must return home to Rathfarnham each evening – for Amelia's sake.'

For some minutes he sat staring into space, then sighed miserably. 'Life can be such a pig of a business.'

PART ONE
1798

Chapter Seven

The horseman reined to a halt at the crest of a hill and sat gazing about him. All around were the mountains of Wicklow, their peaks and hollows a composition of every shade of green. For some time he sat listening to the musical sound of mountain streams running down to the valley, realising he was lost.

Not that he cared overmuch. The early morning all-out gallop had proved a sweet release from his tensions; just the thought of returning to the Castle Rath mansion and being obliged to make small talk over breakfast with scented dandies and coquettish débutantes filled him with dread. And such a waste of time! Precious time that could be more usefully employed studying for his degree exams in the summer.

Down below on the narrow winding road he spotted the red shawl of a country girl. She strolled alongside a grey donkey with two panniers slung over its back filled with chunks of turf, obviously on her way home after a dawn journey to the hills collecting fuel for the fire.

The girl was slim and dark and, although he could not see her face, he was struck by the way she walked. There was a proudness about her, so characteristic of many of her class. She walked like a queen.

His eyes rested on the pitiful donkey that plodded beside her, his shaggy grey ugliness a stark contrast to the sleekness of the girl. The poor fellow's legs were knock-kneed with age, the hoofs turned inwards.

The horse impatiently scraped a well-shod hoof over the grass but his rider remained watching the girl as she continued along the road towards a cluster of ramshackle cabins. Only two had chimneys, all the rest had smoke filtering through every part of the thatched roofs. The inhabitants of these hovels were called cottiers, and he wondered about them; wondered how whole families could cram themselves into those one-roomed huts like so many pigs in a pen, and not go mad. Did that proud girl live there?

Without even appearing to glance sideways at the cabins she strolled on, and eventually disappeared from view. Finally the rider stirred and prodded his horse down the heath to the road, but unlike the girl he looked curiously at each cabin as he slowly rode past.

As he approached the last, two children laughed excitedly as they chased a screaming hen out of the house. They caught sight of him and abruptly fell silent, staring up at him suspiciously. He was a stranger to these parts, and he was gentry. He wore the fine clothes and polished boots of a gentleman.

Robert Emmet was now twenty years old, slim of build but athletic looking, with an aristocratic hint to his features. His black hair, untidy and windswept over the brow, was tied at the nape with a black ribbon. He smiled down at them.

'Good morning.'

The boy, aged about eleven, still stared at him suspiciously, but the girl, a year or two younger, smiled shyly and muttered in greeting, 'Dia agat.'

Of a sudden the expression on the boy's face changed. All hostility fell away as he gazed at the splendid black stallion. His hand slowly came out and reverently stroked the shiny flank.

'Oh, there's a darling boy,' he crooned. 'Oh, he's a grand swanky fella entirely.'

The stallion, over sixteen hands high, stood in complacent fashion nonchalantly accepting his due, but after a few more pats and praises he blew out his nostrils and threw back his head, eager for another gallop.

'What do ye call him?' the boy asked.

'Black Seamus.'

The boy stared at the horse with a desperate longing. 'If I owned a beast like that,' he blurted, 'I'd ride him to the moon!'

Black Seamus snorted, fidgeting to fling himself over the hills in the direction of the moon.

Robert patted his neck and glanced at the girl. She was gazing over his tan riding-coat and fawn breeches with such big and hungry eyes he felt a sort of confused shame. Awkwardly, he took a coin from his pocket and held it down to her. Eyes blinking, she moved forward and stared at the shilling as if it were a crock of gold, then took it carefully in her little fingers. She turned and smiled at her brother who only responded with a resentful glare. A few seconds later the boy was also clutching a coin and laughing excitedly.

It took only a light press of the knees and the horse was off, ignoring the shouts of the children as he rushed over the green grass into the swish of the wind, galloping until no other sound could be heard but the steady drumming of hoof-beats which echoed over the silent hills.

The warm morning turned into a hot afternoon. The sun shone brilliantly for early spring and not even a light breeze stirred the tiny leaves on the trees as the country girl strolled along the winding grey road, her eyes roving over a trail of pine trees edging a path of the Wicklow Mountains.

Anne Devlin had grown from a sturdy tomboy into a feminine girl of eighteen. Her figure was slim, but had a quick-limbed strength to it. She wore a blue petticoat to her ankles, white blouse and tight black bodice. With one hand she casually held a red shawl over her shoulder and, except for the way she walked, she might have been any country girl on her way to market. She walked like a queen surveying her own land.

Her twelve-year-old brother, Little Arthur, ambled beside her. Apart from the green eyes they looked nothing like each other, for Little Arthur had hair as red as a fox and his pale skin was covered in freckles.

Her eyes still on the mountains, Anne breathed in the smells of wild thyme and golden furze and wondered what sane person could ever choose to live in a city after knowing, and growing, in the beauty of Wicklow.

It was almost seven weeks since she had returned from Dublin, but the relief was still with her. Their landlord's wife had approached Anne's mother with the news that her sister in Dublin needed another housemaid – a *hardworking* housemaid. Quietly but firmly, she *suggested* that Anne might go. So Anne was sent.

On her arrival at the big house in Inchicore, the first thing Anne had been made to do was restrict her glossy dark hair in a thick braid which must *never* be allowed to hang provocatively over one shoulder. And if the tiny curls which sprang around her face could not be harnessed under a cap, then they must be greased back with meat-dripping. The mistress was most emphatic on that point.

Anne had hated every minute of being trussed up in starched apron and cap as she stood by the table waiting upon the grand ladies and gentlemen who only stopped stuffing their bellies to moan about *them*. Her blood had boiled to hear them talk about the people as if they were no better than the worms of the earth; useful for turning the soil, but to be stamped underfoot if they attempted to surface from the muck.

After three months she sent a desperate plea to her father, begging him to take her home. He came for her straight away, much to the annoyance of the mistress who had stood sternly by an upper window, watching father and daughter climb on to the trap. Anne had smiled up at her, openly and defiantly, while she yanked at the thick braid of her hair and shook it loose.

As they turned a bend in the road, her brother broke into her thoughts with a sharp nudge. Two undersized old men were sitting on a pile of rocks, smoking pipes and conversing so loudly to combat their bad hearing that their voices could be heard quarter of a mile away.

'He was a gintleman by the looks o'him, and I didn't want to argue wid him, ye understand, but sure, I thought, I'll have to tell him the truth or be damned entirely. So I says to him, I says, if 'tis good bloodstock and grand horses ye want, 'tis not in Kildare ye'll find thim, but right here in the County Wicklow, I says. The very best of thim!'

'True for you, Aloysius. And how did the gintleman respond?'

'He said that nearly ivery horse that won the big races in England last year was reared on the green limestone plains of Kildare.'

'Ah, musha, Devil grill his tongue! And how did ye reply, Aloysius?'

'Well, I didn't want to argue with him, ye understand, but I says— Hoigh! Is that Anne Devlin and little red Arthur?'

Anne nodded a smile at the two ancients. The teller of the tale looked at her with rheumy old eyes. 'Is it into Rathdrum yer going, Anne acquanie?'

'Aye, Mr Moynihan. And I'm late as it is,' she added quickly.

'Arrah, the young can afford to be late. Ye have years to waste. And how is that big strong brother of yours? The one called Michael. The one that's great in the hurley matches.'

'Don't you know well that Michael Dwyer is my cousin and not my brother, Mr Moynihan,' Anne said impatiently. 'And how long is it that you've known him?'

'Faith,' declared the ancient, 'I don't know him at all. What village is he from?'

Anne turned up her eyes, and nudged her giggling brother to move on.

'Will ye stop on the way back, acquanie, and tell us any newses?'

'I will,' Anne called over her shoulder, and knew she would have to, for they would sit there talking all the livelong day unless it rained; and even then they would shift only as far as the shelter of a tree. Now too old for work and considered good for nothing, their daughters-in-law refused to have the ancients cluttering up their kitchens in daytime, and so the two were as much a feature of the Rathdrum road as the rocks they sat on.

'So tell us, Aloysius, what did ye say to the gintleman?'

'Which gintleman would that be?'

'The one who lied about the horses.'

'Well, I says to him, I says . . . Pooh! She's drove it out of me head now with all her talking. Asking me how long I knew her brother! Begor, but women are curious creatures.'

'None more so, Aloysius, none more so.'

'But I once knew a woman even more curiouser than her! She was so curious, d'ye mind, that if she saw a beetle crawling on these rocks now, she would have to know if it was a buck or a doe. My sorrow, she had me married to her before I found out her affliction . . . Faith! are there any good horses in Wicklow? Indeed, says I. The very best of thim!'

Anne and her brother fell against each other with smothered laughter, but their smiles faded as they approached the crowded square of Rathdrum and a strange yet familiar smell reached their nostrils. Anne pushed her way through and stood to stare at the spectacle.

The crowd watched in silent anger as a yeoman stirred a barrel of boiling pitch in the centre of the square. A youth was on his knees next to the barrel, his arms tied behind his back.

'What's he done?' Anne asked a woman.

'Nothing. They're giving it to him just for being a croppy. And look at the bla'guards, scores of them.'

Anne stared at the regiment of red-coated militia, then at the trembling youth who was trying desperately not to show his terror. 'Croppy' was a name given to the young men who wore their hair short. Lord Edward Fitzgerald had returned from a period in France with his long hair cut short in the Revolutionary style. The fashion had been quickly copied by many of the young men as a gesture of dissent. And now the militia, with the consent of government, had devised a punishment for peasant croppies even more agonising than half-hangings or floggings: pitchcapping – a linen cap dipped in boiling pitch and placed on the head.

'Come away, Little Arthur,' Anne snapped. 'Don't they want us to stand and look?'

At that moment a shabbily dressed priest marched into the square, eyes wild and furious, hair straggling down his back. 'Refuse to pay the crippling taxes on your crops!' he shouted. 'Give the same message to His Mad Majesty as the Americans gave to him – no taxation without representation!'

The priest looked more than a little mad himself. Some of the men tried to grab him, to pull him back to the safety of the crowd, but he struggled and shouted louder.

'If George is our noble King, and England our mother country, then why are we treated, not like the *sons*, but the *bastards* of George and England? No, my people! A country ruled by its own takes care of its own, but the conquered—'

The soldiers fell on him, dragging him from the clutches of the men who were lashed back with whips. A stunned silence fell on the crowd as the priest was quickly strung up on a tree at the edge of the square and half-hanged. For one long awful moment he hung in mid-air by the neck, then the order came to release the rope and he fell to the ground. A number of the women ran to his assistance and soon he was conscious again, gasping for air and clutching his throat.

'Long time before he'll shout again,' a yeoman laughed.

Anne turned quickly from the square, pushing her brother before her. Oh, how foolish the priest was – poor man! With all his learning he should have known that freedom of speech was forbidden outside Parliament.

When they returned home to Croneybeag, Anne paused at the bottom of the brown heath and leaned against a tree, gazing towards the thatched farmhouse that was her home. It was due to the hard work of her father they did not suffer the hunger and misery of some of the other people of Wicklow, especially the cottiers, who had no land to farm and survived solely on what they could earn as hired-out labourers. But the Devlins, like the Dywers, were hardworking people of the land. Her da always produced a good yield of crops, paid his taxes and tithes, and was highly regarded by the neighbouring gentry for his good industry and peaceable manner.

Anne pushed away from the tree and followed her brother, a smile moving her lips as she caught sight of a big, black-haired man leaning on the half-door of the cottage, watching her. It was her da, her wonderful da. She grabbed up her skirts and ran towards him.

Anne was too preoccupied with her own angry thoughts to notice the tender sorrow in her father's eyes as he spoke conversationally to her about her journey into the market-square of Rathdrum. When she stepped before him into the house, he wondered if he should tell her the news straight away and maybe ruin her appetite; or wait until she had enjoyed her supper?

The choice was lost to him when Anne continued through the outer room into an inner kitchen where a fire glowed warmly in the hearth. In the centre of the kitchen was a rectangular table on which a spotless but well-darned tablecloth was spread, and where four-year-old Jimmy and five-year-old Nellie

95

were already seated in hungry anticipation. Little Arthur flopped down at the table beside them and sniffed appreciatively at the smell of lamb and onion stew coming from the cooking-cauldron that hung above the fire.

Anne sat down on the settle by the fireside, her anger lulled by the comforting atmosphere of her home. She looked at the kettle bubbling on the hob, at the racks and flitches that hung overhead among muslin bags of herbs, then leant her head back against the wooden settle and closed her eyes, not even opening them when her father sat down beside her.

Mrs Devlin frowned as she eyed her second eldest daughter while at the same time giving a last few stirs to the contents of the cooking pot.

'Wisha,' she said, 'are you going to tell me what's wrong with you, Anne?'

'Not now, Mammy, I'm too vexed to talk about it now.'

'Then you'll be even more vexed when I tell you the bad news so.'

Anne's eyes opened. 'What bad news would that be?'

'Patrick Sarsfield. He's only gone and died.'

Brian Devlin looked at his wife as if thinking she had all the subtlety of a mallet.

'Patrick Sarsfield dead?' Anne cried. 'Ah no—' She broke off at the sound of hurried steps descending the boxed-in wooden stairs that led to the two bedrooms in the loft. When the door opened into the kitchen her elder sister Mary appeared, a frail-looking girl of nineteen. She looked first at her mother, then at Anne's distressed face, then moved to sit timidly at the table.

'Why did he go and die so sudden?' Anne cried in helpless grief. 'And he always such a brave and gallant little hero!'

'He was as old as the hills,' Mary whispered. 'And ugly as sin.'

Anne stared at her elder sister, wondering what she had said. There were times when a mouse had a louder squeak than Mary.

'Now don't start mausying,' Mrs Devlin said sternly when two pearl-sized tears slipped down Anne's face. 'It had to happen sometime. And, despite his grand name, Patrick Sarsfield was no great warrior that fought in the Siege of Limerick – he was only a donkey.'

But so unusual were tears on the face of her strongest and

wildest daughter that Mrs Devlin's heart melted and she nodded in satisfaction when her husband enfolded Anne to his breast.

'Sarsfield loved carrying the turf,' Anne said tremulously through her tears. 'His only happiness was when I took him up the hills for the turf. Made him feel young again, ye see. Made him feel important. My brave and gallant little soldier.'

'If it'll cheer you, alannah,' her father said, 'I'll get out the fiddle and play a few tunes later, as a sort of wake for him.'

Anne sniffed and nodded. 'Aye, Da,' she whispered. 'That would be grand.'

Some thirty miles away from Croneybeag, over on the green limestone plains of Kildare, the kings of the racetrack were lightly stepping the road back to their stables. The majestic thoroughbreds, who lived only for the speed and ecstasy of the race, had had their day. The Curragh race course was almost deserted.

Riding along the wide open road leading away from the Curragh, two very happy young gentlemen were discussing the yearlings, fillies, and stallions that were the heroes and heroines of the turf. Far off against the eastern skyline the Dublin hills lay fold on fold in a purple evening mist.

The two men paused in conversation at the sudden great clatter of horses, then looked round as a party of dragoons came galloping around the bend, the same party who only minutes before had leisurely jog-trotted past them in the opposite direction. The dragoons spurred past them at great speed, almost shying their mounts.

Before either could utter a 'Devil take you!' the dragoons whirled round, and blocked the road. A young officer, a captain, kneed his horse forward a pace and sat staring arrogantly at the two men.

Both men were in their early thirties, both finely dressed, but while one had a face and bearing that was unremarkable, the other was a handsome man who rode in his saddle as if he were some lord of the land, one fist on the reins and the other against his hip – and it was him the dragoons were interested in.

'Well, gentlemen?' the man said with grave courtesy. 'What can we do for you?'

'You can remove your neckcloth and throw it on the ground,' the dragoon officer said coldly.

The man addressed leaned back in his saddle but the fist remained against his hip. He was tall and dark-haired and, although thirty-five years old, still possessed the fresh complexion and clear blue eyes of youth.

'Now, why should I do that?' he said coolly.

The captain smiled scornfully. 'Well, you do speak like a gentleman, you dress like a gentleman, but your neckcloth conveys a very different impression. That neckcloth, sir, is green. A colour that betrays sentiments of sedition. I insist that you remove it at once.'

For a moment the man looked towards the Dublin mountains, as if deciding his response, then he looked back at the captain, calmly and coolly.

'I regret that my neckcloth offends you, but I think you should know that wearing the colour green is not against the law. However, as you seem determined to make it an offence, all I can say is, here it stays, and here I sit, so let any man among you who wishes to try, come forward and take it off me.'

The dragoons looked at each other then at the captain, who seemed somewhat surprised at the cool challenge. But the challenger's companion was not surprised, he was enraged. He also realised that the party of dragoons must be only recently arrived in Ireland, and therefore knew little of the character of his friend who would not allow any man to trifle with him lightly.

'For goodness' sake!' he said sternly to the captain. 'This is hardly the time or place for a scramble between officers and gentlemen. And what is it . . . twelve against two? Not exactly the fair numbers of the cricket teams, eh? But if my friend's neckcloth offends you so much that you wish to make it a point of honour, I suggest the matter can be settled quite satisfactorily if you, sir, were to select a day and a time and another officer as your second. Then we can meet again on more equal terms.'

'What?' the dragoon officer stared at the man wearing the green neckcloth, who now also wore an amused expression as he sat surveying the captain. 'Am I correct in assuming that your companion here is calling me out to meet you with pistols?'

'Why not? For my neckcloth – or for the coat of your uniform – which you insist on shaming with your brutish behaviour.' The amused expression vanished. 'But this is not the first time the noble profession and honourable service of the soldier has been disgraced in Ireland, and it is men like you who disgrace it.'

'By the Devil! Who are you to speak to me like that?'

'Allow me to give you my card. I shall be away for a few days, but I will be back in Kildare from the middle of next week, and shall wait in readiness to receive your communication.'

'And you will hear from me, have no doubts on that,' the captain warned as he reached out and took the card, then turned a sickly shade of pale as he stared down at the name inscribed on it, the same name that General Doyle had mentioned numerous times at the military dinner the previous night.

'Such a brave young creature,' the general had said, recounting one of his many stories of service in the American war. 'I rated him soundly and recommended him to the Commander-in-Chief as a most gallant young officer.'

The dragoon officer was still staring at the card, his bowels stirring dangerously as he recalled one of the stories General Doyle had told about the young redcoat who was then his lieutenant.

'Around our camp the American scouts were becoming more numerous and rendered more patrols necessary. I was a major then, and setting out upon a patrol went to instruct my lieutenant to accompany me, but found he had mysteriously disappeared. I had no choice but to proceed without him, but on entering the forest there I spied him, in combat with *two* of the enemy and giving a marvellous performance in the unequal struggle. He had seriously wounded one when his sword broke in the middle, and the other was closing in for the kill. But my fine young officer whipped out his knife to take him on with such elasticated movements and speed, the Yankee turned and fled.'

The dragoon captain now glanced up at the former British officer who was looking at him with eyes like blue ice.

'Perhaps you will request your men to back-step their mounts and allow us to ride on, Captain. We shall meet again next week I trust?'

The captain nodded meekly, waved his men aside, and the two men rode off at a leisurely pace as if the dragoons had never existed. Before they were even out of sight he could hear their conversation had calmly returned to brood mares and stud stallions.

'Irishmen!' said the young lieutenant at his side. 'If they're not calling you out in a fight they're talking about horses.' He made a braying sound and his companions laughed.

'A plague on your tongue and your arse, you stupid bugger!' the captain snapped. 'Do you know who that man is?'

'No more than you did, sir, before he gave you his card. Who is he?'

'Lord Edward Fitzgerald.'

'What? General Doyle's gallant young officer in America?' The lieutenant stared in shocked mortification.

'Lord Edward Fitzgerald,' the captain repeated. 'Nephew of the Duke of Richmond, and younger brother of the Duke of Leinster – the first peer of Ireland!'

'Well, I'll be damned . . . ! Are you going to meet him next week to exchange shots?'

'What? Exchange shots with a former British major? I'll be hanged if I will!'

'Or shot,' an amused voice ventured.

'Damn you, Partridge!' the captain cried savagely, looking at a sneering young dragoon down the line. 'I'll break all your bones!'

'Oh, save your breath to cool your supper. You picked on the wrong ruddy man and that's the end of it. Or at least, I hope it is. Wouldn't do for some sly tongue to inform General Doyle that his noble young redcoat who not only fought for his regiment, but bled for his regiment, was halted on the Curragh Road and abused like a common peasant, would it now?'

Indeed it would not. The entire party were very subdued as they rode on, the captain looking the most worried of all. Not so much because of the challenge which he had no intention of pursuing, but because of the guilt he suddenly felt at Lord

Edward's remark that his behaviour was a disgrace to the noble profession and honourable service of the soldier.

An old peasant in a hat like a flattened black Christmas pudding came along the road. He looked nervously at the officer leading the party, then politely lifted his hat. An hour ago the captain would have scornfully ignored him, but now he touched a finger to his own hat and endeavoured to move his face into something like a pleasant smile. It was a difficult task, but the honour of his profession was at stake.

Chapter Eight

The following day was Sunday. Robert Emmet returned to Dublin in the late morning, having quit the weekend house-party in Wicklow hours earlier than planned. At St Stephen's Green he rode down the lane at the side of the house to the stableyard, dismounted, and had led Black Seamus into his stable when Lennard appeared in the doorway behind him.

'Why, is it yerself, Misther Robert?' The servant saluted him with a touch of his hat. 'We was not expecting ye back till late this evening, seeing as we thought ye would be having such a darling time with all the young ladies, wha'?'

Robert ignored him and bent to unstrap the girths.

'Well? Did ye dance or did ye not?'

Robert made no answer as he removed the saddle and hung it on the wall.

Lennard bunched his brows in a peevish frown, then exclaimed cunningly, 'Ye did then! Dance with the young ladies, I mean. I can tell ye did. Now feel free, Misther Robert, to contradict me if I'm wrong. Contradict me all the way.'

'Now that, Lennard, is something I would never do. Contradict a clever old rascal like you.' Robert walked out to the yard.

'Ah, wait now,' Lennard cried, scurrying after him. 'Don't go marching off. I only want to know—'

'I know you do, Lennard, and I'm not going to satisfy your insatiable curiosity by telling you.'

'Sure I was only showing an interest out of politeness,' Lennard protested. 'And that's a hard way to talk to a man who's worn himself out all these years showing the same interest in ye.'

'Is Thomas at home?'

'And where else would he be? Last I seen him he was heading up to the nursery with Missis Jane. Now then, going back to what I sez—'

'Too much,' Robert remarked. 'That's your trouble, Lennard, you always sez too much.'

'Oh isn't that a slander!' Lennard cried indignantly. 'Ingratitude of the highest form! Why, if 'tweren't for me always bringing ye out of yerself, ye wouldn't be talking so aisy now. Only Thursday I sez it to Billy the Brogue and he mending me shoes: "Too quiet in himself," I sez. "Needed me to bring him out o' himself," I sez. " 'Tis one thing him being a shutmouth while he's young," I sez, "but what about when he gets old? Why, people'd naturally surmise he had no teeth," I sez. "And who'd be blaming them," I sez . . .' Lennard paused to draw breath, just as the garden door was shut in his face.

'Ah, wait now!' He pushed at the door, and was answered by a slam of the bolt.

Robert found his brother alone in the library, bent over a law book. When he entered Thomas looked up, surprised.

'What brings you back so early?'

'The need to study. This is my final year, you know.'

Thomas eyed Robert with concern as he sat down opposite him. 'You look tired.'

'I feel tired,' Robert admitted, 'tired and frustrated by such a waste of a weekend. Getting my university degree is everything to me, Tom, you know that. Only Thomas Moore could have persuaded me to go there.'

His brother smiled. 'Moore, the young papist poet – I'll wager *he* did not spend the time yearning to study.'

'No,' Robert agreed, 'he spent most of the time yearning

after every maiden there, but in the end even he conceded the weekend's entire conversation was little more than a rhapsody of rubbish.'

'Excuse me, sir.' Simmins made a tiptoed entrance, then paused to stare at Robert.

'Well?' Thomas demanded, looking at the letter in the butler's hand. 'Is that for me?'

'Begging your pardon, Mister Thomas, but I was not expecting to find Mister Robert home so soon.' Simmins held out the letter. 'It's just been delivered. Messenger says it's urgent.'

Thomas took the folded square and stared at the red wax seal bearing the coat of arms of the Duke of Leinster. He waited for Simmins to leave, then ripped it open.

'It's from Fitzgerald,' he said after a moment. 'He's staying at Leinster House and wishes to see me as soon as possible.'

'Has he heard from Tone?'

'He doesn't say.'

Just the mention of Tone's name brought a grim and faraway look to Thomas Emmet's face. In 1795 the Society of United Irishmen, which had continually agitated for constitutional reform, had been suppressed. Shortly afterwards, in what everyone knew to be 'a frame' Tone had been accused of having contact with an agent of the French Republic. The government benevolently declared they would take no action, on condition that Theobald Wolfe Tone left the country.

A few days before Tone's departure, he and Russell had spent a long night in Thomas's study. Tone had discussed his plan to compromise with the government and go into exile only so far as the banks of the Delaware, from where he would continue the great object of the United Irishmen: to make Ireland not three nations but one nation, to abolish the memory of all past dissensions, and to substitute the common name of Irishmen in place of the denominations of Protestant, Catholic, and Dissenter.

Finally the three men shook hands in sad farewell and, having repeated their sentiments of unaltered regard and esteem for each other, parted, agreeing that politics are of a day but friendship is for ever.

The next day Russell gave up his commission in the British army and went back to Belfast to devote his every spare moment to rallying the United Irishmen there. A few months later he had been arrested by agents of the government's Secret Committee, brought down to Dublin, and confined in a solitary cell in Newgate Gaol where he had stayed for the past two years without charge or trial.

For weeks Thomas had gone from door to door, from minister to minister, and from judge to judge, in an attempt to get Russell released. John Philpot Curran sprang to his aid, but all their efforts were futile. Even as they argued their case that there was no crime in a citizen making speeches for the need for reform, other suspected United Irishmen were being arrested and imprisoned.

Sad, sad that the British minister should allow so many young men who had spent years on the battlefields in the service of Britain, ready to stand or fall with Britain, to be treated like dogs in their own country of Ireland! But Britain had allowed it. Britain had made it very clear that she was too busy with her own affairs to trouble with the problems of her subjects across the Irish Sea, who did so often give the impression of being a lot of complaining mendicants.

And so it was that the United Irishmen added two new clauses to their great object of union between Irishmen of every religious persuasion: to subvert the tyranny of our execrable Government – *and to break the connection with Britain*. As soon as Tone learned that Russell and his compatriots were confined in an Irish Bastille, he immediately left America for France.

Thomas folded the letter. 'I'd better go straight away,' he said. 'I'll inform Jane.'

Robert bit down on his lip as he watched his brother stride out of the library, knowing that Thomas was now walking a very dangerous path. Dublin Castle, which had thrived for centuries on the successful policy of 'Divide and Conquer', was determined to destroy the society of men who dared to oppose its rule.

Leinster House, a magnificent grey-stone mansion of countless corridors and over fifty rooms, was the town residence of the Geraldines, less than a ten-minute walk across St Stephen's Green to Kildare Street.

Although Thomas Emmet walked at an easy pace he was eager to see Fitzgerald again, for he liked the young nobleman enormously. More than any man he had ever met, Lord Edward had a singular charm and was the most attractive of the Geraldines.

The ancient Geraldines had once ruled the province of Leinster with almost royal power from the Castle of Maynooth, but now the family seat was the palatial estate of Carton in Kildare. And although the Duke of Leinster was regarded with affection by the common people, it was his younger brother who was the popular hero.

Even as a boy, it was said, Lord Edward had a marked military bent. At seventeen he entered the 96th Infantry as a lieutenant, then exchanged into the 19th to get foreign service. In 1781 at the age of eighteen he was sent to America where he distinguished himself against the forces of one of the toughest American commanders, Colonel Lee.

His skill in covering a retreat soon achieved him the post of aide to Lord Rawdon, then in command of the British forces at Charleston. But during a battle in Carolina, Lord Edward suffered badly, as did his regiment. He was wounded and left unconscious on the field, and would have died had not a Negro, whose only name was Tony, found him and carried him back to his hut where he nursed him back to health. Wherever Lord Edward went after that, he took Tony with him.

He went to Canada, to join his new regiment, the 54th, of which he was made major. Reports came back that, during his time in Nova Scotia, Lord Edward highlighted his very Irishness by encouraging his hungry soldiers to make gardens and grow food (much to their amusement) but, after a long trip to Montreal, he returned to find the gardens bursting with vegetables and the men delighted. His sergeant-major in the 54th, a man called Cobbet, still described him as the only really *honest* officer he had ever known.

He was twenty-five when he received his papers to return home but, instead, accompanied only by his Negro friend Tony, he fulfilled his love for the natural life by setting out on an arduous expedition through great tracts of unexplored wild country to Quebec and into America, meeting only an occasional Indian tribe whose simplicity of life filled him with delight and which he still described as 'a life more sweet than painted pomp'. His love of the Indians was returned in a singular ceremony at Detroit where, at the hands of an Indian Chief, one of the Six Nations, an unprecedented honour was given to the young officer by making him a Chief of the Bear Tribe.

'*No devilish politics here!*' Lord Edward wrote home, but the time came when he had to return to Ireland where devilish politics hung over the land like a stench. He was brought into Parliament by his brother, as the Member for Kildare.

And that was when the change began in Lord Edward Fitzgerald, a radical change.

Sitting in the midst of a corrupt parliamentary system where votes were bargained for and bought by the few in exchange for position and peerages, Lord Edward publicly questioned why the Catholics, seven-eighths of Ireland's population, were not allowed any constitutional rights, not even the right of citizenship in their own land.

The House was appalled at such a question.

The House was appalled at Lord Edward Fitzgerald, who continually insisted on bringing his views into Parliament, not like a fresh wind but an angry storm that greatly discomfited the comfortable members. He accused them of the vilest corruption, placing self-interest before any other. On one occasion, raising the House to uproar by describing the Viceroy and his politicians as 'the worst subjects the King has!', he was ordered to apologise, but refused.

'By God,' shouted his brother the Duke from the gallery, 'he shall not apologise!'

And so the matter was ended, but never forgotten, and never forgiven.

Thomas walked through the open black-iron gates of Leinster House and proceeded up the long drive. The front door was opened by an eagle-faced man whom Thomas presumed to be the head footman, attired in white wig and stockings, black brocade livery and black slippers.

'Please wait hee-ah!' the footman said imperiously, then strutted away, leaving Thomas standing in the main hall, avoiding the eyes of two younger footmen who stood to attention like soldiers but had eyes that darted up and down and over him.

He stood with hands behind his back, head tilted as he gazed up at the exquisite ceiling, scrolls and mouldings picked out in gilt and forming a perfect frame for the blue and pink angelic scene hand painted by an Italian artist.

Thomas wondered if Fitzgerald had brought Lady Edward with him, and the thought made him smile – even in his romantic life Fitzgerald had outraged the establishment. During a trip to Paris six years ago he had visited the theatre to see a performance of *Lodoiska*, but spent the entire evening staring at a beautiful young girl in the opposite box. In response to his urgent inquiries, he was informed that she was unworthy of his consideration – the illegitimate daughter of Madame de Genlis, servant-housekeeper in the palace of the Duke of Orleans. The girl, seventeen years old and named Pamela, had been reared in the palace by the housekeeper, and was employed as companion-in-waiting to the princess in the box.

He married her five days later, and brought her home to the biggest scandal Ireland had enjoyed for years – the son of the twentieth Earl of Kildare and brother of the Duke of Leinster had married a nameless bastard of common blood, the daughter of a servant in the Palais Royal. Lord Edward had been one of the most sought-after bachelors in Irish society and the offended mothers of snubbed débutantes breathlessly clucked and clacked and wondered how the Duke would announce such a *mésalliance* in the Press.

When the announcement came, published in the Dublin and London papers, the people did not believe it, but later examination of the marriage certificate proved that Louis Philippe Joseph (Égalité) had not only attended the private wedding ceremony, but had also signed the certificate. And so the notice of marriage read:

The Hon. Lord Edward Fitzgerald, Knight of the Shire for the Co. Kildare, to Pamela, daughter of his Royal Highness the ci-devant Duke of Orleans.

The marriage made Fitzgerald even more popular with the common people, and even pleased his political enemies – for one reason alone. It kept him away from Parliament House. He declined re-election, insisting he preferred the company of his wife to that of politicians. His particular love of trees and flowers now kept him as much as possible in the green and peaceful country of Kildare with his two little children.

Or so the men at Dublin Castle thought.

The head footman returned, followed by a magnificent tall Negro who radiated an air of special authority. As always there was an attractive vitality in his face, which was smiling.

'Mawnin', Mist' Emmet. You sho came fast!'

'Good morning, Tony. The letter said as soon as possible.'

Tony shot a severe look at the three footmen staring and listening. 'You come 'long with me now, Mist' Emmet. Lawd Eddie says fer me to take you upstairs.' Then, turning towards a seemingly endless corridor off the main hall, he added in a loud, indignant voice, obviously for the benefit of the pompous head footman: 'Huccome you wasn't asked to set down, Mist' Emmet? In Kildare the guests don't git left standin' like lennets. These city footmen got no mo' manners than blood.'

Thomas smiled, his eyes on the splendid dark green suit that Tony wore. But then, Tony always wore green.

'You're a bit of a green linnet yourself,' Thomas said. 'I have often wondered, Tony, why do you never wear any other colour?'

Tony's eyes shot round. 'The colour of mah country, Mist' Emmet. From the fest day at Carton when they come to fet me out with clo'es, I tole Lawd Eddie I'd like to wears green. An' he says, "Sho you can, Tony. Every day ef you like." An so I wears it, every day.'

Tony gave a self-conscious little smile. 'You see, Mist' Emmet, I been in I'land a long time now, long time; an' these days I likes to think of mahself as an Irishman.'

'To be an Irishman,' Thomas told him gently, 'I think you have to be born here.'

'Then huccome the King o' England is a German ginl'man?' Tony's tone was defiant. 'An' from what I hears he don't speak

108

even good English! But me—' Tony's black eyes laughed and danced, 'I can speak English an' Irish!'

'Go on then,' Thomas challenged. 'Speak in Irish.'

'Conas tá tú?' Tony said smugly.

'How am I? Tá go maith. I am well.'

'M'anam!' (On my soul!) Tony cried. 'A thiarcais!' (My goodness!) 'Maith an fear!' (Good man!)

Thomas smiled. 'Excellent!'

Tony's delighted laughing echoed right down the east corridor. 'So you see, Mist' Emmet, I *is* an Irishman now. I's an Irishman jes' like mah Lawd Eddie – septin' he was born in England an' I was born in Georgia.'

'Was he born in England?' Thomas looked surprised.

'Don' mean he ain't Irish jes' 'cos he got dropped someplace else,' Tony explained pleasantly.

At that moment Lord Edward came striding down the corridor, looking somewhat boyish and careless in a cream full-sleeved shirt and buff riding-breeches. 'Thank you for coming so promptly, Thomas.' He smiled warmly as he extended his hand, and it was not the first time Thomas noticed what a handsome man Fitzgerald was.

'Can I gits back now to what I was doin' befo' you called me, Lawd Eddie?'

Fitzgerald looked at Tony; their eyes were of a level and he asked somewhat curiously, 'What were you doing?'

'Mindin' mah own bizness,' Tony said innocently.

'Would you mind mine for a little longer?'

Tony nodded. 'Uh huh.'

'Ask the kitchen to hold luncheon for another hour.'

'Oh, they ain't gonna like that!' Tony rumbled, strutting towards the back staircase. 'They tole me they don't like nuthin' or no one that hupsets the routine o' their ketchen. Not no darkie, not no duke, an' not no dahlin Lawd Eddie – even ef he *is* an Injun Chief.'

Lord Edward laughed; then took Thomas's elbow and led him further down the east passage. Thomas could not help but admire the endless Persian carpets, the Waterford chandeliers, the sheer elegance of Leinster House.

'Bye the bye, what a melancholy house this is,' Lord Edward

said with a sigh. 'Footmen standing like dummies in every passage, staff with faces as stiff as corpses, corridors designed like a maze to confuse . . .'

'You obviously don't find it as awe-inspiring as others do.'

'Leinster House,' Lord Edward replied, 'does not inspire the brightest ideas. You can't imagine how I hate it after Kildare. Tony dreads the place, grumbles incessantly; and a poor little country housemaid I brought with me last time cried for two days – said she thought she was in a prison.'

'Speaking of prisons,' Thomas said, 'I had the displeasure of meeting your most ardent enemy on Friday. I went to the Castle to see Under-Secretary Cooke about one of my clients in Newgate Prison. Lord Castlereagh was lolling on a sofa and never once shifted from his languorous position throughout my entire interview with Cooke.'

'A pox on Castlereagh!' Fitzgerald said grimly. 'We'll talk about him later. But first come up to the Rose Room and say hello to Pamela.'

'Is she well?'

'My dear little wife is very well, goes on delightfully. She continues to grow both broad and tall.' He smiled at Thomas, his eyes twinkling. 'Indeed, she has taken quite a fit of growing lately, as you will see.'

When they entered the small and cosily furnished Rose Room, what Thomas saw was a most beautiful creature of dark Gallic looks dressed in a long flowing gown of the softest blue. 'M'sieur Emmet – *bonjour*!'

Her warm smile and soft French accent quite melted Thomas, and when she rose he saw what Lord Edward had been alluding to: Lady Edward was quite pregnant. He bowed. '*Bonjour*, Madame.'

They spoke conventionally for some minutes until Lord Edward interrupted with an apology. 'Pamela,' he said, 'Thomas and I have business to discuss upstairs, but we shall dine together in here shortly, just the three of us. Yes?' He held her hands as he spoke to her, looking at her with a lover's eyes, and she nodded and smiled like one who knows she is highly cherished.

Do I still look like that at Jane? Thomas wondered.

After the Rose Room Thomas was taken up even more stairs and passages, and as they walked Lord Edward said quietly, 'So, you were forced to discuss your business with Under-Secretary Cooke in the presence of the king spider, eh?'

Thomas smiled at Fitzgerald's description. At the head of the regime in Dublin Castle was the Viceroy, Lord Camden, Lord Castlereagh, his nephew by marriage and Chief Secretary of State, and Lord Clare who had been elevated from the judiciary bench to complete the trinity as their Lord Chancellor – the three Cs who held Ireland in a tight web of power. But the king spider was Castlereagh.

The two men entered a large room which contained a long green-baize table in its centre. From beneath the table Lord Edward lifted out two long billiard cues.

'Organising against the Castle is such a grim and serious business,' he said with a wry smile, 'I thought it might be less so if we talked over a game of billiards.'

Chapter Nine

In the kitchen of The Priory at Rathfarnham, Mrs Jessop stood by the table busily slicing a joint of ham. Sarah Curran sat on a stool beside her, face cupped in her hands as she gave a loud sigh of discontent.

'Well I don't know what you can do, Miss Sarah. What do you want to do?'

'Oh I don't *know* what I want to do,' Sarah cried. 'I just want to do something! Everyone says that life is made for the young, but I have less fun than the old grannies with hairs on their chins.'

Mrs Jessop dug the knife into the ham but through the corner of her eye she looked at the auburn-haired girl of sixteen. She was blossoming into a beautiful maid, as beautiful as her mother; the same voluptuous mouth and huge brilliant eyes. And, added to that, the same timid nature that hid a storm of restlessness. Only Miss Sarah's long dark silences reminded Mrs Jessop of her father . . . her poor father.

Mrs Jessop sighed affectionately as she thought of her master. A lovely man in her book. And a man for the ladies, no mistake. Not that he was the sort to go around whoring, but men is men, wife or no, and a man like the master needed a lady's gentle company now and again.

A gleam came into Mrs Jessop's beady black eyes and her red jowls wobbled. Bless me, she thought with a sniff, but it made you think, didn't it? The mistress running off with the parson like that. Like some gormless servant-maid who didn't know any better. But Mrs Jessop had seen it coming – oh yes! All that whispering and praying together. Mrs Jessop had known what they were thinking – they were the goody-goodies and the master the baddie, just because the poor heartbroken man could not bear his grief. Bloody hypocrites! Whisperers were always sly, sly as the divils, sly as Old Nick himself!

Whenever she thought of it, Mrs Jessop felt she could murder the mistress. But still, the master was well rid of her, for a dull piece she had been for all her beauty; no understanding in her, no laughter, no fire in her blood. And not one bit of pity did Mrs Jessop feel for her now, now the pious parson had thrown her over, deserted her for some other snivelling goody-goody he could whisper his smarmy talk to. Now the mistress lived alone somewhere in England, forbidden to come near or disclose her whereabouts to her children. And now she wanted the master back, was mad to get him back, but too late she had learned that if you sow the wind you may reap the whirlwind; and there were no second chances with John Philpot Curran.

That would teach her! And serves her right, the selfish creature, for whatever her grievances against the master, she had not given a thought to the broken home and broken child she was leaving behind her. Amelia and Richard had coped, sort of; but little Sarah! Oh, would Mrs Jessop ever forget that day? The sight of that poor heartbroken child on the bed, her little body shaking like a leaf, the eyes rolling in her head.

And then there was the little boy she had also left behind,

William Henry, the cuckoo in the nest, tucked away in the nursery with his nurse. God bless him, for it wouldn't be long before he was packed away to school.

No, the master would never forgive his wife, never agree even to discuss the matter with her, and the payments to her would continue only so long as he never – and he had stressed the word when giving his reply to her emissary – *never* laid eyes on her again.

But there were times, Mrs Jessop had lately observed, when his eyes dwelt on young Sarah, that he would suddenly go into one of his . . . silences.

The ham was hacked to shreds now. Lazily, Sarah reached out and slipped a piece into her mouth, a remote look in her eyes.

Mrs Jessop frowned. Young Dr Sheridan – him that took over from old Dr Sheridan – said that Miss Sarah was truly recovered from her illness now, but Mrs Jessop often wondered. Sometimes when you spoke to the girl, she didn't answer, didn't even seem to hear, her blue eyes empty, her thoughts far away. She could sit for hours like that, lost in her own silent world. Most of her time was spent either playing her harp or wandering alone over the hills, sauntering off at noon and sauntering back at dusk. At times she looked so lonely and lost it made you want to sit right down and cry for her.

Then at other times she would get angry and hysterical, like a harnessed young filly chafing at the bit; and it could be quite a job to calm her, quite a job! Bless us all, but it made you think, didn't it?

'Oh the days seem so long when there's nothing to do in them!' Sarah heaved another gusty sigh.

The housekeeper looked at her pityingly. 'Well just think, acushla,' she said gently, 'this time next year you may be going to the academy for a few days a week. Won't that be good?'

Sarah looked doubtful. 'If Papa lets me go. He keeps saying the Celbridge Music Academy is very expensive.'

'Aye, well, it probably is.'

'He doesn't care how much he spends on Richard's education at Trinity though. And he's only studying law because Papa is a lawyer.' She lifted a another shred of ham and slipped

113

it into her mouth. 'But Amelia and I have real talent – my music and Amelia's painting.'

'Oh, aye,' Mrs Jessop agreed, 'even Mr Keegan says you play the harp and sing beautifully.'

Sarah was not used to compliments, her delight at this one brought a smile and bright colour to her face which, in Mrs Jessop's tender opinion, made her look very young and *very* sweet.

'And if Richard had shown the same love of music,' Sarah said, 'Papa would have had him in a music academy years ago. But not me of course. I'm just a worthless female.'

'Worthless is it?' Mrs Jessop chuckled. 'But where in the name of God would men be without us, eh? They wouldn't even be born! And that's what kills them, kills their vanity. They much prefer the story of a woman being made from a man's rib, and just one rib at that, while Adam still had eight or nine to spare.'

'I've often thought about the Garden of Eden,' Sarah mused, 'and in my opinion the whole thing was rather unfair.'

'Rather unfair,' Mrs Jessop repeated, for she was in no mood to disagree with the child. 'I mean, on the sixth day was it, God created man – took a whole day on it, too. But then in a minute out comes a rib and there's poor Eve with only a fig leaf to keep her warm while Adam is covered in glory.' Just the thought of it made Mrs Jessop's cap-ribbons shake with indignation.

'And though it was Eve who plucked the apple,' Sarah said, 'Adam did share in the eating.'

'Scoffed the lot if truth were known, and left poor Eve only the core.'

'And why,' Sarah wondered, 'was it only the poor woman who was punished? In sorrow and travail thou shalt bring forth children . . .'

'Because it was the woman who tempted the poor man,' said Keegan, who had paused at the door to listen, and now walked in.

'Who asked for your opinion?' Mrs Jessop said with a sniff. 'Sure what would an oul bachelor like you know about temptation anyway?'

Keegan's mouth fell open at the audacity of it. For the head

114

of the kitchen to speak to the head of the dining-room like that was not something to be let away with! 'I know all about temptation,' he retorted hotly, 'but 'tis only the dignity of my position that restrains me from yielding to it this very minute.'

'Your position is it? Commander-in-Chief of the knives and forks!' Mrs Jessop put her hands on her hips and laughed.

Keegan spluttered and turned the colour of blueberries while the housekeeper seemed overcome with merriment. At last she gasped out: 'I've not heard the like since my Malachi strutted in and told me he had landed the cream of a position. "Poll," says he, "Poll," he says, "me luck has changed, girl. No more bowing and touching the forelock for me. From this day forth," says he, "I'll be going places!" Turned out he'd landed a job driving an old nag and cart on the dairyman's milk round!'

The housekeeper rocked at the memory, and Sarah wandered out of the kitchen, knowing Mrs Jessop was about to strip layers off the dignity of Keegan's position.

Her mood darkened, her discontent overwhelmed her. She was sixteen, in the spring of her life, the sweetest of her years, and yet unhappiness stalked her every footstep. She was a prisoner in this house with no foreseeable hope of deliverance from the dreariness of her daily life. Her mother's relatives had been banned from entering the house years ago, and not even her father's brothers were given welcome any more, not since they had chosen to shun him after Gertrude's funeral. When they had relented and offered to console him after the defection of his wife, he had simply closed the door in their faces.

Such a quiet and desolate house this was! Even Richard spent most of his time these days in his rooms at Trinity. But she had no escape, for she was rarely allowed to venture further abroad than the surrounding hills where she took her walks, or the twice-yearly visits to the dressmaker in Dublin. Her father guarded his family with a possessive privacy, although he showed little affection to any of them.

Sarah did not blame him. She thought she understood. Underneath the carefree manner he showed to the outside world he was a man wrapped up in his own memories, in his own heartache that would never completely go away, for every few days he placed a posy of flowers on the little grave outside his study window. Even in winter, even in snowtime, he managed to find some flower or shrub to show a watching angel above that her memory still lived, but his favourite flower of all seasons was the forget-me-not.

He would never forget Gertrude, and never forgive the woman who was her mother. And on those two memories, for that's all they were now, memories, Sarah had once thought that an emotional link might have been forged between herself and her father, a sharing. But she had thought wrong. Her father shared his love and his hate with none other than himself.

For a time she tried to make up to him for all his loss, to be as interesting a daughter as Gertrude had been, to make him smile tenderly as her mother had once done, but all her efforts had gone unnoticed or served only to irritate him. Even so, she still loved her father, even though she had to admit that for the most part she was terrified of him. He could cut a person dead with a look of his eye quicker than any parson or judge.

She walked listlessly up the main stairs until she reached her bedroom. From her window she could see Amelia in the adjoining meadow, positioned as usual by her easel, palette and paintbrush in hand. The day was golden and warm, the mountains quilted in yellow gorse and purple heather.

She turned away and threw herself down on the bed, one half of her long auburn hair covering her breast like a shawl. She stared up at the ceiling, trying to quell the familiar feeling of emptiness beginning to swell inside her. It was a feeling like a big black empty hole, swelling more each day, each month, each year, swelling so big she was sure one day it would swamp her so completely that eventually all that people would see when they looked at her, was an empty space.

She closed her eyes, for she had long ago learned that sleep is nature's protection against grief. And although she had not risen until just before noon, within minutes she was sleeping as soundly as a tired child.

Chapter Ten

Inside the Chancery Court, Counsellor Leonard McNally awoke from a doze, yawned, and pushed a finger under his wig to scratch behind his ear. His legs, one shorter than the other, were stretched lazily under the defence table. He caught the judge glancing in his direction and quickly jerked into a pose of rapt attention; his squat, ugly face straining to grasp the proceedings.

'I think we will adjourn there for today,' his lordship announced to the prosecution, then smiled at the leading counsel for the defence.

'Have you any objections, Mr Curran?'

John Curran returned the smile. 'None whatsoever, my lord.'

McNally observed the warm exchange between his colleague and the new Lord Chief Justice. No fractious Lord Clare here. Lord Kilwarden was the most popular judge in the land, and for years had been a bosom chum of John Curran. And McNally approved the friendship, for in all the world Jack Curran was the only man he could truly say he liked.

As they left the court McNally's body felt stiff, his limp even more pronounced than usual. 'Come along, Mac,' John Curran called, 'I told Dr Emmet we would be there by five.'

McNally shuffled behind him, grumbling as he pulled himself into the waiting carriage, 'It has taken Thomas Emmet long enough to invite me to meet his father, don't you think? Still, I suppose I must consider it an honour to dine with the eminent doctor.'

Although John Curran ignored the remark, he felt great sympathy for the crippled barrister. McNally might practise at the Irish Bar but he had never been fully accepted on a social level by its members. Part of the reason was his physical unattractiveness and somewhat gross manners. McNally insisted it was simply because he had once sold groceries in Dublin before going to the Middle Temple in London to study law. His reputation was further tarnished by reports that, whilst in London, he had spent some time employed as an actor.

The carriage rattled over the cobblestones of Bridgefoot Street into Thomas Street, a poor but colourful quarter of

Dublin known as the Liberties, so called since the year 1171 when King Henry II came to Ireland with his army, still grieving in his heart for his most-beloved friend and archbishop who had been murdered in his cathedral by the King's own knights. After a few days Henry rode out to St Catherine's Church and pointed to the land all around it. 'Here,' he commanded, 'let this site of land be dedicated to our holy martyr Thomas à Becket!'

Then he gave a special liberty to the people and the monks of the area, decreeing they would owe allegiance to none other than God and the King. From then on the land received royal grants, and became known as the Liberty of Thomas Court. Later, King John supported Henry's Liberty and drew up a charter to its effect.

And so the area had prospered, and the people had thrived in relative happiness, until four hundred years later when another King Henry, the Eighth, sent his army to seize the Liberty land and its assets which were simply handed as a gift to his Treasurer in Ireland, William Brabazon. Instead of royal grants, high rents were imposed by the Brabazons, who later became the Earls of Meath. By the end of Queen Elizabeth's reign, the Liberties had deteriorated into poverty-stricken slums, the worst in the western world.

Deep in thought, John Curran watched the pavement scenes as the carriage rolled slowly down Thomas Street. Women in black shawls lined the street beside carts of vegetables and fruit. Men held aloft trays of Dublin Bay herrings and shouted so loudly no one could hear them. Here and there an urchin blew on a flute or did a jig while a friend held out a hat to passers-by.

'Dr Emmet is reputed to be a passionate supporter of constitutional rights for the common people,' McNally said suddenly. 'Some say fanatically so.'

'Perhaps he is a little fanatical,' Curran allowed. 'He is highly skilled in the treatment of fevers, and over the years his work has brought him into intimate contact with the poor. He loves them deeply.'

'Indeed!'

McNally wondered how anyone could possibly love that mass of half-starved filth known as the Dublin poor. But then it was easy to be sentimental about poverty when you had plenty.

Easy not to see the battalions of pickpockets, shoplifters, and every other kind of swindler that swarmed Dublin; easy when you lived in the peaceful serenity of Dublin's stateliest square where a beggar would be moved on immediately.

Both men were silent as they drove past Dublin Castle, just a few streets from Thomas Street. At the entrance to the lower courtyard soldiers stood to attention, while through the high arch leading to the upper yard could be seen the long windows of the state apartments.

It was only when they drove into College Green, where Trinity College and Parliament House faced each other like rivals, that conversation resumed. 'One houses the best of the new young intellects,' Curran remarked. 'The other the worst of the old.'

Up Grafton Street and into the tree-lined square of St Stephen's Green. Although just a few miles, this area was a world away from the narrow streets and clustered houses of the Liberties. These red-brick mansions with black-iron balconies on their first-floor windows belonged to the Protestant nobility and professional classes. The carriage rattled over to the west side of the square and came to a halt outside the Emmet house.

McNally rubbed his palms together. Socially, he was moving up and up and up!

It was almost midnight. Thomas Emmet pulled back a fold of the heavy brocade curtains of the dining-room and looked out on to the square. He watched the man stroll casually along the Green; the same man he had seen every night for the past week. He was now positive that officers of the Castle's secret service were watching the house.

His glance moved to the front steps where Curran and McNally were taking their leave of his father, entering their carriage. It had been for the most part an enjoyable evening. John Curran was always an entertaining guest. A pity the same could not be said for Leonard McNally.

During the early stages of the dinner, McNally had responded in a patronising manner to his father, especially when the doctor spoke about the deplorable living conditions of the Dublin poor. Throughout, McNally had continually reached to pat his father's hand, a gesture which had increasingly irritated Thomas. And when his father went on to discuss the children constantly dying of starvation, McNally had greatly embarrassed everyone by bursting into tears.

Thomas turned back to the table and sat down to finish his brandy. Still, McNally was a true patriot; and, together and separately, he and Curran had defended many of the United Irishmen in court. It was only on a social level he found McNally so tiresome.

And *tired* was how Thomas felt now.

He placed the glass back on the table deciding to leave it unfinished. He had drunk far too much tonight as it was.

McNally limped back into the room. 'Ah, Thomas! I know the hour is late, but I wish to have a little talk with you.'

Thomas stared at him in dismay. 'Did I not just see you enter Curran's carriage?'

'You did,' McNally replied, 'but I sent him on home. I can get a hack later.'

Dr Emmet entered the room, and also appeared slightly irritated by McNally's return.

'Robert is not home yet,' he said to Thomas. 'Do you know where he is?'

'At the Rotunda Rooms apparently. Dining with his friends.'

'Oh, well, he could be out for hours then. I'll say good night, Thomas.' He bowed slightly to their visitor. 'And again to you, Mr McNally.'

As soon as the doctor had left the room, McNally quickly withdrew a copy of the *Press* newspaper from under his cloak and sat down.

'I did not wish to speak to you earlier in the presence of Jack Curran,' whispered McNally. 'He is a passionate supporter of the national cause, as you know, but he will have nothing to do with secret societies. He is not aware that I am . . . involved.'

'Is there something in the *Press* which disturbs you?'

'Not in the least. Quite the opposite. I have some money I wish to invest and, as a measure of support to the cause, I thought to purchase shares in the paper. But even the editor claims to have no idea who is financing it. I ask for your assistance, Thomas.'

'Would your investment not be more profitable elsewhere?'

'It is not profit I am after. I have to be careful, Thomas, very careful indeed. The fact that I have defended rebels puts me under suspicion with the Castle. Did you know the militia searched my house last night?'

Thomas nodded wearily. 'You did mention it this evening.'

'Disgraceful!' Anger sparked in McNally's eyes. 'I have no idea what they were searching for, but I intend to make a full complaint to the Castle personally. They must learn they cannot treat respectable citizens in such a manner – not without some sort of justification.'

He looked so enraged that Thomas offered him a glass of brandy which he eagerly accepted. 'However,' McNally continued on a calmer note, 'the *Press* speaks out for the people against the government and I wish to be a chord in that voice.'

'How much were you thinking of investing?'

'Three hundred pounds.'

'Three hundred!' Thomas sat upright. 'That is quite an investment.'

'And worth every penny, I say.' McNally withdrew another packet from inside his cloak and placed it on the table. 'And every penny is there in front of you, Thomas. Now, who is the man that will say aye or nay to it?'

'If you are only interested in supporting the United cause, why not just give the money as a donation?'

'Oh, come now, Thomas! Three hundred pounds is a great deal of money. A fortune! As much as some men earn in ten years. And although I shall not be looking for a profit, or even a return of my investment, I must confess to a little vanity. To be a secret shareholder in the *Press* would give me a great feeling of satisfaction, and a sense of playing a real part in the United cause.'

The rich claret and heady port was beginning to make Thomas feel dizzy. He put a hand to his brow and tried to concentrate. 'You know the Castle would dearly love to know who is financing the paper. They do not take kindly to having their terrorism constantly exposed—'

'I am well aware of the Castle's opinion of the *Press* newspaper,' McNally told him. 'But if we allow them to intimidate us we are finished.'

'Three hundred pounds . . .'

'Three hundred pounds.' McNally's voice rose impatiently as he repeated the sum. 'What say you, Thomas? Who do I do business with?'

Thomas sighed, then conceded. 'Your investment will be very welcome,' he said.

'Aha!' McNally smiled triumphantly. 'I suspicioned it! For weeks now I've racked my brains and suspicioned you must be the man behind the paper. So now, when will I meet the other shareholders?'

'I will have to discuss the matter with them first.'

'When?'

'Soon. You'll hear from me within the next few days.'

A note of sudden fear crept into McNally's voice. 'My involvement will remain undisclosed to all but those few. I can rely on that?'

'Certainly.'

McNally struggled to his feet and extended a hand. 'I apologise for keeping you up, Thomas. I shall leave the money here and will await to hear from you.'

He turned to the door then turned back again, his face beaming. 'Secret shareholders together, Thomas. You and I will become closer friends now. I'm very pleased about that. Very pleased indeed.'

When Thomas quietly entered his bedroom he was surprised to find the candle burning, the bed-curtains open, and his wife still awake.

'Jane,' he whispered, moving over to the bed, 'why are you not asleep?'

'Waiting for you.'

'Devil take McNally for keeping me then.' He kissed her lightly and gave a tired smile. 'If I had known, I would not have drunk so much port.'

She twitched her nose as he kissed her again. 'Or brandy!'

'Tch! You know brandy is like medicine to us Emmets. My mistake was taking too much claret during dinner and too much port afterwards.'

'Why did you then? It's not like you to drink to excess.'

'McNally's fault. His performance with father was too much to suffer on a dry stomach.'

'Do you dislike the man?'

Thomas considered the question as he removed his cravat. 'Yes, I suppose I do. But I am forced to work with him, both in the courts and in the organisation. I try to be fair to him.'

Jane watched him dreamily. She had been his wife now for six years, had borne him two sons, and loved him every bit as passionately as on the day she had married him.

Illogically, something drew Thomas over to the window. He pulled back the curtain and looked down to where the wrought-iron street-lamp lit the pavement. A cat squatted lazily under its glow. Slowly his eyes moved around the silent and empty square. All the windows of the surrounding houses were in darkness. Jane murmured to him from the bed. He closed the curtains, overlapping the edges.

A sound outside!

He opened a fold quickly. The cat was standing now with its back arched, its tail perpendicular and ears pricked. It suddenly darted from the light into one of the black corners of the square.

Before departing Dr Emmet's house, Leonard McNally's eyes had also scanned the square carefully. The Castle agent he had spotted earlier had disappeared. Satisfied, McNally limped to the corner just in time to catch a passing hackney.

Alighting on Wood Quay, McNally stood and watched the carriage out of sight, then he cut through the narrow streets which led to Dublin Castle.

Edward Cooke, the Under-Secretary of State, did not hide his displeasure at his visitor calling so late at night, but when McNally took the *Press* from his pocket and spread it on the desk, Cooke smiled.

'I have used your money as you suggested,' McNally said matter of factly, 'and have succeeded in becoming a shareholder. The paper is financed by Thomas Emmet and other United Irishmen. I will have the names of the others within the week.'

'You have done well! So many of our informers take our money and give very little in return, but you have delivered as promised.'

'I resent being referred to as an informer,' McNally snapped. 'I am a true Irishman and a loyal subject of the King.'

Edward Cooke managed to hide his scorn. He felt utter contempt for a man whose loyalty had to be paid for, but he did not wish to offend McNally further. The Castle needed all the information they could get if they were to defeat the rebels throughout the country. He opened a drawer and withdrew a hundred-pound note and a secret-service payment ledger which he pushed in front of his informer.

'Please sign as usual, Mr McNally.'

'Do not use my name,' McNally hissed. 'We agreed it would never be used, no matter how safe the situation.'

Cooke apologised.

The barrister signed the book with the initials 'J.W.' then smiled smugly. No one looking through that book at any time could ever trace payments back to Leonard McNally. He carefully placed the money in a pocket under his cloak.

'By the way,' McNally said, 'what was the idea of sending Major Sirr to search my house last night?'

'I thought the raid would have pleased you.' Cooke returned the book to the drawer and turned the key. 'You recently mentioned something about Thomas Emmet having suspicions about you.'

'Oh, that.' McNally shrugged. 'That was some time ago, over a court case. You must have misunderstood me, Mr Cooke. Tom Emmet's doubts have been well taken care of, but I must admit that at the time I was worried. I thought the Crown lawyers handled the matter very badly.'

'Oh, how so?'

'They showed an uncanny knowledge of the strategy Emmet would use in court and were ready for him at every turn. It was blatantly obvious that *someone* had shown Emmet's brief to the prosecution beforehand.' McNally limped towards the door. 'Fortunately for me, there was another counsellor besides myself aiding Emmet. I managed to place suspicion on his head.'

'Then I regret any inconvenience suffered by the search.'

'My wife was greatly distressed. I would be grateful if you would ensure that it does not happen again.'

'Just a moment!' Cooke called as the barrister reached to open the door.

McNally turned, chin and eyebrows raised, and Cooke continued, 'We are informed that a certain nobleman of Kildare is closely linked with Thomas Emmet and his friends. It appears they have had meetings long into the night, and the matters they discuss could be of a treasonable nature. Have you any knowledge of the matter?'

McNally hesitated. The Englishman was asking for more than he had paid for. 'There are various levels within the United Irishmen,' he replied cautiously. 'My role is simply to defend any of their members who get into trouble. I am not privy to the secret discussions of their leaders . . . Of course, the United men do trust me implicitly, and rebel prisoners tell me things they would not normally divulge to any other counsel.' He did not add, 'except Curran and Emmet'.

McNally then gave the Under-Secretary a calculating look. Favour with the Castle could prove very beneficial to him in the days ahead. 'But now that you mention it, I think I did hear a whisper about Lord Edward Fitzgerald. Hmn, what was it now . . .'

Edward Cooke knew the game, knew the ploy. 'You surely know by now, Counsellor, that the Castle is always ready to show gratitude to its friends.'

McNally smiled. 'Oh, now I recall. It seems Fitzgerald has decided to turn his back on Parliament as a means of achieving his aims. He believes the time has come for more revolutionary measures.'

'Does he indeed?'

'Thomas Emmet, on the other hand, thinks Lord Edward is being impetuous and impulsive.'

'Ah, yes,' said Cooke. 'I am told Counsellor Emmet is a cool intellectual. Quite unlike the headstrong Fitzgerald.'

McNally smiled maliciously. 'And were you also told that Thomas Emmet wants a call to arms just as much as Fitzgerald? And that he simply believes it would be more prudent to wait for French assistance.'

'French!'

McNally inwardly relished the nervousness that word

always evoked in the Castle men. 'French,' he repeated.

'What connections have they made with the French?' Cooke demanded.

McNally pulled on his earlobe. 'That I don't know . . . yet.'

'Then please continue to keep your ears cocked in that direction,' Cooke urged. 'We have men posted both here and in Kildare, but your assistance will be appreciated.'

'And rewarded?'

Cooke forced a smile. 'As always.'

Chapter Eleven

In the home of his Trinity friend, Thomas Moore, on Aungier Street, Robert Emmet sat on the window seat of the first-floor drawing-room gazing thoughtfully beyond the lace curtains to the dark and deserted street below.

The sound of rain lashing against the cobblestones had a strangely tranquil effect upon him, and he was glad of it. He had lately considered Sunday to be the most peaceful day of the week, a day free from the grinding study for his degree exams.

He closed his eyes and wondered why, all through this particular Sunday, a sensation akin to impending doom bore down on him. What it was he could not define. Mental fatigue, perhaps, from studying long into the small hours?

Richard Curran and Thomas Moore were sitting at the piano a few feet away. Tom played while Richard happily sang in a voice that could only be described as a bad joke. Robert turned his head and watched in amusement as Tom soldiered on at the keyboard, giving Emmet a weary roll of his eyes as Richard belted out discordant notes way above his range.

Robert smiled at Tom Moore. Since the Relief Act of 1793, a few Catholics had at last been admitted to Trinity, although all scholarships, prizes, and distinctions of any kind were denied to them. Thomas Moore was one of those few Catholics, and his parents worked night and day in their grocery shop below these rooms to pay the enormous fees.

The two real passions of Tom Moore's life were literature and music, so, in respect to the latter, when Richard came to the warbling end of the verse, Tom quickly pounded out a finale before Richard could consider finishing the song. Then, looking at Emmet, Tom suddenly said: 'I say, Robert, will you ever forget that incredible lecture on English literature we had on Friday?'

Robert laughed, for he would never forget the English gentleman who had brought letters to the Fellows of the college, claiming to be a distinguished lecturer in English literature. Before a proposed course of lectures was arranged, the Fellows had invited a small but select group of the senior students to the library to hear him and give their views.

'Do you remember his answer, Robert,' Tom asked incredulously, 'when I said to him – You know, sir, of course, Shenstone's *Schoolmistress*?'

' "Yes, but I ha'nt seen her for some time." '

The two of them spluttered in laughter and Tom continued: 'And when he started to quote that passage from Lucan—'

'The one which he claimed had been counted by some critics as being very helegant and hingenious.'

' "The 'eavens," ' Tom mimicked in a deep voice,' "hentomb im oom the hearth does not hinterr—" '

Richard did not laugh with his two friends, only smiled amiably, for although he had been one of those invited, he did not care deeply enough about literature to make the journey to the library to hear and see the man who had quickly proved himself an imposter.

'Beats me,' said Tom, 'how the fool honestly thought he could secure a post at a university such as Trinity.'

Robert was still laughing. 'He probably thought we Irish were too "hignorant" to know the difference.'

'I say, chaps,' Richard suggested brightly, 'how about another song? I rather enjoyed that last one.'

Tom lost his merriment and stared at Richard in horror. 'Another song?' he said unsteadily. He looked at Robert, who had quickly turned back to the window, and knew no hope of rescue would come from that quarter, for Emmet would never hurt Richard's feelings for the world.

And neither would Tom Moore.

'Another song?' Tom said again, then a slow smile came over his good-looking face as he came up with a *coup de grâce*. 'How about if I sing a song for you, Richard? One of my own compositions?'

And before Richard could reply, Tom tinkled out a sequence of melodious bars, and the atmosphere in the room suddenly lulled into a dreamy stillness as Tom softly sang one of his own compositions.

'The thread of our life would be dark, Heaven knows,
    If it were not with friendship and love intertwined;
And I care not how soon I may sink to repose,
    If these blessings shall cease to be dear to my mind.

'But they who have loved the fondest, the purest,
    Too often have wept o'er the dream they believed;
And the heart that has slumbered in friendship securest,
    Is happy indeed, it was never deceived.

'But send round the bowl, while a relic of truth
    Is in man or in woman, this prayer shall be mine –
That the sunshine of love may illumine our youth,
    And the moonlight of friendship console our decline.'

Tom continued playing softly, his eyes on the keyboard. Richard sat beside him deeply moved; while Robert continued gazing thoughtfully through the window. Even then, Robert knew that Thomas Moore was destined to make his name in the world.

'Sing of Tara,' he said, turning to Tom. 'Would you sing that one for me?'

Tom smiled and changed the tune to a melancholy memory of an Ireland of bygone days. Once again he sang one of his own compositions, which he had written to the music of Carolan.

'The harp that once through Tara's halls
    the soul of music shed,
  Now hangs as mute on Tara's walls—'

Mrs Moore hurried into the room. 'Mr Emmet, there's a man downstairs asking for you. He says you must return home immediately.'

Robert moved to his feet. 'Who is the man?'

'A cranky little fellow with a cheeky tongue,' she answered, bristling. 'I eventually established that he is a servant from your household.'

Down below in the hall Robert found Lennard jumping impatiently from one foot to the other.

'Misther Robert, ye must come home at once! Yer parents and Missis Jane are in an awful state, and yer sisther Mary-Anne is bawling her eyes out worser than Cook when she's doing the onions—'

'What has happened?' Robert demanded.

'Amn't I trying to tell ye?' Lennard looked furtively towards the stairs, then dropped his voice to a whisper. 'There was a meeting tonight of the executive council at the house of Oliver Bond.'

'Yes, I know that.'

'And Misther Thomas was to go, but was very late. And when he finally gets there, Mrs Bond tells him the house had been surrounded only half-hour earlier by the Castle's police and the whole group taken. So what does Misther Thomas do then?'

Lennard paused, as if waiting for Robert to make a guess.

Robert suppressed the urge to strangle him. 'Get on with it! What's happened to Thomas?'

'Arrested!' Lennard yelled. 'He comes back home and minutes later Major Sirr and his red hounds surrounded the house and took him. I sez they had no right to take him out like that. Why, like a common felon, I sez. And then—'

Robert thrust past the little man to the door and began to run up the street.

'Will ye hold on a minute,' Lennard called breathlessly in his wake. 'I haven't told ye all of it.'

Robert stopped running and turned. 'What more could there possibly be?'

'There could be another arrest.'

'Of whom?'

'Of a great and darling man. I heard Major Sirr say he'll get him if it's the last thing he does on this earth. And I sez God thwart him all the way, I sez, for no lower—'

'Devil take you!' Robert cried impatiently. 'What darling man?'

'Amn't I trying to tell ye? 'Tis himself – Lord Edward Fitzgerald!'

The following morning Robert stood amongst the crowd standing across the street from the formerly secret offices of the the *Press* newspaper. Soldiers had dragged out the printing presses and were smashing them to pieces. An example was clearly being made. A show of hard authority.

A few minutes later the editor was hauled out by two uniformed bullies, blood streaming from his nose and mouth. One pushed him so hard he fell down the steps. The other dragged him to his feet and pushed him forward again, towards a waiting coach that quickly took him away; while the destruction of the printing presses went on.

Robert watched helpless, his expression dark and bitter as the printed words of another paper moved slowly across his mind.

Free communication of thoughts and opinions being one of the most precious rights of man – every citizen may, therefore, speak, write, and print, freely.

Chapter Twelve

It was her hair that Robert saw first. Her green cloak blended into the spring scenery as she sauntered up the lane towards the rear of The Priory, but her long auburn hair stood out like autumn gold.

He rode slowly along the shaded lane carpeted with layers of old leaves that had fallen year after many a year, and over the muted sound of the horse's hoofs he heard the echo of her voice as she sang softly to herself in Irish. She was neither tall nor small, a slender figure that seemed more to drift than to walk.

She looked . . . listless . . . lonely. Like a sauntering, singing child who has nowhere to go and no one to play with. She turned her head at the sound of the horse, her eyes scrutinising him as he drew alongside, then her face broke into an astonished smile.

'Robert Emmet! I wouldn't have known you.'

He wouldn't have known her either. The child of his recollection was now almost a young woman. The smile still had a delighted, childish quality, the skin was still cream and roses, but he could not help noticing the changes. Her long green cloak hung open from her shoulders and it was possible to see the slender waist and ripe young bosom under beige poplin. Her mouth was lovely, her eyes large and violet. He just stared and stared at her, fascinated; then colour came to his face as he realised he was staring.

'I'm sorry,' he muttered, feeling foolish, then quickly dismounted and faced her with a slight bow. 'It is a pleasure to see you again, Miss Sarah. You are looking well.'

She was not sure if he was merely being polite but, with a clear memory of her mother, she inclined her head in a gracious movement of acknowledgement. 'What brings you out to Rathfarnham?' she asked, walking on. 'We have not seen you for a very long time indeed.'

'Well, no, that's because . . .' He caught the reins and walked beside her, trying to think of the best way to explain his years of avoiding The Priory. He could not tell her how he dreaded the gloomy atmosphere of the place.

She glanced sidelong at him, assessing the young man against her memory of the boy, wondering if he was still as shy as ever.

'Have you come to see Richard?' she asked.

'No, your father.'

Her surprise was evident. 'So why not visit his chambers?'

'I was informed he had already left, and came straight here.'

'Oh, then your business with him must be important.'

'Yes,' he said quietly, 'very important.'

She stopped by the door leading into the orchard. 'No need to go up to the front of the house,' she told him. 'You may as well come in this way.'

Robert hitched the reins to a horse-ring in the wall then followed her through to the orchard where she was moving at the same easy pace.

'It feels strange to be in this orchard again,' he said slowly, gazing around him. She turned to him with a thoughtful expression.

'The last time I recall seeing you in here was years and years ago. Before the time I went to convalesce in Cork . . . with my lung infection.' An embarrassed flush spread up from her neck to her cheeks as she realised that Richard had probably told him the true cause of her illness.

'Is it really that long?' he asked. 'Years and years? And here was I thinking you must be only about sixteen.'

She looked at him quickly and saw he was smiling. For the first time she noticed he had nice eyes, dark and intelligent eyes, that were also very soft and kind. Her uneasiness vanished.

'I'm nearly seventeen,' she informed him.

'Ah, you will soon be going into society then. We may even have the pleasure of dancing with you at the Rotunda Rooms.'

'The Rotunda Rooms?' She stared at him widely as if he had uttered something wonderful, something magical; then in an instant her eyes darkened. 'If Papa ever lets me go to the Rotunda. Amelia is twenty-three now and she still never goes anywhere. Just mopes around here amusing herself with her paints and easel.'

Simply to prolong the conversation with her, he paused

against a tree and asked, 'Why is that? Why has she not gone into society?'

'Because Papa is so mean and possessive,' Sarah confided. 'He gives us no encouragement to enjoy any youthful pleasures. Our life is confined within that melancholy house.' She wrinkled her nose very prettily. '*We* don't have any of the fun of Catherine Wilmott or Lucy and Anne Chetwood. You must know them. Do you?'

He did. He nodded.

'Of course you do,' she said with an angry flick of her hand. 'Because *they* lead such exciting lives. Dining and dancing at the Rotunda Rooms in beautiful gowns, attending balls and weekend houseparties. But not us, not Amelia and I, nothing exciting ever happens to us.'

He looked at her intently, curiosity in his eyes. She looked young and fresh and fragile, all those things, and he wondered if she would truly find all that pomp and pretence as exciting as she imagined. Something in her eyes told him she would.

She stood for a moment reflecting on her unhappy lot, and he continued to watch her with an interest that was deepening by the second. Then she met his eyes, and completely without guile, she smiled at him, a smile so sweet the effect of it hit him somewhere in the chest.

He smiled back at her, and suddenly the breath of young life had moved on both their faces, enlivening them with the thrill of the unexpected, the excitement of a new discovery.

'*Miss Sarah!*'

She turned, startled; relaxing at the sight of Mrs Jessop padding towards them.

'Whatever are you thinking of, Miss Sarah? Making free with a gentleman alone in the orchard! Her father will call you out, young man,' the housekeeper warned, then getting closer and peering at Robert, 'Glory to God – if it's not the Emmet boy!'

Robert eased himself away from the tree. 'A calling-out will not be necessary, Mrs Jessop. Nobody's honour is at stake.'

'Ah, well, now I know who ye are, I'm sure that's true.'

'In case you haven't noticed,' Sarah sniffed, striding past the housekeeper, 'the Emmet boy has grown up.'

Mrs Jessop gaped after Sarah then turned and raked her eyes

over Robert seeing that he had indeed grown into quite a personable young male. But that was no excuse for Miss Sarah suddenly acting hoity-toity.

'Well, now,' the housekeeper declared to Robert, 'hasn't she discovered an edge to her voice all in a day. I can't believe 'tis yourself that's suddenly greased her tongue so slick.'

'No, of course you can't, Mrs Jessop. Did you not often say when I was younger, that my tongue was as dull as a rusty knife through lack of use.'

The housekeeper's fat face turned the colour of beet. 'Oh, glory be! Did you *hear* me saying that?'

'More times than I can remember.'

He smiled and moved past her, leaving her to tramp after him, eyes narrowed as she watched him quickly catch up with Sarah. They strolled on through the orchard and into the garden, all the while smiling and talking as if they had forgotten she was behind them. Then, to her astonishment, Miss Sarah burst out laughing, laughing in that spontaneous way Mrs Jessop had not heard from her in years. It floated on the air, and Mrs Jessop would never have believed that the girl was capable of such joyous laughter.

'Lord's my life,' the housekeeper muttered, 'I think there's blood in that lad after all.'

When Robert later returned home from his interview with John Curran, he explained the outcome to Jane and his parents. Curran had already been to Newgate that afternoon to see Thomas, and found him in a cell six foot square on a diet of bread and water.

John Curran had then gone to the Castle to see Castlereagh (an interview which had almost led to Curran's own arrest) but the situation was thus:

The Act of Habeas Corpus, under which the authorities must, after a period of forty-eight hours, either make a charge or show a civil judge why a civil person was detained in prison, had now been suspended. Therefore, the Castle could keep Thomas imprisoned for as long as they wished without charge or trial. And until he was officially arraigned, no lawyer could take up his case.

Chapter Thirteen

The noise inside the college dining-hall was deafening, although it was hours before the luncheon hour and no one was eating at the rows of long tables crammed to their seating capacity. Those students not lucky enough to get a seat stood in lines along the walls under portraits of former Provosts and Fellows of Trinity.

Amidst the babble and excitement he sat quite still, patiently waiting, knowing it had come. The situation had to be grave for the Lord Chancellor to visit the college; and the consequences . . .

From the Fellows' table at the top of the hall, Whitley Stokes, a physics tutor, sat carefully watching him, noting the patient stillness and expressionless face of the young man who seemed in supreme control of his body and emotions. Only the dark eyes, slightly narrowed in concentration, betrayed a hint he might be wrestling with his thoughts.

Whitley Stokes had always liked Robert Emmet, respected him. It was years since the University had a student like him. In his previous exams his papers had been so good, especially in science, that the examiners had decided against giving him the customary *Valde bene* and had honoured him with an *O quam bene* instead. Other tutors considered him a reserved, studious young man, and found his polite manner rather attractive. But then – Whitley Stokes smiled – they knew nothing of the other Emmet, the one who attended the private meetings and could raise an entire room of young men to their feet in fevered excitement and foot-stamping applause.

Those were the times when Emmet's real personality came to life. His whole face and figure would change as he rose to speak. Instantly he would lose his reserve and become powerful and inspired. His eloquence and the sheer *boldness* of his opinions shocked a few and thrilled many. And yet, he was not one for spewing out impassioned and fiery rhetoric, but sound, practical theory imparted with utter conviction. Some of his words at the last meeting still sounded in Whitley Stokes's ears.

'When a people, advancing rapidly in civilisation and the knowledge of their rights, look back after a lapse of time, and perceive how far the spirit of their government has lagged behind them. What then, I ask, is to be done by them in such a case? What – but to pull the government up to the people!'

At the sound of the bell a hush descended on the assembly. Everybody stood as Lord Clare, now the Lord Chancellor of Ireland and Vice-Chancellor of Trinity, entered the hall followed by the Provost. As he stepped on to the platform, a grey-haired old doctor of Greek literature standing next to Whitley Stokes on the dais, whispered fretfully, 'Lord Clare is a most violent and bigoted man. Dear me, I do believe he should not be involved in a university such as this. And such a deplorable time to come . . . so many students preparing for exams.'

Once the assembly was reseated, Lord Clare remained standing, looking majestic in a robe of crimson velvet and ermine. His hand rested on the large chain of his office as his small grey eyes ranged over the students.

'An accusation has been made,' Lord Clare intoned, 'that there are, within the confines of the University, men who encourage their friends into feelings of disaffection and rebellion. It is my duty to find out if these accusations are mere rumour, or based on truth. I intend to question each student, under oath, as to their political sympathies and knowledge they may have of any secret societies within the college.'

Whitley Stokes sprang to his feet. 'My lord, interrogating students under oath as to their politics is against every principle of this University!'

The Chancellor glared at him. 'Your name, sir?' he said coldly.

'Dr Whitley Stokes, my lord.'

After a silence, the Provost said, 'Please be seated, Dr Stokes.'

Whitley Stokes kept his eyes fixed on the stony face of Lord Clare.

'Dr Stokes!' bellowed the Provost. 'Please be seated!'

136

He sat down. The doctor of literature peered at him short-sightedly, then whispered fretfully, 'Dear me, a deplorable mistake, Stokes.'

Yes. A deplorable and *rash* mistake. Whitley Stokes felt a small clutch of fear in his stomach.

Lord Clare's face was hatchet sharp as he turned his glare on the body of students.

'I intend to wheedle out every student with disaffected principles! I will remove any member who does not exonerate himself from the treasonable charges made against the University. I will *expel* any student who refuses to place his hand on the Bible and be examined as to his knowledge of, or involvement in, the so-called Society of United Irishmen.'

A murmur rumbled through the hall. The Provost hammered for silence.

'Furthermore,' Lord Clare warned, 'I will personally ensure that any person removed from this college will be barred from any other university in England or Scotland, thereby excluding him from all learned professions. Before the examination, each student will be required to publicly swear an oath of allegiance to His Majesty, George the Third.'

Richard Curran, sitting next to Robert Emmet, had turned quite pale. Expulsion! Barred from all learned professions! All his ambitions to be as great a lawyer as his father destroyed? A future with no higher hopes than *trade*! He would rather die than be reduced to the employment of a tradesman. And what had he done to deserve it? Belonged to an exclusive club where he did little more than drink wine and discuss political theory with his friends ... Patriotism and independence, abstract words that had suddenly lost their fire ...

He turned his head slightly and looked covertly at Emmet. Would *he* go forward and make the oath of allegiance to the King of England?

Richard was not at all sure.

But if Robert didn't go forward and somehow bluff his way through the examination, they would kick him out, bar him from all universities, deny him his degree – and the scandal! Richard had suffered enough scandal to last him a lifetime. First the scandal of Gertrude's burial in unconsecrated ground, then a traumatic court case when he had obeyed his father by appearing in court to support the charge of his mother's adultery. That scandal had rocked Dublin. And now this . . .

'Let me make it very clear,' Lord Clare continued. 'Any student who refuses to come forward and take the oath when his name is called, will, without question or investigation, be expelled immediately from the University, and his name included on the blacklist.'

Not a murmur could be heard in the hall as the Chancellor sat down and the Provost rose from his seat.

'When your name is called,' he instructed the students, 'you will come forward and kiss his lordship's hand, then make the oath of allegiance. When this has been completed, you will again place your hand on the Bible and keep it there during the examination. Obviously, because of the large number of students many of you will not be examined today. Those not examined today must return to the dining-hall tomorrow, and wait here until you are called.'

He looked sternly over his glasses at the assembly. 'And for those students whose surname begins with a Y or a W, let me point out, we shall not be conducting the examinations in alphabetical order. Please stand.'

Everyone stood. Richard Curran turned nervously to Emmet, who simply gave him a brief, understanding smile, then turned and walked out of the hall, followed by Corbett, McLaughlin, and Flinn.

Richard stood staring after him, painfully hurt and deeply ashamed. Emmet *knew*! That brief smile had said it all. Without even a word between them, Emmet had known he would not have the courage or conviction to walk out with him.

When the roll was called there was no answer to certain names. Throughout the day the name of Robert Emmet was called three times but was answered with silence.

The Provost checked with his staff. Yes, Emmet had been present during his lordship's speech, but had left the hall immediately afterwards.

Throughout the following day the name of Robert Emmet

was again called a number of times, but was always answered with silence.

By the end of the third day, the interrogation of the students was almost at an end, and Robert Emmet's name was called for the last time.

It was not until many hours later, when Robert Emmet was clear in his conscience and resolved in his determination, did he step forward to make an oath.

With absolute calmness he looked around at the silent body of serious-faced men in the packed room, and saw they were waiting . . .

He then looked at the man directly before him. His lordship slowly held out a Bible on the flat of his palm. He placed the palm of his own hand on top, then raised his right hand and made the oath.

'I, Robert Emmet, do pledge myself to my country, that I will endeavour to form a Brotherhood of Affection amongst Irishmen of every religious persuasion. And will use all my abilities and influence in the attainment of an impartial and equal representation of *all* the People of Ireland in Parliament.

'I do further pledge, and solemnly swear before God, that I will not consider my life my own if my country needs it, that I am prepared to lay down my life should my country demand it, that if called to do so I will take my place on the field of battle, that I will always hold an aversion to the spilling of innocent blood, that all my actions shall be for the good of the common cause, and to that end I will endeavour to make as many friends and as few enemies as possible. So help me God.'

Lord Edward Fitzgerald smiled at him, and every man in the room seemed to release his breath, for all considered the giving of an oath the most sacred thing. And now, due to Lord Edward, Robert Emmet had been sworn in as the youngest intelligence officer on the executive council of the United Irishmen.

Lord Clare's visitation to Trinity had lasted three full days. On the morning of the fourth day, the Provost read out the verdict, and later that afternoon Richard Curran called at the house at

St Stephen's Green to inform Robert of the result.

'Mr Robert *might* be found down the end of the garden,' Simmins had said in an off-hand manner, and there Richard found him, sitting on the bench with his hands in his pockets and his head down.

Seeing that his approach had not been heard, Richard paused, and swallowed nervously. Over the last three days he had come face to face with the truth of himself. He was not like Robert, could never be. Robert had always possessed an inner strength, would always be his own man, but not Richard. He was weak and cowardly, always had been, always would be. But then, so was half the human race. Better to accept it, then settle to a quiet life and hope the world would pass him by untroubled.

He coughed, and Robert looked up.

'Nineteen in all were expelled, including yourself,' Richard said, getting it over quickly. 'Whitley Stokes was suspended from teaching for three years.'

'Three years? For what?'

'For speaking out, I suppose.'

There was a moment's silence as they looked at each other.

'Did anyone actually name me, do you know?'

Richard's colour deepened. He might have sworn the oath of allegiance and lied his way through the examination, but he would never betray the names of others, and he was gratified to see Emmet knew that too. He sat down on the bench.

'When it was all over, the Provost announced that the United Irish had four committees in the College, the secretaries of which were disclosed to be Emmet, McLaughlin, Flinn and Corbett, and those four names would head the blacklist sent to all other universities.'

On the grass near the bench, a goldfinch was busy tearing the head off a dandelion in between bouts of song. They sat watching it for a time, then Richard said sadly: 'I understand how you must feel, about being prevented from graduating with your degree, and losing all chance of a professional career . . .'

Robert shrugged, but there was a sadness in his eyes. 'A choice had to be made, a price had to be paid. Now I've done both.'

140

After another silence, Richard, desperate to maintain the old friendship, said: 'Why . . . why don't you come along with me now, have dinner, a glass or two of wine . . . ?'

Robert was about to refuse, hesitated, looked at Richard.

'At The Priory?'

'Or in town, if you prefer.'

Smiling slightly, Robert said, 'I prefer The Priory.'

It was Counsellor Curran who did most of the talking over dinner. He talked rapidly with the cheerful relief of a man who learns, after expecting bad news, that everything is well after all.

Every now and then Robert's eyes strayed across the candlelit table to Sarah. He had thought of her often since their encounter in the lane. In her father's presence she seemed extremely timid, contributed hardly a word to the conversation, but occasionally, when her eyes met Robert's, she responded with a shy smile that was always followed by a quick and nervous glance at her father.

Sitting next to her, Amelia looked like a woman who had given up all hope of life beyond The Priory. Unlike Sarah's pretty primrose dress, Amelia's was brown and matronly, her hair scraped back in a severe knot. And unlike Sarah, she had plenty to say, contradicting her father continually. When Keegan glided around the table refilling only the wineglasses of the men, Amelia impatiently snatched the decanter from his hand and refilled her own glass herself, sipping it with relish.

When the time came for the ladies to withdraw, Robert and Richard did the honours of holding back their chairs, while Keegan brought brandy and port to the table.

'A sad day for you, Emmet,' Curran said, but Robert was watching Sarah as she walked to the door.

'A sad day, I said, but then you don't appear very sad, young man. Maybe we were misinformed.'

Robert looked vaguely at the lawyer. 'Pardon?'

'Is it true? They kicked you out?'

Robert was taken aback at the sudden coldness of Curran's tone. 'It is true,' he answered quietly.

'Well? What have you got to say about it?'

'What is there to say, Mr Curran?'

John Curran stared at him as he sat down. 'Do you consider

the premature mnd scandalous termination of your education to be unworthy of discussion?'

'I consider it terminated, sir, that is all.'

'You do realise that without your degree, it will be impossible for you now to follow in your father's footsteps and become a doctor.'

'I did hope to become a scientist. But, yes, I do realise that will be difficult now.'

Curran's anger was stirred by the calm voice. He was used to young men squirming under his questioning, babbling out excuses *why* things had happened, or *because* of so and so. But young Emmet had none of the swagger of those less sure of themselves. Twenty years old and absolutely self-possessed.

'You do know the effect this will have on your parents?' he snapped. 'It will destroy them! Is the imprisonment of Thomas not enough for them to suffer?'

'Father . . .'

It was Richard who was squirming with embarrassment at this unbelievable and unexpected attack on his friend.

'Yes, yes,' Curran said in a tone of mingled contrition and exasperation, 'I realise I have no right to question you on the matter, Emmet. I apologise for my brusqueness and interference. No doubt it is due to the strain of seeing my friend, your brother, in Newgate; the shock of hearing about your father's resignation over Thomas's imprisonment, and now he has the distress of your expulsion to suffer. I was simply thinking like a father.'

'My father supports me totally,' Robert said coolly. 'He fully understood why I could not, and would not, put my hand on any Bible held by Lord Clare. I am extremely fortunate to have a man such as he for a father.'

'Extremely fortunate,' Curran returned demurely, taking a long, reflective pull on his drink.

He was not quite sure why he had turned on young Emmet. Only natural the lad should feast his eyes on a pretty girl; he did so himself regularly. Didn't mean he had designs on them. And he admired what Emmet had done, treating that bastard Clare with contempt by walking out. But next to himself, young Emmet held the strongest influence over Richard, and although he himself was behind the United men, he would not allow his son's future career in the law to be jeopardised. Still, at least Richard was safe at Trinity, even if his young hero was now out on his ear.

Keegan entered looking most indignant. 'Begging your pardon, sir, but Mr McNally—'

McNally shoved the butler aside and limped into the room. 'Ah, Jack! Forgive me for this intrusion but I have news which I knew you would wish to hear as soon as possible.'

'A private matter?'

McNally glanced at the two young men. 'The entire country will know it by tomorrow.'

'Well, then,' Curran motioned to Keegan to bring another glass, 'sit down and tell all.'

McNally waited until he had sampled his drink, then said, 'Lord Edward Fitzgerald, as you know, has disappeared off the face of the earth. The Castle is intent on catching him, but no matter how wide they have cast their nets, they can find no trace of him.'

Curran smiled. 'Three cheers for Fitzgerald, so.'

'My sentiments exactly!' McNally cried. 'But the Castle now believe that so long as he remains free, he will endeavour to lead the country into armed rebellion. And that brings me to my news . . .'

McNally paused theatrically, his black-grape eyes darting to each of the three men in turn. 'As from today, gentlemen, Ireland is under martial law.'

Chapter Fourteen

The imprisonment of Thomas had devastated Dr Emmet. For a number of days he was a broken man, but then he collected his strength and dignity and went to Dublin Castle to hand in his resignation as State Physician of Ireland. And, with that, the last link connecting the Emmet family to the Castle had been broken.

And now Dr and Mrs Emmet decided to remove themselves from town society. A small country estate of thirteen acres out in the area of Casino in Milltown had been looked at, liked, and quickly purchased, and the removal from the house on St Stephen's Green completed within two days.

Mary-Anne, the Emmets' twenty-five-year-old daughter, instantly fell in love with the place. Robert found it charming, as did the servants, all except one.

Lennard grumbled and complained loudly about being transported to this foreign land miles and miles away from his pals and the taverns and card schools in town.

'Five miles,' Robert pointed out. 'Not five thousand, Lennard. And you often enough trekked out to Tallaght from the Green for your card games. A much farther distance.'

'Aye, Misther Robert, but 'tis the nippins of life I'll miss.' Lennard sniffed gloomily. 'Nippins were me only pleasure.'

'Nippins?'

'Nippin' here for a jar, nippin' there for a chat, and nippin' into the card schools. And like I sez to Simmins, the boys'll miss me sorely, I sez. The card games won't be the same without me, I sez. And when all's said and done, I sez, 'tis nothing short of *inhuman* to take a man from his natural, happy, peaceful abode where all his pals are, I sez, and bring him out to this wild wilderness.'

'And so say I.' Robert's voice had a sympathetic tone. 'Perhaps it would be better if you left us, Lennard? It shouldn't be too difficult to find another position in the city. I know my father would give you an excellent reference.'

The little man looked up, startled. 'Eh?'

'The family will understand,' Robert said gently. 'Fond as they are of you, Lennard, they would not wish you to sacrifice your nippins on their account. Shall I inform my father of your unhappiness, and that you wish to leave? Or would you prefer to do so yourself?'

'Leave? Who sez anything about leaving?' Lennard cried fiercely. 'Leave me darling misthress and the doctor! No, 'tis like I sez to Simmins – "Why, the poor dears would break their hearts if I took a notion to leave," I sez. "Like a son I am to them now," I sez. "And what about Missus Jane? Now she's without Misther Tom," I sez, "that lovely creature would fair crumble up if she were without me an' all. And even morer than that," I sez, what would young Misther Robert do without me.'

'You have no mind to leave then?'

'Leave? I'd as lief take the pledge as leave the Emmets for those card-cheating gobshites in the Liberties. No, 'tis like I sez—'

'You are satisfied here at Casino and have no reason for further complaint. Is that what you are saying, Lennard?'

'Aye, I suppose so.' Lennard shrugged, then turned and tramped across the lawn towards the back door of the house, even more disgruntled. 'He wouldn't be talking so aisy now if 'twern't for me,' he grumbled. 'Still be spittin' on his words like a love-sick girl, wha'? And who was it that baited him night and day until he was forced to open his shutmouth and answer? Yours truly, that's who!'

He stuck his hands deep into his pockets and kicked at a stone underfoot. 'Haughty young buck with his smooth-as-cream voice and black-as-black eyes talking to *me* like that! Hinting as maybe I should leave. Me, that's done more for him than any man jack I knows! Why, I've a mind to go back and tell him what I think of him now. 'Troth, I'll soon tell him, quick enough—'

'What, Lennard?'

Startled, Lennard turned his aggrieved face to Robert who had been following close behind. 'Eh?'

'You were saying?'

'Who me?' Lennard stood blinking. 'Why, I never sez nothing, Misther Robert, not as I could hear anyhows. No, as I'm alive, I was just walking along minding me own business and thinking me own thoughts and never a word said. Why, did ye imagine ye heard someone?'

Robert looked at the innocent face of the bushy-browed rascal beside him. 'I imagine I did. Every word.'

'Well ye should watch that,' Lennard warned. 'Imagining ye hear voices saying things ye've no right nor reason to hear could get ye locked up in the madhouse. It has for other poor mortals anyhows.'

He paused to hitch up his breeches, then eyed Robert sagely. 'Now then,' he advised gently, 'if ye were me and I were ye, I'd talk to Dr Emmet about it.'

By a window in Dublin Castle, Edward Cooke stood watching the informer stride across the upper courtyard.

'Here he comes,' he said over his shoulder, then turned back into the room where Lord Castlereagh, the Chief Secretary of State, was sitting in a chair by the fireplace, stroking the head of a full-grown Irish setter at his side.

'Let us hope his information is worthwhile,' Castlereagh said. 'So many of these informers are nothing more than damned opportunists. Tell any lie to gain favour with the Castle.'

Cooke sat down at his desk and prepared a fresh sheet of paper in readiness to record the informer's disclosures, but from under hooded lids the Under-Secretary watched Castlereagh as he leisurely stroked his canine companion.

On first acquaintance with Castlereagh, the first and most remarkable thing Cooke had noticed was that he possessed the most fascinating and engaging personality, with a personal appearance that was extremely attractive. His dress was elegant, his smile charming, and his manners were as polished as silver . . . A political genius, just one notch below the very summit of power, and still only twenty-nine years old.

Edward Cooke was an Englishman sent over by his government to perform a duty of office, but he had been in Ireland long enough to have learned that not all the citizens regarded Lord Castlereagh with the same fascination he did. Indeed, Grattan, Curran, and other members of the Whig Party made no secret of describing him as an execrable Judas who had betrayed the land of his birth and bartered her rights, in exchange for personal advancement and the empty glory of a title.

In 1790, at the age of twenty-one, Robert Stewart had stood for parliamentary election in his home province of Ulster as the representative for Down. He had stood as the Reform candidate against Lord Downshire, the autocratic landlord of the district who had long held the seat. Stewart had campaigned passionately, pledging himself to the unceasing pursuit of parliamentary reform and the rights of the people. After the most obstinate political contest ever seen in Ireland, the Honourable Robert Stewart, hailed by the people as a 'model of patriotism' was triumphantly selected for Parliament, by the support and pecuniary contributions of all the friends of civil and religious liberty, in addition to the expense of £60,000, which nearly ruined his family.

But then this most clever and charming young man was courted by the Tories. His new stepmother's brother was Lord Camden, a member of the English Privy Council. A seat in the *real* chamber of power was discussed, the one in Westminster. And to the horror of his supporters, Stewart turned Tory, deserted his seat in Down, and became the Member for Tregony in the British Parliament.

Cooke chuckled inwardly: such was the game of politics, as dirty as the devil, but now Stewart's days of political delinquency were over. Now known as Lord Castlereagh, he was back in Ireland as Chief Secretary of State, with his step-uncle Lord Camden as Viceroy.

'I have had much fatigue today,' Castlereagh said with a sigh. 'If the scoundrel has come to waste our time with no valuable information on Fitzgerald, I swear he will regret it.'

'I am of the opinion that Fitzgerald has already left the country,' Cooke said thoughtfully. 'Especially after Lord Clare publicly announced that all ports would remain open to him.'

Castlereagh sat back with a puzzled frown. 'I'm not sure if the Chancellor is merely pandering to his friends, the Leinsters, or if, despite everything, he still has some regard for Fitzgerald.'

'I expect Lord Clare was considering our position in this matter,' Cooke said. 'It would embarrass the King and greatly distress the English nobility to hear that the brother of a duke had been hanged. Lord Edward is, after all, the nephew of the Duke of Richmond. And don't forget, the King was once passionately in love with Lord Edward's aunt, Lady Sarah Napier.'

'Be that as it may, publicly inviting the rebel to banish himself from the country may be Lord Clare's way of dealing with the matter, but it is not my way.' Castlereagh suddenly gave his Under-Secretary a guarded look. 'But, of course, you are right, Mr Cooke . . . we will have to be very careful in our handling of the Geraldine once he is captured.'

When the informer entered the office, his thin face registered alarm at the presence of the elegant Castlereagh. All previous meetings of this nature had been conducted in privacy between himself and Under-Secretary Cooke.

'Good afternoon, Mr Higgins,' said Cooke. 'We are eager to hear your information.'

Higgins's eyes slithered from Castlereagh to Cooke. 'It's about Fitzgerald.'

'His whereabouts?' asked Castlereagh.

'Not exactly.'

'Mr Higgins!' Cooke exclaimed. 'You said you had information as to his place of concealment.'

'I do, sir, but not the exact address. I have a suspicion he is here in Dublin, in the Liberties.'

'What? Under our noses!'

'I believe so.'

Castlereagh tutted. 'The Liberties is so infested with rebels and sympathisers we'd never flush him out. We need to know the exact dwelling.'

'I could have sworn Fitzgerald would have gone to Kildare,' said Cooke. 'I was sure he would have made some attempt to see his wife, but our men there have seen neither hide nor hair of him.'

'Oh, but he *has* been to see Lady Edward,' said Higgins. 'On more than one occasion, too. He stayed for three days the last time.'

'How do you know this?' Castlereagh demanded.

'He couldn't possibly have got past my men!' Cooke blurted.

Higgins could not prevent his smile. 'It seems Lord Edward moved freely past your men, Mr Cooke, because he was, er . . . attired in the long curls, bonnet, and dress of a lady.'

'A lady!' Cooke seemed suddenly short of breath. 'How . . . ? Why did you not come forward with this information before?'

148

'I only learned about it last evening,' Higgins replied. 'There is a little amusement that one of your men actually assisted Lord Edward into a carriage and was thanked most graciously, if a little coyly, for his assistance.'

Lord Castlereagh rose from his chair, filled a crystal glass with wine, and presented it to the informer. 'If you know so much, Mr Higgins,' he murmured slowly, 'why do you not know where Fitzgerald is now?'

'Well . . . one may be told where Fitzgerald has been, but never where he is. But I do have a plan that might lead us to him . . . if I may I sit down.'

'Please do,' Castlereagh said.

'Oh, no, my lord, not before you. I could not think of sitting while you are still standing.'

'Then, Mr Higgins, allow me to hand you a chair. And while I lower myself to your level on my own seat, I recommend you to apprise us of your plan.'

Castlereagh resumed his seat by the fire and Higgins angled his long body down on to the proffered chair. He was about to speak when Castlereagh suggested that he might like to partake of a drink of wine. The wine was good, his lordship polite, and for a moment Higgins forgot all his earlier feelings of unease in the presence of Lord Castlereagh. Although he did find the manner of the man somewhat *unpredictable*.

'You are a publisher, Mr Higgins, are you not?' Castlereagh queried.

'I am, my lord.'

'A wealthy publisher?'

'No, my lord, I cannot admit to being a wealthy man.'

'Not wealthy – but ambitious to be so?'

Higgins flushed. 'I am only as ambitious as any other businessman, my lord.'

'Oh, perfectly answered.' Castlereagh smiled. 'Now, permit me to ask you of this plan?'

'Well, I have no direct links with the United Irish, I can assure you of that most earnestly, my lord, and would personally have no way of obtaining the information, but with the help of financial inducement . . .' He glanced at the hound beside Castlereagh's chair, busy scratching a flappy ear with one stiff hind leg . . . 'I could use a setter to sniff it out for me.'

'A setter?' repeated Castlereagh with a sudden quickening of interest.

Higgins smiled as he recalled Magan's threats of suicide the previous evening. 'My contact, you understand, believes I am a sympathiser. He is a solicitor, trusted well by the United Irishmen. However, he is in severe financial difficulties and his practice is on the brink of closure. If I were to offer him a way to financial solvency, I believe he could be persuaded to help himself, by helping you.'

'Fitzgerald's supporters have shielded him so far,' Cooke said, 'even under severe interrogation.'

Higgins shrugged. 'My contact would have to choose between himself and Fitzgerald, between poverty and patriotism, and he has a liking for the good things of life.'

There was a moment's silence.

'Very well,' said Castlereagh. 'One thousand pounds. If his information leads to the capture of the Geraldine, your contact will receive one thousand pounds.'

'A most generous reward, my lord,' said Higgins, eyes slithering back to the Under-Secretary with a questioning glint.

Edward Cooke knew the game, knew the glint. 'A thousand pounds for the hound, Lord Castlereagh, but now our friend wants to know – how much for the handler?'

Castlereagh considered. He had unlimited resources and he badly wanted Fitzgerald. 'A thousand each,' he said.

'And do I still retain all rights to publish government literature?' Higgins queried.

'My, my, my, Mr Higgins,' exclaimed Cooke, 'you drive a hard bargain! Do you not earn anything at all from your *Freeman's Journal*? I heard it was making vast profits for you.'

'You retain the right to publish,' Castlereagh snapped. 'But do remember, Mr Higgins, that the rewards will only be paid *after* we catch the fox.'

When Higgins had left, Castlereagh stretched a hand out to his own setter and thoughtfully stroked an ear.

'Give him a week,' he said coldly, 'then, Mr Cooke, make that reward of one thousand pounds public. There is more than one hungry hound in this city.'

＊　　＊　　＊

In the library at Casino, Robert sat at a desk sorting through the thick sheaf of names that Lord Edward had asked him to list into divisions under county, barony, and parish. He glanced up as a warm breeze fluttered the curtain at the open window.

Some were predicting that a blistering summer was on the wing, for the spring of 1798 was the most glorious and golden anyone could recall. Hedgerows and woodland were abundant in leaf, the gorse in full bloom, and the lanes luxuriant in snapdragons, butterwort, and purple and white foxgloves that would grow as tall as six-foot hussars by harvest-time.

After twenty years living in the very heart of Dublin city, Robert was not yet used to the peaceful silence of the country estate at Casino, but already he had developed a passionate love for the winding paths and green retreats all around. He even enjoyed the sound of the wind curling down from the hills and the cry of the tree-owl at night.

For a moment he sat listening to the silence that was not truly a silence, for the birdsong jingled endlessly, then he worked for almost two hours without pause, until the sound of Jane's sweet and resonant voice drifted in to him from the garden.

> 'O mistress mine! where are you roaming?
> O stay and hear; your true love's coming,
>   That can sing both high and low.
> Trip no further, pretty sweeting;
> Journeys end in lovers meeting,
>   Every wise man's son doth know.'

He stretched sideways in his chair and looked out of the open window. Jane was reading to his mother in the garden. His eyes rested on his mother, the mother to whom he felt such tender devotion, and who still did not look her sixty-three years. But Jane – poor Jane had gone into visible decline since Thomas's imprisonment. He was sure his mother's wish to be read to today was one of her many ploys to distract Jane's mind from the constant anxiety that was preventing her from eating or sleeping to any normal degree.

151

He lifted his quill, dipped it in the inkhorn, and began to make a column of figures, but the Bard's words, so sweetly recited, interfered with his concentration. He laid down the pen and looked towards the hills and mountains piled fold on fold against the blue sky. The image of Richard's sister came into his mind, not the timid and nervous girl at the dining-table, but the ripe young beauty he had met in the lane, all cream and roses and blue eyes laughing. Casino was only a few miles south of Rathfarnham, and Richard had casually mentioned that she spent most of her time wandering alone over the fields and deserted hills.

> 'What is love? 'tis not hereafter;
> Present mirth hath present laughter;
>   What's to come is still unsure.
> In delay there lies no plenty
> Then come kiss me, sweet and twenty;
>   Youth's a stuff will not endure . . .'

Robert got up and closed the window, but then his eyes lingered on the deserted hills.

Vacant in mind and purpose, Sarah stepped slowly out into the shady lane at the rear of The Priory and drifted towards the fields. Behind her in the garden she had left Amelia in silent engrossment doing a water-colour of the lily-pond.

She collected wild flowers as she walked, finally stopping on one of the sunny hills to sit down and look at the beauty of nature. In the distance, about half a mile away to her left, she could see the golden fields of buttercups that surrounded the country houses spread out at a distance along Butterfield Lane. To her right two or three dairy farms could be seen, a number of small cottages, but all else was pasture where the sheep and cattle idled deep in the flower-strewn grass of the meadows.

Oh, it was beautiful, beautiful! This was her world. The silent world of nature where the mind was free to create its own entertainment and visions. She had long ago learned without effort how to repress any thought that disturbed her, and find refuge in glorious daydreams of the future and wonderful imaginings of the past.

She picked at the white daisies on the grass around her and made five daisy chains. In the distance she could see the Wicklow Mountains. She hummed dreamily as she looped a daisy chain around each wrist and the remaining three around her neck, imagining she was back in the pagan days when Celtic maidens covered themselves in wild and colourful flowers and paid homage to the Sun God.

It was a splendid day, but the sun was hot on her face. She sighed and moved to her feet, deciding to walk in a southerly direction towards the shady banks of the Dodder river.

From the ground she lifted her collection of wild flowers, white foxgloves, pink hydrangea, and a thick sheaf of bluebells. She arranged them into a bouquet, then turned towards the river, stopping short at the sight of a young man walking leisurely over the grasslands in her direction. She watched him with innocent interest, then a smile broke on her face as she recognised her brother's friend. She waved to him, and he waved back, then she moved eagerly down the hill towards him.

He approached her slowly, almost casually, allowing the picture of her to sink in. She looked very fresh and slender in a white printed dress decorated only by a cornflower-blue sash around the waist . . . and a number of daisy chains around the neck. Her long auburn hair was undressed and unslung and gave the impression that she might be any country girsha instead of a young lady of the gentry.

'Why, Robert Emmet, what a surprise meeting you all the way out here again! I declare it is quite a surprise.'

He smiled at her, relieved to see that she was clearly as pleased to see him as he was to see her. 'I hope I am not intruding,' he said politely.

'Intruding?' She looked around her at the deserted landscape, then smiled. 'I am quite alone,' she assured him.

'Of course you are,' he said, feeling stupid, but glad to see that the painful timidity she had suffered in the presence of her father seemed to have flown again.

He nodded at the flowers in her hand. 'You have been busy.'

'Yes, I intend them for Mrs Jessop's mantelshelf in the kitchen.'

'Are you walking anywhere in particular?'

'I thought the river.'

'May I accompany you?'

She nodded her assent. 'But,' she said in simple confusion as they loitered towards the river, 'what are you doing so far afield from Dublin? And why are you not at your studies in Trinity?'

'Trinity?' He looked at her in surprise. 'Have you not . . . ? But surely you must have been told by Richard or your father that I am no longer at Trinity?'

'No,' she said innocently. 'I have been told nothing. Richard spends most of his nights now in his college rooms, but even when he is at home any interesting conversation is usually withheld until Amelia and I leave the dining-room. Why are you no longer at Trinity?'

'I . . . was expelled.'

'Expelled?' For a minute she could not believe it, then a shocked, condemning look came into her eyes. In his youth her father had almost been expelled from Trinity – for the crime of keeping idle women in his rooms. He had been called before the Board of Fellows, but after he had insisted that he had never in his life kept any woman *idle* in his rooms, they considered his answer so amusing they had let him off with a warning, although Sarah had never understood their reasoning.

'Why were you expelled?'

'For belonging to a political society opposed to the powers at Dublin Castle.'

'Is that all?' Her face cleared. 'Papa has been opposed to the powers at Dublin Castle for many a long year. But he was almost expelled from Trinity for something far worse than that.'

'I know,' he said, smiling.

'You do?' The solemn look was back in her eyes. 'And you smile?'

'Well, it is rather an amusing tale.'

'Explain how you find it so, when my mother did not. Many a time I heard her remind Papa of it in the severest anger.'

He looked at her in perplexity. 'Then she must have been

misinformed of the incident, surely? For as I heard it, and it is now a famous story in Trinity, John Curran was called upon to deliver an oration in Latin from the pulpit to the entire body of students and the Fellows, which he did, in exquisite Latin, except for the fact that he delivered every word and gesture in a perfect mimickry of Dr Duignan who was then one of the Board of Fellows and despised by most of the students. Duignan jumped up in fury and demanded his immediate expulsion, but the Fellows and Provost were laughing so convulsively, they were forced to let your father off with a warning.'

Once again Sarah's spontaneous laughter rippled over the air, for she had once seen Dr Duignan during a family day at Trinity, a most pompous and sour-faced man who tended to follow every sentence with a disdainful sniff of his long nose.

'I believe my father must have collected many warnings so.'

'I believe he did.'

'But,' she said, still presenting a pretty picture of confusion, 'why did you trouble to walk all the way out here today? To Rathfarnham?'

'We are now country people, too, you know. Or did you not know that either?'

She shook her head. 'Where?'

'We moved to a house at Casino some weeks ago.'

'But that's—'

'Only a few miles or so across country,' he said. 'Quite a short ride but rather a long walk.' He turned to her abruptly. 'Would you like to come and visit us there? Tomorrow?'

'Tomorrow?'

'It is the only day I have free for at least a week. We could ride there, if you wish?'

The excitement in Sarah's eyes dimmed. 'I no longer have a horse. I used to ride every day,' she explained, 'but just over a year ago I tried to take a hedge and tumbled, suffered no more than a fractured wrist, but my poor mare had to be put down. Papa has never thought to replace her.'

'I will bring you a horse, if you wish.'

'Oh, I wish!' she cried, her eyes beaming. Suddenly the summer ahead took on a brighter aspect, for she knew with all certainty that it was not only the loan of a horse he was offering, it was friendship.

Night was falling when Anne Devlin rode away from the farm-house at Croneybeag. She rode at an easy pace, the rein of the halter held loosely in one hand, while the other pressed down on a goatskin bag balanced carefully in front of her on the horse; it contained a pot half filled with broth and a loaf of soda bread; they were for her father's brother over in Cronebyrne, Uncle Pat Devlin, alone in his cottage and badly ill with the fever.

Sighing impatiently at the mare's docile pace, she regretted now that she had left her errand so late, but the work at home had to be done and, of all her brothers and sisters, she was the only one who could ride a horse without disgrace.

As she rode over the pastures towards Cronebyrne she heard a loud whinnying and sat alert as she turned down the bohereen leading to her uncle's cottage, riding quietly and slowly through the weather belt of trees.

She came out into bright moonlight and abruptly reined in, her eyes wide as she stared at the house. Red flames from six or seven torches licked dangerously close to the thatch as a detach-ment of militia hammered on the door, then kicked it in.

The mare almost reared, her tail lashed against her sides and she pawed the ground with her fore-hoofs. Anne passed a calming hand up and down the velvety long neck, whispering, whispering until the threatened whinny was silenced and the mare's neck turned sideways, her nostrils wide and twitching.

Anne stared towards the house. The militia had now crashed their way inside. So this was it – martial law. The uniformed ruffians who delighted in persecuting the country now had control of the country. Only from the recently arrived High-land regiments had the people observed humane and orderly behaviour.

No longer caring whether the broth in the pot spilled, Anne twisted the rein into a double loop around her palm and wheeled the horse round, spurring back the way she had come, circling her uncle's farm until she reached the field at the rear of the house.

Still clutching the bag, she slipped from the mare and

tethered her to a tree with a whisper and a pat. She hid the bag behind the bole, then sprinted fast and silently across the field and slipped over the low stone wall, bending low until she reached the back of the cottage where she crouched beneath the small window.

Slowly she lifted her head to peep inside. Uncle Pat lay in his bed. Three men stood over him, their backs to the window. She could hear the voices clearly.

'Where are your sons? We know they're out drilling and training with Michael Dwyer. So where is Dwyer?'

She recognised the speaker as George Manning of Ballyteigue.

'I don't know . . . I've not . . . I've not seen any of the lads for days.' Patrick Devlin tried to rise from his bed but Manning shoved him back with the butt of his musket.

'I swear to God, I've not seen them in days and . . . and . . .' His head flopped to the side, eyes closed.

'Let him be, George,' said a yeoman. 'You can see he's badly ill with the fever. They're not here, so let's go.'

George Manning sneered at his companion. 'You're too soft, Saul. He knows where the rebels are training, sure enough. We stay until he tells us.'

'He'll tell you nothing.'

The one called Saul had bent to peer at the man in the bed. 'He's unconscious. And if we stay here much longer, we'll likely catch the fever ourselves.'

'Are you sure the bastard's not shamming?'

'I'm sure. Let's go.'

Anne ducked as George Manning turned and led the men out. A moment later, she peeped into the room again, just in time to see a yeoman raise his torch to the low ceiling as he left.

Sparks flew into the sky as part of the thatched roof caught fire, and inside her Uncle Patrick lay unconscious. Anne was rooted to the spot. Nausea rose up from her stomach as she realised he was about to be burned alive. Her mind was a mass of confusion; if she tried to help him, they would shoot her, and they might only do that after they'd had their sport with her.

She started as the one called Saul rushed back in, dragged her uncle from his bed and through the smoke-filled room to the door. Thank God! She ran across to the barn and waited. The sky was aglow now, like a sunset. Smoke thickened the air and she clutched her throat to stop herself from coughing. Voices cheered as the flames rose higher and the thatch crackled loudly.

When there was no other sound but the crackling of embers, Anne released her hand from her throat and coughed convulsively until the heaving in her chest subsided, then she moved towards the smouldering remains of the cottage.

Her Uncle Patrick lay a few yards from the front door. She ran and kneeled down beside him, pressing her ear against his chest. He was alive – thanks to the one called Saul. She quickly removed her cloak and draped it over him.

Stinging tears ran down her face as she stared at the black skeleton of her uncle's home. 'God damn them to hell!' she screamed. 'Cead mile curses on their heads.'

It was almost dawn when she rode towards home, having stayed with her uncle most of the night until she was sure he was resting easy and comfortable. She had called on a good and trusty neighbour who had immediately got out his cart and brought Uncle Pat back to his place where he had been slowly revived, then nurtured with broth before he collapsed again.

Her anger had reached burning pitch, but now exhaustion overwhelmed her. The sun was about to rise. She slowed at the top of a hill and sat looking over her beloved Wicklow. Hers was not an easy face to read these days, but sitting there on her horse, dark cloak falling around her, her fiery green eyes and black tousled curls would put many an Irishman in mind of the ancient tales of Gaelic pirate queens.

Everything dark and Celtic was in Anne Devlin. At a very early age she had learned the way of things, but she had never learned to accept them. At an early age she had trailed alongside her cousins Michael Dwyer and Hugh Vesty Byrne when they travelled for miles in search of the Shanachies, and from these historic scholars they had learned all the tales of the Gaels and Fianná warriors of old.

Not a man was taken into the Fianna nor admitted to the great Gathering of Tara, until he was a poet versed in the twelve books of poetic composition. Nor till his hair was inter-woven into braids and after being tied to a rock and using only his shield, emerged unscathed after standing before the nine warriors chosen to let fly their spears at him.

Not a man was taken into the Fianna until he had run through Ireland's woods, pursued by warriors but without being caught or wounded. If he could not jump a pole level with his brow, he was not taken. If he could not stoop below one level with his knee, he was not taken. If his weapons quiv-ered in his hand, he was not taken. This was the spirit of the ancestral Irish, the Gaels, as told in the tales of the Fianna.

She had often listened, and listened well, to the tales of her ancestors, the Clan O'Devlins who had belonged to the Castle of O'Donnell, Prince of Tyrconnell. 'Never forget, Anne,' her father had once said, 'we may be lowly tenants now, but we come from a great and noble ancestry.'

Vengeance rose like a hot flame within her. Cromwell had also tried to burn them out – sitting astride his horse on Tara, waving a Bible in one hand and signalling the extermination of the Irish with the other. Well, that warty old devil had failed, and soon the army of the Gael would rise again, rise to victory. And in victory they would stand once more on the Hill of Tara – Tara of the Irish Kings.

As the sun climbed higher the sky softened in tone. Lennard was out early, sauntering along towards the village in the quiet morning and with the empty road all to himself. Some yards ahead, from out of the woodlands, a pheasant darted across the road.

As quick as an impulse, Lennard picked up a stone and hurled it, missing his game by yards and a detachment of four Highlanders who came round the bend by inches.

'Eh!'

'Ye missed – and lucky for ye tha'ye did, mon,' one of the Highlanders said.

'I was aiming at the pheasant, not ye!' Lennard declared indignantly, while his eyes roamed suspiciously over the four brawny and lengthy Highlanders, who all had fine strong legs, and whose regimental dress he was not yet acquainted with.

'Begor, but yiz must be in a devil of a hurry wherever yer going,' he cried, 'that yiz didn't wait to put yer breeches on!'

The four Highlanders looked down at their kilts, then at the horrified little man who was still staring at their naked knees. 'Are ye jessin' us, Pad, or are ye serious?' one of them asked in astonishment.

'And what's them dead skunks doing hanging over yer vitals?' Lennard demanded, pointing to the Highlanders' sporrans.

'Och, ye bluidy fool!' a Highlander said dismissively. 'Have ye no' seen t'Highland costume before?'

'Well,' Lennard said, lifting his hat to scratch his head, 'I seen it now, if that's it entirely. But in faith and troth I reckon ye lads 'ud better watch out, for if ye insist on marching around showing yer naked knees like that – why, ye'll likely have many a poor Irish girl spinning around in a rare oul didley, and no mistake.'

The Highlanders thanked him gravely for the warning and marched on laughing, while the sun broke up the last few fleecy clouds then shone brightly over the pastures, promising another warm and sunny day.

Although Robert was early, Sarah was waiting for him in the lane. He had brought Jane's horse, all fitted out with side-saddle. They rode out to the farthest regions of the Dublin hills, galloping and cantering, before turning back towards Casino. As they cantered across the fields Sarah was like a bird set free from a cage. By the time they slowed to a trot on the avenue leading to the house, her hair was tousled, her face rosy, and her eyes sparkling with enjoyment.

A short time later she was wandering around the grounds of the small estate expressing her genuine delight at the garden. From the large lawns laid out at the back of the house, the garden suddenly narrowed into a strange twisting shape with a maze of little arches and fairy nooks of flowers everywhere.

While they strolled they talked as they had never talked before, interested in every small detail they learned about the other. Even when the Emmets' housekeeper served them after-noon tea on a white wrought-iron table under a cherry tree,

Sarah chattered away through crumbed lips asking incessant questions about the various functions at the Rotunda Rooms.

'I can't wait to go there,' she said. 'I've even been practising my dancing with Mrs Jessop.'

'Mrs Jessop!'

Sarah laughed. 'She does a wonderful jig. You should see the way she swooshes her skirts. She also taught me the reel.'

'They rarely jig or reel at the Rotunda, Sarah.'

She looked at him widely. 'What do they do?'

'The main one now seems to be the German waltz.'

Sarah said nothing for a moment, a frown on her brow. Mrs Jessop would definitely not know that one. Then a darker look came into her eyes. 'My father doesn't like me, you know,' she said suddenly.

He was amazed at her capacity for abrupt changes of thought and mood. She was like the waters of a lake, one minute all light and sparkling, the next all still under shadow.

'It's true,' she said. 'And he seems to dislike me more as I get older.' The hand toying with her cup shook a little.

'Why do you think he dislikes you?' he asked softly.

'I'm not sure,' she whispered, 'but I think . . . I think he resents the fact that I'm not Gertrude. He would have preferred any of us to die instead of her.'

For a moment he just stared at her, horrified that she could believe such a thing. But she did believe it, he could see it plainly in her eyes. He thought of the one person everyone knew John Curran hated: his wife. And in looks, Sarah was very like her; clearly her mother's child.

And then again, a swift change of mood as she smiled, and the sun shone on the lake again. 'Will you show me the trout stream now?' she said.

Sarah crouched alone by the stream, watching two red-finned trout swimming side by side. She waited until they had disappeared upstream then gently stirred the cool water with her fingers and gazed towards the mountains. She felt released and wild hearted in this new place where the world seemed larger and the waters whispered with the movements of the trout. And she was so very thankful that she had made a friend.

She turned and looked at Robert sitting up the bank, his hands locked around one knee, absorbed in contemplation of the same mountains. She would have given anything at that moment to know the thoughts of his deep reverie.

He was thinking of the number of secret cavities he had discovered in the new house. Old ropes and pulleys suspended between floors, but the most interesting discovery was the one he had made last night: a cavity beneath the library floor. He had been stacking some of the piles of his father's medical books on to the shelves in the far corner, when, bending down, he noticed the thin outline of a square in the floorboards.

Curious, he had pulled back the carpet square and, with the prising of a knife, had discovered it to be a trap door. His investigations had taken him down to a small cavity which led on through a tunnel out to the garden. The secret cavity was just big enough for a man in a sitting position.

He felt her eyes upon him and turned his gaze from the mountains to look at her. She smiled up at him, and the sheer charm of the smile made him even more glad he had pursued her, and persuaded her to come back with him today. And today all the family were at the seaside of Donnybrook, doing their best to cheer and bring colour to poor Jane. And so he had Sarah all to himself.

He lost his mind in watching her as she strolled up the grassy bank towards him. Lovely, she was, so lovely it did something to his insides just to look at her.

'The stream is *full* of trout,' she said.

He nodded. 'Apparently this house was once owned by an Englishman who came to Ireland solely for the joy of fishing. Long before that it was used as a hiding place by one of the chieftains of the Wicklow clan of O'Byrnes. He was captured here by the stream, and incarcerated in Dublin Castle where he died of starvation.'

'Poor man,' she said, sitting down beside him, 'I should prefer to be killed straight off than be left to starve away. Wouldn't you?'

Her eyelashes were long and reddish-brown against her creamy skin. 'I think my only preference would be to live,' he said.

162

Overhead the sun was radiant, its rays shimmering on the waters of the stream. 'This society you belong to,' Sarah said, her eyes curious. 'What is it called?'

He tried to think of an answer simple and evasive, but the enchantment of the girl and her nearness were all against him. The last thing he wanted to even think about today was politics. In the silence he looked at her, his breath suspended as his gaze moved down to the curve of her red lips, wondering how they would feel and taste. He had never yet kissed a girl, never even wanted to, not until now . . . Then one of his worst dreams came to haunt him.

'Yer not disturbing the trout, are ye, Misther Robert?'

Robert glanced irritably over his shoulder, then called back, 'No, we are *not*, Lennard!'

'Are ye shoower now?'

Sarah turned to see a little man sidling towards them. 'Who is he?' she whispered.

'A problem I have lived with since I was six years old,' Robert murmured. 'Trouble is, my father is excessively fond of him.'

Sarah could not help noticing Lennard's bulbous plum nose as he tipped his hat to her. 'Is it Miss Curran?' he asked. 'Simmins sez it is.'

'It is,' Robert snapped. 'Miss Sarah.'

'Well, I only came to remind ye of the time,' said Lennard, moving past them to the water. 'I think this is the particular time of year that no gentleman would disturb the trout.'

'So you decided to disturb us instead?'

'Ah now, Misther Robert, don't be like that! No, like I sez, I was only thinking of the poor trout.'

'If you care so much about the poor trout,' Robert asked, 'why were you cremating one over a fire down the bank last evening?'

' 'Twasn't from the stream!' Lennard cried indignantly. 'I won that trout playing cards with Johnny the Hat.'

'And where did Johnny the Hat get it?'

'Ah now, Misther Robert,' Lennard said in a chiding tone, 'when ye won that prize at the college last year at yer examinations, did ye ask them where they got it? No, and same goes for me and Johnny the Hat's trout!'

Robert looked at Sarah and sighed. 'We may as well go. He'll carry on like this for hours if he's let.'

'Don't ye move, miss!' Lennard shouted, then gave Sarah a toothy grin. 'Sure isn't that a grand sight entirely? A comely young colleen with a dark youth at her right knee, and a big croaker at her left.'

Sarah's glance shot down to an enormous frog crouched beside her. Lennard let out a spray of laughter. 'Mebbe they're both waiting for ye to give them a kiss and turn them into princes, wha'?'

'Devil grill your tongue for a rasher!' Robert snapped in an attempt to quell the gardener's insolence, and thinking how right Lennard was, about himself anyway, if not the croaker which had just leapt off down the bank. He turned to apologise to Sarah but her head was flopped over her knees in laughter.

'At least *one* of the quality has a sense of humour,' Lennard commented.

'And *one* of the servants has no sense at all!' Robert replied.

Sarah thought Lennard the most brazen and delightfully cheeky servant she had ever come across. So different from the formal Keegan. 'Have you come across any leprechauns in the gardens here?' she asked him.

Eh?' Lennard lost his grin and looked at her suspiciously. 'Leprechauns, did ye say, miss? Leprechauns?'

Robert was looking at her, a shadow of disbelief in his eyes. In the silence Sarah's smile faded, her cheeks began to colour like ripe peaches.

'Sure isn't the place overrun with them!' Lennard complained. 'Why, this place is worse than me own country of Tipperary for them that's in it! And faith, there was many a night in Tipp when I couldn't stir a foot for them!'

Robert muttered something under his breath, but Lennard saw he had an appreciative listener in the young miss, her eyes wide and delighted.

'Oh now, let me tell ye, miss, out here in Casino there's been a night or two lately when I've heard their music. Music so magical 'twould lull you to sleep and keep you awake until ye didn't know where ye were. But the cream of the milk was the time I spied two of them *wrestling*! In Tipperary that was, many years ago, about a week before Hallentide, and as God is my judge I was—'

'Drunk as a brewery rat.' Robert jumped up and helped Sarah to her feet. 'I'll not be held responsible to your father for allowing such nonsense to be fed to you by this master of codology.'

Sarah was clearly disappointed at their abrupt departure from Lennard. 'Why is his friend called Johnny the Hat?' she asked as they walked back to the garden.

'God knows! He has another friend called Johnny Fortycoats but I'll swear the man does not possess even one!'

Lennard sat down by the stream tee-heeing to himself. There was nothing he enjoyed more than annoying Misther Robert. Oh, it was funny, wha'? The expression on his face when she asked about the lepos! And funnier still when he furiously jumped to his feet. That was the trouble with these college boys, all brains and learning and no sense of humour. And where had his brains and learning got him? Kicked out of Trinity for being a rebel. And that was the trouble with rebels, all pride and patriotism and no sense of self-preservation. Not like that lily-livered Richard Curran who had bobbed and bowed and lied his way out of it.

Pride goeth before a fall, and Misther Robert was too proud by half. Now where was he? Kicked out of college while that mealy-mouthed mollycoddle came prancing round here in his Trinity uniform, the buckles on his hornpipes shining like the moon. And himself showing not a trace of resentment when the other threw down his books and complained how hard the studying was.

Now Lennard was suddenly angry. Young Misther Robert might be too proud by half, but he had wanted that university degree so bad, had studied hard and long for it, dreamed of the day he would get it; then had thrown it all away without a word. For what? If he was a Catholic it would be easier to understand. But he was a Prod! They were all Prods! The leaders of them anyway.

On the night Misther Tom had been arrested, and everyone in the house seemed to be crying, the females anyway, and Lennard had drank half a bottle of poteen that made his own eyes water, he had asked young Misther Robert what it was all about? Why they were doing it, Misther Tom and his friends? Putting themselves in danger and getting themselves arrested, for what?

'What we want,' Misther Robert had answered in his quiet-like way, 'is what the English have always enjoyed and the Americans have recently gained – the right to govern ourselves in our own land, with equal rights for men of every religious persuasion.'

Lennard shrugged. It was more than he could understand, Protestants fighting for the rights of even Catholics. And troth, he should have known – long before the trouble at Trinity – he should have known that Misther Robert was involved in the whole shebang right up to his neck, every bit as much as his brother.

It made Lennard want to laugh now, whenever he remembered how the doctor used to fret about the boy, fearing he was too quiet and reserved to make his mark on the world. But Lennard had always suspected that his quiet ways concealed a wild imagination and passionate dreaming. He had first started to bait him to draw him out of himself, now he did it purely from habit. Oh, bejabers, there's a trout leppin' now!

Lennard quickly moved on to his knees and crouched forward, slipping his hands beneath the water, towards the trout that had lodged under a rock.

'Come on now,' he whispered, knowing fish were deaf, 'come and get yer darling belly tickled.'

As they rode over the land of Rathfarnham and came near to the lane at the rear of The Priory, Sarah drew rein and asked Robert if she might be allowed to walk the rest of the way, alone.

He looked perplexed. 'Why?'

'My father might have returned early,' she said. 'He usually comes home around six, but he has been known to return by five.'

'Did you not tell him you were coming over to Casino today?'

She looked at him, her eyes clouded. 'He would not have

166

allowed me to go,' she said. 'Not until I was at least eighteen. And not without Amelia as chaperon. What time is it now?'

He withdrew his father's fob-watch. 'Twenty after five.'

'Then, please,' she said in sudden nervousness, 'help me down and let me run on home at once.'

He dismounted and reached up to lift her down. She slid from the saddle into his embrace, flushing slightly when he reluctantly released her.

'Does this mean that I shall not be allowed the pleasure of your company again?' he asked, as if desolate. 'Until you are at least eighteen?'

'Not unless,' she smiled impishly, 'you were to bump into me accidentally while I was out walking for pleasure – as you did yesterday.'

'I shall bear that in mind,' he said, smiling back at her.

'Thank you for a *lovely* day,' she said, and moments later she was gone.

Chapter Fifteen

When Robert entered the White Bull Tavern on Thomas Street, the landlord acknowledged him with a slight nod of the head, but his eyes moved in the direction of the back staircase. Robert slipped through the crowded saloon and swiftly ascended the stairs. As he approached the dark landing he heard a clicking of pistols.

'Robert Emmet,' he said quickly.

'Pass on.'

A shaft of light lit up the two armed sentinels as one opened a door and ushered him inside. The room was packed and heavy with tension. About twenty men stood around a large table at which sat ten more. This was the new Executive Council of the United Irishmen. All were professional men of class, and

167

dedicated to the man standing at the top of the table.

His aristocratic rank and military experience demanded respect and deference, but it was Lord Edward's character and personal charisma that most men admired and many loved. He was flanked by two bodyguards, a Kildare lieutenant named Patrick Gallagher, and Samuel Neilson, a giant of a man who was capable of killing with his bare hands anyone who endangered the chief.

Lord Edward looked tired and, indeed, felt so. Not only was he busy organising the underground movement and struggling to avoid arrest, he was preoccupied with worry about his pregnant wife. He consoled himself that Pamela was young and healthy, still only twenty-three.

Henry and John Sheares, two young lawyers and very revolutionary, were arguing for immediate action. The situation in the country was such, they insisted, that delegates from county committees now believed there was no choice left but immediate insurrection.

'Systematic terrorism by the yeomanry and military is being carried on throughout the country,' said Henry Sheares, 'with the knowledge and approval of the government. Half-hangings, floggings, pitchcappings, rape, and murder. You have all read the order issued by Sir Ralph Abercromby, chief of the army,' he snatched up a paper and read aloud: ' ". . . calling attention to the many complaints and irregularities in the conduct of the troops in this Kingdom. Every crime, every cruelty that could be committed by Cossacks or Calmucks has been transacted here in Ireland . . ." '

He flashed a glare at Lord Edward. 'Even the British commander was horrified at the actions of his own troops! And, for daring to speak out, the Viceroy has forced him to resign. Now, in his place, we have General Lake, a man who only last week restored peace and order to Ulster by mass executions and turning Belfast into a bonfire!'

Robert Emmet stood silently by and watched the faces of the men around the table, grave faces. Some spoke together in lowered tones, but John Sheares, the younger of the two brothers, could contain himself no longer.

'I put it to you plainly,' he said, 'that if no definite order comes from the executive soon, there will be a split in the organisation.'

All eyes seemed to be on Lord Edward, but Lord Edward, standing with arms folded and eyes half closed, seemed deeply set in his own thoughts. He had fought hard against the suggestion of action before the arrival of the French, but now he had received word from the French Government, refusing to make him a part-payment advance of the five thousand pounds he needed immediately, but they would make payment in full of the entire fifteen thousand in August, and *not before* August. The word 'pounds' being a code for men.

Dammit! Lord Edward thought, could they even trust Bonaparte? At times he wondered if the French were merely toying with the Irish in order to worry the English.

'Foreign aid cannot be relied upon,' Lord Edward said finally. 'And I think our foremost concern should be the existing circumstances throughout the country. A persecution of the people accompanied by gross acts of ferocious cruelty is now raging throughout the land in scenes of horror that threaten to rival the days of Cromwell. Neither age nor sex is enough to elicit mercy, much less afford protection. The government's only answer to the complaints of the citizens is to let loose the army and mobs of militia bands to subordinate the people in whatever way their prejudices direct them. And this is no exaggerated picture of the Castle's reign of terror. The statement of the British commander, Sir Ralph Abercromby, bears this out. *Every crime, every cruelty, that could be committed by Cossacks or Calmucks has been transacted here in Ireland.*'

He looked around the room. 'For my part, gentlemen, I believe we can wait no longer.'

There was a murmur of assent. Lord Edward turned and looked at Robert, who moved forward and handed him a paper. Lord Edward studied it for a minute, then said: 'Here is a list of returns of all sworn United Irishmen throughout the country, from Ulster down. These returns show that three hundred thousand men may be counted on to take the field.'

'My lord,' said a thin man sitting halfway down the table, 'it is one thing to have three hundred thousand men on paper, and another in the field. Three hundred thousand men on paper

169

may not furnish fifty thousand in the array. You know for what objects we joined the United Irish, and what means we reckoned on. *Fifteen thousand Frenchmen* were considered essential to our undertaking.'

'Would you attempt nothing without those fifteen thousand Frenchmen?' asked Lord Edward. 'Would you not be satisfied with ten thousand?'

'I would, my lord, if those fifteen thousand could not be procured.'

'And if even ten could not be had, what then?'

'I suppose . . . I would be forced to accept an instalment of five.'

'But we cannot get even those five thousand,' said Lord Edward, fixing his eyes with great earnestness on the man. 'And when you know that we cannot, will you desert our cause?'

Everyone turned to the thin man, awaiting his answer.

'If we had a sufficient number of French officers to head our people, even only *five hundred*, perhaps we might be justified in making an effort for independence. But what military men do we have of our own to lead our people against a disciplined army? You, my lord, are the only true military man amongst us, but you cannot be everywhere. And the misfortune is, you delegate your authority to those whom you think are like yourself, but they are not like you.'

Lord Edward ridiculed the idea of there being anything like discipline in the army.

'My lord, you must not be deceived! They are disciplined. We are not. Who is there to reform our people once our lines are broken? And once in disorder, the greater our numbers the greater the slaughter.'

'We cannot sit and wait until Bonaparte stops sparring with Nelson!' cried John Sheares. 'We must do it alone.'

A tense silence fell on the company, then Lord Edward said quietly, 'I suggest we put it to the vote.'

The moon was high and the sky peppered with stars when Robert Emmet walked home later. His role on the Executive Committee was a minor one, but demanded maximum trust. So far he had done nothing more than give messages to emissaries from the county committees, and help Surgeon Lawless arrange new houses of concealment for Lord Edward.

The protection of Lord Edward Fitzgerald was a task of the most anxious concern, for apart from the personal attachment that every man felt for him, and despite the reservations of the thin sceptic at the table, everyone knew that Lord Edward's presence alone would be enough to marshal thousands into arms. Such was the powerful influence that he possessed, the love and unbounded confidence he received from the people, that if Lord Edward himself were to ride out carrying the standard of liberty, the powers at the Castle would be unable to stand amidst the tumult that followed.

His place of secret residence was frequently changed, usually in the middle of the night, and usually in disguise. Two nights before he had been moved from a house in Harold's Cross, to a house on the banks of the canal. Lady Edward was proving a problem. Only the previous night, sometime after midnight, Robert had been in conversation with Lord Edward when one of the bodyguards showed Lady Edward into the apartment, swathed from head to shoe in a sable cloak, and escorted by a black man whom she introduced as 'Edward's favourite, Tony'.

While Lord and Lady Edward entered into close conversation by the light of the fire, Robert and Tony had retired to a distant part of the room, where they talked about incidents in the American war, then amused themselves looking through a social journal on the sideboard which advised ladies on ways to capture a man's heart and hand.

After half an hour or so Lady Edward rose to leave, embracing her wedded partner with such passion that Robert and Tony had looked away. Apparently light-hearted and in good spirits Lord Edward bade her farewell, but when he embraced Tony, as closely and fondly as a brother, raw emotion showed on his face. He entreated Tony not to search him out again, not until the contest was over, as his black-skinned face was too well known in a land of few Negroes.

Robert had been prevented from seeing or hearing Tony's response, for at that moment Lady Edward put a hand on his arm and spoke to him with dark imploring eyes. 'You are Irish?'

'Yes,' he replied. 'I am Irish.'

'You are good Irish,' she said in a sweet voice but imperfect English. 'My Edward is good Irish. You will look after my Edward. All you good and brave Irish must look after *my Edward.*' Then Tony came to escort her out, gently but firmly, and the tears flowed down her face as she strained to look back once more at her lord, with a love she made no effort to conceal.

'I could find no words to admonish her for coming,' Lord Edward said softly when the door had closed. 'Not when she is with child.' Then, after the few minutes he seemed to need to recollect himself, he answered Robert's question and explained that the reason that 'favourite' had become attached to Tony's name was because, of all the men he knew or had ever known, Tony was his favourite; and if ever he knew that he was dying, the face he would most wish to see after the faces of his children and his cherished Pamela, was Tony's face. He shrugged. 'And there it is.'

Surgeon Lawless had come into the room then, his face grave and his voice stern. 'You cannot stay here now, my lord. The risk is too great. We must leave immediately.' And so he had been removed within minutes to another address near the Cornmarket.

Well out of the town now, Robert passed through a small village on the road to Casino, pausing momentarily before a shop doorway which had nailed to it a government proclamation offering a reward of one thousand pounds for information leading to the arrest of Lord Edward Fitzgerald.

He walked on, a wry expression on his face. The proclamations had been up on every door and gate for over a week now, but even the very poor people of the Liberties had scoffed at the Castle thinking they could get such a cheap bargain.

One week after the meeting of the Executive Council in the upper back room of the White Bull, Robert succeeded in his attempts to see his brother in Newgate Gaol.

Thomas was ushered into the small room where the turnkey on duty usually ate his meals. He looked pale and gaunt and appeared to have lost stones in weight.

'Well, Tom,' Robert said softly.

'Well enough,' Thomas answered, the blue of his eyes highlighted by the thin whiteness of his face. 'But a day or two of Mrs Simmins's home cooking might restore my good looks.'

'Sit down,' Robert almost pushed his brother on to one of the two chairs in the room. 'Have you been fed at all since coming here?'

'Jane,' Thomas said urgently, 'is she well?'

'Yes. She sends her love, and bade me tell you: "Till death us do part, not prison walls." '

For a long moment Thomas sat staring at the wooden table between them then whispered, 'What's to do with our friends?'

In a hushed voice Robert told of his visit to the White Bull. 'Some short time after I left it was raided by Major Sirr and his men. Patrick Gallagher, Neilson, and the rest of the bodyguard put up a tremendous defence while Lord Edward escaped. It seems Major Sirr was almost foaming at the mouth and ranting at his men for not securing one arrest.'

Thomas smiled. 'Especially Fitzgerald's.'

'But Castlereagh went crazy when he heard Lord Edward had escaped. The riding school of John Beresford in Marlborough Street was immediately turned into a flogging arena. Anyone even suspected of being United Irish was introduced to the cat-o'-nine-tails until their bones showed.'

'Where is Fitzgerald hiding?'

'Oh, I dare not disclose that. Not even to you, Tom.'

'Did he give you a message for me?'

'Yes.'

Anguish and fear spread over Thomas's face as Robert conveyed Lord Edward's message about the rebellion.

'There's a great flaw in the plan that Fitzgerald in his modesty cannot see,' Thomas whispered. 'He's the only true military man we have. Tom Russell is as good as he but he's here in Newgate. Fitzgerald must have the assistance of officers, *French* officers.'

'He says the French cannot be relied upon. They're going it alone.'

Thomas made a sound like a groan. 'Madness!'

His chair made a screech as Thomas abruptly moved to his feet and walked up and down for a minute thinking about it.

'Listen,' he said, coming back to the table, 'once martial law was proclaimed it was clear as day that the government had declared war on the people in the hopes of provoking a rebellion *before* French assistance would be procured – which would therefore be easier to defeat. If the executive order a thrust now, prematurely, they are playing right into the hands of the Castle.'

Thomas's voice was strained by dint of keeping it low. 'Through the sleight of hand of a visitor, Tone has managed to get a message in here to Russell. At this very moment he is finalising the details of a French expedition with General Humbert. Go back to Fitzgerald and tell him I strongly urge him to wait! He must not make a move until the French are sighted off the Irish coast.'

A primitive rage engulfed Robert as he strode up Bridgefoot Street. He had not been prepared for his brother's physical deterioration. And there was nothing he could do about it. There was nothing anyone could do about it, not even Curran. Not as long as the Habeas Corpus Act was suspended. Thomas could be left to rot there for years.

And then he remembered – Lord Edward was going to do something, and soon! The thought made him quicken his steps towards Nicholas Murphy's house on Thomas Street. His brother was right. It was better to wait just a few more months – and win.

The sun was setting as he turned into Thomas Street and stopped dead in horror. Major Sirr and his men were outside Murphy's house. Two soldiers held a struggling Pat Gallagher while another tied his arms behind his back. Nicholas Murphy was also being bound. The front of the house was entirely blocked off by soldiers.

Robert sprinted across the street and shouldered his way through the swelling crowd. Major Sirr's assistant, Major Swann, came rushing out of the house holding out a hand dripping with blood. 'Oh, I am killed! I am killed! See what he has done to me. Fitzgerald used his dagger on me! Oh, I am basely murdered!'

'He's definitely in there, then?'

174

While Major Sirr questioned Swann, a local yeomanry officer, Captain Ryan, ordered the soldiers to take Gallagher to the Castle, then rushed inside the house. A few minutes later Mrs Murphy came running out screaming:

'He's killing him! They're both rolling down the stairs and Lord Edward's killing Captain Ryan!'

Major Sirr and four more soldiers charged into the house while Mrs Murphy shouted louder to the crowd. 'Hard? They don't come no harder than Lord Eddy! Captain Ryan's sword-cane just bent like a reed against his ribs.'

The crowd fell silent at the sound of a pistol being fired.

Everyone waited.

The silence was broken by loud shouts and angry screams as Major Sirr emerged from the house, followed by soldiers shoving out Lord Edward. He was without a coat, the shirt covering his right shoulder was in blackened shreds revealing a large gaping wound. Blood gushed down his arm and side as they roughly shoved him up on to a horse.

Major Sirr smugly held aloft Lord Edward's revolutionary uniform – a bottle-green suit with red cuffs and cape.

The crowd went berserk at the sight of their hero bound up with ropes. Men lashed out at the soldiers in an attempt to reach Lord Edward's horse and pull him off.

Major Sirr thundered above the uproar: 'If you let him get away this time, it will be your heads that will swing!'

The mounted soldiers kicked viciously at the crowd while another detachment of militia arrived with a carriage and Lord Edward was hurriedly transferred and taken away.

Major Sirr remained outside the house watching the crowd charge after the departing carriage and soldiers. His smug smile changed into a grimace of irritation as he turned to Major Swann, still holding his hand and moaning. 'Stop bleating about your bloody hand and get help,' he snapped. 'Captain Ryan has been severely wounded.'

'But I only heard one shot.' Swan looked puzzled.

'One shot be hanged – Fitzgerald didn't surrender without a fight! Your hand may have caught his dagger, Swann, but Captain Ryan got it in the gut, more than once!'

*　　*　　*

The turnkey tapped on the cell door and waited for Thomas to appear at the grille. 'Mr Emmet, they've lifted Lord Edward.'

'*What?*'

'On Thomas Street. Someone must have sold him for the reward. I'm told they're bringing him here later tonight.'

'Have you told Tom Russell?'

'Not yet, but I will.'

Thomas moved slowly away from the grille, then turned back quickly. 'Thank you, Foster.'

'You're welcome, sir.'

Thomas watched Foster sit down on his chair a few feet away, a strongly built Englishman getting on in years, from the East End of London.

'Ain't right what those buggers at the Castle are doin',' Foster had said when confiding he was a sympathiser. 'A load of bleedin' ruffians in fancy dress if you ask me.'

Foster had proved his sympathetic leanings by carrying information to and fro amongst a small number of the prisoners. He also kept Thomas informed of all developments outside the gaol.

Thomas slumped down on to the layer of straw which served as a bed and leaned back against the stone wall. If Lord Edward was taken, then all plans for a rebellion must surely be postponed.

Late that night he was awakened by the sound of metal clanging against metal, then voices. Thomas pulled himself to his feet and peered through the grille. Two soldiers were carrying an unconscious man down the corridor, and as they passed, Thomas stared down at the white face and bloodstained torso of Lord Edward.

Major Sirr followed pompously in their wake. He stopped and smiled at Thomas. 'Well, sir! There you see your great leader. He doesn't look in much of a state to defeat the King's army now, does he?'

'Where are you taking him?'

'Where? To his cell of course.'

'Not the rat hole across the way?'

'No, Counsellor Emmet, the room right next door to

176

you – the one with a bed. So now you and your friend will be able to communicate with each other. Rat-tat-tat on the walls perhaps, or even amuse yourselves occasionally by discussing plans for a rebellion.' The major allowed himself a small laugh.

'Will he be given medical attention?' Thomas asked.

Sirr stroked his moustaches. 'The Castle have given no orders for such.'

'Then he will die. But that's what you and that murderous lot at the Castle want.'

The smile that had been on Major Sirr's face vanished. 'Don't you talk to me in that self-righteous voice about murder, Emmet! You and your friends have been planning war in this country. And only this afternoon your great leader killed my captain!'

He turned abruptly and marched back down the corridor. Thomas heard him shout, 'The Castle orders sustenance of bread and water for the titled prisoner. Make that the same for Emmet.'

Thomas sighed. Only yesterday he had been taken off bread and water and put on proper rations.

During the following hours Lord Edward regained consciousness. Thomas shouted through the grille to him, but the response was often so weak he could not distinguish the words.

Thomas inquired of Foster: 'How is he?'

'Not good, Mr Emmet, not good at all. That wound in his shoulder is bad. Nobody's allowed to see him but the Castle men.'

The turnkey scratched the balding dome of his head. 'And listen to this – when Lord Edward was brought in here, he said he wanted to make his will and asked for his solicitor, but even he was not allowed inside the walls. He had to stay in his coach and the Governor carried out what Lord Edward said, then carried back what the solicitor said, then out again with what Lord Edward said, then back with the paper to be signed and witnessed. A bugger of a farce! At the end of it all, Lord Edward passed out.'

'They're not taking any chances, are they?'

'Not with his lordship,' Foster replied. 'I suppose now

they've found him, they've no intention of losing him again.'

Foster started down the corridor, then turned back. 'Oh, there's another thing, Mr Emmet. I mentioned that business with the major to the governor and he said you were to be put back on proper rations. Said he takes his orders from the Castle, not Major bloody Sirr.'

Thomas smiled. 'Thank God for small mercies – and you, Foster.'

The news of Lord Edward's arrest spread through Dublin like wildfire. Members of the Ascendancy were seen nervously rushing out of theatres before the end. Others left dinner parties and hurried home, issuing orders for bags to be packed immediately. The fear of some mass public reaction inspired many to take a holiday in England. That night, the streets of Dublin were shrouded in darkness. No lamp-lighters turned out to light the lamps. When the militia were ordered out to light the streets, they found water had been mixed with the oil to prevent the lamps from burning. And so the city remained in darkness.

The Castle responded by taking its vengeance on the Liberties. City magistrates assisted by seven hundred of the Dublin militia set out to disarm the city. Nicholas Murphy's house was burnt to the ground. Other houses were torn apart, the furniture thrown into the street. Lamp-lighters were tied to the lamp-posts and flogged. Over twenty men were hanging up on triangles in the Castle courtyard as huge caches of pikes and weapons were brought in.

The Executive Council had no choice but to send out the news to all county committees – Dublin was done.

Three days later, in the Emmets' house at Casino, Robert ate sparingly of the large lunch Mrs Simmins had prepared, but James McGucken, a Belfast attorney, devoured everything placed before him, talking non-stop and scattering food over the white linen cloth. When his appetite was finally satisfied, McGucken insisted that Robert show him over the thirteen acres of the small estate.

Robert was anxious to get on with the business, but acquiesced to the wishes of the Ulsterman, thrusting his thumbs inside his belt and sauntering silently beside McGucken as he lavished praise on the land, on the trout stream and the mountain view; stopping every so often to thump his chest and breathe in the air.

Back in the library, McGucken talked more as he drank brandy after brandy while Robert silently sifted through a number of papers. 'I do not wish to be rude, Mr McGucken,' he said finally, 'but I have an appointment shortly and the business must be attended to.'

McGucken inclined his head in acknowledgement. 'Of course.'

'I will take care of the messages sent down from Connaught,' Robert said, 'but any from Ulster must be sent to James Farrell at 33 Paradise Row. Anybody with reason to come down to Dublin must also be sent to Paradise Row. They are to ask for Edward Hewson.'

'Who is he?'

'Farrell. Hewson is the code name.'

McGucken twirled the drink in his glass, feeling slightly aggravated. He had brandy in his hand, brandy in his stomach, and young Emmet was a poor drinking companion. He was too disciplined for one so young, too tense in his idealism, too unwilling to bend a little and relax.

He tossed back his drink. Funny how this quiet young man had suddenly risen so high in the ranks – an officer on the Executive Council no less! No private's oath for him, no lieutenant's oath, but straight in as an executive officer, sworn before forty of the top men, before Lord Edward himself. All reports declared his dedication and discretion beyond dispute.

'Have you fully considered the risk you are running by organising against the Castle?' McGucken said suddenly. 'You are very young to centre your life around the cause.'

The answer was dispassionate. 'Others are younger.' Robert suddenly looked up and smiled. 'We have better hopes of French assistance now.'

McGucken grunted. 'Do you really think the French will bother with us?'

'They did two years ago, when they tried to help Tone, in ninety-six.'

'Ach, it was General Hoche who organised that. And now Hoche is dead. Napoleon hated him.'

'Well Tone has General Humbert behind him now, and Humbert is one of Napoleon's favourite officers.'

McGucken sipped from his glass, then grinned slyly. 'The Castle thinks Dublin is done – finished. But wouldn't it be a real stinger for them to know the Jackeens are still going strong, underground, and just waiting for the French.'

Robert lifted his eyes from the papers and stared coldly at McGucken. 'It would be a stinger for *us* if they did know,' he said.

Later that night, Robert stood by his open bedroom window peering through a telescope. For the past three nights signal fires had been burning on the Wicklow Mountains to the south. They were burning again tonight, varying in intensity, as if sending messages. For a time he watched the fires intently, then eventually lowered the telescope. Then he heard a familiar voice singing merrily on the air.

'The boys will all be there, sez the Shan Van Vocht,
The boys will all be there, with their guns in good repair
And Lord Edward will be there, sez the Shan Van Vocht.'

Robert threw down the telescope and ran swiftly and quietly down the stairs and out through the front door. Lennard was leaning against the hedge clutching a stone poteen jug under his arm. Robert heard a tramping sound in the distance. For a moment he ignored Lennard and peered into the darkness as the sound drew nearer. He could see the glow of torches, but the rest was indiscernible.

'The French are on the sea, sez the Shan—'

Robert shoved his hand over Lennard's mouth. 'You gossoon! It's past the curfew. Do you want to be clamped in manacles and dragged off to gaol?'

'Will ye go way owa that!' Lennard shook himself free. 'Is it to shmother me ye want, wha'?'

'You're as drunk as a bishop!' Robert said with disgust.

'I'm nosh at all!' Lennard showed his teeth indignantly. 'I drank only enough to keep meshelf shober.'

The tramping drew closer. Robert could now see the advancing group. He pulled Lennard behind the hedge and shoved him down. The servant slid into a sitting position, stretched out his little legs and lifted the poteen jug to his mouth.

'Don't make a sound!' Robert rasped, peering over the hedge and watching as the artillery train clattered along the dirt road fifty yards away. By the light of the torches he estimated the column of redcoats to number about five hundred. Heading south.

When the procession had passed he slumped down next to Lennard who looked at him from under his bushy brows, then held out the jug.

'Have a drink,' Lennard said.

Robert took the proffered jug, took a gulp and almost choked.

'Have another,' Lennard said, slapping him on the back. 'Second is always smoother than the first. No? Can only be doing with your expensive brandy, is that it? No mountain dew for ye, me fine young college boy.'

His breath returned, Robert said: 'Where have you been until this time? The curfew is ten and it's after midnight.'

'It's my day off, too. And into Dublin I've been. And I learned quite a few things there an' all. Did ye know, Misther Robert, that a man called Horish tried to burn down Parliament House this afternoon.'

Robert stared at him, and Lennard nodded. 'Aye, but he was caught redhanded and clobbered.'

'Horish the chimney sweep?' Robert said. 'What happened to him?'

'The last I seen of him, which was this evening, about the time of eight o'clock, he was up on a triangle in the lower Castle yard getting the fire lashed out of him.'

Lennard took a swig from his jug. 'But wasn't it a terrible thing they done to the darling Lord Eddie, flinging him in prison and he wounded badly. But howsomever, his health is being drunk all over Dublin and the cry is the same everywhere: To Lord Eddie and Liberty and a pox on the Castle.'

181

Lennard looked around him with a glassy eye, then began to sing in a low menacing voice:

'The French are on the sea, sez the Shan Van Vocht.
The French are in the Bay, they'll be here without delay.
And the Castle sure will pay, sez the Shan Van Vocht.'

He squinted a wink at Robert then lifted the jug to his mouth. 'Slaaaaaawnche!'

'How can you drink that stuff so easily?' Robert said. 'It's got the kick of a mad mule.'

'A mad mule?' Lennard wiped his mouth. 'Now that reminds me of Jackser Brady of John's Lane – strange man – and what he did only this morning to Major Sirr's horse. You see, poor Jackser was mortal sore after being flogged for not lighting the lamps the night of Lord Eddie's arrest. Troth, the whip left him so bent that when the major rode past, Jackser's vengeful eyes could see no higher than the horse. 'My friends,' he would say to all in the tavern, 'my friends, my friends, my friends . . .'

Lennard frowned, narrowing his blurred eyes as if trying to remember what Jackser said next. He lifted the jug to take another drink but seemed to have difficulty finding his mouth.

'Don't you think you've had enough?' Robert asked.

Lennard looked round as if he had forgotten him. 'Wait now, wasn't I telling ye something?'

'About Major Sirr's horse.'

'Eh?'

'My friends . . .' Robert prompted.

' "My friends, my friends, *my friends*," ' Lennard continued as if he had never left off, ' "is that horse – which is of the best Irish bloodstock – a traitor for humping a Castle tyrant around on his back," sez Jackser, "or is he not a traitor?" '

Lennard cocked an eye at the moon. 'Now then, I sez he was a traitor, but others sez he wasn't, but in the heel of the hunt and whatever their politics everyone agreed with Jackser that the horse was indeed a traitor, just to humour the poor man.

'So then, lo and behold, this morning when the major rode past, didn't Jackser only ups and shoots the bastard's horse!

182

"God sakes," sez I, when the men told me, "God sakes," I sez, "wouldn't ye think he'd've aimed a bit higher and shot the real brute and not the poor horse, wha'?"'

This time the jug found its destination and Lennard wiped his mouth.

'So, like I sez, over the beast's head the major went, landing on his bum and not his bonce. Suffering only a sore rump instead of brain damage. And now poor Jackser is like a beast himself, locked in the metal cage in the lower Castle yard and all the passers-by pointing and laughing at him.'

Robert decided he had heard enough. He pushed himself to his feet and reached for Lennard. 'We'd better get inside. The curfew patrols are passing every few hours, there'll be one along shortly.'

'They'd betther not come near me then!' Lennard cried. 'I'll soon show 'em who's ready to shtrike a blow!'

He turned belligerently on Robert. 'And ye may have walked out of Trinishy, me young hero, but that's all ye've done! I don't see ye shtriking no blows for Ireland's freedom. Not like Lord Eddie, not like Misther Thomas, and not like me!'

'You?' Robert stared at the servant. 'What in God's name have you done?'

'Nothing yet,' Lennard admitted on a grudging note, 'but if them soldiers was to come here-along now, ye wouldn't see me running indoors. Why, I'd give them a puck in the gob first.'

Robert looked at the squat little drunk with a jug under his arm. 'Would you even reach that high?' he murmured indistinctly.

'But there ye go,' Lennard said, giving his shoulders a shake and plodding uncertainly towards the house, ' 'tis not for all men to be fearless. And 'tis not always the bravest wears the warrior's uniform—' The jug slipped from under his arm on to the ground.

'Now look what ye done!' he shouted, bending down to lift the upended jug and finding there was no stopper and the liquid seeping into the ground. ' 'Tis all spilled out,' he cried, shaking the jug then pawing at the dark ground like a blind man. 'Me lovely jug o' potcheen that cost me an afternoon's cards has all spilled on to the ground! All of it!'

'Not all of it,' Robert returned. 'It was less than quarter full when I lifted it.'

'Well a quarter is a quarter,' Lennard shouted furiously. 'Less than a half but more than none. And I've none left now!' He grabbed at the jug and put it to his mouth, head back. 'Not a drop. O Holy Mother! Not a drop of comfort to comfort me at close of day and start of night.'

'Well, don't glare at me,' Robert said. 'It was you who dropped your precious illegal brew, not me.'

'Aye, aye; 'twas me at fault,' Lennard said sadly, turning away. 'Didn't put the stopper back in.'

By the glow from the lamps outside the front door, Robert watched him plod miserably towards the passage at the side of the house that led down to his room above the stables. He shrugged and moved into the hall, about to close and bolt the door when Lennard's furious voice rose up in the silence.

'Bad bloody cess to me father's only son!'

Chapter Sixteen

'When is the insurrection due to take place? What plans have been made with the French? Dammit, man! You can achieve nothing now! You would do well to consider your family.'

Thomas woke with a start. The voice came from Lord Edward's cell.

'I warn you, Fitzgerald, if you do not co-operate you will not be the only one to suffer; your wife and family will also. Speaking of which, your wife gave birth, prematurely I believe, to your daughter last night. Now how do you think your little Jacobin wife will fare if we confiscate your estates and render her penniless. How do you think your three children will fare?'

'My children are *Geraldines*! You cannot take away their heritage.'

'Indeed we can, but you can avert such an extremity by giving us information of any impending French landing.'

'I know nothing of a French landing.'

'Very well, have it your way – for now.'

Thomas heard a second voice, a voice he knew well. It belonged to Lord Castlereagh, and it trembled with disgust.

'You have not only degraded and betrayed your family, Fitzgerald, you have betrayed your entire class.'

Thomas watched as the Castle officials marched past his cell, then he shouted through to Lord Edward. 'Don't worry about your family, Edward! To confiscate your estates they would have to get a bill of attainder, and Curran would fight them all the way.'

Lord Edward gave a strained response. 'For the sake of my children, I pray God you are right.'

'It is only a threat,' Thomas shouted. 'And you will survive this.'

A sudden ferocity crept into Lord Edward's voice. 'By God, Thomas, if it can be done by self-will, I'll not give them the satisfaction of seeing me dead unless they hang me.'

Officials from the Castle interrogated Lord Edward every few hours, but he refused to name the men who were conspiring a rebellion. He continually asked for medical attention but the answer was always the same: 'When you give us details of your planned campaign.'

Thomas could hear him moaning in agony but they gave him no respite.

'Damn you to hell! You'll get no help from me!'

'It is you who needs help, Fitzgerald, and we can give it to you, if you will just see reason. You surely don't believe your friends have any chance of *winning*, do you?'

They finally allowed him to sleep. Thomas begged of Foster, 'Do something, man! If his wound is not treated he will die of blood poisoning. If you could even clean it.'

'I daren't, Mr Emmet—'

Foster turned, startled at the sudden clanging of doors and a rushing of feet. He pressed himself against the wall as redcoats shoved him aside to line the corridor. Two positioned themselves outside the open door of Lord Edward's cell.

'Why is the door open?' a soldier asked.

'Hell, he can hardly move,' Foster said. 'And there's little air in there. He needs air on his wounds.'

'Do your business, turnkey, and lock it at once.'

'What's going on?' Foster asked as he locked the cell door.

'Rescue attempt. We've been informed his friends are going to try and storm the gaol.'

The word soon spread. An eerie silence descended over the prison. Thomas knew that every member of the Leinster Executive of United Irishmen in Newgate was alert and waiting.

From outside in the distant streets the drums of the militia were spasmodically heard, but nothing else disturbed the tension within the walls of the gaol.

It was a long, very long night, but finally the greyness of dawn crept into Thomas's cell. He looked up to the small grated window without glass. His eyelids drooped heavily but he fought off sleep.

The rustle of rats in the corners of the cell distracted his attention. They had moved closer, attempting to eat his straw mat. He kicked out at them violently – his mat was the only source of comfort within his miserable cell. They scurried away towards two of the five ratholes he had counted. The rodents in Newgate vastly outnumbered the prisoners.

Foster arrived with his rations, shaking his head silently. Thomas concluded the rescue attempt must have been abandoned.

Later that day the soldiers were curiously withdrawn. Only two remained in position at the entrance to the corridor. Thomas peered through the grille looking for Foster, but his chair was empty.

Foster was in the process of carrying out a letter from another state prisoner also confined in Newgate, Matthew Dowling, an eminent solicitor of Dublin, who had been an agent of Henry Grattan. The letter was addressed to His Grace the Duke of Leinster. '*Your brother, Lord Edward, is dangerously ill. Surely some attention ought to be paid to him. But I think seeing any member of his family or even a friend would be more conducive to his recovery than fifty surgeons.*'

Lord Edward had been in prison a number of days now, but

not a member of his family or friends or servants had been allowed in to see him.

Sometime that afternoon, a surgeon-general came to attend on Lord Edward, Samuel Stone, a lieutenant of the Derry militia. In the hours that he stayed with his patient, removing the bullet and bandaging his wounds, Thomas realised that this gentleman was carrying out the duties assigned to him with much humanity and kindness, and Lord Edward's sufferings were greatly soothed by the affectionate interest that Stone showed to him.

Shortly after the surgeon had left, Foster returned, his face beaming as he held up a tray. 'Look at this lot!'

Thomas stared at the golden roasted chicken, the fresh crusty bread, the fruit full of tartish juices to be swallowed down with the jug of wine. He could feel his own juices swelling under his tongue, thickening up, forcing his mouth open.

'For Lord Edward,' Foster said. 'I'm told his mother the Dowager Duchess Emily has returned from England, but before she left it's said that she implored the Prince of Wales and the Duke of York to help her son. It's also being said that Charles James Fox the Whig leader has threatened to come over himself and personally remove Lord Edward from prison into a hospital – and bedamned to the Tory junta at the Castle.'

'Charles James Fox is a cousin to Lord Edward,' Thomas said. 'That's why Lord Edward's little boy is named Edward Fox Fitzgerald. Is the Duke returned from England?'

'That I dunno. But I do know that Lady Sarah Napier and Lady Louisa Connolly are doing everything they can to try and see Lord Edward, but Camden and Castlereagh won't allow it on any grounds. But myself, I fancy they're beginning to soften, with sending the doctor and this food and all. Castlereagh has even ordered that his bed be turned to face the window so he can draw in the air and lighten his spirits.'

The smell of the chicken was beginning to make Thomas dizzy. He stared at the golden-skinned white meat. It had been a long time since he had been consumed by such hunger, such *lust*! He champed down on his saliva as Foster moved away with the tray.

Unconsciously Thomas's hand moved over his stomach, attempting to assuage the agonising pulling and tugging there. The sight of the food called his mind back to the table at home: beef, pheasants, legs of ham! He remembered how he had once sat down hungrily to a huge helping of game pie, swallowing it with resentment when his father chose that succulent moment to announce that he had only two hours previously covered the face of a four-year-old boy, a victim of starvation.

But his father was right! Now he understood why he was driven to such an extent that even his friends called him a fanatic. Hunger was the most cruel of life's afflictions; the slowest, most agonising. How could the politicians ever understand the plight of the hungry multitudes when their own bellies were always full.

Thomas had learned all about hunger during his first weeks in Newgate. First the constant gnawing at the pit of the stomach, then the wild ravenous hunger which made children stuff grass down their throats. Then the draining of the juices, followed by the awful lethargy. It was when the jaws of hunger finally closed, and the tongue dried up, that all hope was gone.

Lord Edward's voice brought him out of his reverie. 'This is a surprise! But a pleasant one. Please give the wine and some of the food to Mr Emmet.'

'Oh, I daren't, m'lord. The soldiers at the end of the corridor will see me.'

'Then apart from half a glass, drink the wine yourself, man. You will enjoy it more than I.'

Thomas pressed his brow against the grille. Except on special occasions, Fitzgerald had always been abstemious when it came to drink.

Minutes later, Foster returned to the corridor wiping his mouth. 'I'll be going off duty in a minute, Mr Emmet. I'll see you in the morning.'

'No doubt,' Thomas said.

'Oh, I was nearly forgetting . . .' Foster moved closer and muttered, 'They brought in a few more prisoners this morning. One was a man named Neilson, and two brothers named Sheares.'

Thomas only nodded, and when Foster had gone he slumped

down on to his mat and began to count the number of bricks on the opposite wall, tediously working out their cubic dimensions. He used this trick whenever he wished to shut out his thoughts. Swiftly, the lack of sleep and the tension of the night before worked together with the monotony of his mathematics. He slid into a lying position and welcomed the waves of blackness.

They were in the four-poster bed, the morning sun was shining through the chinks of the window-drapes, through the cream lace of the bed-curtains. Jane was asleep beside him; chestnut hair plaited in two thick braids like a girl. He whispered her name. Green eyes opened. She smiled. He moved his body closer, hands reaching for her – then he felt the sudden sharp nip at his leg. He scrambled up with a shout, and the rats scurried towards their holes.

The shout continued, long and agonising, but it took Thomas a full minute to clear his head and realise it was not his own voice that rang in his ears, but Lord Edward's.

He stumbled towards the cell door and tripped over his morning ration plate on the floor. He had not even heard Foster place it there earlier. Damn! Damn! Damn! The rats had eaten every crumb.

He could hear Foster in the cell next door attempting to placate Lord Edward whose shouts had subsided into low groans. 'Oh, they're swines, Lord Eddie, swines! But don't let the buggers beat you. This is how the Castle wants you to react.'

'What's happened?' Thomas shouted. 'Foster!'

Not long after, a shaken Foster walked back to Thomas at the grille. 'They've erected a makeshift gallows outside his window,' Foster said. 'One of his friends is hanging from it.'

Thomas stared at the turnkey who wiped a hand over his face. 'I think it's killed his reason, Mr Emmet. He was in a bad enough way before, but when I left him just now, he was lying there staring at the window with eyes wild and mad looking. His health can't take it. The wound in his shoulder is festering so bad it looked like gangrene to me!'

'Damn them!' Thomas cried angrily. 'And damn you, too, Foster! Why do you serve these monsters?'

Foster looked at him with the same sympathy and honesty of expression that had first made Thomas trust him. 'If I don't do it, Mr Emmet, someone else will. I just try to make things a bit easier in my own way.'

One of the soldiers came marching down the corridor. 'What's all the shouting about, turnkey?'

Foster pointed to Lord Edward's cell. 'Take a look through his window.'

The soldier paused for only a moment in the room. On his return he looked directly at Thomas. 'The price of anarchy,' he said.

Thomas waited till the soldier had strutted back to his post before whispering, 'I'm sorry, Foster.'

'It's all right, Mr Emmet. I understand.'

'How can they do it, Foster? Fitzgerald is the noblest of men. He has no deceit – he stood up in Parliament and spoke openly about the issues he is fighting for now. He has no selfishness, no duplicity of nature. Yet he is the one the Castle hate most of all.'

Foster nodded. 'It's what they said when he first came in here, ain't it. They think he's betrayed his class.'

'*Ready the flag and strike the drum!*'

The two men jumped to attention at the authority of the voice.

'*Pikemen into smart trot! Muskets prepare to fire!*'

Realisation dawned on Thomas. He stared in horror at Foster.

'*Fire!*'

Foster moved quickly towards Lord Edward's room. The two soldiers rushed down the corridor thrusting their bayonets before them. Thomas reeled back against the wall of his cell and put his hands to his head.

'*Come on, damn you. Come on!*'

'Lie down again, Lord Eddie,' Foster cried. 'Lie down or you'll hurt yourself.'

There were sounds of commotion as Fitzgerald struggled with the soldiers who endeavoured to restrain him, his voice mocking.

'Soldiers? Call yourself soldiers? You, dear fellow, don't feel big enough to hold your musket . . . Oh, damn my eyes . . . my eyes . . .'

The three men finally restrained him, then the two soldiers rushed back down the corridor murmuring to themselves as Lord Edward continued the battle in his mind, still commanding his army.

'*Close in! Close in! Pikemen close in! Don't let the strength of their army intimidate you! Closing in makes their powder and ball useless! All their superiority is in fighting at a distance! So close in!* Oh, damn my eyes . . .'

Some minutes later a flustered Foster appeared at the grille.

'It's not only his mind that's gone, Mr Emmet, so has his eyes. He's gone blind.'

Thomas made no answer, just turned away and slumped down on his mat. He stared hard at the bricks on the opposite wall, counting each brick row by row while desperately trying to shut out the voice of his dear friend as he feverishly rallied his army. In the maelstrom and mists of his delirium, Lord Edward Fitzgerald was at last commanding the War for Independence he had planned for so long. A war he would never now see.

For many hours Lord Edward was without his senses. The Castle sent a keeper from the madhouse to attend on him.

Thomas was still staring at the bricks when Lord Edward's fatigue quietened him, when the keeper eventually left, when the doctor reluctantly left, when Foster said Lord Edward was sleeping, when the familiar clang of metal against metal was followed by a haughty voice in the corridor.

'You must understand this is not officially allowed. It is only due to my friendship with your mother, the Duchess Emily, and the respect the Leinsters still hold in England, that I have left my supper to escort you personally to see your brother.'

Thomas moved to his feet.

The voice belonged to the Chancellor, Lord Clare. As they reached his cell Thomas saw that his two companions were Lord Henry Fitzgerald, Edward's younger brother, and his sister Lady Louisa.

'As Castlereagh refused you access, I could find myself in a very awkward position,' said the Chancellor. 'And if the Viceroy, Lord Camden—'

'Lord Camden!' cried Lady Louisa vehemently, quite unlike the sedate, tranquil lady she usually was. 'I who never before kneeled to anyone but my God – humbled myself in the dust and *grovelled* at that man's feet in vain!' Then, her composure barely returned, she added, 'But I do thank you, Lord Clare. Now, may we see Edward?'

'Of course.'

Thomas pressed his ear against the grille and listened.

'Edward?' It was Lord Henry.

'My dear, dear, Edward,' Lady Louisa said gently.

Lord Edward responded with a calm lucidity, his senses returned. 'Henry? Louisa? It is heaven to me to see you . . . only I can't see you . . . Come, embrace me.'

'O my darling,' said Lady Louisa. 'How pale, how very pale you are. What is wrong with your sight, dear?'

'Louisa? Henry? Listen to me! I have made my will. Everything I possess must go to Pamela. See that she and our children are protected . . . Also my poor Tony . . .'

'Edward,' said Lord Henry, 'Pamela is incapable of venturing out. The child—'

'Is born, I know. A girl. Now I am the proud father of a son and two daughters. Are they well? Mother and child?'

'Both are well.'

'And the children, too?'

His voice weakening, he continued to ask questions about the children he so tenderly loved, a subject very dear to his heart. No man was more truly happy in his family circle than Lord Edward. And in possessing Pamela for a wife he felt that he possessed kingdoms.

'Is there any message you wish us to give to Pamela?' Lady Louisa asked.

A long pause. 'No, no, thank you, nothing. Only . . . break it to her tenderly.'

'Nonsense, dear fellow,' Lord Henry said quickly. 'We will get you out of here, get you well again.'

For a moment there was silence, then Lord Edward began to utter words about his wife with a catch in his voice that was something like laughter. Once again the mists were falling over his mind and memory. 'Such a lovely girl. Couldn't describe the place to her . . . white house surrounded by elm trees and, of course, my flower gardens . . . It does not describe well, my love. You will have to wait until we get off this boat and reach there. I hope you will like it, for it has . . . oh! all the things that mean beauty to me.'

'He's talking about his own private lodge in Kildare,' said Lord Henry. 'Frescati.'

'Frescati?' said Lord Edward. 'My dear wife adores it, and indeed, becomes it. She was made for Fres—' A great convulsion of coughing stopped him.

After the long, long silence that followed, the sudden cry of emotion from Lady Louisa told Thomas that Lord Edward was dead.

Foster came into view, a sad spectacle to behold. He sniffed and pulled at his fob-watch. 'The doctor will want to know the exact time of death,' he said quietly.

Lord Henry's voice was far from quiet; it rose up in anger and quivered with grief.

'I lay my brother's death at the door of Dublin Castle and the men in high places who denied him the solace and assistance of his family, even though he was severely wounded! Denied him his Negro friend to attend upon him, who was willing to share his imprisonment, and who could have been depended upon to keep his mind free from agitation. No, no, Lord Clare, you may refuse responsibility, but to his death you and your cronies pursued him. To his death, through madness, you and your cronies persecuted him!'

'Lord Henry—'

'Nor, my Lord Clare, shall I hesitate to tell the world – I wish I could tell the four corners of it – that amongst you, your ill-treatment has murdered my brother as much as if you had put a pistol to his head!'

'Lord Henry . . . Your brother – was bent on treason.'

'And why? Why does a noble man of the first family of Ireland, with his own fortune, a beautiful wife and family of lovely children, decide to turn his mind to the emancipation of his country? I will tell you, in the words that Lord Holland used only the other day. *Because his country is bleeding under one of the hardest tyrannies our times have ever witnessed*. And you, Lord Clare, are part of that tyranny.'

'Lord Henry . . .'

Lord Henry strode back down the corridor followed by his sobbing sister. Lord Clare remained in the death cell, alone with Lord Edward. An extraordinarily long time passed before he emerged, and followed at a slower pace.

'Hell and damnation to you, Fitzgibbon!' Thomas cried, words and tears smashing out together. 'Hell and damnation!'

John Fitzgibbon, the Earl of Clare, paused to look at him, but made no answer. Astonished, Thomas saw the Chancellor had been crying, the tears still wet on his face.

'Oh, what's this?' Thomas sneered. 'Is this what the turn-keys will tell all Dublin? Lord Clare, after seeing the dead Fitzgerald, emerged crying like a woman! *Damn your hypocrisy!* May it kill you!'

'I gave Lord Edward his chance of escape,' Lord Clare blurted. 'I publicly hinted that his friends should get him out of the country. He would not have been stopped at the ports. I would have seen to it. Fitzgerald was too worthy a man to be allowed to rot on the dungheap of his worthless cause.'

The Chancellor sniffed, looked as if he might release more tears, and Foster chose that moment to ask quietly, 'Shall I send for the prison doctor, sir? Dr Trevor. He likes to be called quickly after a death . . . to do the certificate.'

'Bugger off!'

Foster stood astonished at Lord Clare's sudden and vicious temper.

'You damned beggar!' Lord Clare flashed out. 'How dare you stand and listen to the private conversation of the Lord Chancellor! Now bugger off this instant or I'll have you flogged until your bowels show!'

Foster threw a glance at Thomas, who appeared not in the least surprised by the outburst.

Foster moved off, Lord Clare looked at Thomas, and resumed his private conversation. 'But now that Lord Edward *is* dead, I'll make sure that you and your kind never win. This country belongs to the English Crown and always will.'

'Tell that to the people.'

'I'm telling you, Emmet, damn fool that you are. You had admirable talent and intellectual abilities that had not gone unnoticed. You could have been a great adornment at the Bar. Had you played your cards wisely, you might well have been on your way to Solicitor-General by now. But you threw it all away for a piece of American claptrap about all men being born equal. How could men like you and Fitzgerald believe such a lie? Lord damn me if I'll ever understand why decent Protestants—'

'That's something you'll never be.'

'You insolent bloody bastard!' Lord Clare glared with naked malevolence. 'But this is not the end, Emmet, only the beginning. By the time I am finished I will have made the people of this country *as tame as cats*!'

Lord Edward's body lay in its cell for two days, during which time the Castle allowed the United prisoners in Newgate, one by one, to see their dead leader.

Thomas Emmet was the first to enter the room and look down on the slender, white-faced corpse but, like every other man who later entered that room, he did not emerge with an air of defeat or intimidation, as the Castle hoped, but with a face grim with defiance and anger.

The procession was finally over. All had seen him. The Castle ordered that the funeral take place in the middle of the night, a secret affair. No daylight procession followed by millions of mourners, including, possibly, some of rank and noble blood. A secret affair, quickly done, quickly forgotten.

Lady Louisa was again in the cell with Lord Edward when Lord Clare came with the order. She responded with that particular dignity that Thomas often found more usual in women than men in times of sorrow.

'I am seeing to the arrangements,' she answered coldly. 'And, despite the heartbreaking circumstances, I shall instruct my sorrows to be proud. Lord Edward despised all outward show, and to run the risk of shedding one drop of blood on this occasion would be the thing of all others that would vex him most.'

'It is for the safety of his body the Castle fear. His enemies—'

'He had none but those of his country!'

And so she had gone, early that morning. And now it was night and the corridor was quiet, the oil lamps burning dimly, and all waited for the hours to pass when the body could be removed and handed over to the Fitzgerald family.

In the silence of his cell, Thomas listened to the clanging of the corridor door, and the slow dragging of Foster's footsteps on the flagstones. Slow, slow steps that made Thomas sit up. Too slow for Foster. Even in fatigue the turnkey had quicker movements than these.

He stood up and pressed his face to the grille, watching until the owner of those tired feet came into view. And when he did, Thomas caught his breath.

He had changed from a tall, strong man of indeterminate age, and shrunk into a spare old Negro. He wore a long black great-coat; his head was down, his arms hung loosely at his sides.

'Tony . . .'

'Yessuh.' His head stayed down.

'It's me. Thomas Emmet.'

'Yessuh.'

'I share your grief. You know that.'

'Yessuh.'

'Is the Duke returned yet from England?'

'Yessuh.'

'Lift up your head, man. I can barely hear you. Is the Duchess . . . ?'

'No, suh. I ain't gonna lef mah head to no man eve' again.'

'What?'

'No, suh, neve' again. Soon they gonna put mah Lawd Eddie down in the ground, an' that's where I'll be lookin' from now on, 'cos there sho ain't no better man above it. No, suh.'

He looked so helpless, so broken, and although the black head was down, Thomas saw the jaw muscles trembling and knew that he was crying.

'Tony . . .'

' 'Scuse me now, Mist' Emmet, but I got to go'n see mah Lawd Eddie before they takes him away for good an' gone.'

196

He moved on at the same slow pace. Thomas remained standing at the grille, waiting with dread for the expected sounds of Tony's grief, moaning and wailing. But those sounds never came.

At length Thomas turned and sat down on his mat, leaned his head back against the wall and listened with eyes closed to the soothing tone of the black man's religious voice as he crooned quietly to himself.

In the full hour that Tony stayed with Lord Edward, Foster sat on his chair for most of the time, listening with thoughtful face to the low, melodic rumble of the black man's voice as he sat by the open coffin, stroking the dead man's hand and consoling himself with the songs of an enslaved race.

> 'Go do-own, Moses.
> Way down in Egypt land
> An' tell ole Pharaoh
> To let mah people go . . .'

'Mr Emmet,' Foster whispered, 'I'll have to tell him to go himself now or I'll get into trouble. They'll be coming soon.'

Thomas nodded; moved to his feet.

When Tony came into view, head still down, Thomas said gently, 'Tony, I know you are bowed down with your grief, but Lord Edward would expect you to be strong, to take care of Lady Edward. She will need all your support now.'

'No, suh, she don't need me no more 'cos she is gone. Gone with her two chilrun an' the lil baby only born.'

'Lady Edward gone? Oh lift up your head for a minute, man!'

'No, suh.'

'Then explain, explain.'

'The mawnin' after Lawd Eddie died, they comes with an order from the Castle an' tole her to git outa Ireland an' back to France. They say all the Irish gentry is against her. Yessuh, they gave Lady Edward twenty-four hours to git! An' they say they gonna take his estates an' ever'ting he owns.'

Just for a brief flash Tony lifted his red-rimmed eyes. 'You see, Mist' Emmet, mah Lawd Eddie may be dead now, but they ain't finished punishin' him yet.'

Thomas could not believe it, he was too stunned to speak. His eyes moved from Tony to Foster, then back to Tony.

In the silence the sound of a key turned in a lock, the door at the end of the corridor clanged open. A military escort had arrived for Lord Edward.

'Oy! What's that nigger doing in here?'

Tony gave no reaction, his indifference was total, as if nothing they said or did could hurt him now.

And, looking at him, Thomas realised with a sudden surge of grief that the secure and privileged life Tony had known since leaving Georgia had come to an end.

Chapter Seventeen

The 1798 rebellion, the bloodiest war in Ireland's history, began suddenly, and without warning.

Kildare, the home of the Geraldines, was the first county to send up the war cry and spring to arms, but within weeks over 50,000 had risen in revolt.

'A Popish plot! A religious war!' the Viceroy had written to London in explanation of the uprising. But how could that explanation be accepted when it became clear that the leaders of the revolution were, in the main, Presbyterians and Protestants.

'As much Protestant as Popish,' admitted Castlereagh, who had not expected the rebellion to reach such formidable proportions. Lord Clare raged and considered the whole affair thoroughly disgusting. Protestants and Catholics fighting shoulder to shoulder under the flag of United Irishmen. Cromwell would turn in his grave!

'Jacobins,' the Viceroy explained hysterically, 'seeking a republic on the French model. Not Protestants – atheists – the whole boiling of them!'

The city of Dublin remained quiet due to being under heavy military guard, soldiers on every street and corner, the guards doubled in and around the Castle. But all reports coming into the city claimed the United confederates were fighting with military principles and proving the superior force. They had taken control of Kildare, Carlow, Kilkenny, and Arklow. Huge cheers went up all over Dublin when news came in that the Green Flag was flying on the Hill of Tara.

Heavy patrols were sent to guard the bridges and all roads leading into the city. The administration at the Castle was on the verge of hysteria. There was only one way to destroy the popularity and strength of the United Irishmen: old prejudices would have to be revived, old fears and hatreds restored – Divide and Conquer!

The cat was swiftly let loose among the pigeons by way of whispered statements that spread like wildfire throughout the country.

'Armed Papists will have their revenge and eventually cut Protestant throats!'

Banners hanging from Protestant windows bearing the words 'Liberty and Equality' were hastily pulled in.

'Protestants motivated by Jacobin principles are using the rebellion to bring about the final destruction of the Papists!'

'The real enemy are the Dissenters! Only from the Government and the British forces can the Catholics expect protection from Presbyterian fanatics!'

Only the rebels fighting side by side on the battlefields were unaware of the old poison resurrected amongst the formerly united people of the towns and villages. But then came the news that thrilled the people and terrified the masters at Dublin Castle: Wexford had fallen to the United lines. Wexford had been declared a republic.

William Pitt, the British Prime Minister, was forced to act quickly.

Lord Camden was dismissed from his post as Viceroy of Ireland. In his place Lord Cornwallis, a veteran of the American Revolution, was dispatched from England accompanied by massive reinforcements of troops and artillery.

To the people it seemed the rebellion lasted all summer. But after six weeks the revolt was finally crushed, ending in the most horrible massacre on Vinegar Hill in the county of Wexford.

The United confederates were not an official army, just rebels in arms, and therefore the strict codes of war need not apply. With this in mind, General Lake, Commander in the Field of the British reinforcements, sent out a command to his officers: '*No prisoners!*'

Two Catholic captains, Michael Dwyer and Miles Byrne, stood back to back with their Protestant compatriots as the United Irish desperately fought government troops on three sides. All day the fighting raged and cannons thundered around Vinegar Hill. But courage was no match for armoury, and as the day wore on the rebel dead numbered over 12,000.

The battered remnant of the United army knew they were defeated. They were covered on all sides but the west, and to the west they made their retreat from the battlefield. The superior strength of the imperial British army, aided by regiments of German Hessians, had triumphed.

When the guns had finally ceased, and a cloud of smoky silence hung over Vinegar Hill, any wounded found on the battlefield were, contrary to the code of war, instantly shot. *No prisoners!*

In the aftermath, 30,000 United Irishmen of every religious persuasion lay in dead and unburied heaps all over the smouldering countryside of Wexford and other counties in Leinster.

In Ulster the counties of Antrim and Down, which had also risen, were also defeated, and now in flames. The commander of the Ulster Division of United Irishmen, a wealthy young Presbyterian named Henry Joy McCracken, described as one of the handsomest men in Ireland, was hanged by the military in the centre of Belfast.

The unusually hot summer of 1798 finally broke with three days of non-stop rain. Robert Emmet walked alone in the drizzle along Dublin Bay in grim thought. He stood to gaze down at the waves washing over the rocks. He used to come here in the summers of his boyhood, to the hills overlooking Dublin Bay, and always the sun had blazed.

Had it really blazed, he wondered, or did one always remember childhood through sun-drenched memories? He turned and stared towards the Dublin hills shrouded in a watery greyness, the dark mists sweeping over the Wicklow Mountains. Death and disillusionment hung heavy in the air.

No other place in the entire world could know the present sadness of Ireland. A sadness that seemed to ooze out of every hill and cliff, every narrow street, and it was well that it rained. Now all the brave men who were too manly to cry for their dead compatriots, could openly weep for them without anyone noticing.

A sudden wind blew a wet chill over him. He shivered and turned back towards the city, the rain sliding down his face as he stared over the sea.

The high death rate of the Irish rebellion had seemingly not affected England overmuch, receiving no more than a mid-section mention in the English papers. The news over there was the usual preoccupation with Napoleon, the continual battle between Fox and Pitt, and now the suspension of the Act of Habeas Corpus in England as well as Ireland, due to the threat of a revolution by the English lower class.

He turned back towards the city, a city that looked more like a military camp than a civilian town. Before martial law had been declared in the spring, there had been 18,000 regular troops in the country and 44,000 militia. Now the army returns showed a sum total of 114,000 effective bayonets employed in Ireland.

He had not been called to take his place on the field of battle, for no man in Dublin was able to make a move, such was the military strength in and around the city. Every house had to have a list nailed to the front door giving the names and ages of every occupant, so that, if searched, the militia would know if the numbers were one or more too many. Every inhabitant was compelled to retire inside his house by sunset, and forbidden to emerge until after sunrise. Any appearance on the streets outside these times, without a written warrant from the Castle, was prohibited under a warning of the *severest* penalties. Any person found in possession of Thomas Paine's *The Rights of Man* would suffer the same consequence as Thomas Muir and the

Scottish radicals who had advocated Paine's views: transportation to the Antipodes.

So tight was the restrictive hand of authority on the people that Lord Moira was moved to protest in the British House of Lords: 'I have seen, my lords, a conquered country held down by military forces, but never did I see in any conquered country such a tone of insult as has been adopted by Great Britain toward Ireland.'

The rain continued to pour, as wet as water, as Lennard would say. Along the road an old woman in a black shawl came sauntering towards him, as unhurried by the downpour as himself. As they drew close, the eyes in her wizened brown face narrowed while she took a good look at him, then she nodded solemnly.

'A fine day to ye, young sir.'

A fine day? He stared at her, then held out his hand and deliberately watched the raindrops bouncing off his palm.

'Arrah,' she chided, in the way of the old with the young, 'what's the matter wid ye? Sure the day's only half through and the sun could still have a change of heart!'

Robert walked on, a twist to his lips as he glanced up at the black sky. Like everything else in Ireland, hope was green.

Even after the defeat of Wexford, a small army of insurgents encamped on the Wicklow Mountains, under the command of Michael Dwyer, one of the most noted rebel captains of the United army, was still keeping up a resistance against the redcoats. But the revolt in the main had been crushed, and now the most urgent task of the militia was to mete out punishment to the defeated.

From behind the small crowd gathered in the square of Rathdrum, Anne Devlin watched the drum trials. They brought out a young man from Caille-a-cullen to be shot. He was ordered to kneel in his coffin for the purpose. Anne watched as he obediently walked up to the coffin, then jumped in it furiously until he had smashed it to pieces. For this act of defiance he was beaten severely before being executed.

'Not even a trial,' a woman whispered to Anne, 'just a sentence.'

With brooding eyes Anne watched the soldiers. For months Wicklow had been covered in soldiers. A fair number she had encountered had been undeniably gentlemen, especially those under the command of General John Moore; but others were the scrapings of England's bucket, and the worst were not in the lower ranks. The Highland regiments were the best of all. Already the kilties had earned the distinction of being the most humane soldiers in Ireland, exhibiting strict discipline and soldier-like conduct. In contrast the German Hessians were brutal beyond description, the main victims of their shameful cruelty being the poor females of the land, while the Irish militia regiments gratified their revenge on the males . . .

The drums rolled as another young man was led out. This one was to be hanged. He walked on to the fair green with head high, then shouted to the crowd that he would die innocent of the crime of which he was charged: a traitor to his country. A noose was flung on to the sturdy branch of a tree.

Anne could not bear to witness the hanging. She turned and fled to the hills, sat on a crag overlooking the valley, and wept. The terror which had reigned in Paris under Robespierre could not have been worse than that which now reigned in Ireland.

It was almost sunset when she returned to the farm and sidled up to her father as he brushed down the mare. ' 'Tis bad, Da,' she whispered, 'and getting worse.'

Brian Devlin kept brushing and gave no answer. Unlike many other men in Wicklow, he had never had time for secret societies or talk of rebellion. He was a peaceable family man who enjoyed nothing more than tending his farm, sowing and reaping, or helping his big-eyed cows to calve.

'I keep wondering when they will come to take you,' Anne said in a troubled voice.

'They have no reason to take me, alannah. And even if they attempted it, Mr King the magistrate would vouch for my peaceable character. He's known me well and long.'

' 'Tis Mr King that's holding the mock drum trials and stringing everyone up,' Anne cried.

'Ach, we can't hide in our houses jittering. 'Tis near harvest-time, and the land has to be seen to. And if *we* are seen to be carrying on with our business, they will leave us alone.'

They came for him that night. It was bedtime, the family were kneeling around the hearth finishing their prayers when the cottage door was near kicked off its hinges and a party of the Rathdrum militia marched in.

'Are you Brian Devlin?' asked an officer.

'You know very well that I am . . .' Brian Devlin stood to stare at the soldiers. 'Why are your men ripping my house apart?' he demanded. 'What are they looking for?'

'Pikes and guns.'

'What would I be doing with pikes and guns? I'm well known in the barony as a peaceable farmer. I'm no rebel.'

'But your nephews are notorious rebels,' said the yeoman. 'Michael Dwyer, and your brother's son.'

'My brother Patrick is dead,' said Brian Devlin coldly. 'Due, no doubt, to the treatment he received at the hands of your militia when they attempted to burn him alive and he unconscious in his fever bed. If his son is a rebel, and if my wife's nephew, Michael Dwyer, is a rebel also, it is nothing to do with me.'

'Perhaps not, but you're bloody well under arrest anyway.'

'You've no right or reason to take my father,' Anne cried. 'He's done nothing wrong, nothing at all!'

'Where are ye taking him?' Mrs Devlin wailed. 'Not to the barracks at New Geneva in Waterford!'

'No, you bloody whore. He'll be going nowhere beyond Wicklow.'

'On what charge?' Anne stormed. 'For doing what?'

'Supplying guns to rebels. Now come along.'

While his hands were being tied, Brian Devlin said with dignity, 'I did think that if a man minded his own peaceful business he would be respected, but it seems not. If the charge is guilt by relation, then why was the Duke of Richmond not arrested when Fitzgerald was arrested. Lord Edward was *his* nephew.'

'Oh, stop your growling, dog, and come along.'

Brian Devlin turned to his family and gave instructions about the tending of the land and the coming harvest before being pushed outside.

At the door Anne stood beside her mother and watched her

father being marched away down the heath. A hand clutched hers tightly. She looked down at her twelve-year-old brother, red curls over his eyes, his face behind the shower of freckles stark white.

'It will kill him,' Little Arthur whispered. 'Taking Daddy away from the land will destroy him entirely.'

As the weeks went by, the people, to their astonishment, discovered the new Viceroy, General the Marquis Cornwallis, to be a humane man who believed in justice and fair play. Lord Cornwallis was a true soldier, with a soldier's solid belief in discipline. He was enraged at the report of one general who said the Irish militia put under his command on the march to Wexford had behaved in a disgraceful fashion; continually breaking away from the column to set fire to houses on the side of the road.

Cornwallis announced that he would end once and for all the daily practice of indiscriminate hangings by the militia and country magistrates. No more suspected rebels were to be put to death without trial. All drum trials would cease, and no sentence was to be carried out in a rural court without the authority of a British general.

The seventy-seven United prisoners in Newgate were moved to the more spacious cells of Kilmainham Gaol and classed as *State* prisoners, as opposed to common felons. Thomas Emmet and other members of the gentry were given first-class privileges which included beds, clean linen, candles, writing materials, and books.

Out of those seventy-seven men, it was decided that the fourteen members of the Executive arrested before the rebellion at Oliver Bond's house would not be tried – yet. But of the sixty-three remaining rebels set down for State Trial, each requested only one man for their defence: John Philpot Curran.

As his carriage rattled along the road from Rathfarnham towards Harold's Cross, an attempt was made to murder John Curran. Shots were fired from behind a hedge, but went through both windows. He assured his driver he was unharmed and ordered him to drive on.

He sat back and looked thoughtful, melancholy eyes dark and troubled. An occasional murder attempt would not be the only price he would have to pay for undertaking the defence of the United Irishmen. He would be even more hated and despised by the Establishment, would lose the affection of many of his friends, and now a judicial seat on the bench would never be offered.

A special commission of five judges was appointed for the State Trials. The two rebel lawyers, Henry and John Sheares, were the first to be tried.

Arriving at the Four Courts to defend them, John Curran was threatened by armed soldiers as he entered the Great Hall. When the case commenced, three times he rose to speak and three times he was stopped by a clash of arms.

It became clear to all that the life of the defence lawyer was in danger. And for the ladies fluttering their fans and gentlemen sipping wine in the spectator benches, this simply served to heighten the excitement.

When he was again interrupted by a man brandishing a pistol, John Curran turned on his opponents with a freezing dignity. 'Assassinate me you may – intimidate me you shall not!'

Lord Carleton pleaded with him to resume. 'We will take care, Mr Curran, that you shall not be interrupted again.'

Only one witness was called by the prosecution, Captain Armstrong, who told the court that he had met the Sheares brothers in a bookshop. They had shown friendliness, and he had later gone to see Lord Castlereagh who advised him to accept the Sheares's hospitable invitations and report on them.

In cross-examination Curran was able to get Armstrong to admit that before, during, and after the rebellion, he had committed sadistic brutalities, but his credibility with the judges and jury remained unshaken.

Curran put no veil on his disgust in his speech to the jury.

'The witness, Captain Armstrong, admits to you that he got his evidence by the fortunate occurrence of meeting three peasants on a road. One he shot, the second he hanged, and the third he tortured until he got a confession out of him. Gentlemen! Is it possible that you are prepared to accept the testimony of such a man and allow him to stand as an accuser?'

206

The jury took seventeen minutes to bring in a verdict. The Sheares brothers were convicted, sentenced, and executed the next day. And although John Curran fought each case fiercely, every day following a State Trial, another execution took place in the yard of Kilmainham Gaol, in view of the other prisoners awaiting trial.

Inside Kilmainham, Thomas Emmet sat on his bed watching his new cell mate kneeling by the fire in the corner, heating a poker.

'Where the blazes is Tone?' said Russell, pausing to inspect the poker then sticking it back in the heat. 'That's what I'd like to know.'

Thomas shrugged. 'That's what everyone would like to know.'

'Well, if you ask me,' Russell said, 'the French have reneged on their promises to Fitzgerald. August they said, and now here August is almost gone, but where are the French?'

Thomas made no answer as he watched Russell lift the poker from the fire, spit on it, then hearing the sizzle, begin to curl his already curly black hair with careful concentration. Two years of prison had not changed Tom Russell one bit. Before his imprisonment he had fallen in love with a girl in Newry named Betty Goddard, and still cherished hopes of marrying her; and the continual care of his glorious head of black curls was simply his way of keeping his appearance splendid and his heart optimistic.

During the long nights in their cell they talked often about Tone. Neither had seen him since he had left Ireland in 1795, but he had come back to Ireland in the winter of 1796, with a French army.

Earlier that year Tone had written to say that he had great hopes for assistance for Ireland, now that the terrorists in France had been truly overthrown and the original Jacobins who had begun the Revolution were back in power. He had undergone many interviews with the French Government, pleading Ireland's case, until finally the French supplied an expeditionary force of 15,000 under General Lazare Hoche, twenty-eight years old and second only to Napoleon. Tone immediately joined the French army in order to take an active part, and left Brest in the company of seventeen ships of the line, destined for Ireland.

Their main fear had been the superiority of the British fleet, but strangely they met no obstacle other than the weather. '*Bad weather, Master Noah!*' Tone had complained to General Hoche. '*We may not only miss the English in this fog, we may miss Ireland.*'

But Hoche brought them straight on course until they were in view of the rugged coast of Bantry Bay, lying open and without defence. The French ships sailed close to the Irish coast, '*close enough to toss a biscuit ashore*', but unable to land due to a heavy gale which made an immediate landing impossible.

As Tone explained later in his letter: snow covered the mountains and for three days gale-force winds ripped and rolled the ships, '*almost within reach of my native land, but unable to set foot on it*'. Finally all hopes of a landing in the continuing storm were relinquished. The ships were forced to turn for France, with a heartbroken Tone standing on the deck of the *Indomptable* wearing the blue surcoat of an adjutant-general, staring back at Bantry Bay.

But Tone's hopes had not died, and he had taken back with him a favourable opinion of the French. '*Gallant fellows! I never liked the French half so well. To judge the French rightly, or at least see the bright spark of their character, you must see them not in Paris but in the camp. It is in the armies that the Republic exists. Had we been able to land the first day, we should have infallibly carried a coup de main.*'

And so also, Thomas thought, might they have altered the last two years of Ireland's history and prevented the deaths of Lord Edward Fitzgerald and over 30,000 others, not to mention the United Irishmen who were now walking daily up the steps of the gallows as a result of the legal carnage that was taking place in the courts: condemned by juries whom even Curran knew to be hand-picked by the Castle.

The key turned in the lock, the cell door opened, the governor entered and stood looking at the two men. Thomas exchanged a glance with Russell, who stood up and smiled wryly at the governor.

'Well?' Russell said brightly. 'Which of us is the great lawyer going to defend now? And is the court, like the jury, packed?'

'Mr Emmet,' said the governor, 'would you please collect all your personal effects and follow me.'

'Collect all his personal effects?' exclaimed Russell. 'He hasn't even been tried yet, let alone convicted. Why must he collect all his things?'

'As soon as you can, Mr Emmet.'

The governor talked politely as they walked down the long corridor, ignoring the prisoner's expression of surprise when, instead of being led out of the main door and placed inside a coach destined for the courts, he was led up the stairs to the next floor and along the passage to one of the more private, spacious rooms at the back.

'Lord Cornwallis has ordered that you be moved to more comfortable accommodation,' the governor said.

'And what persuaded him to do that?'

'The persuasion of a lady it seems.' The governor smiled as he paused outside a door, opened it to a delicious smell of spiced food, then left Thomas to go inside alone.

She was spreading a cloth on the table for dinner as if she were in her own home, except in her own home she rarely had to set the table. Her cloak lay on the bed, her valise on the floor.

'Jane!'

He half turned as the door was locked behind him, then stared at her again. Jane just stood there, a nervous smile on her face.

'I've come to look after you,' she said softly. 'Like the woman in the Bible who pestered the judge until he finally gave in to her demands just to get rid of her, Lord Cornwallis has agreed that I can share your imprisonment, if that is what I wish.'

'Jane!' he said again. 'Jane, are you mad?'

'About you? Yes. And this, I think, is the only cure for my sickness. I have tried everything else. Sleeping draughts, sedative potions, but all to no avail. Even your father failed in his administrations . . .'

Seeing the expression on his face, she said quickly and nervously: 'The children will hardly notice my absence. Your mother dotes on them, and they will have their nursemaid at

209

night. And His Excellency has given permission for me to return home two afternoons a week. No more, for fear of upsetting the routine of the place, you understand. And look—'

She bent and lifted a bottle of wine from the floor. 'Already I have discovered that prison can have its comforts if one has money to pay for them. Dr Trevor, the superintendent here, runs a frisky business in illegal sales. Sold me this bottle of canary for only five times the normal price, and arranged for this delicious food to be sent in from one of the cookhouses at only a slightly exorbitant charge . . .'

When he continued to stand and stare at her, she turned away quickly and lifted up her cloak. 'Perhaps it was a foolish enterprise after all. I shall leave if you wish.'

'Jane,' he moved behind her, his hands on her shoulders, 'my dear, *dear* Jane.' He put his lips on her neck and moved his arms around her waist.

She turned in his arms and he kissed her with a hunger and passion that left her breathless and smiling. 'The food,' she whispered, 'will go cold.'

'You do know what this means?' he said, still holding her close. 'Cornwallis allowing you to lodge here with me.'

'That despite his gruffness, he is a very kind man?'

'That he knows I shall be confined here either for a very short period, or for a very long time.'

Chapter Eighteen

The following morning, on 22nd August, the morning broke clear and fine up in the north-west county of Mayo. In the fields women worked heroically beside their men in preparation for the harvest, while small boats fished in the bay, and bare-legged girls climbed over the rocks collecting salty piles of seaweed.

Many looked up from their toil and placed a shading hand

over their eyes as three frigates came into the bay, flying British naval colours. The people watched curiously as small boats were lowered from the ships and soldiers began to disembark, not redcoated soldiers, but soldiers in blue uniforms trimmed with red and white. Barrels of gunpowder were then unloaded, and crate after crate of firearms. By the time the small boats of soldiers reached the shore, a crowd had gathered.

A dark-skinned, black-eyed officer walked towards them, smiling smoothly.

'Who are ye?' It was spoken by an old man who was the sage of the community. 'Ye are not English.'

General Humbert was thirty-one years old, and one of Napoleon's favourite officers. He smiled at the Irish peasants and waved his hand towards the column of soldiers behind him.

'People of Irlande!' he said loudly. 'Behold – Frenchmen arrive amongst you. The moment of breaking your chains has arrived. Liberty! Equality! Fraternity! Such is our shout. Let us march together, People of Irlande! Our hearts are devoted to your cause. Our glory is in your freedom!'

The people at first looked stupefied, then as the words sank in, they waved their hands in the air and cried out in joy, 'The French! The French!'

Many rushed forward and threw themselves down to kiss Humbert's black boots. The French saviours had arrived at last, just as the song of the Shan Van Vocht always said they would. And not an English soldier in the whole of Mayo!

General Humbert proceeded to stroll up the hill, followed by his soldiers and the crowd, towards the small castle which dominated Killala and was the residence of Bishop Stock. The bishop stood waiting for him, a kindly Protestant gentleman not disliked by the people.

General Humbert removed his hat and bowed. 'M'sieur, I regret I must take over this castle as a base for my officers.'

'By whose authority?' the bishop demanded curtly.

'By the authority of the People of Irlande.' The more he smiled, the more threatening Humbert was.

Eleven hundred men had sailed from La Rochelle with General Humbert. They were the first instalment of a French expedition of 8,000 destined for Ireland. Later that day the waiting crowd stared in tearful wonderment as the British flag over the castle was lowered, and General Humbert raised a Green Flag bearing the Irish harp – without the Crown! Embroidered in gold silk with the words *Erin Go Bragh* – Ireland for Ever – the flag had been entrusted to Humbert by Theobald Wolfe Tone, who was following from Brest.

General Humbert spent the next two days attempting to turn into soldiers the crowd of Irish peasants who had left their potato fields and fishing boats. He laughed to see a merry young French marine, whose job it was to hand out helmets to the delighted peasant puppies, standing on a barrel and furiously thumping a helmet on to the head of a great hulking youth until it fitted.

'*Voila!*' the marine cried, giving the helmet another thump for luck, and with no obvious care of how it would ever come off again.

On the third day Humbert set off with his Irish allies on a ten-mile forced-march to Ballina. As they marched past the fields farmboys turned to stare at them, then jumped the walls to join them. Women threw themselves on their knees as they passed along, holding out their hands and wishing them success.

At Ballina, General Humbert was amazed as he witnessed the fearless enthusiasm of his Irish allies against the militia who were swiftly defeated. Ballina was taken, and established as the second base of the new Irish republic. Then Humbert pressed on into the interior, towards Castlebar, the county town of Mayo.

As they advanced, a young gentleman rode towards them, a United Irishman, and warned Humbert that 3,000 English soldiers, under General Lake, were on their way to meet them at Castlebar.

General Humbert smiled. 'English soldiers! *Bon*! And now I find my Irish boys are made of the same good stuff as ourselves. *Allons, mes brave camarades!* On to Cazeelbarr!'

Dublin was shocked and incredulous when it learned of the French landing. Members of the gentry rushed to the Castle and demanded to know if reports were true that, at the first sight of French soldiers, the redcoats had flung their weapons and reputations behind at Castlebar. Vehement arguments buzzed in taverns and streets as each piece of news reached the city. All had it on *sound* authority that Napoleon himself was leading the march.

Lord Cornwallis was furious! He called together his generals and prepared to set out to meet the Frenchman.

At Casino, standing by the trout-stream, Lennard looked deeply anxious, his bushy brows knotted over his worried eyes like the brushes of two old foxes. 'That General Blownapart may be a big man in France,' he said to Robert, 'but from what I hears, Lord Cornwallis has only ever lost one battle.'

'Yes,' Robert agreed with a smile. 'America.'

But Cornwallis was determined not to lose Ireland. Leaving Dublin with a force of regiments overwhelmingly superior in number to the Jacobin and his Irish spalpeens, he headed towards the river Shannon.

General Humbert had been in Ireland over two weeks and was now master of the province of Connaught. He marched on towards the midlands, crossing the Shannon at Balintra, then on in the direction of Granard. Just outside Granard, at a place called Ballinamuck, the two armies met.

Finding the road blocked with twelve cannon and ten thousand men, Humbert smiled in a French sort of way. He knew he was defeated, but he had to put up a bit of a show – for the sake of his poor Irish allies. He called his French troops into the front line of battle, ordering them to give it an hour or so, but no more. Their first duty was to die in the service of France, not Irlande.

After a hard burst of fierce fighting, Humbert decided to call a halt. He had lost over eighty French soldiers in twenty minutes, and that was enough for the Irish allies. He placed his hat on his sword, in accordance with the practice of war, and held it high in surrender.

Less than half an hour later, Humbert was on his way to Dublin, accompanied by Lord Cornwallis and his military entourage. General Lake and Major Crauford were the only superior officers left on the battlefield at Ballinamuck.

The low-ranking French soldiers were ordered to separate from the Irish prisoners, then General Lake and Major

Crauford sat astride their horses, gazing towards the huddled masses of unarmed Mayo farmboys.

Where was Tone? Every United Irishman in Kilmainham was asking the same question. What had happened to Tone?

A week after General Humbert's expedition had left La Rochelle, and after a series of frustrating delays at Brest, Theobald Wolfe Tone, still a serving officer in the French army, sailed towards Ireland on board the flagship the *Hoche* accompanied by eight more French men-o'-war.

As they approached the coast near Donegal, they found the British fleet waiting for them. Tone fought fanatically, manning the guns and taking such reckless risks that his comrades feared for his life. The French officers on board tried to persuade him to board one of the other ships and make his escape. If the *Hoche* was captured, they pointed out, they would be returned to France after an exchange of prisoners of war, but Tone might get a very different reception.

Tone refused to leave and continued manning the guns. 'Shall it be said that I fled while Frenchmen were fighting the battles of my country?'

The topmast and rigging of the *Hoche* was in tatters and after six hours of British fire twenty-eight of her guns were out of action. Finally, with most of her crew either wounded or dead, and water rising in the hold, the *Hoche* was forced to strike her colours. Five of the nine French frigates had managed to turn back to France.

Tone was taken off the *Hoche* where Sir George Hill, a commander of the British forces who had known Tone as a young lawyer, came to greet him.

'Mr Tone, I am very happy to see you.'

'Sir George,' Tone answered pleasantly. 'How are Lady Hill and your family?'

'In excellent health, thank you. I shall tell you all about them on our ride to Derry Gaol.'

Robert Emmet sat at a small table at the back of the White Bull tavern in Thomas Street, talking quietly with the landlord and his wife, Mr and Mrs Dillon.

'Did Major Sirr say why he had taken Billy?' Robert asked.

'Oh, aye,' said Mrs Dillon, a handkerchief to her eyes, 'he said he had proof that Billy was a rebel leader and had guns hidden somewhere.'

'Imagine!' snapped her husband. 'A sixteen-year-old being a leader!'

'Aye, my brother was sixteen only last week,' Mrs Dillon sniffed, 'and he as quiet and harmless as a sparrow.'

'*Misther Robert! Misther Robert! Wait till ye hear!*'

Lennard's noisy entrance silenced the conversational murmur of the entire tavern. All eyes turned to him curiously as he stood panting before the back table.

'Oh, 'tis the divil a clip of news I bring ye!' Lennard cried, then seeing he had an audience, shouted sombrely, 'news that'll bring every man in this room – savin' yer presence, Mrs Dillon – up on his brogues!'

Men began to rise from their seats and move towards the back table.

'What news?' Mrs Dillon urged. 'Is there bad tidings in it?'

'Oh, mortal bad,' Lennard cried, 'but sure me heart is thumping so fast and me throat is that dry . . .'

Robert pushed his untouched glass of brandy across the table towards Lennard.

A voice said: 'Out with it, man!'

'Amn't I trying to tell ye?' Lennard gulped the brandy thirstily. ' 'Tis like I sez, I was collecting the fish order from the fish man on the quays when I heard some others shouting it. "Is it true?" I sez. "I don't believe it," I sez. "Why," I sez when they told me again, "if that be truth," I sez, I'd better get up smartish and—'

'If someone doesn't beat it out of him quick I'll be forced to do it myself,' an impatient voice cried.

'Ye couldn't beat yer granny!' Lennard retorted angrily, a red flush coming to his cheeks as his temper flared. ' 'Troth, it near kilt me rushing all the ways back up here to inform ye! Now then, do ye want me to tell ye or not?'

Robert said: 'We do, Lennard, we do. So tell us slowly and plainly.'

'Who was it,' Lennard shouted furiously, 'that, nigh on

three years ago, left his country so he could free his country? Was it the darling Theobald Wolfe Tone? It was! And now, after a week in a northern gaol, he's being brought down to Dublin, back to the city of his birth – in chains!'

He lifted the brandy glass, drained it, then darted backwards. 'Well, what are youse waiting for? They say he'll be in the city within the half-hour!'

It was on King's Inn Quay, outside the Four Courts, that Robert first caught sight of Tone and his huge military escort as they rode towards the barracks. The thirty-four-year-old founder of the United Irishmen sat calmly astride his horse, dressed in the red cape and blue uniform of a French officer, his hands chained in front of him.

As the procession passed the courts, many of Tone's former colleagues at the Bar were coming out. Like the rest of the crowd, they stood to stare at him. Tone smiled down at them without any sign of embarrassment.

'Would ye look at the cool-as-cream smile on him,' Lennard muttered to Robert. 'But then, he's had a long journey, God knows, and plenty of time to consider his fate.'

It seemed as if every prominent citizen had endeavoured to get a seat at the court martial of Theobald Wolfe Tone, held in the Dublin Barracks, before a bench of seven British officers. John Curran was too agitated to sit. He remained standing at the back of the room. His adoring lackey, Leonard McNally, stood beside him.

Tone stood calm and dignified in the dock. He admitted all charges and requested to address the court.

'What I have done,' Tone said, 'has been clearly from principle and the fullest conviction. I wish not for mercy. I hope I am not an object of pity. I anticipate the consequence of my capture and I am prepared for the event. The favourite object of my life has been the independence of my country. My only desire was to raise three million of my countrymen to the rank of citizens.

'But I hear it said that this unfortunate country has been a prey to all sorts of horrors. I sincerely lament it. I beg, however, that it may be remembered that I have been absent some years from Ireland. I designed by fair and open war to procure the separation of the two countries. For open and manly war I was prepared; but if, instead of that, a system of private assassination has taken place, then I deplore it. Atrocities, it seems, have been committed on both sides. I do not less deplore them; I detest them from my heart; and to those who know my character and sentiments, I safely appeal to the truth of this assertion. With them I need no justification.

'But success is *all* in this life. In a cause like this, success is everything. Washington succeeded in America, and Kosciusko failed in Poland. Now we, too, have failed. But I have done my duty and no doubt the court will do theirs. My only request is that I should die the death of a soldier, before a firing squad.'

The request was denied. He was sentenced to death by hanging within forty-eight hours.

John Curran fumed all the way back to his chambers. McNally limped beside him trying to keep pace.

'I ask you, Mac, is it fair that Tone should have been separated from the other French prisoners of war and imprisoned as an Irish civilian on the charge of high treason?'

'Most definitely not, Jack.'

'How can Cornwallis consider it just and lawful to charge Tone as a civilian, then try him as a soldier under court martial? He was even dressed in the uniform of a French officer.'

'It's nonsense,' McNally agreed. 'If Tone is classed as a French soldier then he should be returned to France with the rest of the French, according to the code of war. But if they are charging him as an Irish civilian, then he is entitled to a fair *civil* trial before a judge and jury.'

'Exactly my point!' Curran cried. 'Martial law and civil law are governed by different rules.'

'Cornwallis is a man alone,' McNally said, 'trying to fight a fair fight against the clamour of a bigoted ascendancy and a savage militia. They want Tone's blood. And if they don't get it, they will start baying for Cornwallis's instead.'

Curran turned and stared at McNally, a smile dawning on his face. 'There's a way out of this, Mac. Why did I not think of it before?'

'Think of what?' McNally looked totally confused, but Curran had marched on, his pace quickening by the second.

McNally panted as he limped along trying to keep up. 'There's no time to do anything,' he said. 'Tone could be executed in the morning.'

'And there again they contradict themselves!' Curran cried furiously. 'Tone is tried by the military under court martial, but refused a soldier's death by bullet and sentenced to a felon's death by hanging.' He stabbed the air with his finger. 'But there is still one man in Ireland who is not putrid with prejudice and distributes justice according to the law. We'll see what Arthur Wolfe has to say about this!'

McNally lost his patience and grabbed Curran's arm. 'Would you stop for a minute and tell me what you are planning to do?'

'Who reigns supreme, Mac? Even over the Viceroy and the army?'

'Why, the King of course.'

'And that's the card I shall play,' Curran said. 'The King!'

Arthur Wolfe was Lord Kilwarden, a man who, for over twenty years, had been a close and much-loved friend of John Curran, and was now Lord Chief Justice of the King's Bench.

The following morning, accompanied by Tone's aged father, Curran appeared before the King's Bench. He presented an affidavit to Lord Kilwarden stating that Theobald Wolfe Tone had never served in the British army and therefore was not amenable to trial by court martial.

It was an ingenious move. A British military court had no jurisdiction over an officer in the French army, nor did a military court have the power to sentence a civilian while the Court of the King's Bench still prevailed.

Lord Kilwarden agreed with Curran. He ordered a writ of Habeas Corpus to be prepared immediately and instructed that, once served, Tone was to be brought before the court.

'My lord,' said Curran apprehensively, 'my client may be executed at any time, even while the writ is being prepared.'

Lord Kilwarden turned to the Sheriff. 'Mr Sheriff, proceed immediately to the barracks and inform the Provost-Marshal

218

that a writ is being prepared suspending Mr Tone's execution
– and see that he is not executed.'

The Sheriff left. John Curran and the Tone family waited in
nerve-racking suspense.

Some half-hour later the Sheriff returned and stated that the
Provost-Marshal had said he must obey Major Sandys, and
Major Sandys had said he must obey Lord Cornwallis. A few
minutes later, the clerk who had taken the writ to the barracks
returned and informed the Court that General Craig had
refused to obey it.

'Mr Sheriff,' Lord Kilwarden cried furiously, 'take Mr Tone
into custody! Take the Provost-Marshal and Major Sandys into
custody! And show the order of the court to General Craig. An
order of the Court of the King's Bench cannot be overruled by
law martial!'

Again they waited and, while they did, Curran considered
the beneficial effects the suspension could have. It would give
Cornwallis time to reconsider deporting Tone back to France
as an officer captured while in the French service. It would give
Bonaparte time to parley for the exchange of prisoners. According to the French commander, General Humbert, now residing
in comfortable imprisonment at Dublin's Mail Coach Hotel,
Napoleon would be furious about the trial of Tone.

The wait seemed interminable. Then the Sheriff returned
and informed the Court that it was too late. Mr Tone was at the
point of death. He had attempted to commit suicide in his cell
by cutting his throat.

'No!' Tone's father gasped. 'No!'

John Curran slumped back in his seat, this final defeat
crushing him completely. In his time he had played every card
in the pack in his fight for the United Irishmen, but since the
rebellion, it was impossible to win. Justice had died of prejudice. The days of acquittals were over.

The blade had missed the carotid artery. For a full week
Theobald Wolfe Tone lay on a mat in his cell in agony, refused
all contact with family or friends. Only the military surgeon
who had sewn up the wound was allowed near him.

On the seventh day, the surgeon repeated his initial

command to the turnkey. 'He must not be allowed to speak to you. If he speaks, he dies.'

Tone opened his eyes and smiled. 'I thank you for letting me know, sir,' he whispered. 'It is the most welcome news you could give me.' And Tone died.

Chapter Nineteen

Now that the French epilogue to the 1798 rebellion was over, Castlereagh was determined to flush out the underground network of United Irish in the capital.

A few United men endeavoured to secure their personal safety by turning informer. One of these was James McGucken, the Belfast attorney. He sent a personal letter to Edward Cooke at Dublin Castle, naming one of the most 'active' rebels at large in the capital.

'If young Emmet is not at home,' he wrote, 'search his father's house most minutely for papers, particularly all the leaves of the books in the library on the right-hand side as you go in. Let the officers take up every man in Belfast whose name is written up in any letter signed "Americus" – the code name young Emmet uses. Take W— – he will tell all.'

When the elegantly dressed young man realised his protestations of innocence were getting him nowhere, he burst into tears.

'Oh, come now, Mr Wright!' Lord Castlereagh's voice was derisive. 'You are a revolutionary! Avowed under oath to liberate Ireland! Are you crying because you failed, or because you were caught?' He smiled.

Wright withdrew a handkerchief and wiped his face. He was exhausted: his interrogation had gone on all day and he had held out as long as he could, but now, with the onset of night and the hopelessness of his situation, he was terrified.

'All I ask, Lord Castlereagh, is to be allowed to exile myself from the kingdom under the Banishment Bill. I'm prepared to put up a surety that I will never return to Ireland.'

'Your request will be considered, as soon as you have given a full written confession as to the names and activities of your friends.'

'Must I . . . name names?'

'Oh, indeed you must.'

Wright hesitated, then accepted the inevitable. 'Very well.'

Lord Castlereagh smiled again as he filled three glasses with wine. The first glass he presented to Edward Cooke, the second to Wright. 'You appear weak and fatigued, sir,' he said. 'I suggest you take a little respite. Please excuse me for a moment.'

Castlereagh left the room, and while Wright needily drank his wine, Edward Cooke apologised to him, in the most dignified manner of an Englishman, for the long and painful inquiry he had been subjected to.

Wright could only stare at Cooke in astonished silence.

Castlereagh returned, followed by a servant carrying a tray. 'A slight repast to lighten your fatigue,' Castlereagh said, kindly pressing Wright to partake of the food.

Wright's feelings of terror withered in the kind attentions of the two men. Now he had agreed to co-operate and supply a confession, they appeared to have cast aside the cold, calculating and severe manner which they had displayed earlier. Castlereagh was extremely genial. Secretary Cooke poured him more wine.

'You are young,' Castlereagh said. 'And I am disposed to believe that the passions and impetuosity of youth, though misguided, soon fade.'

When Wright made no response, Castlereagh continued gently: 'We are not monsters, you know. We are simply trying to uphold the power of government. But, in this instance, we are prepared to concede much to the impetuosity of youth. We will not hold you responsible for any of your past actions. You may have no fear of prison, but, under the circumstances, we naturally cannot allow you to stay in Ireland for fear of further contagion. Bad company, as St Paul says, encourages bad morals.'

Wright sat in the warm conciliatory glow of Castlereagh's gentle words. Perhaps he had been mistaken in the reputation of the man. When not assuming the cold character of his office, he appeared a most charming gentleman. 'I am deeply indebted for your humane consideration towards me, Lord Castlereagh,' he said sincerely. 'Deeply indebted.'

'We have always believed in mild measures,' Castlereagh assured him. 'And those who are our friends will not hear a word against us. Now permit me to ask you, sir, the name of the United traitor who holds the military books of the United Irishmen?'

'Emmet,' Wright said easily.

'The younger Emmet – expelled earlier in the year from Trinity?'

Wright nodded and sipped more wine. 'He went straight from Trinity on to Lord Edward's staff.'

'Indeed? Then he was personally attached to the late lamented Lord Edward . . . ? Pray, Mr Wright, have the kindness to tell us more.'

'Well,' said Wright, wiping his mouth with the linen napkin, 'up until that time Emmet was only a member of the civilian part of the United Irishmen. But some time before that the leaders in the Society had decided their only hope of throwing off the yoke was to do like the Americans, and turn to arms. A military organisation was started up as well as civilian. All members of the inner circles of the military division were bound by oath, after Theobald Wolfe Tone went to France. And Tone and Lord Edward, if I may be allowed to say so without offence, are considered by us all to stand unrivalled as patriots. Lord Edward loved his country above his king, and Tone's adventures to negotiate the aid of France, his efforts to help his Catholic and Presbyterian countrymen—'

'Hold . . .' said Castlereagh. 'Let us leave the dead in their graves and return to the living. It is the younger Emmet that interests me at the moment. Are we correct in believing that his code name in the United movement is *Americus*?'

'Yes, all the military staff use a secret name when referring or writing to each other. I never could find out Lord Edward's code name. That was protected with the greatest secrecy. Only his staff knew it. I only knew Emmet's code name because I was entrusted to pass messages to him.'

'Americus . . .' Castlereagh exchanged a glance with Cooke.

'Emmet has always believed fervently in the views of Washington and Jefferson,' Wright explained. 'Especially Jefferson: "All men created equal by their Creator," and so on.'

Castlereagh heaved a sigh. Now that Wright had started, his tongue was running as fast as a river-rapid. He poured him more wine. 'So while Emmet was philosophising, Lord Edward was arming?'

'Well, yes. He was a military man, and obviously thought that was the best and only way he could help his country.'

'And now we must presume that young Emmet is cherishing a secret and hostile revenge on those who imprisoned his brother and later Lord Edward. Are we correct in presuming that?'

'Indeed, no!' Wright's face was flushed with fraternal indignation as well as the effects of the wine. 'Robert Emmet, I admit, still passionately cherishes the principles of *liberty* deep in his heart, but he is incapable of any base desire for some cruel *revenge*.'

'You seriously expect us to believe that?' Castlereagh returned crisply.

'I would expect you to believe it,' Wright answered, 'if you knew Emmet.'

Castlereagh and Cooke exchanged another glance; they expected to get to know Emmet – very shortly.

The night was still but for the light breeze which gently hushed over the waters of the stream. Robert sat with his back against a boulder gazing at the mountains washed in green moonlight. He wondered how the men in Kilmainham had taken the news of Tone's shoddy death. His brother and Thomas Russell, he knew, would both be heartbroken.

The day following Tone's death had passed in a kind of stupor, until the welfare of his young wife and three infant children, still in Paris, became an immediate concern.

Deprived of Tone's support, they would be reduced to poverty and misery. But before any discussions could be held on the matter, General Humbert sent an announcement from on board the *Van Tromp* which was preparing to take him back to France, that the welfare of Tone's wife and children would be secured by the French Republic. An Irishman he may have been, but he had enlisted in the army of France, had died in the uniform of France, and the care of his family would belong to France.

Beyond the stream the land lay silent. A smell of autumn lay over the fields and meadowland. The harvest had been reaped; the corn cut and stooked, the hay gathered and stacked in the haybarns, but there had been no haymaking this year. No one could celebrate their grain harvest when the Castle's human harvest had been more abundant.

In the dark stillness of the night Robert's gaze moved in the direction of Rathfarnham, and he entered into that isolated part of his mind where he could flick Sarah up like a picture to gaze at and think on. Everything between them had stopped that afternoon in the early summer. The week following, Lord Edward had been arrested, and then the rebellion had flared. There had been no time for thoughts of romance that summer when so many comrades were dying. But still he could see her walking over the grasslands of Rathfarnham, wearing a white printed dress and carrying an armload of foxgloves and bluebells as she came down the slope towards him, smiling like an angel in his dream of love.

The sound of horses in the distance jerked him out of his dream and into alertness. It was after midnight, too late for visitors. He sprang to his feet and ran back towards the house. As he reached the arch, the glow of a shaking lamp lit up the shocked paleness of his father's face.

'It's the militia!' his father said. 'I saw them through the window. To come at this hour can mean only one thing! Quickly, get yourself to the library and I'll try to delay them.'

Robert ran through the house to find Lennard by the library door, holding aloft a candle and jumping from one foot to the other. 'Quick as ye like,' he whispered anxiously, then lit the way into the library and held the candle low as Robert pulled back the carpet and lifted the boards of the trap door. Lennard withdrew a knife from inside his belt. 'I'll go out to the garden,' he said, 'and if any of them try to take ye from that end, I'll run them through with this!'

Robert eased himself down into the cavity and Lennard lowered the trap door over him. When the hammering came on the front door, Dr Emmet sent the sleepy-eyed butler back upstairs before opening the door to Major Sirr.

'I hope you have a very good explanation for waking my household at this hour, Major?'

'I apologise for the intrusion, Doctor, but I am here by order of the Castle. I have been instructed to take in your son.'

'My son? But you already have my son, confined in Kilmainham Gaol. And you, Major, were the very man who took him out of my house.'

Sirr stroked his moustaches. 'I refer to your youngest son.'

'Robert! Why on earth should the Castle want Robert?'

'That is not for me to discuss, Dr Emmet. Perhaps you would rouse him, and ask him to accompany me at once.'

Dr Emmet braced his shoulders and shook his head, 'I cannot do that, Major. My son left for Europe two days ago. Now that he has finished at the University, he has embarked on the Grand Tour.'

The two men stood staring at each other for a moment, then Major Sirr shrugged. 'I still must search the house.' He withdrew a document from his tunic and waved it in Dr Emmet's face. 'I have the necessary authority.'

The major moved aside to let his officers pass into the hall. 'Search the entire premises,' he ordered, 'including the servants' quarters.'

A few minutes later, Mrs Emmet and Mary-Anne descended the stairs followed by the bleary-eyed servants.

Mrs Emmet said nervously: 'What is going on?'

Her husband put a protective arm around her shoulders and spoke to the servants in hushed tones. 'Major Sirr has called at this devil's hour to take Robert into custody. I have informed him that my son left for the Continent two days ago.'

Mrs Simmins, the housekeeper, gave the doctor a confidential nod, then glared sternly at the other servants. 'Sure, didn't I wave goodbye to him meself?'

'Oh, you did! You did!' said all the servants in unison.

It seemed an eternity before Major Sirr and his men strode back into the hall after their search. The major stroked his moustaches and gazed towards the huddled group. 'Well, this is the nest,' he said slowly, 'but it seems our bird has flown.'

'Gesh yer filthy hands off me, ye Castle toerag!'

A soldier dragged Lennard into the hall by the collar of his coat. 'I found this one in the garden, Major.' The soldier held up Lennard's knife, 'He pulled this on me! Tried to kill me.'

'Will ye go way owa that!' Lennard cried. 'Don't mind him atall! Sure wasn't I just sitting and minding me own business and innocently peeling an apple when this uniformed ruffian comes along and attacks me.'

'What were you doing in the garden at this hour?' demanded Sirr.

Lennard shook his collar free of the soldier's grip. 'Like I sez – I was peeling an apple.'

'In the pitch dark?'

'Bejabers, do ye think I'm mad altogether, wha'? Only an eejit would peel an apple with a blade in the pitch dark.'

'But you said you were peeling an apple,' Major Sirr cried impatiently.

'And so I was, yer honour, but not in the pitch dark. No, like I sez, 'twas by the light of the moon. Isn't there a darling full moon out tonight?'

'Our gardener is very fond of the outdoor life,' Dr Emmet put in quickly. 'He has spent many a summer night sleeping under the stars.'

'True for you, Dr Emmet!' Lennard cried amiably. 'Sure, who wants to be stuck in a stuffy oul room when they could be out with the—'

'Enough!' cried Major Sirr angrily. 'We are not here to listen to your codswallop, man.'

Dr Emmet took a tentative step forward. 'Perhaps if you have finished now, Major, you will leave and allow us to return to our beds.'

'We must first search the library.'

'The library? But . . . but your men have searched in there already. The library contains all my medical volumes. I'm sure they would be of little interest to the Castle and I cannot allow you to touch them. Some are very valuable.'

'I am merely carrying out my orders, Doctor, which are to search the library for papers belonging to your son. We will leave once the search has been completed. In the meantime, I suggest you send the rest of the household back to bed.'

Mrs Emmet's face had turned the colour of ash, her hand clutched her throat. 'If you will excuse me, Major, I think I will retire to the kitchen for a hot drink.'

'I will make it for you, Mamma,' said Mary-Anne, running after her.

Mrs Emmet clung to her daughter as they descended the stairs to the kitchen where she collapsed heavily on to a chair by the hearth. The fire had been banked down for the night. She reached for the poker and whispered harshly, 'Major Sirr! I remember the night he took Thomas out of Stephen's Green, gloating with pleasure and licking his whiskers with delight.'

She stoked the fire and thoughtfully watched the small turquoise flames spluttering to the surface . . . Dublin was now a city dominated by fear and military authority, but the real carnage was going on in the courts of law. Even the inimitable advocate himself, John Philpot Curran, was breaking under the strain, his health suffering from the fatigue of his battles in the State Trials, but he soldiered on. He was a remarkable man; over the years the Crown lawyers had continually been left to gape in astonishment when, inflicted with last-minute disclosures, Curran had yet managed, at a moment's notice, to rebut evidence which had been considered conclusive to the conviction of the prisoner.

He was winning no acquittals now, of course, but his hard-hitting and merciless tactics with informers were making many refuse to go into the witness box. He had even managed to get one to confess to many of his own crimes, the court learning that the witness had murdered his own mother-in-law. Now cases were being postponed for lack of witnesses . . .

The sound of boots tramping around upstairs distracted Mrs Emmet from the dark pool of her thoughts; she glanced up.

Mary-Anne handed her a cup of tea. She sipped it in silence and thought about her own personal world, and her son Thomas, still in prison. One of the nobles who stalked the corridors of Dublin Castle had suggested a simple time-saving remedy of having all the political prisoners in Kilmainham taken into the yard and shot as a crowd by a platoon of grenadiers. The suggestion had been supported by some of the hireling scribes who perpetuated religious rancour and racial spite under the auspices of journalism; but Lord Cornwallis, to his honour, had been outraged. Even Castlereagh had declared that such a violent and unlawful measure could not be permitted.

But who could tell what would happen?

And now the Castle wanted Robert in Kilmainham ... Elizabeth Emmet loved all her children, but Robert was ... 'The blood of my heart,' she whispered.

Mary-Anne was speaking to her, but she continued to stare with bitterness into the fire. God had taken Christopher away in sudden death, Major Sirr had taken Thomas, and now he was here to take Robert, too. Oh, it was too much, too much to take. She crashed down her cup. Well, neither God nor man was taking this son without a fight!

She moved to her feet with uncharacteristic agility and walked across the stone flags of the huge kitchen. After a moment's astonishment, Mary-Anne lunged after her, managing to grab her arm and hold her back from going through the door. 'Mamma! For heaven's sake, where are you going?'

'To get your father's pistol.'

'Pistol? Don't be silly, Mamma.'

'Silly?' cried Mrs Emmet, her breast heaving with the swell of the storm raging within her. 'That man barged into my house once before waving a Castle warrant as his right of entry. Well, if they are bent on driving the people to destruction, or *madness*, then let them take the consequences!'

'Hush! Someone is coming down the stairs.'

Dr Emmet appeared a moment later. 'They've gone,' he said, 'taking with them a few books which I'm sure they chose at random.'

'Oh, thank God,' said Mary-Anne. 'Mamma was just about to take a pistol to Major Sirr.'

Dr Emmet looked stunned but, after a moment, he smiled. 'So! This is who my sons get their defiant spirit from, is it?'

Tears of relief had begun to run down Mrs Emmet's face. 'Mary-Anne,' she said, with an effort at calmness, 'go and tell Robert to come down here at once . . . He will have to leave Ireland,' she added when Mary-Anne had gone. 'Whether we like it or not, he will have to go.'

Dr Emmet nodded. A lifetime's training had taught him to accept the inevitable. 'But he will need to stay in hiding for a week or two until an opportunity can be found to get him out of the country. Lennard can scout the grounds and make sure the place is not being watched.'

Mrs Emmet's mind was racing in all directions, then she remembered her dear friend who had fled Paris during the Terror and sought refuge with the Emmets in Dublin.

'France,' she said, 'that's where Robert should go. The Marquise de Fontenay will give him great welcome if he goes to Paris. She remembers him well from his childhood days and still asks about him in her letters.'

The following morning a brief letter was delivered to Casino addressed to Robert:

You have been informed against (by O'Hanlon) and should fly.

J. McGucken.

The day was humid and still as Anne Devlin rode towards Glenealy. She had risen before dawn, filled with the bleak dread she always felt on visiting days. The very sight of her father in that awful prison tore her heart apart.

Streaks of grey had appeared in Brian Devlin's black beard which was now long and straggly. He pushed aside the clean linen in the bag and pulled out the chicken, tearing off a piece and stuffing it hungrily into his mouth.

Anne watched her father savagely attack the fowl and thought her heart was going to break. 'Should you not save some for later, Da?' she murmured.

He gave her a look of startled realisation. The pleasure from the food turned to angry humiliation as he turned away. 'Aye.

I'm sorry, daughter, but starvation was never known to have good table manners.'

'What about your rations, Da? You were never hungry like this afore.'

'Rations inagh!' Her father gave an ironic little laugh and stuffed the chicken back into the bag. 'I'm supposed to get rations, right enough, but there's a new little game of tyranny being played inside this place. The head gaoler is a villain of a man named Carr. He's now decided that any person who has means enough to support himself, must do so. That way he gets ration money for prisoners who are fed by their families and makes a tidy little sum for himself.'

'Faith! But the man should be exposed for what he is. Why can't the men speak up for their rights?'

'What rights? You only have to look around this place to see they consider us no better than animals. Musha, isn't that what they've always called us – savages.'

Anne looked at him candidly. 'You've changed since you came in here, Da. You're talking like a rebel.'

'Talking like a rebel? I'm being *treated* like a rebel! Me, who spent all his days tending the land peacefully and keeping out of trouble! No one ever saw me at any secret meetings. No one ever found pikes stored in my house; yet I end up being dragged out of my home like a dog and get thrown in here. I'm telling you, daughter, 'tis an experience to change a man.'

Anne bowed her head and stared at her hands.

'Still, I have been lucky, mind,' he said. 'A lot of the men have been sent to the barracks of New Geneva in Waterford; the worst hell-hole on earth, surely.' He reached across the table and lifted her hand. 'And what about you, alannah? You're looking pale.'

'Oh, I'm well, Da. We all are, thank God.'

'Is it true what the turnkeys are saying about the French, that they were massacred at Ballinamuck?'

' 'Tis not true at all!' Anne declared angrily, ' 'Twas only the *Irish* that were massacred at Ballinamuck!'

'Musha, how can that be? The French were leading the Irish were they not?'

'I only know what the travelling men have been saying, and

there have been many different stories about the French, but they all tell the same tale about Ballinamuck.'

'Then tell me,' he said.

'The French and Irish had made their stand on Shanmullah Hill,' she said, 'but it was after the battle was over, after the surrender, that the dirty business took place; after Lord Cornwallis had ridden off with General Humbert and General Moore, and left General Lake in command.'

'General John Moore is a gentlemen,' her father said. 'The best British soldier ever to set up camp in Wicklow. If all the soldiers were like General Moore—'

'Well, they're not,' Anne snapped. 'And they proved it at Ballinamuck. The Irish prisoners were ordered away from the French prisoners. Irish to the west base of the hill, French up on the eastern slope, both standing in separate groups, waiting to be led away as prisoners of war, waiting for a long time.

'Then the mounted redcoats made their move towards the surprised Irish group, roaring their lungs out as they made charge after charge. The people said you could hear for miles the ferocious shouts of the soldiers and the terrible screams of the poor unarmed Mayo farmboys as they were slashed to death by the sabres.'

Her father's hand went to his beard, pulling at it angrily. 'What about the Frenchies? What did they do when all this was going on?'

'What could they do? They were unarmed and up on the hill. 'Tis said they all turned their backs to the slaughter.'

'Then shame on them,' Brian Devlin said, his voice half strangled. 'And let them take that shame with them back to France.'

'What are you saying, Da?' Anne looked incredulous, confounded. ' 'Twould have been callous and inhuman for the French to have stood and watched them being killed after weeks of sharing camp with them.'

'That's how you see it, but not I. The French brought the guns. The French put those guns into the Irish farmboys' hands. The French led them in the march away from the west and down towards the capital under the promise of Irish liberty and French fraternity. So the French should *not* have turned their backs on the Irish boys at Ballinamuck – they should have seen it through to the bitter end and watched them die!'

Anne averted her eyes and stared at the wall, then turning back, 'Da, it grieves me sorely to hear you speak like this. The French are our allies. Twice now they have tried to help us. They are still our only hope against the British.'

Brian Devlin took a breath and expelled it slowly. 'We will never beat the British,' he said wearily. 'Even if we were to beat them in arms, they would still kill us with their sneers. The Devil produced the first sneer and the British perfected it. At the end of the day it is always their final weapon.'

Oh, he had changed. Anne could not believe how much her father had changed. Gone was the gentle and big-hearted man who faced the world peacefully and smiled and sighed as he tended his land and his soft-eyed cows. He sat staring at the table with eyes full of hard bitterness.

'Oh, Da,' she whispered in torment, 'and you were such a *good* man.'

'Time's up!' shouted the turnkey.

Hesitantly, Anne and her father moved to their feet. 'Now listen carefully,' he said, and Anne listened as he gave her messages for her mother and the children. She wrapped her arms around his waist and clung to him. 'I can't bear to see you in this awful place, Da. I pray every night they will let you home soon.'

'They'll have to let me out one day,' he said in simple faith, 'for I've done nothing wrong. And when they do, we will leave this county. Go to Dublin maybe.'

She stepped back a pace, staring at him. 'What are you saying, Da? Leave Wicklow!'

'Aye. From now on life will be no good for us in Wicklow. We are branded as a rebel family, and the militia will never leave us alone. They'll torment us with searches and every other kind of abuse. But now listen. I've not worked like a slave all these years for nothing. I have something put by. We can rent another small farm around Dublin County, or maybe Cill Dara.'

'I don't want to go to Dublin or Kildare!' Anne cried. 'Our *home* is here in Wicklow. I'll die if I have to leave the vales of Wicklow.'

'Well, let us wait until the time comes,' her father said tiredly. 'Then we will see what's to be done.'

In the drawing-room of The Priory, Sarah was seated at her embroidery frame and no sound save the crackling of a burning log in the grate broke the peaceful splendour of the room – until Richard swept in, still dressed in riding garb and white-faced with shock.

'Drat me if this isn't the last straw,' he cried. 'I've just been over to Casino and was told that Robert has gone to Europe. My own friend, my very best friend – gone without a word of farewell!'

The words were like a thunderclap. Sarah stared at Richard, the colour driven from her face by dismay. 'Europe – when?'

'Now that is the question that still begs an answer,' Richard said in puzzlement. 'I was unable to see either the Doctor or Mrs Emmet as both were indisposed, Mary-Anne also, and none of the servants seemed to know exactly when Robert had gone. I thought Lennard would know for sure, but when I found him, all that little rascal could do was complain non-stop for ten long minutes that Robert hadn't said farewell to him either, but had slipped away to Europe while he was busy lighting his pipe – though which day and which smoke that was he couldn't recall.'

Sarah looked down to her embroidery, her memory recalling all the days she had spent wondering when he would come again. Every day, every walk for pleasure, had been lived in expectation. Then the question, Why did he not come again? Of course, there had been a rebellion, and there had been fighting in several counties, but Dublin and its outlands had remained quiet.

She stuck the needle into the embroidery and realised her foolishness in spending so much time recalling the pleasure of those two days in early summer. With the innocent heart of inexperience, she had been sure that a warm attachment had sprung up between herself and Robert Emmet but, if so, it had not lasted long, because he had never come back. And now he had gone on the Tour of Europe, a period of travelling considered essential to a gentleman's education.

'My eye,' said Richard suddenly, 'but Robert never said anything to me about taking the Tour when I saw him two weeks ago. Rot me if there isn't something beneath wind and water in this, Sarah, something fishy. And it's confounded odd the way Lennard was so vague about everything except his complaints. Very little in the Emmet household escapes him. He usually knows as much about what's going on around him as a bear in a pit.'

Two mornings later, Lennard looked around him furtively as the cart he was driving rattled over the cobblestones of Townsend Street at the back of the Quays. He whistled loudly as he climbed down and looped the reins, then whispered to the pile of sacking in the cart. ' 'Twill be best if we walk it from here, wha'?'

Robert slipped out of the cart and quickly brushed himself down while Lennard lifted a cloak and hat from under the bench. Robert threw the cloak on his shoulders and pulled the hat low on his brow.

Every moment on the journey to the docks Robert expected to feel a hand on his shoulder, but he consoled himself with the thought that few people knew his appearance. Even if he came face to face with Sirr, the major would not know he was Robert Emmet.

'How long will ye be gone?' Lennard muttered.

'Who knows? We will have to see how matters turn out here.'

'I still can't figure out why ye have to go to England,' Lennard said.

'It's the only way. The boats smuggling wool to France have stopped since the arrival of the French. The entire Irish coastline is being watched. My only way is through England.'

'How will ye get over there from England?'

'A number of the boatmen in Hastings run a successful smuggling racket between England and France. They are all radicals, and a few of them are in our pay. Once I get to Little Hastings I shall be all right.'

'Will ye then be crossing the Channel alone?'

'No. Two other United men are waiting for me.'

'Ah, that's good. 'Twould be terrible for ye to be all alone

234

over there with them foreigners who speak only gibberish.'

Robert glanced sidelong at the little man: he was wearing the prized black hat he had finally won in a card game from Johny the Hat. It had a low crown and wide brim which turned down at the front and back. The hat sat on Lennard's head like an oversized crown as he trudged along carrying the valise, his lips sucked in under his bulb of a nose as if he was contemplating a bad card hand.

The sight of the docks and the three-masted ship sent a wave of depression surging through Robert. Everything he cherished was here. He did not want to go.

The quayside was thronged with people bidding farewell to passengers. Two policemen stood by a table on which were papers and pen and ink; they appeared to be writing down the names of each passenger that embarked.

At the sound of the ship's bell, Robert took the valise from Lennard and managed a weak smile. 'Well, old man, this is where we part company.'

Lennard stared at him, a hurt expression on his face. 'I'm not old! I'm not yet fifty. Leastaways, I don't think so.'

'You know what I mean, Lennard.'

Lennard nodded, but kept his eyes averted from Robert as if the goings-on around him were more to his interest. 'Aye, well off ye go then.'

They stood for a moment in silence. 'You can go back now,' Robert said.

Lennard continued to watch the other people on the quayside. 'I've loads of time. No, I'll watch ye on, then I'll go.'

Robert nodded, then moved towards the crowd. He had walked only a few yards when Lennard came running after him, his normal ruddy colour pale, his tongue flicking around his mouth as if searching for lost words. 'I betther stay close behind in case the dock police bother ye,' he muttered. 'Maybe I can cause a bit of a diversion, wha'?'

'You old gomadan,' Robert said affectionately. 'It won't choke you to give me your blessing.'

'Aye, well it might, Misther Robert,' Lennard said quietly. 'When I was a youth leaving Tipperary, me oul da came running after me, but *his* blessing stuck in his throat. He couldn't

235

make himself say it. Not to me, not to his only son.' He gave a little sniff and surveyed the crowd, 'O' course, I left of me own accord. I wasn't on the run like ye.'

The clang of the ship's bell again brought a loud murmur from the crowd on the dockside. Robert gave Lennard a quick farewell pat on the shoulder then turned and walked towards the ship.

'May God bless ye and go with ye on yer journey!' Lennard cried. 'And the Divil take whoever stands in yer way.'

Robert smiled as he pushed his way through the crowd, but he did not turn round. He strode past the two policemen who were occupied in restraining a sobbing woman in a black shawl from going on board. Swiftly mounting the gangplank, he was crossing to the far side of the deck when a voice rose up behind him.

'Excuse me, sir! Hold on there a minute!'

He turned to see one of the policemen step on to the deck and march towards him, holding out a sheet of paper.

'I presume you are addressing me?' he said in his haughtiest voice.

'Yes, sir. I need your name for the list. All passengers leaving Dublin must now be on the list. So, if you'll give me your name?'

Robert could see Lennard squinting up at the front of the crowd, jumping from one foot to the other like an alarmed grasshopper.

'I asked your name, sir.'

'Trebor,' he replied, giving his first name backwards.

The policeman looked down at his paper for a moment and gave a groan. 'Oh, damn and blast, but isn't the pen and ink back down on the quay. You'll have to come back down so's I can write your name on the list.'

'But they're just about to weigh anchor! Surely you can remember my name for a few feet of gangplank?'

'I could, sir, but I have to check it against another list of names.'

A bugle sounded on the dockside. The policeman looked confused. 'All right,' he said, 'but next time you travel to England, sir, kindly have the decency to wait until your name is checked before you board.'

'It will not happen again,' Robert assured him.

'Good, good,' the policeman muttered, turning and rushing back down to the Quays.

As soon as the topsails of the ship began to unfurl in great white billowing sheets, the traditional cries of sad farewell rose up from the crowd, but the only cry meant for Robert was the one sent up by Lennard: 'Fast winds and fair weather to ye, avic!'

That same morning a communication was sent to the Castle from one of their secret agents in Belfast named John Pollock, containing urgent information from the informer who frequently travelled up and down between the two cities, James McGucken:

> Emmet is concealed and will leave the Kingdom at the first opportunity.
> Beard lives in a lane at the end of Paradise Row near to Dorset Street.
> Take up Coyle as soon as possible, and then those that are in custody and those that have fled, have for the present broken up the whole.
> Dublin is done.
> The heads of the South are given in.
> I'll answer for the North.

As the ship sailed away from the Dublin docks, Robert walked over to the far side of the deck and rested his arms on the ship's rail, watching the ocean stretching between him and his homeland.

Was there anyone in Ireland, he wondered, who would ever forget this year of 1798. He knew he would never forget. Lord Edward dead. Tone dead. So many dead. But perhaps the saddest death of all was that of Fitzgerald's favourite Tony, the poor heartbroken Negro who had died in Kildare from his own grief. He had never once held up his head after Lord Edward's death, and now had followed him in death . . . Weep not for the dead, not for the peaceful weep. Whose country's ruin troubleth not their sleep. Their quiet memory dreams not of the past, their journey through eternity is fast . . .

Who had said that? Then he remembered. It was his sister, Mary-Anne Emmet, who had written it. Although the first line was definitely from the Bible.

Dublin Bay was drifting further away.

'*Let us look to Ireland* . . .' The Duke of Bedford's plea to His

Majesty roared amongst the flapping white topsails. '*When I speak of that country, I know not in what terms of reprobation to express my abhorrence of the system which the Ministers have pursued. We earnestly solicit His Majesty to give to the people of Ireland the strongest proof they can receive of His Majesty's disapprobation of that system of treachery by which the present discontents of that country have been fostered; and of His Majesty extending, to men of all descriptions, in that oppressed country, the blessings of the Constitution under which they were born.*'

Well said, the Duke of Bedford.

Stone deaf, George of Hanover.

Dublin Bay was drifting further, and further, and further away. Robert looked towards the hills in the direction of Rathfarnham, and thought of Sarah, the young exquisite he must now forget. Logic told him that time would diminish her image in his mind, and she would become no more than a vague and distant memory of an embryonic first love that circumstances had not allowed to take root and grow.

He thought of all those he was leaving behind: Thomas and Jane in their prison cell; all his friends, his sister, his mother and father . . . Only at the time of final parting does one truly feel the sorrow that comes with the leaving of home and the breaking of tender ties . . . Weep not for the dead, but weep, weep sore, for them that go into exile and return no more. They go, they go from their beloved home, they go in distant dreariness to roam . . .

The sun was rising over the Wicklow Mountains in almost unbearable beauty, turning them from misty blue to a dusty green. He locked the vision in his heart until the day of his return – one day, some day. But for now he said a sad and silent farewell to Ireland, his own lush and beautiful little corner of tragedy.

As the ship lost sight of land, an old and plaintive song from his motherland drifted over the waves . . . Come back to Erin, avourneen, avourneen. Come back aroon, to the land of thy birth. Come back with the shamrock in springtime, avourneen. Come back . . .

PART TWO
1802–1803

Chapter Twenty

Paris was at its gayest amidst the joyous celebrations in honour of the end of the Anglo-French war. It was March 1802, and the peace treaty between Britain and France had been signed at Amiens.

At a table outside a Paris café, Robert Emmet sat biting his lip as he wrote a letter to the Marquise de Fontenay. During his early days in France he had become very intimate with the Marquise, her husband, and her daughter, but, on return from a trip to Hamburg, had decided he could impose no longer on the family's generosity. He had taken an apartment on the rue de la Loi which he shared with his friend, Malachy Delaney, a former lieutenant in the rebellion of 1798.

'*Voilà*, m'sieur!' said the café owner, bringing him a new bottle of ink. Robert murmured his thanks, requested more brandy, then continued the letter:

> . . . I have just learned by a letter from London, that the principal motive that influenced the British Government in making the peace with France was the declaration by Lord Cornwallis, that if ten thousand Frenchmen landed in Ireland the country would be infallibly lost. I have also been informed by a gentleman coming from London, that it is the intention of the British Government to proclaim a general amnesty and system of conciliation in Ireland, so that, if we have not yet found friends to acknowledge or appreciate our service to them, we found enemies at least capable of estimating our importance to them.
>
> I have therefore determined on returning home, but I am not, in any case, to leave until time shall show us

241

more clearly the intention of the British Government.

I am in want of nothing, my dear Madame. If I were, I am quite convinced of the friendly interest you take in me; apart from the affectionate manner in which you write me, but in this respect my father's generosity has left me in want of nothing.

Your sincere friend,
Robert Emmet

He sat reading over the letter while the cool breeze dried the ink, looking up when Malachy Delaney appeared from nowhere and sat down on the chair opposite.

'Have I got good news for you, dear fellow!' Malachy was grinning from ear to ear.

'Well?'

'All the Irish prisoners have been released from Fort George!'

Robert stared at him in disbelief. At the end of 1798, Lord Cornwallis had sent all those United Irishmen not arraigned for trial to Fort George, a lonely prison in the Highlands of Scotland. Thomas had been confined there for nearly four years, and Jane had chosen to go with him.

'Malachy,' said Robert. 'Say it again, slowly.'

'All the United prisoners have been released from Fort George,' Malachy repeated, 'and put aboard a ship destined for Amsterdam.'

'But why Amsterdam? Why not Ireland?'

Malachy withdrew an English newspaper from inside his coat. 'It's all in here,' he said. 'All have been sentenced to permanent exile from the British Isles. A condition of their banishment is execution if they ever return. They should reach Holland any day now.'

'M'sieur! M'sieur!' the café owner shouted, '*Cinq francs! Cinq francs!*' But the young man to whom he had graciously given the paper and ink was running down the rue de la Loi with the other young man in his wake.

He spotted the ten-franc note on the table, lifted it and smiled. Ah, *les Irlandais!* They were all crazy!

*   *   *

The transition from spring to high summer was barely noticeable in Ireland. The rains fell softly, but relentlessly, resulting in a failed harvest. In many rural areas the people were on the verge of famine. In response to their plight, the government did nothing to help them. Taxes on Irish corn and wheat remained impossibly high, and rents on farmlands were mercilessly increased.

By the first leaves of autumn, an old proverb was once again whispering through Ireland. 'A country ruled by its own takes care of its own . . .'

It was October in Dublin city. On the bridge between Merchants' Quay and King's Inn Quay, John Curran stood gazing down to the slushy green waters of the River Anna Liffey. Up and down each quayside crowds were flocked in happy chatter, occasionally waving and cheering as the procession rolled slowly past them.

From under the bridge a family of white swans emerged, gliding on towards Ormond Quay with no apparent interest in the excitement above. A tremendous cheer rose up. John Curran lifted his head and watched Lord Clare's procession draw nearer. From this high centre of the bridge, his view was unobstructed.

Three men, it was said, had been responsible for the reign of terror in Ireland which culminated in the 1798 rebellion, Lords Camden, Castlereagh, and Clare. The first two were now lording it in England, and the news was that Castlereagh was receiving great acclaim as a Westminster politician.

John Curran sighed a long sigh.

But what of Lord Clare? His procession was close now. Again a tremendous cheer rose up from the crowd; and John Curran, standing watching on the bridge, could not have known that this Irish crowd were giving Lord Clare the same send-off the English people would later give to Castlereagh – one young man jumping on a wall and shouting almost the same words the English would later shout about Castlereagh:

'*People of Ireland, rejoice! The Earl of Clare is dead!*'

And as the hearse moved along, and as the people remembered the dead man's oft-repeated boast that he would make them as tame as cats, an exultant yell rose up when someone threw a dead cat on to the Chancellor's coffin.

John Curran smiled. O poetic justice, if nothing else!

But it was strange, he thought idly, how this event, the sudden death of his most hated and long-time enemy, should have made him feel happy, triumphant even; and yet he felt nothing, nothing at all. If Lord Clare was dead now, then so was Ireland.

In Westminster, 'the Irish problem' had raged on as usual, and, as always, discarded for more important matters at home. Although the rebellion had made William Pitt realise that some concessions would have to be made to the Catholics if disaffection was to be contained in that troublesome land. Lord Cornwallis wholeheartedly agreed with him, but both knew concessions would never be granted so long as the privileged minority held power. There was only one solution – the same solution taken with Scotland – a parliamentary union with England.

And so, after a great deal of financial bribery, the bestowing of many English peerages, and the creation of thirty more Irish peerages, the vote to secure the Union was passed. And on 1 January 1801, after sitting for seven centuries, the Irish Parliament was dismantled, the Irish nation dissolved, and the country ruled direct from England, via the old administration at Dublin Castle, where only the leading personnel had changed. The new Viceroy was Philip Yorke, the Earl of Hardwicke, who seemed a decent gentleman. And England had a new Prime Minister.

Two months after the passage of the Act of Union, King George refused any suggestion of the Irish relief measures which Pitt proposed, becoming so enraged at the idea of Catholic emancipation that he fell into yet another bout of insanity and had to be restrained in a straitjacket. Pitt resigned in a fit of pique. The King was glad to get rid of him. King George had always disliked the way Pitt ruled Parliament and England as if *he* were the monarch. Pitt was replaced as head of the Tory Party by Henry Addington, the choice of the King.

The crowds on the quayside were dispersing, the path to the Four Courts clear. John Curran turned and strolled on towards his chambers, still quite youthful at fifty-two, still able to take his drink well, still able to enjoy the pleasures of his mistress, still able to put up a good fight in court, but no heart left for the patriotic fight.

The long bloody drama was over, all the leading players gone. Ireland was more shackled than ever, with no hope of rescue. Curran had fought hard against the Union with Britain for many reasons, one being that without an election it was unconstitutional, not to mention the fact that without a Parliament the Irish Whigs would no longer have a governmental platform in their own country.

He had fought fanatically hard, knocking on doors, organising meetings, and rallying the Bar. When the seat for Kilbeggan became vacant through the previous holder's sudden death, he had even presented himself as the Whig candidate in the hope of becoming one more vote against the Union. His old friend Henry Grattan had come out of retirement to champion him.

Another person had also supported him in the fight against the Union, by way of a privately printed pamphlet that had not so shocked and outraged the Castle since the days of Theobald Wolfe Tone. So clever was the method used by the writer of the pamphlet that at first Curran had not even bothered to read it, for on its cover it promised to set out *why* it was ridiculous to oppose the Union, and every pro-Unionist was eager to read the pamphlet entitled: *An Address to the People of Ireland*.

. . . You are called upon to oppose the Union, and preserve your rights. Now I ask the men who call upon you, what rights you have to preserve? I ask Parliament what rights *they* have not wrested from you? They call upon you to resist – *what*? Not *oppression*, it has been *protected*. Not *injustice*, it has been *legalised*. Not *cruelty*, it has been *indemnified*. You are called upon to resist a Union by which you would lose – a name.

If I am to bend to the altar of British supremacy, if I am to wear the chains of everlasting slavery, it matters not to me whether I wear them as an Irishman or as a West Briton – it matters not to me whether my fetters are forged in London or Dublin. If you had but one unalienated right left to you, I too, would say to you, never submit to the Union – never, never, never . . .

The Castle had sworn vengeance against the unknown writer. Agents of the secret service had worked day and night to bring him in for sedition, but they had never found him, and never would; for the unknown writer, he now knew, was Mary-Anne Emmet, a very pretty young lady who, in a male-dominated world, was forced to wear a simpering smile and a fancily ribboned bonnet to conceal her unladylike intelligence.

And maybe her pamphlet had helped him. He had won the seat of Kilbeggan in time to enter Parliament and cast his vote against the Union, but all to no avail against the purchasing power of the Castle.

Twenty-two of his colleagues at the Bar were given judgeships; others, elevated to the Bench of Bishops. Scores of others had been given peerages in return for their Parliamentary seats. '*What? My country for a bag of gold and my soul for an Earldom? Rather!*' The political seduction had been performed openly and unashamedly, until:

By perjury and fraud,
By slaves who sold their land for gold,

the Union and the Castle had won.

Oh, bitter bitter memories of the smug self-satisfaction of those Tories who had laughed with glee at the sight of a fifty-one-year-old man with egg all over his face. The great legal defender of the United Irishmen had finally decided to fight his case, *his Whig case*, in the Irish Parliament, only to find, when he went to take his seat, that the Irish Parliament no longer existed! And no matter how savage his legal rhetoric, how powerful his speeches of eloquence, all his words would do was bounce off the walls and bring the plaster crashing down from the rococo ceiling on to the deserted floor of an empty chamber.

Ha, ha! Back to the villains in the Four Courts, Jack!

All an exaggeration, of course, but who would listen to the

awful truth when the comedy of malicious humour was more palatable.

And so, while Castlereagh was proudly taking his seat in the Westminster Parliament, Curran went back to the Four Courts. But now the time had come, he decided, for every man to look out for himself. The game of politics and self-advancement was open to all players who could rough the scrum, and he had banged brains with the worst of them. But he was still a brilliant lawyer, the best in his field, and he was determined finally to collect the rewards to which his talent entitled him.

Inside the King's Inn refectory he sat down for an early lunch, at his usual table by the window, facing the door, and ordered beef and roasted potatoes.

He had only lifted his knife and fork when a deputation of young attorneys came into the refectory. On seeing him, they immediately rushed over and begged his charity. One of their colleagues had died penniless, and they had decided to solicit a subscription of one shilling each from every member of the Bar and Judiciary to pay for his funeral.

'It is the least we can do,' a young attorney said sadly.

'It is,' Curran agreed, and gave them fifteen shillings.

William Conyngham Plunkett entered then, and the attorneys ventured towards him. Curran eyed Plunkett coolly. He had been a close friend of Thomas Emmet, as well as an arch-opponent of the Union. Plunkett had even given a rousing speech to the Bar, declaring that, before he would sell out his country, he would *fling the British connection to the winds*! But now the battle was lost, even Plunkett was making servile approaches to the British connection at the Castle.

Ah well, if you can't beat the unscrupulous, at least keep a watchful eye on how they play their hand.

The door flew open and a loud and bombastic presence marched into the refectory: Lord Norbury, one of the most sadistic and heartless devils ever to wear ermine, and commonly known as the 'hanging judge'. Although some were now fearing that Norbury was losing his touch. Out of the last one hundred men that he had tried, he had hanged only ninety-seven.

247

But he did his job cheerfully, roisterously cracking jokes in his gallows humour as he sentenced young men to death. He was also called Puffendorf because of his habit of blowing out his face while thinking.

John Curran watched him blow out his cheeks as the deputation of attorneys appoached him to solicit a subscription towards the funeral of their colleague.

'What! Only a shilling to bury an attorney?' exclaimed the judge. 'Here's a guinea, go and bury twenty-one of them!'

When the deputation had sullenly moved off, Norbury sailed over to Counsellor Curran's table. After all their battles on the field of justice, it was clear as daylight to anyone who had eyes to see, that Curran despised and detested the hanging judge. But heartless as he was, Norbury had no sensitivity to other people's feelings.

'Well, Jack?' he said cheerfully to Curran. 'Celebrating the demise of your old sweetheart, Lord Clare, what, what?'

When Curran deigned no answer, just continued to eat his lunch, Lord Norbury looked down the wide landscape of his stomach which started just below his neck, and curiously examined the meat on Curran's plate.

'Is that hung beef?' he inquired.

Curran lifted an ironical eyebrow. 'It will be if you try it, my lord.'

Some two miles down the Quays, Lennard and another carriage driver stood leaning over the north wall of the Dublin docks, idly watching the ship as it drifted towards them. There had been little wind in the night and the packet boat, normally due in around six, was almost six hours late.

'Isn't it a funny thing,' remarked Lennard's companion, 'that from these docks here, the floor of the world gets lower and lower.'

'It does,' said Lennard, 'because everyone knows that the farther ye go out to sea, the deeper the water gets.'

'Did I ever tell you of a man I once met who told me the world was not square at all, but round.'

'Then he was a stupid man entirely!' Lennard sniffed. 'Sure any fool would know that if the world was round, all that water out there would spill over the side and soon douse Lucifer's fire below.'

The man stared at Lennard as if he had just discovered something incredible about him. 'Aren't you right!'

'Sure I am,' said Lennard impressively. 'And if ye were to ask the young misther on that ship out there, he'd tell ye the same, and he a college boy! Not that a body would need to go to the college, mind, to know a simple thing like that. Now then, if ye want to be educated, think on this – the four corners of the earth – isn't that what people sez when they talk of the great travellers, they went to the four corners of the earth?'

'They do, true enough.'

'And when has anything round had four corners?' Lennard said sneeringly. 'Answer me that? No, 'tis like I always sez, there's too many daft ideas abroad and even more fools to heed them.'

Gulls screeched overhead, sweeping in low, wild circles, but the two servants were solemnly contemplating the swish of the green water below.

'How deep would you say it was?' muttered Lennard's companion.

'Well now,' said Lennard, looking down at the water, 'it's that deep, that a man I once knew fell into it and sank.' He nodded his head gravely. 'Sank out o' sight and we never heard from him again. Not until months later when he gave a letter to a man coming over from America, asking his mother to send him a set of dry clothes. His other set had shrunk.'

'America?' Lennard's companion grinned. 'Do ye think I'm stupid altogether? America?'

' 'Tis true,' Lennard insisted. 'As true as my seven brothers are farmers in Tipperary.'

The other man resumed his contemplation of the water for some moments, then murmured on a cunning note, 'Letters from America to Ireland always have money in them. Was there any money in the letter?'

'Well, if there was,' said Lennard, fixing his eye on a seagull hovering dangerously above, 'the Yankee robbed it.'

The gull missed, squirting his refuse an inch past Lennard's hat down into the water. 'And Lord Clare being buried today, wha'?' Lennard said suddenly. 'Gone down to his maker.'

'A devil of a man, he was. And a bastard of a judge. The only good and fair judge I ever heard of was Lord Kilwarden. A sweet-natured man, they say.'

'As sweet as sugar,' Lennard agreed. 'And loved by all the friends of justice in Ireland. An awful pity he retired as Lord Chief Judge. Now we have that bloodthirsty mongrel Norbury in his place.'

'Norbury?' the other man shuddered. 'Begor, I think I would swap him for Lord Clare again even.'

'Then ye'd only be swapping a mad donkey for an insane mule,' Lennard said dismissively. ' 'Tis a known fact that, apart from Lord Kilwarden, all judges are mad. They're not allowed to be judges unless they can prove to the Castle that they're mad, truly and incurably mad. 'Tis a known fact.'

'Then how come I never knew it?'

'Same reason ye didn't know the world was square. But even ye must know of the judge called Judge Baron?'

'Judge Baron? Was he the one that kilt himself in the River Liffey?'

'That was him, poor man. Kilt himself in the Liffey. A judge. And as mad as George of Handover himself.'

'Ah, wait now . . . we have to be fair and honest about the dead in all cases. Ye can't say the judge was mad just because he kilt himself.'

'Gesh along!' Lennard cried. 'What else would ye say about a judge that sets out in the rain to drown himself, and as he makes the walk down to the river with a firm step, holds up an umbrella to keep himself dry!'

Robert rested his arms on the ship's rail and gazed towards the Wicklow Mountains, a smile on his face. He was going home.

Behind him on the deck a number of his friends were passing the journey in enjoyable debate, jumping from topic to topic and no longer caring if any of it made sense. Irish conversation often becomes a game; a cut and thrust battle of eloquence and humour, poetry and pugnacity, a verbal riot of contradictions and codology to confuse all but themselves. A game to be enjoyed.

Dublin Bay drew nearer. A story about Napoleon was told; about his habit of expressing his gratitude to his officers by slapping them hard across the face with an affectionate laugh, and the red-cheeked, tear-stung Frenchmen humbly thanking '*Mon Général*' for the honour.

A roar of laughter rose up behind him. It was all very clannish. The Paris exiles would soon be home.

Inside Dublin Castle, Alexander Marsden, the new Under-Secretary of State, was seated at his desk reading through a file. He was an elegant, smooth-mannered man, still in his thirties, a former Crown lawyer who had gained his position through the help of his close friend, Lord Castlereagh.

Marsden read slowly, although he knew most of the details. The reports in the file revealed that, whilst in France, Robert Emmet had been employed as the United Irish envoy in Paris, replacing an Edward Lewins in that position. He had mixed in the Irish, Polish, and American communities there, and was highly regarded by the radical element.

The reports had been sent to Marsden by a prominent United Irishman on the Continent, Samuel Turner, who was also a Castle agent.

Reading through more pages, Marsden wondered irritably why Turner relished giving so much of the trivial details. The Castle was not interested in Emmet's social life, although it was not surprising to learn he spent more time in the salon of the writer, Germaine de Staël, than the more frivolous salons of Parisian society. The lady might have a penchant for surrounding herself with young men, but only the very élite of the intelligentsia were allowed to attend her salon gatherings. And by all accounts, politics interested the great de Staël more than philosophy.

And, according to Turner, Robert Emmet had not only attended those gatherings frequently, he had also been granted a number of interviews with Bonaparte's aide, Talleyrand, followed by a personal interview with Napoleon himself.

Marsden sat back in his chair, his crystal-grey eyes half closed. Now ... what did young Emmet have to say, he wondered, that was interesting enough to gain him a personal interview with the leader of the French nation?

The ship's bell was ringing, sails were hauled in, and the anchor finally dropped. A wild buzz rose up from the dockside but now the Paris exiles were strangely silent as they waited to disembark.

Lennard ditched his companion and pushed his way through the gathered groups, his movements quick and excited. He had instantly and joyously recognised the dark-haired young man talking with others not far from the gangway. He pushed forward even more violently, turning his head twice to shout a few choice words to those who protested.

The little man's curses attracted Robert's attention. He smiled, said farewell to his companions, then moved towards Lennard.

Seeing the smile on Robert's face, Lennard composed his own features into an expression of blithe indifference. He was still wearing Johnny the Hat's hat and now touched a finger to it.

'Is it yerself, Misther Robert?'

'It is, Lennard.'

'Ye took yer time, wha'?'

'How so?'

'Coming back. The amnesty was granted months ago, and yer poor father here waiting and watching for ye. Ah, like I sez, yer poor father . . .' Lennard shook his head gravely and lifted the valise.

'How is he, Lennard?'

'Not good, Misther Robert, not good at all. But he'll be all the bether for seeing ye, as long as he's had to wait.'

They had reached the carriage. Lennard opened the door and pushed the valise inside. 'Was it because of Misther Tom ye stayed on in Paris?' he asked. 'To get him settled? They tell me nothing up at the house.'

'I would like to get home as soon as possible, Lennard.'

'Aye.' The little man stood looking at him, waiting for an answer to his question.

'Well?' Robert gestured with an aloof movement of his head

and eyes up to the driver's bench. 'Shall we go?'

Lennard continued standing for a moment, then his face opened up in a toothy grin. 'Ah, Misther Robert, yer as *haughty* as ever! 'Tis going to be grand having ye back! Now in ye get and I'll have ye home in a shout.'

As the carriage entered the vicinity of College Green, Robert leaned out of the window and called up to Lennard to halt. When Lennard obliged, Robert gazed contemptuously across the street to the new Bank of Ireland.

The object of the 1798 rebellion was for Ireland to become a Union of Irishmen of every religious persuasion, a nation independent of England. But now Ireland was nothing more than a western province of Britain, with no government of its own. And the building which had for centuries been the Irish House of Parliament had now been turned into a blasted bank!

'There's little difference in the business carried on there when you think about it,' Dr Emmet later said to Robert. 'At least now the money changing hands will be legitimate transactions, not bribes.'

They were in the garden at Casino. Dr Emmet in a chair with a blanket around his knees, and Robert on a chair beside him.

Robert's first sight of his father had been hard to accept calmly. He had never thought of him as being old; he had never thought of him beyond simply being his beloved father, but the pale gaunt man who rose shakily on his feet to greet him had looked like a stranger.

'Now you are home, Robert,' his mother had said, 'he will start to get better. Wait and see.'

Robert spent the greater part of each day of the following week with his father, who did get better. The look of intense weariness disappeared from his eyes, replaced by a lively enthusiasm as the two men discussed everything from Thomas and Jane, medicine and science, and the politics of Ireland, England, and France.

Thomas's and Jane's children had been cared for at Casino during their parents' imprisonment in Scotland, but now that Thomas had bought a house on the rue du Cherche-Midi, the children had been sent over with a chaperon.

'What will Thomas do now?' Dr Emmet asked.

'I think he will stay on in Paris,' Robert said. 'At least until the children are practised in French.'

'It's better than America, I suppose. Not so far away.'

Robert nodded, knowing that even France was too far for his father to travel in his enfeebled health.

Dr Emmet sat gazing towards the mountains, then turned to Robert with an almost childlike appeal. 'Will I ever see my son Thomas again?'

Robert reached out and gently covered his father's hand with his own.

No, he almost answered truthfully, not as long as Ireland remains under British rule . . . But then he remembered one of his mother's old Irish proverbs from Tralee – 'Promises of hope are better than gifts of despair.'

He smiled, and squeezed his father's hand in a gesture of hope.

The Devlin family of Wicklow now lived in County Dublin. After spending two and a half years in gaol, Brian Devlin had been released a very different and bitter man. Determined to quit Wicklow, he had journeyed to Dublin where he eventually rented a small dairy farm in Rathfarnham.

In the kitchen of the farmhouse, Anne churned the butter so vigorously that perspiration began to dampen the clump of black curls which escaped the red kerchief around her head. She paused to mop her brow with the back of her hand, and it was then, as her eyes strayed to the window, she saw her brother sitting idly on the field wall. She wiped her hands on her apron and ran out to the yard.

'Little Arthur! Is it dreaming you are? I asked you to put the eggs under the hen. She'll go off the cluck if it's not done soon.'

Her brother continued staring towards the peaks of the Wicklow Mountains.

'Little Arthur! Is it deaf you are? There's dreaming and there's working, but only one pays the landlord.'

He sighed wistfully. 'Aye, I'm coming along now.'

She stood to gaze at him. Although still only sixteen he was losing his boyish looks. A hint of manhood was forming around the line of his jaw and the soft blue of his eyes had turned deeper. She loved him, but there were times when she despaired of him. It was almost two years now, and still he had not been able to settle. She turned her gaze in the direction of Wicklow and remembered the day they had left there.

'Think of it this way,' her da had said, as they walked the Dublin road accompanied by two horses and six cows, 'in Dublin County we won't have to put up with the militia kicking down our door every other night.'

Anne had expected a dirty, noisy city, but Rathfarnham had turned out to be a quiet country place on the outskirts, and she had to admit that it was not so bad. The Dublin hills were close enough to ramble, even if they were a poor substitute for the mountains of Wicklow.

'Dublin is our home now, Little Arthur,' she said. 'Will you not try and make the best of it?'

'Dublin inagh!' he rasped. 'Wicklow is our true home.'

'Aye,' she said, trying to be patient, 'I know 'tis hard to get used to level land when the mountains have been your playground.'

' 'Tis only Michael Dwyer's playground now. Musha, but you have to admire him, Anne. 'Tis a merry dance he's led the militia these past four years. They've tried every trick they know but can't catch him.'

Anne smiled as she thought of her tall and happy-go-lucky black-haired cousin. In 1798 the Castle had offered a reward of £500 to anyone who would bring in the rebel captain of the Wicklow Mountains; and since then he had become famous for his ingenious escapes. He could outrun, outshoot, outsmart any militiaman or bounty hunter. And the people loved him for it.

Little Arthur sighed wistfully. 'I sometimes have a yearning to go and join Michael,' he murmured.

'You never will!' Anne cried. 'You're needed here to do the work! You cannot even think of leaving it all to Da.'

Little Arthur flushed as he looked at her. She was telling him he was not doing his share, and she was right. He turned away, wishing he could rid himself of his homesickness. They were faring a lot better here in Rathfarnham than they had ever done in Wicklow. Their dairy business was doing well, and they owned several horses which they hired out to the local gentry. And now they had a slated two-storey house instead of the thatched cottage in Croneybeag. But, oh, how his heart yearned for the wild mountains of Wicklow and the silent scented peace of the lush green glens!

'I know how you feel,' Anne whispered. ' 'Tis terribly tantalising to be forever in sight of your homeland but not close enough to stray there.'

'You loved Wicklow, too. Every bit as much as me, I think.'

'Aye, I did. I do! But fate has brought us here, and what's more, has been kind to us.' She turned back to the house. 'Now come along, Little Arthur, there's no more time for dallying.'

He jumped off the wall and fell in step beside her. 'I don't know why you still call me *little*. I'm taller than you now.'

She smiled at his indignation. 'Arrah, 'tis just habit. You were always called that because of your cousin, Big Arthur Devlin. But seeing as it offends your manly pride, I'll try to check me tongue so.'

A pale November sun shone down on Sarah as she strolled over the fields, but despite the sun the air struck sharp and fresh. She lifted the hood of her cloak and draped it over her hair, wondering whether to continue on to the river, or turn back.

She carried on. No point going back yet, she decided. Amelia would still be weeping in her room and refusing to see anyone. Poor Amelia! After months and months of helping Reverend Harding with his parish activities, and finally securing a proposal, Papa had furiously, and without any reason, refused his consent to the match.

'He still don't like parsons,' Mrs Jessop had said. 'He's still plagued by divils from the past.'

But that did not appease Amelia who had retorted, 'It's horribly unfair!'

Sarah had to agree, it was very unfair. Because although Amelia was twenty-seven, and over the age of consent, without Papa's approval she would have no dowry, and Reverend Harding had little money.

The sun now disappeared behind a cluster of small clouds, changing the afternoon to a bleak grey. She walked around a belt of trees towards the river, pausing at the sight of a lone figure standing motionlessly on the bank – a young man in a dark cloak with his back to her, looking down at the water.

She stood irresolute, filled with a sudden urge to slip away but fearing to attract his attention with a hasty movement. He appeared to be absorbed either in his own thoughts or something in the water.

With a sudden movement the young man threw the front drapings of his cloak over his shoulders and crouched down, dipping his hands into the water and splashing it over his face, still unaware of her presence.

Sarah frowned. An action like that was common in the warmth of summer, but not in this autumnal chill. When he took out a handkerchief and began to wipe his eyes, she wondered if he had been crying.

Gripped by a compelling urge to flee, she looked around her; the ground was strewn with bracken. She had been lucky to miss it on her approach, but she would have to move carefully on her retreat.

She turned and gave a last look at the young man. He had lifted his face from the handkerchief, his head now turned sideways as he gazed down the river. She stared at him in sudden recognition. Even with his back to her she felt she should have recognised him. It was the black hair which was different; not long and tied at the nape in a black ribbon, but shortened to the collar in the French style.

Robert became suddenly conscious of not being alone. He turned his head and looked over his shoulder, eyes slowly widening as he gazed at her. For years he had wondered about her, and on any other day, at any other time, the pleasure of seeing her again would have thrilled him, but today his pain was too deep to feel anything else.

She let out a long slow breath. 'I . . . I heard you were back.'

He rose to his feet, pushing the handkerchief inside his cloak. 'Yes, three weeks ago.'

'Is your father any better?'

'He died this morning.'

'Oh, Robert . . . I'm so sorry.'

Silently they stood looking at each other, and Sarah's face flushed with an ever-increasing embarrassment. As soon as Richard had told her Robert Emmet had returned to Ireland, she had been curious to see him again. But to stumble upon him in his private grief! And it was plain he had no desire for conversation. She turned and took a few sauntering steps away from him.

He stood looking after her for a moment.

'Are you going home?' he asked.

She turned her head and nodded.

'May I accompany you?'

She hesitated, then nodded mutely.

They walked at an easy pace, each thinking about the other. After four years there was so much to say, so many questions to ask, but neither knew how to begin; and now was not really the time.

The silence spun out until Robert suddenly paused by a hedge, now barren of blackberries, and picked at a withered leaf. He said: 'I don't know why people say autumn is beautiful, do you? I have always hated it.'

'Why so?'

'It's the dead season. Just look around you, Sarah. The entire natural world is either dying or dead.'

Sarah shivered with the chill as she gazed around her. The day was grey and cheerless, stretching far and desolate. The stately oaks had lost their summer green foliage and now stood almost leafless. It was so that he saw the world today, faced with death, and seeing it reflected all around him. Unhappily, she understood his sadness, but not trusting herself to express the words adequately she simply reached out and touched his arm.

His eyes moved over her face, then to the auburn hair which no longer hung undressed, but fell in gathered ringlets down each cheek. He had known young ladies in France, charming young ladies, but time had never diminished the image he carried in his mind of a certain young mademoiselle, back in Ireland.

Then he saw that she was shivering and took her elbow,

leading her on and around a large fallen branch in their path. They walked the rest of the way in silence and turned into the leafy lane where the evergreens stood undefeated. At the orchard door Sarah faced him.

'Would you care to come in for some refreshment?'

'No, thank you.'

There seemed nothing else for them to say. Then he said: 'I look forward to seeing you again, soon. Richard has already invited me over.'

She looked at him, still shivering, but her thoughts had turned – there was still something dark and magnetic in the other's eyes, and the attraction was still there. Then her thoughts turned again, and there was a very tender note in her voice when she said: 'I am sorry about your father, Robert. He was a kind man, and always so to me.'

'And to me.'

He reached a hand to the iron latch, and opened the orchard door for her.

'Goodbye,' she said.

'*Au revoir,*' he answered softly, as she disappeared through the door.

It had been a strange meeting, Robert thought, as he walked over the fields in the direction of Casino, nothing at all like he had envisaged whenever he had allowed his imagination to dwell on seeing her again.

He jumped over a ditch then stood for a moment gazing about him. It had been a strange day! First an ending – a spasm of pain flitted across his face – then a beginning.

He walked on. A beginning?

Maybe.

259

Chapter Twenty-One

Christmas Eve and everything was ready. A turkey was roasting on a spit over the fire, slowly changing from pink to gold. A leg of ham which had been smoked the day before now hung from a hook in the ceiling beam. The plum pudding which had been stirred for the required three hours was steaming in a pot craned above the fire.

Mary Devlin sat by the long table putting the finishing touches to the three blue cloaks she had made from the roll of woolcloth her father had brought back from Dublin. 'There now,' she said, holding up a cloak. 'We may not be gentry, but people will think we are tomorrow.'

From where she sat on the settle, Anne fired a contemptuous sniff at her sister. 'And what's so great about the gentry?'

'Well I wouldn't mind looking like them,' Mary said. 'All those lovely satins and silks! God, I'd be in my element.'

'Satins and silks, if you please!' Anne scoffed.

'Ah, Mammy, tell her!' Mary cried. 'She always goes at me when I speak of the quality. 'Tis not fair!'

Mrs Devlin looked long at her eldest daughter. Mary had none of Anne's dark fire in her looks, tall and straight with long brown hair that only sported a curl after she had knotted it with linen strips before retiring to bed. A body would never believe she was twenty-three and a year older than Anne. Always dreaming of fancy things and saying as how she would love to look like a lady. At least Anne's head was down on her shoulders, but Mary! Mary had the longest neck in Ireland, so high was her head above the clouds.

'I learnt all about the well-born when I worked those months in the big house in Inchicore,' Anne said. 'Quality inagh!'

'Some of the gentry are nice,' Mary insisted.

'How would you know?' Anne asked. 'You've only seen them from the road.'

'Oh, for the love of God!' cried Mrs Devlin. 'Why is it that whenever you two argue it's always about the blasted gentry? Now come on, Anne, get the tub in front of the fire for the bathing. We all have to be scrubbed pink for Christmas morning.'

Brian Devlin walked into the kitchen with Nellie and Jimmy shouting beside him in a babble of nervous excitement.

'You two! Get ready for the tub,' Mrs Devlin ordered.

'Will you hush for a minute, woman,' said Brian Devlin. 'The childer are telling me something. Now, a man in uniform you say?'

'Aye, Da!' said Nellie. 'And asking for Brian Devlin, but we said we'd never heard tell of that name. They're not going to take you away again, are they, Da?'

'No, child. What kind of uniform?'

Nellie was not sure.

'Sailor's uniform,' Jimmy said.

The sailor was sitting on a boulder by the road, his head in his hands and his back to the house. 'Holy Mother!' cried Brian Devlin. 'Would you look at that mop of red hair? 'Tis me brother's son!'

The sailor turned at the sound of the voice, stared at Brian Devlin, then gave a yelp and jumped into the air.

'Big Art!' Anne cried, racing towards her cousin. 'Oh, is it really you?'

'Aye, 'tis me all right,' Big Arthur Devlin laughed, 'and glad I am that I found you at last. I've tramped it all the way from Wicklow in the cold.'

The sailor was hugged by everyone except Nellie and Jimmy. Big Arthur pulled a sugar bar from his pocket, broke it in half and handed a piece to each. 'Musha!' he said. 'No wonder you didn't know me. Weren't you both little childybawns when you last seen me?'

Jimmy gave him a scrutinising stare. 'You look a bit like Little Arthur.'

'Aye, and that's why they call me Big Arthur. Sure when your brother was only baptised, wasn't I as big as yourself?'

Being the baby of the family, and now eight years old and not too tall, Jimmy's face beamed at this reference to his height. A cart pulled into the yard and the driver gave a loud shout. 'Well, damn my eyes! Is it Big Art?'

Little Arthur sprang down from the bench. Within seconds the two cousins were hugging each other and drawing back their heads and laughing.

'I can't believe 'tis the same cousin I left behind,' Big Arthur said. 'Sure you could have a peep over a cloud the size you've grown.'

Little Arthur shot a smug look at Anne before turning a smiling face back to his cousin. 'Aw, 'tis great to see you, man! Come in to the fire and let's hear all your news.'

'We will escort Big Art inside,' Brian Devlin said sternly to his son. 'You see to the horse and cart first.'

'Aye, I will, Da,' Little Arthur cried excitedly. 'I will that.'

The ham was taken down and sliced for the evening meal. When the plates had been cleared away, Mrs Devlin placed a pot of tea on the table, as well as two glasses and a bottle of poteen before her husband.

'Now tell us, Big Art,' she said. 'We knew you had left Michael and the mountains, but why did you have to go and join the British fleet? I don't think your da would have liked it, God rest Pat's soul.'

'Sure I never did join the fleet, Winnie. I won this uniform last week playing cards. I thought 'twould make a good disguise while I searched Wicklow for my cousins.'

'But why do you need a disguise?'

'I'm a deserter from the British army.'

'What?' Anne turned startled. 'You left Michael Dwyer fighting in the mountains and signed up for the King's shilling and a red coat!'

'Oh, 'tis easy to see you've not lost your temper, Anne Devlin! But before your tongue lambasts me further, let me tell you, 'twas Michael Dwyer himself who suggested I join the army.'

'And what was his thinking in that?'

'He thought I was useless with a gun,' Big Arthur smiled. 'No, the truth is that some of us found life as rebel fugitives on the mountains a bit tough, especially in the freezing winter. And there were others like me, whose homes had been burned down by the militia. We couldn't stick it on the mountains, we had no homes to go to, and we thought surrender was the only alternative, until Michael suggested a better one.'

Big Art then explained how he and twenty other Wicklow

262

rebels had joined the regular army using false names, and were sent to the south of England.

Big Art smiled. 'Model soldiers we were.'

Brian Devlin drew on his pipe and blew a circle of smoke in the air. 'So why have you deserted now?'

' 'Twas where we were stationed in England, in Southampton. We met a party of Irishmen returning from France. One of them was a Mr Emmet. Oh, just hearing them talk made me homesick. The heart was pulling out of me.'

Mrs Devlin looked puzzled. 'Is it Thomas Emmet you're talking about? The famous United Irishman who was exiled? Sure he could never return here.'

'It was his younger brother, Robert Emmet. They were sitting at the back of a tavern and talking Frenchie. I heard the word *Irlande* a few times and I knew what that meant, right enough. Then I heard one of them call this dark young man, Emmet, and I knew that name, too. So we got talking to them, and when Mr Emmet heard I was a cousin to Michael Dwyer, he bade me sit next to him and asked me questions about Michael. Oh, he was full of admiration for his defiance and skill in evading capture. Ach, he's a fine man entirely is Robert Emmet. He don't speak long or loud, but when he does, you listen.'

Mary pushed a strand of hair behind her ear and moved forward on her chair. 'Big Art, isn't Mr Emmet one of the gentry?'

'Aye, he is.'

Anne couldn't be bothered to get annoyed with Mary's obsession with the gentry.

'And what was he like?' Mary asked. 'Did he wear the tight cream nankeen breeches most of them are wearing?'

Big Art threw back his head and laughed. 'Well, I'll tell you, Mary, 'twas black whipcord breeches he wore, with high boots that would cost a soldier two months' pay.'

'Mary! Will you shut up owa that!' Mrs Devlin snapped. ' 'Tis not the man's cloth we want to hear about. Go on, Big Art, if ye've nothing else to tell, tell us of Mr Emmet.'

'There's little more to tell, except, after he'd gone, a number of us got to talking. Then we deserted and followed him over here.'

Brian Devlin took the pipe from his mouth. 'Why did you do that?'

Big Arthur made a face. 'I don't know just why. But when Emmet talked, he talked true.'

'Is there something in the air?'

'There is, Brian.' Big Arthur grinned slyly. 'Sure now, isn't Christmas in the air?'

'And you lot have not seen the tub,' said Mrs Devlin to the children. 'Into the parlour now.'

'Ah, Mammy!' Jimmy groaned. 'There's no fire in the parlour.'

'There will be in a few minutes.'

Big Arthur topped up his glass with poteen and watched Anne as she stood staring thoughtfully into the fire. She had grown into a fine-looking maid. 'Twas a puzzle to find she'd not been snapped up by some lusty farmer.

Anne turned and met his eyes, her own eyes shining with a startling brilliance. 'There is something in the air, Big Art,' she said, 'and it's not only Christmas, is it?'

A guilty flush darkened her cousin's freckled face. 'You'll have to wait and see, Anne acree,' he said. 'Who knows what the New Year will bring?'

The New Year brought two weeks of unseasonal mild weather and a winter sun that shadowed the shrubby face of the Dublin mountains. Only a mile from The Priory, in the Yellow House tavern, James Hope sat alone drinking a jug of porter. Nobody paid much attention to the fair-haired man sitting in the corner. They knew him to be a weaver who now and then popped in for a jar whenever he delivered cloth to one of the big houses in Rathfarnham. They also knew from his accent that he was an Ulsterman.

James Hope looked around the tavern; three men sat round a barrel playing cards; two more were having a heated discussion with the tapman by the fireplace. He chose that moment to take the letter from his pocket and read it again.

> If you are up – by the edge of Harold's Cross Green
> tonight at six, you will meet a friend.

'Who do you think it can be from?' he asked his wife, Rose, as he sat down that evening to a plate of mutton stew.

Rose moved her stool a little closer to the fire and changed the baby to her left breast. 'You've been asking that question since the letter dropped in this morning, Jemmy. I'm as ignorant as yourself, but you'll be wise soon enough. The letter said six, did it not?'

'Aye, six. On the edge of the Harold's Cross Green. I wonder why there?'

Rose pushed a lock of red hair behind her ear, her blue eyes straying to the clock on the dresser which said five after five. She had been asking herself the same questions all day and the wondering was driving her demented.

Jemmy Hope reckoned it was not quite six when he approached Harold's Cross. The street-lamps were aglow but the Green was deserted. He stood peering around him for a number of minutes, then wandered over to sit on a wall by a clump of trees.

He was telling himself for the tenth time that he was a right eejit to pay heed to a letter with no name at its end, but that very thing had been the bait – it was like the letters he used to get in the old days – and did it not even use the word of the United Irish? 'If you are *up*?'

His body stiffened alert as he saw the figure of a man strolling across the green; a young and sprightly man, his black greatcoat hanging open over black boots.

'Do I know you?' he called warily as the figure approached.

'You should know I,' the young man answered.

Jemmy's face moved into a smile. There it was – 'You and I' – the greeting of the United Irish.

The moon had risen but Jemmy had to wait until the young man was almost upon him before he recognised the face, then gave a cry of surprise, 'Well damn my eyes, if it isn't young Emmet!'

Robert was smiling too as he clasped the proffered hand. 'Hello, Jemmy.'

'When did you get back? I never heard a word. And why did you choose here of all places?'

Robert sat down on the wall next to Hope. 'I have entered

the leather trade, Jemmy, with John Patten, the brother of my sister-in-law Jane. We have taken over a tannery in the Liberties. If I have business in town I occasionally lodge at the house of Mrs Palmer across the Green.'

'Mrs Palmer? I hear she's a grand woman.'

'Yes. One of ourselves.'

'Now that I didn't hear.'

'I bring you news from a friend, Jemmy.'

Jemmy stared at him. 'Not . . .'

Robert smiled. 'Yes, from the devil-may-care exile.'

A lump came into Jemmy Hope's throat as he thought of his much-loved friend from the old days. God! There was many a night when he longed for just an hour or two in his company over a jar. An hour with a friend was better than a lifetime with a host of acquaintances. And Tom Russell was the best friend Jemmy ever had.

They talked about Russell: right back to the days when he had given up his commission as an officer in the British army; of the many times Jemmy, Russell, McCracken, and Tone had enjoyed up in Ulster. And as they talked, Jemmy assessingly eyed Robert Emmet. He must be twenty-five or -six now, about ten years younger than himself, he reckoned. He'd been just a youth when he had last seen him, but he was the brother of Thomas Emmet, and in '98 Lord Edward had trusted him to be his personal confidant.

'What does Russell say? I wouldn't have thought he had time to remember Jemmy Hope with all those French women to occupy his mind.'

'He remembers you well and often, Jemmy, and his mind was not on women when I last spoke to him. He bade me to ask you a question.'

'Aye?'

'Are the fires of ninety-eight still burning? Or has the Union stamped them out?'

Now Jemmy turned his head and openly scrutinised Emmet's face. It was still fresh enough, but there was an unwavering directness in the dark eyes which Jemmy liked.

'No, Robert Emmet, the fires of ninety-eight are no longer burning.' Jemmy turned away and stared across the Green.

'But they are not out! They're just smouldering, waiting for a fresh wind to blow them into flame again.'

Robert smiled. 'Russell will be pleased to hear that.'

'And what good will his pleasure do him?' Jemmy cried. 'Russell was never happy unless he was in the field. But 'tis French fields he'll march through now, for it'll be a trip up the long ladder and down the short rope if he ever came back here.' He shrugged. 'No, as far as Ireland is concerned, Tom Russell can only ever be a spectator from now on.'

Robert placed a hand on Jemmy's shoulder. 'I would not be too sure about that, my friend.'

The following night Robert was at The Priory enjoying a musical evening. He paid little attention to the other guests, preferring to sit quietly and watch Sarah who was getting ready to play her harp.

A hushed silence fell on the room as she placed her fingers on the strings. The candelabrum which stood on the fortepiano behind her threw a soft glow over her lovely face, highlighting the golden glints of her auburn hair. And then, like the fluttering of a gentle bird, her hands moved over the strings and the exquisitely beautiful strains of 'Eileen A Roon' drifted through the candlelit room.

Robert watched her with a fascinated intentness, she looked totally lost to everything but the music, her eyes dreamy and darkly dilated with some undefined pleasure that was finding expression beneath her fingertips. He recalled her once telling him, 'If nothing else, I have my harp. I would *die* without my harp.'

The lilting notes of 'Eileen A Roon' ended. The guests called for more, and this time they demanded that she sing. Sarah smiled shyly, but it was plain she was delighted with the attention. She moved her fingers over the strings again, then in a soft pure voice began 'The Song of Conary More'.

Robert turned his head to lift his brandy from the small satinwood table at his side, reflecting bleakly that she had given him no real signs of encouragement, no little hint that she might feel anything more for him than mere friendship. He paused in the act of lifting the glass, and instead lifted the music book which lay near the edge, bearing in bold print the name of 'Miss Sarah Curran' and underneath in a proud but dainty hand, *l'Académie de Celbridge*.

He smiled: so typical of her to use the French form. She had spoken to him earlier in the evening, almost boastingly, about her year attending the Academy in 1799.

Absently he opened the book and saw a number of sketches drawn on the flyleaf. There was a facial sketch of a lady which underneath bore the initials 'AC'. He glanced over at Amelia, deciding it to be a very flattering sketch, for in all kindness but truth, Sarah's sister was as plain as a blade of grass.

There was a larger sketch in the centre of the page of a girl in a long sweeping gown which was unmistakably Sarah. Then, in the bottom corner of the page, he noticed a head-and-shoulder profile of a man. He peered closer, and as he did, his eyes widened. Underneath the profile she had pencilled the initials R.E. And again underneath, she had written R.E. a number of times.

R.E.
R.E.
R.E.

He looked up from the book and stared at the girl playing the harp. The initials were his, they had to be! A slow unconscious smile spread right over his features.

All the time Robert had been watching Sarah, John Curran had been watching Robert, a smouldering anger burning inside him. Now he understood why Emmet had been visiting The Priory more than his friendship with Richard justified. Now he understood why Emmet disturbed him more and more as the days went by. From his very first visit since his return, and by small indications which had not escaped his own skilful observation, he had suspected that Emmet was actuated by some strong passion which it was lately costing him a perpetual effort to conceal.

John Curran looked at Sarah. And now he knew what that passion was. Well, he could do nothing about Richard's attachment to Emmet, but allow his youngest daughter to become enamoured of a listed rebel? Never! Like his brother, Robert Emmet was a political reformer, would always be associated with radical groups, always trying to achieve the impossible, and the end was always the same – personal ruin.

Painfully, his gaze moved over his daughter, an emotionally unstable and immature girl. Oh, but she was lovely! Any man would be proud to have such a daughter, and he *was* proud, but whenever she turned those big dark-blue eyes on him, a brooding melancholy possessed him until he had to brush her aside and shake it off.

Damn, damn, damn! If only Sarah had not turned out to be the image of her rotten slut of a mother.

At last it was over, but the guests took a good half-hour to drift out of the drawing-room and into the hall, their voices high and merry as they said their farewells. Sarah was the last to leave the room, having stayed behind to gather up the music sheets and place them neatly inside the piano stool.

When she entered the hall she was surprised to find it empty, the front door open, and the sound of carriages trundling down the drive. A shaft of light came from under her father's study door which was firmly closed. She looked towards the open front door again. She had scarcely expected the McNallys to wait and say farewell to her, but Lord and Lady Kilwarden . . . and R.E. The winter night air blew coldly into the hall and she suddenly understood their haste. She shivered, about to turn back into the warm drawing-room when she heard the sound of hurried feet on the front steps.

She glanced over her shoulder, expecting to see Keegan. But it was Robert who stepped into the hall and walked towards her.

'Sarah,' he said quietly, 'I have something to ask you.'

She made a slight puzzled movement with her head. 'Where is Keegan?' she asked.

'Employed in a heated discussion with my driver and Richard.'

'About what?'

'Hurling,' he replied. Then, after a pause, the words at last came out in a rush. 'Sarah, I am considering asking your father for his permission to court you. How . . . how would you feel about it?'

269

It was not how he had meant to say it and inwardly he cursed his gaucheness.

'Would it please or displease you?' he said quickly. 'I won't approach him if you would rather I didn't.'

Sarah's eyes were fixed for a long agonising moment on the hat he held in his hands, then she raised her eyes, an expression of clear delight on her face. 'It would please me very much,' she said.

He felt weak with the relief. They smiled together.

'When?' he asked. 'When would be the best time for me to speak to him? Tonight or tomorrow?'

'Tomorrow, I think. He's usually in a good mood before his Saturday evenings in town.'

Keegan's voice rang down the hall. 'Mr Emmet, would you be good enough to ask that man of yours to keep his voice down and stop lecturing poor Mr Richard about hurling. To hear him talk anyone would think he invented the game.'

Robert smiled at Sarah. 'Tomorrow then?'

'About three o'clock is the best time,' she whispered.

'Three o'clock,' he repeated, then turned and nodded at Keegan before moving down the hall and front steps to where Richard was standing by the open carriage door, grinning up at a chattering Lennard.

As he climbed inside the carriage, Richard said: 'Will you be playing in the hurling match at Donnybrook on Sunday?'

'Yes – but not in your team.'

Richard laughed. 'Then you can be sure to lose, Master Emmet.' He closed the carriage door and stepped back. 'See you on Sunday.'

'And remember what I told ye,' Lennard shouted down to Richard. 'If ye follow my tips and do like the Tipperary Shinsmashers, ye'll win no bother.'

For the third time Sarah poked her head outside the orchard door. Still no sign of him! She stepped out and began to walk quickly down the lane. At the turn-off to the fields she saw the cloaked figure and black horse cantering towards her. She waved, then ran over to a tree and stood waiting under its branches. Robert rode up to her and drew rein, his eyebrow raised in mute query as he dismounted.

'It's after three,' she said. 'I thought you were never coming.'

'Why? Is something wrong?'

'There's no point in calling on Papa,' she told him bluntly. 'He says you're not to be made welcome at The Priory again.'

'What?' Confusion washed over Robert's face. 'Why?'

'I can't imagine! This morning he was in a devil's fury and called us all into the drawing-room. He said there would be no more social gatherings at The Priory, and in future . . . any welcome to you must cease.'

Robert passed a hand across his eyes, questions whirling chaotically through his mind as he stood there, speechless.

'It doesn't make sense,' Sarah said. 'All your trouble with the Castle is over now, so it can't be that.' She glanced nervously over her shoulder. 'I have only a few minutes. Amelia and I are going into Dublin. She has an appointment with the dress-maker at four.'

As the moments passed Robert appeared to retreat into him-self. 'Then all that remains for me to do,' he said in a with-drawn voice, 'is to renounce my former approach to you, Sarah.'

'I'll soon be twenty-one!' she said mutinously. 'Past the age of his consent as to whom I am friendly with. I'm tired of him always treating me like a child. He always treats me like a child! And look what he did to poor Amelia. She's twenty-seven and Reverend Harding was her first and last hope of getting away from that house. Now all she has is her painting, nothing else, nothing else!'

'You know you could not openly defy him,' he said quietly. 'As long as you are maintained in his house, he will expect you to abide by his rules.'

'No, I could never openly defy him,' she finally got out, disappointment choking her. 'Oh, Robert, I've *never* been dancing! And I was so looking forward to going dancing at the Rotunda. You would have taken me to the Rotunda, wouldn't you?'

'If it would have pleased you.' He sighed. 'But it's all in the wind now.'

The silence that followed was broken by the sound of the village church bells in the distance, ringing out the half-hour.

271

'Amelia will be raising the demons,' she whispered. 'I'd better go.'

'Yes.'

She stared at him for a moment, eyes faintly surprised and hurt; then turned away swiftly, tramping furiously over the grass and into the lane. So that was that, she thought. Well, that would teach her! She could have simply sent him a note informing him of the altered circumstances. Or allowed him to arrive at The Priory and face her father's wrath. And he *knew* that. But after his initial surprise, not a sign of regret or disappointment, not a hint, not a flicker.

The resentment she had worked up against her father was now turned on R.E. She repeated his words in a sneering tone inside her head. '*Then all that remains is for me to renounce my approach to you, Sarah.*' No utterances of regret. No declarations of a broken heart. No offer to kill himself. She marched towards the orchard door muttering soundlessly, 'Well as Mrs Jessop would say, bad cess to him, *bad rotten cess to him!*'

Lost in her anger and humiliation she didn't hear him behind her on the soft path until his hand caught her arm. She stumbled around and stared at him.

'Sarah . . . could I see you anyway?'

She smiled unsteadily, feeling an enormous relief. 'You mean . . . go against Papa's orders?'

'Well, yes, I suppose so.'

'Meet without his knowledge?'

'If that's the way it has to be.'

'That's the only way it can be . . . at the moment.' An impish smile had lit up her face.

'We won't be able to go to the Rotunda,' he said warningly. 'Or any of the fashionable dining houses.'

Sarah hesitated, still desperately disappointed about not being able to dance at the Rotunda. 'It doesn't matter,' she decided. 'When Papa gets over his mood and changes his mind we can go to those places. But we will have to meet in daytime – when Papa is in chambers. Will you be able to get away from your business?'

'Yes,' he said, 'but I shall still give you a week to consider. Next Friday, I shall come here to the lane. I will wait an hour, until noon. If you have not appeared by then, I will know you have changed your mind.'

She nodded. 'Very well – but I won't have changed my mind,' she assured him.

Robert could not move. He wanted to touch her, touch her lips, seal their secret pledge with a kiss on the mouth like lovers, but for a man to kiss a girl he was not officially courting was against every expectation of a gentleman, in Ireland anyway.

The orchard door creaked open behind them and Mrs Jessop's fat face popped out, her cap-ribbons dancing with agitation. 'Miss Sarah acquanie ... Miss Amelia is going ma—'

'Yes, yes, Mrs Jessop,' Sarah snapped, waving the housekeeper back inside. 'I'm coming now!'

Mrs Jessop peered suspiciously at Robert, then at Sarah, then back and forth at the two of them. 'Lord's my life,' she whispered, in sudden understanding, 'sure it's as plain to me now as that summer evening when my Malachi came strolling by and I milking the cows in the field.'

'Mrs Jessop!' Sarah moaned.

'Aye, that's me name,' Mrs Jessop said, and grudgingly shut the door. As soon as the cap-ribbons had disappeared, Sarah turned back.

'Next Friday,' she said.

'I'll wait from eleven until noon,' he reminded her.

She nodded, then without any more preamble she put a hand to his shoulder and leaned to kiss him on the lips.

He might well have been surprised. Peering through a crack in the door, Mrs Jessop let out a gasp as she watched young mouth touch young mouth, only for seconds, before Sarah turned and fled from her own daring initiative, banging clumsily through the orchard door and sending the unknown presence of Mrs Jessop tumbling into the empty flower bed along the inside wall.

Robert was smiling with delight as he watched Sarah vanish through the orchard. Her lips had been cool and soft, and with them she had sealed a relationship that had no authority to begin, and nothing would prevent from continuing.

Some seconds later the bulky figure of the housekeeper

staggered into view, her cap askew and rubbing her rear. 'For the love av God,' she whispered in a daze.

Then regaining her breath and senses, 'Why is it whenever you happen along I get put down one way or another!' She pushed at her cap. 'Well, I'll have no hand or part in it,' she warned him. 'I'll not be a party to her secret meetings with ye. Not even if she does come and curl up on me bed counter,' she added, moving away stiffly.

Still smiling, Robert turned back down the lane, wondering if he had ever been happier than he was now. Then he remembered his horse that he had left untethered in the sudden dash after her. He started to run, and found Black Seamus where he had left him, happily cropping the grass, reins hanging loose.

On the ride home he sobered his thoughts and began to think curiously about her father's sudden objection to him. It couldn't be because of his politics. John Curran might never have been a rebel by actions, but he had certainly been a most prominent rebel with words – battering, mocking words that had embarrassed and outraged the Castle time and time again. And how many times in court had he defended the United Irishmen?

He wondered if Richard knew the reason. If Richard did, then Richard would tell him. And then, he decided, he would work out a way to rectify the problem and somehow persuade her father to agree to the match.

Richard's right leg was sorely bruised after the Sunday hurling match. The scent of leather from the bookshelves around the walls of the Casino library had a pleasing effect on his nostrils as he sat sipping brandy, his eyes fixed intently on Robert's face.

Robert was lounging in one of the green leather chairs, his head resting back. He appeared to be silently examining every inch of the ceiling panels as he considered Richard's explanation.

'You must understand,' Richard said, 'that he is a bitterly disappointed man. He sacrificed a great deal defending the United Irishmen.'

'That never mattered to him before.'

274

'True. I think he just got tired of always fighting on the losing side.'

Robert sighed. 'My brother would never believe what you have just said. Not of John Philpot Curran.'

'John Philpot Curran is on his own side now,' Richard said quietly. 'Dedicating himself to his career. His ambition now is the bench, and then hopefully, Lord Chief Justice.'

'And he doesn't want anyone shaking his ladder.' Robert's voice was a shade derisive.

'He is convinced you could be politically dangerous to his career and mine. You will always be the younger brother of the rebel Thomas Emmet, and he doesn't believe the Castle will ever forget that.'

After a silence Richard shifted uncomfortably in his seat. 'There is something else . . . It seems that on Friday night, during the musical evening, he detected something in your manner towards Sarah. He states emphatically that he does not wish your present acquaintance with her to ripen into a greater degree of intimacy.'

Robert stared at him. 'Does Sarah know that?'

'No, he spoke of it to me after the girls had left the room.'

'And that is the true reason he has withdrawn my welcome,' Robert said, suddenly angry. 'To prevent my seeing Sarah.'

'I believe it is. What will you do?'

Robert fixed his eyes on the glass in his hand. He had no wish to deceive Sarah's father, but what else he could do? He *had* to see her again.

'Is there any point in my attempting to discuss the matter with him?'

Richard shook his head. 'Not yet. He's not to be reasoned with at the present. But once you have settled down into your tannery business . . .' Richard coloured slightly, still embarrassed that his friend was reduced to trade, 'and . . . and once he sees you are posing no political threat to his or my career, then he will reconsider. You see, my dear Robert, you must prove to him that you have put the United Irish behind you. Show him you are concerned only with leather – not liberty.'

A slight twist to his mouth, Robert changed the subject. 'Will you stay for dinner?'

Richard relaxed, glad the subject had been broached and now over. 'I'd be delighted.'

'But are you quite sure, my dear Richard, that your father would not object?'

'Makes no difference if he does,' Richard answered, ignoring the sarcasm. 'I made it very clear to him yesterday – he can keep my oldest and dearest friend away from The Priory for the sake of our precious careers, but that is *all* I would agree to.'

Robert smiled. 'A noble and loyal sentiment, especially for a man whose team have just been well and truly massacred at hurling.'

'Damme you, Emmet,' Richard muttered with a scowl, not at all amused.

Chapter Twenty-Two

Miles Byrne stood by the office window above a builder's yard in New Street and watched the people battling along in the cold January wind. He was a tall, fair-haired young man with clean-cut features; from under thick flaxen lashes his blue eyes looked thoughtful.

The Dublin streets, which had once seemed so alien to Miles, were now almost as familiar to him as his home in Wexford, the home to which he had not been able to return after the 1798 rebellion. The dream of liberty was dead now, but not for him, never for him. He had seen too many of his friends die on Vinegar Hill.

But, for him at least, life went on; and so he had endeavoured to fit into the normal run of city social life, as partial to the company of a pretty girl as any other young man.

He suddenly remembered, with embarrassment, a night in March last spring, one week after the news of the Treaty of Amiens. He had been invited to dine with a Mr and Mrs Byrne of Townsend Street. After dinner they had asked him to accompany their niece, a Miss Lawless, to see the illuminations throughout Dublin. The illuminations angered Miles, but he decided he could not repay the couple's kindness by refusing.

Miss Lawless had been a sprightly girl who took great pains to show him all the public buildings blazing with light, but throughout their journey his heart was sick. The gay lights represented only one thing to him – the French allies had made peace with the enemy.

Miss Lawless had smiled and chattered, but he was cast down and dull; his spirit sunk, hopes gone. She then quipped that she was sorry to see the rejoicings did not amuse him overmuch, and he felt ashamed of his behaviour and offered her refreshment; but as soon as it was decently possible, he took his leave of her. He had never cared much for drinking to excess, but that night he went home and drank himself numb by the kitchen fire until the dawn. The Peace of Amiens inagh!

'A good morning to you, Miles!'

He turned from the window as Phineas Norris, a young man expelled from Trinity College in '98, and who now worked at John Patten's nearby tannery, entered the room.

'What has you out so early?' Miles asked. 'On such a bad morning, too.'

Norris grinned as he turned down his coat collar. 'Do you remember that long conversation we had about Mr Patten's relations, the Emmets?'

'Aye.'

'Would you like to meet the younger brother, Robert Emmet? The one recently returned from France.'

Miles gave a cynical little smile. He was a farmer's son, his youth spent sweating in cornfields, not browsing in college rooms.

'We hardly mix in the same social circles,' he said wryly. 'How could I meet him?'

Norris grinned. 'Emmet asked me the same question about you, Miles.'

The meeting took place that afternoon in the offices of the Emmet and Patten establishment on Thomas Street. Miles was immediately struck by the reserved, unaffected manners of Emmet; and then later by those dark, dark eyes which could be either warm or penetrating in an instant.

Miles positioned himself comfortably in a chair by the fire, but Emmet sat perched on the edge of his desk. They talked for some minutes about the defeat of Wexford five years previously, the dreadful consequences on the people of that county; and while they did, they weighed each other up.

Miles only knew what everyone else knew about the Emmets, and that mostly about Thomas Emmet, except for the little Norris had told him about the younger brother expelled with himself from Trinity.

But if Miles knew little about Emmet, Emmet knew all about Miles Byrne: twenty-three years old and a Catholic, the son of a Wexford farmer; educated by one of the secret band of scholastic priests; and in 1798, although only eighteen considered such a crack soldier by the United Irish that, like Michael Dwyer in Wicklow, he had been ranked up to captain before he had even reached Vinegar Hill.

Following the rebellion he had spent a period in the Wicklow Mountains with the intrepid Michael Dwyer, waiting for the French. But after that failure he had made his way to Dublin to seek lodgings with his stepbrother, Edward Kennedy, who had readily taken him in and given him employment in his small building firm. Here Miles had spent the first twelve months working diligently as a book-keeper from Tuesday to Saturday. On Sundays and Mondays he was forced to remain concealed in the house in order to avoid the Wexford and Wicklow militia who generally searched the streets for rebels on those days. He had been in Dublin just over a year when he was at last informed that the hunt for Wexford rebels in the capital had ceased.

Emmet had no doubts that Miles Byrne could be trusted. He came straight to the point and explained the reason for the meeting.

When he had finished, Miles was staring incredulously at him.

'Another thrust?'

'Yes.'

'Why?' Miles asked directly. 'Why now?'

278

'If Lord Edward and his associates felt justified in seeking to take the field,' Emmet said, 'what must be our justification now – now that we are left with not a vestige of self-government in consequence of the Union?'

'The Union!' Miles almost spat the words.

'Until that took place,' Robert went on, 'from time to time, and in spite of corruption, useful local laws were enacted here in Ireland. Now the three hundred seats of the Irish Home Parliament are reduced to one hundred at Westminster. And that hundred go there on behalf of only *one-eighth* of the population – to further the interests of only *one-eighth* of the population, while the remaining majority are given no voice, and have no right under constitutional law to send a member of their body to represent them in the British Parliament.'

'You speak like a politician,' observed Miles.

'No, I speak the truth.'

'You belong to that privileged one-eighth,' Miles reminded him. 'What do you hope to get out of all this?'

'Our own free parliament. One which is democratically elected and freely returned by the people it is supposed to serve.'

Miles sat back in his chair. 'I once heard another man speak like you,' he said quietly. 'He was not a politician either. He was a Bostonian. One of the original Sons of Liberty, or so he said.'

If Emmet was surprised by Byrne's outward lack of enthusiasm, it did not show on his face. 'The Americans won – in the end,' he said.

'And if you get your free parliament,' Miles asked, 'what will I get?'

'What you fought for in ninety-eight.'

'Survival?'

'Justice.'

'Justice!' Miles made a *moue* of cynical disbelief. 'And will that justice include the abolishment of church tithes? My father worked his back crooked to make a tolerable living, but part of his sweat had to go in tithes to the overfed parson. Will your Protestant friends in the free parliament abolish those?'

'Church tithes, I imagine, would be the first thing to be

abolished. The fairest system is that employed in America – each man is free to abide by the religion of his conscience, and pays his own pastor.'

'My God, you do have it all worked out . . .' Miles stared at him. 'I think you really do intend to organise an insurrection!'

Emmet frowned. 'You doubted me?'

'Ach,' Miles shrugged. 'I've met others who organised meetings and talked about rights and rebellion, but when it came to the reality of battle, they were nowhere to be found.'

He looked at Emmet curiously. Emmet had explained that he had returned to Dublin due to private and not public matters. He had received a letter in France saying that his father was seriously ill, which resulted in his urgent journey home. But within days of his father's death, communications had been made to him, supported by returns and details, which gave him assurance that the populations of seventeen counties would be prepared to act if only one successful effort were made in the metropolis. The communications had been made by men of the highest rank and distinction; men who were prepared to finance the rebellion, but they could take no actual part, and their identity must remain secret. They had asked Emmet to organise the effort in Dublin, and, after long deliberation, he had eventually agreed.

'When you say "organise",' Miles asked bluntly, 'does that mean you intend to join the fight? Or, like your investors, just procure the bullets for other men to fire?'

Emmet went very still. 'I would not ask a man to do what I was not prepared to do myself. In 1798 I swore the officer's oath of the United Irishmen. Now I have been asked by higher-ranking United Irishmen to take my place on the field of battle, and I intend to do that. I seek only to serve the interests of my country. And to that end I am resolved to risk my life.'

A silence hung in the room.

'So,' Miles said, as if to himself, 'not a politician after all, but a dedicated idealist. And even prepared to put his life on the scales.'

'Believe me,' Emmet said firmly, 'if there was any way we could ameliorate the present degraded condition of Ireland by the reforming power of reason, by political negotiation, or by constitutional agitation, I would be the first to discourage any idea of the use of arms. But we are not allowed to reason, to negotiate, or even to *protest* by freedom of speech. Castlereagh smashed the free printing press and it has never been replaced. All we have now are government-edited newspapers and journals.' He looked at Miles, his eyes cold. 'Such are the methods of unashamed oppression.'

Miles was doing his best to resist Emmet, but it was difficult. He was finding it impossible to make any objection to him. His language and reasoning all clearly came from the heart. Then Emmet began to speak of what Ireland could expect from France.

'France be damned!' Miles cried.

'Under Bonaparte? I doubt it.'

'Aye, well you'd know more about Boney than me. What is your opinion of him?'

'An egotistical little man. For our part, I would prefer Humbert in his place. But Napoleon is undoubtedly the greatest living commander in the world. A master of military strategy – even the British credit him with that. France is now governed almost solely by him. And he has promised to help us.'

'What about the Treaty of Amiens?' Miles looked perplexed. 'Boney made peace.'

'His only reason for making the peace was to gain time to rebuild his depleted supplies after his losses at Alexandria,' Emmet explained. 'Nelson knows that. Even Addington knows that. And so they, too, are taking the time to rebuild their arms and supplies. It's all a game, Miles, this false peace. Hostilities will certainly recommence shortly. It only remains to be seen which side declares war first.'

Miles could scarcely believe it. 'And Napoleon has personally agreed to help us?'

'On one condition: that the people show they are prepared and ready. He insists he will not have a repeat of General Humbert's experience in ninety-eight.'

'If the French failed in ninety-eight,' Miles said hotly, 'it was their own bloody fault! Only a thousand actually landed, and then too late – when the rebellion was over, and most of our army dead.'

Emmet could not dispute it. 'But you try to get Napoleon to accept that. I certainly couldn't. In his view, the French did not arrive too late, the Irish moved too early.'

'So why did he not send a force as soon as he heard of Lord Edward's arrest?' Miles said.

'He says he did not know about it. He was busy at Malta, sparring with Nelson.'

Emmet then explained that his brother was now the United Irish representative in Paris and had already become friends with General Humbert and the French War Minister, Berthier; as well as consulting with different members of the French government. When Miles queried the possibility of Napoleon wanting Ireland for himself, Robert shook his head.

'He has given us positive assurances that in the event of a French army landing in Ireland, it would be an auxiliary one, and they should be received as General Rochambeau and his army were received by the American people in their war for independence.'

While Miles digested this, Emmet withdrew his fob-watch, glanced at it, then looked hard at Miles as he put it away.

'I have no more time,' he said. 'I need your answer now. Will you join us?'

For the first time since the meeting began, Miles Byrne smiled, a smile that moved into a broad grin. 'I will join you,' he said. 'And there are over two hundred Wexford lads working in the city who were active under my command in ninety-eight. All would be willing to work with me again.'

'Yes,' Robert said, 'I know.'

For an instant Miles's face registered surprise; then he laughed. 'The intelligence machine is active again so. Well, Mr Emmet, what now?'

'I wish to acquaint myself with all those who escaped in ninety-eight. Men whose trust has been proved, and who still enjoy the confidence of their people.'

'And there are many,' Miles said. 'When do you intend to start?'

There was sudden smiling humour in Emmet's eyes. 'I have started already, Captain Byrne.'

* * *

Despite the thick carpet of snow that greeted the inhabitants of Dublin County on Friday morning, Sarah was punctual to her appointment at eleven. Halfway down the lane, beneath a row of evergreens, Robert and Lennard stood waiting beside a carriage which, minutes later, was trundling on its way towards the Globe Coffee House on the edge of the city.

As soon as the carriage halted in the yard behind the coffee house, Lennard scurried off to the nearest tavern, barely stopping to tip his snow-covered hat.

'The owner is a friend of mine,' Robert whispered to Sarah as they entered through a private door at the rear.

A serving maid appeared, bobbed a curtsy, then led them down the hall and showed them into a private parlour. A huge fire burned in the grate; refreshments of brandy and sweetcakes were already laid out. On the fireflag of the hearth a pot of coffee simmered aromatically.

They stayed by the fire for over three hours. Sarah insisted he tell her everything about his travels in Europe, listening so attentively she munched through five cakes and drank almost a full glass of the warming brandy without realising she had done so.

He told her about his visit to see his brother in Fort George in Scotland in 1800. It had distressed him sorely, even though Thomas and Jane seemed to be bearing their imprisonment stoically. But in the same way that the Highland regiments, of all the King's troops, had acted with the most humanity towards the Irish people in 1798, so in Fort George the Irish prisoners were treated with as much humanity as duty allowed by their Scottish guards. The Lieutenant-Governor of the prison, Sir John Stuart, had shown immeasurable kindness, allowing the Emmets many privileges once he learned that Jane was pregnant.

Sarah almost choked on a cake. 'You mean – she birthed a baby in a prison cell?'

Robert nodded, then hastily moved on to tell her of the day he had been sitting in a Paris café when Malachy Delaney gave him the news that all the Irish prisoners in Fort George had been released and put aboard a ship for Amsterdam. And how he had run excitedly down the rue de la Loi, waving to every

283

carriage that passed, and jumping over two dogs while Malachy and the dogs followed in his wake. He had set off for Amsterdam that same day, and it was only during the journey it occurred to him that the English newspapers often took weeks to reach France. Thomas could have landed already and be on his way to find him in Paris. On reaching Amsterdam he went straight to the main post office and asked the clerk if there was a letter for Mr Emmet?

The clerk pointed past his shoulder and said, 'That gentleman has just asked the same question,' and he had turned to see Thomas standing forlornly next to Jane, who was holding a baby. And beside them Thomas Russell; all three looking very much at bay.

Sarah still looked scandalised. A woman giving birth inside a gaol! And not one of the vulgars normally associated with prison life, but the very elegant Jane Emmet!

Robert smiled as he remembered the scene in the post office. 'You should have seen the faces of the *mynheers*, Sarah. They just stood and gaped at the sight of two Irishmen hugging each other and shouting for joy in the middle of the great hall. Then a little man in a uniform sidled up and discreetly informed us that in Holland, it was customary for gentlemen to *remove their hats* when they embraced.'

'Tell me about your friends in Paris?' she said.

One of the first houses Robert and been invited to in Paris was that of the Polish rebel, Tadeusz Kosciusko, now the American Ambassador. There he had met Joel and Ruth Barlow, a Yankee couple who had decided to settle and secure their fortune in France by selling Ohio land to Frenchmen, but gracious enough for all that.

The Barlows became good friends, and it was in their large hospitable house on the rue Vaugirard that Robert had met Tom Paine, the revolutionary author of *The Rights of Man*. But, unquestionably, his closest friend outside the Irish community was the house guest of the Barlows, a young American named Robert Fulton. In Fulton, he had found a friend with as deep a love of science and invention as himself. Fulton was in the process of inventing an underwater vessel which he called a torpedo diving boat. And through Fulton, Robert became friends with the famous French chemist, Vauquelin. The two had on occasion sat with Vauquelin into the small hours, discussing scientific experiments.

But Sarah was not interested in Americans or scientific experiments. The brandy was having a strangely daring effect on her tongue and with a note of impatience she asked, 'What about your other friends?'

'Which other friends?'

'The decadent French ones. Richard told me you often frequented the salon of a notorious Frenchwoman who once chased a young Irishman all over the Continent. The one Napoleon calls "an intellectual in petticoats". '

His eyes flickered in amusement. 'Germaine de Staël is considered to be one of the most interesting women in Europe.'

'And, according to Papa, rather plump.'

'Rather ugly, too, but she has an amazing intellect.'

'A bluestocking!'

'I never did see the colour of her stockings.'

At Sarah's pink-faced declaration that he should be ashamed of himself, he agreed, and reached over to where his greatcoat was draped on a chair and presented her with a long narrow package.

'I purchased this last Saturday morning, and intended to give it to you last week,' he said, ' . . . after I had spoken with your father.'

Sarah stared at the package in his hands, but kept her own tightly clasped.

'Please take it, Sarah. I chose it for you.'

She took the package and tugged carefully at the silver-paper wrapping which revealed a white velvet box. The room was dimming. A spurt from the fire sent a glow of light towards the gold Louis XVI locket and chain on a layer of white satin. The locket had a delicate lace-like framework, but Sarah's eyes were riveted on the blue flame which flashed from the diamond encrusted in its centre.

'Do you like it?'

Did she like it? Never in her life had she received such a present! Never once had she received a gift that was not *practical*. Only Mamma's gifts had ever been personal and extravagant, but that had been so long ago.

She lifted the locket and held it suspended by the chain, letting it spin slowly in order to catch again the fire's glint on the stone.

'Oh, Robert, it's lovely, lovely, thank you.' She jumped up and tripped over to the mirror above the mantel, standing on tiptoe as she fastened the locket around her neck.

He watched her as she admired herself in the glass.

'But I won't be able to wear it in front of anyone,' she said fretfully, 'especially not at home.' She frowned at herself in the mirror then sent him a sidelong glance from under her lashes. 'Not until Papa changes his mind about you.'

'If he ever does,' he said softly.

And then she was beside him again, holding his hand tightly. 'Oh, but he will, Robert. If you make him. If you work hard at your leather business and make lots of money and prove to him what a very respectable young gentleman you really are.'

He should tell her the truth now, he thought. She was risking her father's fury in order to be with him, so it was only fair that she should know everything about him now. Otherwise, later, she might feel he had betrayed her trust in him.

Her eyes smiled at him, violet blue. She was full of innocent provocation, and he saw that the mouth turned up to his was soft and lovely. He said nothing, for suddenly all he wanted to do was kiss her, as surely as she was inviting him to.

Their lips touched, soft and warm upon each other, parted and then met again more certainly. His arms slipped around her soft young body and he kissed her the way he had always wanted.

Not yet, he thought desperately, he could not tell her yet. But he knew that whatever happened, however he would sort it out, he would not risk losing her.

A week later, Robert turned in out of the cold street and whistled as he ran up the stairs to his office. It was not long after eight o'clock, and if he could get the saddles for McPhelan arranged, and then write a letter to his brother in Paris, he should be away in plenty of time to meet Sarah. And now that Thomas had managed to obtain some disclosure-wash from Robert Fulton, he could tell him at length all about the leather business, but it would be the blank lines in between which contained the real message.

He was halfway through the letter when Miles Byrne knocked and popped his head inside the door. Robert looked up and smiled. As he had to pass the timberyard every morning, he had taken to dropping in on Miles and now the two were almost friends.

Miles sat down at the desk. 'Red deal would be better than ash for the pike handles,' he said without preamble. 'Deal would be easier to get in quantity. Is that all right?'

'If you say so.'

'Another important question. Shifting thousands of pikes through the streets is going to be a problem. Do you have a solution?'

'A hardy camouflage is the obvious solution.' Robert unlocked a drawer in his desk, withdrew a sheet of paper on which a number of sketches were drawn and laid it on the desk. 'I've devised a hollow beam for the purpose of transporting the pikes from one place to another without easy detection.'

Both bending over the paper, Robert continued, 'What we will need are pieces of timber about eighteen inches wide and ten feet long. Each beam will need four sheets of timber. Three sides should be nailed together, but the fourth side – which will serve as the lid – should be screwed, not nailed. Then, if mud is carelessly splattered over the joints, no one will suspect the beams are hollow – or in this case – packed.'

Miles looked up and grinned his approval. 'It's a sweet plan,' he said. 'The timber carts can roll back and forth through the streets under the very nose of the Castle.'

'Exactly. But you have your work cut out for you in the months ahead, Miles. Do you think you can manage it?'

'Aye, the team is growing by the day. And we have plenty of time.'

'Yes,' Robert said. 'We have plenty of time.'

Chapter Twenty-Three

The snow of January and icy rains of February were followed by the cold winds of March. But everyone consoled themselves with the old and true saying that when March roars in like a lion, it usually trots out like a lamb.

And so it did.

Big Arthur Devlin had procured employment with Mr Grierson, a printer in Rathfarnham. Since he worked so close, and as the job was only afternoons, Anne had looked forward to enjoying more of her cousin's company, but his visits had been few and far between.

She now came through the kitchen to the hall to find Big Arthur standing by the parlour door whispering to her father.

'Big Art, to what do we owe this honour?' Anne said sarcastically. 'It was St Patrick's night when we last saw the back of your head.'

'He's brought company,' her father said. 'Mr Emmet.'

'Shall I ask him in, Brian?'

'That will be my privilege,' Brian Devlin told his nephew. 'And with all your whispering what will he think of the Devlins at all? Being kept out in the yard like a beggar!'

Anne followed them out to see a dark-haired young man in a blue velvet coat bending down in conversation with Nellie and Jimmy, both smiling shyly and mutely nodding their heads, not at all used to being asked questions by one of the gentry. And standing behind the stranger was the most beautiful black horse Anne had ever seen.

Her father walked over to the stranger and held out his hand. 'Brian Devlin at your service, and, if I may say so, 'tis a pleasure to have one of the brave Emmet family visit my home.'

Robert straightened with a smile and clasped the proffered hand. 'It is a pleasure to meet you too, sir.'

Mrs Devlin and Mary turned in from the roadway carrying two empty milk churns. 'This is my good wife,' said Brian Devlin. 'Winnie,' he called, 'we have the company of Mr Emmet.' He then proceeded to introduce everyone. Anne met the eyes of the stranger with cool appraisal, but Mary flushed a deep red when Robert gave her a slight bow. His face showed his surprise and embarrassment when Mary responded by curtsying to the ground.

He turned away quickly. 'Mr Devlin, I was hoping to hire one of your horses for the day.'

Brian Devlin looked over at the black horse. 'What's wrong with his majesty?'

'Hurt a fetlock, I think. He began to limp on the right fore during the journey from Casino.'

Brian Devlin moved over to the horse and ran his hand reverently over the black glossy coat then slid it down to the right fore, examining first the area at the back, then lifting the hoof.

'When was he last shod?'

'This morning.'

'Fetlock's all right. 'Tis the shoe. It's been fitted too tight and too short. No wonder he limped! I'll have him seen to if you like. You can take one of mine and his majesty will be ready for you by the morning.'

Mrs Devlin bustled forward. 'Will you come in now for some refreshment, Mr Emmet? Please do.'

When the refreshments had been served, in the parlour, Anne sat in the corner and listened silently as the conversation ranged from horses to the new men at Dublin Castle and the dismantling of the Irish Parliament. Mr Emmet appeared genuinely sympathetic as her father launched into his experiences in Wicklow Gaol.

Anne decided she liked him. He had none of the usual condescension of the gentry, and in particular she liked the way he displayed extreme deference to her da. She liked his manner with the children. Nellie seemed quite taken with him, and he with her, allowing her to stand with her small grubby hand moving silently up and down his coat sleeve. And she liked the way he turned to listen in earnest when Jimmy gave him a long rundown on the lessons he was learning from the new hedgemaster. She looked for signs of wearied strain on his face as Jimmy, wriggling with pride, gabbled on, but she had to admit there was none.

Finally, Mr Emmet rose to leave, thanking them for their hospitality.

'Any time, any time,' said Brian Devlin, 'and I'll see the horse is properly shod for you.'

Robert picked up his gloves and crop. 'Perhaps you could help me further, Mr Devlin?'

'If it is in my power, I will.'

'I'm looking to take a house in Rathfarnham. A large house, away from the main road. Have you by chance seen any vacant houses in the area?'

'Now isn't that a funny thing?' said Brian Devlin. 'There's a house just as you describe on Butterfield Lane. Aye! I was only talking about it to Winnie last night. 'Tis empty now for nigh on six months.'

'Butterfield Lane?'

'About a mile over the back fields from here. You can't see it from the road itself because it's set so far back, and there's a wall of trees in front of it. I wouldn't have known about it meself but for the childer running in there.'

'Do you know who the agent is?'

'Not offhand, no. But his handbill will be tied to one of the trees. You'll get it from that.'

When Mr Emmet took his leave, the rest of the family wandered back to their natural habitat in the kitchen, but Anne remained standing behind the curtain of the parlour window, watching with dismay as her father led the mare into the front yard. Oh no! Not the mare! She bit her lip and told herself she had a mean spirit, and wasn't it only for a day.

She waited until her da and Big Arthur had said farewells and disappeared down the lane at the side of the house, then, lifting her skirts, she ran through the parlour. He was turning the mare around when she rushed into the yard.

'Mr Emmet?'

He glanced over his shoulder. She was reaching out to touch the mare and staring up at him. 'The mare,' she said. 'She's mine.'

'I beg your pardon?'

'She's not usually hired out to the gentry,' Anne blurted, 'or anyone else for that matter. She belongs to Da, true, but she has always been considered to be mine.'

He looked down at her, recalling his earlier impression of

this dark husky girl with a haughtiness about her that had nothing to do with class. She wore a plain cotton dress, home-made, with an open neck that revealed a tanned throat. His eyes moved over the black curls cascading carelessly over her shoulders like a Rom gipsy, finally meeting the intent gaze of her green eyes.

He said: 'Perhaps your father has another horse I can use?'

'Oh no!' She had a startled expression now and her cheeks flamed. 'I didn't mean you couldn't have her! I only meant that you should take good care of her. She can be very nervous at times.'

He leaned forward and stroked the mare's neck. 'She's a fine horse. Does she have a name?'

'No.'

'No? Why not?'

'She's never had a name. She's always been the mare. Has your horse got a name?'

'Certainly – Black Seamus.'

She made a face. 'I can understand the black part.'

'Miss Devlin, I think I should ask your father for another horse.'

'No! Take her. Da wants you to have her.'

'But you don't.'

'Oh, phizz!' she said impatiently. 'I only want you to be kind with her. She doesn't like high hedges or walls or anything like that.'

The sound of the village clock striking noon made him frown suddenly. He looped the reins over one hand. 'Don't worry,' he said, pressing his knees into the mare's flanks, 'I'll take good care of her.'

Anne stared as the mare sprang into flight like a young filly: her ears pricked and her tail swooshed. Ah no! After all he had promised he was heading for the field wall! It was quite low but the mare had become too nervous even for that.

The mare cleared the wall with a foot to spare. Anne blew out a sigh of relief, then her relief turned to indignation. The mare was as bad as Mary! Some females couldn't help rising above themselves in the company of the blasted gentry!

That same night, as Anne stretched comfortably in bed, Mary twisted the last piece of hair into a curl with a strip of linen and climbed in beside her. Anne had often mused about Mary's hair being so straight when her own was as curly as Da's. She gazed drowsily over her sister's head bobbled with white linen knots, reflecting that it was a good thing for her that it had not been the other way around. For if ever a man took Mary for a wife, he'd be forgiven for thinking it was a mop lying in his bed.

'I thought Mr Emmet was nice,' Mary whispered.

'Why, because he's gentry?'

'Don't be stupid!' Mary turned over in a huff. A minute later she turned her head again and whispered, 'Did you *see* the way he bowed to me?'

Anne pretended to be asleep.

The following morning, Robert sat in the Hopes' kitchen, his eyes straying yet again to the clock on the dresser. 'What can be keeping them?' he asked Rose Hope.

'Sure they'll be here any minute now, Mr Emmet. Didn't Jemmy say about ten? 'Tis only half past. Will you have a bite of breakfast while you wait?'

Robert shook his head. 'The packet boat usually gets in to the north wall between five and nine,' he said. 'And there was a good wind last night.'

'Aye, but don't you know they'll have stopped to oil their whistles somewhere along the way. And Jemmy will be pumping Pat Gallagher for news of Russell.'

At twenty minutes to eleven, Jemmy Hope and Patrick Gallagher arrived at the house on the Coombe. Rose rushed to greet them at the door, ushering them in with a sudden gravity, quickly taking Gallagher's cloak and removing herself to the bedroom where the baby had started to wail.

Patrick Gallagher was a well-dressed '98 man who had spent the last year in Paris. He proceeded to give Robert messages from Thomas and Jane and news of other members of the Irish community.

'Russell is ready and eager to return,' Gallagher said, 'but he is badly in need of funds.'

'A messenger was dispatched to Paris a few days ago with money for him.'

'Can I ask how much?' Gallagher asked.

When Robert revealed the amount, Jemmy Hope rocked back on his stool. 'Sure he could buy Paris with that!'

'Russell can't travel on the Beresford packet as I did,' Gallagher informed Jemmy. 'He'll need to hire a vessel to bring him over, and the French smugglers are a cunning lot. They know half the Irish over there are exiles and they are now asking an exorbitant sum to smuggle them back.'

Jemmy rubbed a knuckle over his jaw. 'Then how did you travel on the packet?'

'Ah, now me,' Gallagher said, 'I'm just one of the also-rans, but Russell is a different kettle of fish. The Castle know him well – they should do – they had him in gaol for six years.'

'If the messenger got to Paris without much delay,' Robert said, 'Russell should be here by the end of April.'

'And where will he lodge?' Jemmy asked. 'He can stay here with us. 'Twould give me no greater pleasure than to have Russell back in my kitchen, like the old days.'

'No!' Robert said emphatically. 'It would not be safe for him to lodge with anyone even suspected of being a United man. Once he reaches Dublin he has been instructed to make his way to the White Bull tavern. Mrs Dillon will shield him until I have been contacted.'

'He will need a safe house,' said Gallagher.

Robert nodded. 'I'm seeing to that at the moment.'

'This Mrs Dillon,' Jemmy said, 'are you sure she can be trusted?'

'Mrs Dillon can be trusted,' Robert said. 'Her sixteen-year-old brother was hanged by Castlereagh's mob in ninety-eight.'

Michael Quigley, a lean, hollow-eyed man, stood peering through the window of his room in Corbett's Hotel on Capel Street. Quigley had been one of the Kildare captains in '98, and he, too, had just returned from Paris.

He spotted the dark-haired young man striding along the far pavement and moved to get a better look. Aye, it was the younger Emmet all right.

A few minutes later, Quigley opened the door to Robert and shook his hand vigorously. 'Did you see Gallagher?'

'I did, this morning.'

Refusing Quigley's offer of a drink, Robert sat down on the bed and listened as the Kildare man told him of the incident which had led to his return to the old country.

'I was working off and on as a brickie and a mason, but this particular day I was up a ladder setting bricks when I heard a voice behind me. "Come down from there you old reprobate of a Jacobin's tool! Your energy is needed for the building of a more worthy cause." '

Robert smiled. He didn't need to be told whose voice it was.

'I looked down,' Quigley continued, 'and there was the two of them, Tom Russell and William Hamilton. Both grinning and leaning on their canes as if they were the new French aristocracy. They took me to a café where Russell gave me money and told me I was to get back to Ireland quickly and give you as much help as possible.'

'Did Russell say when he will be coming?'

'Soon. As soon as he manages to hire a vessel.' Quigley rubbed his hand along his thigh and grinned. 'So, Mr Emmet. Here I am. What do you want me to do?'

'I want you to go back to your own county first thing tomorrow.'

'Kildare?'

'Yes. Find out how many of the ninety-eight veterans are willing to join us. Russell sent two more of your countrymen back last week. Thomas Wilde and John Mahon. They will go to Kildare with you.'

Quigley flushed slightly and swallowed. 'I'll er . . . need money, Mr Emmet.'

It was almost two o'clock and the April afternoon was soft and warm and full of the fragrance of spring. But for Robert, as he steered his horse towards the Dublin hills, his thoughts were in a turmoil of guilt over Sarah. For months they had met regularly, at least twice a week, and he was more in love with her now than he had ever been.

But just a week ago Major Sirr and some of his red rascals

had paid a late-night visit to Casino demanding to see him. He had taken the precaution of disappearing beneath the library floor, for it was not unknown for the militia to take a young gentlemen in for questioning late at night, but conveniently lose him to a press gang on the way, and he had no intention of serving involuntarily in His Majesty's Fleet. Despite the protestations that he was away from home, Sirr had searched the house, then asked his mother and sister Mary-Anne so many questions as to his activities and friends that a valise had been packed instantly in readiness to get him away to France.

Nothing had happened since. He had stayed away from the city and John Patten reported no government official had visited the tannery. Now they were coming to the conclusion that Major Sirr had called simply because he had little to do these days, and no doubt was still chagrined about Robert escaping arrest before the amnesty.

'Sure wasn't ninety-eight their hey-day,' John Patten had said. 'Rebels on every corner. But now they've nothing to do but pull in the drunks. Must be very dull for them.'

It was when Robert thought he might have to run again that he decided the time had come to face Sarah with the truth. If her fate was ever to be linked with his, she had to know the risks. How was he going to tell her though?

As he approached the hills an old man plodded in front of him, herding a small flock of sheep with the help of a black and white dog which looked as old as the man himself. The old shepherd glanced up and tipped his hat to him as he rode by.

Robert rode to the crest of a hill, then over to a clump of trees halfway down the other side. They had decided to dispense with Lennard and the carriage, preferring to take long isolated walks, or meet in a small wooded dell in a lonely area on the edge of Rathfarnham. Sarah had discovered the dell on one of her walks, and it was becoming their special meeting place. But now that her father had gone to Drogheda for four days, she had suggested a picnic on the open hills while the sunny weather lasted.

He dismounted and waited for her, standing with both hands on the saddle. He had spent the past three days being his own prosecution and defence. Had he deliberately waited until it was too late? Until he was sure she was too involved with him to judge the situation rationally? Or had he not told her because he thought he could keep the two most important things in his life apart, separate, having no influence upon each other?

He turned his head and gazed blankly around him. But could he even trust her? He had no choice, he decided. He would have to take her on blind trust and tell her. But what if she asked him to abandon his plans? He could never do that. As much as he loved her, another passion equally consumed him. The cause of his country's liberty stood paramount, he was sworn to it, and nothing but its victory would satisfy him. He had made the oath on his life.

She appeared on the crest of the hill ten minutes later carrying a basket and waving. He remained standing by the horse, watching her run down to him. 'I got held up,' she cried. 'Dr Sheridan called to see how I was—'

He hushed her with a fervent kiss, dreading it must be his last.

Sarah drew back, a smile on her face. 'Come on,' she said, 'let's eat. Mrs Jessop packed lunch for us, not supper. And if I let you have your way we would kiss until nightfall.'

He pulled a bottle of claret and a corkscrew out of his saddlebag and followed her across the sunny slope. 'Does Amelia ever wonder where you go to?' he asked.

She knelt down, lifted a linen cloth out of the basket and spread it over the grass. 'I told Amelia all about us ages ago.'

He opened the claret and sat down, his eyes fixed on her face as she began to unpack the small parcels of food. 'What did she say?'

'She was a little shocked at first, that I should go behind Papa's back, but then she raved on again about his attitude to Reverend Harding, and agreed his similar attitude towards you was very unfair.'

Robert bit his lip.

The cold meats, cheeses, and soda bread which Mrs Jessop had packed would normally have tempted him, but no matter how he tried, Robert found it impossible to stimulate his appetite. He drank two glasses of wine, hoping its drowsy effect would unwind the tight coil of dread in the pit of his stomach.

'What are you dreaming about?' she asked. 'You're miles away. Miles and miles away.'

Robert turned his eyes and looked for the sun. It was moving westwards. Time was marching on. 'I had a birthday anniversary a few weeks ago,' he murmured, 'my twenty-fifth.'

'Oh, Robert! Why did you not tell me?'

'I only remembered it today.'

'Poof! Men pay so little heed to the progression of their years while women think of nothing else. I shall write a poem for you.'

He lifted an auburn ringlet from her shoulder. 'There is a present you could give me, a lock of your hair. Just a small curl so I can have something of you in the time we are apart.'

She smiled impishly. 'And only last week you had the nerve to chide *me* for being a hopeless romantic!'

'Only when you romance about unromantic things.'

'Such as?'

'Ireland and her wretchedness.'

'Well that's where you're wrong, O knowledgeable Trinity boy. Even in her sadness Ireland has great beauty and romance. Why else do men sing about her? Fight for her? Die for her?'

'The thousands that died five years ago?'

'Yes, them, and great men from our own Lord Edward Fitzgerald right back to King Brian Boru.'

'Sarah,' he said softly, 'I have something to tell you. Something I should have told you at the very beginning, but now there is a possibility I may have to quit the kingdom at a moment's notice.'

At Sarah's confused expression, he lifted her hand and continued quickly, 'I know you believe my work is the leather trade, but it is not, it's only a part. Since shortly after I returned to Ireland, my real work . . . my real work . . . has been the preparations for an uprising.'

She stared at him like a child whose face has been suddenly and unexpectedly slapped. She looked around her slowly in bewilderment, then reached for her wine, her hand shaking as she raised the glass to her lips. Then she stared at him again, her head moving slowly from side to side.

*   *   *

The old shepherd and the dog had been sitting on the crest of the hill for some time now, watching the young colleen and buachaleen. He had little else to do while the flock of sheep grazed contentedly a few feet away.

The old man scratched his face as he pondered on what it was like to be young. Arrah! That was something he could the divil a bit remember!

He dug into his pocket and pulled out his clay pipe, poking his finger inside the bowl. Sure what was she saying to him now? His hearing had always been bad, but now he was as deaf as a garden gate.

He fidgeted inside his other pocket, withdrew his tinderbox and lit his pipe, raising his hand to swipe away the smoke which clouded his view.

Musha, she was on her feet now, her hands in her hair and sobbing like a childybawn! And would ye look at himself – gripping her shoulders and bending his face to hers as if he was pleading with her. Must have told her he was already wed, or asked her to wed him and she's not too keen. Looks like she's shouting something. Pooh! Women always did that when they were foxed.

'If Mr Pitt could not understand,' Sarah was shouting, 'how do you expect me to understand?'

Robert looked utterly perplexed. 'What do you mean?'

'I may be just a stupid female, Robert, but I listen to what's being said around me. The problem – is that not how Mr Pitt always referred to us? The Irish problem!'

'That's how Mr Pitt *dismissed* us! That's how the English have always *dismissed* us! Even after the blood sacrifice of ninety-eight when thousands died in the fight for freedom, it meant nothing to them, *nothing*! We were still waved aside and dismissed as the Irish problem – something to be sorted out when the price of wheat goes down.'

His voice broke up into a softness. 'Sarah, please try and understand.'

'And what about me? Where do I fit into your plans?'

'You're not in my plans, you're in my heart! I love you, but it's only fair to tell you the truth. And if you want to stop seeing me then . . . well then I must accept that.'

298

'Would you give up your preparations, if I asked you to?'

'No, Sarah. I could not do that. I am pledged.'

'Then there's nothing more to be said, Robert.'

'Sarah . . .' His hand moved over his eyes, he looked desolate. 'I can have no personal happiness without you.'

'No!' The tears were coursing down her face. 'I'm all for the cause of Irish freedom, but a rising – no! It's too awful even to think about!' She tossed her head in frustration. 'Why does it have to be you? Why you?'

'Why anybody? Did Tone not say that when we look at the hand that rules us with a rod of iron, we must search for the solution among ourselves?'

'How should I know what Tone said? And where's your rod of iron? You've lived a privileged life so far.'

'I'm not talking about me, I'm talking about our country! But I was kicked out of Trinity for having the audacity to decide my own political views. O, Sarah, have you never read those words of Jefferson that inspired the Americans in their fight for independence? All men are born equal. All men! And that means Protestant, Catholic, black, white, labourer or lord! Our people are like the Jews under the whip of the Roman Empire. And the principle of the rights of man was not decided by Thomas Paine – Christ himself preached equality—'

'There's no need to be profane by bringing Christ into it,' she shouted. 'And I don't *care* what Tone or Jefferson said – what will my *father* say? He'll never change his mind now. Not when he finds out he was right about you all along.'

Her eyes sparked with such a genuine rage that his face went white.

'He'll say you are not a respectable gentleman after all, just a low-down bloodthirsty rebel like your brother! And you had the nerve to think of approaching my father about courting me for marriage. For what? So I could end up visiting you in prison until I'm a withered old woman that's never been dancing at the Rotunda!'

'Sarah, please—'

She lunged forward in an attempt to run past him but his hands reached out and grabbed her. His entire body was shaking with shock. She struggled so violently he eventually released her.

The old shepherd jumped on his perch. Oh, tunder-an-potcheen, she's off! Well he wasn't making after her. More power to ye son! But the divil a clip ye should be downhearted. Lift yer dark head up owa that. Oh, betther and betther, heading for his horse. A horse was a truer friend than a woman any day of the fair.

Begorra, what was he doing at all? Just standing there clutching the bridle. Mind! A handsome brute that shtallion, handsome.

Oh, the curse of mankind – she's coming back to him! And he staring at her like an eejit instead of making his escape. Musha, 'tis the divil of wild behaviour for two of the quality to be carrying on with!

She walked slowly towards him, feet dragging as if she carried a heavy weight on her back. Robert eyed her warily as she approached. Her face was white and tear-streaked as she stood before him, her voice alarming in its softness.

'You forgot to tell me one thing. What if you die in your rising?'

'Then I die. Those who fight for Ireland always know the risks.'

'And you're prepared to take them?'

'Sarah,' he said, 'I can be no more and no less than what I am.'

'And what is that? I hardly know you. You're like a stranger to me now.'

'An Irishman,' he said, 'whose patriotism and love of his country is as true as any Englishman's. But there is the cut of the double-edged sword. What is patriotism in England, is treason in Ireland.'

She stood before him floundering in bewilderment. 'Oh, Robert, I understand and I don't understand. Ireland to me is these hills, the green meadows, and the Irish music I cherish so. What happens outside The Priory and Rathfarnham is all vague to me. But . . . but I don't want to know about your *rights of man*! Men have all the rights, women none. The only thing I understand, is that I have been brought up to do and understand nothing.'

Her eyes went past him, narrowed on some vague distant horizon. 'I don't really like the world,' she said. 'The world is a cold and lonely place. And I sometimes think God can be as cruel and as prejudiced as those you hate so much. Why else are some given a life glutted with happiness and others nothing more than a handful of shadows?'

She looked at him. 'But you too, Robert, are your dreams anything more than a handful of shadows? Will Ireland really be the free land you dream of, or just a lush and beautiful grave for your dreams, like it is for so many others who had dreams?'

He could only stare at her, at her brooding face. It was she who was the stranger now. Her wide tragic eyes had the remote and misty look of one who spends long periods in silent reflection. A voice in his heart raged against the fire of patriotism which burned in his blood as fierce and as strong as his love for this strange and lovely girl.

Her voice and her stillness disturbed him more than anything she said, although everything she said had shown him how little he knew her.

'I spoke the truth when I said I loved you, Sarah.'

'Then you may find that I'm a very dangerous person to love,' she said dully. 'You could end up forever lost. You see, I have a habit of losing people. First I lost my little sister, then I lost my mamma, and sometime after that I lost my father. And for a while,' she tried to smile, 'it seems I even lost my mind.'

In a moment he had her in his arms, holding her close until a semblance of life and warmth came back into her stiff body. She started to shiver uncontrollably. He moved her over to a sunny strip and sat her down, cradling her head into his shoulder as his arms slipped around her.

He sat holding her, staring into space. Oh, how his father would have understood Sarah! How he could have helped her with her black despairs. Why had he never realised that she was still a sick girl, sick with a lonely sense of inferiority which had started way back in childhood, deserted by her mother, ignored by her father, which had resulted in a conviction of her own unimportance.

He remembered his own boyish timidity: how his father had often despaired of him, encouraging him to be more forthright, finally helping him out of it with a mixture of sternness and gentleness. But even though he had chided and admonished, his father had always been there, been involved, showing by his impatience with the boy that he cared about the man.

A red haze of anger suddenly flamed up before his eyes, focusing like a beam on Sarah's father, cursing him silently for the cold and heartless man he could be.

A number of times Sarah had confided to him her bitterness against her home life, complaining about her father's cold indifference towards her, bewildered by his sudden inexplicable jibes about her appearance, jibes about her quietness which he seemed to regard as slyness. But was it any wonder Curran did not look for any warmth or affection in his home? He got all the affection he needed in his other home where he kept his mistress. Dublin was a small place, and in certain circles it was common knowledge that Curran's mistress was now expecting his child.

Publicly, Curran was a great man. A great lawyer. He had once even been a great patriot. Like the times he had openly and defiantly lashed out against the government at the State Trials. But that had been in 1798. What the damnation had happened to him since?

Shadows from the west were stretching out beside him, the air had lost its warmth.

'Sarah?' he murmured.

Receiving no response, he moved his head sideways and peered at her. Astonished, he saw that she was asleep, fast asleep. How could she do that, he wondered, fall asleep on a cooling April afternoon sitting on a hill?

'Sarah,' he said again, and she stirred, lifted her head and looked at him vaguely.

The old shepherd gave a resigned sigh. The colleen and buachaleen were moving now, getting to their feet and walking slowly towards the horse. Ah well, to every ram his ewe lamb!

The dog sprang to life as the old man struggled to his feet and plodded down the hill to his sheep. 'Did you see that, Brian Boru?' he chuckled. 'Never once did that pair of mad lovebirds look up at us. If they had o' done, I would have given them the tip of me hat, for 'twas an interesting afternoon they gave us.'

Robert drew rein at the turn-off to the lane, dismounted, then lifted Sarah down. To his amazement she smiled at him, smiled in that artless way he knew so well, as if the events on the hill had never happened.

'When will we meet again?' she asked.

He blinked. 'Do you want to meet again?'

'Don't you?'

He had to tell her no. But where was his strength? He now needed every ounce of strength he possessed to say no and walk away. For her sake.

'Oh, I do,' he said. 'Any time you say.'

She quirked her brow as she considered. 'Tomorrow? Can you get away from your tannery business tomorrow?'

'What about . . . my other business?'

Her eyes darkened. 'Oh, that . . . your rising for the rights of man.'

He stood waiting, waiting for a seeming eternity for her next words.

'Will it be like ninety-eight?' she asked. 'Lots of blood and death?'

'It will be nothing like ninety-eight. Hopefully, a short bloodless coup.'

'And when? When is it due to take place?'

'I don't know just when. We are still in the early planning stages.'

'How long were Lord Edward and his men planning their rebellion?'

'About two years.'

She gave him that blinding smile again, as if the sun had suddenly come out in her mind. 'Oh, well, that's a very long way off,' she said brightly. 'Years and years.' She was laughing now, relieved.

'Tomorrow,' she said, and brushed a finger over his cheek.

She swung the basket lightly as she walked up the lane. He stood watching her, thinking her violent struggling had left her looking unusually disarrayed; long auburn tendrils had escaped her ringlet bunches and hung down her slender back.

As she sauntered on slowly her voice drifted back to him, singing softly to herself in Irish. His heart twisted painfully.

Inside Dublin Castle, Alexander Marsden adjusted his frilled cuffs with delicate application as he responded to the Chief Secretary.

'I can assure you, Mr Wickham, if Major Sirr called at the Emmet household, he did so of his own volition and not in response to any direction from me.'

'Young Emmet was not at home?'

'Fortunately.'

Wickham's eyes furtively scanned the room as if he suspected someone to be lurking behind a piece of the furniture. 'We cannot have oafs like Major Sirr unnecessarily disturbing the citizens. Have you seen the way he parades through the streets with his men?'

Marsden's crystal-grey eyes twinkled with amusement. 'He revels in thinking the people are terrified of him. His glory in capturing Fitzgerald is wearing thin. I suspect he is looking for a new fox to corner.'

'Idiot!'

Marsden cocked an eyebrow. 'Oh, come now, he is hardly that. Our Major Sirr can be a very clever fellow.'

'Yes. Too clever. That is why he must be kept under control.'

Marsden smiled slyly. 'Rest assured, Chief Secretary. I have warned the major to leave young Emmet to go about his business undisturbed.'

Chapter Twenty-Four

Robert Emmet had visited the Devlins' home twice after returning the mare, but on each occasion Anne had been abroad delivering milk or eggs.

'What did he want?' she asked Mary.

'How should I know?' Mary answered shortly. 'He spent all his time closeted in the parlour with Mammy and Dada and Big Art. Every time we went near Big Art started whispering.'

Anne frowned. 'Why was that?'

'Don't ask me. Mr Emmet didn't speak to us at all. Not even once.'

'Not true, not true!' Nellie cried. 'He talked to me and Jimmy. He brought us sugar bars an' all.'

'Mr Emmet likes me and Nellie,' Jimmy supported. ' 'Tis just Mary who makes his face go red.'

When Mary had stomped out of the kitchen, Anne sat at the table pondering on Mr Emmet's visits. Big Art was whispering was he? She chewed her knuckle thoughtfully. Something was in the wind, and she'd tip her hat to Old Nick to know what it was.

She found out two nights later.

As soon as Big Arthur had arrived at the house, Brian Devlin summoned his children into the kitchen, all except Nellie and Jimmy who were in bed.

'What I have to say concerns us all,' he said. 'Mr Emmet is going to be a neighbour of ours. He has taken the house on Butterfield Lane.'

Mary looked puzzled. 'But Dada, all this whispering? Why was it such a secret that Mr Emmet has taken the house on Butterfield Lane?'

'Because Mr Emmet has not taken the house on Butterfield Lane,' said Big Art, who was standing by the hearth. 'Mr *Ellis* has.'

Brian Devlin then explained that Robert Emmet and his friends were planning to make another strike for liberty, not on the widespread scale of the '98 rebellion, but confined to a small military-style coup on the Castle, which if successful,

305

would lead to the entire country rising up the day after. Only the leaders knew the actual plan, and only the leaders would be allowed to know it until the day before the action. Thousands had been sworn into the movement in Lord Edward's day, and so had treachery in disguise – the Irish informer, a breed of being who was ready to sell not only his country, but his friends with it, for a price.

The house on Butterfield Lane was to be their headquarters; and he and their mother had committed themselves to giving him as much help as possible.

After a babble of excited questions from Little Arthur and Anne, Brian Devlin noticed Mary sitting silently twisting the cloth of her skirt into a knot. She had not uttered a word since the announcement.

'What say you, Mary?'

Mary lifted her eyes and flushed to see all eyes upon her. 'I'll do whatever you ask, Dada . . . for the sake of the cause. But I don't want no part of – you know – guns.'

Her father laughed. 'Ah no, asthore, you won't be involved with anything like that. In fact, you won't be involved at all. 'Tis just that there might be some coming and going between here and Butterfield Lane, and you'll all have to know what's going on, if we're to act normal like.'

Big Art shifted uneasily on his feet. 'There's still the matter of the housekeeper, Brian.'

'Oh, aye.' Brian Devlin rose and reached for his pipe, then having lit it, stood with his back to the fire. 'Mr Emmet will need a housekeeper. He has asked Big Art to find him one. He may be highly educated, but I doubt if he knows the skin of a potato.'

'Oh, not me, Dada,' cried Mary. 'I don't want to be a servant!'

Anne smiled and touched Mary's hand. It was to be a *lady* in some gentleman's house that Mary had always dreamed of, not a skivvy.

'Mr Emmet says—' Big Art screwed up his eyes as if trying to remember the exact words, 'He says she must be one in whom we can place implicit confidence in every respect.'

He opened his eyes. 'He asked for you, Anne.'

'Me?'

Big Art nodded. 'Yourself.'

Anne beamed at the thought of it. She had been a helpless spectator in '98, but now she was being asked to play a real part in the cause. She looked at her father. 'Do you think I should, Da?'

'You're over age now, alannah. The decision is yours.'

She turned to her mother sitting silently by the hearth. 'And you, Ma? What say you?'

'Like your da says, Anne, the decision is yours; but my thoughts are these . . .' Mrs Devlin placed her hands on her knees and went on, 'We were forced to leave our beloved Wicklow because we were stamped as a rebel family – well if we have the name, we may as well play the game so! And from what I've seen and heard, Robert Emmet will plan his rising no matter what. So he may as well have our help while he's at it.'

'Will you do it, Anne?' asked Big Arthur. 'The housekeeper job?'

'Aye, I will, and gladly,' she said.

Big Arthur smiled at her. 'I'll be off so. Mr Emmet will be waiting to see you at Butterfield Lane tomorrow morning. Ten o'clock.'

Anne stared at her cousin. 'You mean . . . you told him already that I'd do it? Without even asking me?'

'But sure I knew you would,' Big Art reasoned, then disappeared smartly out of the door.

The following morning, Anne and her father set off for the house on Butterfield Lane. It was a grey-stone double-fronted house of three storeys with a large black front door. Anne reflected that it was not as grand as some of the other houses in the area, not like The Priory, all yellow bricks and geraniums on the windows, but it was nice just the same.

So engrossed was Anne in her inspection of the exterior of the house, she did not notice her father had stopped to investigate an overgrown patch at the side. She wandered through the open front door and was instantly filled with dismay. The place was filthy. Dust everywhere. Through the open doors of the downstairs rooms she could see pieces of furniture draped in sheets.

'Damme!' The voice came from a room down the hall. She

knew it was Mr Emmet, his black horse was tied outside. She wandered along the hall and found him in the kitchen trying to light a fire. Anne couldn't help laughing. 'You'll never blow life into the turf with your lips!' she said.

He turned his head. 'Miss Devlin!' He rose to his feet looking sheepish. 'I thought to heat water for the making of tea.' He nodded towards the long table where a bag of tea and a bag of sugar lay next to his saddlebag.

'This is what you need,' Anne said, spotting a pile of old newspapers lying in a corner. She lifted a sheet then knelt down and held it across the fireplace. ' 'Twill be burning in no time.'

He stood behind her rubbing turf dust from his hands. 'Did you just happen to be passing this way?'

She turned her head and stared up at him. 'Passing? I thought you wanted to see me at ten o'clock.'

'You! Do you mean you are the housekeeper?'

'Big Art said you asked for me.'

'Oh, no, Miss Devlin. I asked for a housekeeper, and Arthur said he had found the perfect person, but I didn't realise it was you.'

She looked as much hurt as surprised. 'What's wrong with me?'

'Well you're too young for one thing. I had thought of someone much older, someone from the Liberties.'

'Some old rip who'd be a mother figure,' she quipped. 'And why someone from the Liberties?'

'Perhaps I should have said, someone who was committed wholeheartedly to the cause.'

'I'm committed wholeheartedly to the cause.'

'I'm sorry,' he said quietly. 'We have both been misled.'

The fire was burning now. She let the paper fall on top of the turf and stood up. 'Big Art's a vexatious liar,' she said, 'but you still need a housekeeper.'

'Yes, I do, but . . . Miss Devlin, much of the business transacted here will be at night. So the housekeeper will have to live in, naturally. And it will not be just myself living here but three or four more, all men.'

Anne thought she knew his fear. The respectable young Protestant gentry never dishonoured their ladies before marriage, and it was common practice for many of them to turn to the lowly servant girls instead. Oh, she had seen it in the big house in Inchicore, and heard the tales of maids from the other houses when they visited the kitchen. True, most of the girls had no choice, it was a case of obey or lose your livelihood, but there were those other brazen straps who cared nothing for God nor laws and considered it a great privilege to capture the interest of the masters or their gentry sons.

'I see,' she said, her anger growing, 'you think I might try and distract these men from their business?'

He turned and looked at her. The thought hadn't actually crossed his mind. His reluctance was based on the idea of having one pretty young girl living alone with a group of men. It just didn't *seem* right.

'Are you always so forthright?' he inquired.

She looked at him long and coolly. 'Yes, Mr Emmet, I am. And while I'm being so, let me tell you this. If 'twere for my last crust I'd never be a skivvy to no young Protestant gentleman. But I was told the business to be carried on here was for the cause, and it's to the cause I offer my service.'

He looked so astonished she gave a mirthless little smile.

'I'm not as young as you may think, Mr Emmet. I'm twenty-two! and well able to look after myself. So tell me now before Da comes in, do you want me to come as housekeeper or not?'

He bit thoughtfully on his lip. 'I am inclined to say no, but in view of what Arthur said about you, I suppose I should say yes.'

'And what did that great liar say?'

'The lives of a thousand men could be trusted in your hands.'

'Of course, sometimes he does speak the truth,' she said, lifting the kettle. 'Where did you get the water from?'

'From the pump out the back.'

'Oh, that'll be handy, won't it? We have to rely on rainwater or go and fetch it from the stream or the River Dodder.'

He folded his arms and watched her set the kettle on the fire. Women were the strangest creatures, always acting the way you least expected them. She had seemed quite meek and simple the day he borrowed the mare, but now she had an edge to her tongue that could slice a man in two.

'Do you dislike Protestants?'

Her head swung round. 'Why do you ask that?'

'You said you wouldn't normally be a servant to a Protestant gentleman.'

'Would it matter if I did?'

'It would matter a great deal. All the men living here will be Protestants.'

She looked at him candidly. 'No, it's not Protestants I dislike; some of the greatest and bravest men in the ninety-eight rebellion were Protestants. It's just the landed gentry I hate. The ones that own all the land, *our* land, the land they stole from us.'

Before Robert could reply Brian Devlin strolled into the kitchen. 'Them's strawberries growing out there, Mr Emmet. If they're cultivated now there'll be a fine showing in the summer. Ah, good, Anne's started a fire already.'

He then proceeded to tell Robert the house must be given the appearance of normal life and business. To that end, he would send over a cow for milk, a cart, and a few hens.

Robert nodded. 'You can inform me later as to the cost.'

'Oh, no, Mr Emmet,' Brian Devlin shook his head emphatically, ' 'Twill be my personal contribution. And as for my daughter Anne, she's here because you asked for her, and because she wanted to come.'

Robert avoided Anne's eyes. 'But I insist on paying you for the hens and such.'

'Not at all! And let me make it clear, Mr Emmet, that Anne is not here as a hired servant either. We want no wages for her, not a penny.'

Robert looked flabbergasted, but Anne's face radiated with pride. She ran over to her father and hugged him. 'Oh, Da, you're so fine.'

Brian Devlin chuckled. 'Now stop your mythering, alannah, and make Mr Emmet some tea.'

Robert finally found his voice. 'I don't know what to say, Mr Devlin.'

'Say if you like your tea strong or weak, Mr Emmet.'

'Oh, look, Da,' Anne cried, 'Mr Emmet's brought sugar. 'Twill be like Christmas having tea with sugar in it.'

Brian Devlin continued to give Robert his advice on what should be done with the grounds outside while Anne made the tea. When she was ready to pour, she discovered there were no cups. She looked questioningly at Robert.

'I didn't think about cups,' he confessed sheepishly.

'That's why you need a housekeeper,' she replied, smiling sweetly at him.

They closed up the house a short while later, agreeing to return the next day. Robert told Anne he would have a set of china and other necessities delivered from Casino if she would make up a list. At the door, Robert pressed the bag of sugar into Anne's hand.

'Happy Christmas,' he said.

'Aw, I can't take this. You'll just have to bring more tomorrow.'

'I will arrange for groceries to be delivered.'

While her father knelt to examine a handful of soil he had lifted from under a mossy patch, Anne took a last glimpse down the hallway.

'It's not very elegant, is it?' Robert said.

She was inclined to agree, but shrugged, 'It's a lovely house, 'tis just suffering from neglect. Ach, I'll have it looking like a palace in no time.'

'My friends will only be expecting a bed under a dry roof.' He pulled the door shut.

'These friends?' Anne asked. 'Who might they be?'

'Friends from across the Channel.'

'Oh, not Irishmen?'

'Yes, Irishmen.'

He stood with his hand on the doorknob. 'Until the money we have been promised materialises, I must finance everything myself. All but what is necessary for running the house must be used for the purchase of ammunition and arms. There won't be much comfort here at Butterfield Lane. It won't be anything like keeping house for a wealthy gentleman. I think you should know that.'

She looked down at her hands. He was still trying to put her off. He really wanted someone older, more responsible looking. 'What are you trying to tell me, Mr Emmet?'

'That it won't be all sunshine.'

'And this sugar,' she snapped, holding up the bag. 'Do you

think I'm like this sugar? That I'll dissolve at the first drop of rain?'

He opened his mouth to speak but she jumped into it. 'Or do you think I'm like one of your silly gentry misses and swoon at the slightest thing?'

'No, Miss Devlin, I don't think you're at all like sugar. On the contrary, I would have said *salt* was a more apt comparison.'

Her black eyebrows shot up, but the smile on his face checked her. 'All this nonsense about comfort,' she said, tossing her head. 'I thought 'twas a rising you were planning, not a gentry houseparty.'

'You would be leaving a very comfortable home for an indefinite period,' he said, 'and it was by way of apology I sought to warn you of the conditions here. I'm sorry if I gave you the wrong impression.'

She hesitated, then smiled weakly. 'I'm sorry too, Mr Emmet. We seem to have got off to a very bad start, don't we?'

'Whatever makes you think that?' he answered dryly, then strolled over to Brian Devlin who straightened and said, 'All this soil will have to be dug and turned over, Mr Emmet, but Big Art will know what to do with it.'

Robert again thanked him for his help and generosity to which the older man waved him aside. ' 'Tis something I owe that lot, Mr Emmet, and 'tis yourself that's going to deliver it for me.'

As he turned Black Seamus towards the Dublin road, Robert sat for a moment and watched father and daughter stroll arm in arm back to the dairy. He smiled as he prodded his horse on. The Devlins were turning out to be quite a family.

For five days Anne scrubbed floors, dusted walls, and polished furniture until the house on Butterfield Land did indeed look as clean, if not as elegant as a palace. But she had not done it all on her own. Her mother and Nellie had helped in the cleaning, and even Mary had arrived with a needle and threads to mend the curtains.

Robert was astounded at the transformation in the house, and as Anne chattered away he asked her to stop calling him Mr

312

Emmet. 'Are you forgetting, Anne? The gentleman who took this house is called Mr Ellis.'

'Aw, I can't call you that!' she stood for a second as she pondered the problem. 'I'll call you Mr Robert,' she decided, 'like the little man who brought the things from Casino.'

She followed Robert as he wandered into the drawing-room and surveyed the sparse but polished furniture. Two big old chairs sat each side of the fire. They looked comfortable enough in their red velvet plumpness and matched in colour the sofa that sat in the middle of the room.

'You've done a grand job, Anne,' he said, 'truly grand.'

He followed her upstairs to the bedrooms. She had washed the curtains of the two large rooms to the front of the house, but the windows of the two smaller ones at the back were bare. 'The curtains for these are drying on the back hedge,' she said.

'Have you decided which shall be your room?' he asked her.

'I thought the small room downstairs off the hallway. It will be nearer the kitchen in the mornings.'

'Then this room here shall be mine,' he pointed to one of the large front rooms, 'and the one opposite will be Tom Russell's. This one at the back can be for Hamilton, and the upper rooms for any others who stay.'

'But Mr Emm – Mr Robert, what about the beds?' Her eyes moved past him to the room he had claimed for himself: it contained the one bed she had found in the house. 'That's the only bed in the entire house!'

'Then you must have it.'

'But what about you . . . and the others?'

Robert shrugged and turned to the stairs. 'Arthur will be delivering a number of mattresses tonight, after dark. And Lennard will bring clean linen and blankets. We can't have the neighbours wondering why a gentleman like Mr Ellis and his guests sleep on mats and not beds.'

'But,' she started down the stairs after him, 'are you not going to buy more beds?'

He turned and leaned against the banister. 'I have told you, Anne, there is no money available for comforts such as beds, not at the moment anyway.'

'Well, I can't take your bed. 'Twouldn't be right! A mattress will do me.'

He waved a hand dismissively and ran down the stairs. 'I'd better go and see what the manager of the property is up to.'

For the purposes of the outside world, Big Arthur had been given the job of managing Mr Ellis's property, and Big Arthur had nominated Little Arthur as his assistant.

Robert came through the front door to see the two Arthurs crouched down by the mossy patch at the side. He was about to join them when he spotted two women in black bonnets peeping around a tree. He stepped back quickly from view.

Big Arthur had also seen the women. He straightened up and assumed a businesslike attitude. 'Now, young man,' he said loudly, 'all these weeds must be dug away entirely, and no slacking either.'

Little Arthur gaped up at him.

'And another thing, young man, when you plant in the patch around the back, don't forget to use plenty of mulch.'

Little Arthur stared incredulously at his cousin. 'You don't have to tell me! I've been living on a blasted farm all my life, Big Art!'

'Aye,' Big Arthur kicked his cousin's shoe, 'A big heart I'm reputed to have, but I'll still not tolerate any slacking on the master's property. So get on with it now.'

Little Arthur turned his head and saw the black bonnets by the tree. 'Yes, sor!' he cried, tipping his forelock. 'I'll get to it right away, sor.'

'That's the job!' Big Arthur bellowed. 'You see to your business and I'll see to mine. For isn't it a terrible thing when people don't mind their own business and stick their long noses into others. We don't want anyone like that around here, do we now?'

'No, sor!'

'And what's more! Mr Ellis is very particular about his privacy! 'Twould make him awful mad if he discovered people weren't minding their own business. Fact, if he found anyone snooping or trespassing on his property, he'd kick up an awful stink, to be sure. He might complain to the militia. He might even complain to his friends at the Castle!'

'Indeed he would, sor!'

Big Arthur then put his hands behind his back and whistled loudly as he sauntered towards the trees where the two women were hiding. A few seconds later they heard the rustle of skirts and the scurrying of feet.

Robert stepped out from the doorway as Big Arthur turned back, both men laughed while Little Arthur fell back on to the ground in fits of mirth.

'Now, your honour! Mr Ellis,' Big Arthur yanked his hat down until it almost covered his eyes, 'is there something I can do for you?'

Robert's face straightened in mock solemnity. 'Nooooh, Mr Devlin. Carry on your business, my good man.'

'Right you are, O noble sor!'

'Oh, you can do one thing,' Robert said. 'Have the bed in the first-floor bedroom moved down to the small room off the hallway.'

'Indeed, I will, your eminent honour.'

Robert was still smiling as he strolled around to the stables to see Black Seamus. The horse brushed him a nuzzle, but a sniffing sound from the back of the stables made him turn his head quickly. He moved stealthily over to the far corner and pulled back a pile of straw. A small tear-stained face stared up at him.

'Nellie! Why are you hiding in here? And why the tears?'

' 'Cos I'm sad. And I'm mad.'

'You're sad and you're mad? Now that's a terrible combination.' He crouched down in front of her, thinking she looked a smaller version of Anne. 'Do you want to tell me what made you mad?'

Nellie sniffed. ' 'Cos I hate boyeens, they always stick together. Jimmy doesn't want to play with me no more since we got Patsa.'

He eventually established that Patsa was a dog and gave a sympathetic smile. 'Well, we will just have to see what we can do about that.'

'You won't get him away from Patsa,' she wiped her face with her dress, 'nobody can.'

'We will have to think of something else then. Something to stop you feeling sad.' He reached to take her hand. 'Come away now into the house.'

315

Nellie kept her eyes on his face and a tight hold of his hand as they walked across the yard. 'I like you, Mr Emmet,' she said finally.

He tilted an eyebrow. 'But you said you didn't like boyeens, Nellie.'

'I like you.'

'Will you do something for me then?'

'What?'

'Don't call me Mr Emmet.'

'What shall I call you?'

'Your sister calls me Mr Robert.'

'Then I'll call you Mr Robert, too. And you can call me Miss Ellen if you like. That's my real name.'

He smiled down at her. 'Nellie suits you better.'

'Do you think so?' Her eyes were shining. 'Do you *really* think Nellie is a nice name?'

'Very nice.'

'Jimmy doesn't think so,' she said slowly. 'He calls me smelly Nellie.'

Later that day, Brian Devlin arrived with a cart filled with sacks of potatoes, eggs, and flour. Mrs Devlin strolled behind him pulling a cow, while Mary rode Anne's mare.

'There you are, Mr Emmet,' Brian Devlin announced. 'This will give the place an appearance of business. I've painted the cart fresh.'

Robert stood in the doorway, smiling and shaking his head.

'What's the matter?' Brian Devlin asked. 'Don't you like the colour of the cart? Of course, blue is a bit bright, but 'twas all the paint I had.'

'The colour is grand, Mr Devlin, but I can't take advantage of your generosity. You must allow me to pay you.'

'Now we've spoken about that afore, Mr Emmet, and I don't like repeating myself. Did Big Art bring the sleeping mats?'

'Not until tonight, after dark.'

'You'll be set then, once the mats arrive?'

'Yes, we'll be set. As from tonight, I can take full-time residence of Butterfield Lane.'

* * *

It was the following day, and John Patten was extremely worried about his brother-in-law's finances. John was five years older than Robert and had a sound business head on him.

'You can't pay for everything yourself, Robert. Your inheritance from your father was not that big. Not as big as it should have been, but Tom's imprisonment cost a small fortune in the end as you know. And there's the money you've put into this business. The returns will give you only a reasonable living at best. You will have to hold on to some of your capital.'

The conversation was interrupted by a tap on the door. 'Well, think on, Robert, think about what I have said.'

John Patten exchanged a few brisk words with Miles Byrne before going down to the tannery. 'What's wrong with him?' Miles asked.

Robert shrugged. 'A business matter. What news?'

'The jointed pikes,' Miles said, pulling over a chair and sitting down, 'how important are they?'

'Very important. A jointed pike can be folded in the middle and carried under a man's greatcoat. Why? Is there a problem?'

'No problem. They just take longer to make than the plain ones. We now have almost a thousand plain, but only a hundred jointed.'

'What about the gunsmith?' Robert asked. 'Have you seen him yet?'

'I'm seeing him tomorrow.'

'Good. We will want a number of pocket pistols. The barrels must be only four inches long, and the calibre to admit a soldier's musket cartridge.'

'Right. I'd better get back now or Edward will be after my blood.'

'You are still coming to share dinner with me tonight at Butterfield Lane?'

'Aye, seven o'clock you said?'

Robert nodded. 'About this gunsmith, Miles. Is he safe?'

'Aye, he's safe. He's the type of man whose curiosity would never lead him to inquire if the firearms were for smugglers or privateers.'

'An unusual man,' Robert said.

*   *   *

Robert rode into the front yard of Butterfield Lane to find Anne busily polishing the front-door brass. She turned her head and smiled coquettishly. 'Good evening, Mr Ellis.'

'Where is Nellie?' he asked.

'I haven't seen her for a while but she's probably sulking somewhere.' She flicked her cloth impatiently. 'She asked if she could come and keep me company today then spends all her time sulking. 'Tis Jimmy that's upset her as usual.'

Robert rode down the side of the house to the stables at the back where he found Nellie. 'I've been waiting for you, Mr Robert,' she said as he dismounted. 'I saved you a bit of cake. Mammy made a lovely cake today and gave me some before I came over.'

She scrambled over the straw and pulled a piece of cake out of the pocket of her dress. 'Here, you can have it all.'

Robert stared down at the mushed-up lump of cake in her hand. 'Before I take it, Nellie, tell me if you and Jimmy are friends again?'

'No, I'll never be friends with him ever again.'

'And do you still feel sad?'

'Aye, a little bit.'

Robert sat down in the straw beside her and put his hand inside his coat. 'I've brought you a little friend,' he said. 'All for yourself.'

He gently lifted out a tiny black kitten and handed it to her. 'Seeing as you don't like boyeens, this is a girl kitten.'

Nellie squealed with delight. 'Oh, she's lovely, Mr Robert! Oh, let me hold her. Here, take the cake.' He placed the kitten into her lap and reluctantly removed the squashed lump from her hand.

'Oh, won't Jimmy be raging when I show him. Won't he just be scratching himself with murder when I tell him you got it for me an' all!' She nuzzled the kitten to her face. 'Aw, Mr Robert, you're so fine! What shall I call her?'

Robert looked down at the kitten. 'Well, she is a purty little thing.'

Nellie laughed excitedly. 'Shall I call her that then? Purty?'

'Yes. Purty suits her well.'

Nellie kissed the kitten over and over, then looked at Robert curiously. 'I was thinking last night, Mr Robert. When I'm sixteen, how old will you be?'

'That depends on how old you are now, Nellie.'

'I'm ten.'

'In that case, when you are sixteen I shall be thirty-one.'

'Is that old?'

'I wouldn't say so.'

'Could you and me get married then?'

Robert turned his head quickly to hide his smile. 'By the time you are sixteen, Nellie, I shall probably be already married.'

'Oh, will you?' She swallowed her dismay and bent her head as she stroked the kitten. She silently pondered what she could do now. Now she had confided to Anne that she was so in love with Mr Robert. *Devoted!*

'Are you going to eat the cake?' she whispered.

Robert was about to say he would save it until after dinner, but the glimmer of tears in her big eyes forced him to be brave. He looked down at his palm and sighed, 'Yes, Nellie. I'm going to eat the cake.'

Miles Byrne looked up from his books with a grin as Robert slipped quietly into the little office over the timberyard.

'How did you get on with the gunsmith?' Robert asked eagerly.

'Fine. He can do the pocket pistols to your specifications.'

'What about blunderbusses? We shall need a vast number of short blunderbusses.'

Miles walked over to a cupboard and unlocked it. He took out a short blunderbuss and handed it to Robert. 'As you can see, the locks and barrels are perfect. The polish could be better, but the price is low because he concentrates on performance rather than appearance.'

Robert examined the gun. 'When are you seeing him again?'

'Whenever you want.'

'Order one hundred pocket pistols and three hundred blunderbusses for now. The barrels of the latter to be of the same metal as the pistols, no brass ones. As you say, performance is more important than appearance.' He handed the blunderbuss back to Miles and turned to leave. 'Can you drop in for the money in the morning?'

'Aye, but he says you needn't pay until the order is ready.'

Robert hesitated. 'Are you *sure* about him?'

'Very sure. Apart from anything else, he's a Wexford man, and he lost two sons in the ninety-eight.'

Robert sighed and moved to the door. 'Say no more.'

An hour later, in the room at Corbett's Hotel, Robert stood with his back to the window and listened carefully to the three men as they reported on their visit to Kildare. Thomas Wilde and John Mahon sat silently as Michael Quigley consulted a paper in his hand.

'Thomas Daley, one of Lord Edward's generals,' Quigley said, 'has been assigned the job of preparing the men, together with Michael and Andrew Flood.'

'But Nicholas Grey must have top command,' Robert said quickly.

Quigley nodded. 'Then there's Thomas Frayne and Michael Dalton, they have asked to meet you. They'll be coming to Dublin next week.'

Robert had already decided that only the leaders would be allowed to know about the house on Butterfield Lane. 'I'll have to find a suitable place to meet people,' he said.

Thomas Wilde said: 'Now the Grand Canal is open, the packet boats take care of the traffic between Kildare and Dublin. Many of the men go straight to the White Bull to wet their whistles after the journey. 'Tis an ideal meeting place.'

'Yes,' Robert mused, 'and there *is* the room at the back. It has two exits.'

Quigley looked a shade embarrassed. 'I'll have to look for lodgings, Mr Emmet. This hotel is beyond my means.'

Robert stared at him. 'Are you short?'

'You could say that.'

'I gave you ample funds before you left.'

'Aye, but you know how it is, looking everyone up and discussing business. There was a lot of entertaining involved.'

Mahon and Wilde exchanged glances. 'You were acting the

320

blasted rich man with Mr Emmet's money!' Thomas Wilde snapped.

'What the Devil are you talking about?' Quigley demanded. 'I saw you two boyos cutting me dirty looks in Fitz's tavern, and don't think I didn't.'

Robert withdrew some money from his pocket and handed it to Quigley. 'Get yourself lodgings in the city tonight. The Liberties is cheap. But remember, the well is not deep and there is a floor to it.'

'Aye,' Quigley said. 'I'll get work part-time as a mason or a brickie to keep me going. And don't mind that boyo, Mr Emmet. Michael Quigley is not looking for no free ride.'

'No?' Wilde shouted. 'And who's been footing your bills so far?'

Robert could see the trip to Kildare had caused a strain of hostility to develop between Quigley and Wilde. He suggested to the latter that he accompany him back to the White Bull in Thomas Street.

Once outside, Thomas Wilde frowned at Robert. 'I tell you, Mr Emmet, there's nothing I find more sickening than having to sit and watch someone acting the big shot – with another man's gun.'

Chapter Twenty-Five

Anne wandered into the dining-room to check the table settings, smiling as she glanced over at Robert who stood leaning against the window and gazing on to the front drive. He took out his watch and glanced at it.

'They don't go any faster by looking at them,' she said. 'The minutes. Every time I come in you look at your timepiece.'

He put the watch away and continued gazing out to the drive. Anne went back to the kitchen. Everything was ready and she, too, was feeling the length of the day. She sat down on the settle at the side of the hearth and replaited her hair into a thick braid. She had started to wear her hair in this fashion from her first day at Butterfield Lane, hoping it would make her look more prim. She held her black braid over her breast and sighed heavily as she stared into the fire.

Robert entered a few minutes later and sat down at the table. He glanced up to the mantel. 'You need a clock in here,' he said.

'Ah, for heaven's sake, Mr Robert. They won't be here until after dark. 'Tis only about five now.'

He took out his watch again. 'Half past. What are you preparing for dinner?'

'Well,' she gave him a triumphant smile, 'I've made four fruit tarts, but I thought you could start with pork and apple, then lobster, then—'

'Lobster! Anne, you are threatening to jeopardise this project entirely.'

She looked perplexed. 'What do you mean?'

'First of all, the money we have is for arms, not banquets; and secondly, fat men become lazy. Miles could hardly rise from his chair last week after the five courses you served him.'

'Well that's the sort of food the gentry ate in the big house in Inchicore.'

'Never mind the gentry in Inchicore. We will eat the way the Devlins eat in Rathfarnham. Simple food will be fine. You don't have to waste your time on all that preparation.'

'I was told Mr Russell was an aristocrat,' she said, flushing hotly.

'Who told you that?' Robert smiled. 'He may act like one, but I can tell you this – when you put your lobster on the table in front of Russell tonight, if at the same time I was to lay a musket beside it, I know which would make his eyes shine the most.'

Anne's cheeks were flaming with indignation. 'Well as for eating like the Devlins – we often have lobster ourselves! Only a few weeks ago Mammy served lobster and none of us could finish it. As Mary rightly said, it can get to be a very boring dish. Even Patsa turned his nose up at our leavings. Imagine that! Even dogs can get bored with the same old thing. And he's now thoroughly *sick* of swan.'

Robert knew she was making it up as she went along. But he felt guilty; he had been tactless with her. She thought he was putting down her efforts to do her best by him.

'I know for a fact that Russell loves lobster,' he said quickly. 'He ate it whenever possible in Paris. On second thoughts, Anne, you couldn't have made a better choice for his first meal back in the old country.'

Anne was not fooled by his efforts at capitulation. She stood up and haughtily flicked an invisible crumb off the table as she passed him. 'I think I'll pass the time by taking the mare out for a breath of air,' she said.

'Good idea. I'll join you.' But she had already marched out of the kitchen.

She was leaving the stable as he entered the yard, breaking into a trot without giving him a glance. Robert stared after her, he had forgotten that peasant girls didn't ride side-saddle.

He rode Black Seamus slowly down the path at the side of the house, out to the leafy greenness of Butterfield Lane, and on towards the fields. In the distance he spied her figure astride the trotting horse and set out to join her. Glancing back, she dug her heels suddenly into the mare's flanks, galloping as if the Devil himself was after her. Black Seamus rapidly closed the distance and raced alongside, easily keeping pace for pace until they reached the Dublin hills where both horses dropped to a canter, a trot, then halted.

She turned the mare round, then looked at him, cheeks flushed. 'My mare gave your stallion a run for his money,' she said in a tone that was half surprised, half delighted.

'Black Seamus was simply being a gentleman,' he explained. 'Ladies first.'

'Is that right?' Her eyes danced mischievously. 'Well, like myself, the mare is no lady, so if your beast will stop being so noble, maybe we can find out which one really has the quality.'

'How so?'

'First horse back to the house gets a saucer of sugar and is accepted as the best horse on the place.'

He was about to laugh, then saw she was deadly serious. Unconsciously his eyes moved over her: she was wearing a white cotton blouse that clung to her body and a navy skirt ruched up by her straddled position, revealing a slender ankle.

'Well?' she said impatiently. 'The gauntlet is down, Mr Emmet. Are you going to lift it – or is your horse nothing more than handsome?'

Robert responded with the same seriousness. 'The gauntlet is lifted, Miss Devlin.'

She plunged forward, head lowered to the mare's neck. Robert grinned as he followed at a slower pace, allowing her to hold the lead; she had obviously forgotten he had ridden the mare.

At the trees she glanced back and he heard her laugh. The mare's legs were now stretched to the limit, but slowly the stallion gained until they fell in stride together. With a swift motion she raised her whip and brought it down in desperate fury; he allowed her the lead again.

The road was coming up; she jerked the reins, swiftly manoeuvring the mare down to a sheep path, lengthening the distance between them.

Robert continued straight ahead, riding rapidly as he set his horse at the stone wall. It was not a high jump, but too high for the mare.

Anne turned her head as the stallion easily cleared the wall. 'Devil use his tail for a wig!' she muttered furiously.

When Anne trotted back into the yard he was bent unstrapping the girths. 'You cheated!' she cried. 'You knew the mare couldn't take that jump!'

'You said the race would decide the question of quality,' he retorted.

'She was out in front of your beast loads of times!'

'Ah, yes, but once a gent, always a gent, don't you know.' He cast a sympathetic glance at the poor mare, her neck lathered with sweat. 'And I didn't need to use the *whip* on mine.'

He laughed soundlessly as he led his horse into the stables, not exactly sure what it was that Anne muttered after him, but it didn't sound very ladylike.

* * *

324

Later that night Anne opened the door to Jemmy Hope, William Hamilton and Thomas Russell. She felt a great sense of occasion at meeting the handsome Russell. This was the man who, together with Theobald Wolfe Tone and Thomas Emmet, had founded the Society of United Irishmen; and he did indeed look like an aristocrat, and such a lovely head of black curls.

Russell bowed to Anne with great courtesy and she liked him at once. She felt more at ease with the weaver, Jemmy Hope, but William Hamilton was a different kettle of fish. Although he was as courteous as Russell, she detected a facetious flirtation in his manner which she did not like.

Anne later learned that William Hamilton had served in the French army, and had been with General Humbert when he landed in Mayo in 1798. Unlike Tone and Bartholomew Teeling, he had not been recognised as an Irishman, and together with other French soldiers, had been exchanged for English prisoners of war and sent back to France. He was still in General Humbert's confidence, and the two often discussed taking another crack at Ireland. She also learned that under Hamilton's sophisticated façade he was every bit a soldier, and dedicated to the cause.

They began discussing business as soon as they sat down to dinner. At one point Russell fell silent when Anne walked into the room but Robert waved a hand and told him to speak freely. 'Anne is one of ourselves,' he said.

Russell beamed when Anne carried in the lobster. 'Young woman! It is a feast fit for Napoleon himself you have prepared.'

Anne smiled sweetly. 'Are you sure you would not prefer a musket, Mr Russell?'

Robert shot her an amused glance as Russell laughed, 'By God, it's good to hear the Irish wit again, although the devil a bit of me can understand that one.'

'And I don't blame you,' Anne said, keeping her eyes on Russell, ' 'tis just a little piece of Mr Robert's nonsense.'

Russell's news was not cheering. Bonaparte's promises to send another expedition were vague. Preparations of the French fleet were proceeding at Brest, but Russell thought they could well be for an invasion of England, and not help for Ireland.

'An insurrection could succeed without the French,' Russell insisted, 'especially if we have the north with us.'

'Ulster is your province,' Robert said.

As the night moved on, it was agreed that Jemmy Hope should be sent to the north as soon as possible, to search out the men Russell named and see if they were as ready as ever to fight for their country's freedom. William Hamilton pleaded fatigue from the journey and announced he was off to bed. Robert informed him where his room was situated. 'Anne will have put your valise in there,' he said.

Russell refilled the glasses and brought up the subject of the money which had been promised to Robert by the secret men of rank who were financing the insurrection.

'Money has started to filter through to me,' Robert said, 'but not from the people I expected. Philip Long forced me to take a thousand pounds last week, and other contributions have come from men who can ill afford it.'

'So what do you think?' Russell asked. 'Are our influential friends becoming faint-hearted, eh?'

Robert studied the wine in his glass. 'There are many who will passionately profess to serve a cause with life and fortune,' he said, 'but when called to redeem their pledge, contrive to do it with the lives and fortunes of others.'

'My dear Emmet,' said William Hamilton walking back into the room, 'I have managed to find my room, but, search as I may, I cannot find my bed.'

Robert smiled. 'Did you look on the floor, William?'

'I did. And there were sheets, and there were blankets, but there was no *bed*!'

The three men at the tables burst out laughing. 'That *is* your bed,' Robert told him. 'A new fashion in Irish mattresses – rebel's repose – no bed to fall out of when the militia call.'

Hamilton sniffed. 'I was looking forward to a good night's rest. Do *you* have a bed, Emmet?'

'Certainly not. There's only one in the whole house.'

'And who, may I ask, has that?'

'My horse. He won a race today so I had it moved into the stables.'

Hamilton looked unamused as he waited for them to stop laughing. 'I don't think it's at all funny, dear fellow. Are you seriously asking me to sleep on the floor?'

'We have no money for beds, William, and the one bed there is I gave to Anne. You don't begrudge her, do you?'

Again Hamilton sniffed. 'Oh, very well, but I suffered enough on that blasted boat. I think I'd better take a glass of comfort up with me.'

He filled his wineglass, then gave a slow and exaggerated bow, and left the room.

Russell laughed and placed his hands on his chest. 'He's the devil for his comforts, but I'd risk my life on his courage when it's needed. Oh, I nearly forgot,' he withdrew a letter from inside his coat, 'your brother handed this to me a moment before I boarded the Paris coach.'

Robert ripped open the letter and scanned through the contents quickly, pausing to smile at a sentence here and there. 'That's the family news,' he said at length, 'I'll need the discovery-wash to read the rest.'

He returned a minute later with a small bottle, painted fluid over the letter then held it near the light of a candle, slowly reading aloud the words as they emerged:

'Thomas has seen Berthier, the French War Minister. They are planning to send arms, money, and an expedition of twenty-five thousand men to Ireland, but not before November. Berthier insists the Irish must not act until then.'

'Tch!' Russell curled his lip. 'The French must learn we will take their help, but not their orders.'

'Thomas was right in ninety-eight,' Robert said. 'It is better to wait, and win.'

'And we could use the time the French give us,' Jemmy said. 'November gives us only six months or so.'

The moon was high when Robert accompanied Jemmy Hope down the drive. Jemmy had travelled with the others in Mrs Dillon's covered chaise, but he refused Robert's offer to stay in one of the empty rooms.

' 'Tis a warm night, and 'tis a warm woman I have waiting for me,' Jemmy chuckled. 'None of your rebel's repose for me! You lot may be happy to cuddle up on your mats with a hard gun at your side, but give me a soft bed and a soft wife anytime.'

'I'll see you when you get back from the north.'

'Aye, goodnight now.'

Robert watched Jemmy saunter down the lane, then ran after him. 'Jemmy.'

'Aye.'

'The names of those men of rank and fortune we spoke about tonight – I gave them my pledge of secrecy. Only my brother, Russell, and yourself know who they are. Promise me you will never breathe their names to a soul.'

'If that's what you want.'

'Do I have your oath on that?'

'As God is my judge,' Jemmy said, 'their names will not pass my lips, and I'll go to me grave before I break my oath to you, Robert Emmet. Unless you release me from it.'

Robert put a hand on Jemmy's shoulder and nodded. 'Good man.'

The house on Butterfield Lane kept Anne busier than she had envisaged. As well as Messrs Emmet, Russell and Hamilton, an elegant young gentleman named Dowdall often slept there. But despite the labour of looking after four men, Anne felt happier than she had ever done in her life.

She had even grown to like the flirtatious William Hamilton. He had a beautiful singing voice, and not a day went by when the house was not brightened by his melodious renderings.

Thomas Russell was a great joker, always laughing and teasing her, and always showed the same tender interest in Nellie and Jimmy as Mr Robert did. She wondered how old he was and put the question to Robert.

'Thirty-three.'

'Why has he never married?'

Robert smiled. 'Oh, there has been many a young lady who has shared a hopeless love affair with Russell.'

'Why hopeless?'

'Because it was hopeless for any of them to hold on to him long enough to get him to the altar.'

'But has *he* never loved anyone? I mean, truly loved someone?'

'Yes, I believe he did once, in the long ago.'

'What happened to her?'

'She married someone else. During his long internment in gaol.'

'Was he very hurt?'

'I doubt if he will ever consider marriage again.'

After that, Anne felt sorry for Russell and fussed over him with great kindness whenever possible.

If Anne was happy in her new life in Butterfield Lane, Little Arthur was even happier. In the beginning he had carried out his minor duties in assisting Big Art to maintain the property, but then one day, searching in the dining-room for Robert, Little Arthur discovered something which changed his life. He discovered books. The books Robert kept in a bookcase there. Some were in strange languages which he later discovered to be Greek and French, but others were in English and he started to read.

He read tales of the days when Ireland was a land of poets and princes. Of the days when the harbours were filled with ships from all over the world, eager to trade for Irish marble and wool. He devoured the tales of the past High Kings of Ireland, drinking in every word about the Irish princes who had almost succeeded in taking back their land. He read of Owen Roe O'Neill who, a century earlier, had returned from Spain to the land of his fathers, and at the head of an Irish army had attempted to overthrow the English. He read of an Ireland he never knew had existed. An Ireland which had been prosperous, which had sent its scholars to be tutors all over the world. An Ireland where each man had his chance, not destined from birth to poverty and ignorance because of his creed.

'Is it really true,' he asked Robert one afternoon as they sat perched on the field wall at the back of the house, 'that Ireland once sent its scholars all over the world?'

'Very true. There was a time in the past when most of the brilliant teachers in Charlemagne's palace school were Irishmen. There was even a time when English princes considered it prestigious to be educated in Ireland. And it was not only our scholars who enriched Europe, but our philosophers, writers, and poets.'

'And why were Irishmen called "the wild geese"?'

'That was a name given to the thousands of Irishmen who left this country to seek a better life and fortune abroad. They filled the Continental armies and led their campaigns. But most of the exiles carried three things across the water with them: their love of Ireland, their unique sense of humour and pathos, and their dream of liberty.'

'And their wildness. Is that why they were called the wild geese?'

'No!' Robert laughed. 'In the early days when many of them stowed away in the hold of French ships, they were booked down in the logs as so many wild geese, to escape detection.'

'I think I'd like to travel over the water and see the world,' Little Arthur said slowly, 'just as long as I could be sure of coming back. I'd learn everything there is to learn, see everything there is to see, make my fortune and come back a rich man. And then I'd find me a beautiful girl with golden hair and build me a mansion in Wicklow.'

'And what would you do in your mansion in Wicklow? Apart from those times you were not admiring your wife and her golden hair?'

'What would I do?' Little Arthur repeated the question incredulously. 'I'd do what any gentlemen would do – I'd read books!'

Robert soon discovered that Anne's brother had a quick and penetrating mind; although his education was only tolerable, given the time and difficulty Catholics had to obtain it. Before long Little Arthur became Robert's aide-de-camp, attending on his person, and slowly writing the letters Robert patiently dictated to him. They occasionally sat for hours discussing the English language, the correct use of words and their alternatives. Robert would give Little Arthur a subject and leave the composition of the letter to him. He laboured over each sentence, never satisfied until Robert assured him it was correct. His handwriting was plain and businesslike and improved rapidly.

Robert's delight in his protégé's progress was tainted with a sadness. He should be at Trinity, he thought. He's a natural-born scholar.

Jemmy Hope returned from Ulster with heartening news. Every United Irishman he had contacted had bared their teeth with pleasure at the news that Russell was back.

'If he is here, we will follow him,' some said. 'If Dublin will move first, we will not be the last,' others said.

'So,' Russell said, 'that takes care of my province. We have Ulster.'

'But we still need Wicklow,' Robert said.

Miles Byrne had joined them for dinner. He looked questioningly at Robert. 'Michael Dwyer?'

Robert smiled. 'The Wicklow Captain himself.'

Anne was ladling heaps of fortifying vegetables on to Russell's plate when Robert glanced at her. 'What say you of your cousin, Anne?'

She shook her head vaguely. 'I cannot say about Michael, no one can. He has always been his own man.'

'It's incredible how Dwyer and his men have withstood such a vigilant militia for five years,' Russell exclaimed. 'Incredible!'

Miles suddenly laughed. 'Michael Dwyer has a most peculiar talent. He has this ability to disguise himself by a sudden change in his expression and walk. In a second, he looks a different man.'

'Aye,' Anne chuckled, 'I've seen him do it.'

'There was one occasion,' Miles continued, 'when Michael went into Baltinglass. Suddenly the militia were everywhere, shouting that Dwyer was in the streets. So, using the strange talent that he has, Michael pulled his hat low and changed his facial expression and walk. A group of militia ran up to him, demanding to know if he had seen the rebel.

' "Have I seen him?" ' Dwyer said furiously. ' "The blatherumskite nearly knocked me down – and me with a gammy leg! After him, lads! I've just seen the varmint slipping into the house there of the chief of police."

'Then Michael sits on a wall a few feet away, tranquilly

enjoying an apple as he watches the furious militia kick in the chief yeoman's door and charge inside like raging bulls.'

Russell roared a laugh. 'So what happened when the militia discovered he had lied?'

'Ah, well,' Miles grinned. 'Michael also has the ability to disappear like a ghost.'

'I *have* to meet him,' Robert declared. 'We must have a man like that with us.' He turned to Anne. 'Where is Big Arthur?'

'He went over to see Da. Shall I go and fetch him?'

'Yes, tell him we wish to speak with him at once. Tell him he must prepare for a journey to his kinsman.'

The following morning Big Arthur and Jemmy Hope set off on horseback for Wicklow. Robert stood beside Anne as she watched them leave, her eyes bright with yearning.

'I can see you would have liked to go with them,' Robert murmured.

'Oh, I would, Mr Robert. Sometimes I miss my homeland so much. The mountains and glens where I used to roam. And the Wicklow people . . .' She paused, staring into the distance.

'The Wicklow people,' he prompted.

But she made no response, just turned and walked back to the house. How could a Trinity boy, brought up in the chandeliered drawing-rooms of Dublin, ever understand the friendliness of the mountain people or the cosy warmth of a thatched cottage?

That same afternoon, Robert paid a visit to Rose Hope and asked her if she would visit the house on Butterfield Lane occasionally to give Anne some female company.

'It can't be bright for her,' he said to Rose, 'surrounded only by men who talk of little else but rebellion.'

Rose smiled. 'Sure I will, Mr Emmet. Anne is a brave girl, for she must know in the end she runs the same risks as the men, if things go wrong.'

'Pray God they don't, Rose.'

Chapter Twenty-Six

Anne was preparing the evening meal when Big Arthur stomped into the kitchen. 'Where's himself?'

'In the drawing-room.' Her eyes strayed to the dejected figure of Jemmy Hope behind him. 'Did you see Michael?'

'Aye, not much good it did us though.' She followed them through to the drawing-room where Robert and Russell were bent over a map.

'Well?' Robert asked.

'He's not convinced,' Jemmy said. 'He's not prepared to risk his men or the people of Wicklow in another rebellion.'

Miles Byrne could not believe it when he arrived later for dinner. 'Dwyer is dedicated heart and soul to the cause. I can't believe he refuses to join forces with us.'

'Oh, he didn't say that,' Robert answered wryly. 'He said he would have to consider the situation carefully, after discussions with us.'

'So? When is he coming?'

Jemmy snorted. 'He wouldn't even tell us that! It seems he never makes prearranged appointments with anyone. He said it would be himself who picked the day and the hour. Maybe in a month or two.'

Big Art stuck a potato into his mouth and waved his fork in the air, saying finally, 'I told him as I mounted my horse. I said, "Michael, can you not understand that Messrs Emmet and Russell want to see you badly?" '

'And what did he say to that?' Anne asked.

Big Arthur shrugged. 'He just gave that smile of his and said, "Tell Robert Emmet he will see me when he sees me." '

Anne's heart was heavy as she undressed for bed that night. She should have known Michael would not be easy to persuade. How many troublemakers had tried to use him in the past to fight their private feuds for them, under the pretence of striking a blow for liberty.

She climbed into bed and pulled the covers up to her chin. The sound of the trees outside rustling in the soft wind calmed her spirit a little and she closed her eyes in thought. Very few could fool Michael Dwyer, but Emmet and Russell – he must know they were risking everything, surely. Russell only had to be recognised and he was a dead man.

Of a sudden her body stiffened; she turned her head, ears straining towards the window: she had lived too long in the country not to recognise a footfall. She tried to still her breathing as she listened again. Then she heard what sounded like the soft clomping of a horse – more than one horse. She jumped out of bed and pulled a dress over her chemise.

She crept through the dark hall and up the stairs. Russell's room was in darkness but a glimmer of candlelight peeped out from under Mr Robert's door. She tapped on it urgently.

He was at the door in a matter of seconds. 'Mr Robert,' she whispered 'there's someone outside.'

'Are you sure?'

'I'm sure 'twas a footfall I heard. Do you think it's the militia? They always come acreeping late at night – before they kick the doors in.'

Robert ran back into the room for the candle and lit the way down.

' 'Twas at the back of the house I heard them,' Anne whispered.

He blew out the candle at the foot of the stairs. Anne crept behind him down the hall and into the narrow corridor that led to the back door. She stood at his side as he pressed his ear against the panels of the door. 'Do you think it's Major Sirr's militia?' she whispered again.

He made no reply. In the long silence the only sound was their breathing. He moved his face close to hers and whispered, 'Are you sure you heard something?'

'I . . . I thought I did.'

Outside and within the silence spun out until Anne decided she must have been imagining things. 'Perhaps 'twas my imagination after all,' she said in a normal voice. 'I was—'

Robert had reached for her in the darkness and clamped a hand over her mouth.

Startled, Anne stared up at him although she could not see him in the darkness, her ears straining for sounds outside while she tried to ignore his breath on her cheek. A sudden scraping of a stone outside made him drop his hand and pull her away from the door.

'Quickly,' he said. 'You wake Dowdall and Hamilton. I'll get Russell.' She ran after him down the hall. 'But even if they search the place,' she whispered, 'they have nothing on Mr Ellis.'

'Are you forgetting, Anne? We have *Russell* here. A banished rebel.'

He bounded back up the stairs and within minutes, the two Williams, Dowdall and Hamilton, were positioned at the front of the house. Robert and Tom Russell covered the back door, while Anne hovered by the kitchen window. All were armed with muskets, except Anne, who stood by the window clutching a pocket pistol in both hands. She almost dropped it when a hand rapped on the back door. Robert hissed through to her, 'Come out here, Anne.'

The rapping came again.

'Ask who it is,' Robert told her.

'Who are you?' she called.

'King George the Third,' an amused voice replied.

Anne clutched at Robert's arm. 'It's him!'

'Who?'

'My cousin Michael! He doesn't know the password. Open the door.'

He was leaning against the frame when Robert opened the door, his smile bright in the darkness.

'You wanted to see me, avic?'

Seconds later Anne was lighting candles while Emmet and Russell stood in the kitchen shaking hands with the Wicklow Captain and his three companions: Hugh Vesty Byrne, John Mernagh, and Martin Burke.

Robert was smiling at Dwyer with instant liking. He was tall and somewhere in his late twenties. His voice had the musical lilt of the mountains, not broad like the Dubliners. There was a cool confidence and reckless humour in his face that belied the hard and hunted life he led, which seemed to have left him quite undamaged. Indeed, he looked like a hard, fit young man who truly owned himself in every way.

'What did you do with your horses?' Robert asked.

'We led them one by one into your stables,' Michael said. 'After we had carefully inspected the place.'

Anne's eyes proudly took in the manly frame of her cousin, from his high mountain boots to the curly tips of his black hair. His hazel eyes were now smiling merrily at her, and she meant to smile in return, but a delighted giggle escaped her. She should have *known* Michael would come.

Dwyer turned quickly as Hamilton and Dowdall entered the kitchen. Russell introduced them.

The Wicklow Captain responded in a friendly manner to Hamilton, but there was cynical humour in his eyes as he looked long at the dandified Dowdall, clothed in a red silk dressing-gown. 'A newspaper man, you say?'

'And a patriot of the ninety-eight,' Dowdall added grandly.

Dwyer seemed to find this very amusing. 'Sure every mother's son you meet these days claims to be a patriot of the ninety-eight,' he said dryly.

'Well I am!' Dowdall insisted, looking affronted. 'And it was men like Thomas Emmet I worked with.'

'Oh!' the Wicklow Captain looked hugely impressed; then glancing down at the musket in Dowdall's hand, observed quietly, 'Lucky for you, avic, that we were not the militia.'

'Why so?' Dowdall looked down at his musket.

'The doghead is missing,' Michael informed him, 'so is the flint. And I've yet to find a musket that will fire a bullet without a flint.'

Dowdall turned very white under Dwyer's mocking gaze and looked to Emmet for moral support, but Robert and Russell were staring at him in disbelief.

'You fool!' Russell exclaimed. 'Where did you get that musket?'

'From the drawing-room,' Dowdall answered. 'I grabbed the first one that came to hand.'

'And that is the one I was cleaning earlier this evening,' Hamilton told him. 'Imbecile! A mistake like that could get you killed.'

'I'm not used to muskets,' Dowdall cried. His face was now the colour of his dressing-gown, but he was spared from further humiliation when Emmet said in his defence to Dwyer:

'Dowdall was a close friend of my brother. He may be no expert with a gun, but he is very loyal, and has spent time in prison for being a United man. He secured the lease on these premises, and does all our paperwork.'

At that moment another knock came on the back door, followed by the password.

'It's Jemmy,' said Russell moving out to the passage, then, when he had opened the back door, 'What the blazes has you back at this hour?'

'Sure hadn't I got as far as the Terenure Road when I discovered I'd left—' Jemmy's mouth dropped open when he entered the kitchen and saw Michael Dwyer. 'Good God! I know you said you'd pick the day and the hour, but you didn't say you'd be right behind us.'

Michael grinned. 'Like the Devil.' Then, turning to Robert, 'Are there any more of your friends lurking upstairs or wandering hereabouts?'

'No,' Robert assured him. 'We are all here.'

'And I believe you wish to talk business?'

'That is true.'

'Then let us get on with it, avic. I must shortly return to Imaal.'

Later in the dining-room, after the Wicklow men had eaten the bread and cheese supper Anne had prepared, Robert asked Dwyer his views, as a front-line fighter, on the failure of the '98.

Dwyer ran silent and deep for a moment, and when he spoke there was not a tinge of emotion in his voice. He spoke with a quiet authority, a man experienced in battle and used to command.

'There was more than one cause for our failure,' he said. 'Kildare flew to arms and the affair exploded without a proper signal. We had not enough officers sufficiently qualified, and we were in great need of arms and ammunition. We might have won, if the business had gone as Lord Edward planned. The whole of Ireland was supposed to rise, but when it happened, the province of Leinster was left to fight alone. And, although the business was organised in Dublin itself, Dublin itself made little show.'

'Dublin was crippled by a huge military presence,' Robert said. 'You know that.'

'Ach,' Michael said dismissively, 'the Dublin committees had too many grand meetings and made too many fine and bold speeches for all to hear. They might as well have sent out a public warning to the Castle saying "Here we are, getting ready to take the field against you, unless you speedily stop us." '

No one could disagree. The arrests of the Executive Council before the rebellion proved the careless lack of caution and secrecy by men belonging to the Dublin committees.

'And that is why I tell you now,' Michael went on, his voice deadly serious, 'that Wexford and Wicklow have resolved never to be the first in the field again. They suffered the heaviest losses, even worse than Kildare; half of their young men wiped out. It would be cruel to bring them out again, without guaranteed support from elsewhere.'

'Well,' Robert said, 'this time it will be Dublin that makes the first move. And both Ulster and Munster have pledged to support us.'

Emmet suddenly felt swamped with gloom. Somehow, because Dwyer had fought with such valour in 1798, and still kept up a resistance in the glens, he had been sure the Wicklow Captain would jump eagerly at the chance of joining them. Now he was not so sure. This cool, realistic Wicklow man was as cautious as a fox. But he was also an excellent commander and, even more importantly, he was an honourable fellow who upheld all the beliefs of the United Irishmen. Despite his long resistance, it was an acknowledged fact that he had never committed an unmanly act, or tolerated any faction-fighting or unacceptable behaviour from his men. Dwyer's best friend in '98 had been a Presbyterian soldier named Sam McAllister and, like many another in Wicklow, he truly honoured the name of General John Moore – even though he had faced him in battle.

He was also known to be wholly uncontaminated by any animosity towards Englishmen. Although, like every United Irishman, he despised and detested their politicians at Dublin Castle. He was a man to have on your side. William Wickham had recently announced that his capture alone would be like the capture of an army to the Castle. So far, Michael Dwyer had proved unbeatable.

Suddenly, William Dowdall, eager to wipe away their initial bad start and establish a camaraderie with Dwyer, said: 'The massacre on Vinegar Hill – that must have been brutal for the rebel army. Will you tell us about it?'

'God, no!' Michael answered. 'That was a dirty business. If it's the tragic and gory details you want, then you're talking to the wrong rebel.'

He leaned back in his chair and fixed his eyes on Emmet. 'You asked for my opinion on the last rebellion; I have given it. Now, I ask about your venture. A swift bloodless coup, Big Arthur tells me.'

Dwyer's face showed no reaction as he listened attentively to Emmet outlining his plan.

'The Castle are so confident we have been wiped out,' Robert said, 'their security is minimal. The gates of the Castle stay open far into the night and it is only half garrisoned. The Viceroy and the Secretaries travel with hardly any protection. There are fewer troops in Ireland now than Kildare alone had to contend with in ninety-eight. And once the war between Britain and France resumes, many of those troops will be shipped back to England.'

'It's the Trojan Horse idea,' Russell added. 'There is always some sort of entertaining going on in the Castle banqueting rooms. The soldiers don't even bother to halt or check the occupants of carriages.'

'So, our first small detachment enters the Castle in carriages and dress-cloaks over their uniforms,' Robert continued. 'Once they are safely inside, the second detachment moves in. Other detachments will be waiting at strategic points around the city. Once they see the signal flare, the Viceregal Lodge, the Pigeon House, and the Artillery Barracks will be taken.'

Michael thought about it. 'Even if your plan worked, they would send a large force to retake the Castle.'

'Yes, but they would have to take it from an equally large army of men. And even if a huge force of troops marched on Dublin, from whatever direction they came, they would be caught between our men advancing from north and south.'

Hugh Vesty was smiling. 'I've got to hand it to you, Robert Emmet, you're a cool boyo to dream up that one. Taking the mighty Dublin Castle! Man, you're daft!'

'No, he's not,' Dwyer said slowly. 'It's been proven many times that a small man can knock out a giant if he—'

'Has the element of surprise,' Robert finished.

Dwyer smiled. 'That was the strategy we used at Ballyellis,' he said. 'One of our better victories in ninety-eight.'

He lost his smile. 'But taking the Castle is one thing – how do you intend to hold the city against the troops until you receive back-up support from elsewhere? Have you worked out a strategy?'

'I have,' Emmet replied. 'It is very similar to the strategy worked out with Lord Edward Fitzgerald in ninety-eight.'

They talked for an hour. Anne listened attentively, and much of the strategic detail made a great deal of sense to her.

'It is well known,' Emmet was saying, 'that any officer of skill would be cautious in bringing his troops into a large city in a state of insurrection. First of all his troops, by the width of the streets, would have a very narrow front. And no matter how many troops he has, only four men deep could be brought into action, which even in the widest of our streets, cannot be more than eighty men, as space must be left on each side of the street for the men who discharge to retreat to the rear, so that their places may be occupied by the next in succession who are loaded. Therefore, even if he has a thousand men at his command, not more than eighty can act at any one time.

'In the next place, in those parts where our men would be positioned but not engaged in any action, they would be busy unpaving the streets, so as to impede the movements of horse and artillery along all avenues where government troops are likely to pass. Numbers would be engaged forming barricades at every twenty or thirty yards, which should impede the progress of the troops getting into the city.

'At the same time, our men in the neighbouring counties would rise, and engage the troops in their vicinity, and prevent a junction or passage to any army intended for the city; they would tear up the roads, and barricade at every convenient distance with felled trees and implements of husbandry, etc.,

etc., while at the same time lining the hedges, walls, ditches with men armed with muskets who could defend their positions.'

He looked at Michael Dwyer for his reaction, but Dwyer was leaning forward to look at the map on the table.

'It is a fact,' he said to Emmet, 'that however well exercised armies are by sham battles, they are never prepared for broken roads or enclosed fields in a country like ours. They were not prepared at Arklow, Oulart Hill, or Ballyellis, and that is why our regiments carried the fields there.'

'The most important act of all,' Emmet said, 'is the fall of the Castle. The symbolic effect of that would be as powerful as the fall of the Bastille – although we intend no murder, not even if the three Cs themselves were there. The oath of the United Irishmen must be upheld. Ideally, we hope to be able to put the underlings of George of Hanover on a very comfy vessel and send them sailing back whence they came.'

'And you think the British Government would accept that?' Dwyer asked.

'They would have to accept it eventually, if only on the broad historical statement that their rule was imposed by conquest and not the will of the people, has never succeeded, and therefore cannot indefinitely survive. During six hundred years there have been five major rebellions, and if we fail, there will be more. It would be a blessing from heaven if we were not constantly driven to the last stage of desperate resistance, and the will of the people was considered. But no! The only solution effected is an Act of Union passed by a Parliament notoriously bribed, who sold while they still had a country to sell, before another rebellion finally snatched it from them. But, Act of Union or not, *without* the will of the people, a ruling government can only maintain power by a constant reliance on military force. It is the same in Poland – listen to Kosciusko speak about Poland and your heart would break. You would think he was speaking about Ireland.'

Michael Dwyer was looking at Emmet with a new respect. If he had feared so before, he now knew for certain that Emmet was no dilettante playing at revolution, he was as determined as Lord Edward and Tone had been.

'So what is it to be, Dwyer?' Russell said suddenly. 'You have heard Robert out. Now, are you willing to join forces with us?'

From under his lashes Michael threw glances at his comrades, then looked Russell fully in the face, but gave his answer to Emmet.

'Yes,' he said, 'and glad of the chance.'

Robert suddenly realised he had been holding his breath. He exhaled with relief; for without Michael Dwyer in command, no man in Wicklow would make a move. Miles Byrne had assured them of that.

For the moment everyone seem satisfied, then Russell bit his lip thoughtfully and set his glass down. 'What finally persuaded you?' he asked Dwyer curiously. 'Which part of the plan?'

Michael shrugged. 'No part in particular,' he said, then broke into a wicked smile. 'We had already decided before we left Wicklow to assist you in any way we could.'

'Oh, you bastard!' Russell said with a laugh.

'But we'll not strike the first blow,' Dwyer repeated to Emmet. 'As I've already said, the whole of Ireland was to rise once before, but Leinster was left to fight alone. If you succeed in your attempt, and get inside the Castle, then we will be waiting on the outskirts as a back-up force ready to move in and assist you.'

Emmet and Russell smiled at each other with delight; and Anne, who was sitting with the men around the large table, beamed with joy at the successful outcome of the meeting. Her warm eyes embraced them all. Michael first, her cousin whom she had adored since childhood, then nice Mr Robert and nice Mr Russell, amorous young Hamilton, sturdy Jemmy, and even pompous Dowdall. Her eyes glistened with sudden love for them all.

'And on that happy note,' said Jemmy Hope, 'I'll take myself home. I'll get a couple of hours sleep if I'm lucky.'

Within seconds Hugh Vesty Byrne and Martin Burke were standing in front of the door barring Jemmy's exit.

'Nobody leaves before we do,' said Hugh Vesty.

'Are you codding?' Jemmy turned to stare at Dwyer. 'Surely

to God you can trust me? I can't stay here! I've a business to see to in the morning.'

'And so you shall,' Michael said. 'We will leave before the cock crows.'

'If you trust us then you trust Jemmy,' Robert said, astonished. 'He's as safe as a rock.'

'Rocks are known to slide,' Michael informed him, then looked at Jemmy who protested, 'I have a wife waiting for me at home.'

'I understand your problem,' Michael said, 'but I understand my own better. We cannot move as freely as you. There is a price on each of us, and we rarely take chances. I mean no offence to yourself, man.'

'None taken,' Jemmy said, 'not if you let me go now.'

After a moment's hesitation, Michael waved his men aside. 'But when we call in future,' he said to Emmet, 'I would ask for your guarantee that no man leaves until after we do.'

'You have it. But you will not be betrayed by anyone here. Russell runs as great a risk as yourself.'

'Well,' said Dowdall airily, having decided now that he loathed Michael Dwyer's cool arrogance. 'I find all this mistrust thoroughly offensive! To listen to you, Dwyer, anyone would think we were a bunch of ruddy informers!'

'Oh, mind your tone, avic,' Michael answered quietly. 'I've not kept my freedom for five years with half the army and every bounty hunter on my back by trusting easily, not even United Irishmen.' His eyes slanted over Dowdall's flamboyant red silk dressing-gown as he leaned forward, his voice soft and confiding, 'Not even patriots of the ninety-eight.'

Jemmy Hope suddenly bolted out of the room. Anne ran after him and caught him at the back door. 'You're not angry are you, Jemmy? Michael intended no personal insult to you.'

When Jemmy turned to face her, she saw he was laughing. 'Did ye see Dowdall's face!'

After a few seconds, he patted her arm to reassure her. 'Dowdall is Emmet's devoted fop but he's no traitor. Still, Michael Dwyer is wise enough to know that it is Irish traitors who have ruined this land as much as English foes. And if more of the commanders of ninety-eight had been like Michael

Dwyer, we wouldn't have been betrayed so much and so often.'
Jemmy scratched his head and laughed again. 'Boys, o boys,
now there's a man if ever you need one.'

Anne turned as Robert came down the hall and moved into
the yard to exchange a few quiet words with Jemmy. When he
stepped back inside, she said anxiously, 'Are you happy, Mr
Robert, that Michael is joining you?'

'Happy?' He smiled and lightly flicked her chin. 'I'm
delirious! With the Wicklow Captain backing us, I just *know*
we can do it.'

Miles Byrne was also delighted with the news of Michael
Dwyer's recruitment. He advised Robert that depots would
now have to be found to store the pikes, arms, and ammunition.

Michael Quigley was instructed to lease the vacant
malthouse at the back of the White Bull in Thomas Street. It
would be used at the time of the rising to arm the men from
Kildare. Robert inspected the walls of the depot, then drew up
designs for false walls to be erected around each room, behind
which the arms could be stacked.

A week later Robert instructed a Scots carpenter by the name
of McIntosh to take a house in Patrick Street, for which he
provided the necessary money. McIntosh immediately took the
lease in his own name, paying six months' rent in advance, and
set to work making changes in the design of the house, according to Emmet's instructions.

On the morning of 16th May, Robert dropped in to see Jemmy
Hope who was having his breakfast. 'Is Gallagher ready?'

Jemmy nodded. 'His valise is packed.'

'Then tell him to come to the house this afternoon for the
letter. Impress upon him, as I will, that he must hand it personally to Thomas. If he cannot place it in my brother's hand, he
must destroy it.'

'Gallagher will only need to be told once.'

Back at Butterfield Lane, Robert wrote to Thomas:

Organisation on a new and closer plan has been carried to
a great extent upon the United Irishmen. There is close

344

communication between north and south. Kildare and Dublin are in a forward state. Wicklow is pledged. The government have no suspicions of the preparations, but we are keeping as low as possible. Our biggest difficulty now is lack of money. Contributions filter in from unexpected sources, but that which was promised I fear will not now come and my resources are dwindling. I cannot raise the money here by subscription for fear of making the business public. We have one hope left – you must raise the money from the Irish community in Paris and the Americans.

Send home McP, S, and McD – particularly the last – communications with his county are worse than elsewhere.

Robert sealed the letter, and lightly pressed his signet-ring on to the wax. The following morning Gallagher left Ireland for France, the letter sewn inside the knee of his breeches.

That same day, on 17th May 1803, France declared war on England.

Chapter Twenty-Seven

Miles Byrne struggled to curb his exasperation as he watched Robert bent in concentration over a table in the Patrick Street depot. He had already made his objections plain enough: what money they had should be spent on the ordinary weapons of battle, not scientific experiments.

Six other men stood watching Emmet. The Scottish carpenter, McIntosh, looked utterly bemused. 'I've never seen anythin' like this,' he said, 'rawkets ye call them?'

Robert held the iron tube of the rocket in his left hand, lifted the hammer with his right, and said, 'We must check exactly how many blows are needed to drive in the clasps . . . one, two, three.'

He looked at each of the men. 'Always use a hammer of the same weight as this one. Always weigh your hammer before using it. And remember, three blows will do the clasps.'

'That stuff in the jug,' Miles said, 'it looks like runny mortar.'

'All you need learn is the assembly,' Robert told him, 'I will make the mixture.' Then as he carefully poured the substance into the tube, added, 'It's a mixture of gunpowder, nitre, sulphur, and other substances.' He finished by plugging the explosive down into the tube. 'And there it is!'

Miles looked dubiously at the tube.

'My dear Miles, you can make the next one,' Robert said. 'And it will be yours we will use when we are ready to test. Then, after everybody has made one, we will discuss the business of care and safety.'

Miles, still looking doubtful as he handled the iron tube, slowly assembled the rocket under Robert's supervision, his face intense with the attention he gave to each detail.

'Good man,' Robert said, smiling. 'Now it is your turn, Mr McIntosh.'

On the journey home Robert let the reins hang slack as he pondered the decisions made by the council the night before. Now that France and England were at war again, a meeting had been called for all leaders of each county in the Leinster province.

As in 1798, a system of military discipline was to be upheld. A general for each county, a captain for each barony, and a number of lieutenants for each parish. Tailors were to be instructed to make green uniforms for the leaders. Ranks were decided. Russell and Hamilton would command Belfast and pick their own lieutenants when they reached the north. Robert chose Miles Byrne as his captain, with Stafford, Quigley, Mahon, and Wilde as lieutenants.

Robert sighed as Rathfarnham came into view. So many problems still to sort out. So many things to do. And what wouldn't he give for a good night's sleep in a decent bed for a change.

Inside the kitchen of Butterfield Lane he found another problem waiting for him on the settle by the hearth.

'Ah, me boy!' Lennard cried. 'I was wondering when ye were coming back.'

'Lennard! I told you never to come here unless I sent for you.'

'Aye, ye did. But I got fed up waiting. So here I am.'

'Is my mother well?'

'Yer mother is well. Didn't ye see her only last week? Now then, where's me instructions?'

Robert glanced over at Anne standing by the sink, her head bent low as she peeled potatoes which she washed in a bowl then dropped into a massive cooking cauldron.

'What instructions, Lennard?'

'For the rising, o' course! Ye don't think I'm not going to be there when ye shtrike a blow do ye!'

Again Robert looked at Anne, who met his eyes. 'A rising?' he said to her. 'A rising – for pity's sake! Have you ever heard such nonsense?'

Anne pressed her lips together and shook her head mutely, her eyes bright with amusement.

'Nonsense is it, wha'? Who sez it's nonsense? Ye may say it's nonsense, but I know it's not! I didn't come off yesterday's cabbage leaf, I was a wise old butterfly long ago. Ye can't fool me—'

Robert ignored him. 'Is anyone using the hip-bath?' he asked Anne.

'Mr Hamilton took it to his room half an hour ago. He must be in it now. Can't you hear him singing?'

'I'll just have to wait then,' Robert said. 'I'll fetch a bucket of water for the fire in the meantime.'

'Now hold on there,' Lennard cried. 'Say what ye have to say to me first, then I'll fetch the water for yer wash.'

'I've nothing to say to you, Lennard.'

'So why do ye have these boys here,' Lennard demanded, 'if 'tis not for the plan of a rising?'

Robert sat down beside Lennard on the settle and bent to remove his boot. 'These are my friends, Lennard, and, true, we may discuss Ireland's problems, but no one has said anything about a rising.' He tilted an eyebrow. 'The very idea!'

'Gah! So ye don't want to tell me! Is that it?' Lennard was on his mettle now. 'Ye think I'm too old. Me, who long suffered yer youth! If it weren't for me always bringing ye out of yerself, ye wouldn't be talking so aisy now. Ye'd still be shpitting on yer words like a lovesick girl!'

'Well, here, ye do some shpitting on that,' Robert held out his boot, 'I no longer have Simmins to shine them for me.'

'What!' Lennard was almost frothing at the mouth. 'I'm not yer man! I was never yer man! And I'm not going to be yer man now!'

Robert turned in bewilderment to Anne. 'Why is it that other gents command such respect from their staff, but I get only abuse?' He turned back to Lennard and smiled coaxingly, 'Will you not reconsider polishing my boots?'

Lennard muttered a curse, then sat glooming like an injured parent. Robert shrugged and pulled his boot back on, then, looking carefully into Lennard's face, inquired, 'Are ye going into Dubbelin, wha'? Or are ye shtaying to have a bite?'

'Oh, now!' Lennard declared with a sniff. 'So you think I might be good enough to eat in yer kitchen with yer handmaiden, do ye? Well let me tell ye something here and now—'

'He's definitely staying,' Robert said over his shoulder to Anne. 'Throw another potato in the pot.'

'Who was it,' Lennard wailed with extravagant self-pity, 'that stood guard over ye in the garden that night? Whooo risked life and limb getting ye to the docks? Whoooo looked after ye like a son when Mr Christopher was the shining light and ye were just a small shadow? Whoooooo was it . . . ?'

'Enough!' Robert groaned. 'I give in, Lennard. I have enough on my mind without a performance from you.'

Lennard jerked round and peered at him from under his bushy brows. 'Are ye going to let me join ye then?'

'Yes, but I warn you, Lennard, if you breathe one word to Johnny the Hat, Billy the Brogue, or anyone else, I swear I'll tie your tongue in a knot.'

'Ah, me boy! Ye know ye can trust me!' Lennard's teeth were bared with delight. 'Sure, didn't I know ye were planning to strike a blow. And may the Devil eat me tongue if I open me gob about it. Now then – what do ye want me to do? Run them in with a pike or blow their brains out with a gun?'

Robert's face was drawn in intense concentration as he stared at the floor. Anne carried the cauldron over to the fire, then, like Lennard, she waited silently for his answer.

'There are many important jobs to do in an insurrection, Lennard,' he said quietly, 'and although he may not be in the front line, a man must do his appointed task with noble dedication, for the sake of his country.'

'Oh, aye,' Lennard agreed solemnly.

'And on the night in question, there will be various groups around the city waiting for the signal to move.'

'Aye, aye.'

Robert frowned. 'I did hope Russell himself could do this job, but unfortunately he will not be to hand, so I shall trust it to you, Lennard.'

Lennard could hardly control himself. 'Aye, go on, go on!'

'Precision is very important,' Robert went on. 'The signals must be set off at exactly the right time. The head signalman – that will be you – must position himself in a strategic point overlooking the city.' Robert's eyes widened as an idea came to him. 'The garden of my mother's house at Casino. It is the ideal place, Lennard!'

'Do ye think so? Well, go on.'

'Then the head signalman – which will be you – must watch carefully, and write down the time each flare goes off. He must note down exactly how many minutes there are between flares. That way we will know afterwards if every man did his job properly. And believe me, Lennard, woe betide any man whom you report—' He stopped as Anne ran out of the kitchen.

Robert looked back at Lennard. 'Oh, how could I have been so tactless, Lennard? I completely forgot Anne had asked to do that job. But this house is not placed as well as Casino. She doesn't seem to understand that correct positioning is essential.'

'Gah!' Lennard grunted. 'Ye don't want no blathering woman doing a man's job, Misther Robert.' He gripped his knees and pursed his lips solemnly. 'Now then, I'll need a timepiece, won't I?'

* * *

Anne was sitting in the straw chuckling when Robert strode into the stable ten minutes later. 'Is Lennard happy now?' she asked.

'Happy as a bee in a honeypot.'

'How did you dream that one up?'

He lifted his cloak off the stall. 'I don't know what you are insinuating, Miss Devlin. I've been looking for a man for that job for over a month.'

'What's Lennard doing now?'

'Discussing the matter with *Misther* Russell. And that gentleman, after slapping the new soldier on the back a number of times, has insisted that Lennard should be furnished with a military-style hat and a telescope as well as a watch.'

Anne flopped back on to the straw in laughter. 'Ah, God! 'Tis too much for me in this house.' She jerked up again. 'Did you know that Mr Russell curls his hair with a heated poker? I've seen him doing it many a morning.'

Robert adjusted the cloak on his shoulders. 'Every man has his weakness, Anne, and Russell's hair has always been his pride and joy.'

Her smile faded as she stared at him. 'Where are you going? I thought you wanted a bath.'

'Hamilton refuses to shift himself,' he answered, walking away. 'I'll have one later.'

'So where are you off to now?' she cried, jumping up. 'You're always disappearing for hours and no one knows where you go.'

He turned sharply and looked at her.

Anne knew the moment had come to ask the question that had puzzled her for weeks. He kept her informed of all his movements, except those times when he disappeared for entire afternoons, two or three times a week.

'Where do you go?' she murmured.

Robert moved over to the black stallion and fondled its nose. Something deep inside him refused to allow his secret meetings with Sarah to be known to anyone, especially this country girl who could be so abrasively mocking about young ladies of the gentry.

'Do you go walking?'

'Sometimes.' Robert was evasive. 'Other times I ride out to the hills.' He patted the stallion's flank, then turned away. 'But now I'm going across the fields to have a few words with your father about the equipment for Dwyer.'

'Can I come with you?'

Robert stared at her, surprised at her request. 'What about the preparation of dinner?'

'Oh, 'tis done! All it needs now is to sit and simmer for an hour.' She waited for him to say something. 'Can I come with you then? 'Tis a while since I've seen Ma and Da.'

He shrugged. 'If you wish.'

Anne flashed him a smile. 'I'll get my cloak, so.'

Robert talked quietly and earnestly as they walked slowly back from the dairy across the back fields to Butterfield Lane. The shadows of evening enveloped the trees and all the natural world was folding into a silence.

'America showed us the way,' he was saying. 'When she achieved her independence, Jefferson and Adams drafted a policy decreeing that a section of land be set aside in every thirty sections of land, and used for the building of school-houses to educate the people.'

'Oh, now you are getting greedy!' Anne said with a laugh. 'Ireland's independence is one thing, but schoolhouses everywhere, too!'

'Democracy *needs* knowledge to succeed,' he insisted. 'As Jefferson said – "If you expect the people to be ignorant *and* free, you expect what never was, and never will be." '

She looked into his dark eyes with their serious, intellectual expression, and thought him to be a very clever, but innocent young man. His dreams were moving from the revolutionary to the romantic. Schoolhouses indeed! Did he honestly believe that all the children of rural peasants would march off to school when there was so much work to be done on the land? Work that paid the rack-rents. Work that meant survival.

'If we all went off to school and did less work,' she said, 'how could the gentry live off our backs?'

'In a democratic land,' he told her, 'there would be no gentle-men who did nothing, and lived in expectation of doing nothing.

Every man would be whatever he could make of himself by his own industry.' He smiled. 'You see, Anne, the entire world is changing. The seed of liberty was first planted in America, it shot into bud in France, but one day it will bloom all over the world – even in Ireland, even in Poland. Freedom for every nation to rule itself will be a reality.'

'What about religion?' she suddenly demanded. 'Da says that men who read Tom Paine have no religion, only a fill of something—'

'A philosophy.'

'Well, you have a book in your room by Tom Paine, yet you claim to be a Christian. You even have a Bible.'

'It is possible, Anne, for a man to have a belief and still embrace the finer parts of another philosophy.'

'So what is this filoss—'

'It is a philosophy that man is responsible for his own actions, and free to choose his own development and destiny.'

'Oh, I see,' she said, not seeing at all, and thinking that everyone knew that only God and fate could decide a man's destiny.

'And that the human rights of the common man take precedence over property and privilege. Equality and fraternity. Government by the consent of the governed.'

'Da also says that a lot of the French revolutionaries turned their back on God, and Tom Paine does not believe in religion.'

'Maybe not in any one particular religion, but Paine does say, every religion is good that teaches man to be good.'

She could find no answer to that.

It was just after dawn, one week later, when Robert set out for the Dublin hills accompanied by Russell, Hamilton, Dowdall, Miles Byrne and Jemmy Hope. As soon as they had dismounted, and while Robert and Jemmy proceeded to knock two supports into the ground, Miles made his fears known to Tom Russell.

'Some of the Wexford men do not approve of Mr Emmet's scientific experiments. Neither do I, if for no other reason than the expense of it all.'

Russell gave a small laugh, hiding his own apprehensions.

352

'The Wexford men have only experienced the cheapest weapons of battle, that's why they have always been defeated.'

Miles's mouth twisted bitterly, unable to deny the defeat. They both fell silent, curiously watching Emmet as he laid a board against the supports to make a trestle. Then, fastening the rocket to a pole with wire, he placed the pole against the trestle and set light to the fuse.

Everyone waited, then stepped quickly back, their breaths held as they watched the small flame twist its way up the fuse. The rocket went off like a thunderbolt, carrying the pole with it. It rose, screaming and hissing into the air, throwing flames and fire behind it. They all sprang into a mad run after the rocket, trying to keep up and gaping in astonishment as it descended, continuing to tear up the ground until the last of the substance with which it was filled was finished.

A stunned silence fell on the other men as Robert crouched down to examine the tail of the rocket.

'The fuse didn't communicate the fire quick enough,' he murmured, 'but that can be remedied by using stronger liquid.'

'What exactly will you be using them for?' Hamilton asked.

'Initially as signal flares. But if detachments of cavalry enter the city by the various roads, and there are not enough men to stop them, one of these will do the job a damned sight better. The flames alone will rear the horses and disorganise them.'

'Bloody marvellous!' Miles exclaimed.

It was then they heard the thunder of hoofs in the distance. They turned quickly to see William Dowdall galloping away over the crest of a hill as if the Devil himself was after him.

The men all laughed uproariously. 'Come on,' Hamilton cried, 'let's celebrate and go for a swim in the river.'

Robert was looking after Dowdall and grinning. 'And then back to the house for a good breakfast,' he said.

Miles and Jemmy still stared at the remains of the rocket and the scorched hole in the ground. Robert put a hand on Miles's shoulder. 'Come along, my friend, you must be the first to celebrate. It was yourself who made that rocket.'

'Did I?' Miles asked, ingenuously surprised. 'Is that the one I made?'

Robert nodded. 'The very one.'

'Fancy that!' Miles's blue eyes were jubilant. 'Just think, man! If we'd only had a few of those on Vinegar Hill.'

'You'd have torn the ground from under them,' Jemmy said, then let out a 'Whooooop!' and ran after Russell and Hamilton as they strode back to the horses.

Miles looked sheepishly at Robert. 'Ah, I take back everything I said about you and your blasted experiments.'

The two young men smiled at each other with open liking and friendship, then fell into an easy stroll behind the others.

The old shepherd sat on the hill smoking his pipe. The summer days were getting longer and the young gentry couple were back on their camp near the tree. It would be amusing to watch them again.

She looked a lovely young thing with her auburn hair falling down over her green frock. 'Twould remind ye of the burnished autumn leaves, falling on to the green grass of all seasons.

At length the old man sighed with disappointment. The young gentry couple were having a quiet peaceful afternoon, none of the shenanigans of the last time they were here. Almost an hour had passed and they had hardly moved, just sitting with their heads together and talking as if starved of the nourishment of conversation for years.

The old shepherd swiped at the pipe smoke before his rheumy eyes to get a closer look. Oh, tunderturf, what's he doing now? Stealing a kiss! Putting his heart into it an' all. *Acushla!*

That's right, avic – steal a kiss, steal her heart, steal her money, then steal away. Ah, musha, would you look at the way he's stroking her hair. Sure what's Romeo to that? *Acushla!*

Arrah, they're standing up, departing. Ah well, to every shoe its road, to every foot its blister!

The old man rose to leave and laughed as he plodded down to his sheep with his dog at his heels. 'Did ye see that, Brian Boru? All lovey-dovey they were today, and ye and me hoping for another good disagrayment! Ah well, to every bee his flower.'

Robert discreetly visited the arms depots in the city by day and by night. Preparations were progressing satisfactorily, with everyone exercising the greatest caution. Each group concentrated on their own work and often did not know the names or the allotted jobs of others. The men in the Patrick Street depot rarely mixed with those from the Thomas Street depot. Only the lieutenants were allowed to move freely from one work station to the other.

'My God!' said Rose Hope as she sat down opposite Anne in the kitchen of Butterfield Lane and lifted her cup of tea. 'No wonder Jemmy and Miles refer to this place as The Palace. There must be a hundred coming to dine tonight with the food that we've prepared.'

'There'll be thirty,' Anne said. 'The leaders from each district are having another council tonight.'

'And where are the men now?'

'Away in the mountains since before dawn yesterday. Mr Russell is training all the leaders to reload their muskets in forty seconds flat. He says he won't have fifty or sixty. It has to be done in forty, like the British.'

'And no doubt they'll all be famished when they come back. Mind, there's enough food there to feed an army.'

'I wouldn't have managed without your help, Rose.'

Rose chuckled and sipped her tea. 'Aye, well, when Mr Emmet asked me to come out sometimes and keep you company, he did me a favour, too. Jemmy's not a mixer at all.'

Anne put down her cup and looked at Rose in surprise. 'It was Mr Robert who went and asked you to come and keep me company? Why did he do that?'

Rose shrugged. 'He was worried you might be lonely with only men around. And he wants to involve your mother and sisters as little as possible.'

'Fancy that . . .' Anne was smiling. 'Doesn't he think of everything?'

'Aye, he seems to.'

Anne leaned forward conspiratorily. 'Did you know, Rose, that Mr Robert designed the United Irish seal in ninety-eight?'

'Is that right?'

'Aye, Mr Russell told me. It was when his brother was running things. He wanted a letter-seal for the United leaders, so Mr Robert designed a special ring. Have you not noticed that himself and Russell wear them?'

'I have not,' Rose said.

'And did you know, Rose, that Mr Robert can speak Irish like a farmer and French as good as a Jacobin.'

'Imagine,' Rose replied with a wide-eyed sarcasm that was lost on Anne. 'And yet to myself he speaks only the language of an Englishman.'

'And he writes poetry! When I was tidying his papers I saw this poem about a sad and beautiful young girl with long auburn hair playing lilting tunes on her harp. Ireland the Queen, of course. Isn't she always described as sad and playing her harp?'

Anne took a quick sip of tea. 'And there was another poem about the shamrock and the London pride. It told how the shamrock had for so long grown under the dark shade of the London pride, but whenever the poor shamrock tried to see the sun and raised her head, the roots of the mighty London pride encircled her and *crushed* her dead.' The last was emphasised with a quick twist of her hand into a fist.

'Imagine that now,' Rose said. 'Wouldn't you think Mr Emmet had more important things to do with his time than write about plants?'

But Anne was not disposed to question it, so Rose rested her elbows on the table, sipped her tea and listened patiently as Anne confided that Mr Robert was so *kind*. Warned her to be thrifty, then turned around and was generous to a fault. And he never really treated her like a servant, was nothing at all like the jumped-up gentry.

'But he is gentry, Anne.'

'Aye, but he's not like the most of them.'

For a moment Rose gazed thoughtfully at the rim of her cup. 'I'm just wondering,' she said slowly, 'if Robert Emmet has any faults at all?' Anne stared at Rose and Rose went on, 'I mean, only a saint could be that faultless, not like the rest of us poor sinners.'

Anne's cup crashed on to the saucer. 'What are you saying, Rose?'

Rose pondered the question and the thoughts which had lately troubled her so. Could she tell Anne she was heading for heartbreak? That apart from Anne being just a servant and he a gentleman, Jemmy had said twice in the past week that he was convinced Robert Emmet had a woman somewhere. Jemmy was always right about that sort of thing. Always! And if he did have a woman, it would be serious. Himself was not the sort to fool around.

'I'm saying that if Robert Emmet ever gives his heart to a girl, Anne, it will be a highly placed one. Someone from his own class.'

'Rose! How can you even think such a thing of me!' Anne ran her hand over her hair. ' 'Tis true, I will admit only to you, I'm devoted to Mr Robert. But – 'tis not his person! 'Tis what he stands for.'

' 'Tis what Russell and the others stand for, too. Are you devoted to them?'

Anne cast down her head. 'Aye, I am,' she said softly. 'Each and every one of them.'

Rose looked sadly at the girl across the table, a good-looking girl of the gypsy kind, fiery and passionate one minute, soft and laughing the next.

Rose carefully set her cup down then lifted Anne's hand in both of hers. 'You're a brave lass, Anne Devlin, and a fine one. But, God love you, girl, I'm only warning you because I couldn't abide to see you getting hurt.'

Anne lifted a lazy eyelid and surveyed Rose with a bored expression as she removed her hand. 'And how do you imagine I could get hurt, Rose?'

Rose narrowed her eyes and said firmly: 'You know right well what I'm saying, Anne.'

'Do I?'

Anne finished her tea and looked at the other woman with an air of stern reproof. Clearly she had nothing but contempt for the suspicions swirling around in Rose's head.

'You disappoint me, Rose,' she said coldly. 'You think like a fishwife and talk like a fool.'

Rose flushed a deep pink and gaped as Anne marched out of the kitchen. If any other female had spoken to her like that she might have jumped up and slapped her face. But she had come to know Anne well enough to learn that she didn't always mean what she said in anger. In a minute now she would be back in the kitchen, putting her arms around Rose's shoulders and whispering an apology.

A minute later Anne came back in and walked over to where a basket of laundry was waiting to be hung out to dry.

'Now, listen here, Anne,' Rose said quietly, 'it doesn't do to get on your high horse so often. You may get away with bossing Mr Emmet and the men around, but not me. I'm sure you didn't mean what you said, but nevertheless—'

But Anne had turned and walked out of the kitchen as if Rose wasn't there.

Chapter Twenty-Eight

Robert leaned against a tree at the turn-off to the lane that led to The Priory. His stomach felt empty but he ignored it. He had been too knotted up with excitement at the prospect of seeing Sarah again to partake of a bite at luncheon. She had been unable to meet him for six days due to her father's confinement at home with illness. His week was not the same if he did not see her at least once. The days seemed long, making him tetchy; and last night even Russell had noticed that his attention kept wandering.

Two hours later he gave up the ghost and wandered miserably back to Butterfield Lane. There was always tomorrow, he supposed. Although if she did not show tomorrow, he decided, he would go to the front door and ask for her – and to hell with Curran!

Anne was standing by the long table filling a basket with foodstuffs when he strolled into the kitchen of Butterfield Lane. Nellie stood beside her watching the preparations.

'We're going on a picnic, Mr Robert,' Nellie said. 'Me and Anne.'

'What are Russell and Hamilton doing?' Robert asked idly,

his eyes fixed on the food which Anne was packing, feeling suddenly famished.

'Mr Russell is in the drawing-room, drawing a map,' Anne replied. 'And Mr Hamilton is upstairs having a rest.' She slapped away his hand as it moved to lift a slice of pie.

'Oh, where's your pity, Anne?' he pleaded. 'Ta ocras orm.'

'The hunger is on you, is it? So why did you leave the luncheon I prepared untouched?' She smiled sarcastically. 'Or is that where you've been – out to look for your appetite and found it under a tree?'

'Why don't you come with us on the picnic,' Nellie said. 'We're going to the stream.'

Anne caught the embarrassed expression on Robert's face. 'We'll be back in a few hours,' she said coolly. 'Come on, Nellie. You carry the jug.'

Robert lifted the brown jug from the table and removed the stopper to sniff the rim. 'What's inside?'

'Lemonade.' Anne took the jug and handed it to Nellie. 'Nothing to tempt a gentleman.'

'Won't you come with us, Mr Robert?' Nellie pleaded.

'You won't be coming yourself if you don't move now,' Anne said irritably, pushing Nellie out of the kitchen.

Robert wandered through to the drawing-room to find Russell, and found him asleep on the sofa, a pile of papers and a half-drawn map on the side-table. Robert removed his jacket and sat down in a nearby chair to stare disconsolately at Russell, annoyed that he should be sleeping like a hound when he himself felt so restless. He coughed loudly and moved forward a little to see any signs of facial movement, but Russell slept on.

Robert sighed ruefully, knowing his resentment towards his friend was unreasonable. Russell and Hamilton had spent hours discussing Ulster the night before, not retiring until almost four, but still up for breakfast at eight.

Rising abruptly he strode out of the room and down the hall. He needed desperately to get out of the confines of the house, so he might as well give Anne a shove off her high horse by joining them. He paused in his tracks and grimaced. *Lemonade!*

* * *

He found them beneath the shade of a willow tree where they had settled to enjoy the basket. Nellie let out a squeal and ran to greet him, but Anne just looked at him blandly as he approached.

'You can have some of the food now,' Nellie informed him.

'Thank you.' Robert looked warily at Anne. 'That is, if you don't mind?'

She shrugged. 'Help yourself. It was your money that bought it.'

'It's a beautiful day,' he murmured. 'Why do you have to spoil it by being so touchy?'

Her face remained impassive. 'I'm not touchy. No one touches me.'

'And is that surprising?' he asked, placing a bottle of claret between his knees and opening it. 'When you possess a tongue a man could shave his face with.'

Anne's sudden throaty burst of laughter sent Purty jumping from Nellie's arms and the child scampering after her down the bank. 'Why did you only bring one glass?' Anne asked. 'I would have shared my lemonade with you.'

'But you have always said you don't drink wine.'

'Have I?' Anne lifted her unused cup from the basket and held it out to him. 'You know what they say – yesterday's truth can be today's lie.'

'My mother often says something like that,' Robert murmured as he poured, 'one of her Tralee proverbs: "Today's cream is tomorrow's cheese." '

'She must have been talking about a woman then. Some vain thing who preened herself publicly, not taking into account that even the finest roses of summer fade with the season.'

A small bird had been singing a silvery jingle from a branch above their heads. It paused for a moment, then sang another few notes down to them.

'Do you know what he's just sung to us?' Anne asked.

'No,' Robert lifted a slice of pie from the basket, 'but I have a notion you're about to tell me.'

'A little piece of bread and I'll sing you another little song.'

She threw a tiny piece of bread on the ground and waited for the small bird to fly down, hop around the bread, then cock its head in her direction. She cocked her head in like manner, laughing softly when the bird flew back to the branch with its picnic in its mouth.

A long melodious warble came from a tree a few yards away. 'What's that bird singing?' Robert asked. 'And now it's time for a little sip of wine?'

Anne lifted her own wine and took down a gulp before croaking, 'That's the mating call of the thrush.'

The mate's answering call a second later was high and vibrant like a flute. Nellie came running back to them clutching her kitten. 'She ran up a tree and I climbed after her, but I tore me frock.'

Anne looked at the torn hem around Nellie's ankles. 'Mary will be very vexed about that,' she said. 'Sit down and make some daisy chains.'

'I'll make you a fairy crown, then I'll crown you queen of the meadow fairies,' Nellie cried, running off again.

Robert had moved to lean his back against the tree, his knees up and holding his glass loosely between them. They sat in an unusually companionable mood, recounting with amusement Hamilton's lecture over breakfast that morning about the latest fashion for gentlemen.

According to Hamilton the vogue was now for an untidy, carefree look. Greatcoats had to be worn dashingly open, whatever the weather. And when Anne had said that if he cared so much about fashion, why did he always look so untidy, Hamilton had looked deeply offended, declaring he had just spent half an hour before the mirror, rumpling his hair and tugging his cravat in order to achieve such a carefree and seductive slovenliness.

Anne chuckled as she refilled her cup and gulped thirstily.

'Steady on,' he warned, 'that stuff is supposed to be sipped, not gulped.'

She waved a dismissive hand and took another gulp. 'Sure it's just like cordial, and drink has never had any effect on us Devlins. Have you seen the way Big Art downs the potcheen? Like water!'

They began to talk of random times and people, exchanging incidents about Lennard, Hamilton, Michael Dwyer, until they were both shaking with laughter. Overhead the sun was radiant. The bleating of lambs sounded in the far distance, the clanking of a cow's bell a little nearer.

She gazed up and around at the long drooping curtain of green branches which shaded them. 'The weeping willow is well named, don't you think? It certainly looks as if it's in mourning.'

'The Jews have a legend,' he said, 'that after King David married Bathsheba, he was so penitent at having sent her first husband into the front line of battle, like a lamb to the slaughter, that he sat alone in the garden and wept so profusely that streams of tears ran from his eyes down to the ground, and where the tears sank, there later sprang up a small willow tree. The legend says the willow weeps in memory of David's sorrow.'

He turned his eyes in time to catch her looking at him in a peculiar manner. 'Did you just make that up?' she asked. 'Or is it true?'

'The fact of the legend is true.'

'It's a beautiful legend!' she said. 'Sad, but beautiful. Oh dear!' She put her hands to her flushed cheeks and gave a lazy laugh. 'I feel as if there's a thousand bubbles inside my head, big pink bubbles.'

'I did warn you that wine should be sipped,' he said in a wry tone.

'The crown is ready now,' Nellie cried, running over to them. 'Here, Mr Robert, you hold Purty while I crown Anne Queen of the Meadow Fairies.'

Robert made a face as Purty dug her claws through the sleeve of his white cotton shirt. Nellie held a garland of blue, white, and yellow wildflowers with a number of green leaves sprouting downwards.

'Are you ready, Anne?'

Anne seemed to be sitting in a contented mellowness as she allowed Nellie to undo the thick black braid of her hair and arrange it over the shoulders of her blue linen dress.

Thoroughly bemused, and feeling instinctively that the two girls had played out this scene many times before, Robert watched as Nellie placed a single daisy chain on her own dark head and whispered up a solemn 'Hush!' to the small songbird. Then she called out in whispers and beckoned with her hands to the imaginary fairies, before reverently placing the garland of flowers over Anne's dark curls, and singing in a sweet pure voice:

> 'A floral crown we offer thee
> 'Tis nature's richest treasure,
> We lead thee forth
> Our queen to be
> To rule our days with pleasure.'

A whimsical smile on his face, Robert wondered if he was glimpsing back to some mysterious Celtic world where the archangels of the land were Magic and Nature, working together to weave enchanted spells over a wild and innocent people. A people of long past, whose young men dreamed of finding and riding the elusive horses with wings; and harpers who sang lusty songs of love and life and the richness of the earth. And maidens who swam innocently naked in bright lakes they believed to be enchanted by the tears of Eithne: the beautiful invisible princess who had lost her way back to the Land of Faery and spent hundreds of tearful years searching for the path which would lead her home.

A musical, enchanted, dreaming people, whose beliefs fell to dust when Patrick came over the seas to march amongst them, preaching that the Land of the Ever Young was called Heaven, and the Land of Shadows was a roasting Hell, and there were not many Gods but only one God, whose footstool was all Creation, and the Prince of Light was not Lugh, but Christ, Son of God and High Shepherd of Man.

He blinked, coming out of his thoughts to see Nellie and Anne smiling at him. 'Did you like our crowning?' Nellie asked.

Robert looked at the colourful garland on Anne's dark head. He was feeling strangely light-headed, the warm air and the heavy red wind pressing down on him. 'Tell me,' he said lazily, 'did Eithne ever find the path back to the Land of Faery?'

Anne sat with head bowed for a moment while the songbird

above them sang another silvery jingle in the summer silence. Then suddenly she looked up with a smile and said: 'A white songbird found it for her. After hundreds of years her father, the King, sent the bird to find her, and show her the path home which started at the rainbow's end. And there she found a silver unicorn who told Eithne to climb on to his back, and he flew away with her, over the rainbow and back to the Land of Faery.'

He was smiling at her. 'You've just made that up.'

'No.' She tilted her head upwards. 'The bird has just sung it to me.'

'I heard him sing it, too,' Nellie confirmed.

Robert looked up at the songbird. 'He's got plenty to say for himself for one so small. I suppose he could tell you all about Finn and the Fianna. Why bother with books when you have birds to teach you?'

'Books don't truly tell the legends,' Anne said, 'people do. Ireland will always have her legend-tellers – the Shanachie. And we Devlins come from a long and noble ancestry. Our forefathers hunted with Irish Kings and fought with Irish Princes. The Gaels may now be no more than trampled weeds, but we were once as tall and as proud as the trees – O!' Her hands went to her face. 'O, my face is roasting and my mind is fogged with all those pink bubbles – I must have water.'

She grabbed her cup and ran to the stream, crouching down and drinking thirstily, then splashing handfuls of water over her face. Nellie joined her and soon they were splashing water over each other and laughing. Robert felt as if they had forgotten his presence. He felt sure that if he stood up and walked away, it would take some time for them to notice his absence.

Anne stood with her back to him, hands on hips as she gazed up to the sky, the crown of flowers still on her head. He saw her framed against the summer greenness and the shimmering hills. Something about her intrigued him. She had a cutting tongue and a simple way with her at times, but there was also a lightness and gaiety about her, in the way she walked, in the way she could always laugh at herself.

But it was her eyes that disturbed him most of all. A number of times he had caught her looking at him, a strange musing

364

expression in her eyes, and always he would feel she was going to burst out laughing at any moment.

She raised her hands above her head and clasped them together, stretching her body like an awakening cat, then dropped her hands back to her hips and squared her shoulders.

And it was then that he realised what it was about her that had always intrigued him. He had thought of it at first as no more than her insufferable arrogance, but now he suspected that somewhere deep within her there was an inner strength and a magnificent pride that could be indomitable. Her people might be conquered, but not Anne, never Anne. She had the body of a woman but the spirit of a warrior.

She was bending down and laughing with Nellie again. He decided to get up and take his leave, return to the more logical and sobering influence of the men. He glanced down at Purty who was stretched on his thigh in sleep, her small black paws crossed on his updrawn knee. He stroked behind the furry ear a few times, glancing up to see Anne standing before him, her hands behind her back, her face gravely serious.

'Will you be my man?'

He stared up at her, not sure what she was asking.

'Will you be my man?' she repeated.

'No.'

'Will you carry my can?'

'No.'

'Will you fight the fairies for me?'

'No – ahhhhh!' He sprang to his feet as the cup of water went over him. The kitten scampered away in fright while Anne and Nellie stood laughing like delighted children.

He shook his wet hair angrily, refusing to be enticed into any more of her childish little games.

'Ah, don't be such a cranky sourpuss,' Anne laughed. 'Can't you take a jest? You shouldn't have come out to holiday with us peasant folk if you can't take a little jest.'

He stared at her. She really had to be the most audacious creature ever born. A sudden '*bjerr-err-err-err*' and loud flapping of wings shattered the air above his head. He spun round and stared up to the tree in time to see the bloodsplattered little songbird gripped within the hawk's fierce claws.

He silently groaned in dismay as he watched the hawk soar up to the sky, his eyes following its flight as it carried its lifeless prey back to its plucking post.

The strangled cry made him turn and look at Anne. The hands over her mouth were trembling, her face stark white. He walked over and put his hands on her shoulders, not understanding at first the words mumbling out of her, then he realised she was stammering. Strangely, it shocked him. She seemed too sure of herself to stammer.

'Stop that!' he said harshly, suddenly grasping what she was saying.

'It-t-t's an omen! The small b-b-bird slashed by the big hawk. *It's an omen!*'

He knew instantly what she meant and it infuriated him. 'It's rot!' he snapped. 'Evil superstitious rot!'

'The b-b-bird—'

'The bird was one of many killed every day by hawks. A sad fact of life, of nature, nothing more.'

Her trembling continued and he moved her over to the tree and sat her down, then sitting down himself a few feet away, he stared grimly at the stream. After a long silence he turned and looked at her.

'I'm sorry,' he said softly, 'but I detest superstition.'

She whispered: 'Why so?'

'It weakens, cripples, can even destroy people. I've seen people caught in its power. An evil self-inflicted bondage which subjugates the mind and will to a level of infancy.'

'Oh, I see,' she said, not seeing at all. 'Did you think our crowning ceremony was evil then?'

'Oh, no, that was nice . . . That was just silly girls playing at folklore,' he added.

Fortunately for him, Anne had not heard the last part. Of course, he was right, she thought, birds were killed every day by hawks. It was the shock of the sudden attack, and the sickly Jacobin wine which had given her the deliriums. In her mind she saw again the fierce eyes of the hawk as it left the tree with the bird in its claws.

She shuddered.

'The poor little songbird. He sang so lovely to us. It was such a nice afternoon until the hawk spoiled it.'

'The double face of nature,' he said, looking around him. 'Where's Nellie?'

Anne had a faint recollection of Nellie running off a moment after the hawk attacked. She sprang to her feet.

'We'd better find her,' Robert said, standing. 'The kitten's probably taken her up a tree again. She could break her neck one of these days.'

Anne's hand flew to her mouth. Was that the message of the omen? *Nellie!* She choked back a cry of relief as Nellie came sauntering round the bush clutching the kitten.

'She was hiding up the same tree so I found her easy. But I tore me frock again.'

Anne stared at the large rip from hem to waist. 'Oh, Nellie! What's Ma going to say when she sees you? 'Twill be me she'll give the lambasting to. And another thing, never let me hear tell of you climbing any more trees!'

She suddenly turned on Robert. 'It's all your fault! You should never have given her that kitten! Or given me your Jacobin wine that shook me with the deliriums!'

Robert stared at her, then started to laugh.

'What's so funny?' Anne demanded hotly.

'Nothing's funny, but I have to confess, it's a great relief to see the old belligerent Anne Devlin back again.'

She spun on her heels and marched back to the tree, hastily shoving cups and the glass into the basket.

Robert came up behind her, still smiling. 'Do you intend to wear that crown serving dinner tonight, I wonder? Hamilton will be charmed, I'm sure.'

She slung him a venomous look. 'Now you're being vexatious again. Come on, Nellie!'

Dinner was an hour later than usual that evening, due to Anne's sudden disappearance and her finally being discovered fast asleep on her bed. 'How many glasses of claret did she drink?' Russell asked.

'Nearly three full cups,' Robert answered, 'and downed as if it was water.'

Later, looking very pale as she chopped vegetables, Anne

turned shame-facedly to Robert when he entered the kitchen. 'Oh, Mr Robert, I think I got overfamiliar in my joviality today. Will you try and forget it?'

'Surely. I just came to say that I'll be back in an hour or so.'

'Aw! Where are you off to now?'

Across the back fields to see her father, but he did not tell her so. He picked up a slice of raw carrot, popped it into his mouth and gave an enigmatic little smile.

'Well?' she demanded. 'Where are you going?'

'To find the rainbow's end, Anne. But I should be back for dinner.'

'And may it *choke* you!' she muttered after he had left the room.

Russell and Hamilton were quite concerned about her; even helped her to peel the potatoes, until she waved them out of the kitchen with an imperious hand when she surveyed the mess they had made. 'Honestly! There's more potatoes on the skins than there is in the pot.'

She was standing by the fire tiredly stirring the contents of the huge cooking cauldron on the crane when Robert walked back in.

'Something smells good,' he remarked. 'What is it?'

Anne eyed him sullenly. 'Coddle,' she answered, then explained: ' 'Tis what you gentry would call an Irish peasant dish. 'Tis like a stew, but 'tis not a stew; 'tis made with bacon and sausages and onions and vegetables and lots of herbs.'

'Sounds appetising.'

'It's delicious! Especially the way I make it. Are you hungry?'

'Famished,' he answered, walking to the door. 'So when will this wonderful peasant dish be ready?'

She veiled her eyes as she stirred. ' 'Tis ready now. And I know you'll enjoy it, Mr Robert. I've put a pig's head in to give it extra flavour.'

She looked over her shoulder, and, seeing the greenish hue on his face, gasped in concern, 'Oh my dear vexatious Mr Robert – has something unsettled you?'

He left the kitchen without another word. Anne turned slowly back to the cooking-pot, shaking with silent laughter.

'Butter?' Rose Hope said in surprise.

'And eggs, for your breakfast.' Anne's face was full of contrition. 'I didn't steal them from Mr Emmet,' she added quickly. 'I ran over to the dairy and got them from Da this morning.'

'And he just gave them to you? A dozen eggs?'

'Well, not entirely. He gave me six though!'

Rose, almost moved to tears by the gesture, pushed a lock of red hair behind her ear as she stood considering the basket Anne held out to her.

'Oh, Rose!' Anne touched Rose's arm. 'I can be very mean at times, can't I?'

'You surely can,' Rose agreed. 'Mean as a cat!'

'Take the basket, Rose.'

Rose took the basket, then glanced up and down the row of adjoining cottages on the Coombe. 'Come in and have a cup of buttermilk,' she said.

'I can't,' Anne said. 'I have to get some provisions on Thomas Street and head straight back. Why don't you come out to me . . . this afternoon?'

Rose shrugged petulantly. 'Oh, I don't know about that,' she said slowly. 'There are those in that Butterfield Lane who give themselves too many airs, I reckon. There are those in that Butterfield Lane who swan around the kitchen as if they were the mistress and not the maid of the house. And there are those in that Butterfield Lane who don't know when they are being given good advice and will call a friend a fishwife. Go out there? Oh, I don't know about that . . .'

Anne smiled in a mischievous way. 'When you come out, Rose, suppose I make us some lovely hot soda bread dripping with salty butter – how would that be?'

'Oh, that would be grand,' Rose laughed. 'I'll be out around two.'

As Anne strolled away Rose stood thoughtfully at the door. No words of actual apology had been uttered, but the eggs and butter had said it just as well. In fact, to Rose's practical Ulster mind, a whole lot better!

Rose sighed. An unpredictable lot those Wicklow people!

Tender and smiling one minute, arrogant and proud the next; and Anne Devlin was the proudest piece she had ever clapped eyes on. A warm-hearted girl deep down, and a lovely girl she could be, too, if she would just tilt her head down a bit and stop acting so sassy!

Michael Dwyer and his three companions made another visit to Butterfield Lane. This time they stayed for two days. After dinner the first night, Anne was busy cleaning up in the kitchen, listening to the laughter of Russell, Hamilton, and Mr Robert, and wondering what Michael was saying that was so amusing.

Thomas Russell came out to her later, shaking his head and grinning. 'You ought to be proud of your cousins, Anne, they are certainly clever fellows.'

'And why shouldn't they be?' she said indifferently, but secretly delighted.

'Michael Dwyer,' said Russell, 'is a man of vast capacity, and truly original! Is it true what Big Arthur says about him? He can do anything with a gun short of making it sing?'

Anne smiled. 'Well, I don't know about that. But I once saw him shoot the hat off a man without touching a hair on his head. And another time, on his father's farm, he shot the eye out of a hawk who was marking a wandering hen from the yard.'

Russell laughed. 'A real son of a gun! And neither he nor the others seem to know or care anything about danger.'

Anne wondered if she should tell Russell that the only thing she had ever known Michael Dwyer to be frightened of, when a lad, was the superstition of the wailing banshee and her deathly comb. She decided Michael might throttle her if she did.

When the time came for Dwyer and the Wicklow lads to leave, the men of the house desperately tried to persuade him to stay longer.

'I can't stay, avics,' Michael said seriously. 'My lovely wife worries herself into a fever when I'm missing for too long.'

As they prepared to mount their horses, Anne drew Michael aside in the moonlit yard. 'Will you be coming to Dublin on the day of the rising?' she asked.

'No,' he said. 'We have our own part assigned to us.'

'I'd be greatly relieved if you did come, Michael.'

'Why?'

'So I might have your protection in case of danger.'

'Emmet and his friends will protect you,' he told her. 'Or do you want me to send someone to lodge here with you on the day?'

'No,' she murmured after a moment. 'No, I'll be all right. It was just a sudden fancy I had, wishing you'd be in Dublin on the day.'

'I should be in Dublin on the night,' he said with a smile. 'Anyway, 'tis still some time off. November, Emmet reckons. You'll be seeing a lot more of me before then.'

'Will I?' This cheered Anne enormously, and even more so when he said, 'Listen, Anne, my sister Cathy and John O'Neil are leaving Wicklow at the end of the month. They've taken a lease on a small dairy on the Coombe in Dublin. Will you call on Cathy when you go into town for provisions? She's likely to feel a bit lonely at first, a country girl among city folk.'

'Aye, I'll call on her,' Anne assured him. 'And I'll introduce her to Rose Hope, too. She lives on the Coombe.'

She breathed in the warm night air, her eyes bright in the moonlight. She folded her arms across her breasts and rocked happily on her heels.

'What do you think of Robert Emmet,' she whispered lightly. 'Do you like him, Michael?'

Michael, who had moved to mount his horse, turned and gave her a long, cool look. 'Do you?'

Anne was taken off guard by the question. 'I like him well enough. No more or less than the others.'

'Be careful, Anne, and don't be a fool.' His voice was as quiet and as low as hers. 'Dark maid rarely ever became fair lady.'

'Aw, Michael! What nonsense are you saying?'

He put his hands on her shoulders and looked straight into her face. She saw in his eyes the tenderness and affection he felt for her. She was his cousin, his blood; their mothers were sisters.

'I'm saying, Anne, that it's only the needs of his *house* that Robert Emmet wants you to serve. If he wanted more, another man would see it, and I've been watching him.'

'Oh, don't be so vexatious, Michael!' she snapped. 'And you are not so smart as you think. 'Tis the cause he wants me to serve. 'Tis the cause that *I* want to serve!'

'Is that a fact?' he said softly, smiling at her.

'That is a fact!' she insisted.

He turned and swung up into the saddle. 'Then keep your head down and stop blinding people with the stars in your eyes so.'

Three days later Alexander Marsden was preparing to leave his office at the Castle to attend a luncheon at the Viceregal Lodge in the Phoenix Park.

'Yes, what is it, Mr Jones?' he said sharply when his secretary entered.

'This letter has just been delivered, sir. The gentleman said he had to rush to catch the Belfast mailcoach, but he insisted that the letter received your attention as soon as possible.'

Marsden waited until the door had closed before he ripped open the note from James McGucken.

> Emmet and Hope have taken an arms depot at 26 Patrick Street.

Chapter Twenty-Nine

The rain came suddenly. A hard belting rain that fell without warning.

'Come on!' Robert tugged at Sarah's hand and ran with her across the field towards the woodland trees. He held back the thick drooping branches, then followed her inside the green leafy dell. Sarah was laughing. Her dress was wet and the rain dripped from her hair on to her cheeks.

Robert stood for a moment, looking at the life in her face and happiness in her eyes, and knew it was one of her happy days, knew that she was pleased to be free to roam again, but most of all he knew that he would risk anything for the chance of even an hour with her. She was as fragile and elusive as a rare and beautiful butterfly, but he was the one caught in the net.

She was wearing a thin, short-sleeved blue summer dress which the rain had dampened. He saw how it outlined her slim body and clung to the sweet beauty of her ripe young breasts. He lost his mind in looking at her as she put up her hands to push back the ringlet that had come loose from its bunch in the flight across the field. To his eyes she had never looked more ravishing. The skin on her neck and shoulders and arms was like smooth and pale honey; delicious.

'It's dry over there,' she said, turning towards a dry emerald corner of the glade. He followed her willingly, as he would to the other side of the globe.

'Let us sit here for a while,' she suggested. 'It will be over soon, like all summer showers.'

The rain drummed around them but the part where they sat was completely dry. For a few moments they listened to the rain in silence, watching it force its way through the gaps in the trees on the far side of the dell. He looked up at the canopy of thick ancient branches above them, then smiled at her with all the confidence of a cottager who had just inspected his newly thatched roof.

'Continue with what you were saying about Butterfield Lane,' she invited.

'No, not now.' He shrugged. 'I have no wish to even think about Butterfield Lane.'

'No?' She looked disbelieving. 'Not want to talk about your great plans and fine comrades? Robert! Why, Robert! You *surprise* me!'

He smiled at the sarcasm in her voice; he was well used to it, and knew there was no genuine ill humour behind it. She had long accepted how things were, and now said she only prayed for his safety and success.

'You've quite *startled* me,' she continued. 'I was sure your plans and comrades were *all* you ever thought of. Why, Robert! I'm so surprised I believe you have taken my breath away.'

'Oh, I think not.'

She laughed quietly; and he looked around the woodland dell. 'We seem to spend all our time walking on hills or sitting under trees,' he murmured. 'What I wouldn't give to be in a room with you for a change – a room with solid walls and soft furniture, even other people – normality!'

She sighed wistfully. 'Myself also.'

'Do you still regret not being able to go to the Rotunda?'

'Desperately.'

'You could still go,' he said hesitantly, deciding to bring up a discovery that worried him greatly. 'Richard tells me that your father has given permission to a lawyer named Huband to formally pay his addresses to you, and that after dining at The Priory, he arranged to call on you last week. Did he?'

Sarah made a face of disinterest. 'Yes, he did. And if he had suggested taking me to the Rotunda I might have been tempted. But all he suggested was that the two of us might take a stroll over the meadows of Rathfarnham together. I did not tell him I already had a walking companion. I told him I had a headache.'

'But if he suggests the Rotunda?'

She frowned across the glade and there was silence except for the sound of dripping rain. 'Then I truly might be tempted to go,' she said.

'And if he then proposed his suit of marriage?'

'Then I would definitely not be tempted,' she assured him. 'He is extremely full of himself, leers at me in the way I imagine a fox leers at a chicken, and he says "what, what?" after every sentence. When he dined with us, Richard drank too much wine and ended up behaving most ungraciously and declared to Mr Huband that if he was forced to listen to one more gentleman say "what, what?" just because King George always says "what, what?", he would vomit!'

'Good old Richard,' Robert murmured with a smile. 'And what did Huband say?'

'He said – "I say, dear fellow, that's a bit below the table, what, what?" '

They looked at each other, and with one accord erupted into laughter. 'So even under the glittering chandeliers of the Rotunda, you would not be persuaded to marry him?'

'No.'

He took her hand and sat for a moment looking down at her palm. 'If and when you marry,' he said quietly, 'I hope it will be to me.'

'I hope so too,' she whispered.

He stroked her palm. 'We were meant for each other. I believe that. Don't you?'

'Yes,' she agreed simply.

'So you agree to marry me? After the rising, whether your father consents or not?'

'Yes.'

He paused for a second, then stared at her. 'Sarah! O my darling girl, do you mean it? Are you *serious*?'

'Yes, I seriously mean it,' she said seriously.

He couldn't believe it! For months he had lived in a dream of marrying her, but had never dared to mention it.

'Then you do love me?' he said uncertainly. 'Even though you have never once said it.'

She looked away, swallowed, looked at him again. 'I *must* have said it.'

'No, Sarah. Not even once.' He was quite positive. 'I have told you at least a thousand times, but you have never uttered it to me.'

She looked away briefly, then looked at him again, her face embarrassed. 'Then *why* do I meet you in secret so often? No one forces me to come. And *why* do I allow you to kiss me so often? And *why* have I agreed to marry you? Now why?'

'Yes, why?'

'Don't jest with me, please.'

'I assure you I am not jesting. I simply yearn to hear you say it.'

'Say what?'

'The reason why?'

She stared ahead of her. It was not easy for her to say it. She came from a family where there had been very little happiness and even less love. Display of emotions were not the form in her household, and expressions of endearment were unheard of. To utter one would be like . . . like taking off one's clothes and standing in nakedness to be laughed at.

She looked once more at her brother's friend. 'I love you,'

she told him for the first time, a hint of vulnerability in her voice.

He smiled like a man whose dream had just come true. He put his arms around her, and she dropped her head on his shoulder. 'I will do everything I can to ensure your pleasure and happiness,' he said gently, breaking the silence. 'You will have no regrets.'

'But . . .' she said in sudden bewilderment, lifting her head, 'the rising is a very long way off. Years away.'

'No, it's not years away,' he told her, uneasiness in his tone. 'Only months. Four or five at the most. Probably sometime in November.'

'Oh . . . and do you mean, if Papa refuses his consent, we would elope?'

'Why not? Even Tone eloped. I don't care how we do it so long as we are married.'

'Tone eloped!' Sarah smiled her astonishment. 'Why?'

'Because he was passionately in love with a beautiful young girl called Tilly, Matilda that is, but she was only sixteen and he but a few years older. So, one glorious July morning, without asking consent of anyone, they ran off together and got married.'

'What happened when they returned to face her family?'

'Well, after spending three passionate days in Maynooth, they returned to face the uproar. But once the initial outrage was over they were forgiven on all sides, and the happy couple settled down in their love-nest very pleased with themselves.'

She looked at him, a flicker of fear in her eyes. 'I don't think my father would be so forgiving . . .'

'So why care? He pays you no attention now. If everything you have told me is true, it will take months before he even notices you are gone.'

That was true. She nodded in agreement, then smiled and asked happily, 'What about my betrothal ring?'

'Oh, yes, a ring – I'll get you one tomorrow.'

'There's really no point,' she said after a moment. 'I won't be able to wear it in front of anyone, especially not at home.' Her fingers clutched the gold locket around her neck. 'I wish I could wear my beautiful locket all the time. Wouldn't Lucy Chetwood be *desperate* if she saw it?'

His eyes moved down to the locket he had given her. 'Wait,' he said smiling, 'I have an idea.'

He drew up his knee, withdrew a knife neatly sheathed inside the top of his boot, and urged her to sit still while he cut a small lock of her hair. 'That's for me,' he said, twisting it into a knot and shoving it into his breeches pocket.

Sarah looked bewildered as he cut another, much finer strand of her hair and carefully placed it on his knee, then realisation dawned as he cut a strand from his own hair, and entwined it with hers.

'Our betrothal ring,' he said, 'a ring of entwined hair which you can wear inside your locket.'

When she had closed the little door of the locket, he smiled. 'Now we are truly betrothed,' he said. 'You have promised yourself to me.'

Hot tears were prickling behind Sarah's eyelids. 'Oh, Robert avourneen,' she whispered. 'Can I truly believe heaven is promising happiness at last?'

'Yes,' he said, 'believe it.'

But how long would that happiness last? Sarah wondered as something stirred and swelled and came to life within her, the old and never quite absent conviction of her own inferiority and worthlessness.

'Perhaps you should take further time to reconsider,' she whispered. 'To . . . to examine your doubts.'

'Doubts? About you? I have no doubts!'

She rolled the locket between her fingers, then the words came out in a rush. 'Sometimes I think you are only in love with the girl you imagine me to be, but I may not be the person you fancy I am at all. I have a distorted nature that is very distrusting and can never make up its mind what it wants. My habits and disposition can be very retiring. Richard told me that when you first came back to Ireland you went straight back into society, dining often at the house of young Lord Cloncurry, and a gentleman who lives on Marlborough Street and is known as the Duke of Marlborough because of all the wonderful parties he gives – but my limited experience of entertaining makes it very difficult for me to please or amuse those who are indifferent to me. You might find that after the honeymoon haze has lifted that . . . I can be very dull.'

Looking at her serious face, he could do nothing else but

smile with relief. Then his smile faded, and he took her face in his hands and said softly and slowly: 'I have known you since we were children, Sarah. And I have loved you quietly since the first time I saw you with the eyes of a man, on a spring afternoon in the lane at Rathfarnham many years ago. I carried your image with me into exile, and I have spent nights in Paris, Hamburg, Rome, and Amsterdam, thinking of you. I have never loved anyone else, and I never will.'

She looked into his eyes so dark and so loving, and all her fears evaporated. She knew that he would always love her, whatever her faults. It was his nature to be constant and true to whatever or whoever he gave his heart. Constancy was in the nature of all the Emmets, for had she not seen it that day she had visited the house in Casino, a silver platter above the mantel in the drawing-room, bearing the Emmet coat of arms and the motto *Constans*.

'I love you,' she said again to her brother's friend. 'And I will marry you, if you wish.'

'Oh, I do wish,' he said, and gently kissed her forehead and her eyes. Then he kissed her lips, drew away, and kissed them again hungrily. His hands began to move over the soft skin of her neck and shoulders. And once he had begun, he found he couldn't stop, touching her arms, her breast, her waist, her thighs. He was faintly surprised when she made no protest, only curved her arms around him. He buried his face in the soft warmth of her neck, tasting the honey skin with his lips. He felt her give a deep sigh and they lay back on the grass which was soft and dry.

And so utterly absorbed were they in each other, neither was aware that, outside the wood, the hammering of the rain had eased and grown softer.

The leaves on the trees and hedgerows shone wetly as they walked hand in hand in companionable silence over the grasslands towards The Priory. The rain had stopped, the day was brighter, and there was a wonderful newly washed smell on the air of Rathfarnham. The wheat and barley stood high in the summer fields, the ears on their green stalks refreshed and ripening. The birds had begun to sing again, and the streams

378

gurgling along the ditches joined in the harmony.

At the turn-off to the lane they paused in reluctant farewell, and agreed to meet three days later, on Monday. Then, all words said, their lips met in a long kiss of mutual love and frustration, the last raindrops dripping unheeded around their straining bodies, until, at last, they broke apart with a sigh.

He watched her run up the lane, pause and wave, then disappear from view.

He glanced up at the sky, at the rolling black clouds that would soon pour again, but he didn't care. He walked at an easy pace back towards the yellow fields that surrounded Butterfield Lane, silently reflecting on every wonderful, passionate, frustrating moment of the afternoon.

His thoughts suddenly turned him back to a candlelit night in days now gone, full of laughter and wine and the warmth of male friendship, and the chuckling of his Trinity friend, Thomas Moore, as he wondered if he would ever dare let the world see such a wonderful but youthful little ditty of a poem, which he himself had immediately copied down. Slowing his pace, he smiled to himself as he mentally murmured those words penned by Tom Moore, which now seemed so appropriate.

> 'Twas a new feeling – something more
> Than we had ever dared to own before,
>   Which then we hid not;
> We saw it in each other's eye,
> And wished, in every half-breathed sigh,
>   To speak, but did not.
>
> She felt my lips' impassioned touch –
> 'Twas the first time I dared so much,
>   And yet she chid not;
> But whispered o'er my burning brow,
> 'Oh, do you doubt I love you now,'
>   Sweet soul, I did not.
>
> Warmly I felt her bosom thrill,
> I pressed it close, closer still,

379

And still she chid not;
Till – oh! the world hath seldom heard
Of lovers who so nearly erred,
And yet, who did not.

He was still smiling as he walked up the gravelled path to the house on Butterfield Lane. He passed by the front door of the house, for only strangers entered there, and walked on round to the back, feeling a new contentment within himself and with all the world. God was in his heaven, and Sarah had promised to be his wife, and all around the land was green and growing.

Not even a life-long bad dream could disturb his equilibrium as he entered the kitchen and a voice rose up: 'Ah, me boy!'

'Lennard, my dear fellow, how delightful to see you.'

'Eh?' Lennard gaped at him in astonishment, gaped at Anne, gaped round the room, then gaped at Robert again. 'Do ye mean, that for the first time in yer life, yer going to admit that ye really are . . . happy . . . to see me?'

Robert sat down beside him and smiled blissfully. 'Yes, Lennard, I am happy. Very happy indeed.'

'Well by the hokey . . .'

Anne could only stare, and stare at Lennard. Only an artist with genius and paints at his hand could have portrayed Lennard's expression at that moment, for it was beyond description.

Brian Devlin and Little Arthur had been given the job of transmitting military stores to Michael Dwyer in the Glen of Imaal. Beneath the timber and pikeheads in their cart lay a quantity of ball cartridge and powder not made up.

The night was dark as they proceeded to cross the River Slaney. It had rained non-stop that day and the waters were still swelled. 'We have to carry on,' Brian Devlin shouted as the cart stuck, 'we have to carry on!'

Soaking wet and pushing and pulling, they eventually reached the other side where Little Arthur pointed to a black shape about fifty yards away.

'What's that, Da?'

Brian Devlin grunted. 'The new military barracks they're building.'

'Military barracks?' Little Arthur shuddered. 'I don't think Michael will like that at all. A military barracks so close to Imaal.'

' 'Tis probably because of Michael they're building it. Now let's press on. We don't want Misters Emmet and Russell to think we're sluggards, do we?'

When they finally reached Imaal the two Devlins groaned in dismay. All the powder in the bottom of the cart had got soaking wet.

The following morning broke clear and fine. Deep within the glen, Michael Dwyer stood looking at the wet bags of powder in the cart.

Brian Devlin muttered sheepishly, ' 'Tis all wasted.'

The Wicklow Captain was not in the least perturbed. 'Maybe not all,' he said, glancing up at the blue July sky, then to a ridge of broken rock above them. 'The sun is in the east, but it will soon be overhead.'

'So?' Brian Devlin looked perplexed.

'Up there,' Michael said, pointing to the ridge, 'is a solid granite platform. Much of the powder might be saved if we carry up the bags, then lay the powder out on a blanket and allow it to dry in the sun.'

Chapter Thirty

One week later, on the morning of Saturday, 16 July, an explosion blew out the windows of the depot on Patrick Street.

'What the blazes *happened*?' Robert demanded later in the Thomas Street depot. 'The rules of safety were drilled into everyone!'

McIntosh exchanged glances with the other men. 'We be discussing that, Mr Emmet, an' all we can think is that it must've been Johnstone. He an' McDaniel were testing a fusee in one o' the inner rooms and came out to the one where the composition matter was. Johnstone must have had a spark still smoulderin' on his shoes.'

'Three of our men in hospital!' Robert exclaimed, walking to the back of the room. He was still standing there five minutes later when Miles Byrne arrived with a dark-haired young man named Denis Lambert Redmond.

'I've just bought a house on Coal Quay,' Redmond said. 'It's for when I get married later this year, but you can use it to store the pikes and ammunition, Mr Emmet.'

'What's the point?' Robert answered bleakly. 'Three of our men are in the hospital, at the mercy of government agents who by torture and other means could extort from them all our plans.' He turned as Big Art marched into the room. 'Have they shown yet?'

'Not a hint of a uniform in sight, Mr Emmet.'

'Then go back and wait until they do show.'

'Mr Emmet,' said McIntosh. 'You're verra wrong about the lads in the 'ospital. They'll nae talk to the polis.'

'What about the arms?' Robert asked. 'Did the partition walls stand?'

'Aye, they b'fine.'Twas mair noise and blast than fire. The damage to Keenan was caused by the glass when he fell back through the window.'

'What's the condition of the depot?'

'I came along after the explosion,' Miles said. 'McIntosh and the boys had managed to get it cleaned up before they left. All there is to see is the carpenter's timber.'

'How well did you tidy it up?' Robert asked.

'Och, like a new pin,' McIntosh assured him.

'Oh, fine!' Robert exclaimed. 'Now the police will discover a house in which, although there has been an explosion, there is no debris to allude to an accident with oil or some other innocent combustible substance.'

McIntosh scratched his head. 'We dinna think o' that. We just wanted to clear away any evidence.'

'But if there's no evidence *at all*, it must lead to speculation.'

Miles gave Robert a calming pat on the shoulder.

'There's something strange about this,' Robert said. 'In

ninety-eight a man only had to sneeze and the police were out in force. Now a damned *explosion* and four hours later they have not made an appearance!'

'Och! Ye bluidy fancy-dan!' McIntosh cried to one of the men. 'Mr Emmet! Berney here has just remembered that he ran back int' the depot to get his tools, and left down a bag containin' a pouch o' gunpowder.'

'You eejit!' Miles Byrne shouted at Berney. 'You blatherumskite of a blasted *eejit!*'

'Well, that should end their conjecture,' Robert said grimly.

Sometime later Big Art came running back into the depot. 'Major Sirr's been to the house, Mr Emmet. He searched it from top to bottom. He had a bag in his hand, and he was shoving something inside his tunic.'

'How did he appear?'

'Raging! He was ranting to one of his men about them all having being sent on some wild-goose chase to Tallaght.'

'This gets stranger by the minute,' Robert murmured.

'Then Major Sirr questioned the crowd, asking who had taken the men to Steevens Hospital. They told him it was the carpenter and his men.'

'Are you sure he didn't discover the arms behind the wall?'

'Nay, but I tell you this, Mr Emmet, he looked as if he needed a scratch for a fierce itch.'

'Well, thanks for keeping watch, Arthur. Now you get back and inform Russell of what has happened. I'll follow you shortly.' Robert turned to Miles. 'Have two men watch the depot to see if the police return, then send out messengers to as many leaders of the surrounding counties to attend a meeting at headquarters tomorrow evening.'

As he was about to leave, Miles caught his arm at the door. 'Are you thinking what I'm thinking?'

'What else? Who has deserted us, Miles? Who?'

Miles shook his head. 'It looks as if the Castle must have known about the depot, but, if so, why have they made no arrests? Why have they done nothing?'

'Maybe they have done something,' Robert said.

When he had gone Miles stood in contemplation of the

situation, then strolled back into the room to delegate two men to watch the depot.

'That young man just gone out the door,' declared Denis Lambert Redmond solemnly, 'is the most noble and inspiring thing ever to walk through Dublin.'

'Dear God!' Miles cried. 'If you start romancing about him again you'll force me to hit you.'

'Now, now!' Redmond cried. 'The devotion I have for Mr Emmet is the same as I had for Lord Eddie! Two brave patriots! 'Tis their self-sacrifice and dedication that inspires me so.'

'Our whole world could be about to crash around our ears,' Miles cried, 'and you're talking soft. *Shut up!*'

'Begob,' Redmond said, 'aren't you the tetchy one today? You nearly ate Berney without waiting for the salt earlier.'

Major Sirr put a hand inside his tunic and withdrew the book he had found in a desk at the depot. He smoothed down his moustaches as he read the title: it was Thomas Paine's *The Rights of Man*.

'There's a Jacobin in this somewhere!' he muttered.

'Nonsense!' Alexander Marsden scoffed later. 'Major Sirr, you are getting carried away with all this.'

'Well, something is going on, Mr Marsden. Something I don't know about! I've been watching that place, and yet you have ignored all my reports. Now we discover it is a gunpowder manufactory!'

'Gunpowder manufactory? Oh, come now, Major Sirr, a small pouch of powder does not mean a manufactory.'

'And what about that Wexford lad, Hogan? I found him in possession of a firearm and had him arrested, but you liberated him this morning.'

'I had no alternative, Major. I was certain that in the course of a day or two he would have got a judge to liberate him, thereby exposing our want of powers – now the Habeas Corpus Act has been restored.'

'The damned Habeas Corpus! It's like a wire round our wrists.'

Marsden rose from his chair and poured two glasses of brandy. 'If you were to follow my instructions, Major, we might get rid of the Habeas Corpus sooner than you think.' He smiled as he presented a glass to Sirr. 'Was it not the policy in ninety-eight, Major, that if you gave the disaffected enough rope, they might very well – hang themselves?'

Major Sirr stared at Marsden, took a gulp at his drink, then stared at him again. 'Mr Secretary, I must say, you suddenly put me in mind of Lord Castlereagh.'

'I communicate with him regularly.'

The major lifted his glass to his lips, lowered it again, eyes narrowed. 'Who's the fox?'

'A young man with an old dream.'

'Does he kick in my stable?'

'That we don't know. He quit his mother's house and his business in the early spring to disappear off the face of the earth. We only know that he is responsible for certain activities in the city.'

Robert sat on a crate amongst his men in the depot and gazed sadly through the window at the black sky. 'Poor Keenan,' he murmured.

McIntosh sniffed. 'Aye, and he never uttered a word about the depot. Not even wi' Major Sirr standin' o'er him an' questionin' him as he died.'

'One of our men dead,' Robert said, 'and we have not yet struck a blow.'

' 'Twas the window glass,' McIntosh said quietly. 'It cut through an artery.'

'And McDaniel and Johnstone were just released? No questions?'

'Och, they were questioned all right, but their answers were accepted. Our guess is they'll be watched from now on, so Captain Byrne has discharged them from all duties. He's no' letting them work wi' us again, but they understand.'

Miles Byrne entered the depot with the two men who had been on look-out duty in Patrick Street and spoke earnestly to Robert.

'Incredible!' Robert exclaimed. 'No search has been made in the Liberties. No questions asked in the taverns, and the depot is left unwatched and unguarded.'

'Unless,' said Miles, 'they have just accepted it was an accident.'

'What about the pouch of gunpowder?'

'Sure, don't they know Dublin is rife with smugglers; and they also know a lot of men can only earn a few shillings if they go over the Channel to work as mercenaries. They could be thinking Keenan was a mercenary working for the French, and, with the war back on, that's why he didn't talk.'

Robert sat in silent thought for a moment as he considered the situation. 'Right!' he said at length. 'McIntosh leased the premises ostensibly as a carpenter's workshop. Send two men over there with McIntosh to board up the windows. Once that is done, we will put all the pikes and arms inside the hollow beams and remove them to Redmond's house on Coal Quay. There's no room left behind the walls here.'

'What if anyone gets nosy?' Miles asked.

'If anyone approaches the depot, the arms are back behind the false walls before they are allowed to enter. McIntosh then says he was merely sorting matters out before the resumption of business.'

An extremely handsome young man named Nicholas Stafford, a baker from Thomas Street, went with McIntosh to see to the boards. When they returned, Robert lifted an old greatcoat hanging on the wall and asked, 'Who does this belong to?'

Michael Quigley claimed the coat as his. 'I use it as a cover when I'm sleeping overnight.'

Robert pulled on the coat. 'Then you won't mind if I borrow it? May I also borrow your hat, Mr McIntosh?'

Miles grinned. 'You look like Mahaffy the pedlar.'

'That's the idea. You don't think I can just sit here while you men are doing all the work. We'll go in pairs. Quigley – you come with me now.'

When they had left, Denis Lambert Redmond turned to Miles. 'That young man is the most—'

'Shut up!'

The removal operation went on for most of the night. The value of the hollow beams had been proved and now Miles saw the value of the jointed pikes. Men walked casually in twos, carrying the jointed pikes inside their greatcoats. Others strolled at a distance as bodyguards, carrying blunderbusses under their coats.

They met no obstacles, and when there was nothing left to convey but a casket of cartridges and flints, Miles was too exhausted to object to a big lad named Murphy carrying it away on his shoulder.

Miles and three others were returning to the Thomas Street depot when Murphy came charging back with blood running down his face. 'Six watchmen! They took the barrel of cartridges!'

'Get up to Thomas Street,' Miles ordered, 'and tell Mr Emmet what has happened.' Then he and the others ran back down Thomas Street and caught up with the watchmen outside Coulson's Brewery in St Augustine Street. Two of the watchmen were carrying the cask and four others guarding them. The four turned, then stepped out ready for combat.

'On no account use your firearms,' Miles whispered.

Redmond frowned. 'Why not?'

'Don't let them know you have any.'

'If you insist, Captain Byrne.'

Then Miles stood and watched the four watchmen being knocked down and out with fists and boots.

'In the name of God,' Miles cried, 'where did you learn to fight like that?'

Denis Redmond grinned. 'On the streets of the Liberties, Captain, on the streets – in 1798. If a man couldn't protect himself against the militia in those days, he was dead.'

The other two watchmen had dropped the cartridges and run for their lives. Michael Berney hoisted the cask on to his shoulder and they headed back to the depot. Minutes later a shout rose up behind them.

'It's the two watchmen that got away,' Stafford said. 'And they've three more with them.'

'Berney,' Miles whispered, 'take the cask and dump it with the dairyman round the corner for tonight. We will take care of this lot.'

'I warn you!' Miles shouted to the advancing group. 'This is our property and we intend to keep it. We've been promised a lot of money for this across the channel in Bordeaux.'

'Filthy smugglers!' the watchmen shouted. 'Boney's lackeys!'

'I warn you again,' Miles shouted. 'Take another step and you advance at your peril.'

They advanced, at their peril. One of the watchmen fell to his knee and aimed his musket. A flying kick from Miles's boot sent the gun flying into the air.

Emmet came running down the street followed by four others. He stood and stared at the sprawled watchmen. 'Are they dead?'

'Not at all,' said Redmond brightly. 'They'll have a good sleep and just feel a bit sore in the morning.'

'And wonder where their teeth have gone,' Robert murmured, bending over the face of a watchmen.

It was dawn when they returned to the depot. All the men assembled were exhausted and glad to return to their homes. Only Robert, Miles, and Redmond sank down on to the sleeping pallets at the back of the first-storey workroom. Denis Lambert Redmond was soon snoring softly.

Smiling, Miles whispered to Emmet the power of Redmond's fighting skills.

Robert raised his head and looked over at Redmond's sleeping face. It was the face of an artist, finely cut and sensitive. 'You wouldn't think so to look at him,' he whispered.

Miles spluttered a laugh. 'That's what the poor watchman probably thought, before Redmond downed him in one.'

Robert lay back on his pallet and stared at the ceiling. 'You know what all this means, don't you?'

'Aye, I do. Did you come to any final arrangements with Dwyer?'

'Yes. We agreed on most things – except the method of signal for him to move. I suggested that once we were in the Castle we would give him the flare of a rocket. He said the devil could take my rockets. Only one thing would make him advance – the sound of the Castle cannon. Then he would know we were definitely inside.'

'I can see his point,' Miles said. 'Michael went through the ninety-eight, saw it all, held out and kept fighting when defeat stared him in the face. Man! I could tell you tales of Michael Dwyer that would send your blood racing. He commanded at the Battle of Hacketstown even after Wexford was crushed, fought strong for ten hours, refusing to leave the field until every bit of his ammunition was gone.'

Miles smiled. 'And the irony is that, afterwards, he was offered a commission in the British army.'

'Did you send for him to attend the meeting tomorrow night?'

'No point. Michael never attends prearranged meetings. You should know that by now. And anyway, he's not a man for talking round a table. All he will want to know is when to be ready to make his strike, and when he does, he will strike fast.'

'That's gratifying to know,' Robert said with a tired smile. 'Come on, let's get a few hours' sleep. It's been a pig of a day.'

On Sunday morning, Rose Hope was sitting on the settle in the kitchen in Butterfield Lane, chattering away to Anne as her baby fed at her breast.

'It's something I've had to learn to live with,' Rose said, 'well, since I married Jemmy. Keeping only to those who are of like thoughts, and always watching you don't let something slip in the wrong company.'

'But would you change it, Rose? Would you change Jemmy for some other who was happy to sit on his dungheap?'

'Nay! I'd as lief change my babby for a bag of oats as change Jemmy for another.'

Anne sat down at the table and sighed, 'My heart hasn't stopped pounding since I learned of the explosion. If only Mr Robert was here to calm it for me with that voice of his – it always calms me.'

Ten minutes later Robert marched into the kitchen and Rose quickly turned her feeding baby away from him. Robert made an about-turn and called Anne into the hall. They stood just outside the kitchen door and Rose cocked her head to listen for his news.

'Did you sleep in the depot last night?' Anne asked.

'Yes, and I've not much time. I must go straight back into town to visit some friends.'

'I have clean clothes all ready for you.'

'Thank you, but can you do something else for me? Do you know a house in the area, The Priory?'

'Aye, I do. I used to deliver the milk and eggs there to Mrs Jessop.'

'Could you carry this letter there for me? It's very important.'

'Sure I will, Mr Robert. Is it for Mr Curran? He's the United men's lawyer, is he not?'

'Mr Curran is the one person who must *not* see this letter, Anne. It's for his daughter. You must release it to no one but her.'

A pause.

'Which Miss Curran. There are two as I recall.'

'Miss Sarah.'

Another pause, then Anne's voice became high and child-like. 'Who is she? Miss Sarah? She's not in the conspiracy! What is she to you?'

'She is . . . my future wife. Now listen, Anne. I'm supposed to be meeting Sarah tomorrow, but I may not be able to get away. She will be—'

'Do you love her?'

'What?'

'Do you love her?'

'Oh, yes, I do, very much.'

When it came, Anne's voice sounded small and defeated. 'Well . . . in that case, I'd better take this to her straight away.'

His voice sounded warm, as if he was smiling. 'When you meet her, Anne, I know you will truly like Sarah. She is—'

At the sound of Anne running through the hall, Rose twisted her mouth and thought how true it was – class always sticks to class in the end. And wasn't Jemmy right again!

She lifted the baby, fastened her bodice, and walked out of the kitchen. He was leaning against the wall and staring at the floor with a small frown on his face.

'Would you like a cup of tea, Mr Emmet?'

He looked up. 'No, thanks, Rose.'

'Well I'm afraid you've put me sorely in need of one, God save you!'

By ten o'clock that night, most of the Leinster leaders were assembled in the dining-room of Butterfield Lane. Russell was now convinced that if not the police, then *someone* at the Castle knew about the arms depot.

'What we must decide,' Russell said, 'is what we are going to do now.'

After a long silence, Hamilton suggested, 'We take Robert's element of surprise a step further – and move now.'

Robert stared at him. 'Now?'

Excitement crept into Russell's voice. 'Yes! They will expect us to lie low after the explosion, so we move now – set the rising to take place immediately.'

'But could we organise in time?' Jemmy asked.

Robert looked at the Kildare commander. 'Is your county ready, Mr Grey?'

Nicholas Grey replied quietly: 'Kildare is always ready.'

Each man vouched his county was ready.

Robert looked around the table. 'Well, I don't think we are near ready. But I move to put the suggestion for immediate action to the vote.'

The majority carried the vote – immediate action.

Russell turned to Robert. 'When?'

Robert leafed through the papers on the table and drew out a newspaper cutting. 'Saturday is the best day. Dublin is packed on Saturdays with farmers from the counties coming up for the market. Our men can assemble in the city under cover of the crowds. And, according to the papers, Littlehales is hosting a gala dinner at the Castle next Saturday night. Our men will enter in the carriages, ostensibly to participate.'

'I'll send three hundred Kildare men to help you take the Castle,' Grey offered.

Robert nodded. 'But it is essential that no county rises until Dublin is secured. If things go wrong, we don't want a repetition of ninety-eight. Once the Castle is taken, the rocket flares will be lit, and the messengers dispatched to the other counties in the midlands and the north. It should take forty-eight hours maximum, after Dublin, for the rest of Ireland to rise.'

The following Saturday, 23 July was voted as the date for the rising. It was agreed that Russell, Hamilton and Jemmy Hope would leave the following morning for Ulster.

'We need more ammunition,' Miles put in. 'Especially blunderbusses and muskets. Will your friends help you with more finance?'

Robert glanced at Miles, but made no answer.

'Well, will they?' Russell demanded.

Robert shook his head. 'They're pulling out. This afternoon I informed them the explosion had changed matters. There was now a possibility we might have to move on our own. They say they'll supply no more finance unless we wait for the French. They will have nothing to do with any plan which does not involve the French.'

'That settles it then,' Russell said. 'We go it alone.'

As the meeting came to a close, Russell gave them all a final few words. 'There is treachery abroad,' he said slowly. 'From which direction it comes, we do not know. But we are now caught in the vortex. If we swim ashore, let it not be through innocent blood. If the people of Ireland are true to themselves, we have an overwhelming force. If the people are not true, we fail, and our lives will be sufficient sacrifice.'

The next morning, with a heavy heart, Anne packed Russell's and Hamilton's green uniforms. Then, standing in the drive next to Robert, she smiled bravely as they took their leave, accompanied by Jemmy Hope.

Each man embraced Robert and wished him victory, and, to her surprise, each embraced Anne also. Even Hamilton's warm embrace was without flirtation. Jemmy clutched her arm and said urgently, 'You'll keep your eye on Rose for me, won't you, Anne?'

'Aye, I will, Jemmy.'

She stood with her fingers pressed over her lips as the three men drew away in the covered wagon that was taking them to the fields. They had become her friends, good friends. And who was to say which one would die in the impending battle? Maybe all of them.

Robert put a hand on her arm, and together and in silence they turned and entered the house which suddenly seemed big and empty without the others. In the kitchen, Anne sank down on the settle, tears coursing down her cheeks.

Robert was at a loss as to what to say to her. 'Shall I make you some tea?' he asked.

She looked up into his face and fresh tears bubbled.

'Come now, Anne,' he said softly, putting his hands on her shoulders, 'it's not that bad.'

'Oh, it is, Mr Robert,' she sobbed. 'You've tried it afore and you near poisoned me.'

Robert stared at her. He had been referring to the departure of the Ulstermen.

In the week that followed, Robert visited Butterfield Lane every day to exchange letters with Sarah through Anne, but each night he slept on a pallet in the upper loft of the Thomas Street depot. He ate in the taverns or had food sent in from the cookhouses. Miles Byrne became his closest aide and confidant and lived in the depot with him, together with the lieutenants: Nicholas Stafford, Michael Quigley, Thomas Wilde, John Mahon, and Big Arthur Devlin.

Miles spent a great part of the first few days going through the city contacting the men they counted upon at their various lodgings, instructing them to get prepared and hold themselves in readiness – the die was cast, the day and hour fixed for the attack on the Castle.

Anne and Little Arthur were in the middle of a heated argument which ceased abruptly when Rose entered the kitchen. Little Arthur, his face flaming, ignored Rose's greeting and stormed out through the door.

'What was all that about?' Rose asked.

'He wants to join the others in the rising,' Anne said, 'but Mr Robert has already told me he will pack him straight home if he catches sight of him anywhere near the Liberties on the day.'

Rose tutted and sat down. 'I've done the upstairs rooms for you. Mind, there was no cleaning in it with them all gone.'

'Aye.' Anne sighed bleakly. 'I'll get the water for some tea.'

Rose waited until Anne had returned and was setting the

kettle to heat. 'You haven't mentioned her, Anne, Miss Sarah. What is she like?'

Anne sat down and said quietly, 'She is about medium height, her figure is slender and her eyes are large. He was right about her . . . you couldn't see Miss Sarah and not help liking her. She is not handsome, but she is more than handsome. Do you understand what I mean, Rose?'

'No,' her friend confessed, 'I can't say I do.'

'Oh, Rose,' Anne whispered, 'she has the mildest, and the softest, and the *sweetest* look you ever saw.'

Alexander Marsden was greatly irritated by the visit of Mr Edward Clarke of Palmerstown on Thursday morning.

'Please state the nature of your business quickly, Mr Clarke. I am already late for an appointment.'

'Well, sir,'tis something I believe you should know straight away. I have been fortunate enough to overhear a lot of my workmen talking, and believe me, sir, there is something seditious going on.'

Marsden sighed irritably.

'Whatever it is,' Clarke insisted, 'all of my workmen are involved.'

'Perhaps, Mr Clarke, you could explain exactly what you mean by "something seditious". '

'An insurrection of the people, sir.'

Marsden shoved back his chair and rang the bell. 'I have quite enough on my Under-Secretary's plate, Mr Clarke, without having to deal with all the insurrections that are supposed to take place in this city every week.'

'But, sir—'

'Escort this gentleman out!' Marsden shouted to the secretary who had answered his ring.

'But, sir,' Edward Clarke stammered, 'I can assure you—'

'Mr Clarke,' Marsden said impatiently, 'please understand that while Mr Wickham is in London attending Parliament, and Lord Hardwicke is at the Viceregal Lodge, I must deal with every complaint made to the Castle. I receive reports such as yours every day of the week! Now please be kind enough to return to your business.'

Clarke stood fidgeting with his hat until Marsden cried, 'You may *leave*, Mr Clarke.'

When Clarke had gone, Marsden sat down at his desk and put a finger contemplatively to his lips. He unlocked a drawer and withdrew the letter he had received that morning from his new Dublin informer.

> Dublin and Belfast are to rise Saturday night.
> Emmet is the leader of all.

Marsden sat back, a smile on his face.

Robert was sitting at the back of the depot making slow fuses for the rockets. He dipped strips of hempen cord into a mixture of saltpetre and other substances, then separated these into two boxes: one simply marked *fuses*, the other marked *slow fuses*. When he had finished, he moved over to the slant-topped desk and made a list of the work he still had to do:

Bore the beams.
Pound the Roisin and make the balls.
Send for cramp irons and bars.
Make 10 ládders, 1–30 feet long and block them.

He looked down the depot at the men working flat out already. There was so little time, and so very much to do. He withdrew Sarah's latest letter from the pocket of his waistcoat and read it for the fifth time.

> . . . I am sorry to hear you are not quite well. I long to hear from you again, and hope the messenger will have a letter if she comes this day. I hate to desire you to destroy my letter, as I know I should find some difficulty in complying with such a request from you. I believe it is on the principle that the last child is always the favourite that I would not give up your last letter for all the others. Do not let this be any encouragement to you. Indeed, I see you are plainly turning out a *Rebel* on my hands; but be assured, if I could lay hold of my handywork, as you

call it, it should be anything of a moment of delight to you.

I must tell you that I heard a great many things lately which in your wisdom you did not tell me of, which adds to my resentment, and I long to see you for the purpose of mortifying you. I enclose a bit of Ribbon which was not *originally intended* for a willow, but which may break with dumb eloquence my inconstancy. I intend shortly to make a worthy man happy with my heart and hand, which unhappily for you, do not always go together.

Adieu, my dearest friend, I hope that you will forgive my folly, and believe me always the same as you would wish.

He knew very well that she was teasing him, but he bit his lip anxiously. He had not told Sarah about the imminence of the rising, or that it was to be on Saturday night. And clearly she was piqued at him being unable to meet her, without being able to say why. He had quickly ridden over the lands of Rathfarnham in the hope of seeing her and explaining matters personally, for he could not commit to paper a matter that endangered not only himself, but all the other people involved with him. He had not seen her, and had been unable to spend time waiting around for her . . . It must have been Anne who had told her that he was not very well.

He withdrew a sheet of paper, lifted his quill and wrote an immediate reply to her.

Whatever account you may have heard of my not being well, be assured that I never was in better health or spirits, nor looked forward with greater hopes to the accomplishments of all my wishes. I called two or three times to the same place in the hope of seeing you, and would have continued but for the circumstances of which the bearer may inform you. If, however, I have life, I will see you the day after, and prove to you that however other objects may for a time occupy my mind, the ultimate object which I look forward to for my happiness is that which I now seem to neglect . . .

He looked up as Miles Byrne arrived with some food for their lunch. He glanced down and quickly read over the letter, then frowned. It was not very satisfactory or very clear; and he doubted if Anne would reveal to Sarah the truth of Saturday night, even if Sarah showed her the letter. Anne objected to anyone knowing about the conspiracy except those involved in it.

Miles was speaking to him. He looked again at the letter, then folded it; it would have to do.

'I heard the strangest thing this morning,' Miles said. 'It seems that late last night, two men visited a number of the taverns in the Liberties, and were quietly talking rebelly to some of the drinkers.'

Robert shrugged. 'Nothing strange in that. You will always find bar-stool patriots wherever you go.'

'These two were different,' Miles said. 'They spoke in French accents.'

Robert's eyes shot up. 'French?'

'Aye. One was overheard to say they were *friends of the cause*!'

That afternoon Robert entered the kitchen of Butterfield Lane to hear Anne banging pots and pans in the pantry. 'Hello,' he said, poking his head around the door.

She looked around and nodded mutely, then continued banging about in grim-faced silence.

Robert bit his lip, wondering whether he should make a hasty retreat. Throughout the past few days she had been distant and uncommunicative. All his attempts at conversation had resulted in her wandering out of the room.

He moved back into the kitchen, sighing as he sat down on a chair, wishing she would stop being so unfriendly to him.

He had given her change of attitude long thought, and worked out that it had started from the day he had told her about Sarah. At first, he had wondered, then dismissed the idea, chiding himself for such vanity. She was devoted to them all. Look how she had grieved when Russell and Hamilton had left!

But, on two occasions in the past days, he had caught her

397

looking at him with such disillusionment in her eyes, he was now sure she *was* annoyed about Sarah. Anne was devoted to the cause, and no doubt she felt he was being disloyal and careless by allowing himself to be sidetracked from his duties.

A loud clatter came from the pantry.

He hated it when she was like this. He missed the old joking Anne who could turn a tantrum into a laugh in a second. Her tongue had been sharp on occasions, but now its silence was as deadly as a strike from a cobra.

She came out of the pantry and lifted her shawl from a hook on the back of the door, keeping her head down as she crossed it over her breasts and tied it at the back.

'There's a letter for you,' she said, walking over to the mantelshelf. 'You'd gone when I brought it back yesterday.'

She held the letter out to him. 'If you want me to carry another, just leave it on the shelf. I'll deliver it later.'

He took the letter from her hand but his eyes were on her face. 'Where are you going?'

'Home, for an hour or so. Jimmy is feeling sickly.'

'What's wrong with him?'

She shrugged. 'Jimmy denies it, but Mammy thinks he's been eating the berries again.'

His eyes followed her to the door, and he continued to gaze at it long after it had closed behind her.

On Friday afternoon, Mr Edward Clarke of Palmerstown paid another visit to the Under-Secretary's office.

'Mr Clarke! What is it now?' Marsden snapped.

'Well, sir. It seems you were right. After I left you yesterday morning, I went straight back and asked my men outright what was going on. They assured me that I had been misinformed and nothing was going on. They all insisted they were loyal subjects of the King.'

Marsden sat back and glared.

'I could tell by the straight and honest look on their faces,' Clarke continued, 'that they were telling me the truth.'

'Good day, Mr Clarke.'

Clarke looked sheepish.

'Good day, sir.'

PART THREE

Chapter Thirty-One

The Morning

The cocks had not long announced the break of day when Anne sauntered into the kitchen. She knelt to stoke the banked-down fire, lifted the bellows and blew up the embers. The house felt lonely and empty. She watched a flame splutter to the surface and thought how nice it would be to suddenly hear William Hamilton singing on the floor above.

She stood and ran her hands through the mass of black hair which hung over her shoulders. Every morning she plaited it neatly into a braid, but today she couldn't be bothered. No more looking like the prim and proper housekeeper. She was Anne Devlin, country girl, and that's how she would look from now on.

She placed her forearms on the mantelpiece and rested her face on them, feeling tired, very tired, missing the sleep she had lost in the night. She felt a strange churning sensation in her stomach and knew what it was – the fear and tension which had kept her awake. She wondered if all the men around the city felt the same as her, if they, too, had lain awake wondering what would be the outcome of tonight's action.

Without warning, all the silent tears she had kept bottled up inside her came bubbling to the surface. She pressed her face into her arms on the mantel. Even during the long hours of the night she had refused to succumb to tears, and now here she was, crying like a childybawn, because any one of those she loved could be dead by this time tomorrow.

As the minutes passed, her tears subsided. She gave a sigh that shuddered through her entire body. She must be calm; calm and ready to face the men with an encouraging smile when they came later today for the ammunition.

She closed her eyes, and, just as she had done as a child, she calmed herself by drowsily pondering on one of the stories of the Gaels: the story of Deirdre and Naois, and how poor Deirdre and her hardy hero Naois, had suffered so at the hands of her betrothed:

And the beauteous young creature, Deirdre, lived hidden away in the mountains with her mother, until Connachar, the King of Ulster, was told about her beauty. And on finding the sixteen-year-old maiden, Connachar thought her the fairest creature that ever was born in Erin and begged her to marry him. Deirdre agreed, but asked him to wait for a year and a day, and so Connachar, King of Ulster, became her betrothed.

And then one summer day, Deirdre met Naois, the young hunter whose hair was as black as the raven, and her face went into a crimson blaze of fire. And Naois gave Deirdre the love that he never gave to thing, to vision, or to creature but herself, and he took Deirdre away with him, and the lovers were pursued, through meadow and stream and forest, by the warriors of Connachar, the King of Ulster, her betrothed.

And one morning, Deirdre said, 'I had a dream, Naois, and will you interpret it for me?

'There came three white doves out of the south
   Flying over the sea,
And drops of honey were in their mouth
   From the hive of the honey-bee.

O Naois, son of Uisnech, hear
   What was shown in a dream to me?

I saw three great hawks out of the south,
   Come flying over the sea,
And red blood dripped from their mouth . . .'

What did Deirdre say after that? Anne wondered. She moved her face tiredly over her arms and found the rest of Deirdre's words were gone.

But Naois said:

'It is nought but the fear of a woman's heart
And a dream of the night, Deirdre.'

When the hand touched Anne's back she near jumped out of
her skin, swinging around so fast her foot slipped to the fender.
Robert had to reach out and grab her to stop her stumbling on
the floor.

'Have you been crying?' he asked, looking at her red swollen
lids.

'Crying?' She gave a small nervous laugh and passed a hand
over her eyes. 'Oh don't be so vexatious so early. I got a midge
bite on my eyelid yesterday in the field, and . . . now both eyes
are irritated.'

He peered curiously into her face. 'Is something wrong with
you, Anne?'

'Wrong? What could be wrong with me? I ask you, what
could be wrong with me?'

'Oh, is it a game?' he asked. 'A guessing game?'

She suddenly smiled but he said tiredly, 'I have no time left
for games, Anne. Are we friends again or not?'

'So what makes you think we're not friends?' she murmured.

'So what made you, whenever I asked you a question in the
past week, always give the answer to the wall or some invisible
person in the next room, but never me?'

Her laugh was so infectious he smiled, feeling some of his
tension evaporating.

'Are you sure you were not upset about something earlier?'
he said. 'Is Jimmy any better?'

She shrugged. 'He didn't look too hale yesterday. No, it's the
rising. I was just edgy over the rising.'

He moved past her to sit down on the settle. 'Yes. I suppose
we have all been a bit edgy this week over the rising.'

Robert felt as weary as he looked, lounged there on the settle.
It was only then Anne noticed the dark shadows of fatigue
under his eyes.

'Would you like some tea or coffee?'

'Tea would be . . .' He stretched his legs and closed his eyes,
'. . . very nice.'

She set the kettle to heat then sat down beside him. Neither bothered to speak, just listened silently to the sounds of the dawn chorus which came through the window. The silence spun out, a tired quietness between the two of them, until the kettle hissed furiously.

She glanced at him as she scooped tea into the pot, concern in her eyes. 'You look like you died last night but nobody had the heart to tell you about it,' she said.

'No one would have had the time.'

'Have you had much sleep this week?'

'Last night was the first time in the week that I slept for more than two hours.'

'Did you sleep badly?'

'Well enough, considering.'

'Considering what?'

'Considering . . .' he opened his eyes, 'a rock-hard pallet and six other restless men tossing and turning around me. Would you do me a favour, Anne?'

She looked darkly at him over the steam as she tipped the bubbling water from the kettle into the teapot. 'A letter to Miss Curran?'

'No. Big Arthur came home to Rathfarnham last night, to your father's house. Would you go over and tell him that I wish to see him?'

She handed him his tea with a smile. 'Sure I will.'

When Anne returned with Big Art, Robert was scrubbing himself under the pump. 'Did you want me, Mr Emmet?' Big Arthur asked.

'Yes, Arthur. Can you ride out to Carey in Rathcoole, and the Doyles in Athgoe. Collect Kennedy and take him with you. Tell them things are going forward as planned and they are to repair to Dublin with their friends tonight.'

'Aye, I'll go now, General.'

Robert laughed. 'General!' He rubbed his face with the towel. 'Generals are the ones who usually stay behind the lines. I wonder if General Fox has to stay up all night making his own cartridges?'

'Oh, once a week, don't you know,' Big Art grinned, strolling away.

'It must have rained in the night,' Anne said when he entered the kitchen. 'The shirts I had drying on the hedge are still damp. Shall I bring one to you later, at the depot?'

Robert shrugged his jacket on. 'The city will be packed today.'

'It will give me something to do. It's going to be a long day, and the waiting here will be hard.'

'All right, if you want to; but I must get back now.'

She walked with him to his horse. 'Now don't forget,' he said, 'a couple of the men will be coming out about five for the rest of the arms here.'

There was impatience in the way she nodded her head. 'Big Art was saying you must have the constitution of an ox,' she said anxiously. 'He doesn't know how you have suffered the fatigue and lack of sleep this past week.'

He looked at her absently, then smiled. 'Goodbye, Anne.'

She made no answer as he swung into the saddle, stepping back as he turned the horse round, moodily staring after him as he rode out of the yard.

It was just after eight when William Dowdall, John Allen, and William Putnam McCabe called at Denis Redmond's house on Coal Quay. After checking the arms and pikes stored there, the three men walked to the second lock of the Grand Canal where John Allen pointed to a field just beyond.

'A number of our people will assemble in that field tonight,' he said. 'It is the best vantage point for taking the Artillery Barracks at Islandbridge.'

They then strolled to a tavern run by Mr Nason Browne, and enjoyed a good breakfast.

Alexander Marsden arrived at his office a little after nine on Saturday morning. His first visitor was a Mr Nason Browne, informing him he had overheard three men talking in his tavern.

'It sounds as if there's going to be arising in the city tonight, Mr Marsden. I heard them say half past nine.'

'I will have the matter investigated, Mr Browne. Thank you for your prompt action.'

Marsden's second visitor was a one-eared man named

Rafferty. He was a Castle informer of long standing, and now said he had heard a 'whisper' of an insurrection before the day was out.

Rafferty stood under Marsden's gaze pulling on his one ear. The other had been cut off in '98 by rebels when it was discovered Rafferty had passed on secret information he had overheard. Marsden found Rafferty's scruffy mutilated appearance too gross to tolerate so early in the morning. He got rid of him quickly.

Another informer swiftly followed Rafferty. 'They intend to take up arms at dusk, Mr Marsden.'

Marsden's last visitor that morning was Mr William Atkinson of Belfast. He had just arrived from the north with the information that Thomas Russell was in the northern province and an insurrection was planned, possibly for that very night.

Marsden treated the Ulsterman with great courtesy, arranging for him to dine in the Castle before he caught the mail-coach back to Belfast. When Mr Atkinson had disappeared through the outer door, Marsden turned to his secretary.

'Mr Jones, please ensure that I am disturbed by no more visitors until after luncheon.'

The streets of the Liberties were thronged with farmers from the surrounding counties up for the Saturday market. More and more men forced their way into the depot which rang with the beat of hammers and the grinding of saws and planes. Robert stood at the back of the depot and wondered if he would ever know peace again.

'It's bloody deafening,' said Miles Byrne, coming up to him.

'It's worrying, too. Major Sirr and his men must realise the noise coming from here is not normally associated with a malthouse.'

'Well, lucky for us, the major is nowhere in sight. I have sentinels in disguise posted around the depot. The men are arriving from Kildare like swarms of bees, and people are meeting in each other's houses all over the city.'

Robert gave a satisfied smile, but Miles's next words wiped it from his face. 'We have more important problems than Major Sirr. The rammers for the cannon have not arrived, and the smithies have not yet sent the cramp irons for the scaling ladders. If they don't send them soon, we'll have only one scaler by tonight.'

Robert frowned. 'If they have not arrived by noon, send someone to chase them up.' He took out his watch. 'Are any of the lieutenants free?'

'No, they're all out in the streets meeting with the men.'

'I need to get some money from Philip Long. Can you go?'

Miles shook his head. 'I have a meeting with some of the Wexford men in Redmond's house in ten minutes.'

'Then I'll have to go myself,' Robert said, rising to his feet.

Miles caught his arm. 'No! It would be dangerous for you to be seen in the streets today.'

'I'll go for you, Mr Emmet.' Michael McDaniel was standing next to a crate a few feet away.

'McDaniel!' Robert exclaimed. 'I thought you had been relieved of all duties after the explosion.'

McDaniel cast a nervous glance at Miles Byrne. 'Aye, I was, Mr Emmet, but sure I only got a few cuts and bruises. And after all the work I've put in, helping to wind up the clock, I think it's only fair I should be there when it strikes.'

Robert looked questioningly at Miles, who in turn eyed McDaniel for a moment. 'Captain Byrne!' Denis Redmond came rushing up to the desk. 'The Wexford boys are waiting for you.'

Miles grinned. 'Early and eager as usual. Tell them I'll be along in a few minutes.' McDaniel watched Redmond running off then turned to Robert. 'Shall I go for you, Mr Emmet?'

Robert considered McDaniel's earnest face, then nodded. 'Yes. Will you go to Philip Long's place on Crow Street. Tell him I need as much money as he can spare, as soon as possible today.'

'Aye, Mr Emmet.'

'And McDaniel . . . tell him it *must* be cash.'

When McDaniel had gone Miles asked, 'Why do you need money?'

'Oh, more problems. I have just concluded a long and tiring argument with Felix Rourke.'

He then explained that while Quigley was having breakfast in

407

the White Bull, John Fleming, the ostler, told him Felix Rourke had arrived from Kildare with a group of men. He was in the Golden Bottle and demanding to see Emmet.

'So, I sent for Rourke to come here. He insisted on seeing the arms. I showed him the thousands of pikes stacked behind the walls, the bushels of musket balls and the rockets. Rourke then insisted that every Kildare man had to be furnished with a firearm. They wanted no pikes.'

'*What?* He must have been joking.'

'That was the last thing he was doing. I then agreed that as we had been promised blunderbusses at two guineas a piece by Tomlinson of Chapel Street, I would buy more. But I have no funds available. That's why I have sent to Philip Long.'

Miles gave a bemused look around the depot, a sudden indignant anger rising in him. 'Fancy that bloody Rourke to come up with that! Demanding you find the money to provide guns for him at a moment's notice. I wonder does Nicholas Grey know about his attitude?'

'That's not all. Rourke then suggested we take the barracks before the Castle, but he got short shrift from me on that one.'

The Afternoon

Alexander Marsden's first visitor after luncheon was Mr Edward Clarke of Palmerstown.

'I tell you, Mr Marsden, something seditious is going on! All my workmen came to me this morning and asked to be paid up. I had no choice but to pay them, but I gave an extra sovereign to one of them who eventually told me they were all going into Dublin, to take part in a rising.'

'You have changed your mind very suddenly,' Marsden cried. 'Yesterday they were all loyal subjects of the King! You even vouched for their honesty.'

'Yes, sir, I know, sir, but 'twas their straight faces. Bad cess to them.'

Marsden stood thoughtful. 'Oh, very well, Mr Clarke. I will report the matter to the Viceroy and General Fox. I will send for you when I have their views on your report.'

'With all respect, Mr Marsden, I think you should send a troop out to stop them coming into the city. They were heading for the river road on foot when last I saw them.'

'If the Viceroy thinks a detachment of troops should be sent to impede the progress of your Palmerstown rebels, then one will be sent. Meanwhile, Mr Clarke, please wait for me to send for you.'

Edward Clarke stuck out his bottom lip, then shrugged. 'I'll wait in my Dublin warehouse,' he said.

Anne was amazed at the crowds in the streets of the Liberties. She pushed through the mass of people on Thomas Street and made her way towards the depot, clutching against her chest the parcel containing Robert's clean linen.

Seeing the pretty girl moving amongst them, some of the young farmers started to joke with her until she felt she was being pulled and hauled in every direction. She spotted Nicholas Stafford coming out of Marshalsea Lane and frantically waved to him.

'All right, lads,' Nicholas Stafford grinned, 'get back to your sheep and your pigs, and leave the young colleen alone.'

Some of the men grinned back at Stafford, admiring his height and incredible good looks. He was a baker from Thomas Street, and many a breathless old matron had been heard to wonder aloud how any girl could look on Nicholas Stafford without falling in love with him.

'Is it for yerself ye want her, big fella?' a voice shouted.

Anne stretched over the crowd and handed the packet to Stafford. 'Can you give this to himself?' she shouted.

As Anne stretched, a man rubbed his hand down her thigh. She swung around and gave him a whack of her hand against his head. The man snorted with laughter.

'Ah, well,' she said angrily, pushing her way out, 'what else can you expect from a pig but a grunt!'

She was passing a group of men outside the White Bull when a fragment of their conversation reached her ears. 'Aye, 'tis true. They've changed all the plans. We're to come back next Saturday instead. The Gen'l himself has given the order!'

She grabbed the speaker's arm. 'What are you saying?'

'What's our conversation to do with ye?' the man snapped. 'Get away with ye!'

Anne was so stunned she moved on, but as she passed the Golden Bottle she heard someone else saying it. 'Aye, you're wasting your time. The Gen'l and Cap'n Byrne gave the order half an hour ago.'

She pulled her shawl around her and cut down a side street to where the mare and cart were stabled. The rising was off! But why?

'Where is Anne now?' Robert asked when Stafford handed him the package.

'Gone. After fighting off most of the lusty farmers down there.'

Miles Byrne marched up to them, glaring with anger. 'Dowdall!' he cried. 'Instead of being here where he is needed, I found him carousing with a girl at Hevey's.'

'Did you order him over here?' Robert asked.

'Aye, but he insisted on having a long sentimental farewell with her first.'

Robert and Stafford exchanged smiles but Miles was not amused. 'We'll have plenty of time for women afterwards. But now every man should be at his post.'

'Just a minute,' Stafford said slowly. 'You say it was *Hevey's* you saw Dowdall carousing?'

'Aye.'

'And the girl? Who was she?'

'How the blazes should I know?'

Stafford's voice became impatient. 'Was her hair the colour of golden corn on a summer afternoon?'

'No!' Miles shouted. 'It was as black as a witch's hat on Hallowe'en.'

Stafford blew a sigh of relief, then turned to Robert. 'If it's all right with you, Mr Emmet, I think I'll go over there and see what those fancy boys are up to. You'll see me in ten minutes.'

Miles gaped. 'What the devil was all that about?' he asked Robert.

'Stafford is courting Hevey's young sister and hopes to marry her.'

410

'God! Only Irishmen would concern themselves with women on the day of battle!'

'I wonder,' Robert mused aloud, 'who Edward Kennedy was talking about when he told me he was having a terrible job keeping his young stepbrother from day-dreaming over the books about a certain young Miss named Meghann?'

Miles smiled reluctantly. 'But *not* on the day of battle!' he insisted. His expression sobered again as he sat down. 'I fought on Vinegar Hill. I saw thousands of my countrymen massacred. It was only five years ago and the memory is still fresh. We all risk our lives tonight, and in the fight for liberty, a man must be a soldier first and last.' He looked curiously at Robert. 'Has McDaniel come back yet?'

Robert frowned. 'Not yet. I've sent another messenger to find out what's happened to him.'

'Are you *sure* Long will you give you the money?'

'Positive.' Robert sat thoughtfully looking into the distance for a moment, his brow furrowing, his teeth down on his bottom lip as if trying to solve a puzzle.

'What's up?' Miles asked.

'McDaniel,' Robert murmured, 'there's something troubling me about him.'

'He shouldn't be here at all, not after what happened in Patrick—'

'That's it – Patrick Street!'

'What?'

'Keenan dies,' Robert said slowly, 'Johnstone is severely wounded. But McDaniel, who was working *inside* the room, gets nothing more than a few scratches . . . God in heaven, Miles! Before he died, Keenan told McIntosh that he saw McDaniel standing *outside* the doorway a moment before the place exploded!'

Miles stared at him. 'And where has McDaniel got to now?'

'You get down to Crow Street immediately,' Robert said.

'I'm there already.'

As Miles edged past three men sawing wood near the exit door, part of their conversation reached his ears, making him swing around angrily.

'What was that you just said?' he demanded.

The three men exchanged glances, then one piped up, 'We were just commenting, Captain Byrne, that yourself and Mr Emmet are a bit young to be leading a revolution.'

'Is that right now?' Miles lifted his chin and looked at each man. 'And how old do you think Napoleon was when he helped to take Paris and form the French Republic?'

'Sure what do we know about Boney?'

'He was *twenty*! Younger than both Emmet and myself.'

The three men gaped after the young captain as he marched out of the depot. 'Sure, isn't he right?' said one, ' 'tis young blood that runs the fastest.'

'And the hottest,' laughed another. The three men went back to their work, quite satisfied their doubts were unfounded.

As he strode down Marshalsea Lane, Miles glanced over his shoulder at Big Arthur Devlin who galloped past him into the depot. 'That Devlin must never have learned how to walk,' Miles muttered to himself.

'Mr Emmet, I'm a bit worried about Red Mick,' said Big Art as he came up to Robert. 'He should have been back from Wicklow by now.'

'When did you send him?'

'Thursday. He could not go before then. And Michael can often prove difficult to find.'

Robert frowned. He knew that only the Devlins and a few trusted Wicklow boys would ever get through to wherever Dwyer was hiding in the mountains. 'Are you sure you picked the right man?'

'Aye, but that's the trouble with some of the Wicklow boys, Mr Emmet. Once they get back to the glens they hate to leave them.'

'Would he have got to Dwyer by now?'

'Aye. His arrival in Imaal would have been speedily conveyed to Michael, who would then make an appearance in his own good time. But the Divil eat Red Mick, he was told to return straight away. He's probably decided to wait and come back in with Michael.'

'Just so long as Dwyer is in position tonight,' Robert said anxiously.

Big Art rubbed his hands together and grinned. 'Oh, I can't

412

wait to see Michael in action again. 'Twill be just like old times.'

Barney Duggan's orders were to be positioned outside the Castle gates all day and report anything untoward happening there. Barney had kept to his post, except for the number of times he had slunk off to the nearest tavern to calm his nerves and had missed seeing practically every visitor that entered.

Barney now pulled himself to attention and watched with eyes alert as Mr Edward Clarke of Palmerstown marched through the lower yard.

Marsden's secretary gave Clarke a haughty look and waved him aside. 'I regret, Mr Clarke, but the Under-Secretary has the Viceroy and General Fox with him at the moment. He can *not* be disturbed.'

'Ah, so he has done that much?' said Clarke, 'sent for the bigwigs! About time, too. He told me he would send for me, but I can't sit in my warehouse all day. What are they talking about in there?'

'None of your demned business, Mr Clarke!'

Alexander Marsden faced Lord Hardwicke and General Fox. He had a mass of information about the plans of the rebels, but he could not let Lord Hardwicke or General Fox know that. It would lead to a series of awkward questions.

'I can assure you, my lord,' said Marsden, 'there are indications of some form of trouble tonight, but I doubt on a scale that has been suggested.'

'You say you had a letter from a Mr McGucken, a former rebel?'

'Yes, my lord, but I suspect McGucken's friends no longer trust him. He informed us that certain people had taken a house in Patrick Street as an arms depot, but when we investigated his information, we found it was completely unfounded.'

'How so?'

'The property was leased by a Mr McIntosh, a Scotsman residing in the city whose trade is that of carpenter. When the premises were searched, we discovered only sheets of timber.'

'But was there not an explosion there?' said General Fox.

Marsden waved a hand. 'An accident with some of the carpenter's oils. You must understand, gentlemen, a lot of these informers made a great deal of money in 1798. I suspect that for some, funds are now running low. Why, just this morning a Mr Nason Browne called to see me to say he had overheard a few men talking rebelly in his tavern. Then this afternoon, he had the audacity to send me a note asking for payment for his information.'

Lord Hardwicke leaned forward on his cane. 'What about this Belfast gentleman, Atkinson? To travel down from Ulster! He must have been alarmed.'

'The Ulster loyalists are always panicking about risings, my lord. And as far as I could ascertain, Mr Atkinson's information was not even second-hand, but third!'

Mr Edward Clarke of Palmerstown sighed impatiently as he paced outside Marsden's office and watched Mr Jones make a scrutinuous examination of his finger nails.

'Mr Marsden said he would send a troop to stop my lads,' Clarke said, 'but sure they must have reached the city hours ago.'

Mr Jones also gave a sigh but did not lift his eyes from his examination. A sudden movement of chairs from the inner office made them both jump to attention.

'And you are quite sure there is no reason to be alarmed?' asked General Fox. 'We cannot have any disturbance in the capital.'

Again Marsden waved a hand. 'A few of the boys are most likely planning some trouble, but I don't believe it is anything serious. And even if there were something more serious amiss, I don't think any alarm should be raised. If this bunch of rebels were made aware their plans were known, then we could not take measures to frustrate them.'

Lord Hardwicke frowned. 'I don't think I understand you.'

'My lord, if a group of rebels *are* planning some mischief tonight, it is too late to prevent their preparations now. And if these rebels are to rise, is it not better they do so now, without aid from France, and not later, when their mischief would be much greater?'

'But you said it was just a few of the boys!' snapped General Fox.

'And that is what I believe, General. I believe some sort of disturbance is planned, but, at worst, nothing more than a small riot involving the local militia.'

General Fox looked unsure. 'I have an engagement this evening but, nevertheless, I think I should return to the city tonight to make absolutely sure. What time were you informed there would be trouble?'

'Ten or thereabouts,' Marsden said.

'Very well, I shall return at ten.'

Marsden nodded. 'With due respect, General Fox, I think it would be prudent if you were to take the precaution of sending a small number of reinforcements to the Bank, the Castle, Kilmainham Gaol, and the Viceregal Lodge in the Park.'

Lord Hardwicke agreed. 'Yes, that would be a very wise precaution.'

'I also think it would be unwise, General, to issue orders to your officers about what measures should be taken,' Marsden said, 'until after half past nine. The troublemakers may have friends in the barracks.'

General Fox frowned. 'Thank you, Mr Marsden, but I am quite capable of deciding how I will deal with my own officers.'

Marsden looked contrite. 'Forgive me, General. I merely wished to stress the importance of not causing our citizens any undue alarm.'

Mr Edward Clarke of Palmerstown bowed low as the door opened and the Viceroy and General Fox strode past him.

'Ah, yes, Mr Clarke,' Marsden snapped, 'I shall send a number of soldiers out to Palmerstown to investigate your apprehensions immediately.'

'But Mr Secretary—'

Clarke turned to Mr Jones. 'Now isn't that a fine thing to do? Slam the door in my face!'

Robert stared at Miles in disbelief. 'That's the truth of it,' Miles said. 'When McDaniel reached Crow Street, Mr Long was not there, but he came back at half past twelve. Mr Long then sent his nephew, David Fitzgerald, to a merchant who owed him money and requested five hundred pounds. The merchant gave the nephew a draft for the five hundred pounds, but by that time the banks were closed. Mr Long managed to get the money from some of the bank runners, and gave it to McDaniel . . . And that's the last we know of it.'

Robert's eyes blazed with fury. 'So Philip Long sent the money to me as I knew he would, but McDaniel has absconded with it.'

'The last time I saw McDaniel,' said Nicholas Stafford, 'he was heading in the direction of the Kildare canal boat. If I had known—'

'You bloody well would have done if you hadn't gone chasing round to Hevey's,' Miles snapped.

'The Kildare canal boat,' Robert said, 'with five hundred pounds in his pocket. Hard-earned money that was donated to the cause.'

'McDaniel is a dead man,' a voice said coldly.

Robert looked round to the two men standing a few feet away. 'We will get the next canal boat to Kildare, Mr Emmet,' one said in a low voice, his eyes dangerous.

'No!' Robert rasped. 'No murder!'

'McDaniel can't be allowed to get away with it, Mr Emmet. Men are risking their skins while McDaniel steals our money.'

Robert's hands tightened into fists on the desk. 'He won't get away with it! McDaniel has a number of questions to answer, but it will be the Executive Council who questions him, no one else!'

The man's face remained hard, his voice low and sneering. 'You're too soft for this game, Mr Emmet.'

'It's not a game!' Robert snapped. 'What do you think I am?'

'You're a Trinity boy! Playing by college rules! What're you and your executive council going to do with McDaniel? Rap him on the knuckles?'

'Shut your mouth,' Miles shouted, 'or I'll shut it for you – and quick!'

The man looked levelly at Robert. 'I've nothing against you, Mr Emmet. I respect what you're doing. But like yourself we've worked hard without sleep, while McDaniel rests up after his scratches. Now he walks away a rich man. It's hard to take.'

'The discipline of the ninety-eight leaders *must* be upheld,'

Robert said. 'Meanwhile, we will send men to Kildare to find McDaniel – but not you two.'

The two men walked away, muttering angrily to themselves. Robert sank down on to his chair while Miles walked over to a group of three men and talked quietly to them. The men nodded gravely and reached for their coats.

Another man came up to Robert and complained. 'Mr Emmet, there's too many men in here. We've hardly room to work.'

Robert gave him a strained look. 'I know, I know. But just try and manage as best as you can. We've lost the Patrick Street depot, and those men have come from Kildare to help us. I can't order them out.'

The man shrugged and moved away. Miles returned and said, 'Philip Long is very distressed, but he doesn't see how he can raise any more money for you today, not with the banks all closed.'

Robert pressed his fingers against his eyes, the pain behind them was agonising. 'There's nothing we can do about it now,' he said. 'If Felix Rourke wants arms, tell him that he will find more than enough inside the Castle tonight. Now, let us call the lieutenants and go over the plan one last time before we go and get some dinner.'

Michael Quigley, Nicholas Stafford, Thomas Wilde, John Mahon, Pat Finerty, Owen Kirwan, Henry Howley, Ned Condon, Pat McCabe, and Arthur Devlin sat on their crates, listening attentively. The plan was so simple it had every chance of success. If it did there was no need for bloodshed, just a strong display of men and arms.

'We make our move at half past nine,' Robert said. 'Miles, you will have several hundred of the Wexford men assembled inside Redmond's before dusk. Pikes and ammunitions to be distributed in readiness.'

Miles nodded.

'Ned, you will take men to the carriage rank and hire six carriages and bring them here. Myself, Stafford, Wilde, Mahon, Kirwan and Howley, all wearing greatcoats or cloaks over our uniforms, will set out for our night at the Castle. In each coach, there will be two additional armed men.'

'Will I not be in a coach?' Quigley asked.

Robert shook his head. 'The walk from here to the Castle takes no more than a few minutes. Yourself and the others will follow at a distance, walking casually behind us. Then, when the carriages pass the point nearest to Coal Quay, Miles and his men will fall in behind and assist with the attack on the Castle.'

'I will send men to stroll the Castle yard at regular intervals from the Ship Street direction,' Miles said, 'to ensure all remains quiet there.'

'Three separate attacks are to be made,' Robert said. 'First the Castle, followed by the Pigeon House, then the Park Battery. Big Arthur will assemble his men at Costigan's Mills, and, as I understand it, over two thousand men in and around the city will assemble at the Mills once the rocket is set off inside the Castle. Brangan is already organising Irishtown—'

'Mr Emmet!' They all turned to see the towering figure of Henry Hevey loping towards them. 'Mr Emmet, I insist that you let me supply you with a few horses. No battle looks right unless you have a cavalry.'

Robert exchanged smiles with the men. 'Thank you, Mr Hevey, but we hope to take the Castle by surprise. We would not do that if we had a cavalry of men riding down Thomas Street in green uniforms.'

'Are you sure now? You'd look a real general mounted on one of my stallions with a sword raised in your hand.'

'I'm quite sure, Mr Hevey. Thank you all the same.'

Barney Duggan was the next to make an appearance. 'Mr Emmet, oul Clarke of Palmerstown has been to the Castle!'

'And?'

'I don't think they could have paid much attention to him because Lord Hardwicke has gone back to the Viceregal Lodge and General Fox has sallied out in the carriage, dressed in civilians.'

'Nevertheless,' Robert said promptly, 'we can't take any chances. Barney, set a steady group of men to guard the various roads from the Castle to where the artillery is at Islandbridge. Also the road from the Royal Barracks to the Castle. No one carrying expresses to and from the Castle is to be allowed through.'

Duggan smiled. 'You can rely on me, Mr Emmet.'

Miles shoved back his chair. 'I'll tell you, this waiting is killing me! Come on, let's go and get something to eat.'

'At least when the times does come,' Stafford said, 'hopefully it should all be over within a few hours.'

As they strolled through the depot and along the private entrance to the White Bull, Robert murmured, 'I wish I could put my finger on just what it is that's stabbing me in the gut.'

'Hunger,' Stafford said.

The Night

The clock of St Catherine's Church had just chimed the seventh hour. Robert checked his watch. Two and half hours still to go! Each man had been ravenously hungry when they entered Mrs Dillon's back room at the White Bull, but none had managed to finish their dinner. Their stomachs were too knotted with the tension of what lay ahead.

All heads shot up as Henry Hevey burst into the Dillons' back room without knocking. 'No, Henry,' Stafford cried good-humouredly, 'we've not changed our minds about the horses.'

John Allen and two other esquires followed Hevey into the room. 'Is it true what I'm hearing, Mr Emmet?' Hevey asked. 'The rising's been postponed?'

'What?'

'Well, that's what I've been told. I've just met a lot of the Naas men on their way home. They said they were told the rising's off until next week.'

'They were told a lie then!' Robert cried. 'Who told them? Did they say? Or have they just turned coward?'

'Oh, I don't think that, Mr Emmet. You know they've always been as ready to fight as anyone.'

'Then tell them everything goes forward as planned.'

Hevey swallowed nervously. 'It's too late, they've gone.'

John Allen faced Robert. 'Well, Emmet, what do you say we do now?'

'What do *you* say we do, Allen?'

'I say we go on, as planned.'

Robert nodded. 'So say I.'

'Let's all get to our stations,' Miles said, rising. 'Once the leaders are in command, the men will remain disciplined.'

Outside the depot Miles turned to Robert. 'The next time I see you, hopefully it will be inside the Viceroy's office. God grant you life and victory.'

By eight o'clock, Miles Byrne had almost three hundred Wexford men packed inside the large house on Coal Quay, and every few minutes the door was opened to yet another soldier. Miles changed into his uniform of white breeches, white waistcoat, and green military jacket with gold fringes. He left his hat lying on the table until it was time to leave.

At that same moment, Robert was staring at Michael Quigley and listening to the hiss of a slow fuse as all his plans threatened to blow up in his face. '*You've done what?*'

'It was an accident, Mr Emmet. I don't know how I did it.'

'Do you realise what you've done! Now you have mixed the ready fuses with the unfinished ones, and the ordinary with the slow ones, we won't know which to attach to the rockets. All our labour has gone for nothing!'

'It's all the crowds in here, Mr Emmet. And I put the box of fuses for the grenades down for a minute, and next I looked it was gone. I've searched everywhere but—'

'You mean you have *mislaid* the fuses for the grenades, too?'

'Somebody must have moved it.'

Robert clutched the desk while he struggled to hold on to his temper. 'Go to Devlin at Costigan's Mills,' he said, 'and get as many ready fuses as you can from him.'

Thomas Wilde pushed a glass of brandy into Robert's hand while Stafford poured out four more. 'Quigley's tired,' Stafford said. 'We all are. Too much to do in too little time.'

'Yes, you're right,' Robert answered wearily. 'Time I should have spent checking the arrangements has had to be employed in work.'

The next bombshell was a man running into the depot saying he had seen a lot of the Kildare men heading for the canal boat home. 'They were told it was off until next week, Mr Emmet. They say they're coming back next week!'

'Who told them?' Stafford demanded.

'That's what I asked them. They said they were told the

leaders, even Nicholas Grey had given the order. But Felix Rourke and some of his men are still here. They say they'll take the Castle on their own if they have to.'

Robert put his hands to his head, walked to the back of the depot and sank down on a crate. Nicholas Stafford followed him. 'Something's not right, Mr Emmet.'

Ten minutes later, Big Arthur Devlin galloped into the depot like a horse and bounded up to Robert. 'Red Mick! I've just seen Red Mick – he's been nowhere near Wicklow! I charged after him but the cowardly swine ran for his life. I've just found out he's been hiding in the Liberties all along.'

'What the devil is going on?' Stafford demanded.

Robert felt as if he had been kicked in the stomach. 'You mean . . . Michael Dwyer knows nothing about the rising tonight? He won't be positioned on the outskirts or anywhere near Dublin tonight?'

'Not if no one has told him to be.' Big Arthur looked very pale.

'Call the whole thing off,' said John Mahon. 'Fate has turned against us. Most of the Kildare men supposed to work with us have gone. Dwyer and the Wicklow men haven't a clue the rising's tonight. The fuses are mixed. We only have one scaler and the rammers are—'

'It's as if we're being sabotaged,' Stafford said, 'but I don't think we should call a halt. Not now. It's too late!'

Robert pressed his fingers to his eyes and tried to quell the panic and desolation now swamping him. He had to keep calm. The men were getting frustrated and enraged. *He* had to keep calm.

'If we leave quietly,' said John Mahon, 'no one will be the wiser. We can rise at a later date.'

'Quigley mixed and mislaid the fuses,' Robert said slowly. 'He would hardly sabotage us. No man has worked harder in the past weeks.' He looked around. 'Where's Ned Condon?'

'Gone to get the coaches,' Stafford said.

'What? But he was supposed to wait until just before dusk.'

'Aye, but he's been itching for action all day.'

A spark of hope flared in Robert's breast. 'Our plan can still work. We have all the Dublin men, also a detachment of

Wexford men on the Quays. Besides, we are pledged to Munster, Ulster, and the other districts that will be waiting tonight.'

'Put it to the vote,' said Thomas Wilde.

Nicholas Stafford called the vote of the two hundred men in the depot. He returned to Robert with a smile on his face. 'The vote is unanimous – we rise tonight. Come on, while we wait for Ned's men and the coaches, we may as well change into our uniforms.'

At the sound of one hard rap, Miles opened the door of Redmond's house and pulled Pat Ford inside. 'How was it?'

'The Castle is as quiet as a cemetery. All the gates are open and only the normal guard on duty.'

'Great. Now you go up to Thomas Street, Pat, and tell Mr Emmet that everyone here is ready.'

'Aye, and I've just seen Condon hire the six coaches.'

Miles frowned. Condon was a bit quick off the mark. The coaches were not due to move down Thomas Street for almost another hour.

Robert smiled with relief when he heard Pat Ford's message. Trust Miles Byrne to be as reliable as clockwork.

'When Ned returns,' he said, 'we must still wait until the allotted time. The coaches can stay around the back.'

'Are the coachmen with us?' asked Thomas Wilde.

'Yes, they know their part. But for the sake of the men waiting around the city we must keep to the agreed time. They'll not be watching for the rocket flares for another hour.'

Robert moved over to his desk and lifted the lid. The letter which he had intended to give to Anne for Sarah was lying next to two of the letters she had sent to him during the week.

He lifted his black cravat and looked long at the auburn curl which Colgan the tailor had sewn inside for him, then wrapped the cravat around his neck.

Nicholas Stafford approached him, looking absolutely splendid in his green and white uniform. Robert smiled. 'Now we are suitably dressed,' he said, 'I think it is time to read out the Proclamation of the Provisional Government to the men.'

Ned Condon sat on top with the driver of the first coach and nervously looked around him as they proceeded over Queen's Bridge.

Ned was a hardy Dublin man of almost forty years. He had known all those connected with Tom Emmet and Lord Edward in '98, and was now equally devoted to Robert Emmet. He had been impatient for the fight, but he was now realising his mistake. Robert Emmet had told him to wait until just before dusk, and dusk meant the falling of night. Ned looked around him – it was still too light!

An officer of the Guard appeared from nowhere. He rode up to the first coach and ordered the driver to halt. Ned recognised him as Colonel Browne of the 21st Regiment.

'Where are you going with so many coaches?' Colonel Browne demanded.

Ned didn't know what to say. He chose the only way out of the situation he could think of. 'Begging your pardon, sir, but I'm desperate hard of hearing.'

Colonel Browne asked the question again.

Ned could feel his panic rising. ' 'Pon me word, your honour, but I can't hear a word you're saying atall!'

Browne's voice now rose with anger. 'I will ask you one more time! Where—' Before he realised what he was doing, Ned had withdrawn his pistol and fired.

The coachman looked at the officer sprawled on the ground and took fright. He pushed Ned off the bench and shouted over his shoulder to the other drivers. 'Come on! Get out of here!'

Ned shouted a curse as he fell to the ground. The impact stunned him for a moment. He opened his eyes and looked at Colonel Browne lying unconscious next to him, a bleeding wound in his chest. He pulled himself to his feet and began to run back to the depot, gaining momentum with each step.

Robert gaped at Ned. 'You were told to take five men with you and space out the carriages. Did you kill the officer?'

'No . . . at least . . . I'm not sure.'

'If Miles Byrne was here, he'd call you a bloody *eejit*!' Nicholas Stafford shouted.

'Come on through! Come and meet our General.' Thomas

Wilde was smiling as he escorted a dark-skinned man over to Robert. 'This gentleman is French,' said Wilde. 'He and his companion, whom he seems to have lost, were with the Kildare men today. They have come to Ireland because they are *friends of the cause*!'

'Monsieur,' said the Frenchman nervously, 'we 'ave come to 'elp you.'

Robert spoke a few words to him in French.

'No, no! Speak plis, Anglais.'

'Do you hear that, lads?' a voice shouted, 'the French are coming to help us. *Oh, the French are on the sea, says the Shan Van Vocht!*'

Robert detected a glimmer of fear in the Frenchman's eyes as he gazed around the packed depot. He lifted a glass and the half-full bottle of brandy from the table next to his desk.

'A glass of cognac, M'sieur?'

'Yes, merci.'

Robert hesitated, his eyes fastened on the Frenchman, then he gave a friendly smile. '*Ta mère est une putain,*' he said, as he slowly filled the glass, '*et ton père est un con.*'

The Frenchman nodded and smiled as he reached for the drink.

Robert tilted the glass and let the brandy spill on to the floor.

'Which playhouse were you recruited from, *M'sieur*?'

'What?' Stafford and Wilde stared at the Frenchman who had turned pale.

'This is no Frenchman,' Robert said. 'I have just told him his mother is a whore and his father worse – something any Frenchman would kill me for – but he just smiles and nods. He didn't understand a word I said.'

Stafford and Wilde grabbed the impostor roughly. 'Who put you up to it? You better tell us or we'll drop you here and now!'

'I don't know . . . a man . . . he came to the playhouse and paid me and my friend.'

'Who was he?'

'I don't know. He paid us a lot so we didn't ask questions.'

'Take him to the end of the depot and tie him up for now,' Robert ordered.

'He should be dropped,' a voice shouted. 'We can't let stag

424

informers get away with it. We wanted to drop Farrell when we caught him snooping around earlier, but you made us tie him up too! What d'ya intend to do with them atall?'

'We will do no murder!' Robert shouted, ignoring the voice that shouted he was 'too bloody soft'.

Desperation and fatigue lined Emmet's face as he turned to the lieutenants. 'It's no use. It would be foolish to carry on now. Wicklow, Kildare, coaches, fuses – everything has gone too wrong! Now this proves there are hostile agents at work. It would be irresponsible to risk the men now.'

'Aye, I suppose you're right,' Stafford said in a defeated voice, 'but the men will be disappointed. They've been waiting for this for months.'

Michael Quigley gaped at Emmet. 'What are you talking about? We move tonight as planned. Otherwise all our hard work will be wasted.'

'Not wasted,' Robert answered. 'The rising is only postponed.'

Quigley was not appeased; he began to plead with Emmet to carry on, finally turning away in fury. 'Ach! I'm going out to get some air.'

Stafford caught his arm. 'Then take off your uniform or put a coat or cloak over you.'

Quigley yanked down a cloak from the wall and draped it around him. 'I'm only going down to the lane,' he said sulkily.

Robert felt sick as he sank down into his chair and gazed blankly at the floor. If he had been on his own he might have wept there and then. After all his meticulous preparations, everything had gone ridiculously wrong. But why? Why had the messenger not gone to Dwyer? Why had someone sent the Kildare men home? Why had the men in Hevey's been told it was off? Why?

'Just a minute,' said Ned Condon kicking something near his foot. 'Just a bloody minute.' He pulled away the pile of sacking next to a crate and stared at the box of grenade fuses. 'Well damn my eyes! It looks as if they've been deliberately hidden under here.'

'*All is lost! The army is out in force and advancing!*' Quigley screamed, running into the depot. '*The army is out in force!*'

425

Robert's defeated expression vanished. He sprang to his feet. It was at this moment, some said later, that the true Emmet revealed himself. Gone was the studious, soft-spoken gentleman who made plans with mathematical precision, and in his place stood a defiant young man as angry as a caged lion.

'Well, what are you waiting for?' he shouted to the stunned men. 'We might as well go down fighting as be trapped in here!' He pulled the strap of his musket over his shoulder, withdrew his sword and ran through the depot shouting, 'Turn out! Turn out! Don't let them trap you inside!'

He felt released! Free! And it was a wonderful, *glorious* feeling! A feeling like soldiers must have after spending long tense hours in the ditches waiting and keyed up for battle, before the enemy appears and they at last rise to make their charge. For so long had his indignation and anger been kept under rigid control, not wishing for release in violence, but gratification in an outright and bold challenge; like the slave who longs to grab the master's whip and thrash him back!

Stafford, Wilde, Mahon and Condon followed in his wake with a host of the men charging down the stairs after them.

As Robert emerged from the lane at the back of the depot, Quigley caught up with him and the other lieutenants. Two young men strolling up Bridgefoot Street stopped to gape at the young men in green uniforms running like madmen at the head of a few hundred others. Within seconds, they had pikes in their hands and followed the chase.

They ran into Thomas Street to find it already packed with a mob carrying pikes. Most of them appeared drunk, staggering as they waved their pikes aloft and cheering.

'Where the devil did they come from?' John Mahon shouted.

Robert stopped dead in his tracks, staring in bewilderment down Thomas Street. 'Where's the army?' he cried.

Stafford, Mahon, and Wilde also stared, dumbstruck.

Robert turned to Quigley. 'Where's the army? *There's not a soldier in sight!*'

Quigley began to stutter. 'I saw soldiers . . .'

'How many soldiers did you see?'

'Well, someone told me the army were coming, then I saw two soldiers, and I thought—'

426

'You saw *two*,' Stafford cried, 'you stupid—' But before anyone could say another word, Thomas Wilde had punched Quigley in the face.

Confused and not thinking straight, and in a rush of nervous energy and desperation, Robert said, 'We can still do it if we move fast enough. We can still take the Castle. Get these damned drunks out of the way!'

A man shoved his chin into Emmet's face. 'And who are you calling a dhrunk, Misther Gen'l?'

Robert shoved the man aside and proceeded to move down Thomas Street which was now filling up with men from Meath Street and John's Lane. All were tavern men who had nothing to do with the conspiracy. Robert looked around him in desolation, then felt something evaporating inside him. This was not simply a mob, it was an *organised* mob, and they would never get through it.

'Get our men off the streets!' he shouted. 'Fall back! Fall back!'

'They can't fall back,' Stafford shouted. 'A load are coming from the James's Street end.'

Emmet, Stafford, and Wilde shouted to their ranks in an effort to pull them together. 'If you are not disciplined, when the soldiers do arrive they will cut you down!'

'It's a riot, boys! And look at the young soldiers in their uniforms leading us! Come on lads. *Erin Go Bragh!*'

'*Up the rebels!*'

'*For God and Lord Edward Fitzgerald!*'

Emmet made a last desperate attempt to control the men around him. 'You are playing into their hands! No riot ever won anything!'

'It's no use,' Thomas Wilde shouted. 'Every drunk, thief, and bullyboy is on the streets, and all intoxicated. Where did they get the money and the pikes?'

'O God!' Robert cried as he heard the shattering of glass. 'The drunks have started to loot and pillage.' He looked around him wildly, seeing the mob were clamouring at the fore and pressing at the rear, sealing them in. No disciplined advance or retreat could be made.

The stench of drink was nauseating. Robert recalled the

words he had written himself in the Manifesto of the Provisional Government:

> We call upon you, to carefully avoid all appearance of intoxication, plunder, or revenge; recollecting that you lost Ireland before, not from want of courage, but from not having that courage rightly directed by discipline.

'The Castle gates are slamming shut!' someone shouted. 'They're rolling out the cannons!'

The mob converged around them. A small number of the bullyboys were surreptitiously gathering around Emmet, isolating him from his men, but he did not notice as he realised the dream of liberty had turned into a nightmare. It was finished! Every plan they had made was now stamped into the gutter together with the Green standard someone had dropped.

They were pressed forward as the mob moved towards the Cornmarket and Cutpurse Row. 'Damn the Castle!' someone shouted. 'The city will be ours in half an hour!'

A young woman had pushed her way through the crowd and now appeared at Emmet's side. She glanced at the epaulettes on his green coat and threw her arms around his neck with a smile, pulling him further into the group of roughs. 'Are you the one they call the Gen'l?'

Robert stared at her. She was obviously a Lame Lane prostitute. 'Now why would a young man like yerself waste your energy on all this nonsense—'

Stafford, Wilde, and Mahon had appeared from nowhere, pushing through the men with their swords and closing around Robert.

Nicholas Stafford shoved the woman aside roughly, his eyes darting over the bullyboys around them, positive something shifty was going on. 'Try anything and we'll fecking kill ya!' he shouted viciously.

'If our men can't fall back,' Robert said, 'make them fall to the sides.'

'Most of them are getting out already,' Stafford said, grabbing his arm. 'It's yourself we must get out of here now.'

428

Before Robert knew what was happening, a number of lieutenants were dragging him through the crowd into Francis Street.

A group of pikemen came marching towards them heading in the direction of the Castle. A minute later a large force led by Captain Wilson charged into the bottom of the street from the Coombe end, firing their muskets into the group.

'Fall aside!' Robert shouted to the crowd. 'Make way for the firearms!'

The pikemen fell aside as Robert led his men forward with a run. When he called 'Halt!' each man raised his musket and fired. The air was swamped with the acrid smell of gunpowder as they quickly reloaded from cartridge boxes at their waists and fired again. The soldiers were now advancing. They withdrew their swords and moved forward with the pikemen pressing behind them.

'Get their damned general!' a voice shouted.

An explosion, then a musket ball ripped past Robert's ear. The man standing just behind him fell dead at his feet. Stafford grabbed his arm and pulled him to the side of the crowd who were now swallowing up the soldiers. Shouts, curses and struggles erupted around him.

Someone screamed. Robert glanced back to see blood gushing from the back of a man's legs as a result of a bayonet slash.

Captain Wilson lunged forward and grabbed Emmet's shoulder, pushing him flat against the wall. For one frozen instant the two uniformed men stared at each other, then Wilson drew back his bayonet. Emmet swiftly twisted sideways and thrust his sword into Wilson's stomach, savagely shaking himself free as the captain fell over him. The pikemen were rapidly scattering as the redcoats began to fire indiscriminately. He ran to join Stafford who was furiously shouting to the others.

'Take cover in the doorways,' Stafford ordered. 'Use your firearms!'

They exchanged volleys for over ten minutes until the soldiers were distracted by the arrival of Big Arthur Devlin and his group coming at them from their rear, firing muskets and blunderbusses.

'Let's get out of here,' Thomas Wilde shouted above the sound of gunfire.

'We must assist Devlin's men,' Robert shouted back.

`No!' Stafford cried. 'More armed troops will come from the Coombe within minutes and we'll be boxed in on both sides. There are too few of us.'

They ran down to the corner of Limerick Alley. There, Robert turned and looked back. 'Did I kill Wilson?'

Stafford also looked back. 'No,' he answered. 'He's wounded but they're helping him to his feet. Don't you fret about him. Wilson is as big a croppy hater as Castlereagh.'

They carried on through Patrick Street and Kevin Street, in the direction of the Dublin hills and Butterfield Lane.

Chapter Thirty-Two

In the Castle banqueting-room, Sir Edward Littlehales, Military Secretary to General Fox, was hosting a dinner for thirty officers when Alexander Marsden burst in. 'Call out the troops! A murderous mob are on their way to the Castle!'

Sir Edward sprang to his feet calling out orders as two soldiers helped a sobbing young woman into the room. 'Lord Kilwarden!' a soldier said. 'The mob stopped Lord Kilwarden's carriage and piked him.'

'They've killed my father!' the woman screamed.

'And they spared you?' Marsden spluttered.

' "Don't hurt the woman," ' she sobbed, 'that's what they kept shouting as they did their foul deed, "Don't hurt the woman." '

Marsden ran through the Castle corridors like a rabbit and crashed into Mr Edward Clarke of Palmerstown as he turned the corner. Marsden was about to shove him aside when he saw the blood pouring down Clarke's face.

'It was Barney Duggan, Mr Marsden! I was on my way home and he accused me of taking a message to the barracks. Then the bla'guard shot at me! I warned you this would happen, Mr Marsden. I warned you! And for my trouble I was nearly killed!'

Marsden was breathless when he entered Major Sirr's office in the lower yard. He stepped back as Major Swann and three soldiers carried in Lord Kilwarden and laid him on a bench. Major Swann knelt down beside the dying man. 'My lord?'

Kilwarden opened his eyes. 'Swann?'

'Yes, my lord. Your daughter is safe.'

'We have the four who did it,' a soldier shouted from the doorway. 'What shall we do with them, Major?'

'*Execute immediately!*' Major Swann shouted back, jumping to his feet and following the soldier out.

Lord Kilwarden slowly raised a hand, not appearing to see Marsden standing over him. 'Oh, no, my dear Swann, we had enough of that in ninety-eight. Let the wretches at least have a fair trial.' His hand fell down as he sank into death.

Down on Coal Quay, Miles Byrne was anxiously awaiting the return of the messenger whose duty it was to watch for the coaches passing along Thomas Street. Redmond's house was packed beyond its capacity, and the tense atmosphere inside was stifling.

Miles opened the door again and scanned the Quays which were strangely deserted. 'Something's wrong,' he whispered to Denis Redmond. 'Pat Ford should have returned well before this. And Emmet should be moving down Thomas Street now. Why has the messenger not arrived with word of the coaches?'

Miles had no way of knowing that both Pat Ford and the messenger had joined in the premature affray.

'It's not like Pat Ford to stay up there when I told him to come straight back,' he said to Redmond. 'You go up to Thomas Street, Denis, find out what's happening then come straight back. If you have not returned in fifteen minutes, I'll go up there myself.'

Michael Berney shouldered his way through the men to Miles. 'What's the reason for this delay, Captain Byrne? The men are getting very edgy.'

'I've sent another messenger to Thomas Street.'

'What do you think has happened?'

Miles had a bad feeling in his gut, his voice was low and troubled. 'I think something perilous has happened to Emmet, that's what I think.'

'How do you mean? Perilous?'

'I don't know. They could have simply been delayed somehow, although Emmet has continually stressed the importance of timing.'

'I think we should go up there now.'

'No, we could ruin everything by appearing on the streets too soon. We'll wait another fifteen minutes and no more.'

Fifteen minutes later, Miles quietly led his men through the now darkened streets. He had thrown a greatcoat over his uniform and stood on the corner of Thomas Street, staring in disbelief. Pikes were strewn all over the ground; the Standard of Liberty was trampled into the gutter, but the street was deserted.

Holding his hand up for the men to remain where they stood, he moved cautiously down Marshalsea Lane to the back entrance of the depot. It, too, was deserted, the floor covered in trails of gunpowder where barrels had been knocked over.

He returned to the men and said grimly, 'Whatever happened here, happened long before the time of half past nine. It must have happened just after Pat Ford came up.'

'While we were down on the Quays doing nothing!' said Michael Berney.

It was then they heard the heavy tramp of troops coming from the direction of James's Street. They ran down Thomas Street into Meath Street and met a small group of watchmen whom they easily put aside.

'We must get intelligence,' Miles said to Redmond. 'Go to the houses and see what you can discover as to what has happened to Emmet. And when you find out, take the intelligence out to Anne Devlin in Butterfield Lane. After that, lose yourself!'

The marching of the soldiers drew closer. 'Separate!' Miles commanded. 'Go to your homes or the homes of your friends as quickly as possible.'

As the men silently scattered, Miles pulled Michael Berney

into a doorway and rapped on the door. The door opened a crack: a man's face peeped out.

'United Irish,' Miles hissed. 'We don't wish to be seen on the streets.'

The door opened wider. 'Quickly then.'

Less than an hour later, Denis Redmond met up with Big Arthur Devlin on the Coombe. After a few minutes whispering, the two men knocked on a cottage door two streets away. A man nervously opened the door a few inches.

'United Irish,' Redmond said.

'Well you can't come in here,' the man grunted. 'Me wife's in bed.'

'We're not asking to climb in beside her.' Redmond shoved his foot in the door. 'Stand aside.'

The threatening undertone in Redmond's voice frightened the man. He held the door open and let them pass through. The man himself, although big and sturdy, walked unsteadily and reeked of whiskey.

'No, don't light another candle,' Big Arthur said, smiling slyly. 'One will be enough.'

The man looked at the two young men guardedly, his eyes resting for a moment on Big Arthur's green uniform, then he lifted a bottle of whiskey from the floor.

'Will youse have a drop?'

They both refused. Two wooden chairs were placed by a table in the centre of the room. The big man sat heavily down on one and poured himself a drink. 'Well, God, I tell you this, I need a drink after all the trouble out there tonight.'

'Oh, so you were there?' said Redmond.

'I was. I seen the judge murdered, too.'

'And weren't you also one of those who led the mob?'

The man's head shot up. He ran his tongue nervously over his lips as he looked at the dangerous gleam in Redmond's eyes. He struggled to his feet but Big Art shoved him down again.

'We just want to have a little talk with you,' said Big Art, clamping his hands on the man's shoulders and holding him down.

'From what I can gather,' said Redmond, 'someone has been

piling up the shit to throw at a certain young gentleman. And by all accounts, you were one of the bullyboys inciting the mob tonight.'

'No! It wasn't me! I was only an onlooker! Honest to God!'

'You see,' Redmond continued, 'my friend and I have a problem. We are in a great hurry. And if you don't spit what you know in the next five minutes, we'll be forced to take care of you before we leave.'

'Take care of me?' The man's eyes bulged out of his head. 'Surely to God, you don't mean . . . ?'

Redmond withdrew his pistol and rammed it against the man's temple. 'I mean I'll blow your fecking brains out! Now *talk*!'

It had been a lonely and confusing day for Anne. Within an hour of her return to Butterfield Lane, around the time of five o'clock, two Wexford men had arrived to collect ammunition stored at the house. They stared at her in bewilderment when she asked if the rising had been postponed. As far as they were concerned, the rising was very much on, otherwise they would not have been sent out to collect arms.

Then, just after six o'clock, her mother had arrived in a desperate state, wringing her hands and sobbing because Little Arthur had gone into the city to join Mr Emmet.

'What does a lad of just seventeen know about swordfighting or guns?'

'Mr Robert will send him home again,' Anne had said as she lifted the kettle to make tea. 'He said he would.'

By the time the tea was drunk her mother was mollified. She returned home after agreeing to send Nellie over to keep Anne company.

Once alone, Anne gave vent to her own panic about her brother. It was always the innocent that got it. If anything happened to Little Arthur it would kill her she knew. Rage surged through her against her brother for defying instructions. Fighting indeed! Even Mr Robert said Little Arthur was a born scholar. His hands were made to hold pens, not guns!

Anne had hoped that Nellie's innocent prattle would help to

434

dissipate her gloomy thoughts, but when Nellie arrived she was in a tearful mood, wailing that Jimmy was even sicker.

Anne cuddled Nellie on the settle and told her one of the stories of the Fianna, the story of Oisin in Tir Na Nog. Every time she paused in the telling, she wondered what was happening in the Liberties to her darling brother, to Mr Robert, to Big Art, to all her friends.

Her limbs felt heavy as she sauntered into the kitchen after tucking Nellie up in bed. She glanced at the clock – just after eleven. The next time she looked it was four minutes past. And wasn't she the one who had told Mr Robert the minutes don't go any faster for watching them?

Ten minutes later she heard footsteps outside. She ran to the back door and hastily bolted it, then to check the front door was still locked. She held her breath as she stood in the hallway. It couldn't be Mr Robert and the men – it was too soon!

Someone called the password but in her panic she didn't recognise the voice. She hesitated: too many strange things had happened today. The password came again. 'Who are you?' she shouted.

'It's me, Anne.'

'Oh my God!' She flew to unbolt the door, standing back as Robert, Stafford, Wilde, Mahon, Hevey, and Quigley walked in. Her shoulders sagged in relief, then as she gazed over their dejected faces she knew the worst had happened. *Again!* It had happened again! The blasted Castle had won *again!*

Then she saw that neither her brother nor Big Art were with them.

'Oh, what have you done?' she cried at Robert. 'My bad welcome to you! Have you destroyed the whole kingdom and all belonging to me? Are my kinsmen among the dead?'

She stood only inches away from him. 'And what has become of all your grand preparations?' she stormed. 'Are they all gone and lost? Is the cause lost? *Again!*' Her hands were slapping him hard across the face, angry hands that lashed out in refusal to accept it had all been in vain.

'Leave him alone!' Stafford cried, wrenching her away. 'He's suffered enough mischief this night without you turning on him!'

435

Robert stared at her, too shocked to speak, the whiteness of his face stark against the red marks of her hands. He turned and walked out of the room.

'What's got into you, Anne?' Thomas Wilde cried. 'You're kicking a man when he's bloody down. You wouldn't do that to a dog!'

The room was deathly quiet, so quiet her harsh breathing sounded like a bellows. She looked into the shocked face of each man in turn, then whispered, 'O God! What happened? What went wrong?'

The men all threw looks at Quigley, but none said anything.

The rage within her suddenly vanished, replaced by a sharp ache in her breast as she realised what she had done: given him her bad welcome, and savagely turned on him because he was not a conquering hero after all. But how could she even rejoice in their safety when her brother could be lying dead somewhere?

She turned and ran from the room, down the hall and up the stairs. No light shone from beneath his door. She knocked but received no familiar call to enter. She opened the door and walked slowly into the room. He was standing by the window, his hand high on the pane, his face turned down on his arm. His still figure in the green uniform was lit up by the brilliance of the moon beaming through the glass.

She stood beside him, trembling, 'Mr Robert?'

He lifted his head and looked at her, tears spilling down his face. 'Cead mile failte,' he whispered.

A slash from a knife could not have hurt her more than his good Irish welcome. 'I didn't mean it,' she choked. 'My bad welcome, I didn't mean it.'

He tried to smile, to reassure her that it was all right; to let her know that his grief was nothing to do with her, even though she had so unexpectedly rubbed a stinging salt into the wound, but after a few seconds he just nodded his head slightly and looked away from her.

It was the expression in his eyes which swelled the ache under her breast to piercing, an expression of naked shame. *Shame!* He who had spared neither himself nor his wealth for the sake of the cause! He who could have lived off the fat of the land if he had chosen to – was now feeling shame because he had failed to achieve what trained military men like Fitzgerald and Tone had failed to achieve.

He was staring out at the night, the hand on the glass trembling, the tears continuing to run silently down his face. She had never seen him like this; so off-balance, no longer in control of himself.

She stood watching him until she could stand it no longer. 'I didn't mean any of it,' she cried wretchedly, her hands going to his shoulders and pulling him round to face her. 'Don't you know I would never deliberately hurt you for the world!'

In a moment her arms were around him, comforting him with all the tenderness of a mother with her son.

For Robert it was like being a child again, those very young days of childhood when the terrifying images of the black night would vanish in the glow of a candle, and the relief of hearing his mother's gentle voice as she held him and assured him it had all been a nightmare.

He closed his eyes and felt the conflicting emotions of the night falling away, felt her warmth and softness and comfort seeping into him. Even her smell was reminiscent of childhood, not heady and fragrant like the flowers of the season, but cleanly fresh like the plain green grass . . .

Suddenly his physical and mental exhaustion cleared and he abruptly moved back from her. He stared at her and she did not speak, just lifted a shaky hand to wipe her own eyes.

'Will you come down now?' she asked at length.

'No . . . not yet.'

'I'm so very worried about my brother,' she whispered.

'Jimmy?'

'Little Arthur. Mammy says he went into the city after you. Did you see him?'

He shook his head. 'Not once. He came nowhere near the depot. But I shouldn't worry, the men will have sent him home.'

She turned to go, then hesitated. 'What went wrong?'

'Everything.'

'You're not the first leader to fail.'

'But not one of them failed so completely, so pathetically as I did.'

'The insurrection—'

'The *insurrection*!' he spat out the word. 'I couldn't even give it the respectability of an insurrection. It was nothing more than a drunken riot.'

'Lord Edward couldn't do it,' she cried, 'nor Wolfe Tone, nor Rory O'More, nor Shane O'Neill the Lion of Ulster, nor—'

'Oh, stop it, Anne!'

'The fight for freedom,' she whispered frantically, 'can be tried again.'

'The fight for freedom *must* be tried again, but not led by me. Who would follow me now?'

'The men,' she said. 'The ones who call themselves your staff – Miles Byrne, Stafford, Wilde, Mahon . . . And Big Art . . . when he comes back.'

'It was all such a chaotic mess,' he said in a cracked voice. 'A ridiculous farce.'

'What happened? Tell me.'

He passed a hand over his eyes as he tried to unravel his thoughts. 'First of all,' he said, 'three hundred Kildare men were to come to Dublin today, but it seemed as if half the county turned up. Many of them tried to wait inside the depot instead of the various houses, public and private. For a time it was impossible to move inside the depot; tired men became irritated. I had finished making the fuses, but the box was mislaid later. The Kildare men who were to act – particularly with me – went off again to the Canal harbour around six. It was given out by some treacherous or cowardly person that the rising was posponed until next week.'

'I heard a man telling others the rising was postponed when I passed the White Bull,' she said.

'Did you? What time was that?'

'About three.'

'Well, add to incidents like that a whole series of mistakes and disappointments. We needed money for muskets and blunderbusses, but the one I sent to Philip Long absconded with it. Quigley had the management of the depot, yet he mixed the fuses. Money was finally sent in to me at Mrs Dillon's just before seven, but it was too late to buy the guns. A whole number of things went wrong, but I felt to change the day was impossible, for I expected the other counties to act and feared to lose the advantage of surprise.'

He gave a small ironic laugh. 'Surprise! A herd of mad cattle could have sprung a better surprise than we did.'

He looked at her intently. 'But had I another week, Anne, another thousand pounds, another thousand men, I would have feared nothing. But tonight there was deficiency in all – plan, preparation, and men.'

'It's just like ninety-eight all over again,' she whispered. 'I watched my cousins and the other lads of Wicklow, full of fire and enthusiasm, convinced after so long it was going to be Ireland's first year of liberty. Then the pain and despair of defeat. Some of those that weren't killed returned from Vinegar Hill half insane. They had seen their comrades blown to pieces. One man used to get the shakes at the sight of anything red. He picked up his fowling piece one day and shot down a poor old woman wearing a red scarf. He didn't mean to kill her – he just wanted to blast the red away. When he realised what he had done, he took all his money and gave it to the woman's family, then he turned the gun on himself.'

Again she wiped a hand over her eyes. 'That's what I was doing when I struck you – hitting out at them, the tyrants at the Castle – not at you.'

'Not today, Anne,' he whispered, 'but one day, some day, we will beat them.'

'Oh, we will,' she breathed, longing to believe him. 'We will.'

He moved over to the table and began to sift through the papers. 'I'd better destroy anything incriminating. They'll be looking for us now.'

Anne shuddered at his words. Yes, they would be looking for them now.

She took a few steps towards the door, then paused.

'Was it because of the fuses the men all looked at Michael Quigley when I asked what went wrong?'

'Quigley?' He turned to her, a puzzled expression on his face. 'Quigley ran into the depot shouting that the army were out in force, so we went out to meet them. But there was no army – except an army of drunks and corner-boys. He'd seen no more than two soldiers. Only for that, we would not have made a move tonight. We had already decided to wait until a later date.'

Her voice flared with anger. 'Wait till I go down there!'

'No, say nothing. Quigley feels bad enough as it is.'

She considered him for moments, as if she was seeing him for the first time. Funny how failure can change a hero into a human and lay bare the true weakness of a man. And in this case, his was a very dangerous weakness for a revolutionary.

'Do you know what's wrong with you, Mr Robert?' she said quietly, 'You're too soft-hearted, and you trust others too easily.'

Once again he found himself staring at the door for a number of minutes after it had closed behind her.

When she entered the kitchen the men were arguing over what had gone wrong. Michael Quigley sat alone staring into the fire. He lifted his eyes to Anne but her answering glare froze him. Then the men told her their version of every little thing that had gone wrong. Some were plain honest-to-God accidents, but others!

A rap on the door was followed by the password. She ran into the passage and opened the door to Big Arthur and Denis Redmond.

'Big Art! Oh, thank God you're safe! But . . . but where is my brother?'

'Safe in his bed, I hope. I sent him home around seven in the company of two stout lads who were instructed to take him all the way to his door. Ah, but Anne—' Big Art's shoulders slumped as he sat down. 'Half the boys that came back to Ireland with me are now lying dead on Francis Street.'

'Where's Mr Emmet?' Redmond cried, walking through to the hall. 'Mr Emmet!'

'Will you keep your voice down,' Anne hissed. 'My little sister is asleep, and there's no Mr Emmet lives here. Only a Mr Ellis.'

Robert came into the kitchen a few minutes later carrying a bundle of loose papers which he threw on to the turf flames.

'Mr Emmet,' Redmond said, 'you've been deceived and betrayed. *Agents provocateurs* were out tonight.'

'Do you mean the two Frenchmen?' Stafford demanded.

Robert just looked at Redmond who continued, 'Men acting

440

on orders of the Castle were in Thomas Street today, and tonight they were even in the depot.'

'The depot?'

'Aye. They were instructed to go to the depot dressed as country labourers who wanted to join the insurrection. They were paid to take up arms and join the Standard of Liberty at an appointed hour. Then they were to rush forward and create confusion by calling out the corner-boys and the drunks and arming them – they were told to shout, "Do not be delaying all night". '

'How do you know all this?' Robert asked.

'I went seeking intelligence, and I tell you, Mr Emmet, it's all coming out now! The money they were paid is swilling in their bladders and loosening their tongues. One man was crying his eyes out when he realised what they had done.'

'Who paid them?'

'Sure, they don't seem to know themselves, just men they say. I found a corner-boy in a hallway. He said he was told the call to take up arms before nine was from the young gen'l in the depot.'

'But why?' Henry Hevey asked.

'It's not hard to guess,' Robert said slowly. 'In ninety-eight they provoked a premature rebellion before the French arrived. Perhaps their reason is the same now – explode what is left of the United Irishmen before the French land.'

He shook his head irritably. 'God, what fools we were! We've played right into their hands.'

'It was the explosion in Patrick Street,' Wilde muttered. 'It was that brought everything forward.'

'What's the situation in the city?' Robert asked Big Art.

'Small outbreaks of trouble all over the place. About two hundred men attacked the barracks just before midnight, but the military were waiting. They shot into the crowds. A few of our men died, but many were wounded.'

'And on our way here,' Redmond said, 'we hid in a hallway because a detachment of troops were on the street. We heard their commander giving them orders. It seems Nicholas Grey has been spotted in Athy.'

Robert nodded. 'Grey took a house in Athy so that he could

lead a contingent of Kildare men into Dublin after the main attack. What did the officer say?'

'That Nicholas Grey and three more were dressed in green uniforms, which makes Grey's position in this trouble very clear. And that earlier, in Kildare, five others were seen in the same uniforms and the whole county was on the boil. Large detachments of troops are being sent there.'

Redmond and Big Arthur exchanged glances, then Redmond looked at Robert. 'There's something else you should know, Mr Emmet. Myself and Arthur visited the house of one of the mob ringleaders. He said they were told to ensure a rising, but in particular – to detach *Emmet* from his followers.'

'They know all about you,' Anne cried. 'You must get out of here, now, this minute!'

'She's right,' said Thomas Wilde. 'If they know who you are, your chances of leading another rising are finished.'

Stafford banged his fist on the table. 'So that's what those bastards were up to! And if the Castle do know you're the leader, they'll have every man jack and soldier out looking for you. Come on!'

'Over to the dairy,' Anne cried. 'Da will give you the protection of his house until other arrangements can be made, but you must get out of here now.'

Big Arthur rose tiredly to his feet. ' 'Twas a bad business all the same. After the killing of Lord Kilwarden the troops managed to round up a lot of the men including Felix Rourke and about—'

'Lord Kilwarden!' Robert stared at Big Arthur, as if praying he had misheard. 'Lord Kilwarden was killed?'

'Aye, it seems that when his carriage came near Thomas Street, the mob thought he shouted that he was Lord Norbury, the hanging judge. They pulled him out of the carriage and piked him.'

'He was *murdered*?' Horror and revulsion contorted Robert's face as he moved back into the room. 'O my God,' he whispered, 'Lord Kilwarden . . . the finest, most decent man . . . O my God.'

'It was not *your* fault,' Anne cried. But the guilt and grief on his face said it was.

'Lord Kilwarden,' he said wretchedly, 'was the only judge amongst all the other hangers who ever played fair with the United Irishmen. It was *Kilwarden* who issued the writ suspending Tone's execution when Curran pleaded with him . . .'

His knees appeared to buckle under him and he sat down. 'O God, Lord Kilwarden was John Curran's best friend . . .'

Anne pulled roughly on his arm. ' 'Tis not the time to think of that now. Get away over the fields to the dairy.'

As Anne made to shut the door behind them, Robert pushed it open again. 'You can't stay here alone, Anne. You must come with us.'

'No! Who knows that Miles Byrne or Michael Dwyer or any of the others will show up. And Nellie's asleep. 'Tis best I stay.'

'But if the militia—'

'They won't harm an ignorant serving-maid.' She almost pushed him off his feet. 'Now, for the last time – go!'

At the edge of the field, Denis Redmond announced he was going back to his house on the Quays to collect his things, then he would journey to friends in Newry.

'Why Newry?' Robert asked.

'From Ulster I can take a ship to America, and that's the place you should head for, too, Mr Emmet. The Yankees won't hold it against a man for trying to do what they've just done themselves.'

Robert's thoughts began to race as he ran after the others across the dark fields. He could not remain in Ireland after what had happened tonight. The fate of Ireland was now for other men. He was done. He would have to get away to France, and then maybe over the western ocean to America.

He collided with Hevey who had stopped to catch his breath. 'I can't see a damned thing in this darkness,' Hevey whispered.

Robert grabbed his arm and pulled him on, almost being knocked to the ground as he helped the cumbersome Hevey over the bars of the stile.

But then, Robert thought as he ran on, he could not leave Ireland before he knew the fate of Russell, Hamilton and Jemmy Hope. He would not have anyone say he had run to save his own skin and left his friends to take the consequences.

He stopped suddenly, making Hevey stumble with a curse.

He gazed in the direction of The Priory. What would she think when she heard of his humiliating failure? Would she still want to marry him? Go away with him?

'This is no time for stargazing,' Hevey panted. 'You know the way to the Devlins' place, but I don't. Now lead on.' Hevey added coaxingly, 'And if you don't mind, at a more regular pace now.'

Chapter Thirty-Three

The following morning, red-coated soldiers and yeomen swarmed the streets and houses of the Liberties searching for rebels. They smashed and burned furniture, making huge bonfires in the centre of the streets. The city trembled with fear, for the violence of the soldiers was more terrifying than the insurrection of the night before.

Mr Cody of the *Dublin Post*, who was drawing a government secret service allowance of £400 a year, sought a private interview with Alexander Marsden and asked for instructions as to how news of the insurrection should be reported.

'Although it would be untrue to call it an insurrection,' Cody said.

Marsden glared. 'It is not what they did, Mr Cody! It is what they *intended* to do! A full-scale revolution is what they intended, and would have got it if their plans had not been thwarted.'

'So how shall I report it?'

'Make much coverage of the murders of Lord Kilwarden and Colonel Browne, and what terror the events of last night have created. The so-called rebels were nothing more than a murderous rabble.'

'And the leaders, sir? Do we have names?'

'The leaders! Oh, yes, you must say *much* about the leaders.

Make it very clear that *the leaders* were men of bloodthirsty appetites! Hell-dog reformers only interested in murder and plunder.'

'But do we have any names, Mr Marsden?'

Marsden hesitated. 'No names. Not yet. Not until you have let the entire kingdom know all about those murdering thugs who dared to dream they could take Ireland from the Crown.'

Mary Devlin's coyness with the house guests quickly disappeared under their friendly banter. She thought Nicholas Stafford, with his chestnut-brown hair and eyes, to be the most gorgeous man she had ever laid eyes on, and expended all her energy vying for his attention.

All had revived their good spirits, all except Robert who hardly spoke, but he did manage to smile when the others laughed at the sight of Henry Hevey helping Mrs Devlin to churn butter with an apron around his thick waist.

Without warning the latch on the kitchen door was raised and a neighbour walked in without rapping as she was used to do. The woman stopped short at the sight of the men sitting around the room in their green uniforms. She gazed about her with an air of stupid vacancy and stuttered, 'Oh, Mrs Devlin, what on earth could I be thinking of? Wasn't it Mrs Shaughnessy I intended to call on, but sure my mind is miles away. Well, sorry for disturbing you. Good evening to you.'

Mrs Devlin had frantically been thinking of something to say to the woman, but when she managed to open her mouth the woman had disappeared through the door in a flurry of skirts.

'Who was that?' Nicholas Stafford asked.

'Mrs Coates. She's as dozy as an old cat and probably didn't even notice youse. But wait now, I'll lock the door while ye have your meal.'

Half an hour later, someone else fiddled at the latch on the kitchen door which was now locked. 'Who are you?' shouted Brian Devlin.

'O'Hanlon.'

Brian Devlin looked back at the men inside the room. 'O'Hanlon is butler to Mr Grierson, the printer. He's a friend of Big Art.'

He opened the door and O'Hanlon pushed his way breathlessly inside. 'Where's Arthur?'

'Having a sleep, Mr O'Hanlon. Why are you looking for him?'

' 'Tis that Coates woman. She's been to see Mr Grierson. He was having dinner with some of his friends and the wine was going round and toasts being pledged and thanks sent to heaven for the preservation of all the King's loyal subjects, when the Coates woman pushed her way in. I was waiting by the sideboard and I heard her say she had just that minute seen fifty French soldiers in the Devlins' kitchen.'

'God bless you, Mr O'Hanlon, for bringing the intelligence,' said Brian Devlin. 'And how did Grierson respond?'

'He didn't seem to believe her. "How could *fifty* soldiers get into the Devlins' kitchen?" he asked. But then after discussing it with his friends, he assured the woman he would set off after dinner and take her report to the Castle.'

'There's no time to be lost,' said Brian Devlin to Robert. 'We'll have to find another place for you quickly.'

It was almost dark. Robert was standing by the parlour window when Anne sidled up to him a short time later. 'You'll be moving on so?' she said.

He nodded. 'Yes, into the Dublin mountains.'

Mrs Devlin came in. 'Mr Emmet, I wonder ... did you learn anything at all about sickness growing up in the house of a doctor?'

Robert gave her a questioning look. 'Jimmy?'

'Aye, I have him tucked away in bed these past few days but he's getting worse all the time. Will you have a look at him for me?'

Robert followed Mrs Devlin up to the bedroom where Jimmy raised his head and peered at the visitor. 'Hello, Mr Robert,' he said weakly.

'Hello, young man.' Robert sat on the side of the bed, his eyes examining the rash on the boy's face. 'Jimmy, your mammy thinks your skin rash is from the berries. Will you let me look at your arms and legs?'

When Jimmy nodded, Robert pulled back the cover and

peered at the small pimples of pus beginning to form on the boy's arms and thighs, then quickly moved back slightly. He forced a smile as he covered Jimmy up again. 'I suppose you are tired of being cooped up in bed,' he said.

Jimmy nodded. 'Aye, I don't like being sick.'

'You'll be up and about in no time,' Robert told him gently. 'But you must rest easy and do everything your mammy tells you.'

When they returned to the kitchen, Mrs Devlin looked at him in mute anxious query. 'Smallpox,' he said.

'Ah, no! I feared it could be that, but I was hoping it was the berries.'

Robert said: 'A great many children survive smallpox, but Jimmy must be kept in strict isolation from the rest of family. It is also important to keep a close watch on his eyes. Even when his body is clear, any ulceration around the eyes could lead to blindness.'

'Is there no medicine we can give him?' Mary asked. 'Something to make him better more quickly?'

Robert shook his head. 'The apothecary probably has something which will relieve him, but there is really nothing other than time, and the body's natural resources to fight it off. Just before my father died, he told me that a man named Edward Jenner had discovered an effective vaccine for smallpox as recently as 1796, but it will probably take a long time for it to reach the people.'

Stafford came in and informed Robert that a man named James Commons was waiting to take them to Jack Doyle's house in Ballynameece. 'Mr Devlin is getting a number of his horses ready for us out the back,' Stafford said.

Mrs Devlin pulled herself together, thanked Robert and gave him her blessing as he left the kitchen. 'May God go with you,' she said.

Outside the house, Robert noticed Anne standing alone against the end wall, her arms folded about her waist, her head down. He approached her casually.

'It's time to go,' he said quietly. 'Are you returning to Butterfield Lane?'

'Aye.' She looked up. 'It's the only place the men will know to bring intelligence. If I can, I'll try and let you know what's happening.'

'How will you know where we are? Doyle's place is only for a night.'

She looked past him, fixing her eyes on the men as they sorted out their mounts. 'I'll find you.'

'If any of the men from the Liberties turn up with my horse, will you give him to your father.'

'Black Seamus?'

'Yes. He can keep him.'

They looked at each other, both conscious that his time in Ireland was nearly over. And once he went, he could never come back. He had no more need of the horse.

He looked away and found himself staring hard at a small rough square of a garden to the side of the yard which was full of flowers, although he was not really seeing them. Anne followed his gaze and smiled wryly.

'Mary did that. She's always wanted the nice things ladies have. Silks and scents and gardens full of flowers.'

'Have you not?' he asked quietly.

'Oh, me,' she choked a small laugh. 'I rarely get what I want. Sometimes I think I must have been born on a rainy day or a starless night. Looking back, nothing has ever really worked out for me.' She shrugged a shoulder carelessly. 'Except my family. I have a nice family.'

'Yes.'

'Well, off you go,' she said curtly. 'You don't want to keep the men waiting.'

Nellie ran up and tugged at Robert's arm. He smiled down at her. 'And how is little Miss Purty?'

'You know I'm not called Purty. Only me kitten is called Purty.'

He put a finger to her pretty face. 'Well, you should be called Purty, too.'

Nellie beamed, but as quickly her smile faded. 'Me and Purty are very unhappy, Mr Robert, because Jimmy is sick and the soldiers are after you. But don't worry,' she said determinedly, 'Purty and me'll scratch their eyes out if they come anywhere near you.'

'Now listen, Nellie,' he said firmly. 'If anyone asks you questions about Mr Emmet or Mr Ellis, you don't have to lie, just keep your mouth tightly closed and say nothing. Better still, try and forget you ever knew me.'

Nellie stared at him, her eyes dark with sudden understanding. This was not a game of soldiers and rebels – it was serious, grown-up business, and Mr Robert was in bad trouble. If they caught him they would lock him in a dungeon for years, just like they did to her da.

Her mouth twisted. She dropped Purty and her small face began to crumple. 'I could never forget you, Mr Robert! Me and Purty could never forget *you*.'

When she began to cry he knelt on one knee and gently held Nellie's shaking form as her arms clung tightly to his neck, sobbing hiccuping threats against the soldiers. Over her head he smiled at Anne who did not smile back, just stood there staring at him, looking like some wild gypsy girl with her black curls hanging over her shoulders.

Nellie's sobs became louder. He stroked her hair and murmured soft, encouraging words to her, but all the time his eyes were on Anne, held so long by her watery green gaze that for one timeless moment he was not sure which Devlin girl he was holding, or to which Devlin girl he was speaking.

Big Arthur touched his shoulder. 'The horses are ready and time's a-flying.'

Robert stood up, patted Nellie on the cheek, then held out his hand to Anne. She gently placed her own in his, and for a moment their fingers clutched and held fast. Then he turned and walked to where Little Arthur stood holding a horse.

As they rode away, he glanced back, just in time to see the mane of her black hair and quick-limbed figure running across the fields in the direction of Butterfield Lane.

Beneath a tree in the field at the back of Butterfield Lane, Anne threw herself down breathlessly on the cool grass.

'The pursuers are coming!' said Deirdre.

'Yes,' said Naois.

But word came to Connacher, the King of Ulster, that the company he was in pursuit of were gone.

449

The King then sent for Dunan Gacha Druid, the best magician in his court, and said to him:

'Too much wealth have I expended on you, Dunan Gacha Druid, to give schooling and learning and magic mystery to you, if these people get away from me today, and without power to stop them.'

'I will stop them,' said the magician, 'until the company you send in pursuit return.'

And the magician weaved his spell and placed a forest before them through which no man could go. But the sons of Uisnech ran through the forest without halt or hesitation, and Deirdre held on to Naois's hand.

By the time the men had arrived at the house of Jack Doyle, they had been joined by six more rebels, swelling their number to fourteen. James Commons warned Robert that although Jack Doyle boasted of being a notorious rebel in his day, he could not be trusted completely, and advised caution with him.

Jack Doyle was a big burly man with a round moon face. He opened the door to Commons's knock and gazed over the group of armed men, his eyes lingering on the six dressed in green uniforms.

'These are all French soldiers,' Commons said. 'They need your protection for the night.'

'Frenchies? I only help Irish lads!'

'But these French boys bravely came here to help us,' Commons explained.

Robert stepped forward and gave a low bow. 'Monsieur Doyle, *nous vous sommes très reconnaissants de nous permettre de séjourner chez vous, merci.*'

Doyle stared at him. 'Sure you might as well be talking rubbish for all I can understand ye. Come in then. Enteray.'

While the ale was served no one spoke to Doyle except James Commons, and whenever the big man directed a question at one of the men, they stared at him mutely and shook their heads.

'Not one can speak a word of English,' Commons explained.

'I have no spare room, you know,' Doyle said to Commons. 'These Frenchies will have to sleep on the floor. There's just

450

this room, and me own bedroom back there.'

Stafford signalled to Robert with a droop of his eyelid; both men casually stood up and strolled to the door.

'Ah, here! Where are they off to?' Doyle demanded.

'Sure, isn't it the ale, Mr Doyle,' Commons said. 'You know these Frenchies are only used to wine. 'Tis just to the necessary they're going.'

Robert and Stafford inspected the outside of the house and the barn. They discovered Doyle's bedroom had a door out to the backyard. They went back inside the house, making Doyle scratch his head in amusement when they both bowed low to him.

'Are you sure ye have no spirits?' Doyle asked again, and again James Commons shook his head.

'Then I'm off to me bed so,' Doyle said sourly to Commons. 'They'll just have to spread themselves out as best they can. Nobody warned me I'd have a load of Frenchies coming to camp on me floor. I hope Boney is prepared to do the same for me if I ever need it an' all!'

As Jack Doyle stood by the open door of his bedroom, the men could see a huge four-poster bed in its centre. Doyle took another long look at the Frenchies, then slowly shook his head and closed the door.

A half-hour later, everyone was asleep except for the two men on guard outside, and Robert and Stafford who were sitting with their backs against the wall talking in whispers.

'I don't trust him,' Stafford said.

'Neither does James Commons, but this was the only place at such short notice.'

'You know that Doyle's nickname is Silky Jack?' Stafford whispered. 'As slippery as a silkworm.'

'And that door out to the back . . .'

Stafford nodded. 'That door out the back could interfere with a man's sleep.'

They rested their heads back against the wall, closed their eyes and tried to sleep. A few minutes later Stafford whispered, 'You wouldn't be thinking the same as I'm thinking, would you?'

Robert shifted his body on the hard floor. 'I'm thinking it's the biggest blasted bed I've ever seen.'

'And Doyle is in it all on his own.'

'With no one to know if he slips out of it in the dark of night.'

The candle was still burning, and Jack Doyle still awake, when Robert and Stafford entered the room. Doyle's mouth dropped open as he sat up and stared at the two Frenchmen. 'Eh! What d'ya think yer up to?'

'*Mon cher* M'sieur Doyle,' said Robert silkily. '*Tous mes regrets*, but we zee you 'av a grande bed.'

'*Grosse!*' smiled Stafford, taking off his green jacket.

'Now hold on just a minute!' Doyle shouted. 'Ye can't sleep with me! What's wrong with the floor out there?'

Robert draped his jacket over the chair. 'Augh! It ees so 'arrd!'

Doyle drew in his breath at the sight of their pistols. 'Vo! Vo!' he moaned.

'Vo! Vo!' cooed Stafford with a smile, climbing into the bed beside him.

Jack Doyle's eyes were bulging as Robert lifted the covers and slipped in the other side. The two rebels exchanged glances when they saw Doyle was still dressed in his top clothes, including his jacket.

'God blast ye!' Doyle shouted as they made themselves comfortable. 'Ye still have yer boots on!'

Stafford sat up, lifted his pistol, pointed it at Doyle and said indignantly, 'M'sieur Doyle! 'Av you ever 'ad a French General-all and a French Colon-all in bed weeth you before?'

'Honest to God! I never have!' Doyle wailed, staring down the barrel of the gun.

'So!' Robert smiled. 'Boots ees no probleme. *Sink of zee 'onair!*'

'Ah, yes, yes.' Doyle groaned. 'Sure didn't I once share a bed with an old goat, but that was only because the poor fella was sick, and there's no honour in that!'

'*Bonne nuit*, M'sieur Doyle,' Robert murmured.

Stafford put down his pistol, then rolled his eyes roguishly and grinned into the big man's face. 'Bon drims,' he crooned.

'Faith!' Doyle moaned. 'A man's no longer safe in his own bed!'

Silky Jack lay nervously between the two men, knowing they had him trapped. Eventually he fell asleep. He awoke just after dawn and opened one bleary eye to see Stafford fast asleep beside him. He closed his eyes tight as he remembered the invasion of the Frenchies.

He opened an eye again and peeped at Stafford – dead to the world! He opened the other eye and peeped at Robert. Blast! This one was lying on his front with his face turned away.

Doyle turned his face to Robert. 'Mis-yoor?' he whispered. 'Mis-yoor?' He let out his breath. The two of them were sleeping like babes.

He painstakingly lifted the bedclothes and moved down the great bed on his knees. Finally he had opened the door and was in the living quarter where men lay asleep all over the floor. He counted seven, including James Commons. He crept out to the barn and found another three had moved out there. All were asleep as if they had not lain down for a week.

Doyle moved stealthily down to the gate, stopping dead when the two men on guard duty stepped out from behind a tree, holding muskets. They looked suspiciously at Doyle and raised their guns.

'Ah, Mis-yoors,' Doyle cried. 'I was wondhering if ye would like some break-a-fast?'

The two men exchanged glances, then nodded mutely at Doyle.

Later that afternoon Michael Quigley told Robert that he and Big Art had been talking in the barn when they noticed Silky Jack hiding in the straw and listening to their conversation. When they challenged him, Doyle said he was looking for a sovereign he had once lost there.

'He knows we're not Frenchies now,' said Quigley. 'Devlin called him a lying blatherumskite.'

From that moment, everywhere Silky Jack went, two men followed close behind.

At nine o'clock that night, a man named Loughlin called and whispered to Robert that another hiding place was ready for them. They left a relieved Jack Doyle shortly after and travelled deeper into the mountains to stay with a Mrs Bagnall.

As soon as they had left, Silky Jack rode over to the land of Mr Richard Jones, a gentleman farmer who held a very respectable station in life, and who was also a tenant of Mr Finlay, the banker.

Silky Jack wanted to keep in Richard Jones's good favour. It was through the intercession of Jones that proceedings had been dropped against a son of Doyle's when he had been accused of robbing Mr Ormsby of Tallaght.

'The two in bed with me,' said Doyle, 'they were Frenchies all right, but some of the others were as Irish as the shamrock. Then in the barn, I heard the tall one tell the red-haired one that, "*Anne gave him a bad welcome*". The red-haired one got very upset about that.'

'Their uniforms were green you say?'

'Ah, yes, a lovely green with gold fringes on the shoulders and those tight-fitting white military breeches with high black boots.'

Richard Jones gave a little smile. 'Well, Mr Doyle, after your unnerving experience, I think you need fortifying with another glass of whiskey.'

'God bless ye, yer honour, I do! For it was a terrible ungentlemanly thing those two Frenchies did – getting into me bed with their boots on.'

The rebels had spent two nights enjoying the hospitality of Mrs Bagnall's house in the mountain area known as the Breaks of Ballinascorney. On the second evening Mrs Bagnall ordered a sheep to be roasted. James Commons mysteriously disappeared into the mountains, and returned with two jugs of poteen.

At ten o'clock Robert retired to bed while the rest of the party stayed below and started a bit of a hooley. He lay on one of the mats lined along the floor and gazed through the window at the night sky. The men's spirited voices reached up to him, but he could hear a trace of fear and desperation behind their wild laughter. He had a sudden craving for the feel of air in his lungs and sprang to his feet.

No one noticed him as he slipped through the front door to stroll down to a clump of trees and leaned against a bole. The branches around him were fragrant after the evening rain and the wet earth sent up a damp odour which was pungently rich.

He wondered what was happening to Russell and Hamilton in Ulster. And Miles Byrne? He had let them all down. They had displayed such faith in his plan but it had turned out to be nothing more than a tragic débâcle.

And Anne, dear Anne: he felt strangely tenderhearted towards her now, but he had let her down, too. All her months of tending them in Butterfield Lane had been for nothing.

And there was Sarah, his beloved Sarah. He started to walk. Walking would help to still his tension and fear whenever he thought of Sarah.

He stopped and gazed over the undulating black outline of the mountains under the yellow half-moon. He was alone, amidst the landscape and the sleeping life of nature. He felt such a part of it all – this wild Irish land; such a gigantic love for it; such ineffable communion with it. He wondered if he could truly bear to leave it again.

But he would have to leave if he wanted Sarah – he could never subject her to the arduous life of being wife to a hunted rebel. She was fragile and defenceless. He would have to leave Ireland, take her to some gentle society in France or America. She was all he had now. The one sweet thing left to him after the bitterness of defeat.

Between four and five the following afternoon, a ragged-looking man approached one of the sentries standing guard in the field near Mrs Bagnall's house and asked to have Arthur Devlin sent out to him. He then warned Big Arthur that he was sure the army had been given intelligence they were there.

The man was brought into the house and given refreshment. Mrs Bagnall listened with fear as he told her the word had been spread: anyone found sheltering rebels would have his or her house burned as a warning to others. She begged Robert to take his party away at once. They all agreed they would not wish any person to suffer on their account.

The grey dawn peeped through the branches overhead. They had camped for the night under a small grove of trees in a glen not far from Mrs Bagnall's. James Commons had returned to Rathfarnham with Brian Devlin's horses; they were, after all, part of Devlin's livelihood.

Robert was lying face down on the grass, his head pillowed on his folded arms. He awoke with the sound of a tramping army which suddenly gave a loud roar. The sound rocked through the air and the very ground seemed to tremble. He opened his eyes with a start and looked over his shoulder, expecting to see the barrel of a musket pointed at him, but the land was deserted.

He then realised that the sound had come from Michael Quigley lying beside him, snoring so loudly, so vibrantly, and with such rhythm that Robert could only stare at him in amazement. Then Quigley was seized by some sort of convulsion; Robert watched as he choked and grunted, and relaxed into a shuddering rhythm again.

Robert remembered a time at Trinity, going on a week's trip to Galway, and being forced to share a room with a lad known as 'the snorer of Tralee'. It had been a week of sheer torture, like sleeping in a sawmill. He had spent the last night tossing in his bed, deciding that one day he would get his revenge by inventing a snoring silencer. It would make him the hero of married women everywhere. When they lay down beside their husbands each night, they would look at the silencer attached to his nose and whisper a soft blessing for Robert Emmet, the man who had invented the contraption in the cause of peace.

Meanwhile he had recourse to the old-fashioned method. He reached out and gave Quigley a sharp dig in the side. Quigley gasped violently, snorted, grunted, choked, then was again seized by a convulsion.

Robert wondered, not too despondently, if Quigley was dying. But then the recital struck up once more, steady and vibrant, and now a whistling sound was added to the concerto. Compared in volume and variation with the snorer of Tralee, Robert decided that Quigley was a genius.

He shoved himself on to his knees and looked around at the other men, sleeping soundly and undisturbed by the earthquake around them. Stafford was actually smiling, no doubt dreaming of Hevey's young sister and her corn-coloured hair.

He sat back on his heels and wondered where they would go from here? They had hoped to set tyranny and foreign domination on the run, but now they themselves were on the run. And where would they run to today?

He pushed himself to his feet and flexed his leg muscles, rubbing his arms and thighs to stir his blood and rid his body of the cold and stiffness. He walked past each sleeping man and lightly gave them the toe of his boot, reserving a hard thrust for Quigley who spluttered into a sitting position.

All were chilled from the night air and dew, and suffering from want of food. They had left Mrs Bagnall's before dinner and had eaten nothing since breakfast the day before.

'Ta ocras orm!' Big Arthur moaned.

'The hunger is on me too,' said Quigley dolefully.

'We have money to buy food,' Robert said, 'but we dare not venture into a village.'

Henry Hevey grimaced as he ran his hands over his breeches. 'Let's go to Bohernabreena.'

'That's over two miles back into Dublin,' said Big Arthur. 'It wouldn't be safe.'

Nicholas Stafford grinned. 'By God, you're right, Henry. We *will* go to Bohernabreena. William Kearney has a small public house there and he's a good friend of mine. He fought in ninety-eight and can be trusted as one of ourselves.'

'Let's move then,' Robert said. 'Ta ocras orm.'

The safe house of a friend and chunks of fried bread and bacon had a tranquillising effect on their nerves, helping to dissipate the tension of the past three nights.

William Kearney carried two bottles of spirits to the table where his guests were seated. 'Take your choice, lads,' he said. 'My own mountain dew or the parliamentarian kind?'

They took their time testing the comparative properties of Kearney's refreshment, but all concluded that his own mountain dew was far superior to the parliamentarian whiskey on which duty had to be paid.

Everyone was relaxing comfortably when Henry Hevey, who had been standing guard duty outside, poked his head inside the door and shouted: 'A military party composed of army and yeomen are heading in this direction.'

All sprang to their feet and lifted their guns. Kearney frantically ushered them through to a taproom which had a narrow flight of wooden stairs in the corner. He led them up to a loft which was empty of furniture, the only window being a small skylight.

'You will be safer up here,' said Kearney.

'If one of those redcoats shows his head above that hatch,' Big Arthur cried, 'then my face will be the last thing he'll see, for I won't let them take me alive!'

'The house is low,' Robert said as he closed the hatch door over Kearney, 'but there are too few windows for fire. We have no choice but to make our defence from here.'

'Whatever happens,' Stafford said grimly, 'we will not surrender with life.'

Down below William Kearney prepared for the visit from the army. A number of baskets which were used for bringing turf from the mountains lay by the door.

'Quickly now!' he called to his wife. They threw one basket on the bottom step, then the others haphazardly up the steps to the top. Sweat had begun to form on Kearney's brow. 'Gives the upper room more of an unused appearance,' he whispered nervously.

The tension in the upper loft was silent and thick. Big Arthur knelt down in the middle of the floor, his blunderbuss covering the hatch door. Robert, Stafford, Mahon, and Wylde knelt in each corner while the rest stood along the walls. Each held his gun in his left hand, the forefinger of the right fixed firmly on the trigger; all eyes and weapons trained on the hatch door.

Kearney and his wife stood side by side like mute dummies when Captain La Touche and Lieutenant Shaw stepped inside. They could hear the shouts of the army as they surrounded the house.

'Well, Kearney,' said Captain La Touche, 'are there any strangers here?'

Kearney stared at him blankly. 'No, sir, the place is small and you can easily search it.'

The two officers marched through the house. Lieutenant Shaw pushed open the door of the taproom and peered inside, his eyes pausing on the narrow flight of stairs which led to the loft. He called to Captain La Touche. Kearney and his wife nervously followed them through the room to the stairs.

'Do these stairs lead to an apartment?' Shaw asked.

'Oh, no, sir,' Kearney replied, ' 'tis nothing but a cock-loft up there.'

458

Captain La Touche frowned as he brushed dust from his sleeve. 'Is there anyone up there?'

Kearney dribbled a laugh. 'Up there? Why, no, sir. We make no use of that place at all. 'Tis too weak to bear anything strong on its floor.'

'Indeed,' said La Touche, removing a basket and placing a foot on the bottom step. Mrs Kearney moved hastily towards the captain. 'Oh, I wouldn't take another step, sir. Not if you don't want to be killed.'

La Touche rounded on her. 'What do you mean, woman?'

'Well, sir, 'tis the floor up there, sir. If a fine big handsome man like you was to step on it, you might fall right through and likely break a leg or two, if not your neck. Sure even the steps at the top are rotten.'

Captain La Touche gazed over the strewn baskets and had a sudden fit of coughing from the turf dust. He drew back his foot. 'Yes, they look quite unsafe. Well, no sense in risking my limbs.'

The Kearneys let out their breaths as the two officers strode out of the house. They followed them to the door, biting back their smiles as La Touche shouted: 'To Mrs Bagnall's at Ballinascorney.'

As soon as the men made their way down from the loft and came into the main room, William Kearney poured each a large measure of his mountain dew. 'I don't know about you boys,' he said, 'but I'm sorely in need of this.'

Anne Devlin waited anxiously outside the door of her cousin Cathy's dairy on the Coombe in the Liberties. A few minutes later she had jumped up to the bench of a little pony and trap and smiled at Miss Helen Wilde. She was the sister of Thomas Wilde and as different to her brother as chalk to cheese. He lived up to his name – a wild rebel – but his sister was cute and dainty with golden ringlets and as pretty as a flower. No one would ever believe that Miss Wilde thought of anything beyond hairstyles and fashions.

So much so that when they approached the guards now positioned on all roads leading out of the city, the soldiers only stopped them to give the two girls a few amorous advances which sent Miss Wilde into a fit of feminine giggles.

'I do believe, Miss Wilde,' said Anne, dropping the hood of her cloak as they cleared the city, 'that you should consider a life on the stage.'

'It has crossed my mind, Miss Devlin, on more than one occasion, too. You should see how large my eyes open when people talk about the young men who ran down Thomas Street in *magnificent* green uniforms.' She turned to Anne, her eyes wide and sparkling. 'Who on earth can they be, I ask!'

Anne smiled, deciding she could like Helen Wilde very much.

They were travelling through Bohernabreena when Anne heard a loud whistle. She turned her head to see Big Arthur waving from a hilltop.

The men were sitting at the back of Kearney's house enjoying the sunshine when the two girls approached them. Robert rose slowly to his feet, his eyes fixed on Anne and a smile spreading across his face. Instantly Anne lost all her doubts about making the journey.

'Anne! I didn't expect you to come all the way out here personally.'

She glanced up at the blue sky and shrugged. 'It's a lovely day for it.'

'It is,' he laughed, grabbing her hand and pulling her over to the shade of a tree. When they were seated he begged her for the news.

'Martial law has been proclaimed, and Thomas Street is cordoned off,' she told him. 'I've had a few messages at Butterfield Lane, but I've now sent word to the leaders that all communications in future should be sent to the house of Michael Dwyer's sister on the Coombe.'

'What were the messages?'

'Oh, just some of the men wanting to know how things stand now.'

'Any news from Ulster?'

'Not a bit.'

He frowned. 'And Miles Byrne?'

'In hiding. The Wexford people living in the Liberties are like a silent fortress around him. But there are rumours of

460

trouble all over the country. There's talk that a large body of men led by Nicholas Grey and the Flood brothers have been fighting for days in Kildare. It seems that Nicholas Grey received a message from the Duke of Leinster, informing him that refreshments would be laid out for his tenants in the servants' quarters of Carton on Sunday night, but when Grey and his men got there, they found firearms and cartridges laid out instead.'

An enigmatic smile crossed Robert's face. 'I doubt if the Geraldines will ever forget the death of Lord Edward in Newgate.'

They sat shoulder to shoulder gazing over the sunny slopes. Anne had a sudden sensation of their being totally equal, on a level, no longer master and servant; just two conspirators sharing the one danger.

'How is Jimmy now?' he asked.

'Ah, the poor darling. He feels so sickly all the time.'

'Is your mother watching his eyes?'

'Aye, like a hawk. But now tell me, what have *you* been doing since you left Rathfarnham?'

She convulsed with laughter as he told her about himself and Stafford getting into bed with Silky Jack Doyle; imitating Stafford's French accent when he asked Doyle if he had ever had a French general and colonel in his bed before. Her head flopped on to his arm when he rounded his eyes in mock terror and cried, 'Honest to God, I never have, only a goat! Vo! Vo!'

But when he told her about the visit of the army to Kearney's that morning, her expression sobered.

'It's getting very dangerous,' she said. 'You'll have to get away.'

He shook his head. 'I can't go, not yet. Not until I know something of Russell and Hamilton. It was their confidence in me that brought them back from France.'

He stared ahead of him. 'I know nothing in life is certain, Anne, and I knew there was a chance things could go wrong, but I can't stop thinking that any rabble rouser could have organised what happened in Thomas Street.'

'You were betrayed. You know you were.'

'I was a fool, I know that.'

'Listen,' she said earnestly, 'you can't torture yourself with blame. From what the messengers have told me, none of the men blame you, they all feel sorry for you.'

He gave an ironic laugh. 'Oh, that's all right then. There was a time before the twenty-third of July when I thought I had the men's respect. Now it seems I have their pity.'

'No, no! that's not what I meant! O don't make me feel bad for saying the wrong words, I only meant to cheer you.'

'Dear Anne,' he smiled at her. 'I'm being petulant. Why do you bother with me?' Then suddenly he was up on his feet running over the hedgerow where he picked a small clump of wild flowers. Sitting back down, he held them out to her with a sheepish grin.

'What's this?' she murmured, her face crimson.

With an awkward movement he pushed the flowers into her hands. 'The mountain people call them dilis, the Irish for faithful, and that's what you are, Anne, a true and faithful friend.' He began to feel foolish. 'It was a silly thing to do, but I know of no other way I can ever repay you. You can throw them away if you like.'

She stared down at the flowers in her hand. 'No man has ever given me flowers before,' she whispered.

'Well I'm sure I won't be the last,' he said quickly.

She took two deep breaths before lifting her flushed face. 'I brought your brown coat,' was all she could think to say. 'You'll have to ditch this green one, for, as handsome as it is, it gives you away.'

'Mr Emmet?'

They both turned to see one of the sentries bringing a man over to them. Anne gave a cry of delight, for it was John Doyle of Knockandarragh, Michael Dwyer's brother-in-law. They both stood quickly as he approached.

'Mr Emmet,' said John Doyle, 'I've been instructed to escort you down to the Glen of Imaal. Michael Dwyer promises you his protection there until an opportunity can be found to get you out of the country.'

Robert coloured slightly. 'Please give my grateful thanks to Michael Dwyer, but I cannot go.'

'Why not?' Anne cried. 'You'll be safe there. Michael will

not let anyone get within a mile of you. And the leaders can still send intelligence to you in the glens.'

'I cannot go to Imaal!' he insisted.

'Why not?' Anne demanded. 'Just tell me why not?'

'I could not, for any consideration, go near Dwyer after our failure. I would be too embarrassed!'

'Ach, nonsense!'

'She's right, Mr Emmet,' said John Doyle. 'Some of Michael Dwyer's men have been into Dublin sifting intelligence. 'Tis true Michael feels great anger, but not against you. That's why he wishes to ensure your protection.'

Indecision crossed Robert's face. He would be safe with Dwyer. He had held the glens against the militia for five years. It would be an impenetrable sanctuary where he could hide until his friends arranged a vessel to France.

'Michael has sent Hugh Vesty Byrne and John Mernagh to assist me in being your guide and bodyguard,' John Doyle said. 'They are waiting a half a mile from here in the mountains.'

'No, no; maybe I will go to Dwyer later, but there are people I have to see first.'

Nicholas Stafford arrived to announce that a council had been called. They must decide what to do next. They could not stay at Kearney's for ever. Big Arthur called to Anne. She threw a sulky look at Robert before running over to her cousin.

'Are you going inside, Mr Emmet?' John Doyle asked.

'Not yet. You go on ahead and have some of Kearney's mountain dew.'

'Mountain dew my eye!' John Doyle grinned. 'The last dew I had was like a mountain rockfall on my brain. I'll stick to the parliamentarian.'

Robert watched the Wicklow lad saunter off and drift into Kearney's behind the men. Anne and Big Art had moved inside, too, but Thomas Wilde and his sister were still sitting by the hedgerow talking earnestly.

For some unreckonable time Robert stood staring at the ground, deep in thought. Someone called to him and he looked up, then walked slowly towards the house.

* * *

During the council, John Doyle again pressed Robert to go with him to Imaal but he was even more steadfast in his refusal. Michael Quigley, Mahon and Wilde decided they would return to Kildare. Nicholas Stafford volunteered to go with them.

Big Arthur said he would go with Doyle to Imaal. He also urged Robert to change his mind and join them, but Robert was obdurate. It was agreed that they all went their chosen ways and each man should do the best he could for himself. Later on, hopefully, they would meet up again.

Robert took what money he had from his coat and divided it equally between the men. Then in a subdued manner, they each shook his hand and expressed their wish to serve with him again.

Nicholas Stafford grasped his hand warmly. 'Farewell, Emmet. As soon as we reach a safe house in Kildare, we will send word to you.'

'To Dwyer's sister on the Coombe.'

'Aye, Mrs O'Neil. Anne has already told us. And remember – any trouble and you come straight to us, do you hear?'

Robert nodded, smiled. 'Goodbye, Nick.'

When they had all gone, Robert changed into the brown coat Anne had brought and handed the tunic to Kearney. 'Will you get rid of this for me?'

'I will not,' Kearney exclaimed. 'Such a handsome coat was made for wearing.' He pulled it on and looked down at himself. 'There now, don't you think that suits me grand?'

Anne smiled. 'You're a bit too wide round the waist. The buttons are pulling.'

'It would be dangerous to wear it abroad,' Robert added.

'I'll just have to wear it in bed so,' Kearney laughed, 'for I won't destroy it. Musha, it must have cost a fortune. Can I keep it, Mr Emmet?'

'You saved our lives. I owe you more than a coat.'

Kearney tossed his head with a proud smile. 'And I'll tell my grandchildren it was the coat I wore when I marched down Thomas Street as General Kearney.'

'As long as you don't tell them it was the coat Robert Emmet wore on Thomas Street.'

Kearney looked at Robert in puzzlement. 'And why not?'

Robert shrugged. 'Who could be proud of a man who organised a scuffle?'

'It was not your fault!' Anne cried in desperation.

'It was my insurrection!' Robert snapped. 'It was my responsibility! And the base, degrading result shall be *my* shame!'

'Man,' cried Kearney, 'you're too hard on yourself. Lord Edward Fitzgerald was lounging on his bed reading one of those novel books when Major Swann walked in on him. But that wasn't his fault, it was the negligence of his bodyguard.'

Wishing to be done with remonstrances, Robert gave his hand and expressions of gratitude to Kearney and his wife, then took his leave.

As they left the house, Anne clutched roughly on Robert's arm and pulled him towards the hedgerow. 'Where are you going?' she demanded. 'You can't just walk off in the direction of Dublin where every policeman and soldier is looking for you.'

'Then Dublin is where I should go,' he said. 'One place the eye cannot see, Anne, is directly under the nose. So I shall hide under the nose of the military.'

Her eyes were blazing, her voice exasperated. 'Why? When you could be safe in the mountains with Michael!'

He didn't answer, just stood looking at her, and then she knew why. 'You're going to Rathfarnham,' she said.

'I must, Anne.' His eyes pleaded with her to understand. 'She is my betrothed wife. I must go to Sarah before I can go anywhere else.'

She looked away. 'I wish you every happiness so.'

'Thank you, Anne,' he said solemnly.

Helen Wilde gave a loud cough from the bench of the trap to let Anne know she was growing impatient.

'And what will you do?' Robert asked Anne. 'Will you lock up Butterfield Lane and return to your family now?'

'I suppose so.'

'There's little point in you staying on there any longer. There is still months to go on the lease, but just leave the keys on the kitchen table.'

'I'll go tomorrow,' she muttered through tight lips. 'I must complete my duties as servant-maid. The grates will all need to be cleared out and the place left tidy.'

'I would feel happier if you left tonight. You never know when the militia may call there.'

'If they do, all they will find is a lowly servant-maid whose master has gone away. And all my things are still there. I'll take Nellie over tonight to keep me company.'

'But you will leave tomorrow? Promise me that.'

Helen Wilde coughed again.

'Well,' Anne whispered. 'I suppose this is goodbye.'

'Not goodbye, *au revoir*.'

'What does that mean?'

'Until we meet again. And even if we don't, wherever I may be I would still like to know what is happening to you, to all of you.'

She shrugged. 'If you send word of where you are to the Coombe, I'll bring you any messages that arrive there.' She glanced at him darkly. 'I may no longer be needed at Butterfield Lane, but I'll serve the cause and its people until I die.'

'That's the spirit,' he said lightly. 'I always knew you had the heart of a warrior.'

'I told you in the beginning I was brave,' she said. 'Braver than any man.' But he was walking away.

He walked to the front of the trap. 'Could I ask you to take me halfway to Dublin, Miss Wilde?'

'You are more than welcome, Mr Emmet. You can hide under the sacking in the trap, but hurry, I would like to get home before dusk.' She tossed her blonde ringlets and smiled coquettishly. 'We young ladies have to be so careful now, you know. All these dangerous rebels on the loose.'

'Yes, of course,' Robert answered. 'Worse than savages I believe.'

When the trap stopped on the outskirts of Rathfarnham, Anne remained sitting on the bench, eyes veiled as she moodily watched Robert running swiftly across a field. And while she did, Helen Wilde watched Anne.

'Are you in love with him?' she murmured.

Anne turned and stared at her, mortified. 'Don't be foolish! I was just his servant-maid, doing my job as best I can.'

Helen Wilde nodded and chucked the reins. 'Then I hope

service work suited you well, my dear Anne, because, unlike me, you would never make a living on the stage.'

And so the carriage rolled on. Anne sat in silence. Helen Wilde completely understood, and left her to the peace of her own delusions.

Behind her the hills were turning mauve in the twilight. The first star of evening appeared in the sky, shining down from the all-knowing heavens on the silent and proud Wicklow girl who would never admit, even to herself, that she was as hopelessly in love with Robert Emmet, as he was with Sarah Curran.

Chapter Thirty-Four

He decided to enter The Priory through the garden which led down to the basement and the kitchens, and hopefully to solicit Mrs Jessop's aid in procuring a few minutes alone with Sarah.

He creaked open the orchard door, was about to make a run through the orchard – when he saw Sarah herself standing alone by a tree.

They stared at each other.

'Robert!' she whispered. 'Oh, Robert avourneen . . .' She glanced nervously in the direction of the house, then took his hand and pulled him down to a secluded corner at the end wall of the orchard, where they stood for a moment and stared at each other again.

'You're very pale,' he said.

'I – the shock . . . Sunday morning when I heard . . . I haven't yet recovered . . .'

'I want you to come away with me,' he said quietly.

'O, Robert, please be sensible!'

He took her hand in both of his, his eyes on her open palm. She looked down at his hands, and saw they were trembling.

He said quietly, 'I want to marry you. You promised to marry me. You said you would elope with me after the rising. Well the rising is over. Although it – it actually never began. But that is not what I came to talk about. I came to talk about you and I going away together. To France. Then on to America, if you prefer.'

His eyes were still on her palm, and she stole a glance at the face of the young man who loved her so devotedly. She listened silently as he spoke of their future together.

'I have enough money for us to live on. In America I could resume my studies and follow a scientific career. Although some of my foreign friends believe my niche is truly politics. Before I left Paris, Tadeusz Kosciusko, the Polish rebel who fled to America and is now their ambassador in France, gave me letters of introduction to some of the most respectable and influential persons in New York and Washington, including Jefferson. The Barlows also gave me letters to friends of theirs in Pennsylvania, but I think our heartiest welcome would come from my intimate friend, Robert Fulton of Vermont.'

'Why did they give you the letters?' she asked, puzzled.

'Because they did not want me to return to Ireland.'

'Then why did you come back? Why did you not go to America before?'

'I don't want to go to America *now*. My heart and soul belong to my own country of Ireland. I would not even think of leaving it again, no matter how dangerous the circumstances, if it were not the only way that you and I could have a life together.'

When she made no answer, he said softly, 'Will you come with me, Sarah?'

Sarah lifted her free hand to her eyes. She felt confused in a way that she had not felt in a long time; and tired, tired.

'I could not just run away,' she whispered. 'It would be a cruel way to repay my father who has already suffered the cruel desertion of my mother. And then there are Richard and Amelia to consider . . . he would know they had known about us all along.'

'If I made the arrangements for you, would you follow, and meet me in France?'

A sudden noise shattered the silence of the evening and she jumped. But it was only the screech of a curlew from somewhere near the river. She looked at his face and saw he was watching her, a hint of desperation in his eyes. His hands were still trembling, and still holding her hand, tightly.

'Will you come with me, or promise to come to me, Sarah?'

Sarah was all at bay. She wanted to yield to him, to say yes, but how could she? She looked around the orchard, the orchard where she had grown up, where she had played with Gertrude. She looked towards the house, although from here she could only see the gables. That house, this orchard, and this place of Rathfarnham were all she had ever known. Here she felt safe. No matter how stifled she had sometimes felt, she had also felt safe . . . And even in her dream of marriage to him, she had somehow believed they would live in or around Rathfarnham, somewhere just below the Dublin hills, somewhere peaceful and isolated with an apple orchard just like this one, with a fire burning bright and comforting at night, and the sun rising over the hills in the morning . . . Oh she could so easily *scream* at him now for his failure! He had ruined everything! Destroyed her lovely dream of them both living in happiness together beneath an Irish sky, after his victory.

She had truly *believed* they would win this time. *He* had made her believe it – telling her that it *was* possible. That it had happened before – in Portugal – which had won its independence from Spain by the actions of only forty men.

He said: 'If you come with me, or come to me in France, I will do everything in my power to ensure your happiness. It is not how I dreamed it, living in exile, but we are young, and we are in love, and it can still come right for us, Sarah, my love, my dearest Sarah, my beloved Sarah . . .'

He had even once pointed to a field in the distance of Rathfarnham, a small rectangular field with a small villa at its edge. He had told her the villa had once belonged to his brother Thomas, a small country retreat that he and Jane had bought to live in at weekends, but had been sold shortly after his imprisonment. He had pointed to the field, and said Thomas had also once pointed to the field, and remarked that it was in a very

469

similar rectangular field that William Tell had planned the downfall of the tyranny of Austria.

He said: 'I do truly love you, Sarah.'

She stood there looking at him until a tear ran down her face. In all her life he was the only person who had ever truly loved her; not her mother, not her father, not even Richard or Amelia – their love was preconditioned on the simple fact that she was their sister. Only he had ever loved her for herself alone . . . But even then he only loved the girl he imagined her to be, the girl he usually saw on her happy days, full of laughter and optimism and willing to conquer the world. But she was not always like that, not usually like that, not truly like that at all. She was dull and ordinary with as much bravery in her as a titmouse . . .

So how could she go running off to France where they cut people's heads off. Or to America – where yellow fever was always raging and the climate not congenial to European constitutions. Only the other day when Dr Sheridan had called to give her her usual check-up, she had heard him saying to Amelia that independent of the cholera, it was now an established fact that, after the first two years in America, Europeans generally declined in health, and those that survived were often as not killed by Indians.

She looked at him again and saw he was still watching her, the desperation in his eyes now pleading with her, together with his words.

'I – I want to marry you. I said to you after the rising, and you agreed. You carry the pledge of our betrothal in that locket there. I will not go without you, Sarah. Away from my own homeland of Ireland *and* you, I would live only half a life.'

She made a sound like a moan. A small nerve in her cheek began to twitch. The old thumping was back in her head. She wanted to sit down, lie down, sleep, sleep, sleep . . .

He touched her face with his fingertips, and said at last, 'Do you love me, Sarah?'

Did she love him? She would always love him. He was her first love and her only love.

'Yes,' she said, 'I do.'

'Do you still wish to marry me?'

If they could marry in Ireland, and live in the safe familiarity of Rathfarnham, she would prefer no other man for a husband.

'Yes,' she said, 'I do.'

'Then will you come away with me?'

For the first time in several minutes she looked up at him, and the old familiar feeling of love mounted in her heart and swelled over.

Then she remembered the proverb which says that it is the first step alone which costs us anything. Could she dare to take that step and go with him? Could she go to America – brave the cholera and the Indians? Could she . . . *could* she?

'How soon would we have to leave?' she whispered.

He stared at her. 'Then you might come?'

'Would it make you happy if I said yes?'

'Happy?' he said shakily. 'I think it would make me fall at your feet and weep with relief.'

Sarah gulped, then smiled through her tears and the thumping in her head. 'How soon would we have to leave?' she asked again.

'Oh, not this very day,' he assured her. 'I cannot go until I have made contact with Russell and Miles Byrne and the others. I could not just run to save my own skin. I must ensure their safety first.'

'How soon?' she repeated.

'A week or so.'

'Then . . . can I have that time to think about it?' she asked meekly.

Chapter Thirty-Five

It was the thunder of hoofs in the quiet of Butterfield Lane which awakened Anne the following morning. She blinked as horses halted outside, then heard the sound of running feet, then a terrible din as the front door was kicked in.

Incredibly, the noise had not awakened Nellie who always slept like a dormouse. Anne quickly slipped out of bed, her hands trembling as she pulled on a skirt and blouse. Footsteps thudded through the hall, voices shouting as she pulled on her shoes. She opened her door and moved into the hall to see the militia tossing furniture aside as they searched the rooms.

'What are you doing?' she demanded. 'This is the residence of a gentleman—' Before she could utter another word, two soldiers rushed her into the kitchen, keeping her under guard with fixed bayonets.

She watched contemptuously as every piece of paper was gathered up and brought to the table. She knew they contained not one sentence that could incriminate anybody. Anything Mr Robert had overlooked in the drawing-room, she herself had burned last night.

She maintained a cool gaze as the men given the job of guarding her looked her up and down and subjected her to odious obscenities. Although so early in the day she knew from the smell of their breaths they were drunk.

'You're well oiled for your sport,' she quipped.

A man dressed in civilian clothes entered the kitchen and said, 'Now young woman, I am Mr Bell. I am a magistrate. And I would be grateful if you would save us time by telling us where we can find Mr Ellis?'

Anne stared at the magistrate. Under martial law the militia could do anything they wished so long as they were accompanied by a magistrate.

'How should I know where he's gone? I'm just his serving-maid.'

One of the yeoman smiled lasciviously as his eyes moved over her body. 'And I'll wager you served him well.'

'Come on, beauty,' grinned another. 'Admit you were his whore, his little papish whore!'

'You *filth*!' Anne shouted.

'As his servant-maid,' said the magistrate, 'you would know all that went on here. Now where is he? When did you last see him? Where did he go?'

'I told you, I don't know where he's gone. 'Tis not my place to ask his business. All I care about is that my wages be paid.'

'And his visitors? You must have seen the men who visited Mr Ellis here?'

'No, I always stayed in the kitchen, that was my job.'

'A grocery bill was found in the depot on Thomas Street where the men who led the insurrection of last Saturday night organised. The same depot which was filled with ammunition intended for an attack on the Castle. That grocery bill was addressed to Mr Ellis of Butterfield Lane. Now – if you tell the truth, you will have nothing to be afraid of.'

'I know nothing about Mr Ellis, further than that I was his serving-maid and spent my time in this kitchen.'

'If it is fear of the conspirators that holds your tongue, be assured, we shall give you our protection.'

Anne looked scornfully at the bayonets. ' 'Tis protection from you I need!'

'Young woman,' the magistrate was losing his patience, 'if you do not tell us what you know about Mr Ellis and his associates, you have nothing more to expect than to be publicly hanged!' He nodded. 'Believe me, before this day is out we will have all of the conspirators behind bars, and I give you my solemn oath, you will be hanged with them.'

The harshness of the magistrate inspired the soldiers. They began to goad her, pricking her with their bayonets until blood streamed down her sides and arms. And with each thrust they shouted, 'Now will you tell us what you know of him?'

She cried out in pain, and by the time they had finished she could have scarcely given an answer even if she had wished. Her head hung down on to her chest as she swayed blindly, then a terrified screaming penetrated the fogginess of her mind. She fell back against the wall and opened her eyes to see Nellie being dragged into the kitchen, still in her chemise and clutching her frock.

'No!' Anne gasped. 'Leave the child alone!'

Nellie wailed even louder at the sight of Anne covered in blood. She tried to run across the kitchen but two soldiers held her back. The magistrate bent down in front of Nellie and smiled.

'Now, little girl, there is nothing of be frightened of. Do you know where Mr Ellis has gone?'

473

Nellie's eyes were magnified with fear as she pressed her lips tightly together and stared at him.

The magistrate raised a hand and gently brushed Nellie's hair back, saying in a soothing, hypnotic voice, 'Do not be afraid, little one. Your sister had to be punished because she is a bad girl. And Mr Ellis is a bad man. Your sister and he are two of a kind, as bad as each other. But you look like a good little girl who always tells the truth. So now, tell us everything you know about Mr Ellis.'

'She knows nothing,' Anne shouted.

The magistrate smiled at Nellie. 'When was the last time you saw him?'

'I want to put me frock on.'

'When you tell us about Mr Ellis.'

'I don't know anyone. I only know me sister.'

'Lying little bitch!' A yeoman prodded Nellie in the breast with his bayonet. The two girls screamed together as the blood spurted down the child's chemise.

'O great and brave men you all are!' Anne cried. 'Attacking a ten-year-old child!'

The magistrate was seething with frustration when he turned back to Anne. '*Where is he?*'

'No, you blackguards, I'll tell you nothing! I have nothing to tell!'

An ugly grimace twisted the magistrate's mouth. 'You have tried my patience to the limit,' he rasped, 'and now martial law has been proclaimed my powers are, as you know, limitless. I'm afraid you have left me with no alternative.'

He nodded to the soldiers. 'Take her outside and hang her.'

Anne kicked and screamed as they dragged her out to the back-yard and tied her wrists together. A soldier pulled Nellie behind them, still shaking in her bloodstained chemise and sobbing to put her frock on.

The cart which Anne's father had painted blue stood to the side of the yard. A soldier tilted the shaft back at a high angle, threw a rope over it and looped the end into a noose. Anne struggled in frantic terror as they dragged her under the shaft and placed the noose around her neck.

'What are you doing to me sister!' Nellie screamed. 'What are you doing to Anne!'

The magistrate stood in front of Anne and stared into her face. 'You can still save your own life,' he said, 'if you tell us all you know about Ellis.'

Anne glanced at the soldiers holding the rope's end in readiness to pull.

'We are waiting,' said the magistrate. 'It's your last chance. Where did he go?'

Anne squared her shoulders and tried desperately to be brave, summoning all her courage as she fixed the magistrate with an unwavering stare of defiance.

'You can kill me,' she said quietly, 'but not one word from me will you ever get about him.'

It seemed a long time before the magistrate responded, the eyes in his pudgy face locked with hers. Then he sighed, turned to the soldiers, and raised his hand.

Anne managed to let out a last desperate cry: 'Lord Jesus have mercy on my soul!'

A ferocious shout went up from the militia as they pulled the rope and her body was lifted by the neck, held suspended, then lowered until her shoes scraped with relief on the ground. Instantly she was lifted high again, held suspended, lowered. Then up again, held suspended, lowered . . . on and on the choking agony continued, until a merciful blackness washed over her.

She fell into the grave with a thud. The sound of her body hitting the hard earth was like a thunderclap between her ears. She was dead, and she was being buried. She opened her eyes and saw blurred shadows, heard loud laughing.

Slowly, incredulously, she began to realise she was not dead. She sucked desperately at the air; the effort sent an agonising pain ripping through her chest into her throat and again the thunder clapped like a mighty roar between her ears.

The blackness returned.

She came back to consciousness a second time with the feel of hands lifting her head and pulling at something around her neck. Someone was bending over her. Who was it? The fog began to clear and the face came into focus; a stark white face against red curls. Little Arthur! She tried to say his name but her tongue was stuck to the roof of her mouth. The blue sky twirled around as he lifted her up into his arms and carried her away.

' 'Twas a half-hanging,' said a shaky voice. Mary's voice.

'Evil bastards.'

The next sensation was the soothing touch of a wet cloth on her throat. This time it was her mother's face that loomed over her, red and tear-stained.

'O alannah! O my poor darling! The bla'guards left you lying by the cart like a trussed-up lamb.'

Anne lay still but her eyes moved slowly round the room, her bed had been overturned by the militia, she was on the mattress, on the floor.

She sipped painfully at the water her mother held to her mouth then fell back on to the pillow. A half-hanging! She should have known. The sport of '98. They knew how to tie the rope so the neck would not break, and just how long to hold it.

Mrs Devlin wet the cloth again and wrapped it around her throat, all the while murmuring quiet words of hatred against the militia.

Little Arthur swallowed back his tears as he sat stroking her hair. Then of a sudden, Anne turned to stare at him.

'Why . . . why did they not take me?' She gulped for air. 'Why did they leave me here . . . and not take me to the gaol?'

'I suppose they thought if a girl told nothing with a rope around her neck, she must have nothing to tell.'

'And Nellie? What did they do to Nellie?'

'Nellie is fine,' Mrs Devlin assured her. 'She's gone to fetch your daddy. Mary is out in the kitchen making you some tea.'

'But . . . Nellie was bleeding!'

Mrs Devlin dipped the cloth in the water and began to wash the blood from Anne's arm. ' 'Twas just a small cut, more blood than harm.'

Mary walked in carrying a cup of tea. She paused in the centre of the room and stared down at Anne. 'Those vermin should have their faces shoved in a dungheap before being cut limb from limb!' she cried venomously.

Mrs Devlin and Little Arthur gaped in astonishment at the savagery on the face of their genteel Mary.

Mary knelt down beside the mattress, then setting the cup of tea on the floor, reached out a trembling hand and gently lifted the cloth to look at the purple weals on Anne's throat.

'Oh, Anne,' she said helplessly. 'Oh, Anne.'

Then, for the first time in many a long year, Mary put her arms around her younger sister, and wept.

When Anne's own tears finally came, they were relentless; the sobs which forced their way through the constriction in her throat were like glass in her gullet, great grinding heaving sobs which echoed through the house on Butterfield Lane.

Miles Byrne had been in hiding for over a week when he received word from his stepbrother saying there had been no search for him at home or at the yard. On Monday morning Miles returned to work, endeavouring to assume a businesslike air as he opened up the yard, acting as if nothing had happened.

He continued through the day in an agitated state, wondering what had happened to Emmet. Since he had left Kearney's place in the mountains, no one had heard a whisper about him.

Two days later Miles received a message from Philip Long arranging to collect him by carriage that afternoon.

One hard rap gave them entrance to the house of Mrs Palmer at Harold's Cross. She led them into a large, comfortably furnished back parlour which now served as both bedroom and study for Robert. He was sitting with John Patten at a table near the window, looking much affected and cast down.

The two young men greeted each other like lost brothers, then Robert began to explain the circumstances of what had happened on the night of 23 July, and why the plans agreed between them had failed.

As Miles listened, he could plainly see that Robert was overwhelmed with sorrow and regret as he talked, but he himself felt only anger at the ineptitude and betrayal of the people around Emmet. He also felt a new and deeper respect for this young man, who never once uttered a word of blame against any of those who deserted him.

'You say Dowdall never showed?' Miles exclaimed. 'No wonder Dwyer didn't like the look of him. And did you see the way he ran from the rocket? Huh! He might have been good at doing your brother's paperwork in ninety-eight, but I'll swear that's all he's good for. And what happened to John Allen?'

'I don't know what happened to Allen.'

'But when he came into the White Bull he was raring for action.'

'I've told you,' Robert said in a distressed voice, 'I don't know what happened to Allen.'

Miles bit back the impulse to tell Robert that all the men he had spoken with still had great confidence in him, and many had said they would venture their lives for him.

Instead he said: 'The Castle is glorying in the setting aside of the Habeas Corpus. We have returned to the days of ninety-eight – searches, arrests, imprisonment without charges – the lot! Did you hear they got Denis Redmond?'

'Ah, no!'

'Aye, in Newry, as he was about to board a vessel for America. But he was awful stupid. First of all, he gets rid of the arms and ammo left in his house by throwing them over the back wall – I ask you – *the back wall*! The militia found them within hours and also found that Redmond had disappeared. After ten minutes' interrogation at the Castle, a neighbour revealed that Redmond had relations in Newry.'

'I liked him,' Robert said bleakly.

'So did I,' Miles returned, 'but Berney and I always feared Redmond would do something flighty. When we were walking by the Black Pitts on the twenty-third, he discharged his blunderbuss across a hedge where a horse had made some noise. He could have brought the entire barracks down on us.'

'Are they still holding Felix Rourke and the Kildare men?'

'Aye, and they've taken a number of the Wexford boys, too, but it seems none have disclosed my name.'

Robert smiled. 'Wexford was always true. What's the situation in the Liberties?'

'The Castle have taken everything from the depot. Your desk was lowered down from the window. At first the military didn't want to search inside because the place was covered in gunpowder. They feared it would go up at any minute. But eventually they cleared it and began searching, and they've not stopped searching since.'

'Mr Byrne,' John Patten interrupted. 'You have been a good friend of Robert's for some time now. Perhaps you can assist myself and Mr Long. We have spent the past two days trying to persuade Robert to leave for France, but he refuses to go. Perhaps he will listen to you.'

'I'll not abandon the people implicated through my actions,' Robert insisted. 'And we still don't know what has happened to Russell, Hamilton, or Jemmy Hope. I couldn't honourably leave until I've made contact with them.'

John Patten said impatiently to Miles, 'We have made arrangements with the captain of a Yankee vessel which is leaving for France in two days. Robert has a clear path to freedom and *refuses* to take it!'

'You should go,' Miles said.

Robert was looking thoughtfully at Miles. 'I can't go yet,' he said slowly, 'but I would like someone to be sent to Paris to communicate to the French Consulate, through my brother, the situation in Ireland. Will you be my emissary, Miles?'

'Me?'

'Who better? You have a perfect knowledge of the organisation and the vast preparations being carried on until the explosion in Patrick Street. As you are fully in possession of all the facts, you will be received agreeably by my brother . . . Will you go, Miles?'

'Aye, I'll go. But I've never met your brother. Why should he trust me?'

'I will give you my signet ring. Tom will not doubt you once he sees that.'

Miles took the ring and stood staring down at the onyx seal, engraved with a harp and weeping willows.

'Tell Thomas that if France is to aid Ireland at all, the time must be *now*! And we still have to think of those of our men in gaol. Once you get over there, see if Thomas can get his friends in the French government to agree to parley for the exchange of English prisoners in France for the Irish prisoners here. The French owe us that. Their armies are filled with our men.'

'It makes me livid,' Miles said suddenly. 'If we had succeeded in hoisting the Standard of Liberty over the Castle, those men of rank or fortune who backed you would have hastened there to take their seats on the Provisional Government. Now they keep silent and leave you to the manhunt.'

'What else would you have them do?' Robert asked. 'Make themselves known? Or wait for another chance for Ireland? Their loyalty is to the cause of liberty, not individuals. I let them down. Their involvement always stipulated the arrival of the French – we went against that.'

'We had no bloody choice!' Miles cried. 'As I see it, your friends wanted us to wait for the French, but there were others who didn't. And I'll tell you another thing . . .' Miles slipped the ring into his waistcoat pocket. 'I have talked to quite a few of the men who were on Thomas Street when the judge was murdered. Every single one says the men who did the deed were unknown to them. Strangers! Many are saying that Kilwarden was *not* piked because they thought he was Norbury, but because he was the most humane and popular judge in the land, and killing him would cause the greatest outrage against the leaders and turn the people against us.'

There was a moment's silence, and Miles watched their faces. Robert seemed the least surprised of the three.

'Just get safely to France as soon as possible,' he said quietly. 'France is now our last hope.'

Philip Long glanced at his fob-watch. 'Mr Byrne, I will provide you with the money necessary for your journey. You will also be provided with a sailor's uniform. As soon as you board, you will be met by Captain O'Connor. He will see that you are taken care of and will ensure your safe arrival in France. We must leave now.'

When the farewells were over and Miles had gone, Robert lay down on his bed and allowed his eyes to follow the line of a thin crack across the ceiling. It had been sheer bliss to sleep in a fresh comfortable bed after so many months on a mat. He felt rested in mind and body, and now felt guilty about the relentless way he had implored Sarah to leave with him. Her situation at home was very difficult. If she did simply disappear, where would that leave Mrs Jessop, Amelia, and Richard? Curran would know they had all been privy to the liaison over the months. No, there had to be another way.

He got up and wrote Sarah a letter, opening with a humble

request for her forgiveness. If he left the country, it would have to be for ever. But he now intended to stay in Ireland. A messenger had been sent to France and everything may not be lost after all. It would be safer for her if they did not meet, not for a while at least. All he asked, was that she kept herself well in mind and body, not to lapse into melancholia over matters, and to write to him constantly. He wrote unashamedly of his love for her, and when he had finished and sealed the letter, he lifted a fresh sheet of paper and wrote another letter: this time to Anne.

Philip Long had dropped Miles off at Stephen's Green, and as he strolled back to New Street, Miles saw the new proclamations which had appeared on walls and shop doors all over the city. They offered a reward of £300 each for the arrest of Robert Emmet, Thomas Russell, William Hamilton, William Dowdall, John Allen, Nicholas Stafford and Miles Byrne.

His head shrunk down into his coat as he hurried home. Once inside the house he made his way up to the loft where, influenced by Emmet's methods, he had built a secret compartment behind a false wall.

The following morning he was awakened just after dawn by his stepbrother, Edward.

'Avic, there's a seafaring man downstairs looking for you, and he's in a bad hurry.'

Miles pulled on his clothes and rushed downstairs from the tiny closet to see a tall, ruddy-faced man standing in the kitchen.

'I am Captain O'Connor. I believe you have been told about me.'

'I have, sir.'

'Unfortunately my ship is bound in the Custom House Dock and will not be able to sail for at least a week, but there is another American vessel leaving for Bordeaux this morning. You must be on it. I've just quit the Yankee captain, and as the wind has changed and become favourable he is determined to sail immediately. There's no time to be lost.'

The three men walked quickly towards the Docks, slowing down occasionally so as not to draw attention to themselves.

During their journey, Captain O'Connor told Miles he traded between New York, which was his home, and Dublin. He originated from Wexford, but had long been a citizen of the free States of America.

The American vessel was preparing to weigh anchor when they reached the Docks. Captain O'Connor led Miles over the ribbed deck and introduced him to the Yankee captain.

'He has no sailor dress,' said the captain, 'how can he pass as a sailor in civilian clothes?'

Miles stared at Captain O'Connor. 'Mr Long gave me the money yesterday, but the sailor clothes were to be sent to me this evening.'

Captain O'Connor scratched his head. 'There's only one thing for it, I'll go to my ship and get you a set belonging to one of my boys.'

He returned quickly, and a few minutes later, Miles grinned as he looked down at himself in the uniform.

'He can act as a steward,' said the captain, 'but we must set sail now.'

'Farewell, young man,' O'Connor said. 'France helped America. Let us hope she now helps Ireland.'

Miles drew O'Connor aside and whispered, 'How much should I offer the Yankee captain for my fare?'

'If it was my vessel you would pay nothing,' O'Connor replied, 'but you had better sort that out with him yourself.'

Miles then watched him descend the gangplank and rush along the quay. As the ship sailed out of the Custom House Dock, Miles gazed fondly at his stepbrother who stood forlornly on the quayside. They took their last farewell with many salutes of the hands.

Miles stood lost in a sadness as he watched the ocean stretching between him and his homeland. He knew he could never have left it, but for the hope of returning with a French army.

A voice spoke behind him. 'It always seems to have that effect on Irishmen. Leaving the old country.'

Miles turned his head and saw a smiling young man with cropped blond hair.

'And who might you be?'

'The ship's mate.'

Miles turned his face back to the land and the ship's mate also leaned on the rail.

'Do you have a name?'

'Miles Byrne.'

'Then welcome aboard, Miles Byrne. My own name is Columcille.'

Miles looked at him. 'Columcille?'

'If it's too long for your tongue you can call me Colum, but myself, I prefer Columcille.'

Miles detected a soft twang in the voice. 'Which part of America are you from?'

'New York, but sixteen years ago when I was ten, I came from Connemara.'

'Musha, I should have known with a name like Columcille.' Miles smiled. 'And I see your hair is cut short like my own.'

'Yep, but in New York we're not called croppies. Now, Miles Byrne, it's not your hair but your skin that worries me. It's a healthy colour, but not ruddy enough for a sailor.'

Columcille bent down and rubbed his fingers into the floor of the deck then smeared the dust across Miles's face. 'Go on now, rub some more dust into your face. We may get hailed by an English cruiser and they know the Irish rebels stow away to France on vessels such as this.'

Miles bent and quickly rubbed the deck, smearing dust over his face.

Columcille smiled. 'That's better, and don't wash it for the duration of the voyage.'

'How long will it take us to reach Bordeaux?'

'If the wind keeps up, we should be there in less than four days.'

'Will you take me to the captain now?'

Miles was taken before the captain who told him: 'Your job will be to see to the provisions and help out in any small way.'

'I have been provided with the money for my passage, sir. Can you tell me how much it is?'

The captain sat back in his chair, smiling as he stroked his Vandyke beard. 'Well, nah, it's usually about twenty guineas, but you need only pay nineteen.'

'That's very generous of you, sir,' Miles said in all sincerity.

He took out the money Philip Long had given him, and placed twenty guineas on the table.

It was a very pale-looking girl, shrouded in a dark blue hooded cloak that gave four slow raps on Mrs Palmer's door at Harold's Cross and asked for Mr Hewitt.

'Whatever you do,' Mrs Palmer whispered, 'don't mention the death of Lord Kilwarden. He gets very distressed about it.' Mrs Palmer then knocked and opened the back parlour door.

Robert peered sharply at Anne as he led her over to the couch that faced the fireplace. 'Anne, are you ill?'

She gave him a tired smile and sat down. 'No, but I'm staying down at my cousin Cathy's place on the Coombe, and I've not been sleeping well.'

'What's wrong with your neck?'

'Oh, my scarf?' she gave a hoarse laugh. 'Do you like it? 'Tis the new fashion . . . well, for us country girls anyhow.' Then seeing the puzzled expression on his face, she sighed. 'I have a summer cold and a sore throat, that's all. It will go in a few days.'

'Poor Anne,' he said gently. 'I'll ask Mrs Palmer to bring you some tea.'

When he had left the room, Anne clasped her hands together tightly and closed her eyes. The day after she had left Butterfield Lane the militia had ransacked two of the houses neighbouring on the dairy but, miraculously, the Devlins' place had been left untouched. Her da had come to the conclusion the soldiers must have made a mistake and would be back. He insisted that she go and stay with Cathy for a week or two, hide herself in the crowded streets of the Liberties. If the militia did come back to the dairy and see her, they'd soon put two and two together, and set a spy on her.

She watched Robert as he returned to the room and sat down in the armchair to the right of the couch. He no longer looked the weary and dusty rebel she had left running across the fields, but clean and fresh and every bit the young gentleman again.

She sat up straight and smiled at him, determined he would never know of the degradation of her half-hanging.

Her smile set until it looked more like a grimace. Because, let's admit it, she thought, they'd never have done a brutal thing like that to his delicate little gentry miss.

Mrs Palmer brought in a tray and set it down on the small table in front of the cold fireplace, giving Anne a kindly smile before she left the room.

'Why are you staying down on the Coombe?' Robert asked.

'Cathy's husband, John O'Neil, was a rebel with Michael Dwyer until a few years ago,' she explained. 'But after a visit from Major Sirr on the morning after the trouble in Thomas Street, Cathy made John flee back to Wicklow until we see how things turn out. Cathy is now doing all John's work, so I'm helping her with the milking and such.'

She sipped her tea. 'Why did you want to see me?'

He flushed slightly. 'I'm not sure if I should ask you now, seeing how unwell you look.'

'Oh, I'm fine!' she assured him. 'I've had a lot worse sicknesses in my time than a sore throat.' She momentarily reflected that she had never had a day's real sickness in her life. 'Come on, just say what you want me to do and I'll do it.'

'Will you carry a letter to Sarah for me?'

She stared at him, a white silent stare. 'Did you see her then?'

'Yes. For a few minutes, in the orchard.'

'Has she agreed to go away with you?'

He sat on the edge of his chair, stirring his tea for so long that she feared she might end up grabbing the cup and throwing the contents over him.

'She needs time to think about it,' he said eventually.

'But you haven't any time to give her! You're a wanted man with a price on your head. You must get out of Ireland as soon as possible.'

Her face looked fierce, but he simply shook his head. 'Sarah was upset the other night, shocked and frightened by the outcome of the rising. But once she starts to think about it calmly, she will come with me.'

'*O you poor dreamer!*' she wanted to scream, wishing she could box his ears and knock some sense into him.

She said: 'Are you mad?'

He looked at her with a half-smile. 'Quite possibly.'

485

'Oh, you are the most vexatious man I have ever encountered!' She jumped to her feet. She would not help him. She would leave him to rot here for ever if that's what he wanted to do. But before she could march out, Robert had risen to his feet and caught her arm.

'Miles has gone to France, to my brother. The French promised November, they may come before.'

'They didn't in ninety-eight, did they? They said August and August they came, not before.' She began to shake with impatience. 'Why can't you even wait in the glens? You'd be safe with Michael in the glens.'

He shook his head. 'Sarah must know I am still here and waiting. Waiting near by.'

She wanted to kill him. 'I've got to go,' she said impatiently. 'Give me the letter.'

He lifted his hand and gently touched her cheek with one finger. 'You don't have to take it if you don't want to, Anne,' he said softly.

She dropped her shoulders and forced herself to be calm. 'Of course I'll take it,' she said huskily. 'The back of my hand to Cupid, but let it never be said 'twas Anne Devlin who twisted his arrow around his fat little neck.'

Anne returned the next evening and watched Robert's smile fade when she told him there was no reply to his letter.

The following evening she called at The Priory, but again received no letter in reply.

'According to Mrs Jessop,' she told him, 'Miss Sarah has been unwell. But I'm sure I'll get a letter for you when I go there tomorrow.' She flopped down on the sofa.

Seeing his utter disappointment, she sought to distract him by telling him the story about Lady Anne Fitzgerald, an eccentric old lady who had written a letter to the newspaper stating she was *not*, as some dreadful people had suggested, the aunt of Lord Edward Fitzgerald. And, in consequence, she was *not* harbouring Mr Robert Emmet. This was followed by a second letter to the newspaper complaining that since her first letter, the militia had searched her house and taken away a few deal sticks attached to flowers in her garden, saying they *could* be

486

pike handles. And that her footman was the man in her carriage – not Mr Robert Emmet.

Robert was smiling and she went on, encouraged. 'There was another letter in the paper today in which she insists that not only was she *not* an aunt to the poor unfortunate Lord Edward Fitzgerald, but even her servants had never met Mr Robert Emmet, and neither would she wish them to know such a traitor to the King.'

'Lady Anne has visited my parents' house a number of times,' Robert protested. 'My father once saved her life.'

'She also said that she *did* know Dr Emmet, but she had not seen Mr Tom for a very long time, nor Mr Robert since the day his father was buried, and reports were *not* true that the Emmet brothers dined with her a few days after the insurrection.'

'Is that why Mrs Palmer could not get a paper these last days? Everyone buying it for these letters?'

Anne let out a husky laugh. 'Sold out before the ink is dry! I heard that each tavern sends a runner to fetch the paper, then everyone gathers round while the keeper reads out the latest.'

'Poor Lady Anne,' Robert murmured. 'There was a time when she became very angry if anyone suggested she was *not* related to Lord Edward.' He sighed, then looked at her with a kind of irony. 'Funny how success or failure decides who our friends are.'

Anne was silent.

' 'Tis the way of people, most people,' she said at length, 'always ready to unite their name and opinion with whoever is succeeding, whoever is winning. But failure is usually a lonely affair.'

The next evening she walked into his room with a smile on her face as she handed him the white square tied with a blue ribbon.

Robert also smiled as he took the letter and sat down. Anne watched his hands tremble as he pulled at the little blue bow and opened the square into pages, his teeth down on his bottom lip as he read:

I have been intending these many days to write you a few
lines, but was really incapable of conveying anything like

consolation, and altho' I felt there might have been a momentary gratification in hearing from me, I feared that the communication of my feelings would only serve to irritate and embitter your own. Besides this, I felt a degree of reluctance in writing which, after what has passed, may seem rather inconsistent, but my reluctance was increased when considering the extent of the risk I run . . .

He frowned as he read on, paragraph after paragraph that had left Anne herself confused about Miss Sarah when she had stopped under a tree to read the letter. Clearly Miss Sarah was terrified of her father, and, although she had no wish to break her promise to Robert, she was *very* reluctant to forgo her duty to her father.

And then Anne saw such a look of relief come over his face that she knew at once which part he had come to. Maybe it had, after all, been worth the walk out to The Priory each evening.

. . . I shall never forget the sensation of agony I felt while reading your letter. My head suddenly felt as if it was burning, and for a few minutes I think I was in a fever. You must therefore attribute to mental derangement my wish of seeing you at present. Do not think of it, unless it might be done with safety, which I fear impossible.

I believe you will find I began and ended this letter in very different moods. I began it in the morning and it is now near two o'clock at night. If I thought you were in safety, I would be comparatively happy at least. I shall expect a letter from you to tell me if you are well and in spirits. Try and forget the past and fancy that everything is to be attempted for the first time.

Goodbye, my dear friend, but not for ever.

P.S. *I request you to burn this instantly.*

The letter was unsigned. Robert kept his eyes fixed on the paper, longing desperately to comply with Sarah's wish and find a way to see her, if even for a few minutes. But he knew it would be too dangerous. Better to forgo the few minutes now for a lifetime later. He read through the letter once more, then lifted his eyes and gazed in puzzlement around the room.

Anne had gone.

Chapter Thirty-Six

After three days of deck-scrubbing, sail-shifting, and rope-hauling, Miles decided his face had enough of a weather-beaten hue to wash it. The days had passed cheerfully and they were making five or six knots an hour. But late in the evening of the third day they were hailed by an English cruiser. They had to reef their sail and lie to, while an officer from the cruiser came aboard to question the captain and inspect the ship.

The captain was greatly alarmed because of Miles. He ordered him down below to where a sailor lay ill with signs of smallpox, and told him to lie in the hammock next to the sick man. The English officer passed through each part of the vessel then stopped at the small cabin where Miles lay on his stomach. He turned to the captain. 'What's wrong with those two?'

'The pox.'

'So why do you sail with such a crew?'

'Well, nah, these are two good sailors, and a doctor I consulted said they would have a better chance of recovering at sea than remaining in the Dublin docks where contagion is reigning at the moment.'

The officer hesitated.

'I would be obliged,' said the captain quickly, 'if you would ask the doctor on your ship to come and look at my poor sick sailors.'

'Our ship's doctor has better things to do than attend on Yankees.'

'Well, nah, to show I take no offence at your manner, I would be obliged if you came and joined me in a glass of Dublin's finest whiskey.'

'My good man! I would not partake of anything from a ship that contains sickness, especially the pox!'

Miles let out his breath at the sound of marching feet. When Columcille came to inform him the English officer had left the ship, Miles made his way to the captain.

'Thank you, sir. I know you and your crew had nothing to fear, being a neutral vessel, but why did you invite his doctor to examine us? Surely he would have discovered I was as healthy as himself.'

'Well, nah, it was because I invited his doctor on board that he believed every word I did say.'

'Are we likely to get many more visits from English cruisers?'

The captain shrugged. 'As long as we sail in a direct line for Lisbon we shall be all right, but once we get to the mouth of the Gironde we may meet the cruisers again.'

It was almost evening on the fourth day when they approached the Gironde and reached the station where a French squadron lay at anchor, guarding the river. The captain received an order to go on board the French commodore's frigate.

'Let me go with you,' said Miles. 'I can put myself at the disposition of the French officer in command and ask him to send me in custody to Bordeaux, and then on to Paris.'

'No! I must go alone,' the captain said hastily.

Miles was perplexed by the captain's attitude. More than once was he tempted to jump into the water and make the long swim over to the frigate. As he contemplated doing just that, he saw the captain returning in a small boat, accompanied by an officer and eight marine soldiers.

'What's going on?' Miles demanded as the captain came aboard.

'They are here to guard the ship during the night, and to prevent any communication with the shore. We are not being allowed to proceed further.'

'*What?* Did you tell them you had an emissary from Ireland on board?'

'I didn't get the chance! How was I to know an American ship would be prevented from sailing up to Bordeaux? It's a damned new regulation. Any vessels coming from a country at war with France will not be admitted. England is at war with France, and Ireland is part of the Kingdom.'

'What can I do now?' Miles demanded. 'I *must* get to Paris as soon as possible. I have been trusted to carry out a mission for my country!'

'I shall sail in the morning for Lisbon, which is a neutral port. I will get clearance there and return immediately to Bordeaux.'

Miles marched away. The vexation of the delay was too much for him. Every hour seemed like a day when he thought of the perilous situation his friends were in back home. He had seen the round-ups of '98, and if that happened again, they could all be dead before he even reached Paris.

Later, he sat on deck and thought about his own position. It occurred to him that the marine soldiers would be returning to their ship in the morning. He decided to go back with them, at the risk of his life.

Columcille came up to Miles and told him he would try to persuade the captain to land him safely on the French coast the following night. Miles gave no answer; he was determined on his own plan. His orders were to get to Paris *as soon as possible*, and he would do everything in his power to carry out that duty. And, for some unknown reason, he suddenly distrusted the Yankee captain.

The following morning the American vessel was signalled to be off. Miles had slipped below earlier and changed out of his sailor clothes into his black breeches, black hessian boots, the white waistcoat of his Irish uniform and a black coat. The Yankee vessel might go to Lisbon, but it would go without him.

From his hiding-place at the back of the deck, he watched the French soldiers descend the rope ladder to the boat which would take them back to the squadron. He waited until the last of the soldiers had got into the boat, then ran forward and threw his bundle down to them. The Yankee captain saw him rushing forward and quickly hoisted the ladder.

'No, no! You can't go with them, Mr Byrne. I'll take you to Bordeaux from Lisbon.'

'Lisbon my eye! 'Tis *Paris* I'm going and nobody will stop me.'

One of the crew gripped him by the collar and tried to hold him back. Miles gave a contemptuous smile as he looked down at the little sailor, then threw him halfway across the deck.

'If I can't go the regular way,' Miles shouted to the captain, 'I'll just have to go this way.' He took hold of a rope and swung over the side. He had not spent months in the mountains with Michael Dwyer and learned nothing.

Some of the French marines reached up and grabbed his legs as he lowered himself. They were agog as Miles placed himself beside the officer in the boat and gesticulated wildly to him. He used sign language to make the officer understand that he was placing himself under his care, until they reached the commodore's vessel.

As they approached the French squadron, Miles could see a number of telescopes pointed at the boat. The sight of a man dressed in civilian clothes jumping from an American vessel was enough to arouse curiosity.

Once on board the frigate Miles was greeted by an extremely handsome officer, aged somewhere in his thirties, who took him by the arm and conducted him to a cabin, told him to sit down, and introduced himself as the commodore.

'Now, M'sieur, perhaps you will explain?'

Miles explained. He was on a mission to Paris. He explained the object of that mission. It was immaterial to him in what manner he was sent to Paris, as long as he was sent there quickly.

The commodore smiled. 'I can only arrange for you to be sent to Bordeaux, but once you reach there, you will be put at the disposition of the Marine Prefect. I am sure he will comply with your request and send you to Paris.'

'Ah, thank you,' Miles blurted, then remembering the small bits of French picked up from Columcille said, 'Merci! merci!'

The commodore smiled again. 'Tell me, what do you know about the American captain?'

Miles shrugged, 'Nothing at all, except he is a Yankee and he agreed to take me to Bordeaux. Although he may believe I am someone else, the man who should have taken this trip.'

'You refer to this Monsieur Emmet?'

'Yes. The arrangements and money for the voyage were passed on to me when he decided not to come.'

The commodore raised a brow. 'He remains in Irlande, after his *révolte*?'

Miles nodded.

'So! Why do you think the American captain did not want you to leave his vessel?'

'I haven't a notion.'

'How much did he make you pay for your passage?'

'Twenty guineas, but he only asked—'

The Yankee captain was ushered into the cabin. The Frenchman glared at the American. 'You told me nothing about this Irishman last evening. Although I asked you about each member of your crew, and you knew he wished to go in haste to Bordeaux.'

The captain made no reply.

'I do not say you are in the pay of England, but your conduct on this occasion shows you are not friendly to France, nor Irlande.'

The American licked his lips nervously, but the Frenchman smiled cynically. 'I know your little game, M'sieur. Your game is traffic! You intended to take twenty more guineas from your passenger before you put him at liberty in Bordeaux. Never has the fare from Irlande to Bordeaux been more than five guineas. Refund the balance at once.'

Miles felt sorry for the Yankee captain as he meekly withdrew his purse and began to lay the money on the table. If money was his only object then Miles could not be angry with him.

'You may keep five guineas,' said the commodore, 'but give the remainder to Monsieur Byrne.'

Miles suddenly realised he faced a moral dilemma. He rose to his feet and faced the Frenchman with a tremor in his voice: 'I cannot, in honour, act so unhandsomely to a man who two days ago acted so valiantly on my behalf when his ship was boarded by an officer from an English cruiser. He probably saved my life.'

Miles then explained the incident to the commodore. 'I could not on any account consider taking the money back.'

'That is your affair,' the Frenchman replied crisply, then ordered the captain to take up the money and leave.

The Yankee captain caught hold of Miles's arm. 'You can think bad of me if you wish, but I hope you never thought I intended to betray you to the English.'

'Why not? You have no Irish blood.'

'No, but when I was your age I was one of the Sons of Liberty in Boston, fighting the British for the same independence you seek. Look—' he pulled a chain from around his neck and held it up to Miles, 'here is my Liberty Medal, I still wear it.'

'Are you saying you're not a traitor, just a villain?'

The captain scratched his beard and smiled sheepishly. 'Well, nah, I guess that's just what I am saying.'

Miles turned to the commodore. 'Can I have your permission to accompany the captain to the deck, sir?'

The Frenchman shrugged. 'Very well. *Un vaisseau* will be prepared to take you to Bordeaux as soon as we have breakfasted.'

As they made their farewells, Miles slapped the American captain on the back and laughed. 'At least we part now better friends than when I left your vessel an hour ago.'

The captain nodded and looked nervous again. 'When you return to Dublin, you won't mention any of this to Captain O'Connor, will you? He's like a mad bull when he gets in a temper.'

Miles stood and waved to Columcille as the American vessel sailed away from the squadron, then he took a walk along the deck, waiting for the breakfast hour. As he neared the bridge he saw the French marine who had brought the Yankee captain into the Commodore's cabin heading in his direction. Miles wanted to ask him a question, and gesticulated in sign language which made the young marine double up in laughter.

'Will you stop! My name is James Browne and I'm from Dublin's Baggot Street.'

Miles stared at him. 'Dear God! I'm meeting as many Irish away from Ireland as I did in it. Didn't I hear you speaking perfect French? And what are you doing in a French uniform?'

'What was Theo Wolfe Tone doing in a French uniform? There are many of our men in the French service. I myself have been so for five years, since the ninety-eight.'

'Tell me,' said Miles, remembering the question he wanted to ask, 'have I displeased the commodore by not taking the money from the Yankee captain?'

'On the contrary, the whole transaction did you great honour. It showed you were disinterested and forgiving at the same time.'

'Ach, it was only money he was after, not my life.'

'Well, the commodore has sent me to invite you to join him at breakfast.'

'Will you be there?' Miles asked.

James Browne smiled. 'I don't usually eat with the commodore and the officers, but he thought you might like another Irishman beside you during your first meal in French waters.'

'God, but he's a decent fellow, that commodore.'

'He's not bad,' Browne agreed, 'for a Frenchman.'

They were eight at table: the commodore and five officers, two of whom were from a war brig at anchor beside the frigate, Miles and James Browne.

Miles just gaped at the splendid table in front of him. There were various meats, *viandes* the French called them; eggs, vegetables, and all kinds of fruit, everything the season could afford. It was the first French repast Miles had experienced and it stayed for ever with him for the favourable impression it made respecting French living and manners.

He was surprised to discover that Browne's main duty was that of interpreter to the commodore.

'But you speak excellent English, sir,' Miles said. 'You have no need of an interpreter.'

'Oh, you flatter me! I am sometimes quite at a loss for the English words. It is a good lesson for me to hear your countryman translating into English what I tell him in French.' The commodore smiled. 'Besides, I spent some years in England, as a prisoner of war.'

'A prisoner of the English?' Miles laid down his empty wineglass. One of the other officers filled it up again.

'Oui! I know a great deal about the history of the English statesmen,' the commodore continued, 'particularly Monsieur Fox, Monsieur Sheridan, and of course,' he gave a wry little smile, 'Monsieur Pitt.'

Miles then spent a happy hour talking with the Frenchmen, and when the coffee and liqueurs were served, he could not help thinking how well Robert Emmet would have fitted in with this fine group of men. As if reading his mind, the commodore said, 'M'sieur Byrne, I would very much like to hear more about your friend, Robert Emmet.'

Miles was not sure afterwards if it was all the wine which he was not used to, but when he answered the commodore he did so passionately.

'I can only give you my opinion, which is that Robert Emmet is one of the finest, most talented and noble-minded young men you could ever wish to meet. He has no vanity nor avarice nor awe of wealth whatsoever. He used all his personal fortune to finance our cause and the men who worked for him. He is passionately devoted to our country and its liberty.'

As he spoke, Browne translated rapidly what Miles said to the other French officers. One lifted his glass and said softly, '*Vive l'Irlande!*'

'*Vive Robert Emmet!*' added the commodore.

Miles drank the toast, then said quietly, 'He is also in grave danger.'

'So!' The commodore rose. 'We must get you to Bordeaux very soon. I will conduct you to the vessel that will take you there, and introduce you to the officer in command.'

The wind being favourable, the ship was soon in full sail and steered off. James Browne cupped his hands to his mouth and gave Miles the call of '98: '*Erin Go Bragh!*' Ireland for ever!

As they sailed down the river and lost sight of the squadron, Miles reflected that if the commodore, who had said farewell as if they were old friends, and his officers were an example, then he was already favourably disposed to the French people.

496

Chapter Thirty-Seven

A silence fell after Mrs Palmer had left the room.

'I saw Rose today,' Anne murmured.

Robert looked up from the letters she had brought from the men. 'Has she heard from Jemmy?'

'Aye, he sent word to her yesterday by a travelling man. A United man.'

'What news of Russell?'

'Bad news.'

'How bad?'

'It seems everything went wrong up there, too. Someone sent an anonymous letter to Russell saying that a great force of United men were waiting for him at Loughlin Island, but when he arrived there, the place was deserted. William Hamilton and Jemmy were above Belfast in Ballymena. A messenger told *them* that Russell had left Ulster and returned to Dublin to try and stop the rising here. Of course, they found out later the messages were false. Now they think the person behind it all was a man named McGucken who had volunteered to lead some of the Belfast rebels, but rode all over the place on the Saturday morning telling everyone the rising was off.'

Another silence fell, then Robert said, 'Where's Russell now?'

'Staying with Mary McCracken, the sister of Henry Joy.'

'Hamilton?'

'Got away on a boat, back to France, to solicit aid.'

'One piece of good news at least,' he murmured.

She studied his face. 'Did you get any air today?'

'You know I can only take the air at night, under cover of darkness in the back garden.'

Anne put down her tea. 'Well, it's not dark yet,' she said briskly, 'so why don't you answer the letters? I can send messengers out with them tomorrow.'

'Will you stay and help me?'

Anne was surprised at the request; startled. 'If – if you want, but my writing and spelling is nothing as good as Little Arthur's,' she warned.

Robert didn't seem to care. 'Just so long as it's understandable,' he said, moving to the table by the window. 'The only message to convey to them all is to keep safe but prepared, until we hear something definite.'

They spent the next half-hour sitting across from each other at the table, answering the letters.

'Do you assume, or presume, responsibility?' Anne asked him.

'Assume.'

She continued writing then flourished a line across the page. 'Will you check mine and see if they are all right.'

He lifted her letters and read through them, a finger over his lips pressing back a smile as he read her signature:

I beg to remane, your most humble servant,
Anne Devlin. (Miss).

The letter was to her cousin, Michael Dwyer.

On the second letter, to Nicholas Grey in Kildare, she had written:

Yours, most affecshunatly.

'Did I sign them right?' she queried earnestly. 'I wasn't sure which was the right way, so I did both.'

'They're both perfect,' he said, the smile now on his lips.

She flushed slightly and her eyes, when she smiled back at him, had a shine of pleasure. He returned her look for a moment only, then lifted his pen from the inkstand, dipped, and finished writing his own letter.

Anne sat with her chin in her hands and looked beyond the table to the window. The slanting shadows of evening were now widening towards darkness. It would soon be time to leave, she thought, regretfully, for she always felt a strange kind of peace alone with him here in this quiet, comfortable room.

But how would it end? she wondered. How long could his luck hold out? She wished Sarah Curran would make up her mind either to run with him or be done with him, instead of all this pretty letter writing.

Her thoughts went round and round like the turns of a mangle. She came back to her surroundings and saw that he was watching her, a slight frown on his face.

'Why do you still wear that scarf around your neck?' he asked 'Is your throat not better yet?'

She fixed him with an unwavering stare, racking her brains for a suitable reply. The bruising was barely noticeable now, but still there. 'Yes, better, completely better,' she said it with the slight huskiness she'd hoped had gone. 'But I don't want to chance another chill.'

'Chill?' He was flabbergasted. The past few days had been very hot and even the evenings were overly warm. He himself had stripped to his shirtsleeves. 'At times I think there's no knowing you, Anne. On windy April days in Butterfield Lane you were running around in only a blouse and petticoat, but now, in the heat of August, you are wrapped up as if it is winter.'

'Oh, mind your own business!' she snapped, suddenly belligerent and rising to her feet. 'I don't criticise what you wear do I?'

As usual, her belligerence amused him. 'Come now, Anne, cool down and be reasonable.'

'I am being reasonable. I'm going back to the Coombe before being caught out after the curfew. And Cathy will be waiting for me.'

'Yes, Cathy will be waiting for you,' he said quietly, feeling suddenly lonely and alone. Over the past few weeks they had drifted into an easy intimacy, a natural friendliness, and he had never thought about their friendship or questioned it. But now, as she picked up the letters on the table in readiness to depart, he realised just how much he enjoyed Anne's company.

'Is there anything you want me to bring you tomorrow?' she asked, her back to him as she buttoned the letters inside her bodice.

'No, thank you, nothing.'

She had reached the door when he called her back. He had moved to the chair by his bed and was withdrawing another letter from the pocket of his jacket.

'I hate to ask you again . . . but would you take this to Sarah?'

Anne stared at the letter, at the wax seal prohibiting prying eyes from knowing the private thoughts he shared with only one other. Never once had he given her a letter that was not securely sealed with hot red wax.

She dragged up a smile. 'Sure I will.'

Two evenings later Anne stopped to sit on a wall and read Sarah's letter of reply, which had been handed to her by the housekeeper. She had not seen the young lady herself since before the rising, but she could still see clearly that lovely sweet face, which somehow she could not dislike. Under any other circumstances, if Mr Robert had been a doctor or whatever and not a rebel, himself and Miss Sarah would have been perfectly suited; two gentlepeople of the gentry living the easy life of two happy kittens on a hearthrug. Her with her shyness and sudden blushes and sweet smile. Him so courteously aloof, reading to her with his quiet voice from all his boring novel books, until some handy maid would tinkle a bell and inform them that it was time to dine.

But that was only how it *might* have been, if he had not chosen to forgo such pleasant activities and put his life on the scales along with his convictions. And now he was in grave danger, staying in Dublin when he could be safe in a safe-house in the Wicklow glens, under the protection of Michael Dwyer, while waiting for news from his brother in France. And he *would* go to Michael – if Miss Sarah agreed to go with him. She was sure he would go. That he loved Miss Sarah was as plain as the sky over the hills of Ireland, but did Miss Sarah love him? If she did, then why had she not grabbed up her skirts and run with him, even agreed to share an exile with him if it came to that? But no, Miss Sarah dithered and dallied in Rathfarnham and kept him on a string with her letters all wrapped in pretty blue bows.

Anne sighed in exasperation and flicked open the pretty blue bow, a dry expression on her twenty-two-year-old face as she read:

I feel myself cheered even by the sight of your hand-writing, and find more consolation from your letters than any effort of reason on my mind. Your last, particularly, made me quite happy when I received it.

Since that, however, I have had new causes for anxiety – one which fills me with apprehensions, the return of — from England, which I expect soon. I have not entirely resolved how to act yet, and wish I could apply myself to the proverb which says that the first step alone costs us anything.

I should wish particularly to know from you how matters stand at present (if you would not be afraid); particularly what are your hopes from abroad, and what you think they mean to do. As to the French invasion—'

At the sound of a troop of horses, Anne literally rolled over the wall on to the grass below, pressing herself against the stone as the soldiers rode by. Then, breathing a sigh of relief, she sat with her back against the wall and quickly read through to the end of the letter.

I cannot tell you how uneasy I shall be until I know you have got this. Let me know immediately. Adieu, my dearest friend. I am quite well, except that I sleep badly. My thoughts run almost equally on the past and the future.

P.S. I passed the house you are in twice this day in the hope of seeing you. Again I must bid you *burn* this instantly.

Oh, the thoughtless little ninny! Anne's eyes went back to the part about the French invasion. She doesn't even stop to consider her words carefully, nor the danger she's putting *me* in as well as him. All this insisting he destroy her letters and actually saying *I passed the house you are in twice this day*! If the militia stopped me and found this letter, they'd know for sure there was someone suspicious concealed within walking distance of Rathfarnham!

She quickly folded the letter and retied the blue ribbon into its former pretty little bow, her brow creasing into a puzzled frown. I thought he was her lover – her betrothed? So why did she keep calling him her *friend*?

Anxiety rose in Anne as she took the route across the fields towards Harold's Cross. How could she possibly make him see the danger of these letters without letting him know she had peeped at them? Although she felt no shame or conscience about that! She would carry *his* letters without question, for she was his patriotic comrade, but she never had agreed to act as servant to Miss Sarah Curran!

She would tell him, she determined as she walked on. She would admit she had read the letter and point out that Miss Sarah seemed more concerned with her own safety than his.

But once inside the house, when she saw with what eagerness he took the letter, handling it like something precious and priceless, placing it inside his pocket to be read when alone, she said nothing, just sighed in a resigned sort of way, then went in search of Mrs Palmer and the tea-tray.

Miles Byrne was beginning to think he would never reach the coach house at rue Montmartre where his journey would be terminated. He had been shut up inside the coach for four nights and five days on the long journey from Bordeaux to Paris. It seemed an age since he had said farewell to the French commodore and sailed down the Gironde, followed by a whole week waiting at Bordeaux before the marine prefect had given permission for him to proceed.

Finally, at three o'clock on the fifth afternoon of this second stage of his long journey, the coach drew up in the yard at rue Montmartre. Miles stepped down in relief and bent to rub some life back into his legs.

'Mr Byrne?'

He straightened and looked at the two men standing in front of him. One wore an impressive French uniform, the other was elegantly civilian.

'Aye, I'm Miles Byrne.'

The one in uniform smiled and spoke with an Irish accent. 'Welcome to Paris, Mr Byrne. I am Adjutant-General Dalton, member of staff of General Berthier, the French Minister of War.'

The second man also smiled, and he, too, had an Irish accent. 'We are pleased you have arrived safely, Mr Byrne, but we would have been happier if Robert had travelled with you.'

Miles soon learned that this smooth-voiced man was Dr

James MacNeven, a friend of Thomas Emmet who had also been imprisoned in Fort George.

'How did you know I was coming to Paris?' Miles asked.

MacNeven smiled. 'Your friend, the commodore, sent a communication to us. He was very impressed with your determination.'

General Dalton ushered Miles towards another waiting coach, calling to the driver to take them to the Grand Judge Regnier's hotel in the Place Vendôme.

'But I haven't time to go to an hotel,' Miles said. 'It is imperative that I see Mr Thomas Emmet immediately!'

'Mr Emmet is waiting to meet you in the Grand Judge's study.'

When Miles entered the elegantly furnished study, he knew instantly, without introduction, who the serious-faced man standing by the window was. 'I have come with a message from your brother,' he said.

Thomas Emmet continued to stare coolly at him, without answering.

Miles drew in his breath. Unlike his brother, Thomas Emmet was obviously a man not given to trusting easily.

The Grand Judge looked from Miles to Thomas. 'Do you know this man, Mr Emmet?'

'No, I have never seen him before in my life.'

Miles found Robert's signet ring and held it out. Thomas walked slowly across the room, compared the ring with his own, then looked at Miles with a warm smile.

'Welcome to Paris,' Thomas said, then embraced Miles like a brother.

The young emissary was flabbergasted. He had received nothing but kindness since arriving in France, even the marine prefect at Bordeaux had insisted he stay as a guest in his villa while he waited for clearance, but to be embraced like a brother by Thomas Emmet, friend of Tone and Lord Edward!

'Now, Miles Byrne,' Thomas said, 'tell me about my dear Robert.'

So Miles told him, then added, 'Robert wishes for you to use every means to prevail upon the French Government to parley for the exchange of English prisoners here in France for the State prisoners in Ireland. He also—'

'If I may interrupt, Mr Emmet,' said the Grand Judge, 'I am now satisfied that this man is a true emissary from your brother.' He smiled kindly at Miles, then turned back to Thomas. 'I have been instructed to inform you that the First Consul is eager to have a report on the present state of Irlande as revealed to you by the messenger. I suggest you have it ready first thing in the morning.'

Thomas took Miles to his house on the rue du Cherche-Midi and introduced him to Jane and his children. Jane begged him for every detail of their 'darling Robert', then sent for two more guests to join them for dinner.

Miles felt deeply honoured at meeting Mrs Matilda Tone, the wife of the great patriot, and thought her still beautiful. The other guest was Mrs Hamilton, the wife of William Hamilton, who beseeched him for news of her husband, and of her uncle, Thomas Russell; turning pale and silent when Miles confessed he knew nothing of their present state and whereabouts.

Immediately after dinner Thomas and James MacNeven took Miles to the study where the three men sat down to write the report for Bonaparte. Thomas and MacNeven asked many questions and took notes, while Miles answered and explained the situation as best he could.

It was almost dawn when Miles and James MacNeven retired to bed, but Thomas Emmet remained in his study and, after concluding his report to the First Consul, wrote a summary of the details in his diary:

The Insurrection of the 23rd was forced on by the explosion of the powder manufactory in Patrick Street, but the country in general was not called or expected to rise unless Dublin had been taken.

The Proclamation of the Provisional Government was not to have been published till the next day, and was therefore not signed by the members.

If no persecutions take place, the people will be quiet till the French come, and the instructions to me were to urge an expedition with the utmost speed. But as to arms, if they come they could be concealed, but not used before a landing, and therefore it was useless to run the risk of sending them.

My brother says he is not in any danger, but I doubt that. He says the people's spirits have received a spring by the effort and that if a speedy landing takes place they will act much better than they would have done.

Robert had been in hiding at Harold's Cross for almost a month, waiting, waiting, waiting, and the tension and worry was beginning to get unbearable for all concerned.

A number of men secretly and regularly visited him at Mrs Palmer's house, but his most constant visitor was Anne, who ventured out every evening and continued to carry letters to and fro without a word of complaint.

Passing through the hall one night, Anne heard Mrs Palmer say to her son, 'Why shouldn't she come and visit him? She's his servant, isn't she? Runs all his errands for him.'

Anne stood in the hall beset by a wave of cynicism. Did people really believe Anne Devlin was that simple? That humble? That servile to anyone? Were people really that stupid! She was *not* his servant, she was his comrade.

Inside the back parlour she shrugged off her annoyance and grinned wickedly as she withdrew a copy of that day's edition of the newspaper, which she had brought especially for his amusement, and began to recite the latest about Lady Anne Fitzgerald.

'She has written to the Viceroy,' Anne said in mock gravity, 'telling him she was extremely worried because she knows her avowals of loyalty to King and country have made her a marked victim of the rebels. And she demands round-the-clock police protection.'

'So, as well as her flower sticks, have the police now taken away her clock?' he asked.

They both laughed, then Robert sat at the table and read the letter himself. Anne leaned over his shoulder and murmured, 'Wouldn't it be something if you were to pay her ladyship a visit one of these dark nights.'

'Tut-tut! You are cruel, Anne. She is just a poor old lady convinced the world thinks her a rebel. Probably suffering from aged dementia.'

'And sapping every bit of fame out of the situation, too. People are asking for her signature.'

He looked up at her. 'You're jesting.'

'No! And now she has had posters printed and nailed up all over the city, stating she is *not* an aunt of the traitor Lord Edward Fitzgerald, and avowing her loyalty to the King.'

Robert managed to maintain a straight face while Anne hooted with laughter.

The following evening Robert was in a quiet and thoughtful mood. Anne listened to his anxiety about the uncertainty of everything.

'Miles should have reached my brother by now,' he said.

'How long does it take to get to France?' Anne asked.

'Four or five days, depending on the weather, and a safe journey.'

'Ach, Miles will get there, safe and sure enough. Don't you worry about that.'

They were both leaning out of the parlour window, drawing in the warm evening air. Despite the low garden wall they were free from all eyes, for beyond the back wall lay only acres of cornfields.

'How long does it take to get to America?' she asked.

'It can take up to three months. America is over three thousand miles away.'

Anne stared at him, incredulous. 'Is the world that big?'

'Even bigger.'

'Imagine!' She leaned further over the window ledge and touched one of the wild marigolds growing in a clump beneath the window. 'If I had to leave Ireland, it is America I would go to.'

'Myself also. If I *had* to leave.'

'But you say most of the English people are fine, eh? So why can't some of the nice ones get into power? Then they'd see that we can be nice, too, if they played even-handed, and stopped treating us like the dirt on their shoes. It could all be so different. 'Tis like that poem you wrote about the London pride and the shamrock, about us living side by side, so why not help each other instead of fighting each other, because two . . . two . . .'

Her face flamed as she realised she was giving away that she had once looked through his private papers and writings.

'Two twists will make the strongest cable,' Robert said, not appearing to notice anything amiss as he reached down to pluck a golden marigold then stuck it behind her ear.

'I – I think it was Russell that told me it,' she said quickly. 'So how does it go again? The last bit about big England and little Ireland and the cable?'

'It goes:

> 'Take heed, learn wisdom hence, strong man,
>   And keep a good friend while you can.
> Reflect that every act you do
>   To strengthen him doth strengthen you;
> To serve you he is willing – able –
>   Two twists will make the strongest cable.'

'When did you write that?' she asked.

'Oh, a long time ago. Before I became a revolutionary.'

'Do you still believe it? What you said in the poem?'

He thought for a moment. 'Yes, I do. If only England would realise that a free and independent friend is more caring and reliable than a conquered slave.'

The next day it poured. Anne arrived in the afternoon, hours earlier than usual. She came in, her long hair hanging in black wet streaks over her shoulders. She looked pale and anxious as she stood wiping the rain from her face.

'I can't stay,' she said, moving back when Robert reached to take her cloak. 'I have to go home to the dairy. Da sent word to me this morning to come home tonight. Mammy is busy looking after Jimmy and Mary is finding it hard to cope with the housework on her own.'

'How is Jimmy?'

'The scabs on his sores have nearly all gone.'

'Then he is no longer contagious. Although it will take him some time yet to recover completely.'

'Aye, he still feels very sickly, and now the scabs have gone, the soles of his feet are so tender he can't bear anything to touch them.'

'Will you not remove your cloak and sit down for a few minutes?'

She hesitated, then shook her head. 'No, I wish I could . . . with Da sending for me I really shouldn't have come at all. But I had to see you. I'm that worried for you.'

Robert looked so genuinely perplexed that Anne said, 'Mrs Palmer hasn't told you then? Doesn't she know?'

'Know what?'

'About the new proclamations. They went up all over the city this afternoon. The reward on the others remains at three hundred pounds, but they're now offering a thousand pounds for you.'

She waited for his reaction but he gave none, just turned his head and watched the rain trickling down the windowpane while he digested this information.

'Mrs Palmer says the neighbours here are trusty,' she said, 'but a thousand pounds! A thousand pounds could turn a beggar into a prince. And musha, only thirty bought Judas.'

When he still didn't speak and continued staring at the rain she said more urgently. 'What are you going to do?'

'Think about it.'

'There's no thinking in it! You can't stay here any longer! The new proclamations change everything. You've no other choice but to seek protection with Michael in Wicklow.'

'I can't decide this minute. I need time.'

She knew why he needed time, and said very bleakly, 'God in heaven, I would never have believed you could be so stupid or so stubborn. Don't you care what happens to you? And even if you care nothing about yourself, what about the people who *do* care what happens to you?'

He looked at her then. He knew she was right. He would not leave Ireland, but he would have to leave Dublin. Go to Dwyer in Wicklow and wait there until news came from Miles Byrne.

'Just another day,' he said, 'that's all I need to sort out my affairs.'

'A day? Then you agree to leave here tomorrow?'

'Can you arrange it?' he asked. 'I have no idea where in Wicklow your cousin is. I believe it is very difficult for strangers to find him.'

She stood very still, a glint of triumph in her eyes. 'Little Arthur will take you,' she said, having thought it out beforehand. 'He'll be the best and hardiest one to guide you through the mountains. I'll send him to you tomorrow night, as soon as it's dark. You will make sure to be ready?'

'Yes,' he said. 'I'll be ready.'

She smiled in satisfaction, moving over to the fireplace and tilting her head sideways as she gathered her long hair in her hand and squeezed rain out of it. 'A dry towel and a hot cup of tea would be very welcome now,' she said ruefully, 'but I must go. Da will expect me home before the curfew.'

He knew there was no stopping her, so he walked with her to the door where she turned to him with an amused grin. 'I met Billy Rourke today. He whispered to me that Robert Emmet was away in New York. Said he'd had it from a very trusty and *confidential* source.'

'Is he a stag?'

'Billy Rourke an informer? Never.'

'Pity.'

They stood facing each other in the silence of the room. More raindrops were dripping on to her face, making her look very young and very vulnerable. She blinked at him wetly and he wondered how it was possible to love Sarah so much, and yet feel such affection and tenderness for this girl, too.

'I'll have no rest until I know you are safely out of this city,' she told him, turning to go, opening the door.

He caught her arm.

'Anne,' he said softly.

She turned and looked at him. 'What is it?' she asked, concern in her eyes.

And in that moment, as he looked into her face, pale against the wet black eyelashes and wet black hair, he suddenly saw her for what she was, a brave and wonderful young woman . . . And the truest friend he would ever have on this earth. In that moment, he almost loved her.

'I'll pray God keeps you safe,' she whispered.

On an emotional impulse he took her face in his hands and gently kissed her wet forehead, then her cheek. He spoke softly to her. 'Only as safe as He keeps you, my dear Anne.'

She looked into his face, but did not speak, then abruptly she turned and ran down the hall. He leaned against the door frame and watched her go.

In Dublin Castle, the Viceroy demanded that Wickham and Marsden face him at once.

Lord Hardwicke fumed at his secretaries. 'This is the situation in the country at the moment – reports say the people of Longford are getting ready for a major insurrection and are simply waiting for the French! Men are known to be secretly drilling in Granard! The mail coach was attacked in Maynooth last night by a large body of men. It was heard they were waiting for a *speedy invasion*! Even the county of Meath, usually a quiet place, is now ripe for rebellion.

'It seems a vast secret organisation has existed throughout the country. All are now known to be connected with the Emmet conspiracy! A host of rebels have been taken up in the regions of Limerick and Kerry. Five were ranked as captains and wore green uniforms identical to the ones worn by Emmet and his men. Interrogation of these rebels revealed they were not only in full knowledge of the Emmet conspiracy, but had intimate knowledge of his arms depot in Thomas Street. They were ready to support Emmet once word was received he had struck his blow. It seems that all around the country men had sworn an oath known as *the finisher*! Their aim? – to hoist their green flag over Dublin Castle!'

Lord Hardwicke gripped the edges of his desk in fury. 'Prosperous, Naas, Rathangan, Wicklow, Wexford – all are reported to be waiting for the French. Reports say rebels are gathering near the Shannon, waiting to rise with County Clare, and the fact that Emmet remains free encourages them. He has become the new Fitzgerald, not because of his military skill, but because of his incredible *audacity*! Even the Whigs are refusing to believe he prepared for his revolution right under the nose of the Castle.'

'Your Excellency,' said Marsden, 'I think you give Emmet too much credit.'

'That was your attitude on the day of the twenty-third of July, Mr Marsden. You insisted to myself and General Fox that there was no need for any alarm. That any trouble would be no more than a spot of bother with the local militia.'

'And that is all it was, your Excellency.'

'My dear man, all reports show the entire country is ripe for another revolt. And the implications of the twenty-third of July are greatly worrying Downing Street. An insurrection in Ireland could be just what William Pitt needs to topple Addington and get back into power. And doubtless his friend Castlereagh is rejoicing at this very minute!'

General Fox knocked and entered in a state of great agitation. 'Forgive me for intruding, your Excellency, but I have just had a meeting with a number of my officers from various parts of Leinster. I believe the government has no choice but to now declare the counties of Kildare and Meath as being outside the king's peace.'

Half an hour later, Lord Hardwicke and the Privy Council met to discuss new preparations to defeat a possible insurrection and French invasion. Every person even suspected of being a rebel was to be arrested.

As soon as the meeting had ended, Alexander Marsden issued an order that everyone known to have even talked with Emmet was to be taken up immediately.

Mr Cody of the *Dublin Post* was waiting patiently for Mr Marsden in his office.

'Ah yes, Mr Cody,' Marsden said glibly. 'Please inform the world that peace and safety have now effectively been restored to Ireland. Assure them that the country is truly tranquil again.'

'But that is clearly a lie, Mr Marsden. It will appear as if the Castle is trying to hide the true facts of the matter.'

'Just do it!' Marsden snapped.

'Yes, sir.'

It was almost midnight when a knock came on the door of Robert's room. He opened it to Mrs Palmer.

'Mr Emmet, I have bad news. Proclamations went up this afternoon offering one thousand pounds reward for information leading to your arrest.'

'Yes, Anne told me earlier.'

'Now, as far as we are concerned, you can stay here as long as you like,' Mrs Palmer said, 'but I do think you should get away. The neighbours are true, but nobody around here earns more than twenty-five pounds a year.'

Another knock on the door. A second later young John Palmer popped his head inside. 'Ah, you're here now,' Mrs Palmer said to her son. 'Well, say what you have to say, but don't keep Mr Emmet up till dawn like you did last night.'

Robert could see that John Palmer was in a state of great agitation.

'What has happened, John?'

'I've just come back from the Liberties. Mr Emmet. They're rounding the people up by the hundreds, men and women, and throwing them into gaol. I only got away by the skin of my teeth, but I heard Major Sirr barking down Thomas Street—' John swallowed. 'He was saying that if a thousand pounds got Fitzgerald, a thousand pounds would get Emmet.'

Chapter Thirty-Eight

All the family had gone to bed. Anne remained sitting by the fire, staring into the embers and lost in her thoughts; her body warmed by the hot whiskey toddy her mother had given her. A quiet peace and gentleness lay over her like a blanket and she felt strangely happy.

Finally she stirred and rose from the settle. Upstairs she peeped inside the children's room and saw Jimmy propped against his pillows, the candle still burning as he played with a pack of cards.

'Jimmy!' she whispered. 'I was told you were asleep hours ago, otherwise I would have come up to see you.'

Sitting down on the bed she looked at the red marks on his face left by the smallpox sores.

'Can't sleep at night if I'm in bed all day,' Jimmy said. 'And I miss Nellie in here.' His voice faltered and he looked at her with frightened eyes. 'I had the pox, Anne. Did they tell you? I had the smallpox.'

She caught him in her arms and buried her face in his hair, murmuring that the nasty old infection had all come out now, and the horrid sores had gone.

'Soon you'll be better entirely,' she assured him. He sat quiet and content in her arms. 'I have something to ask you, Jimmy,' she whispered, 'something important.'

His head drew back. 'What?'

'Will you be my man?'

Jimmy smiled. 'Aye.'

'Will you carry my can?'

'Aye.'

'Will you fight the fairies for me?'

'Aye!'

They pursed their lips and blew hard into each other's face in a mock battle with the fairies, and laughed.

Finally he slept. She snuffed the candle and quietly left. Inside her own room she found Mary still awake, and complaining:

'It'll be bad enough with three of us squeezed in one bed, but I don't see why we should allow her blasted cat in with us, too. Lift it out, Anne.'

Anne pulled back the covers and saw Nellie asleep halfway down the bed, the black kitten curled under her chin.

'Ah, leave her be for tonight. We'll tell her tomorrow that Purty will have to sleep on the floor.'

Anne undressed quickly, snuffed the candle here also, then climbed into bed. After a silence, Mary whispered, 'I'm glad you're home all the same.'

'Aye, so am I. Even with three in a bed.'

'Four.' Mary turned away on to her side. 'And wait till the hairy one stretches her claws on you. My legs are reefed from knee to ankle.'

Anne closed her eyes and listened to the rain splashing against the window. Very soon the spitting and splashing sounded a long way off, and she sank deeper and deeper into the soft mattress.

Then she heard them.

She jerked awake, her breath coming short and rapid as the sound of boots and voices drew nearer, then the hammering on the door.

Mary sat up with a cry and clutched at Anne. From the next room their father called out: 'Stay abed! Everyone stay abed!'

They heard him descend the stairs, and through the cracks in the floorboards heard him rousing Little Arthur from his pallet bed in the parlour.

The banging on the door became more insistent.

Brian Devlin shouted, 'Who are you? I cannot admit anyone at this hour. Martial law is proclaimed.'

'It is Mr Walker, the local magistrate. You know me well, Mr Devlin. Please open your door.'

'Is it yourself, Mr Walker? But don't you know that martial law prevents me from opening the door at this time.'

'Come, come, Mr Devlin, you must open the door. We have an authority for insisting on it.'

'Mr Walker,' said Brian Devlin indignantly as he opened the door, 'what business brings you to my house at this hour? If it's about the horse I hired you yesterday—'

A captain of the yeomanry stepped forward. 'Mr Brian Devlin, I have a warrant for your arrest, and the arrest of all your family.'

'Arrest . . . all my family?'

'I must assure you,' whispered the magistrate as soldiers pushed past Devlin, 'it was with the very greatest reluctance that I accompanied them here.'

'And isn't it a good-natured man you are, Mr Walker,' said the Wicklow man dryly. 'First you agree to conduct the militia by the shortest route to my house, and now you wish to obtain a double thanks. One from your captives, and no doubt one from the Castle.'

The soldiers ran through the house. The females were scarcely given time to dress before being pushed down to the kitchen where they found Brian Devlin and Little Arthur standing with hands tied behind their backs.

Anne spied Mary's sewing scissors lying on the dresser behind where her father was standing. She waited until all backs were turned, then slipped her hand under her father's coat and cut the cords.

'Don't draw out your hands in their view,' she whispered.

'Into marching order,' the captain shouted.

Mrs Devlin let out a cry when a soldier carried Jimmy into the room. 'Surely you don't mean to take the child? Out in this weather? Look at his condition!'

'The warrant states the entire family,' the captain said flatly.

'Warrant inagh!' Mrs Devlin cried. 'You would act more manly if you were to *shoot* him!'

Brian Devlin took a step forward. 'No! You cannot take the boy.'

'We must. Now into line!'

Mrs Devlin lifted Jimmy's feet off the ground and bundled him into her arms. 'My poor child! 'Tis early you are marked for the slaughterhouse.'

'Into line!' the captain shouted again.

Anne was surprised to see that the one who held her head the highest was Mary. Poor Mary, who so longed to be a lady, was being marched away like a low felon but holding her chin high with defiance.

'What a hero you are, Mr Walker,' said Mary in a sarcastic tone as she passed the magistrate. 'This night you have helped capture such *distinguished* felons as three women and a child recovering from smallpox. Bravo!'

They marched through the black night by the light of the militia's box lanterns while the rain splashed and bubbled over them. Anne and Mary took turns in carrying Jimmy until they reached the Yellow House tavern where the keeper was roused and ordered to bring out refreshments. The Devlins stood in a small wet group inside the door as whiskey and porter were served to the soldiers.

By the time an hour had elapsed, even the magistrate was well primed with whiskey. The soldiers now pressed Brian Devlin and Little Arthur to partake of a jug of porter. Both stared ahead as if they had not even heard.

'Devlin,' said the magistrate, 'we are minded to hire a man to mind your house and horses for a time – until we see how matters go.'

Brian Devlin stared silently over their heads.

They now surrounded him, pressing him to take the drink,

holding the tankard against his mouth, deliberately spilling it down his coat.

'If it's all the same to you,' said the burly Wicklowman, 'I will hold it myself,' then withdrew a hand from behind his back, took the tankard and drank the contents in one intake.

'The prisoner is not bound!'

'There's a traitor amongst us.'

'Who cut the cords?'

Goaded and provoked as he was, Anne could not blame her father for what he did. She watched as they grabbed him and retied his hands, then proceeded to examine the cords on her brother. A yeoman held a glass of whiskey to Little Arthur's lips and urged him to take a drink. 'It will refresh you for your journey to the Castle,' he said.

Little Arthur gave the soldier a grateful smile, then spat into the glass. An act for which he received the butt of a musket.

'This is a dangerous bunch we have here!' the captain declared. 'We had better take extra precautions.'

He withdrew a knife and slit Brian Devlin's breeches down the back, then did the same to Little Arthur's, forcing both to grip their breeches with the fingers of their bound hands in order to keep them up.

Brian Devlin looked contemptuously at the captain. 'Only a gentleman of refinement and feeling would have considered such an act,' he said.

A dragoon was then sent on ahead to Dublin Castle. 'Inform Mr Marsden that we have this night, at the Yellow House in Rathfarnham, taken some relatives of Michael Dwyer who were found out after the curfew.'

While the captain was issuing this order, the wife of the tavern keeper moved over and whispered to Mrs Devlin, ' 'Tis shameful to see you degraded like this, Winnie. Is there anything you want me to do?'

'Aye,' Mrs Devlin whispered back, 'they have overlooked Nellie in the bed. Will you go and see to her?'

The woman nodded. 'Aye, I will, don't you worry.' Then she put a hand over her mouth. 'Oh, heaven help youse!'

'Move away from there, woman! Now march, quick march!'

It was the hour past midnight when they passed through the

gates of Dublin Castle. Once inside, Jimmy was taken away. The rest were left sitting in a corridor.

'Thank God, they're at least being kind to Jimmy,' said Mrs Devlin. 'He should never have been taken out on a wet night like this. Lord damn the law that says an eight-year-old sick child can be arrested.'

A ferocious-looking man came striding along the corridor. 'Which one of you is Anne Devlin?'

Anne looked at each of her family, then slowly rose to her feet.

'Follow me,' the man ordered.

She was taken to a room at the top of the tower where Major Sirr sat waiting for her behind a small table. He bade her sit on the chair opposite him, then came straight to the point.

'You know where the conspirators are,' he said. 'You will have to tell what you know of them, so save yourself and your family a great deal of time and trouble, particularly your parents, by telling us quickly.'

'I know nothing about them. I had enough to do to earn my bread and preferred to mind my own business.'

'Your father is in fairly comfortable circumstances. It is not usual in this country for such persons to let their daughters go into service.'

'My father has a large family.'

A knock was heard on the door. The ferocious-looking man entered and muttered a few words to Major Sirr, who sprang to his feet.

'Take her to one of the waiting-rooms,' the major ordered as he hurried out.

'My name is Hanlon,' said the man as he led her down a flight of stairs. 'I'm the tower keeper.' His eyes moved over her body. 'And if you know what's good for you, you'll be nice to me while you're here.'

Anne looked sidelong at Hanlon and saw him to be a lecherous devil. 'I won't be here that long,' she replied. 'Servant-maids cannot be blamed for whatever the gentry get up to in their drawing-rooms.'

Hanlon laughed. 'Mebbe not, but many a servant-maid can be blamed for what the gentry get up to in their beddarooms.' He laughed again, very pleased at his own wit.

He stopped outside a door and opened it. 'In there with you.'

Inside the room Anne found Jimmy lying on the bare floor with nothing but a woman's apron over him. He was wet, shivering, and crying.

'Oh, Jimmy! Oh, my poor darling!'

'Don't say one word to the boy.' Hanlon abruptly grabbed her by the hair and struck her across the face. 'D'ya hear? Not one word. And I'll be right outside listening.'

She stood staring at him redly, a hand to her cheek.

As soon as the door closed, Anne lay down beside Jimmy and tried to press the warmth of her body into him. 'It'll soon be over, my angel,' she whispered. 'We'll soon be back home.'

For some unreckonable time she lay holding Jimmy, distracting him with whispered stories of the Gaels until he fell asleep.

At the sound of footsteps in the corridor she moved swifly and quietly to her feet. A guard opened the door.

'Mr Marsden wants to see you.'

In the office of Under-Secretary Marsden, Anne was not requested to sit down. Seated to the right of Marsden's desk was Chief Secretary William Wickham, who viewed her with a superior coldness.

Marsden adjusted his monocle and peered down at a book laid open on the desk. 'Miss Devlin, each member of your family has now been examined. I have their answers written down in front of me.'

He lifted his eyes and smiled at her. 'But perhaps you would like to tell us, in your own words, all you know about the conspirators?'

'I know nothing, other than that I was servant-maid to Mr Ellis.'

Marsden and Wickham exchanged glances. 'Come now, Miss Devlin,' said Marsden. 'You know perfectly well the name is Emmet, not Ellis.'

'Is that right? Well he told me his name was Ellis and I don't think a gentleman would lie about his own name, sir.'

Marsden glared. 'I am sure I need not point out to you that prison life can be very harsh on a young woman, and, indeed, I

518

would not wish to remind you of your parents' suffering and disgrace. When was the last time you saw your cousin, Arthur Devlin?'

'Sometime in July. He has not visited us since.'

'What do you know about Thomas Russell?'

'Who might he be, sir?'

'William Hamilton?'

'I know a Patrick Hamilton on the Coombe, sir.'

'James Hope?'

'Who, sir?'

'You were friendly with his wife. We have her confined.'

' . . . I never met her husband, sir.'

Marsden narrowed his eyes and Wickham glared at her. 'What can you tell us about the Wexford rebel, Miles Byrne?'

'Miles Byrne?' Anne bit her lip as she considered the question. 'I have a cousin, Hugh Vesty Byrne, but he's a Wicklow man. He's not from Wexford country, sir.'

'Nor is your cousin, the notorious Michael Dwyer. When did you last see him?'

'Not for years, sir, not since we left Wicklow. Michael's never been one for keeping in touch.'

'We *know* he agreed to help Emmet.'

'Who, sir?'

'*Robert Emmet!*'

Anne's heart missed a beat at the savagery behind the name. Marsden raised his eyebrows. 'You hesitated, Miss Devlin?'

'Aye. I did, sir,' Anne drew a shaky breath, 'for I think I have heard that name before.'

She pressed her fingers over her lips and tried to stop the trembling of her body. 'Ah yes, sure wasn't it yourself, sir, that told me the name just a few minutes ago?'

Marsden lifted his quill and scolded her as he wrote his notes. 'You are obviously dead to all the fine and noble feelings that usually adorn the character of a woman. Not only are you a most incorrigible girl, you are foolish, very foolish.'

'I'd rather be that than an informer,' Anne muttered.

Marsden looked up quickly and stared at her. 'Did you hear that, Mr Wickham? Did you hear that?'

The interview was interrupted by a knock on the door.

Major Sirr poked his head around it. 'Pardon my intrusion, Mr Marsden, but Philip Long is now ready to be examined.'

Anne began to feel sick. Philip Long! The net was surely moving closer to Mr Robert.

'Take this one out, and show Long in,' Marsden ordered, 'but leave her in the corridor. I have not finished with her yet.'

From under her lashes Anne glanced at Philip Long as they passed each other. She had seen him on two occasions at Harold's Cross but affected not to know him.

From her seat in the corridor, Anne strained to hear the voices from the inner office. Two armed soldiers stood at the entrance to the corridor and she sat alone in the centre. Slowly she edged her way, inch by inch, down the bench until she was right by the door. Marsden's voice, raised in anger, reached out to her.

'We *know* you gave him money! One thousand pounds, followed by a number of small amounts.'

'An investment in his tannery, sir.'

'Who financed him?'

'Financed him for what, Mr Marsden? The Emmets were never poor.'

'Mr Long, in accordance with the normal practice, Dr Emmet left the bulk of his estate to his eldest son, Thomas Addis Emmet. Various other assets were left in trust for his youngest son, Robert Emmet, which would go to him when his mother died. But apart from an annual allowance from his mother's trust, the only immediate money left to Robert Emmet was a sum of four thousand pounds.'

'That's more than most men earn in twenty years, sir.'

'But it is not enough to purchase the vast amount of arms and ammunition we found in the city! And from what we are told, every man who gave up his employment to work for the conspiracy had his food and lodging bills paid by Emmet. Someone gave him financial support, and I believe, Mr Long, that you know who.'

Anne strained her ears in the long silence, then heard the voice of Philip Long.

'Mr Marsden, I am prepared to swear under oath that I gave

him one thousand pounds and other small sums, but as to his financial dealings after that, I have no knowledge. I am prepared to swear.'

'Do you know where Emmet is now?'

'No, sir.'

'Are you prepared to swear to that?'

'About the money, yes sir.'

'And as to having no knowledge of Emmet's whereabouts now, will you swear under oath to that?'

'No, sir.'

'Will you tell us where Emmet is?'

'No, sir.'

'How old are you, Mr Long?'

'Thirty-one years.'

'Then I suggest you consider, very carefully, whether you wish to live to be thirty-two.'

The sound of carriage wheels rolling noisily through the Castle yard made Anne jump up and look through the window. She watched with dismay as John Fleming, the ostler from the White Bull, stepped out. So they had got him, too. She sat down again. The net was closing, closing, closing. And poor Mr Robert would be waiting for Little Arthur to come and take him down to Imaal!

She tried to listen again but the conversation was lost to her. She sat back feeling greatly proud of Philip Long.

A few minutes later, the door of the inner office opened and Major Sirr hauled Philip Long out. He called to the soldiers at the entrance to the corridor.

'Have this one taken to Kilmainham Gaol.'

Alexander Marsden changed his mind about interviewing Anne again. He ordered her to be taken to a room on the upper floor of the tower. As she was led there, she saw the black greatcoat of John Fleming disappearing into a room.

'Who was that?' she asked Major Sirr.

The major looked nonplussed. 'The towerkeeper, Mr Hanlon. Mind your own business.'

She was put into a little closet adjoining the room she had seen Fleming enter. She discovered she could make only three short steps inside it. Throughout the night she pressed her ear against the thin partition wall and listened to Fleming pacing up and down and sighing. At least he could move about, all she could do was sit with her knees under her chin.

She then heard Fleming sobbing as if his heart was rent with anguish and she pitied him from her very soul. She frequently coughed and spoke a word or two to herself to see if it would induce him to speak to her.

Fleming continued his lamentations as if oblivious to all but himself. Anne's pity consumed her. He was just like herself, willing to remain faithful no matter what the consequences.

The following morning, Hanlon, the tower keeper, opened her door a fraction and shouted, 'Are you up?' He burst out laughing. 'Are you *up*! Isn't that what you rebels always say?' He gave another burst of laughter. His delight at his own wit was obviously a habit. 'I want you down in the yard,' he said, 'for a bit of fresh air.'

Another woman was led to join Anne at the door of the Castle yard. Hanlon ordered them to go and enjoy the pure air.

'How could air be pure with him around,' the woman murmured.

'Your voice,' Anne exclaimed, ' 'tis Ulster.'

'Newry. They brought me down yesterday for harbouring some of the rebels.'

'Go on,' Hanlon shouted from the door, 'walk out, walk out.'

Two ponies stood at the left side of the Castle yard. 'Oh, are they not beauties?' Annie cried. 'I wouldn't mind getting an airing on one of them.'

'Come back from there,' Hanlon shouted as she ran over to the ponies. 'Stay in the middle of the yard.'

As Anne glanced over her shoulder, she noticed two men standing by an upper window. One was John Fleming, the other Major Sirr. Fleming was looking at her and nodding his head.

With the coldness of an icy rag across her face, it suddenly struck Anne why Fleming had been in such a state through the night – he'd turned informer!

She moved into the centre of the yard and gave a low curtsy to the two men at the window. 'I think I have been viewed well enough, Mr Hanlon,' she said. 'I suppose I may go in? There's no more necessity for fresh air.'

'Get in with you then,' Hanlon cried, nodding to two turn-keys standing in the passage behind him, 'but you,' he hailed the other woman, 'I want to talk to you, over in the stables.'

It was only then, due to the expression on Hanlon's face, that Anne noticed the woman from Newry was extremely beautiful.

'Oy! Where's he going?'

Anne turned to see a plump, middle-aged woman standing by the door.

'Where's he going with her?' the woman demanded.

'To the stables,' Anne replied innocently.

'You dirty adulterist!' the woman shouted after Hanlon. 'I knew you were panting after that one as soon as she walked in. Do you think I'm going to put up with it? I'll smather you!'

Hanlon marched back to the woman and knocked her down with a thump in the face.

'You great ruffian!' Anne cried in shock. 'Is it proving to the Newry woman how manly you are?' She bent down to Hanlon's wife and attempted to assist her to her feet.

'Don't provoke him,' Mrs Hanlon muttered. 'You're in enough trouble as it is.' She gave a moan as she lifted her hand from her mouth and held up a bloody tooth. 'Oh, if me mother knew what I have to suffer now she'd jump up in her grave!' she wailed. 'And me mother had a good and true saying about men – them than bate and rape let the law castrate! And that's what he'll be doing in those stables – raping that woman.'

Anne had no doubt about it – the brute!

'Castrate?' she said to the woman. 'What does that mean?'

' 'Tis what they do to horses when they want them to ride races not mares.'

Anne's face flamed with embarrassment, and Mrs Hanlon explained, 'My dear father used to breed racing horses.' She looked at the tooth in her hand, then threw it away.

'Is your little brother all right?' she asked. 'Poor wee bairn! All I could do to warm him was put my apron over him, before that dirty adulterist dragged me away.'

'It was you then who put the apron over Jimmy?'

'Aye, I would've liked to have done more for the child, but as I said—'

'You,' said one of the turnkeys to Anne, 'you're wanted upstairs by the major.'

She was ushered roughly along the passage and up the stairs. As they turned into the corridor where Major Sirr and Fleming still stood by the window, she heard the major say, 'Do you know her brother and sister?'

'No,' Fleming replied.

Major Sirr turned to Anne, and attempted to assume what God had denied him – a gentle countenance. He gave her one of his very best smiles. It made Anne think of a panting bulldog.

'Do you know this young man?' he asked.

'I do not,' she replied.

'Oh, Anne,' Fleming cried, 'there's no point in this work now. Admit you know me very well. I was deeply engaged in the conspiracy, but against my will. I was young and seeking employment and could not obtain the work unless I also joined the conspiracy. But I know what to do now – and so should you.'

'That's right,' said the major. 'You are an honest man, Mr Fleming. No wonder she did not instantly recognise you, so worn down are you with your treason and treachery and anxiety of mind.'

Fleming stared Anne in the face as if forcing her to recognise him. 'Well, Anne, don't you know me yet?'

She turned away, greatly agitated.

'Tell them what you know, Anne,' Fleming pleaded. 'Tell them about Em—'

She swung round and seized Fleming by the throat. 'You'd have me swear away my life – but I'll have yours first!' She twisted her hand tightly around his cravat.

Fleming's face turned red, spluttering until he was almost choked. It was only when she realised Fleming was not lifting a hand to stop her that Anne loosened her grip, but she did not let go until the turnkeys grabbed her and managed to prise her fingers loose.

Major Sirr declared she was obviously mad. No knife or destructive weapon should be left near her. 'Take her away!' he shouted.

Anne narrowed her eyes in warning at Fleming, then allowed herself to be dragged off as the major cried, 'Fleming! Fleming! Stop coughing and listen to me now. I want nothing from you but the truth. Lies won't buy your release!'

She was taken to yet another room and introduced to Dr Trevor, the head superintendent of Kilmainham Gaol and all gaols. He was a small, plump man with a downturned mouth in a round face.

'I think you should know,' he said, 'that we took most of the conspirators last night. They acquired wisdom before the dawn and are now telling all to save their lives.'

Anne stared at him widely but did not reply.

'Several of them have made disclosures about the whole plot.'

'And what plot would that be, sir?'

For a long silent moment Dr Trevor studied her, then rose to his feet and left the room without another word.

Minutes later Major Sirr came into the room. He gave her the same bulldog smile as if the incident with Fleming had never happened. He sat down at the table and embarked on a long rigmarole about how unpleasant prison life could be on a young woman, and such a pretty one, too.

Anne solemnly studied the small panes in the window as he continued about how fine it would be if she were given her liberty, along with her family, and could return home to be well protected and provided for.

'You know, Anne,' he said in a voice he hoped sounded fatherly, 'obstinacy never did anyone any good, and so many mistake it for virtue. Now, this man who was your master in Butterfield—'

'Mr Ellis?'

'If you wish to call him that. Were you . . . fond of him?'

After a pause, she shrugged negligently. 'I never really paid him that much notice, sir. I spent most of my time in the kitchen.'

The major sighed. 'If you will just stop this foolishness, and be a good girl and tell us what you know of Emmet and his associates and any information as to where he might be now, then you need not mention a word about yourself or your relatives. All we want to know is where the conspirators went from Butterfield Lane. And to show our gratitude, we will give you the sum of five hundred pounds – a fine fortune for a young woman.'

'I know nothing,' she said flatly.

'What! Your family acted honestly about what *they* knew. And for such were liberated this morning.'

Relief flooded over Anne to such an extent she almost smiled at the major, who nodded and said. 'Yes, yes! And we have even been told about the bad welcome you gave to Emmet on his return to Butterfield Lane.'

Anne was puzzled. None of her family knew about that.

'Don't be a fool now,' the major said quickly. 'Five hundred pounds is a handsome fortune. Look to yourself and be your own friend. Don't refuse it.'

'If my only way of getting a fortune,' she said quietly, 'is to get one from blood money, then I shall be without one all the days of my life.'

'Blood money? What do you mean by blood money?' The major jumped to his feet. 'You are a desperate young woman,' he stormed. 'You are the most obstinate person I have ever met with. I have sent your father and mother home because they were honest. They are all upright except you. I will keep you in gaol all the days of your life as a pattern to other women like you!'

Later that afternoon, Anne was transferred to Kilmainham Gaol. Here she was informed no cell was ready for her yet, and ordered to sit on a bench with two other women. One of them she knew as a Mrs Egan from Thomas Street; the other a Mrs Stockdale. Both had been taken in the indiscriminate round-ups the night before and were about to be released.

Anne signalled to them both with her eyes. The women understood. Mrs Stockdale started a strange and rambling conversation with the turnkey while Anne whispered to Mrs Egan.

'When you get back to Thomas Street, make haste in telling Mr and Mrs Dillon at the White Bull that Fleming has turned informer.'

Mrs Egan nodded. 'I'll go there first thing.'

Anne looked towards the turnkey who was trying desperately to shut Mrs Stockdale up.

'Do you think they'll put you in with your family?' Mrs Egan whispered.

'My family were released this morning,' Anne whispered back.

'Oh, no, my dear.' Mrs Egan shook her head positively. 'Your mother and sister were brought in here about an hour ago. I left them only ten minutes since. They've been put in with Rose Hope and her child. I believe your father and the little boy are in the men's side, and the older lad has been sent to the Provost prison.'

Anne stared at her. 'But he told me they were liberated! Major Sirr told me he had sent them all home.'

'Sure, don't you know what a lying cur he is,' said Mrs Egan.

Anne later discovered that each of her family, including Mary, had been as staunch in refusing to give information as herself.

'Ninety-eight,' a turnkey said to Anne. 'You are to be kept in solitary, and while you are here you will be known as number ninety-eight.'

Anne's depression was total now. Ninety-eight had been a very bad year for Irish patriots.

During the time that Anne was being transferred to Kilmainham Gaol, Simon Doyle, a son of Silky Jack who kept the Half Moon public house near Harold's Cross, rode with extraordinary haste to his father at Ballynameece. He rode back at the same pace and his neighbours anxiously whispered and wondered if 'something be in the wind'.

A very short time later a silent troop of soldiers hid themselves behind every earthly cover while Major Sirr sent his man, an old pedlar selling brightly coloured hair-ribbons, to knock on Mrs Palmer's front door.

A small face appeared at the window, and before anyone could stop her, Mrs Palmer's ten-year-old daughter Jemima rushed to open it.

The soldiers charged.

Neighbours who knew where young Mr Emmet was hiding, and had not succumbed to any of the rewards, realised what was happening and ran furiously towards the house, but it was too late. The soldiers had gained entry, some remained on guard in the front garden, others had run round the back.

A woman let out a scream as they heard an order given to fire.

'He must be making a run for it through the cornfields at the back,' a man shouted. *'More power to ye, son!'*

A detachment of Highlanders appeared on the scene and moved in to hold back the swelling crowd.

A loud booing rose up as Major Sirr strode out of the house, smoothing down his whiskers and puffing out his chest.

'Ah, no! They've got him!'

Minutes later, Emmet was led out, hands tied in front of him. Blood from a head wound trickled down his face.

The crowd watched mutely as a soldier suddenly stopped Emmet by the gate and said something earnestly to him. Emmet appeared to summon a dignified smile as he answered the soldier.

A carriage drew into the street and the prisoner was ordered inside. It then moved off, surrounded by the military and followed by most of the crowd shouting abuse at Major Sirr.

'Well, would you credit that!' gasped a woman standing near Mrs Palmer's gate. 'Didn't the soldier just apologise to young Emmet for the necessity of having to be so rough when restraining him!'

'Nay, he never did!' A group of people gathered round the woman.

'Honest to God! And betther still. Didn't young Misther Emmet just look him in the eye and say, "All is fair in war." '

'Begob! A gentleman to the bloody end.'

'God save him!'

'And the Devil eat the tongue that betrayed him.'

By midnight, Alexander Marsden was feeling pleased enough with the day's events to allow himself a final glass of Madeira before retiring to his apartment in another wing of the Castle. The corridors without sounded quiet, and for the first time in weeks Marsden faced the prospect of bed knowing he would sleep. For, safely confined in the tower, was the leader of the conspiracy.

Marsden laid down the glass, sat back in his chair and stretched the last of the tension out of his body. He locked his hands behind his head and smiled as his eyes rested on the open pages of the secret service payment ledger.

> Finlay and Co. Bankers. Account of Richard Jones. (To be replaced to the account hereafter)   £1000.

And knowing Richard Jones as he did, Marsden doubted if Silky Jack Doyle would ever see a penny of it.

Chapter Thirty-Nine

The following evening the prisoner was brought down for examination before the Privy Council – the Chancellor Lord Redesdale, the Attorney-General Mr Standish O'Grady, the Chief Secretary of State William Wickham, and Alexander Marsden.

Marsden lifted his pen in readiness to record the details of the interview for London, then looked at the prisoner.

He had received a head wound in the struggle to resist arrest, a hard blow from a musket butt had left him with a gash above his left eye which he had refused to let Dr Trevor suture.

Silently the Privy Council took in every detail of the young man standing quite relaxed before them; only his wrists were chained.

'A very *polite* young man,' each of his former Trinity tutors had said about him when questioned, 'and definitely not the type to rejoice in violence.'

He was requested to sit on the chair facing the table.

'What is your name?' the Attorney-General asked.

'Robert Emmet. And having now answered to my name, I must decline answering any further questions.'

Each man stared at him.

'You have been brought here,' Lord Redesdale informed him, 'in order that you may have an opportunity to explain that which appears suspicious in your late conduct.'

'I am very much obliged, but I must still insist on declining. If I answered one question and not another, an invidious distinction could be drawn.'

'You are aware that by refusing to answer, an unfavourable conclusion *must* be drawn?'

'I hope no unfavourable conclusion can be drawn as to the point of honour.'

'Honour is important to you, Mr Emmet?' asked Marsden.

'As it is to most men. Although, with notions of honour, people may have different principles.'

'Have you been in France within the last two years?' asked the Attorney-General.

'I have already said that I refuse to answer to you.'

The men behind the table exchanged glances.

'Continue,' Marsden snapped at the Attorney-General.

'When did you first hear of the Insurrection of the twenty-third of July?'

'Were you in Dublin that night?'

'Have you corresponded with any persons in France?'

'Have you ever used the name Robert Ellis?'

'Did you, in the spring, lease a house in Butterfield Lane under the name of Robert Ellis?'

'Whilst residing at the house of Mrs Palmer, did you go by the name of Mr Hewitt?'

'Did you ever see a Proclamation purporting to be a Proclamation of the Provisional Government?'

'Have you seen it in manuscript form?'

'Are you prepared to give an example of your handwriting?'

The questions went on and on. Lord Redesdale sighed impatiently. 'Mr Emmet, is it futile then, to put any further questions to you?'

'Yes.'

After a silence, Marsden lifted up two letters. 'Mr Emmet,

these letters found on your person by Major Sirr . . . by whom were they written?'

Emmet stared at the letters, then at Marsden. 'Those letters could have been written years ago,' he stammered, 'and . . . and I held on to them due to sentimental fancy.'

The men behind the table were astonished at the prisoner's sudden loss of composure. The half-smile which had been on Emmet's face throughout the examination was now wiped so completely, his demeanour so changed, they realised Marsden had hit target.

'In point of fact,' Emmet said quickly, 'I do not even admit they are mine. They are not addressed to anyone, are unsigned and undated. I could have been simply holding them for a friend.'

Marsden smiled. 'Oh, come, come, Mr Emmet.'

'You must, gentlemen, realise how disagreeable it would be to one of yourselves to have a delicate and virtuous female brought to notice. I wish every person in Ireland were as innocent as she.'

'Mr Emmet,' Lord Redesdale said, 'there is evidence in passages of those letters which might be used against you.'

'Might those passages be read to me?'

Marsden applied his monocle and began to read:

'I wish particularly to know from you how matters stand at present (if you would not be afraid); particularly what are your hopes from abroad . . .'

Marsden turned to another page.

'As to the French invasion, he thinks it may not take place at all and that the French plan to wear down the English by the expense of a continual preparation against it. He thinks the quiet here is merely temporary. He is very desponding, however, and says the people are incapable of redress, and unworthy of it. This opinion he is confirmed in by the late transaction, which he thinks must surely have succeeded, but for their barbarous desertion . . .'

Marsden looked up. 'Well, Mr Emmet?'

'May I know by what means those letters might be prevented from coming forward?' Emmet asked.

'There is evidence of high treason in those letters,' said the Attorney-General, 'and therefore their production is necessary.'

'And the intimate passages . . . there is no necessity for those to be read out in a court. Gentlemen, a lady's reputation is at stake!'

'Producing some parts, and withholding others, never was done,' said the Attorney-General.

Emmet looked desperate. 'May I be told the utmost limit that I must go to prevent the exposure of the letters?'

'Tell us the names of those who conspired with you and financed you in an attempt to overthrow the government?'

Emmet shook his head. 'Then nothing remains to be done. I would rather give up my own life than trade it for the life of another.'

Marsden closed the book with a bang. 'We knew before you came in that this was the line you would take.'

'I am glad you had that opinion of me!' Emmet snapped. 'May I now have the assistance of legal counsel?'

'Request for counsel is refused until you have been officially charged. Are you aware, Mr Emmet, that these letters form evidence *against* the person who wrote them?'

Emmet paled. 'They . . . are only opinions.'

'So the female who wrote the letters had only opinions, you say?'

'I say it on my honour! I say that a woman's sentiments are only opinions, and not reality. When a man gives opinions, it is supposed he has actions to match. But for a woman in our society, the utmost limit is opinion.'

Seeing the prisoner had now weakened in his resolve, the Attorney-General pressed his questions again. 'Tell us about any other arms depots?'

'I have mentioned the only matter on which I will speak – the letters!'

'Are you prepared now to disclose the names of your associates?'

'No!'

'Perhaps,' he was asked, 'you consider the disclosure of names as inconsistent with your notions of honour?'

'I will not trade honour for personal safety.'

Lord Redesdale sighed. 'Mr Emmet, the government cannot compromise with you, but if you were to render a service to government by making disclosures, some favour may be given the lady.'

They then questioned him about the Palmers.

'Mrs Palmer was under obligations to my family. Her political sentiments were not necessarily the same as mine.'

'Are the Palmers connected to another Palmer on the Coombe? Is he the one who had the gunpowder?'

'I have made no mention of gunpowder.'

'Or was it someone under obligations to you or John Patten?'

'Few people have obligations to me,' said Emmet, ignoring Patten's name. 'May I again request the assistance of legal counsel?'

'Which counsel do you request?' asked the Attorney-General.

'Mr Burton.'

'Is he not a member of Curran's chambers?'

'I believe so.'

'Request refused.'

'Mr Emmet . . . the lady who wrote the letters . . .' said Marsden, returning to the only apparent chink in the armour, 'would it help you if we brought her into the room with you now?'

A silence fell as the implication of Marsden's words sank in with the prisoner. If they could offer to bring the writer into the room, then they not only knew who she was, but had arrested her.

'I repeat, Mr Emmet, would it help you to have the lady brought into the room with you?'

Emmet sprang to his feet and shouted into Marsden's face, '*It might help you better!*'

'Mr Emmet's feelings are a good deal affected,' Lord Redesdale observed. 'Perhaps we should terminate the examination until he has been given more time to consider his situation.'

In the interplay of eyes that followed, Emmet suddenly realised it had all been a trick! The offer to bring in the writer of the letters had been nothing more than one of Marsden's clever tricks which had failed. Because, despite his alarm and anxiety, he had not done as they hoped and blurted out her name, not even her Christian name.

Marsden rang the bell to summon the guards. 'You may return to your quarters, Mr Emmet. For the present.'

Later that night, Chief Secretary Wickham wrote the following report to Mr Pole Carew, Secretary to Mr Charles Yorke in Whitehall.

Secret and Confidential. 28th August 1803.

I send you enclosed copies of the two depositions that affect Emmet the most. The first is by Mrs Palmer, who is the owner of the house in which Emmet was taken – the other deponent is her son. This information was not obtained until the close of a very able and judicious examination of these two persons, which lasted from twelve noon until six.

Mr Yorke will observe that Mrs Palmer says that Emmet wrote several different hands. This is unfortunately too true; and if the prosecution against him should fail, it will probably be owing to his act in changing frequently his manner of writing. We cannot, I fear, convict him without producing *as his handwriting*, different papers written apparently by different persons.

Emmet was very much beloved in private life, so that all the friends of his family, even those who abhorred his treasons, will be glad of any pretext to avoid appearing against him, and we shall be left, I fear, to accomplices in his own guilt, who will give most reluctant testimony against the man who was considered chief of the conspiracy.

The following day, Emmet had another long examination before the Privy Council, but all to no avail. He refused to answer any question put to him, maintaining his silence even when severely provoked.

He was then officially charged with the crime of high treason, removed from the Castle, and placed in solitary confinement in Kilmainham Gaol.

Chapter Forty

Kilmainham Gaol had been built only eight years previously in 1795 for the confinement of political prisoners, and the rigid class structures of society were upheld even inside the prison system, every prisoner being classified in accordance with his status in society. And so, despite the necessity of solitary confinement, Robert Emmet was naturally categorised as a 'first-class' prisoner, and allowed all the privileges his status required – a bed, clean sheets, candles, writing materials, and books. A man might be a traitor, but he was still a gentleman!

The Governor of Kilmainham was a man named John Dunne: a burly Lancashireman with a rough manner, but underneath humane and kind.

Emmet's turnkey was also called Dunne, George Dunne; a man who could walk so quietly some prisoners had nicknamed him 'the Cat'.

It was almost midnight. In the darkness of his cell on the ground floor, Robert was seated on a chair by his table, his hands in his pockets and his head down.

'Mr Emmet?'

The whisper at the grille brought his head up, but he did not stir until the whisper came again.

'Mr Emmet?'

He rose and moved quickly to the door where the turnkey slipped a letter through the grille. 'From your cousin,' Dunne whispered.

'Thank you.'

Emmet had been in prison for just over a week, and when

George Dunne had first confided that he was a sympathiser and offered to help in any way he could, Robert tested him by giving him a harmless letter to take to one of the other prisoners inside Kilmainham. Dunne brought back a reply which Robert knew was genuine.

He then gave the turnkey a letter to take outside the prison, to his cousin, St John Mason, and when Dunne brought a reply, Robert instantly recognised his cousin's familiar hand.

St John Mason was a lawyer, and the nephew of Elizabeth Mason Emmet; Robert's mother. He was convinced that if the turnkey agreed to help, Robert's escape could be effected.

George Dunne agreed to help.

And now, by the light of a candle, Robert read the third letter from St John Mason, who said he had secured a vessel called the *Erin* which would convey him to France should the escape attempt be successful. Everything was being arranged by his friends outside. A large sum of money had been paid to the turnkey, as well as a promise of safe passage to America. The turnkey had been supplied with a blue greatcoat plus a set of spectacles (size five) to facilitate Robert with a disguise. All Robert had to do when Dunne opened the outer doors, was walk briskly beside the turnkey to the coach and four that would be waiting in readiness around the corner from the gaol.

'Have you a letter for me to take back to him?' Dunne whispered.

Robert considered. 'Come back in an hour,' he whispered.

When Robert had finished writing the letter to his cousin, he sat deep in thought for some minutes then slowly and carefully wrote another letter.

At half past one o'clock the turnkey came back, walking so softly on the stone floor of the corridor that Robert did not hear him until he murmured at the grille.

Robert passed through the letter for his cousin, then whispered, 'Will you take another letter for me? To someone else?'

'Of course I will, Mr Emmet.'

'It will mean journeying out to Rathfarnham?'

'That's all right. I'll go by hack.'

Robert made to pass the second letter through the bars, then quickly pulled it back again. 'You must deliver it only into the hands of the lady to whom it is addressed,' he whispered urgently. 'Understand? If there is a chance it may fall into the hands of anyone else, destroy it at once.'

Dunne assured him he would, then took the letter. 'Where in Rathfarnham must I go?'

'To a place called The Priory. It's about a mile beyond the Yellow House.'

Dunne moved beneath the oil lamp on the wall and peered at the name on the sealed envelope, 'Miss Sarah Curran'.

The turnkey nodded. 'I'll go as soon as I've finished my shift in the morning.'

Robert withdrew some money from his pocket which he tried to give to Dunne, but the turnkey shook his head.

'Oh, no, Mr Emmet, your cousin has paid me enough already. And sure 'tis not for the money I do it. Even turnkeys can be sympathisers.'

An hour later, Alexander Marsden smiled as he took the letter from George Dunne.

'At last!' he said.

Marsden had controlled the whole plot, reading every letter which passed between Emmet and his cousin beforehand, allowing the escape plan to proceed and Robert's trust in the turnkey to develop and deepen, until he finally trusted him with a letter to the unknown lady.

Marsden dismissed Dunne, then sat down with a glass of Madeira, sipping slowly as he read:

My Dearest Love,

I don't know how to write to you. I never felt so oppressed in my life at the cruel injury I have done to you. I was seized and searched with a pistol over me before I could destroy your letters.

They offered to bring the writer into the room with me and I was sure you had been arrested and could not stand the idea of seeing you in that situation. When I found this was not the case, I realised they only meant to trick me. Not that they can do anything to you, even if they were base enough to attempt it, for they can have no proof who

537

wrote the letters. Destroy *my* letters so there may be nothing against yourself, and deny having any knowledge of me further than seeing me once or twice.

For God's sake, write to me by the bearer one line to tell me how you are. I have no anxiety, no care about myself, but I am terribly oppressed about you. Do not be alarmed; they may try to frighten you, but they cannot do more.

God bless you, My dearest Sarah, forgive me.

William Wickham later read the letter, feeling greatly disgruntled that Emmet's secret lady had turned out to be the youngest and unmarried daughter of the lawyer Curran, and not some other which would have created a greater scandal. A married woman, for instance, would have exposed Emmet as a low cuckolder, and shown up his cherished honour as sham.

'This hardly ties in with John Curran's new attitude,' Wickham said. 'Just before he left for England, Curran made a long speech in court abusing the French and placing the blame for the insurrection on Bonaparte's shoulders. He also advised the people *as an old friend* against the folly of rebellion. He has made a political turnabout, and now hints at his loyalty to the Crown.'

'I would hazard a guess,' Marsden said, 'that the relationship between Emmet and Miss Curran was conducted without her father's knowledge. Events have forced the great lawyer to finally bow his head in deference to us, but this – this will bring him to us on his knees!'

'We have to handle him carefully though,' Wickham said quickly. 'We don't want to alienate him. And Lord Hardwicke will insist we handle him with the utmost courtesy.'

'Oh, we shall, Mr Wickham, we shall.' Marsden smiled. 'We shall handle Counsellor Curran with velvet gloves.'

Major Sirr was sent for, and ordered to arrest St John Mason immediately and bring him to the Castle. When this had been done, the major was instructed to journey to Rathfarnham first thing in the morning with a letter for Counsellor Curran, but if he was not at home (as Marsden knew he would not be) his youngest daughter was to be arrested and brought to the Castle for examination before the Privy Council.

'The charge?' Major Sirr asked curiously.

'Conspirator to treason.'

St John Mason sat before the two secretaries and listened calmly as they charged him with paying a turnkey to assist Robert Emmet in a plan to escape gaol.

St John had been one of Lord Edward's bodyguards in '98 and had been arrested at the same time as Thomas Emmet. The prospect of prison did not intimidate him, but he was extremely indignant about one point when Marsden questioned him on the matter.

'The turnkey says I paid him two hundred pounds to help my young cousin escape?' Mason exclaimed. 'I most certainly did not! I paid him *five* hundred pounds.'

For almost two weeks Sarah had done little more than lie on her bed staring at the wall and refusing to eat. Guilt clawed at her remorselessly until she was too tired even to sleep.

She heard the sound of horses outside but did not have the energy to rouse herself. She knew it was her father, back from his trip to England, and the thought of having to listen to him expounding at length to Richard about how right he had been to warn him against Emmet was unbearable.

She tried to cry to ease her misery but had no tears left. For almost three days after hearing of his arrest she had abandoned herself to a frenzy of agonised weeping that had done little to remove the guilt and only increased the terrible thumping in her head.

She turned on the bed as someone entered the room. It was Amelia.

'*Your letters from Robert! Where are they?*'

'My letters?'

'Where are they?' Amelia rasped urgently.

Sarah reached under her pillow and pulled out a handful of letters. Amelia snatched them and rushed over to the smoored fire. She was pushing them down into the embers with the poker when the door flew open and Major Sirr marched into the room. His eyes went at once to the splutter of flames.

'So! You tried to prevent the course of justice!' He roughly shoved Amelia aside and grabbed at a handful of the scorched papers.

'*My letters!*'

Sarah was standing by her bed.

Major Sirr turned to her. So this was the beauty that Emmet was in such straits about? He held up a few scorched pieces of paper. 'These letters may constitute evidence against one Robert Emmet, at present confined in Kilmainham Gaol.'

White-faced and trembling, Sarah could only stare at him.

'Miss Sarah Curran,' the major announced, 'by order of the government, I arrest you on suspicion of being a conspirator to treason. You are to be brought to the Castle immediately.'

'The Castle . . .'

Horror stared from Sarah's huge eyes. Like most of the inhabitants of Ireland, Dublin Castle presented only one picture in Sarah's terrified mind – a vast place of secret corridors and secret rooms where interrogation and torture had been carried on throughout the centuries.

'The Castle,' she repeated shakily, then began to scream; a terrified, hysterical screaming that brought Richard hurrying into the room as Sarah was gathered into Amelia's arms.

'She's going into a fit!' Amelia cried, and Richard stood helpless as Sarah's whole body convulsed into a paroxysm of violent shaking and her eyes rolled in her head.

In the ensuing din of confusion the room filled with servants and soldiers, all talking at once, until Sarah slumped against Amelia in a dead faint.

Major Sirr was forced to make a quick decision. It was one thing leading out Fitzgerald and Emmet, but to be seen *carrying* out a young lady of the gentry . . .

'I leave her in your care,' he snapped at Richard, 'until I can discuss the situation at the Castle. But remember, she is under house arrest from now on.'

He glared furiously at Amelia. 'And as for you, miss, you may well be charged as being an accessory! You may *all* be charged as conspirators in Emmet's treason.'

*   *   *

Leonard McNally, who had rushed to meet John Curran at the dockside, now looked at him guardedly as the carriage rolled along the quays. 'Are you going to defend him in court, Jack?'

'Naturally I shall defend him. I have never refused a United man yet. And I owe it to his father and to Thomas. That is, of course, if Emmet asks for me. I have not been very cordial towards him since his return from France.'

'You'd be very unpopular with the common people if you did not defend him,' McNally said. 'They all expect it.'

Curran frowned. 'I find all this very perplexing, Mac. From what I have perceived, the Castle were warned about a possible insurrection and played it down, but now they are blowing it up out of all proportion.'

'How so?'

'Well, you yourself greeted me with the news that they had caught the leader of the rebellion, the man who had almost succeeded in taking Dublin, and would have done so were it not for the sudden appearance of a drunken mob.'

McNally bristled under Curran's mocking tone. 'But the arms and ammunitions found all over the city. There was enough there to supply the whole of Ireland. And what about the death of Lord Kilwarden?'

Curran's face darkened. 'I would gladly help to prosecute the men who did that, but Emmet was not one of them. I have known the Emmets too well and too long. They have always been rebelly to be sure, but they have ethics, morals, and honour.'

McNally sniffed. 'Sounds as if you are preparing his defence already.'

'What the devil—' The carriage had pulled to an abrupt halt outside the Yellow House. John Curran poked his head out of the window to see Major Sirr dismounting from his horse.

'Ah, Counsellor Curran,' said the major coming up to the window. 'I have just come from your home. I have a letter for you from Chief Secretary Wickham.'

Curran took the letter. 'About Emmet's defence, I presume?'

'No, it is about the . . . er . . . young lady of his affections.'

Curran slanted a smile at McNally. 'So, young Emmet found time for wooing as well as warring!'

His expression changed slowly as he read the letter.

Major Sirr gave a little cough. 'It would appear, Counsellor, that the love affair between Emmet and your daughter has been going on for some time.'

Curran's face was rigid and white. 'Please inform the Chief Secretary that I shall visit the Castle within the next few hours,' he said stiffly to Major Sirr, then called up to his driver to proceed.

When the carriage halted outside The Priory, Curran spoke to McNally without looking at him. 'I would appreciate it if you would return to the city, then have my carriage sent back at once.'

'But Jack—'

'If you don't mind, Mr McNally, I would like to enter my home alone.'

When Amelia eventually led Sarah into the study in response to his summons, Curran was standing with his back to the fireplace, still wearing his black cloak and leaning on his cane.

'Papa,' Amelia said, 'I think you should know that Sarah has—'

'Leave!' he rasped. 'What I have to say is for your sister's ears alone.'

Amelia hesitated as she looked at Sarah; her sister was wearing a delicately embroidered white boudoir wrap, the auburn shock of hair in dishevelled tangles about her shoulders. She had never looked so frail, so helpless.

Amelia turned to leave and Sarah stared at her father, her eyes dilated with fear. She attempted to give him an innocent smile but even her lips were shaking. Only once before had she had seen him like this – the day that Reverend Sandys had said he was taking Gertrude away to be buried in the churchyard.

Amelia closed the door quickly but remained standing outside with Richard, their faces stark with the fear that only their father could induce in them. Mrs Jessop and Keegan cowered silently behind them as they listened.

'You deceived me, Sarah.' The voice was loud and angry. 'You went behind my back and deceived me with Emmet. I demand to know why?'

Sarah's reply was too soft to be heard.

'Love! Love! That is what your mother said about that miscreant of a parson who finally threw her aside. And you dare to tell me that you love that miscreant who is now behind bars? That miscreant who some fools in this city are calling a visionary. *Ha!*'

Silence.

'Where did your secret meetings take place? In his house of rebels?'

'No.'

'Where then?'

The questioning went on and on. Outside the door Amelia bit her lip almost to bleeding as his voice became less controlled.

'Oh! You mean to tell me – but then you are a very good liar, Sarah – that although he seduced you into betraying me and shamelessly creeping out of this house to engage in months of *clandestine* meetings, amidst all the excitement of your long conspiracy, he did not succeed in seducing you into anything else?'

'No! No! He had too high a regard for my honour!'

'Honour? What honour has a woman who conducts secret meetings with a man? Every man at the Castle knows about you. Soon the entire country will. You will be a notorious woman! You will make me a laughing stock at the Bar. I trusted you, Sarah, just as I trusted your mother, but you also went behind my back! Where did you get that thing round your neck?'

'The only person you have ever loved is Gertrude!' Sarah cried. 'Years ago I loved you. Always I have been frightened of you. But now I hate you!'

For a moment there was silence, then a sudden high-pitched scream broke from Sarah followed by whacking sounds.

Amelia stared at Richard in horror. 'He's flogging her!'

'Do something!' Mrs Jessop groaned.

Richard pushed in the door and saw Sarah had fallen under the blows. He rushed over to his father. 'Stop it! Stop it!' He grabbed for the cane which lashed down on his arm instead of Sarah's back, making him wince with pain.

Mrs Jessop and Amelia rushed into the room and tried to lift Sarah to her feet. 'Oh, master, how could you?' Mrs Jessop wailed. 'She's your daughter.'

'She is not my daughter! She is her slut of a mother's daughter! *My daughter* is lying under six feet of earth out there!'

'Thank you, Papa,' Amelia said coldly.

Keegan entered and, without even glancing at his master, waved Mrs Jessop and Amelia aside, then lifted and carried the unconscious Sarah out of the room.

'You should be ashamed of yourself,' Richard shouted at his father. 'Ashamed!'

Curran's face was still twitching with his anger. 'You all helped her to conspire with him. Against me! You. Amelia. The servants. All of you!'

'They loved each other!' Richard cried. 'And if you had not withdrawn his welcome, he would have come to you in honour and asked for her hand. Maybe then, just maybe, with Sarah as his wife, Robert would have turned his back on his other plans.'

'His plans!' Curran laughed maliciously. 'His plans to make an utter fool of himself in Thomas Street? No, Richard, Emmet's destiny was marked out for him long ago. Dr Emmet called himself a humanitarian and a reformer, but he was a rebel of the first order.'

'So were you! Until you started kowtowing to the government.'

Curran's anger flared again at his son's new temerity. 'I have never told my sons they should be prepared to sacrifice everything, even their lives, for their principles – as I once heard Dr Emmet tell his sons. Is it any wonder Thomas planned a rebellion, and now his brother tried to do the same?'

'Speaking of doctors,' Richard said coldly, 'I'd better go and see if my sister needs one.'

'And you can tell your precious sister that she is no longer my daughter. She may remain under my roof, but only so long as she never strays into my presence.'

Slowly Richard turned and looked at his father. 'You are disowning her?'

'Yes, but as a parting gift I shall now go and plead her case at the Castle. After that, apart from her food and lodgings, she will receive nothing from me. Nothing! If she needs anything more let her apply to her lover.'

Richard was halfway up the stairs when he heard the front door bang on its hinges.

'I'm sorry, Mr Emmet, terribly sorry. I was just walking away from the gaol this morning when Major Sirr stepped out from a side street. He said he knew I was your turnkey and insisted on searching me. And then . . . he took the letter.'

Robert turned away from the grille without answering and lay down on his bed. God! What a *fool* he had been. And now through his stupidity he had placed Sarah in even greater danger.

The minutes moved into hours, but never once throughout the night did he stir from his contemplation of the ceiling. Then of a sudden he rolled off the bed, strode to the door and called loudly for Dunne. When the turnkey appeared at the grille, he said:

'Ah, so you have not gone off duty.'

'No, Mr Emmet, but I will be in a few minutes.'

'Then perhaps you will do something else for me.'

'If I can, Mr Emmet, if I can.'

'Oh, you can, Mr Dunne, you can.'

He sat down at the table and wrote furiously. Then he sealed the letter and pushed it through the bars of the grille. The turnkey took it with an expression of bewilderment.

'Another letter for you to take to the Castle,' Robert said. 'As you can see, it is addressed to the Chief Secretary. In view of the large sum of money my cousin paid you, I would be obliged if, as before, you would deliver it there immediately.'

'Mr Emmet—'

'Good day, Mr Dunne.'

They had made John Curran wait. Then he was asked to return the following day. He fumed at this indignity, but when he finally faced Marsden and Chief Secretary Wickham, he did so in utter humiliation.

He insisted he knew nothing of the affair between his daughter and that *miscreant*! He called Robert Emmet the most foul names and denounced his daughter with him. He offered the Attorney-General the opportunity to examine his papers. He was prepared to go before the Privy Council and prove he had no knowledge of Emmet's conspiracy. He denounced the conspiracy, the insurrection, Emmet, his daughter, until he had nothing left to denounce.

It was a great victory for the Castle. The great orator and nationalist lawyer who had been a thorn in the government's side for so many years was, at last, brought down. The teeth had been ripped out of the bear. The demon of the Four Courts had turned into a whining pussycat.

They made him wait again. Then they brought him before the Viceroy. Fortunately Lord Hardwicke was a considerate man. He regarded Curran with compassion.

'I must admit, Mr Curran, I find the love affair between Emmet and your daughter a most extraordinary story. It would appear that he turned his back on an earlier chance to escape the country rather than leave her.'

'My daughter is a rather strange and excitable young girl, your excellency. That she should come under the influence of a man like Emmet is deplorable. She is childish, immature . . . but then, you must understand, it is not really her fault; she must be given some excuse; her mother cruelly deserted her when she was still a child. It would have been very easy for a man like Emmet to lead her astray.'

Lord Hardwicke did try to be fair in his dealings with *all* men. 'From the various reports I have had from my secretaries,' he said, 'it would appear that Mr Emmet holds your daughter in a higher regard than his own life.'

'I . . . don't understand . . .'

'Emmet knows the evidence we have against him might not be enough to convict him if it is not substantiated by reliable witnesses, and we have not yet managed to persuade those friends of his in custody to testify against him. But now that he is aware your daughter is known to us, he sent a letter this morning offering to put up no defence at his trial, and plead guilty to all charges – on the condition that she is left alone and her name is not disclosed to public scandal.'

'Did you agree?'

'We made no agreements with him except that of keeping Miss Curran's name secret. London insists on a full trial

546

with the prosecution putting forth a sound case against him. The rebels in this country must be taught a lesson by Mr Emmet.'

'And my daughter?'

'I have read your daughter's letters, and I agree with that said by Mr Emmet at his examination before the Privy Council. They contain no more than a few opinions. I do not believe she was in any way involved with the conspiracy, simply in love with one of the conspirators.'

'The charge against her . . . the warrant for her arrest?'

Lord Hardwicke waved a hand. 'We will forget all about that. From what Major Sirr tells me, your daughter is in no fit state to be examined. I think it best if we leave her to your fatherly care and guidance.'

Curran sat silent, then whispered, 'Thank you, my lord.'

Before he left, Alexander Marsden requested another interview with him. He could not refuse. Although he had saved Sarah, his own position was still on very shaky ground. In the early part of the year Emmet had often visited his house, the house of a man who for years had spoken out in court against the Castle, the same Castle on which Emmet had planned his attack. Oh, yes, a charge of conspiracy could easily be made against the lawyer himself!

'There is just one other small matter on which we would ask your co-operation, Mr Curran,' said Marsden gently. 'Under no circumstances can you agree to represent Emmet at his trial.'

'Of course not!'

'Or the other rebels that have been arraigned. We are informed the briefs for most of them are awaiting you in your chambers. We would be grateful if you would refuse and return all such briefs.'

Curran nodded mutely, his humiliation choking him.

'And as from this day, Counsellor, we would suggest you terminate your long role as defence counsel for the United Irishmen. Please leave their defence in future to Mr McNally or Mr Burrowes.'

When John Curran finally crawled out of Dublin Castle he was a broken man, his independence, which he had maintained for so long, destroyed. He vowed he would never again look on Sarah's face. Thanks to her romantic connection with Emmet, they had him in their power at last.

Chapter Forty-One

Anne was sitting on her straw pallet when the key turned in the lock and Dr Trevor stepped inside her cell.

'Good morning, Anne,' he said softly.

She quickly stood up. Since her arrival at Kilmainham Dr Trevor had treated her very kindly; his mild manner was such a contrast to the turnkeys that at times she feared she might end up actually liking him.

She implored him for news of Jimmy. He assured her that he was receiving medical attention; nodding his head in agreement when she railed against the Castle for imprisoning a sick child.

'And it is shameful to see a girl like you in this place,' he added, frowning as he looked around the cell. 'It is so narrow,' he murmured, then looked at her intently for a moment, a softness in his eyes.

She smiled at him.

He quickly looked away from her, and said slowly: 'Would you like some fresh air and a little exercise?'

'Oh, indeed I would, sir.'

'Then you shall have it!' he said decisively.

He moved out to the corridor and called to the turnkey. 'She must be permitted to go to the yard and have some exercise.'

'Oh, thank you, sir!' Anne cried, but Dr Trevor had marched away.

The turnkey escorted her through the various corridors of the prison, but when they reached the door of the women's yard he pushed her past it.

'You're a solitary,' he said. 'You can't be allowed to mix with the other women. You must take your exercise in the men's yard.'

Anne didn't care which yard it was so long as she could stretch her legs and breathe in the air. They reached the door of the men's yard but now the turnkey stayed her with his hand while he peeped through a spy-hole in the door.

'We have to be sure there are no male prisoners in the yard before we let you out there.' The turnkey smiled sarcastically. 'Dr Trevor wouldn't want you being molested, would he now?'

She looked at him contemptuously. It was the turnkeys a woman had to watch out for, not other prisoners.

'All clear.' He shoved his key into the lock. 'Out you go.'

As she stepped out to the yard her eyes turned to the sky, its colour a delicate blue. She breathed deeply on the fresh air, her gaze wandering around the high walls of the prison, and it was then she spied the faces of Dr Trevor and two other men standing by a barred upper window, watching her intently.

Even before the sudden thudding noise drew her eyes down, instant realisation hit her, swift and hard, like a lash from a whip. She had been tricked!

She looked down to the only other prisoner in the yard, about midway down, with his back to her. He had a racquet in his hand and was hitting a ball hard against the wall, unaware that he was no longer alone.

Oh, yes, she had been tricked nicely, by the turnkeys and by Dr Trevor who had told her about every other prisoner admitted – except this one. She hadn't even been told of his capture.

Panic swamped her so fiercely her pulse began to beat in her neck. She put her hands to her eyes as if momentarily blinded by the daylight, then through her fingers she stole another glance at the window, and saw the men were now eagerly watching Emmet.

Behind her the door slammed loudly. Emmet turned towards the noise, and their eyes met. His stunned expression told her that he also had been kept in ignorance of her imprisonment. He seemed about to speak, but she frowned sternly and flashed a look up at the window.

Instantly he knew something was wrong and checked himself.

He deliberately paused to glance her up and down in the manner of any young buck with a strange female, then turned away disinterested, resumed hitting the ball against the wall.

She strolled down the yard with arms folded. Passing a few feet away, she shaded her eyes with her hand and gazed up to a bird flying overhead. 'We're being watched from the window,' she whispered, and walked on.

At the end of the yard she turned, started to stroll back, and as if by accident, he struck the ball in her direction, and followed it, his back to the window.

'Anne,' he whispered, stooping to pick up the ball, 'confess what you know of me, and obtain your liberty.'

She made no answer, and passed on, her face turned away.

At the top of the yard she paused, then turned back down. Approaching him again, she tripped as if lame, bent to take off a shoe and shook out an imaginary bit of gravel.

'I thought,' she said under her breath, 'that you would be the last man in the world to encourage me to become an informer.'

'I don't mean that,' he said, his back to her. 'Tell of no one but me, for I'm already a dead man.' He slammed the ball against the wall.

She put on her shoe with trembling hands. 'What do you mean, a dead man?'

'My fate was decided at the Castle weeks ago.'

She walked on, gazing around as if thinking of no one and nothing in particular, but she could feel the sweat of fear running down her sides.

After strolling up and down the yard a number of times and giving no sign of knowing him, he slammed the ball again, tipping it slightly so it rebounded past her. She turned her back to the window and lifted her skirt to draw up her stockings, a hussyish thing to do, but she could think of no other ruse.

'There will be plenty of others to swear against me,' he said, coming back behind her.

'We are being watched,' she hissed, drawing up the other stocking.

He bounced the ball on the ground as he walked; a note of pleading crept into his voice. 'Do it for my sake, Anne. I'll not die easy knowing you are in such danger because of me. Tell what you know of me and obtain your release.'

'Not for thousands of pounds,' she swore vehemently, 'not for the whole world, will I swear one *syllable* against you!' She straightened and moved away to the far side of the yard.

She continued her idle stroll for some time without turning her head once in his direction while he continued swinging the racquet and hitting the ball against the wall, seeming to take no particular notice of each other.

At last the door opened, the turnkey beckoned her inside. She stepped back into the corridor to meet the hard slap of a hand across her cheek. She gasped and looked into the face of Dr Trevor, now puce with anger.

'You think we were fooled by your little game? Two people alone in a yard and yet never once acknowledged each other!'

'Who? That fellow out there? He looked gentry. I hate gentry. I never talk to gentry.'

'You have made me look a fool in the eyes of Castle officials!' He gave her the back of his hand this time, all pretence of sympathy and friendship gone.

'My patience is worn to the limits with you, Anne Devlin. Do you recognise that man as the one who was your master in Butterfield Lane? Is he Robert Emmet?'

'What? Have you a man in prison and you don't know who he is? What kind of justice is that?'

Dr Trevor grabbed a handful of her black curls and pulled her back to the cell, all the while shouting that she and her co-religionists were the scum of the earth.

'Because we don't lick the hand that lashes us?' Anne retorted.

He shoved her down on the pallet. 'We don't want you to identify him, we are past that. We have a proposition for you. It will result in your release and the payment of a substantial amount of money, a lot more than Major Sirr offered you. Help us to discover who the other conspirators are, and appear for the prosecution against Emmet at his trial.'

Anne stared at him if he had lost his senses.

'Freedom and wealth,' said Trevor.

'Go to the Devil!'

Dr Trevor did not lift his hand to her, but reduced himself to the point of collapse by describing her in the most obscene and vulgar names Anne had ever heard.

'No charge has been made against me,' Anne cried. 'I demand the assistance of legal counsel. I demand my rights under the Habeas Corpus.'

'Habeas Corpus?' Trevor sniggered. 'Upon my soul, Devlin, those appear to be the first two words you Papists learn on leaving the breast – Habeas Corpus, Habeas Corpus!'

'Aye, because we're forced to learn that under the Habeas Corpus the government must show a civil judge a reason for keeping a civil person in prison, or make a charge against them – no charge has been made against me!'

'Well, the Habeas Corpus is suspended now. Out! Gone! Defunct! We can keep you imprisoned without charge or trial all the days of your life if we wish.'

He looked at her with a mocking pity. 'It is heart-rending to see you so devoted to this man, Anne. I suppose you know he is very much in love with another young lady – loves her to the point of obsession I believe.'

'I know that,' Anne whispered.

'Oh – so you do know about him and his young lady?'

'Whose young lady? Other people's affections matter not to me. I just wish for people to have happiness.'

'And what about your happiness, Anne?'

'I'm happy if I know the people I love are happy.'

Again Trevor sniggered. 'You expect me to believe you are that selfless?'

'What do you mean – selfless? Even if I was given the world and its wealth, I couldn't be happy if I knew my little brother was in pain. Is that selfless?'

Dr Trevor had heard enough. The impatience was back in his voice. 'Will you testify against him?'

'No! Get yourself another Judas!'

'I swear to God, *on my honour*, Devlin, I will send you where you will end up screaming for a friend.'

'If you ever had any honour,' Anne muttered, 'you have surely lost it.'

He demanded to know what she had said or he would lambast her.

Anne shrugged. 'I said that I did not think it decent for you to couple your honour, or lack of it, with the name of God.'

He stared at her with eyes like glaring blue moons. 'I have only seen one woman hanged,' he said slowly, 'and I would not like to see such again. Yet, Devlin, I would go any distance to see *you* hanged. I would feel great pleasure in pulling the rope!'

She gave him a sultry smile. 'I thank you kindly for your good intentions towards me.'

Dr Trevor almost frothed at the mouth. He had never in his prison life witnessed such lack of fear in a woman. He had seen it in some of the United men. He had seen it in Russell, he saw it in Emmet, and now he was seeing it in Anne Devlin. A small strain of respect crept into his utter hatred of her. But he would beat her! If it was the last thing he ever did, he would make Anne Devlin crawl on her hands and knees and beg to him.

'You will be given time to reconsider your decision about testifying against Emmet,' he rasped. 'And, to help you reconsider, I shall have you removed from here to another cell, much smaller than this one. You will be taken off the state meal allowance and given the fare of a common robber – one loaf of bread and two pints of milk a week. You will be confined in solitary all the day round, and no turnkey will be allowed to speak to you.'

'And all that for someone no charge has been made against?'

He marched out, shouting his instructions as to her new quarters and conditions to the turnkey. Anne covered her face with trembling hands and began to pray for courage and fortitude.

From the day of his arrest, Emmet had been kept in strict solitary confinement and allowed no visitors or communications by letter. His sister Mary-Anne wrote to Lord Hardwicke asking permission to see Robert, if only for a few minutes, and in the presence of another person chosen by the State. The request was refused.

In his office in the lower Castle yard, Major Sirr's patience was reaching breaking point. For over a week he had been pestered to persecution by one of the Emmet servants who daily applied for a permit to visit the traitor in Kilmainham.

From the window of his office he had a clear view of the little man in an oversized black hat, who was not only drunk tonight, but insisted on quarrelling with every person who passed into the Castle yard; then when ordered outside, harangued all passers-by.

And now the insolent rascal was abusing him personally.

'. . . And 'tis only in yer own interest that I tell ye the truth about yerself, Major,' Lennard shouted, his arm linked around a bar of the open Castle gate. 'Ye see, mebbe ye think as yer wearing those big whiskers yer the King Cat! Or mebbe ye think as yer wearing that uniform yer a top dog! But truth is, Major, you ain't nothing but a gobshite of a gutter rat!'

'Move along and get home to bed,' a sentry advised with an amused grin. 'You don't want the major to confine you now, do you?'

'Confine me? Ye ignoramus! Haven't I been challenging him all week to confine me, but the bastard won't! What kind of a polisman is he at all? Into Kilmainham he should put me and quick. And who'd be blaming him? Answer me that? No, 'tis like I sez, I'm ready and willing to take me punishment, in Kilmainham. Yiz can even lock me up with the rebel boys and I'll not utter a word of complaint.'

'It might not be into Kilmainham he puts you,' the sentry said, 'but the dungeons of Newgate.'

'Eh?' Lennard peered at the sentry, then exclaimed indignantly, 'And why would he put me in Newgate with the dregs and scum of society? Answer me that? 'Tis a decent rebel I am, not a robber or a rogue! And 'tis only fair and right that into Kilmainham I should go with the other rebels – not blasted Newgate!'

Alexander Marsden did not even notice the little man at the gate as he hurried into Major Sirr's office and handed him a letter.

'Check this out immediately,' he ordered. 'I gather the shop owner in question lets his upper rooms to lodgers.'

Major Sirr took the letter, frowning as he quickly read:

I have the strongest reason to believe that there is a Traitor concealed in Mr Muley's house in Parliament Street.

You know (I dare say) the disaffected character of *Muley*. Two nights ago, he conducted the man I suspect to the room immediately *over* the Drawing Room which lies over his shop; and since then, various people have been spied going in there. And so careful is Muley about the stranger, he brings the man his breakfast every morning himself, and does not allow even his wife to go into the apartment to tidy it. The stranger is there *now*. The window shutters of his apartment are generally kept closed. It is well worth the search at any rate.

P.S. The Stranger's room is the *second room* over Muley's shop.

Sirr looked up. 'Who do you think it might be?'

'It could simply be the paranoiacal delusions of yet another loyal citizen,' Marsden said. 'I am being swamped daily with tip-offs about concealed rebels. But this one sounds worth investigating, especially as it has been whispered to me that Thomas Russell has returned to the city for the purpose of effecting Emmet's escape.'

The major looked at Marsden with quickening interest. 'What's the reward on Russell now?'

'Same as Emmet. A thousand pounds.'

Major Sirr sprang out of his chair. 'If it is him,' he said, 'I'll not take a percentage this time. The whole must be mine.'

'I doubt if it is Russell,' Marsden murmured. 'More than one source believes he is out of the country and back in France.'

'More than one source believed that of Emmet, too, but he also was right here in the city.'

When Major Sirr had collected some of his more burly assistants and sallied quickly through the Castle gates, Lennard was swinging from the post and shouted to the passers-by: 'Now then, my people, now then: see the famous Major Sirr trotting off on one of his hunts. Look at him go, and ask yerselves if ye've ever, in all yer livelong days, seen such a mangy son of a bulldog bitch that was mated with a bandy-legged greyhound . . .'

The sentry was looking over at another and grinning. Lennard's rantings at the major were highly entertaining to them.

'I should watch it,' the sentry warned. 'The major's left you unmolested so far, probably because you're from the Emmet household, but give him much more . . .'

'How much blathering more?' Lennard yelled. 'That's what I in all me weariness would likes to know! All I wants is to be punished fair and square with a few days in Kilmainham Gaol. And *why* take one member of the Emmet household, and not another. Answer me that? Where's the fairness in that?'

'Only one way I can see of you getting into Kilmainham with Emmet,' the sentry said. 'Become the head of a conspiracy and plan an insurrection.'

'Now then, now then, mind that tongue o' yours!' Lennard cried. 'Nobody's proved he planned any insurrection, have they? No, 'tis like I sez, he's just a poor shylike lad with a golden heart that's been mercilessly singled out because he has no father to defend him.'

The sentry chuckled and turned up his eyes. 'Away with you now.'

Lennard decided he might as well go, now that the major had sallied out of earshot. 'But listen, my Castle lackey, I'll be back tomorrow,' he warned.

Daniel Muley was not a wealthy man these days, and in recent months had been forced to let one half of his shop on Parliament Street to a shoemaker.

'Muley is not at home,' the major was told in a whisper, 'but away on an errand for the stranger upstairs.'

Leaving the other men hiding outside, Sirr and one other assistant gained entrance and silently and cautiously climbed the stairs. On the landing below that of the stranger's room, the major stopped and removed the holster containing his pistols and sword and quietly laid them on the floor.

'What are you doing?' the assistant whispered.

'Protecting myself.'

'By removing your weapons!'

The major smiled. He knew Thomas Russell well, and, if it *was* Russell inside, he knew how to handle him.

'Discard your pistols and sword, too,' he whispered. 'Trust me.'

When they burst into the room, the unsuspecting stranger was sitting reading a magazine. He instantly jumped to his feet and lifted the brace of pistols on the table before him.

Sirr quickly spread his arms. 'We are unarmed! See, Mr Russell, we carry no weapons.'

Russell hesitated, cocked the triggers, a gun pointing at each man. But the major had guessed right – the over-ethical Russell found he could not shoot at unarmed men. Seconds later more men burst into the room and Russell was eventually overpowered and taken prisoner.

'Was it your plan to bring about Emmet's escape?' Sirr inquired as they marched back to the Castle.

'With every ounce of energy I possessed,' came the reply. 'And you know I would gladly have shot you dead – if you had faced me with firearms.'

'Well, Mr Russell,' the major said, smiling, 'you may consider yourself a patriot, but I, sir, have always known you to be a gentleman.' He allowed himself a small laugh. 'And that, dear fellow, is the reason why you and Emmet failed so badly. Patriots may win revolutions, but never gentlemen.'

Russell glanced at him wryly. 'You would wish us to be barbarians like your mob?'

'Barbarians, do you say? My dear man, you have been guided and influenced by the greatest barbarian ever born – Napoleon Bonaparte!'

It was another great victory for the Castle. Of all the conspirators, they considered Russell to be the one with the most knowledge of the French connection, and interrogation of him should provide valuable information about the United Irish executive in Paris.

Marsden informed the Privy Council, quite honestly, that Sirr's life had apparently been saved by the accident of him going into the room unarmed, and the rebel had hesitated to open fire on unarmed men.

Nevertheless the next day's newspapers depicted Russell as something close to a savage monster, and gave a detailed report of how Major Sirr had barely escaped with his life, the rebel about to shoot him down in cold blood, had not the gallant major and his men overpowered him by force.

Two days later, inside Dublin Castle, Lord Hardwicke sat listening to the reports of the Privy Council.

'Denis Lambert Redmond has agreed to make disclosures of everything done within his knowledge either in France, England, or Ireland,' said William Wickham. 'But as a preliminary to this, he requires an interview with Emmet for one hour, to settle with him the conditions of such explicit a confession. He says he must have Emmet's assistance thereon.'

'Your excellency,' Marsden protested, 'Redmond cannot be regarded as a reliable witness. He continually declares his support for their so-called cause, and even under the most severe interrogation has insisted on flaunting his adoration of Emmet to a shameless degree.'

Attorney-General O'Grady tutted. 'I have heard his rhetoric about Emmet and I agree with Mr Marsden. Although Redmond has agreed to disclose information, he refuses to be a witness for the prosecution or reveal any names. It is my belief that anything Redmond discloses, after previously colluding with Emmet, will be a lot of facts which they are aware are already known to the government.'

Lord Hardwicke made an entry on the paper before him. 'The proposed interview with Emmet is not allowed. Let the prisoner be informed.'

'Emmet himself,' Wickham put in, 'has sent a number of messages demanding the release of Anne Devlin.'

'Anne Devlin?' Lord Hardwicke looked puzzled. 'Who is she?'

'She was Emmet's servant-maid in Butterfield Lane,' Marsden said, 'and, according to the deposition given by Mrs Palmer, she visited him almost every day during his month at Harold's Cross.'

'She was obviously in his confidence then.'

'Intimately so.' Marsden smiled. 'We believe, in time, she could provide valuable assistance to government.'

Standish O'Grady moved to the next item which was a mere formality that had to be minuted. 'John McIntosh, the Scottish carpenter,' he said, 'was offered his freedom to return to his kirk in Scotland if he agreed to give information against Emmet. When he refused, he was arraigned for trial. That brings the total arraigned so far to fourteen.'

'Have any admitted their guilt or denounced their principles?'

'No, your excellency.'

'It seems to me,' said William Wickham, 'that convicting Emmet is not our most important task. We *must* persuade him to denounce his principles publicly.'

Lord Hardwicke agreed. 'Yes, once their leader does that, I am sure the rest will follow his example.'

'I don't think that will be too difficult,' Lord Redesdale mused. 'On the last few occasions he was examined here, Emmet struck me as rather a gentle young man. And his breeding is still very apparent.'

Marsden laid down his pen with a gesture of impatience. 'It is a common folly, my lord, to mistake gentleness for weakness. I have seen no evidence of any weakness in Robert Emmet.'

'Ah yes, but he has known only the company of his riff-raff over the past months.' Lord Redesdale smiled. 'Once he gets into court and realises he is on view to the world, I think he will see things in a different light.'

Denis Lambert Redmond was very tired. His request to speak with Emmet had been refused, but as 'an indulgence' he had been allowed two visitors that day: his aunt Mrs Hatshell, and his cousin John Redmond.

Redmond rose from his chair and peered through the grille. The turnkeys, as always, would be hovering near Emmet's door on the floor below. Poor Emmet! And they wanted him, Denis Lambert Redmond, to betray him.

Sitting down at his table, Redmond lifted the quill and stared at the blank paper that had been provided for him to make disclosures. His hand trembled as he wrote slowly:

To the Government.

I will repeat again, that there never was such a wanton attack upon any young man as Robert Emmet. He has been deceived and betrayed into a lawless enemy. I do not mean to resort to threats or menaces, for you well know how you stand. You may rest assured there will be retaliation, and that shortly.

O God, will ever that day arrive when the liberty of the citizen is realised? Farewell you tools of oppression. You will soon meet the fate of all tyrants. May God protect all the friends of liberty, and may God deliver Robert Emmet from the hands of his enemies, so I say.

Citizen Denis Lambert Redmond.

Redmond placed the quill back in the cup, then, bending down, slipped his hands inside his boot and withdrew the small pistol which his cousin had smuggled in to him earlier. He closed his eyes, whispered a prayer; then pressed the barrel against the side of his head and pulled the trigger.

The moon had climbed high in the sky, no longer visible through the grated window of his ground-floor cell. Robert lay on his bed fully clothed and booted. He was tired after the long session with Counsellor McNally, but had no wish to sleep. Tomorrow he was due to stand his trial. After which, all the actions of his life would be left to the savage judgement of men.

He knew how readily men would later pronounce judgement on his failure without knowing one of the circumstances that occasioned it. Whether the failure was caused by chance, or any other ground, they would not care. They would make no compromise of errors. Those very same men that after success would have flattered, would now condemn.

So true the words of Sir John Harington:

Treason doth never prosper: what's the reason?
Why if it prosper, none dare call it treason.

He could not help savouring the irony of it. If George Washington had failed, the British would undoubtedly have hanged him for treason.

Later he would be judged by his God and his country, but tomorrow he was to be judged by a jury of men who had already reached a verdict. Well, for his actions he would answer to law and ask no mercy.

But, for the *motives* behind those actions, he would defend himself to the utmost limit. He would use the last of his life doing justice to the reputation that would live after him, and which was the only legacy he could leave to those he loved, and to the country he loved.

Just above his bed, the dawn began to lighten the square of barred window. His eyelids were drooping heavily, he forced them open. By tonight he would be utterly exhausted. Tonight would undoubtedly be his last, the longest of all. And exhaustion would be a merciful soporific.

He lay watching the square of window as it grew brighter and brighter, until the blue sky was tinted with golden rays. It was Monday the 19th, and a September sun was rising over Dublin city.

Chapter Forty-Two

The trial was set for nine o'clock. When the coach and military escort arrived to take Emmet to the Four Courts, he walked calmly along the corridors of Kilmainham. As he passed St John Mason's cell he whispered two words of Latin: '*Utrumque paratus*' – I am prepared for anything.

The courtroom was filled to the four corners. Many of the prisoner's old Trinity friends were there; some dressed in the King's uniform, as well as scores of his other friends, discreetly anonymous. Alexander Marsden and William Wickham sat surrounded by a host of Castle officials and members of the Established Church. It seemed every person in Dublin had endeavoured to get inside. Outside the common people thronged the Quays.

Gowned and wigged, the Attorney-General, Standish

O'Grady, entered the court and sat down at the prosecution table. He was joined by the Solicitor-General and four other Crown attorneys. Opposite them, just below the dock, Leonard McNally and Peter Burrowes sat as lawyers for the defence.

It was a tremendous triumph for Leonard McNally. By agreeing to defend Emmet he had, overnight, replaced Curran as 'the people's lawyer'. In every tavern the previous night he had been toasted as a brave and true patriot. And, upon his arrival at the Four Courts, McNally had accepted their shouts and cheers with great aplomb.

McNally leafed through his papers and chuckled inwardly at his good fortune. Besides the large fee paid by Emmet's sister, he had also received £200 of secret-service money on the day he had accepted the brief, and a further £100 that very morning. Yes, indeed! Today his bread was richly buttered on both sides.

Everyone rose as the three judges entered the court and took their seats. The presiding judge was Lord Norbury – better known as Jack Toler, the hanging judge.

The jury was being sworn, and one by one they filed into their seats in the jury box to the left of the judges' bench. When the Crown and defence lawyers signalled they were ready, the order was given for the prisoner to be brought up from the cells.

The court fell silent when the prisoner stepped into the dock. He gave a dignified bow to the bench, then was ordered to put his hands to the bar of justice – a round iron rod which topped the partition of the dock.

The clerk of the court read out the indictment:

'You, Robert Emmet, stand indicted that, not having the fear of God in your heart, nor weighing the duty of your allegiance but being moved by the devil as a false traitor against our lord and King, George the Third, did, on the twenty-third day of July, on Thomas Street, in the city of Dublin, maliciously and traitorously raise and make a cruel insurrection rebellion and war against our said sovereign lord the King, and to procure great quantities of arms and ammunitions, guns, swords, pistols, gunpowder and shot, for the purposes of the said rebellion.'

The clerk sat down.

The Attorney-General whisked his gown and stood up,

bowed low to the bench, and commenced the case for the Crown.

'Gentlemen of the jury, the first point you must consider, is whether there has or has not existed a traitorous conspiracy and rebellion for the purposes of altering the law, the constitution, and the government of the country by force. And secondly, whether the prisoner has in any and in what degree participated in that conspiracy and rebellion.'

He then went on to make a blazing attack on the prisoner at the bar, outlining the facts which proved him to be the *head and soul* of the conspiracy.

'We live under a constitution we love,' he declared. 'Free, affluent and happy. Rebellion can find no incentive in our present condition. We feel the happy effects of beneficial laws. Of the just administration of those laws there is no colour of complaint, but,' he looked at the prisoner, 'Mr Emmet would have wished to destroy this happy state of affairs.'

Throughout the prisoner had remained impassive, but it was when the Attorney-General reminded the jury of the lamentable consequences of the French Revolution, and hinted that the conspiracy had been fomented in France, and the prisoner was merely an emissary of France, that Emmet was seen to grip the rail of the dock angrily.

'And should it be proved,' O'Grady continued, 'that the prisoner was the prime mover of the rebellion, that he was the spring that gave it life, then I say: no false pity for the man should warp your judgement! You must find him guilty, and discharge your duty to your King, your country, and your God.'

He sat down.

The Crown then called its first witness. Counsellor William Plunkett now took the floor to examine the witnesses.

A Mr Joseph Rawlings testified that he was an attorney and had attended to legal work on behalf of Dr Robert Emmet before his death. He confirmed he had seen Robert Emmet junior in Ireland in November 1802. He had returned from a period of living in France.

Plunkett's eyes widened. 'France?'

The significance of the word was not lost on the court.

Witnesses trailed to and from the chair, continually having to be prompted in their answers. Two were residents of Butterfield Lane. One stated he thought Mr Ellis must be a counterfeiter. He and his wife had gone there one night and listened for the sound of a printing press.

The second stated that he had assumed Mr Ellis was an attorney.

John Fleming, the ostler from the White Bull, took the chair. His cheeks flushed as he met the eyes of the prisoner, then he quickly turned his shoulder to the dock. Fleming answered the questions in a small voice.

'Yes, sir. I saw men making pikes in the depot, and later putting heads to them.'

'Did you see any arms?'

'Blunderbusses, pistols and firelocks at the depot. I saw men making ball cartridges.'

'How many ball cartridges.'

'More than I could possibly describe, sir.'

'Did you see uniforms being made?'

'Yes, sir. Mr Colgan made them.'

'Please describe these uniforms?'

Fleming described the green and gold uniforms, white breeches and waistcoats.

The jury all turned to look at the prisoner. They could see he was wearing a white waistcoat.

Leonard McNally rose to cross-examine the witness, but the prisoner leaned over the dock and was heard to say, 'Don't, the man is telling the truth.'

The next witness was Mr Colgan, the tailor. He insisted he had been kidnapped while drunk; taken to the depot, and forced to make the uniforms.

Leonard McNally pushed himself to his feet. 'Mr Colgan, would you agree that the man who took you to the depot did you a great wrong?'

'Indeed he did, sir.'

'Do you believe him to be a great rogue?'

'He was a great foe to me.'

'Is that why you agreed to testify against him?'

Colgan turned slightly and looked at the prisoner who

returned the gaze without any trace of resentment. 'Ah, no!' he said. 'I only gave information when I was arrested, and then only because the government promised me my liberty back so I could earn bread for my family.'

Patrick Farrell took the chair. Another Crown lawyer, a Mr Mayne, examined him.

Farrell told the court of how he had been caught standing outside the Marshalsea Lane entrance of the Thomas Street depot on 23 July and had been dragged inside by a group of angry men.

'A few said, "Drop him immediately".'

'And did they?'

Farrell stared at the young lawyer as laughter rumbled through the court.

'Well, of course they didn't drop me! I wouldn't be here now if they had.'

Mr Mayne cleared his throat. 'Quite. I gather "dropped" means killed. Do you know why they did not "drop" you?'

'Well, a few of them wanted to, sir, but then they talked among themselves and decided to wait for someone to come in. That someone was the gentleman standing there—' Farrell nodded to the prisoner. 'He came into the depot soon after and said I was to be taken into care and not let out of the depot, but on no account was I to be harmed.'

'Did the men respond to *all* Mr Emmet's directions.'

'Oh yes, sir. They called him the General.'

'From your observations while you were held prisoner in the depot, would you say Mr Emmet held the most superior position of all the men?'

'Oh yes, sir. The ones called his lieutenants, they all did whatever he said.'

Farrell spent another three-quarters of an hour answering questions, during the latter part of which the prisoner leaned over the dock and conversed with his counsel.

McNally rose and addressed the bench, making it clear he was doing so at the request of his client.

'My lords, I do not intend to ask any questions of this witness by way of cross-examination, but, at the express desire of my client, I shall be excused in putting such questions as he suggests to me, and which will be considered as coming directly from him.'

The court agreed.

Before each question the prisoner whispered to McNally.

'Mr Farrell, you say Mr Emmet was the only *gentleman* you saw in the depot?'

'I think so.'

'How many men did you see who appeared to be active men, having command in different situations?'

'There were a good many, and every man very hearty in his business, as I saw.'

'Did not many go in and out who had no residence in the place?'

'There did.'

'What did they appear to be?'

'Some of them country people, and some like citizens, and some well-dressed people.'

'Well-dressed people? Did you see any who looked like esquires?'

Farrell looked nervously towards the Crown lawyers. He had been instructed to make it very clear that only the *rabble* of Ireland supported Emmet.

'I repeat. Did you see any young men who looked like esquires?'

'I cannot say. The only esquire I remember was Mr Emmet.'

'Did you hear any printed paper read?'

'I did; part of it only.'

'What did it state?'

'I can't remember it all, but it appeared as nineteen counties were to rise.'

Amidst the buzz that broke out the prisoner again whispered to McNally, who then asked the witness: 'Was there anything said then about the French?'

'Not the smallest, as I heard. They said they had no idea as to French assistance, but intended to do it themselves.'

The prisoner whispered and nodded to McNally. The lawyer again addressed the bench.

'My lords, my client wishes it to be known that, although he is calling no witnesses in his defence, on no account will any witness be allowed in any way to misrepresent his *intentions*.'

Many more witnesses tramped back and forth from the chair: soldiers, constables and yeomen. The hours drifted by and the weariness of standing for seven hours without respite began to show on the prisoner's face.

Everyone stared at the big cumbersome man who plodded towards the chair. Jack Doyle put his hands to his lapels and stuck out his chest. Mr Mayne invited the witness to tell the court about his visitors on the night of 24 July.

'There was a whole parcel of armed men around me. They wanted me to take some spirits but I refused. Then two of them followed me into the beddaroom and I was scared out of me wits. Well, then they moved me over into the centre of the bed, and they lay, two of them, one each side of me. Then one said I had a French general and a French colonel in bed with me what I never had before. And true enough, I never had!'

The courtroom erupted with laughter.

'Anyway,' said Doyle, revelling in the attention. 'I lay there between them for some hours, between sleep and awake, and then I fell alistening.' He cocked his head and rolled his eyes in imitation of the gesture. 'Then I got up, stole out of bed and I found guns, blunder-bushes and some pistols.'

'These two persons in bed with you? Did you look at them?'

'Of course I looked at them.' Silky Jack laughed.

'Look at the prisoner.'

'Aye, I see a young man.'

'Was he in your bed?'

Silky Jack nodded. 'He was.'

'In which language did he speak?'

'Well, now, it wasn't English, and it wasn't Irish.'

'Mr Doyle!'

'He passed for a French officer.'

Mrs Bagnall was led to the chair, bursting into tears as she looked at the prisoner. She answered the questions as best as she could then burst into more tears.

'It's no joke, your honour. What with having to come to

town in a carriage in the dark of night because my neighbours on the mountains have no time for those who give information to the government. Neither do they like anyone who testifies against the rebels, but I've been bound by a fine of a thousand pounds to prosecute. And what with my servant Tom Duffy being dragged off to Kilmainham, I'm near beside myself. No! I can't describe the green uniforms the men wore!'

The prisoner bowed his head when young John Palmer was led to the chair. Reluctant and plainly unhappy, the witness had also been bound by a fine of £1000 to prosecute.

The Attorney-General rose to examine this witness and John Palmer confessed that a young man using the name of Mr Hewitt had stayed at his mother's house, then left in the spring. He had returned a month before he was arrested, and again used the name Hewitt. Visitors had called at the house asking for him by that name.

'Do you recollect how he was dressed in the spring?'

'Like a gentleman.'

'Do you recollect how he was dressed when he returned?'

'Yes.'

'Mention it.'

'Military style in all but the coat.'

'Pray, Mr Palmer, did he speak of the transaction of the twenty-third of July?'

'He did.'

'Will you mention the details of those conversations?'

'I cannot unless you ask me.'

The Attorney-General shrugged. 'I do not wish to ask you particulars because it might give the appearance of suggesting them to you. I wish you would mention them yourself. Did he say where he passed that evening?'

'He said he passed part of it on Thomas Street.'

John Palmer looked over to the prisoner standing in the dock, then denied any knowledge of every other question put to him. He would not admit that he had ever seen the lodger's handwriting. After a further half-hour of getting nowhere with the witness, the Attorney-General walked up and down the courtroom, then heaved a sigh and approached the chair.

'So, now we come to my final question, Mr Palmer. The lodger in your house who went under the name of Mr Hewitt, is he the prisoner in the dock?'

The courtroom fell silent as John Palmer kept his back to the prisoner. The question was put to him again. Still he gave no answer.

'Mr Palmer, I will put the question to you once more. If you continue to refuse to answer, you will be committed for contempt. Is the man who came to your house dressed in military style in all but the coat, who used the name Hewitt, and who told you he had spent part of the night of the twenty-third of July in Thomas Street, the same man that is standing in the dock?'

A reporter from the *Dublin Evening Post* sitting at the front of the courtroom wrote down the details of the following scene, which were printed in the following day's edition:

> Being called upon to identify the prisoner, [Palmer] turned reluctantly towards him, and the prisoner smiled and nodded his head to him. The witness identified the prisoner.

The last witness was Major Henry Sirr. The Attorney-General directed him to tell the court what had happened when he reached the Palmers' house.

'I had a company of soldiers waiting at the canal bridge. We gained entrance to the house and found the prisoner at dinner. He attempted to escape and I ordered a sentinel to fire. He snapped the trigger but the musket did not go off. Soldiers placed to the back of the house caught the prisoner as he ran through the cornfields beyond.'

'Did he say anything with regard to the head-wound he received.'

'A soldier expressed to him concern that we were obliged to treat him so roughly, but his only reply was that "All is fair in war".'

This concluded the case for the Crown.

It was now the turn of the defence to make its case.

McNally rose and addressed the bench.

'My lords, my client does not intend to call any witnesses in his

569

defence, and does not intend to take up the time of the court by his counsel stating case, or making observations upon the evidence. I can only presume, therefore, the trial is now closed on both sides.'

There was a great stirring in the court; all shocked that Emmet was putting up no defence. But that was the agreement he had made with the Castle, in exchange for keeping Sarah's name secret and free from public scandal.

The Crown prepared to make its closing speeches. In accordance with custom, the prosecution was allowed two closing speeches and the defence only one. The Attorney-General addressed the jury in a speech that occupied nine of the recorder's long pages.

When McNally rose to make the speech for the defence, the prisoner leaned over the dock and said, 'Don't attempt to defend me. There is no point.'

McNally sat down, but Mr William Conyngham Plunkett, a Crown attorney, stood up and requested permission to reply to the speech the defence *might* have made.

Emmet and McNally stared at him in astonishment.

The Attorney-General whisked to his feet and informed the bench that as the prisoner's declining to go into any case wore the impression that the Crown's case deserved no answer, it was at his particular desire that Mr Plunkett addressed the court.

Emmet continued to stare at William Plunkett, who had not only been an intimate friend of his brother, but had also been a violent opponent of the Union; and in 1800 had publicly declared: 'If the wanton ambition of politicians should assault the freedom of Ireland and compel me to the alternative, I would fling the British connection to the winds!'

But now Plunkett took the opportunity of displaying his reformed political sentiments to his new employers at the Castle, while at the same time proving he was worthy of the post shortly to be vacated by the Solicitor-General, and rose to reply to a defence that had not been made.

'My lords, and gentlemen of the jury. You need not fear that, at this hour of the day, I am disposed to take up a great deal of your time by observing upon the evidence . . .'

He then went on to make a speech which exceeded in length that of the Attorney-General, occupying twelve recorded pages.

'. . . why then do I address you, gentlemen, and why do I trespass any longer on your time and attention? Because I feel this to be a case of great public importance; and because I prosecute a man in whose veins the life-blood of this conspiracy flowed.'

He looked at Emmet. 'How wicked – even to think of separating Ireland from Britain! God and Nature have made the two countries essential to each other. Let them cling to each other until the end of time!'

Alexander Marsden was smiling. And those other members of the legal fraternity who saw the smile knew, there and then, that the post Plunkett coveted so badly, would be given to him.

'Gentlemen . . .' Plunkett moved towards the jury. 'I am ready to suppose that the mind of the prisoner recoiled at the scenes of murder which he witnessed, and I mention one circumstance in his favour. It seems he saved the life of Farrell; and may the recollection of that one good action cheer him in his last moments. But though he may not have planned individual murders, that is no excuse to justify his embarking on treason. It is supported by the rabble of the country, while the rank, the wealth, and the power of the country are opposed to it.'

Plunkett glanced at the prisoner, and saw such naked contempt on Emmet's face, he declared angrily: 'But when this unfortunate young gentlemen reflects – that he has stooped from the honourable situation in which his birth, talents, and his education placed him, to debauch the minds of the lower order of ignorant men with the phantoms of liberty and equality – he must feel that it was an unworthy use of his talents. But let loose the winds of heaven, and what power less than omnipotent can control them! So it is with the rabble – let them loose, and who can restrain them?'

He now spoke with very affected sadness. 'It is not for me to say what are the limits of the mercy of God, but I do say that, if the unfortunate young gentleman retains any seeds of humanity in his heart, he will make atonement to God and his country by employing whatever time remains to him in warning his deluded countrymen from persevering with their futile schemes.'

He sat down to murmured congratulations from the Attorney-General. 'A masterly performance.'

The Solicitor-General himself then rose and made a short oration against the prisoner, his principles, and his associates. And so the prosecution rested its case in the bosom of the jury.

It was almost ten o'clock at night. The prisoner had been standing for thirteen hours loaded down with chains and without any refreshment, not even water. Weariness showed plainly on his young face.

Lord Norbury, in summing up, informed the jury he would not detain them longer than necessary, then launched into a long and detailed analysis of the case against Robert Emmet, which concluded:

'No witnesses have been called for the prisoner at the bar, and now you have your duty to perform. If you have any rational doubt, upon the evidence, you should acquit him. If you do not entertain any doubt, you must find him guilty.'

The jury whispered amongst themselves for a moment, and then, without leaving the box, the foreman rose. 'My lords, I have consulted with my brother jurors and we have reached a verdict.'

The clerk rose and said: 'On the charge of high treason, how do you find the prisoner?'

'Guilty.'

Someone at the back of the court cheered, others answered with loud boos; a number of scuffles broke out in the public gallery and a shoe was hurled at the jury. Lord Norbury gavelled for silence and threatened to clear the court if order was not restored.

When it was, to the astonishment of the legal fraternity sitting in the spectator benches, Leonard McNally made no move to request the one day's customary adjournment before sentence which was usually allowed when a verdict was reached so late at night.

And so the Attorney-General whisked to his feet and said, 'My lord, it only remains for me to pray the sentence of the court upon the prisoner.'

Emmet whispered furiously down to McNally, demanding to know why he had not requested an adjournment before sentence? After standing for thirteen hours without even water he was incapable of clear thought, let alone making a defence of his character and motives.

McNally at last rose apologetically. 'My lords, in view of the late hour, I request that the motion for judgement not be made until tomorrow.'

But it was too late, and McNally knew it.

'The Attorney-General has already made the motion for judgement,' said Lord Norbury. 'It is impossible for us now to comply with your request.'

From the back of the court, John Curran bowed his head in shame. No matter how deep his personal feelings against Emmet, he did not wish him his fate. But in the name of law and justice, he would have wished him a better defence than the disgraceful pretence of one made by McNally and Burrowes.

The clerk of the court read the indictment again, then faced the prisoner.

'Robert Emmet, you have been found guilty of the charge of high treason. What have you therefore now to say, why judgement of death and execution should not be passed against you, according to law?'

Darkness had fallen. The glow from the night candles gave Lord Norbury, in his long wig, a sinister appearance. The courtroom was hot and humid; the stench from the sweating bodies crammed into the court moved the clerk to order the doors to be opened. The crowds who had lined the streets all day now clamoured forward at the word that Robert Emmet was about to address the court.

'My lords,' Emmet said slowly, 'as to why judgement of death and execution should not be passed upon me, according to law, I have nothing to say. But as to why my character should not be relieved from the calumnies thrown against it in this court – I have *much* to say.'

Somehow he had shrugged off his exhaustion. He spoke in a manly voice, so perfect in its modulation and cadences, that each word was distinctly heard outside the courthouse doors.

'I stand here a conspirator – as one engaged in a conspiracy for the overthrow of the British Government in Ireland. Were I to suffer only death after being adjudged guilty, I should bow in silence to the fate which awaits me. But although the man dies, his memory lives, and so that mine shall not forfeit all claim to the respect of his country, I seize upon this opportunity to vindicate myself from some of the charges alleged against me.'

There was something in the voice, in the face, that made everyone sit up attentively; and many of his Trinity friends saw again the powerful and inspired Emmet who had once thrilled them with his eloquence and boldness of opinion.

'I am charged with being an emissary of France! *An emissary of France!* And for what end? It is alleged I wished to sell the independence of my country to France! And for what end? For a change of masters? Was this my ambition? No! I am no emissary, and my ambition was to hold a place amongst the deliverers of my country, not in *profit*, not in *power*, but in the *glory of achievement*! Never did I entertain the remotest idea of establishing French power in Ireland! I looked indeed for the assistance of France, but it was not as an enemy that the succours of France were to land. I wished to prove to France, and to the world, that Ireland deserved to be assisted, that the Irish people were indignant to slavery, and ready to assist in the independence and liberty of their country.'

'Mr Emmet!' Lord Norbury shouted, but Emmet ignored him.

'I wished to procure for my country the guarantee which Washington procured for America. Connection with France was only intended as far as mutual interest would sanction or require. We sought their aid, and we sought it, as we had assurances we should obtain it – as auxiliaries in war and allies in peace. The French would come to us as strangers and leave us as friends, after sharing our perils and elevating our destiny. *These* were my objects, not to receive new taskmasters, but to expel old tyrants.'

'Mr Emmet!'

'I did prepare for rebellion – but not for France – for freedom!'

From outside the court wild cheering could be heard, then a clash of arms.

When the noise subsided, Lord Norbury said sternly: 'Mr

Emmet, the massacres and murders committed in one night by those under your command, showed them to be barbarians who imbrued their hands in the blood of the country before you proceeded down Thomas Street boasting that you would take Dublin Castle. No man who has heard this trial can doubt that you are guilty of high treason.'

'I swear by the throne of heaven,' Emmet answered, 'before which I must shortly appear, that my actions were governed only by the convictions I have uttered, and by no other view than that of the emancipation of my country from the super-inhuman oppression under which it has too long and too patiently travailed. And which I hope, wild and chimerical as it may appear, there is still strength and union enough in Ireland to accomplish it. For while that government reigns, which sets man upon his brother, and encourages him to lift his hand, in religion's name, against the throat of his brother who believes a little more or a little less—'

'Mr Emmet!' Lord Norbury folded his hands on the bench. 'You have had a most patient trial. We have listened to you with great patience. At a moment when you are called upon to show the court why sentence of death should not be passed against you, you persevere in making avowals of your principles, which I do believe has astonished your audience! It is an insult to the judges of this land to sit here and listen to your expressions of treason.'

Emmet gave another dignified bow to the bench. 'I say again, what I have spoken was not intended for your lordships, whose situation I commiserate rather than envy. My expressions were for my countrymen. But it is hardly possible for me to explain my motives without mentioning some which must be disagreeable to—'

Again he was interrupted by Norbury who loudly muttered something extremely vulgar about his motives.

Emmet's anger became contemptuously derisive. 'I have always understood it to be the duty of a judge, when a prisoner has been convicted, to hear with patience, and to speak with humanity, his opinion of the motives by which the prisoner was actuated in the crime of which he has been adjudged guilty. That there has been such a judge, I have no doubt. But *where* is the vaunted impartiality and clemency of your courts of justice, if a prisoner whom your policy is about to deliver into the hands of the executioner is denied the legal privilege of exculpating himself from the reproaches thrown upon him at his trial. If I stand at the bar of this court and dare not vindicate my motives, *what a farce is your justice*! If I stand at this bar and dare not vindicate my character, *how dare you insult it*!'

Norbury was flabbergasted. He snapped: 'The charge of high treason has been supported by evidence, and the jury, upon their oaths, have found you guilty. Is there anything in point of *law* that you can urge in your defence?'

'My lord, I did say that I had nothing to offer why the sentence of the law should not pass upon me. But if that is all I am asked, that is not all I am to suffer. It may be part of the system of angry justice to bow a man's mind to the shame and terror of the scaffold; but worse to me, would be the *timid* endurance of such foul and unfounded accusations thrown against me in this court.

'You, my lord, are a judge. I am the supposed culprit. I am a man, and you also are a man. By a revolution of power we might even change places, although we could never change character. And as men, my lord, we must all appear on the great day at one common tribunal, and it will then remain for the Searcher of all hearts to show a collective universe, who was actuated by the purest motives—'

'Mr Emmet,' Lord Norbury shouted. 'We will listen only to points of law as to why sentence of death should not be pronounced upon you.'

Emmet looked at the judge in a very fatigued manner. 'My lord, why insult me, and why insult justice by continually demanding of me why sentence of death should not be pronounced? I know the rules prescribe that you put the question, but the rules can all be dispensed with, and, in fact, so might the whole ceremony of this trial, since verdict and sentence were already pronounced at the Castle before your jury was even empanelled.'

John Curran sat in utter astonishment as he looked and listened to Emmet. Only once before, at Tone's trial, had he ever seen a man cast affectation and pretence so far behind him.

Like Tone, there was not a hint of fear in young Emmet. He had listened with patience while the Attorney-General sneered at him and his insurrection; he had responded only with his eyes when his brother's friend, Plunkett, had sold his political principles for personal position, then fired on Emmet with every sentence enough guilt to have convicted twenty men.

And like Tone, it was truly now, at the end, that Emmet rose to his full stature, as a man and as a patriot.

He spoke in a voice loud enough to be heard outside the courthouse doors, and yet, there was nothing boisterous in its delivery, or forced or affected in his manner. Despite his chains his actions were not ungraceful, his movements greater or lesser in vehemence, corresponding with the rise and fall of his voice. And he was now speaking about his brother's friend, Plunkett.

Curran observed a number of sly smiles amongst his colleagues of the legal fraternity, for whenever Emmet referred to the charges brought against him by Plunkett, he continually used the words, '*The honourable gentleman* said . . .'

And as Curran watched him enforcing his arguments against Plunkett, Emmet's hand was stretched forward, and the two forefingers of the right hand were slowly laid on the open palm of the left, alternately raised or lowered as he proceeded to outline his replies to everything '*The honourable gentleman* said . . .'

And as Emmet politely but scathingly ripped into 'The honourable gentleman', Plunkett's face at this moment was a sight for any of his enemies to behold with joy.

But it soon became clear that Emmet had only contempt for Plunkett. Any real anger he felt seemed to be directed at Lord Norbury. It was as if he saw in Norbury everything he despised, the system he detested. Lord Norbury was, after all, the judge renowned for making a joke as he sentenced a sixteen-year-old boy to the gallows.

'I am charged,' Emmet said to Norbury, 'as being the life-blood and soul of this conspiracy – you do honour me overmuch! You have given to the subaltern all the credit of the superior. You see, I did not create the conspiracy, I joined it. And I know it will go on whatever happens. There are men in this conspiracy who are not only superior to me, but even to *you*, my lord, men who would not disgrace themselves by shaking your bloodstained hand.'

'It is your own hands that are bloodstained!' Lord Norbury had never been so insulted. 'It is you that is responsible for all the bloodshed!'

'What! Shall you tell me – on my passage to the scaffold – that I, Robert Emmet, am accountable for all the blood that has and will be shed in this struggle of the oppressed and the oppressor? Shall you tell me this – and expect me to be so much a slave as not to repel it?

'If I do not fear to approach the Omnipotent Judge to answer for the conduct of my short life, then why should I stand appalled and trembling here – before a mere *remnant* of mortality? And if it were possible, my Lord Norbury, to collect in one great reservoir all the innocent blood that you have shed in your unhallowed legal ministry – you, my lord, could *swim* in it!'

The court was in an uproar. There was another clash of arms as many in the public gallery jumped to their feet, cheering in unison with the crowds outside.

Norbury was still gasping as he gaped at Emmet. Never, in his entire judicial life, had he been faced with such fearless aggression or audacity! All the other rebels had stood in silence, but this one was openly challenging the very foundations of the system, and insulting him into the bargain. Well, he would pay for it! When the noise subsided he snapped: 'Have you finished?'

'Ah, my lord, you are impatient for the sacrifice! But the blood you seek is not chilled by the artificial terrors which surround your victim. It flows warmly and unruffled through its channels and in a little time it will cry to Heaven. But be yet patient, I have just a few more words to say.'

He paused, and looked around the court, his eyes very dark and very tired. He said slowly:

'Let no man dare, when I am dead, to charge me with dishonour. Let no man attaint my memory by believing that I could have engaged in any cause but that of my country's freedom – oh, no, God forbid. My lamp of life is nearly extinguished, my race is run, and the grave awaits me – but I am ready to die. I have parted with everything that was dear to me in this life for my country's sake. And now I have but one request to make at my departure from this world – and that is the *charity* of its silence.

'Let no man write my epitaph; for as no man who knows my motives dares now to vindicate them, let not prejudice, or ignorance, asperse them. Let me rest in obscurity and peace. Let my memory rest in oblivion, and my grave remain uninscribed, until other times and other men can do justice to my character. *When my country takes her place among the nations of the earth*, then and not till then, let my epitaph be written.

'I have done.'

A long brooding silence hung over the court. Even those who did not agree with his principles appeared profoundly moved by this young man, only twenty-five years old, who had faced his judges with such courage, and now faced his death.

The silence broke when a number of former Trinity students, now wearing the King's uniform, suddenly and defiantly surged forward to the dock and reached to shake Emmet's hand.

'*Stop! Stop!*' Lord Norbury shouted. 'How dare you shake the hand of a traitor while wearing the King's uniform!'

It took over ten minutes for order to be restored. The packed courtroom was sweltering. Someone handed Emmet a spray of lavender which he sniffed appreciatively. Lord Norbury immediately ordered the lavender to be taken from the prisoner lest it should contain poison. He then ordered the prisoner to be searched to ensure nobody else had contrived to slip him a blade or some other instrument that would facilitate a suicide.

The prisoner expressed contempt at being searched in the dock. 'It is absurd to suppose that I am capable of suicide,' he said. 'Death is death, but the shame of its manner shall not be mine.'

Lord Norbury had prepared a long eloquent speech which he intended to make before passing sentence; it was to be the high point of his day, but he abandoned it now, deciding it would be an anticlimax. Emmet had taken the stage like a young Hannibal, and won over his audience so completely that it was clear he had the admiration and sympathy of almost every spectator in the court.

But Norbury decided the final great dramatic scene would still be his. He had played it often, but tonight he would concur with the mood of the court, and play it for the tragedy it was.

Very slowly and sombrely, he lifted the black hat, placed it upon his head, and looked gravely at the prisoner.

'Be assured,' he said, 'that I have the most sincere affliction in performing the painful duty which devolves upon me. And let me, with the most anxious concern, exhort you not to depart this life with such sentiments of rooted hostility towards your country as those which you have expressed. Far better sentiments will help to give you courage to bear the dreadful sentence which at this awful moment I must pronounce.'

There was a great gasp in the courtroom as sentence was passed. The atmosphere was pure shock. Not even Tone had been judged so harshly, so barbarically. The system of angry justice had suddenly turned quite savage.

Emmet listened to the sentence calmly, bowing in silence when the judge had finished.

But the last dramatic scene was not to be Norbury's after all. As Emmet turned to leave the dock, Leonard McNally rushed up to him, pulled the prisoner into his arms, and kissed him.

'Remove the prisoner!' Norbury shouted.

And McNally stood and watched him go, with tears streaming down his face.

Chapter Forty-Three

The prisoner was transferred, under heavy escort, back to his quarters on the ground floor of Kilmainham. The English governor, John Dunne, took one look at his exhaustion, at his bloodstained wrists, and ordered the manacles which had cut into them to be removed immediately.

'I've ordered a fire to be lit in your room,' the governor said gently. 'And hot food and some wine. A little comfort might help you to sleep.'

Robert looked at the gruff but kindly Lancashire man. 'Thank you,' he said.

Then taking his arm as one might a dying man's, the governor led him down the corridors and past the cells where his friends stood by their grilles calling out questions to him. Only at St John Mason's cell did Robert pause and whisper, 'I shall be hanged tomorrow.'

The governor glanced at him, admiration in his eyes. There it was: that particular quality of Robert Emmet that marked him, even to the guards, as a likeable and, yes, a heroic young man. No revelation of the gory details, no desire to shock, or stir up a storm of protest. Just a simple statement that told St John Mason all he needed to know. 'I shall be hanged tomorrow.' As if the burden of the rest of his sentence was his alone to bear. Impeccable manners to the end.

Shortly after midnight the guard in and around the prison was trebled. The Castle had been warned of a rumour that Michael Dwyer and his men were in the city and efforts would be made to rescue Emmet.

When morning came the turnkey reported to Dr Trevor that Emmet had spent the night lying peacefully in his bed, and, although his face had been turned to the wall, the turnkey was almost certain he had slept soundly throughout. The prisoner refused breakfast.

The first visitor to his cell was one of two clergymen assigned to accompany him to the scaffold. Alone with Emmet, Reverend Gamble said, 'I am informed you were once a Christian. Are you now?'

'I have never ceased to believe in the redemptive spirit of Christ,' Robert answered quietly.

'Will you not admit to the people that what you have done was wrong?'

'No, I could not do that. I do not believe the motives behind what I did were wrong. I could not confess to a lie.'

'And do you honestly believe, after all the terrible things you

581

have done, that you have any chance of entering the Kingdom of Heaven?'

'My hopes of salvation,' Emmet said, 'are not based on any merits of my own, but through the mediation of the Saviour who died an ignominious death on the cross.'

The clergyman looked as if he had been personally rebuked: two red spots of embarrassment appeared on his cheeks. After a silence, he said: 'Do you ever take the sacraments?'

'Yes, but not habitually.'

'Would you like now to take the sacrament of Holy Communion?'

'Yes.'

The clergyman eventually administered the sacrament of Holy Communion and later admitted the prisoner's behaviour was undoubtedly marked with reverence and propriety.

His second visitor was Leonard McNally, who limped into the cell with hand outstretched. 'Robert! My poor boy!'

Robert ignored the lawyer's hand and made an urgent inquiry about his mother.

'I am greatly worried about her. She is quite old, not strong. I fear she may not be able to endure . . . my fate.'

McNally stared at him, stunned. As Emmet's counsel it had been left to him to inform the prisoner about his mother. In all the excitement of the money, his own fame and the trial, he had simply forgotten to tell Emmet that his mother had collapsed and died three days ago.

Robert repeated his inquiry about his mother. 'Would they allow me to see her?'

McNally spoke gently to him in a paternal voice. 'I know, Robert, that you would dearly like to see your mother.'

'Oh, yes,' Robert said, 'Indeed, I would.'

Even at this last moment, McNally the old actor could not resist a moment of cruel drama. 'Then have courage, my boy, for you will see her tonight.'

Robert's eyes followed the direction of McNally's finger as it pointed upwards. He stood for silent moments, then he reached out, his fingers gripping the back of the chair, evidently struggling hard with his emotions and endeavouring to suppress them. After a while he drew a breath and whispered, 'It is better so.'

He was sitting at his table, writing a letter, when his next visitor entered the cell. Dr Trevor came straight to the point.

'Mr Emmet, do you have a last request?'

Robert looked up slowly. 'Yes, I do.'

'Well?'

'I am informed that William Kearney of Bohernabreena has been arrested.'

'You were informed correctly.'

'And that you, Dr Trevor, now have the green coat of my uniform in your possession.'

'So?'

'My last request is that I be allowed to wear that green coat today.'

Trevor stared at him, aghast. Emmet's execution was to be a public one. If he stepped on to the scaffold wearing his green uniform the country truly would be up in arms, riots everywhere, even the risk of another insurrection. And besides, after today, that green coat would fetch a fortune on the collectors' market.

'Your punishment fits your crime,' Trevor retorted. 'You are to die as a traitor, as a traitor!'

In the ensuing silence Emmet studied his visitor.

Dr Trevor announced, 'Such a request will not be granted.'

'I did not think that it would,' Emmet answered. 'But I would like you to do your duty and record it as my last request.'

The young man's eyes and interest now returned to the letter as he dipped his pen into the ink. Dr Trevor realised that he had actually been dismissed. It was unthinkable. He, the head superintendent of Kilmainham Gaol, habituated to even turnkeys and guards cowering in his presence, had now been dismissed – by a prisoner!

'Your arrogance does not fit your situation,' he told Emmet angrily. 'You are insolent. You are foolish! Like Lord Edward Fitzgerald you are overburdened with notions of duty and honour and patriotism that are laughable.'

When Emmet continued to ignore him, Trevor's voice became high and thin. 'You are insufferable. You are nothing more than a dangerous revolutionary with pernicious ideas. You should have stayed in Revolutionary France, or gone to Revolutionary America. You are a disgrace to Ireland! You are a disgrace to your gentle class! You are a disgrace to all good Protestants! You are . . . you are . . .' Suddenly he remembered and exclaimed triumphantly, 'You are going to die!' And on this note he strode out of the cell.

Robert stopped writing and held the page tilted towards the window as he read over the contents of his letter.

My dearest Tom and Jane,

I am just going to do my last duty to my country. It can be done as well on the scaffold as in the field. Do not give way to any weak feelings on my account, but rather encourage proud ones that I have possessed fortitude and tranquillity of mind to the last.

God bless you and the young ones that are growing up about you. May they be more fortunate than their uncle, but may they preserve as pure and ardent an attachment to their country as he has done. Give the watch to little Robert. He will not prize it the less for having been in possession of two Roberts before him.

I have one dying request to make to you. I was attached to Sarah Curran, the youngest daughter of your friend. I did hope to have had her for my companion for life. I did hope that she would have become one of Jane's dearest friends. I know that Jane would have loved her on my account, and I feel also that had they been acquainted she must have loved her on her own.

No one knew of the attachment until now, nor is it generally known. She is still living with her father and brother, but if these protectors should fall away, and should no other man replace them, then treat her as my wife, and love her as a sister.

God almighty bless you. Give my love to all my friends.

Robert.

He laid the letter down, folded it, addressed it, sealed it with wax, then sat pensive. If nothing else, at least he could be sure that if she did not marry, and ever needed protection, Tom and Jane would welcome Sarah into their home and take care of her, his Sarah, whom he would never see again.

From his waistcoat pocket he removed the curl of auburn hair and sat looking at it for a very long time, then slowly replaced it inside his pocket.

Weep not for the dead, but weep for the promised bride, whose love is quenched within the grave of him that lies – in the fallen land they both prized . . .

And then, with a surge of grief, he thought of Anne Devlin. It was only since his imprisonment, through the turnkeys who had been told it in anger by her father, that he had learned of the torture Anne had suffered in Butterfield Lane. Prodded with bayonets until her blouse was drenched with blood, half-hanged into an agony of unconsciousness . . .

Weep not for the dead, but weep for the brave, the splendid, baffled brave. Bereaved of all they vainly bled to save. Weep, weep, *weep*!

He wept.

But not so the tears would show. No tears would be seen on his face today, for they might be misconstrued, and he could not allow them the joyful delusion of such a mistake.

He turned his thoughts to the more pressing problem of Anne – here in Kilmainham, in solitary confinement, and because of him. He had petitioned Thomas and Jane to help Sarah, but who could he petition to help Anne?

Nobody.

Every one of Anne's family, and almost all of his own relatives and friends were presently lodged in one prison or another. Even his new brother-in-law, Mary-Anne's husband, had been arrested in the round-ups. So had John Patten. So had Edward Kennedy, the stepbrother of Miles Byrne.

Perhaps . . . perhaps the English governor, a truly decent man, would find it in his heart to help Anne.

Almost an hour later the governor himself came into the cell. He found Robert lost in thought, sitting at the table with arms folded and staring into space.

'I apologise for disturbing you,' the governor said.

Emmet looked at him. 'How long?' he asked.

'Oh, you have a few hours yet. Some time this afternoon, they tell me.' The governor's expression softened. 'Would you like me to send down some whiskey, to dull your mind a bit?'

Emmet smiled slightly. 'No, thank you; clarity of mind is all I have left.'

The governor sighed, and flopped down on the chair opposite. 'I've seen so many of you Irish boys take the last walk,' he said quietly. 'The bravest of all was young Billy Byrne from Wicklow in 1798. He'd already been convicted, but Curran was trying to get his sentence deferred. He was a great favourite with the other prisoners, and so handsome, I doubt any female could have looked at him without falling in love with him.'

'I knew him,' Emmet said. 'He was a younger brother to Garrett Byrne of Ballymanus.'

'Yes, that's him. And the two men he cared most about in the prison were Oliver Bond and Thomas Russell. He was having breakfast in his cell with two others when I was given the job of telling him that Curran had failed, and his day had come. I whispered it to him. He just nodded, and standing up, said to his friends, also condemned, "I'll see you again soon," as if he was going off for another interrogation with Dr Trevor. Then, as we walked along the corridor, he crouched down as he passed the cells of Bond and Russell, so they would not see him through their grilles. He knew they would instantly put two and two together, and wanted to spare them the distress of seeing him go to his execution.'

'Why are you telling me this?'

The governor shrugged. 'I don't know just why. But it sickens the shit out of me when I hear the likes of Dr Trevor and others refer to lads like him as Irish scum.'

Emmet looked long at the Englishman; and knew he was the right person to ask about Anne.

In response, the governor shrugged. 'Don't you worry yourself about Anne Devlin. They have no further need of her now. She'll probably be out by tonight.'

'Are you sure?'

'I cannot see why not. The only reason she was being held

586

was in the hope she would testify against you. After today, any use she might have been is over.'

Emmet gave a relieved sigh. 'At least one good thing will come out of today's event so.'

In the silence that followed, the governor looked curiously at Emmet. He seemed completely detached, and uncannily calm about his own fate.

'Perhaps it is not right or decent for me to ask,' he said softly, 'but I have often wondered just what it is you lads think about while waiting to go.'

Emmet smiled slightly, but there was a certain sadness in his eyes. 'Well, when you came in, I was thinking of something a friend once told me; about a young Negro in America, who said as he was taken out to be hanged: "It sho is a hard thing for a young man to die, when he no sick." '

The governor looked down at the table; he had his answer: it was as hard for the likes of Billy Byrne and Robert Emmet as anyone else. They just made a braver show of it.

'I had better tell you why I came,' he whispered, 'for I very nearly forgot. A young man came to the prison this morning, pale and sickly he looked, begging to be allowed to speak to you. Of course, it was more than my job is worth. Not even your sister is allowed in.' He glanced towards the door, then stretched his hand under the table. 'But I eventually agreed to slip this note to you.'

Emmet reached down and took the note.

'You'll have to read it while I'm here. I could not take the risk of it being found on you. I may be the governor, but Trevor is the man with all the real power in here. Just as Marsden is the real power at the Castle. The two of them work hand in glove. Now read quickly.'

Emmet moved back in his chair, unfolded the paper on his lap. When he had finished reading, he passed the letter back under the table. His face was very pale.

'I need some time alone,' he whispered.

The governor nodded, and left him alone. Then Emmet did the only thing he could, and lifted the quill from the inkstand to answer the most heartrending letter he had ever read, from his childhood friend.

587

My dearest Richard,

I find that I have but a few hours to live; but if it was the last moment, I would find time to thank you from the bottom of my heart for your generous expression of affection for me. I have deeply injured you, I have injured the happiness of a sister that you love, and who was formed to give happiness to everyone about her, instead of having her mind a prey to such affliction.

Oh, Richard, I have no excuse to offer, but that I meant the reverse. I intended as much happiness for Sarah as the most ardent love could have given her. I never did tell you just how much I idolised her. I did hope that success would have afforded the opportunity of our union. I did not look for honours for myself – praise I would have asked from the lips of no man; but I would have wished to read in the glow of Sarah's face that her husband was respected.

This is no time for affliction. I have had public motives to sustain my mind, and I have not suffered it to sink; but there have been moments in my imprisonment when my mind was so sunk by grief on her account that death would have been a refuge.

God bless you, my dearest Richard. I am obliged to leave off immediately.

The Sheriff was at the door; they had come for him.

A strong guard of both cavalry and infantry were waiting to escort him to Thomas Street. The place where he had planned and committed his treason was to be the place of his public execution. He was allowed to say farewell to just a few of his companions in the prison. And although he ignored Dr Trevor, he gave a warm smile to the English governor, and shook hands with him.

The governor could not help but stand in awe of his easy politeness. Anyone would think he was a guest saying his farewells to staff at an hotel. This lad was even more remarkable than young Billy Byrne of Ballymanus. By God, even if they were just putting a brave face on it, they were a breed apart!

'What did he say to you?' Trevor demanded as Emmet was led away.

The governor stood watching him go. 'He thanked me for my humanity and kindness towards him,' he answered sadly.

An open carriage and a crowd were waiting when he was led out through the high black gates of Kilmainham. The crowd pressed against the military cordon, shouting words of encouragement to him. He took his seat in the carriage between the two clergymen, who viewed his calmness with some alarm.

Reverend Gamble wondered if he would retain his composure when he reached the scaffold. Very few of them died without a struggle.

Preceded, followed, and accompanied by the military escort, the procession moved off at a funeral pace along the route lined with soldiers. A roundabout route along the Quays, people at every door and window. The Castle wanted every citizen to take a last glimpse of the rebel, and to consider the fate of those who wished to imitate him.

Reverend Gamble spoke gently to him, urging him to give a just acknowledgement and public repentance of the crime for which he was to suffer. How could he possibly reconcile his actions with the Christian principle? How could he possibly sacrifice heaven for hell when his fellow comrades had deserted him? He had been used and deceived. It was enough to arouse resentment in the most honourable of men . . .

Reverend Gamble looked to see if any resentment had been stirred, but Emmet appeared to be absorbed in taking a last look at the city of his birth. He continued his urgings in a louder voice, until Emmet eventually turned his head and looked at him.

'I wonder, Reverend,' he said softly, 'which are you first – a servant of God, or a servant of the Castle?'

The two red spots were back blazing on the clergyman's cheeks. He whipped out his snuffbox, flipped the lid, took a pinch, and sneezed loudly.

The scaffold stood in Thomas Street, outside St Catherine's Protestant Church, directly opposite the building which had been an arms depot. The area immediately surrounding the scaffold was fenced off by a solid line of redcoats, holding back the shouting crowds.

When the carriage drew to a halt and Emmet stepped down, the entire area fell silent. He stood for a moment gazing up at the crude gallows erected overnight, and Reverend Gamble chose that moment to return to the attack.

'Mr Emmet, will you not even now, at this late hour, speak to the people and renounce your principles? It would do much for you in the next world,' he insisted. 'A public cleansing of the soul, so to speak.'

'If I speak to the people,' Emmet said quietly to Reverend Gamble, 'it will be to say that I have never taken any oath but that pledged to the independence of my country, and the Union of Irishmen of every religious persuasion, and to that oath I abide to the end.'

'Such an address would not be allowed,' Gamble explained urgently. 'They would never permit it.'

The bewildered crowd watched the three men stand in conversation for over five minutes. To them it appeared as if Emmet was having a casual discussion with the two clergymen. He did not seem in the least disturbed or agitated, and appeared quite unconcerned that the hangman and the rope were waiting for him.

Reverend Gamble wondered frantically if he should accept defeat. He turned towards the open carriage where William Wickham and Alexander Marsden sat waiting, and slowly shook his head.

When he turned back, Emmet was already mounting the wooden steps to the scaffold. There, he turned and looked down at the people, an immense silent crowd in the great space of Thomas Street, and saw to the front of the crowd a large group of his friends, white-faced and sombre. The whitest of all was Richard Curran, who stared up at him as if in a trance.

Quiet, serene, he gave them a last brief smile. 'My friends,' he said. 'I die in peace.'

Then, turning to the back of the platform, he gave whatever money he had in his pockets to the masked executioner, and removed himself the black cravat from around his neck.

The military drums struck up a thundering roll as he stepped up on to the single plank beneath the cross-beam, then, in the stance of an officer of the United Irishmen, he stood calmly to attention, his face devoid of all expression as he waited for the executioner to carry out his orders.

PART FOUR

Bold Robert Emmet, the darling of Erin
Bold Robert Emmet, he died with a smile.
Saying farewell companions, both loyal and daring,
I lay down my life, for the Emerald Isle.

Chapter Forty-Four

The *Dublin Post* published an account of the event later that afternoon, which was reprinted in the *London Chronicle* in its next issue. Dr Trevor received a copy within half an hour of it being printed. He rushed down the passage to Anne Devlin's cell, pulling her over to the light of the small grated window, barely able to control his delight at her expression as he read aloud:

> In short, he behaved without the least symptoms of fear, and with all the nonchalance which so distinguished his conduct at his trial yesterday. He seemed unaffected by the dreadful circumstances attendant upon him; at the same time with all the coolness and complacency that can be possibly imagined. But even as it was, I never saw a man die like him.

'Can you doubt me now, Devlin, when you see it there in black and white? Oh yes, your darling Robert Emmet is gone – gone on the wind.'

'But even as it was,' she repeated slowly, 'I never saw a man die like him.' She looked at Trevor, trembling with pride and pain. 'And that is the truth of it – he beat them! Even on the scaffold they did not break him.'

Dr Trevor smiled, a nasty smile. 'You,' he said, 'are going to accompany me on a little jaunt.' He turned to lead the way out. 'Come along, my haughty heroine, your coach awaits.'

The curtains on the coach windows were drawn shut. A soldier sat each side of her, bayonet drawn. Dr Trevor sat on the seat opposite with a pair of pistols only partly concealed. The carriage moved off rapidly and Dr Trevor sat back.

'You know, Devlin,' he said thoughtfully, 'Emmet had the most splendid manners. You would do well to learn from him. He, at least, appreciated my efforts on his behalf. Before he left Kilmainham he embraced me.'

Trevor nodded at the soldier who stared curiously at him. 'Oh, yes, he embraced me in his arms and thanked me for my humanity and kindness towards him.'

Anne Devlin did not respond. She appeared not even to hear, had retreated into herself, her eyes fixed on the hands in her lap.

'Do you hear me speaking to you, Devlin?'

'I hear you lying to me,' she replied.

She lifted her eyes and looked dispassionately at him. He saw her regarding him with the same slow revulsion one would feel for a slimy snake. His face changed, became spiteful.

'Ah, we are slowing,' he announced. 'Time for a breath of air.'

The coach came to a halt and he pulled back the curtain and dropped the window down. Through the corner of her eye Anne thought she saw the high, grey-stone building of St Catherine's Church. She pressed her back into the seat and stared at Trevor in disbelief.

He smiled at her, crudely. 'Take a look, Devlin.'

She shook her head.

He reached over and grabbed a handful of her hair, yanked her head around and thrust her face half out the window. The scaffold was empty and deserted, but in the afternoon sun she saw his blood, still shiny and wet on the deal boards.

She turned and stared at Trevor.

'Surely you understand, Devlin,' he said with a hint of cold humour. 'As the leader of the conspiracy, your darling Emmet suffered a much harsher judgement than his followers.'

She turned her eyes back to his blood – young blood.

'He suffered death by hanging,' Trevor explained matter of factly, 'but after the executioner lifted his body down, he laid it across those boards, lifted up a sword and hacked his head from his body, just as the judge ordered.'

'But . . . why?' The words had difficulty coming away from her throat . . . 'What was the point? If he was dead?'

'A necessary formality for traitors.'

She coiled herself inwards, back against the seat like a snail trying to find the shield of its shell. Yes, she realised, they would need to have blood. The agonising writhing at the end of a rope was not enough – a felon's end. It would have to be more, more brutal and bloody. A public bloodletting. An example to others.

'And as you can see, Devlin, your silence did nothing to help him, nothing at all.'

For a moment he saw the cold, piercing glare of her green eyes, then the snail flared into a viper and she lunged forward and spat in his face.

Alexander Marsden was already back at business in his office, contemplating the charcoal sketch drawn by a Wicklow artist. It was of another dark-haired young man, a smile on his face, a large black slouch hat cocked over the left eye and a drawn sword held casually over the right shoulder. Underneath were the words, 'Michael Dwyer, the Rebel Captain of the Wicklow Mountains'.

He laid down the sketch and read again the letter from Lieutenant Sutherland of the 38th Regiment stationed in Wicklow.

> The country is quiet at present, but it is well known to the best informed that Michael Dwyer could, at half an hour's warning, draw to his standard nineteen out of every twenty of the inhabitants . . .

Marsden sat back and considered. Michael Dwyer . . . no easy fox to corner. Adored by the Wicklow people and – he suspicioned – secretly respected by many of the Highland regiments whose valiant efforts had never yet managed to run the rebel captain to ground.

He sighed in irritation and rang his hand bell. Dr Trevor entered with Anne Devlin.

'You may wait outside,' he said to Trevor.

Disappointed, the superintendent threw a chilly glance at Anne, then bowed to his superior.

'Well, Miss Devlin. You have been to Thomas Street?'

Anne silently stared at him.

'Please answer when I speak to you. You have been to Thomas Street?'

She veiled her eyes. 'Yes, sir.'

'Miss Devlin, surely you now realise that it will serve you favourably if you cooperate with us. There were other gentlemen in this conspiracy with Emmet who are not yet known to us. Men of rank and distinction. Tell us any small detail that might lead to their discovery.'

Two persons of distinction had called late one night to Butterfield Lane. One was Fitzgerald, the brother of the Knight of Glynn; the other Lord Wycombe, son of the Marquis of Lansdowne. But all of Anne's wily questions to Mr Robert had led her to believe that, although these two men were part of the conspiracy, they were nowhere near the heads of it.

'I know nothing about any gentlemen of distinction,' she said.

'Did you ever hear Emmet speak of Lord Moira? Or the statesman, Henry Grattan? Or the Duke of Leinster?'

She recalled once seeing an unfinished letter written by Mr Robert, addressed to Lord Moira, but there was nothing seditious in it.

'I know nothing about any gentlemen of distinction,' she repeated.

Marsden rested his elbows on the desk, putting his fingertips together, and eyeing her speculatively. Apart from the dirty dress and untidy dark hair, he saw the same stubborn girl of some weeks ago – Emmet's servant-maid, devoted to her master. But was she, he wondered, as devoted to her famous cousin?

'How are you being treated in Kilmainham?' he asked in a gentle tone.

'Like an animal. My food – if you can call it that – is thrown in to me as if I was a dog in a kennel.'

'But your time in prison could be ended, you know. Why waste your life over a dead cause? After today's event all Ireland knows the revolution is finished. But you, Anne, you can still make a new life, start again. The offer of a substantial sum of money, together with your liberty, still stands.'

While she appeared to be thinking about this he lifted the proclamation offering a reward for Michael Dwyer.

'As you can see – five hundred pounds for the arrest of your cousin, and five hundred for any information leading thereto. If you had the mind, you know you could help us.' He smiled at her. 'A thousand pounds would make a very fine dowry, secure you an excellent marriage far above your present station.'

Anne was having trouble with her breathing. '. . . Lead you to Michael?'

'Not right to his door. We would not wish to endanger you. Our informers are well protected. But if we knew the houses where he enjoys concealment, some of his cavernous hideouts in the mountains . . . perhaps a warning of where he might be at some particular time . . . Could you do that?'

Anne made a swallowing sound.

'Well?'

'I have to be honest and confess to you, sir, that before I'd do that, I'd cut my own throat.'

Marsden sat staring at her, still cool and composed, but now the venom was as dark in his eyes as in hers.

'You'll never catch Michael!' Anne rasped. 'Not in five years nor fifty, and not with all the armies at England's command. *And you know it!*'

It seemed as if Marsden's glare would penetrate right through to the back of her head. She stood before him quivering with grief and anger, her hands down by her sides, clenching and unclenching convulsively.

'The back of my hand to your blood money!' she rasped. 'If you gave it as easily to the starving as you do to stags, Ireland might be a better place.'

His eyes never once blinked from hers as he reached across his desk and rang the bell to summon Dr Trevor, who entered instantly.

'Take her back to Kilmainham,' Marsden said. 'And let her rot there.'

The next man to enter Marsden's office was his immediate superior, the Chief Secretary of State, William Wickham. He looked like a man who had just returned from a long journey down the road to Damascus. His face was white as he sank down in the chair on the other side of Marsden's desk.

'Why?' he said in a bewildered tone. 'Why does an undeniably fine young man, only twenty-five years old, endowed with the gift of scientific genius, the gift of outstanding oratory and intellectual power, and in love with a young girl, to whom he was betrothed to be married, throw it all away and fearlessly and serenely mount the scaffold as if *we* were the felons and not he?'

'The answer is quite simple,' Marsden replied. 'A proverbial answer. He was young and he was vain and he wanted to die a martyr.'

'No, no, Mr Marsden, that will not suffice!' Wickham shook his head angrily. 'Proverbial answers are no longer enough. The death of every patriotic young Irishman cannot be continually and contemptuously dismissed as a vain quest for martyrdom! Not when that young man had everything to live for, and what is more, desperately wanted to live!'

'My dear Wickham, you are simply unsettled by the emotion of the day—'

'No, Mr Marsden, I am disturbed by the brutality and *hypocrisy* of the day. If Emmet had been an Englishman in an England ruled by France, and declared the same avowed intentions to free England from the rule of France, he would now be on his way to a burial in Westminster Abbey with all the honours England could bestow on him. But he is a mere Irishman, and so, we throw his mutilated young body into a cheap shell coffin and order underlings to bury him in the field for criminals behind Kilmainham Gaol.'

Marsden was so astounded he almost laughed. For years William Wickham had served England in Europe, posing as a diplomatic ambassador but in reality Britain's chief spy and the head of Pitt's secret service on the Continent, where Wickham had engineered a spy system bordering on genius. Using thousands and thousands of pounds of British taxpayers' money, he had bribed princes, generals, ministers, mistresses of soldiers, even Bonaparte's secretary. No detail was too small for him or his spies – how else had the Castle collected a file a foot thick on all Emmet's movements in Paris and Hamburg? Every piece of information had been supplied by four British agents who had posed as dedicated United Irishmen, then reported back to Wickham's spy machine, which sent those reports on to Dublin Castle.

And now – after such a long and intriguing career – William Wickham was undergoing a crisis of conscience quite unique, and all because of a deluded young man who deserved everything he got; *everything*.

'I intend to resign my post as Chief Secretary of State for Ireland,' Wickham said quietly.

'Resign?' Marsden sat up in utter shock. 'Oh, surely not – not because of Emmet!'

Wickham looked at Marsden, then through him, and beyond him, at something Marsden would never see.

'I am not yet an old man,' Wickham said softly, 'but I have lived in the world too long to know that no man faces his executioner as Emmet did today, no man calls up that amount of courage, through vanity.'

Marsden was greatly alarmed, agitated to the edge of his chair. When high-ranking ministers suddenly resigned from an administration, that administration usually came under question.

'My dear Wickham – you cannot possibly resign! You are distressed, tired. You have been working too hard with the Privy Council on matters concerning other rebels. I concede, yes, I do concede that no one was expecting Emmet to behave as he did in court or on the scaffold. But that is their game! *Martyrdom!* You must not let it affect you!'

'My dear Mr Marsden, there is no doubt that your sentiments on my behalf are kindly meant,' Wickham said wryly, 'but allow me to form my own judgements on how and why the game is played. I know that Lord Edward Fitzgerald was not seeking martyrdom. I know that Theobald Wolfe Tone was not seeking martyrdom. They cannot *all* have been vain fools. I also know this, Mr Marsden, no man risks his young life and forfeits his young life, *for nothing!*'

'You are ... unwell. After a good night's sleep you will—'

'I shall take further time to consider my decision, of course,' said the Chief Secretary, rising to his feet.

'And if you decide in the affirmative, what reason shall you give?'

Wickham paused at the door. 'Oh, the usual reason that

ministers always give in situations like this one,' he said wearily. 'Poor health.'

Inside Kilmainham Gaol, Anne walked along the dark corridor and turned into her cell. She sank down heavily on to her straw mat, and Dr Trevor looked down at her pityingly. Such a fool if she thought all the shots had been fired.

'Bread and water only,' he said to the turnkey. 'No milk ration until further notice.'

'I had wondered,' Anne said tiredly, 'if it was you, or your government, who intended to murder me by this slow but sure process. Now I know it is both.'

Trevor's voice ranted on, and on, and on, with the usual obscenities and threats but she was no longer listening.

'They are gone,' said Dunan Gacha Druid to Connacher, the King of Ulster. 'I have done what you desired me.'

And the sons of Uisnech were lying dead, without breath of life, on the green meadow plain. And kneeling over, and showering down her tears on Naois, Deirdre said:

'Beloved noble and modest warrior, I cannot eat or smile henceforth. Soon enough, I shall lie within my own grave.'

Trevor was smiling. When they started muttering the tales of the soothsayers, it was a sure sign they were going mad.

He spoke to her again, but she gave no answer. She did not even hear the door close, or his heavy footsteps on the stone-flagged corridor as he marched away.

The rain began to lash down in torrents. Within her cell in the male section of Kilmainham, she lay on her mat, shivering under her one blanket. On other nights she had heard the voices of the prisoners as they shouted to each other, but tonight all was deathly silent.

She passed the hours in her memories. Six months she had known Robert Emmet, just six short months, from March until September. And yet she knew he would remain the very core of her life, and, however long she lived, his memory would always haunt her.

And then, from somewhere down the corridor, she heard a prisoner's voice, raised in plaintive song, lamenting as only the

Irish can lament, and as she listened to the lovely voice, she finally allowed herself to weep.

> 'To numbers sadly sweet and wild
>   Dejected Ireland strikes her lyre,
> She mourns in tears a darling child
>   Whose bosom glowed with freedom's fire.
>
> Neglected through the aerial breeze
>   Her snowy vestments loosely flow,
> O'er Emmet's grave she fondly grieves,
>   And mourns him with a mother's woe.'

The ballads about him had started already; and now they had started, they would go on. Ballads were the only tribute the people had.

It was still dark, but her cell door was being unlocked. She waited, feeling sure they were coming to take her out and execute her in the dead of night.

The turnkey stepped aside and Dr Trevor stood framed in the doorway, holding the hand of a skinny little boy.

'As an act of humanity and kindness, Devlin, I have brought your brother to keep you company.'

Anne scrambled to her feet and reached out to Jimmy. He was shivering, and the large eyes that stared up at her were almost blind. She gazed into his little face, then up at her adversary.

'He has the fever. He's yellow and sweating with gaol fever!'

'Regrettably so,' Trevor replied, 'but perhaps you will take better care of him than your father. He prefers to spend all his time blaming the child's illness on me.'

'Let hell wait for you!'

She snatched Jimmy into her arms and carried him over to her straw mattress where she laid him down. 'He's as light as feather. Have you been starving him, too?'

The door clanged shut and they were left alone. She lay down beside Jimmy and pulled the blanket over them, cuddling him tight within her arms and pressing the warmth of her body into him. The dim lamplight from the corridor shone through the grille to them.

'There now, my darling boy,' she whispered. 'You're with Anne now, and Anne is going to make you better.'

Jimmy put his thin arms around her neck and pressed his cheek against hers, crying quietly.

'Ah, Jimmy,' she whispered, 'will you be my man?'

'Aye,' he croaked.

'Will you carry my can?'

'Aye.'

'Will you fight the fairies for me?'

'Only,' Jimmy wiped his blotched face with his hand, 'only if you tell me a story of the Gaels.'

She thought, then cleared her throat, and began to tell him the story of the Children of Lîr.

'It happened some time ago, in the age of Gods and heroes, and King Lîr had four children; a lovely daughter called Fionnula, and three sons, Aed, Fiachra, and Conn.'

It was a long story, but not too long, yet by the time she had finished Jimmy's little heart and fluttering breaths had stopped.

'Ah, Jimmy,' she moaned. 'Ah, Jimmy . . .' She began to lift him into a sitting position, pressing her lips frantically to his, trying to breathe her own life into him. 'Will you be my man, Jimmy?' she cried desperately. 'Will you carry my can?'

She began to shake him, plead with him, 'Jimmy! Jimmy! You promised to fight the fairies for me if I told you a story of the Gaels.'

And then she was on her feet, staring wildly around her as she wailed out her grief and pain.

In the demented rage that followed, even Dr Trevor was terrified to go near her. She screamed and cursed like a woman insane. Any turnkey who tried to enter the cell to remove Jimmy's body was clawed and kicked until he ran for his life. She would allow no one even to touch him.

In the end, four turnkeys restrained her while Dr Trevor lifted Jimmy's body and carried him to the door. There he paused and looked at her ravaged face.

'You could walk out of here tomorrow, Devlin. If you would just cooperate with us.'

Anne's face twisted with rage. 'You say that while you hold

my little dead brother! God burn you in hell! I'd kiss the arse of Lucifer first.'

After weeks of consideration, William Wickham resigned from his office as Chief Secretary of State for Ireland. But the reason he gave was not, after all, poor health.

> I hereby repeat that no consideration on earth could induce me to remain after having maturely reflected. For in what honours or other earthly advantages could I find compensation for what I must suffer were I again compelled by official duty to persecute to death men capable of thinking and acting like Emmet, for making an effort to liberate their country from grievances, the existence of many of which none can deny and, which I myself acknowledge to be unjust, oppressive, and unchristian.
>
> I know that the manner in which I have suffered myself to be affected will be attributed to a sort of morbid sensibility rather than its real cause, but no one can be capable of forming a right judgement on my motives who has not, like myself, been condemned by official duty to dip his hands in the blood of his fellow men, in execution of a portion of the laws and institutions of his country of which his conscience cannot approve.

William Wickham returned home to England. His resignation was publicly accepted with deep regret, but complete understanding of his need to retire, due to poor health.

Inside the Rotunda ballroom the crystal chandeliers containing hundreds of candles glittered above the swirling dancers, their lights reflecting on the shimmering satins and silks, diamonds and emeralds, worn by the excited young ladies who had spent all day in preparation for the Christmas Ball.

Everyone was in a gay and festive mood. At the end of the hall a white-wigged orchestra was playing a German waltz. Around the walls and pillars of the room, dowagers sat on gilt-edged chairs with quizzing-glasses raised and lips murmuring curiously as all eyes focused on the exquisite young girl who danced around the room in smiling and giddy pleasure, in the arms of the young poet, Thomas Moore.

Sarah Curran was undoubtedly the belle of the ball. Gentleman after gentleman competed for the pleasure of dancing with her, and she accepted as many as she practically could.

The dowagers watched her change from partner to partner, then heaved their well-upholstered bosoms and declared that not only was the betrothed of Emmet recovered, she was vain and frivolous and not, in truth, a very good dancer.

With lips curled, they watched her laugh excitedly as she galloped through an eight-handed reel, gaily dance the gavotte, then swish around in another waltz. But by a pillar at the top of the room, Thomas Moore, her official escort, watched Sarah with sad and troubled eyes. Her gaiety was too gay, her hilarity verging on the edge of hysteria, and he closed his eyes in pain when that which he most feared, finally happened.

She suddenly stopped dancing, apparently unconscious of the world around her, wandering through the room and the dancers with an air of abstraction, until she reached the steps of the orchestra and sat down, looking about her with a vacant air.

The orchestra scraped on, but when a crowd gathered around her, mute and silent, the last bow of a violoncello murmured to silence, and all looked at the lovely but pale and wretched young girl, who was now known simply as the betrothed of Emmet.

All knew her story, for a Crown lawyer named Huband had revealed the secret name of the writer of the letters found on Emmet. After her lover's death she had suffered a mental breakdown which had lasted some long weeks, and had not softened the heart of her father who still refused to look at or speak to her, although she still lived in his house.

The most respectful and cherishing attentions were paid her by young men of wealth and distinction, all friends of Emmet, who endeavoured by all kinds of occupations and amusements to dissipate her grief, and so far had seemed to be succeeding, until this night in the Rotunda.

Thomas Moore pushed through the silent ballroom towards her.

'Sarah,' he said softly.

604

Her dark blue eyes remained wide and unblinking, she seemed unaware of the crowd around her as she began to sing a plaintive song. She had an exquisite voice, and a young violinist in the orchestra could not resist providing her with a lonely accompaniment, for she sang to the beautiful air of Carolan's 'Eileen A Roon', but the words she sang were not those written for the tune in 1793 by Rabby Burns.

And as she sang, many of the young ladies, and even a few of the gentlemen, melted into tears.

> 'The joy of life lies here,
>> Robert Aroon;
> All that my soul held dear,
>> Robert Aroon.
> Love of my heart, this shrine—
> The long last home, of thine,
> Entombs each hope of mine,
>> Robert Aroon.
>
> The night is cold and chill,
>> Robert Aroon.
> My heart is colder still,
>> Robert Aroon.
> But sun will never shine
> To warm this heart of mine;
> 'Tis almost as cold as thine,
>> Robert Aroon.'

A young lady began to sob loudly. Thomas Moore moved forward and reached down to take her hand.

'Sarah,' he said.

EPILOGUE

Chapter Forty-Five

In Westminster, when the Parliamentary session opened after the Christmas break, the Whigs were still demanding an official investigation into the conduct of an administration that had almost lost Dublin to the rebels on 23 July 1803. William Pitt attacked Prime Minister Addington so violently, many said he should have been sitting on the opposite side of the House, next to the Whig leader, Charles Fox.

Alexander Marsden was desperate that no such official investigation should take place. Lord Castlereagh answered Marsden's frantic letters with assurances that he would defend him strongly in the House.

When the House of Commons sat for the first debate on the Irish bills, Mr William Windham rose to his feet and asked:

'Will the King's ministers please let the House know – when they have made up their minds – whether the late insurrection was really a contemptible riot, or whether it had spread to a greater extent and had taken deep root in the entire country? It is absurd to present the rising first as a most terrifying conspiracy, and then as a contemptible riot.'

A member of the Addington cabinet declared it to be a contemptible riot.

'In that case,' replied Windham, 'why does Ireland still need the powers of the Insurrection Act? The Honourable Gentlemen of the other side of the House are seeking to have the benefit of both suppositions. They are like the student, who, when asked whether the sun revolved around the earth or the earth around the sun, said, "Sometimes one way and sometimes the other".'

Sir John Wrottesley, of the Pitt faction, then charged the Irish administration with the grossest neglect in some quarters on 23rd July 1803. He informed the House that 'although the leader of the insurrection had worked only a few streets away from the Castle, and the officials there had been notified of his intentions, the Under-Secretary of State, Mr Marsden, informed the Lord Lieutenant and General Fox, *on the very day*, that there was no need for *alarm*!'

The Speaker called, 'Order!' and Sir John continued:

'It has always been agreed that it is better to *prevent* than to *punish* crimes. Therefore, it is impossible to believe that the government could have intended to wait until the insurrection took place with a view to discovering the authors. To risk every loyal man, to place the lives of His Majesty's subjects, even for the shortest period, in such a state of danger would itself be deemed highly *criminal*, and the impropriety of such a measure could not be more fully exemplified than in the unfortunate occurrence that actually took place – the death of Lord Kilwarden!'

The Whigs and the Pitt faction were jubilant, while Prime Minister Henry Addington was visibly shrinking with age by the minute.

'Was it a contemptible riot,' Sir John continued, 'that had for its object the separation of Ireland from Britain? Was it a contemptible riot, which induces you to pass bills, giving the greatest possible powers to the administration of that country? Was it a contemptible riot, which obliged that administration to put the yeomanry of Ireland on permanent duty, at a cost of four hundred thousand pounds to be defrayed by the two countries? No, sir!

'I therefore move,' Sir John continued, 'that this House resolves itself to a committee to inquire into the conduct of the Irish administration relative to the Insurrection of 23rd July, and the *previous* conduct of that government as far as it relates to the said insurrection!'

Hidden away at the back of the gallery, Alexander Marsden waited for Castlereagh to stand up and speak in his defence.

Lord Castlereagh rose to his feet and pointed out to the Honourable Members that the Castle had acted on the principle of not giving alarm.

'It was very important not to carry out such precautions as to alarm the fears of the rebels, and thereby induce them to delay their project. If patrols had been sent out, if such extraordinary precautions had been taken as would have induced the rebels to lay aside their design, the consequence would have been that the government would have been the laughing stock of the country. No one would have believed that any danger existed.

'And in that case, how could the government of Ireland have applied to Parliament for greater powers? And the suspension of the Habeas Corpus Act?'

Marsden slumped down in his seat. Castlereagh had promised to defend him, but had now practically admitted to the entire House that the Castle had known all about the Emmet conspiracy and allowed it to ripen until they were ready to crush it! And now Lord Hardwicke would know he had kept vital information from him. He had been sold out! *Deserted* by Castlereagh.

He slipped out into the London streets and walked as if in a daze down to the Thames. The Emmet conspiracy was blowing up in his face, threatening to destroy him. It had all seemed so simple in the beginning. Smoke out what was left of the United Irishmen, lead them into an insurrection that would fail so badly that even the most dedicated patriots would think twice about rising again.

And there were the personal considerations. Until the Emmet conspiracy, on the surface at least, Ireland had appeared quite tranquil. But there was nothing like a war, big or small, to bring a politician to notice.

But a *frustrated* rebellion, successfully quashed, could make a politician an outright hero – even bring him into the very cabinet of power at Whitehall.

Now he would be left to rot in Dublin Castle – if he was lucky. Pitt was on his way back to power. And Castlereagh was Pitt's man. And now Castlereagh had deserted him.

Marsden walked back towards his hotel, a dejected figure, brought low by the weight of newly acquired wisdom. Such were the moves on the political chessboard. King and Country might be the game, but – inside the Party – it was every man for himself.

And so Marsden went back to Dublin. Henry Addington was

forced to resign. William Pitt regained his seat as Prime Minister of Great Britain. Castlereagh was given a Cabinet post, later becoming Foreign Secretary.

As time moved on, and William Pitt roused his beloved England to even greater efforts in the war against France in defence of her freedom, no move was made to reinstate the Act of Habeas Corpus in Ireland.

So the Irish State prisoners remained confined in Kilmainham Gaol, without charge or trial.

On a bright sunny morning in 1806, Anne Devlin was awakened by the sound of loud voices in the corridor. She struggled to push her heavy frame up from her mat and, blinking through her dim vision, plodded over to the grille. 'What's happened?' she called. 'Someone tell me why all the voices at this time of the morning.'

Anne was lucky. The turnkey on duty that day was a true sympathiser and for a long time had admired Anne Devlin.

'It's not morning, Anne, it's the monthly visiting hour.'

'Why are those people shouting?'

'The Whigs have gained power in England.'

Anne stared at the turnkey, then as understanding dawned, her hands moved over her face. 'O God . . . ! But . . . but this means we may soon be freed.'

'Aye, you might at that.'

Anne moved back to her mat and sat down heavily, thinking, 'No, girl, control yourself. It's too much to hope for, too much.'

After three years in solitary confinement, Anne had given up hoping. All her energies had been devoted to surviving, and surviving with a sane mind.

But although Anne's mind had remained strong, her body had broken under the torture of being confined in a small place for so long without air or exercise and with a paltry diet. The long winter days and nights of shivering in a cold damp cell had taken their toll.

She had first felt a stiffness around her whole frame, which gradually led to a swelling of her entire body. Her legs had swollen to such a colossal size that Dr Trevor had finally agreed to bring in an apothecary from Thomas Street, who made three incisions in each leg. Anne found the incisions did not ease her suffering but increased it.

After twelve months her sight had started to weaken and symptoms of erysipelas were diagnosed. Now after three years, she was sure it would not be long before she was totally blind.

As the months passed into years, every friend of Robert Emmet who had been arrested and brought into the men's part of Kilmainham Gaol had innocently and foolishly asked if they could see Anne Devlin. All were refused. Word of her cruel and savage torture was sent to people on the outside with pleas to try and help her. A letter complaining of her merciless treatment at the hands of Dr Trevor was sent to the Castle, signed by John Patten and St John Mason.

The only small concession obtained for Anne was her being taken under guard to the spa at Lucan and allowed to soak her swollen limbs in the waters. The light had hurt her eyes at first, but ohhhhh! The air had been the sweetest ever breathed, and the water as smooth as cool silk.

Anne pushed herself up on her feet again. Now that freedom was a possibility, she would have to work on herself. It was time to get prepared. Time to start learning to walk again. She held on to the wall as she took the slow ten steps down her cell. She would try and keep going until the visiting hour was over.

As she walked, she thought over all the events that had taken place since her internment. She had learned a lot from Mrs Dunne, the English wife of the governor who had occasionally appeared at the grille with a few kind and tender words for her. On one occasion, Mrs Dunne had even obtained her husband's key to Anne's cell, and, while the turnkeys were at supper, had unlocked the door and brought Anne up to her apartment. There in the kitchen, the Lancashire woman had sat her down and placed such a wonderful meal in front of her, it was almost cold when Anne had stopped crying enough to eat it.

But Mrs Dunne had just poured Anne her second cup of steaming delicious tea when Dr Trevor walked in. He made Anne pay dearly for that meal and the Englishwoman was watched from then on.

Anne paused and leaned heavily against the wall. Her legs

felt like great slabs of dead meat. No, she must carry on. Think of freedom.

She thought about little Jimmy, and how Edward Kennedy, the stepbrother to Miles Byrne and a prisoner in Kilmainham, had viciously attacked Dr Trevor for his inhumane treatment of the boy.

She thought about Thomas Russell, with his attractive face and laughter – hanged and beheaded in Downpatrick.

And Mary, released after twelve months to find their home and possessions confiscated. Poor Mary, with nowhere to live, nowhere to go, until a kindly United family had assumed responsibility for her.

'*Do you assume, or presume, responsibility, Mr Robert?*'

'*Assume.*'

And Little Arthur, her darling brother: his months of being Mr Robert's aide-de-camp and pupil had been the best thing that had happened to him. Through Mrs Dunne Anne had discovered that, although her brother was still confined in the Provost prison, his learning had impressed the governor there so much that after six months Little Arthur had become his aide, answering all his correspondence and escaping much of the harshness of prison life.

'*You know, Anne, your brother has a natural genius for learning. He should be at Trinity.*'

She thought about Hanlon, the violent tower keeper at the Castle, and how Henry Howley, who had been one of Mr Robert's men in the Thomas Street depot, had gone there and shot Hanlon dead. What the tower keeper had done to provoke this act, nobody knew.

And then she stared hard at the floor as she thought of Sarah Curran, who, last year, had married an officer in the army of George of Hanover.

Silently, and outwardly remote from all passion, Anne had listened as the governor's wife whispered to her all the Dublin gossip about the betrothed of Emmet. The poor girl had suffered badly after his execution, ill for months, finally leaving the house of a father who had irrevocably disowned her to live with a Quaker family in Cork of the name of Penrose. Here she had met Captain Robert Henry Sturgeon in the summer of

1805. Only twenty-three years old then, she could not have been expected to spend the rest of her life pining for a dead lover. But, even so, many who gathered outside to watch the wedding said she had arrived at the church in tears. And rumour had it from Bessie Penrose that, on accepting Captain Sturgeon, Sarah had told him he could have her hand, but that her heart belonged, and would always belong, to Emmet, that she could give to a husband no more than respect and affection, and on those terms Sturgeon was willing to marry her.

Silently, and outwardly remote from all passion, Anne had listened but made no comment. So many young gentlemen in Ireland, but Sarah Curran had chosen to marry a redcoat. Would not go to France with the Irish patriot, but went to Sicily with her redcoat while he fought the French.

To Anne, it was the ultimate betrayal.

Three weeks after the Whigs came to power, the Habeas Corpus Act was reinstated in Ireland.

Dr Trevor appeared in Anne's cell. 'Well, Devlin. Your time here is over. On your feet.'

Anne could scarcely believe her ears. Her breathing came fast and excited as she stumbled towards the door.

'Bring your crutches.'

'No, I want to walk out on my own strength.'

Dr Trevor sighed irritably and motioned with his head to the turnkey. 'Bring the crutches.'

It took Anne a few minutes to accustom her weak eyes to the light outside Kilmainham Gaol. So busy was she gasping the air and smiling that she was unaware of being led up to a waiting carriage until she felt herself being pushed inside. Two armed guards sat beside her. Dr Trevor relaxed on the seat opposite.

'Where are we going?' she asked.

'To the Castle. Although no charge has been made against you, there will still be release papers for you to sign.'

Once inside the Castle, Dr Trevor took Anne to a small closet in the tower. It was the length of the pallet it contained and two feet broader; the only light came from under the door.

'Wait in here for a few minutes,' Dr Trevor said, throwing her crutches on to the pallet.

Anne sat down on the pallet and, covering her face with her hands, alternately wept and prayed in thanksgiving.

The following day, Mr Long, the new Chief Secretary of State for Ireland, requested a list of all the names of political prisoners detained in Kilmainham Gaol without charge. On being presented with the list by Dr Trevor, Mr Long signed the release papers for each of them.

The name of Anne Devlin was not listed as a prisoner in Kilmainham Gaol.

Mrs Hanlon, the widow of the tower keeper, was still employed in Dublin Castle. Although she knew she risked losing her position, Mrs Hanlon presented herself in Mr Long's office and begged for an interview.

'She's been up there eleven weeks now, sir. Eleven weeks! In solitary confinement, friendless and forsaken!'

'I have already told you in my replies to your many letters, Mrs Hanlon, that this is a matter for Dr Trevor, the superintendent of the gaols. It seems there are a number of irregularities in Miss Devlin's case, and he is endeavouring to sort out the matter.'

'But Dr Trevor is the one who put her there,' Mrs Hanlon cried. 'It's slow murder he's after.'

Mr Long looked greatly ill at ease. 'Mrs Hanlon, it is impossible that Miss Devlin's case can be as you present it. It is not possible that this government, or any government, could keep a person, particularly a female, so long confined without any specific charge being made against her.'

'I will admit, sir, I have not presented the facts of her case truthfully, but only because I feared that I might disgust you with the unheard of atrocities she has had to suffer at the hands of Dr Trevor in Kilmainham. Ask any turnkey, ex-prisoner or, better – Mrs Dunne, the widow of the ex-Governor.'

Mr Long was obdurate. 'Mrs Hanlon, I regret—' his face dropped in utter embarrassment. He stared at the woman, appalled. 'Oh, my dear lady, there is no need for this!'

Mrs Hanlon was on her knees, her hands raised in supplication, 'Please, sir, please! If you could just take one minute to come and look at her wretchedness. Just one *look* at her will convince you of her claim to your humanity.'

The Englishman hesitated, then turned and strode to the door and ordered the tower keeper to be sent for. When he arrived, Mr Long asked him to lead the way to wherever in the tower a Miss Anne Devlin was confined.

At the door of the closet, the keeper looked reluctant. 'Dr Trevor, sir, he has given strict—'

'Open the door.'

Anne was lying on the pallet when the door was opened. Her body was now more swollen than ever and her eyes were caked in a yellow pus. For one long silent moment, Mr Long stood gazing down at her, then turned and strode back down the corridor.

Some hours later, the door was opened again. Mrs Hanlon and the keeper helped Anne to her feet and, making her use the crutches, took her to Mrs Hanlon's apartment where the good lady washed her face and combed her hair and changed her rags for fresh linen undergarments and a bright cotton dress. Mrs Hanlon was a stout lady, and under normal circumstances her dress would have been like a tent on Anne's young body, but now with her unnatural bloatedness, it fitted well.

A light meal and a cup of tea followed, and throughout Mrs Hanlon spoke soft comforting words, but Anne remained silent, like someone moving through a dream.

Mrs Hanlon kept an arm around Anne as they hesitantly walked through the upper Castle yard, but at the arch to the lower yard, Anne handed her the crutches.

'I want to walk out on my own strength,' she whispered.

Mrs Hanlon nodded, took the crutches, then put a hand on her arm. 'I'll leave you here, Anne, but I'll come to see you in a few days.' Then, bunching her lips to stop the tears, and pressing Anne's hand, Mrs Hanlon turned and left Anne Devlin to walk out of Dublin Castle alone.

After a few steps, she turned and looked over her shoulder. Anne was still standing there, gazing back at her.

'Go on!' Mrs Hanlon shouted, waving her hand, 'walk out! Remember what that bastard husband of mine once said to you; walk out, walk out!'

Anne turned and slowly walked through the lower yard,

towards the ragged old couple standing waiting for her. Both were stooped and thin with grey hair, and it was not until she was only an arm's length away that she recognised them.

She fell in her pain. She heaved and rocked and cried with a hurt she had not felt since that day in September 1803 in Thomas Street.

And then she was embracing and caressing and lovingly touching the two prematurely aged faces of her parents who wept with her.

The Castle was at the top of Dame Street. They walked from there along High Street to Thomas Street, towards two small rented rooms in Thomas Court; her new home. Nellie and Little Arthur were preparing a meal, her ma said. Mary had died of consumption.

The three huddled Devlins walked in silence up Thomas Street and past St Catherine's Protestant Church. Today was not the day to glance towards the centre of the street where three years earlier an execution had taken place, nor to the building opposite which had once been an arms depot. Today was a day to be happy.

They turned the corner and walked slowly up Thomas Court to a large old house on the right. A loud melancholy sound rang through the air. Anne paused and cocked her head.

' 'Tis just the bells of John's Lane Chapel,' her mother said. 'They toll three times a day for the Angelus. The monks have been warned about it, but still they ring them.'

From that day on, whenever Anne Devlin heard the bells from the old chapel building on Thomas Street, she fancied they were tolling especially for her, rejoicing the day of her liberty.

Author's Note

Afterwards

Robert Emmet's last letter to Thomas and Jane was held by Dublin Castle and never forwarded to Paris. It was not until years later that Thomas Emmet learned of his brother's attachment to Sarah Curran, but by then it was too late.

Sarah Curran died four and half years after Emmet, at the age of twenty-six. She knew that she was dying and wrote to her father requesting to be buried in Rathfarnham. He refused on the grounds that the Church would not suffer *two* of his daughters being buried in unconsecrated ground. Her husband sent her body home to Ireland, where she was buried beside her grandmother in the Curran family plot in Newmarket, County Cork.

Sarah became a heroine of romantic legend in Ireland and America when Thomas Moore's tribute to Robert and Sarah was published. When Moore wrote the song 'She is Far from the Land', Sarah was alive and living in Sicily, but his prediction proved sadly accurate.

> She is far from the land where her young hero sleeps,
>   And lovers are round her sighing;
> But coldly she turns from their gaze, and weeps,
>   For her heart in his grave is lying!
>
> He had lived for his love, for his country he died,
>   They were all that to life had entwined him.
> Not soon shall the tears of his country be dried,
>   Nor long will his love stay behind him.

Amelia Curran left The Priory shortly after Sarah, and went to Rome to study art. She became a close friend of the poet Percy Bysshe Shelley, and her portrait of him now hangs in the National Gallery in London, catalogued under inventory number 1234. She died unmarried and is buried in Rome.

John Philpot Curran lost all desire for political office, but through his outstanding talents as a lawyer he became Master of the Rolls in Ireland and earned a reputation amongst the younger lawyers of the Bar as a kind and honest judge. He was savagely criticised for his treatment of his daughter and Emmet, but he never lost the respect or affection of those who remembered his long and hard fight for his countrymen in the State Trials of 1798.

John Curran had two illegitimate sons by his mistress, Margaret Fitzgerald. They were never recognised by his relatives, but on entering Trinity College, the elder son, Henry Grattan Fitzgerald, changed his name to Curran, and later became a lawyer.

John Curran died in the spring of 1817, and is buried in Glasnevin Cemetry in a tomb which bears the one word: 'CURRAN'.

Richard Curran suffered a severe mental breakdown after Robert Emmet's brutal execution and never totally recovered. He died young in an asylum for the insane.

Thomas Emmet was heartbroken by the news of his brother's death. In his diary he wrote,

> 'I have just received the news of my dear Robert's trial and execution. It is only his conduct on both occasions that consoles me in his loss.'

Thomas retired with his grief to a retreat in St Cloud, then announced that he had no wish ever to see Ireland again. He removed his family to America, whither he was later followed by his friend, James MacNeven. On arriving in New York, contrary to the usual term of ten years, Thomas Emmet was given his naturalisation papers within twenty-four hours. He rose to great eminence at the American bar, earning a reputation for identifying with his case, the most memorable being his magnificent and successful defence of two fugitive Negro slaves who had run away from their tyrannical master. He became Attorney-General of the State of New York. His son Robert became Judge Emmet of the Supreme Court.

On his death in 1824 the members of the New York Bar, together with the Board of Judges of the US Court, voted to suspend the hearing of all cases so they could attend the funeral procession of Thomas Addis Emmet. At a court of general sessions held the following day at City Hall, the members of the New York Bar and the Board of Judges passed a resolution to erect a monument in honour of their 'most distinguished and talented member whose name belongs in the history of his native land, but will always be cherished by the people of his adopted land – America'. That thirty-foot monument still stands today in St Paul's Churchyard, between Vesey Street and Fulton Street, on Broadway. Next to the obelisk is a granite shaft laid in honour of Dr W. James MacNeven who saved New York from the cholera.

Miles Byrne was unable to return to Ireland due to threat of arrest and execution. He joined the French army; served in Spain, Germany, Greece, and at Flushing, earning many decorations including the medal of St Helena. He was made a Knight of the Legion of Honour by Napoleon I, and received the Officer's Cross from King Louis-Philippe. He retired after a long military career to a quiet life in Paris with his wife Frances, the daughter of an Irish exile. An Irishman who became a Frenchman, Miles is buried in the cemetery at Montmartre in Paris.

Michael Quigley – In the Castle's secret-service payment books of that period, a payment is recorded:

2nd May 1803 – Mr Marsden, for Quigley – £40. 0s 0d.

Whether this was Michael Quigley is a matter for conjecture. Quigley was arrested and brought to Kilmainham shortly after

Emmet's death, and, during his three years there, he informed regularly to the Castle on the conversations of the other prisoners. On his release he was able to buy a large farm in Kildare.

Thomas Wilde and *John Mahon* escaped from Kildare to Dublin where they were given refuge in the house of Lord Moira, then put aboard a ship to America. When the war with Britain commenced in 1812, they both joined the Irish Brigade of the American army, and were killed in action.

Nicholas Stafford was arrested shortly after Quigley, spent three years in Kilmainham, but did not become an informer. On his release in 1806 he married his sweetheart, the sister of Henry Hevey, and settled down to a long and quiet life.

Denis Lambert Redmond did not die from his suicide attempt. He was nursed back to health and upon his recovery was hanged.

John McIntosh, the Scottish carpenter, was executed shortly after Emmet, along with fourteen others.

Leonard McNally's treachery was not discovered in his lifetime. On his deathbed he sent for a Catholic priest and asked to resume his faith and make a full confession of all his sins. But old habits die hard – the priest that McNally particularly requested was seventy years old, and stone deaf.

Only when the *Memoirs* of Lord Cornwallis were published did the Irish people learn that McNally had been a long-standing recipient of secret-service money under the initials 'J. W.' Later examination of the ledgers and papers revealed the extent of his betrayal. He had habitually reported on the activities of his closest friends, including Curran; and had even reported the words of gratitude given to him by clients he had helped to send to the scaffold.

Only his family ever suspected him. 'Let him go to Hell his own way,' McNally's son declared on his death.

Lord Norbury clung tenaciously to his reputation as 'the hanging judge' and his seat on the bench. Years later, when eighty-seven years old and requested by the Viceroy's messenger to retire, Norbury responded furiously by challenging the messenger to a duel. Upon the Viceroy's second request, Norbury beseeched time to discuss the proposition of retirement with a close friend and adviser, and after this time was granted to him, announced that the friend lived in India and he would have to write.

It was the lawyer Daniel O'Connell who finally prevented Norbury from hanging on. He presented evidence to prove Norbury had slept through an entire trial, then awoke to pass sentence before the jury had brought in the verdict. This secured Norbury's immediate removal from the bench.

Lord Castlereagh later served in the ministry of Lord Liverpool, renowned for its repressive government and the infamous massacre of Peterloo. It has been said that Castlereagh was 'unfairly' blamed for the excesses of that government, but blamed by the English people he was, and died by suicide in 1822. On his death a leading British journalist posted a notice outside his Fleet Street office reading *People of England, rejoice! Castlereagh is dead.*

Castlereagh was buried in Westminster Abbey. Amongst the pallbearers were the Duke of Wellington and two of the Royal princes. Many fine eulogies were said over him, but the most famous epitaph of all, and the most brutal, was that written by Lord Byron.

> Posterity shall ne'er survey,
> A nobler grave than this.
> Here lie the bones of Castlereagh,
> Stop, traveller, and —!

Alexander Marsden was removed from political office when the Whigs came to power in 1806. He later served as a Commissary Judge in the Slavery Courts; and afterwards as Chairman of Excise until 1817, when he disappeared from public record until his death in 1834.

James Hope lived to a ripe old age but nothing could ever induce him to reveal the identities of the secret men who backed Emmet, insisting that he had given his solemn oath to Emmet, from which Emmet had never released him. Thirty years after the event, he spoke at length to the historian Dr Madden, but in answer to the vital question, Jemmy's reply remained staunch: 'There were persons of distinction in the confidence of our leaders, who kept up communication with them in exile . . . Having been Mr Emmet's constant attendant for some months, many things that I learned from him are sealed up by his request.'

Anne Devlin did not become a heroine of romantic legend. No poets wrote songs about her. She lived a long life in abject poverty in the Liberties of Dublin, her eyesight almost gone, her bravery and patriotism forgotten.

Towards the end of her life she broke her silence and told her story to two men: Brother Luke Cullen of the Carmelite Monastery, and the historian Dr Richard Madden. She described Emmet as 'The best, the kindest-hearted person I ever knew in my whole life'.

Late in life she married a man named Campbell whom she described simply as 'a good man'. He died early and she was left alone to bring up her son and a little crippled daughter. Her son worked hard to maintain her and the girl, but when Anne died she was buried in a charity coffin in the paupers' section of Glasnevin cemetery.

A few years later, due to the devotion of Dr Madden, her body was removed from the paupers' section to a grave in that part of the cemetery reserved for men like Daniel O'Connell, above which is a headstone bearing Emmet's name as well as Anne's. In 1951 President Eamon de Valera paid an official visit to the grave of Anne Devlin, and placed there a tricolour wreath of flowers, from the freely elected government of the Irish Republic.

Immediately after his execution Robert Emmet was buried behind Kilmainham Gaol in the acre of land reserved for all executed criminals, known as the Hospital Fields. During the dark hours of that same night, a secret party of men, accompanied by a clergyman, removed his body to a private resting place 'somewhere in Dublin' where Robert's last request to be left in obscurity and peace could be upheld, and where a stone without any inscription had been laid over him. John Patten, and Michael Lennard, the Emmets' very old gardener, affirmed this to Dr Madden, as did the then governor of Kilmainham Gaol, who had been a turnkey at the time. But up to this day, that final uninscribed resting place of Robert Emmet has never been discovered.

Short Bibliography

The Life of Robert Emmet, including the narratives of Anne Devlin, James Hope, and Bernard Duggan, by Dr R.R. Madden, 1856.

The Pursuit of Robert Emmet, by Helen Landreth, 1949.

The Life of Anne Devlin, as told to Brother Luke Cullen of the Carmelite Monastery. Edited by J.J. Finnegan.

The Voice of Sarah Curran, by Major-General H.T. MacMullen, privately printed.

The Life of the Right Honourable John Philpot Curran, Late Master of the Rolls in Ireland, by his son, William Henry Curran, 1822.

Recollections of Curran and his Contemporaries by Charles Phillips.

John Philpot Curran by Leslie Hale.

Memoirs of Miles Byrne, 2 Vols, Paris, 1863.

Memoirs, Journal, and Correspondence of Thomas Moore, edited by Lord John Russell, 1860.

Correspondence of Emily, Duchess of Leinster, edited by Brian Fitzgerald.

The Viceroy's Postbag: Whitehall Papers and Correspondence of the Earl of Hardwicke, Michael MacDonagh, 1904.

The United Irishmen: Their Lives and Times, Vols II and III, third series, by Dr R.R. Madden, 1860.

History of the Irish Rebellion of 1798: A Personal Narrative, by Charles Hamilton Teeling, 1828.